FROM ASHES TO SONG

HILARY HAUCK

Dear Joyce,
So wonderful to see you —
Keep on writing, & follow
your song always!

Hilary Hauck

MILFORD HOUSE

An imprint of Sunbury Press, Inc.
MECHANICSBURG, PA USA

May 2021

MILFORD HOUSE

an imprint of Sunbury Press, Inc.
Mechanicsburg, PA USA

FIRST MILFORD HOUSE PRESS EDITION: April 2021

Set in Garamond. Interior design by Chris Fenwick | Cover by Chris Fenwick | Edited by Chris Fenwick.

Publisher's Cataloging-in-Publication Data
Names: Hauck, Hilary, author.
Title: From Ashes to Song / Hilary Hauck.
Description: Revised trade paperback edition. | Mechanicsburg, Pennsylvania : Milford House Press, 2021.
Summary: After losing his grandfather and the family vineyard in Italy, 1911, a young Italian composer, who's never ventured beyond his grandfather's pervasive influence, seeks a new start in America. Inspired by true events, a story of unconventional love, hope, and the extraordinary gifts brought to America by ordinary people.
Identifiers: ISBN 978-1-62006-408-5 (softcover).
Subjects: BISAC: FICTION / Historical / Italian. | FICTION / Historical / Biographical. | FICTION / Historical / Cultural Heritage.

Continue the Enlightenment!

For Irene and Susan

"When you're young, you don't care about your history, about where you came from, then all of a sudden fifty years have gone by and it's too late to find out." – John Smylnycky

ONE

Pietro breathed lightly into his clarinet so his song would not travel the length of the grapevines that stretched like lines of music on either side of him. He didn't want Nonno to hear it—not yet. On his oath, he'd make himself play it for him in the next week.

The song was Pietro's first composition—not that anyone could credit him, he had simply captured the sounds of harvest, of the annual tending of plants whose roots had burrowed into the soil long before he'd been born.

Without a specific plan in mind, he had tucked away the beats and notes, adding new rifts each year until this summer, when it had all begun to spread out and rearrange in his mind. The paper-light tremble of leaves had given him the rhythm. It scampered so heartily it might have dissolved into chaos if it hadn't been grounded by fruit held by the improbable strength of the vine. The grapes were a firm, reliable beat.

The only thing that had eluded him had been the ending, but now he had found it, he couldn't imagine it any other way. It brought the music together, so it no longer felt like a rough sketch of a song, not telling the whole story at once as it did now.

He'd found the ending in the celebration that followed the harvest when family and friends gathered around the table heaped with a feast that had taken an entire week to prepare. The culmination of the long season that brought both relief and melancholy for the end of the summer days, even though Pietro could depend on the same cycle beginning all over again next year.

At this year's celebration, he'd wait until the food was gone and glasses filled with last year's wine were raised to this year's grapes, when he, Nonno, and the others gathered their instruments to shroud the night's sky with song—that was when Pietro would play his music.

First, though, he needed the courage to play it for Nonno. Only then would he know if his efforts were worthy.

TWO

San Damiano d'Asti, Piedmont, Italy

Pietro worked the latch on his clarinet case loose, then set the open case on his lap. He pulled the lower joint from its velvet slot, then twisted the bell gently onto it. The barrel came next, and lastly, he eased the mouthpiece firmly onto the barrel. He cradled his clarinet in his palm and the crook of his arm and sat back to wait.

He'd gone through a dozen ways to tell Nonno about his composition as they'd walked the five miles back to town for the harvest mass to bless grapes, hazelnuts, and truffles. Part blessing, part spirit-raising before the hard work of the actual harvest, all the best musicians in the band played at the event, one of the most important of the year.

It may, one day, be an event where people might come to hear his music. First, his harvest song, then all the other pieces that would surely follow. Unless, of course, Nonno called him a fool.

Every family in town had a stake in the harvest being bountiful. They had turned out more devoutly ever since warnings had been posted on every bulletin board and read at every Cooperative meeting about a dreadful disease that was attacking vineyards in France. News that spurred a town-wide chorus of jangling rosaries and murmured prayers.

That had been five years ago, just before Pietro's seventeenth birthday. Since then, no disease had crossed the border, and people had begun to claim that they hadn't truly believed it could attack superior Piedmont vines. Still, even now, the church pews continued to see more activity for the harvest mass.

Soon, the church doors would open and release the congregation. People would speak in hush tones until they were out of earshot of the stone Saints, Cosimo and Damiano, who stood guard on either side of the church door. They would make their way to the piazza, where they would dance as though the most intense labor of the year did not still lie ahead.

From the bandstand, Pietro listened for them. He watched Nonno, issuing animated directives to the servers who scuttled between tables in their black pants and starched white shirts, setting out glasses and straightening chairs. The sounds of their movements had a hollow quality to them, which would change once the piazza was carpeted by people, as though the crowd absorbed a bit of the music they had come to hear.

Nonno hoisted himself back onto the bandstand; his leather-bound music book tucked under his left arm as it always was before a performance. "Hey, *ragazzo*. Are you set for tonight?"

Nonno's question was more of an instruction than something that warranted a direct answer. Instead, Pietro said, "I have something to tell you."

"Make it quick," Nonno said.

Pietro opened his mouth to tell his grandfather about how he'd composed a song, but words couldn't match the way he felt inside. He needed to play the music, not describe it, and of course, there wasn't time for that.

"They'll be here soon," Nonno urged, his voice brisk.

Pietro couldn't hurry, and he couldn't describe the song. He shook his head, no.

"Well, I have something to tell *you*," Nonno said. "Your cousin Giacomo is making his debut tonight. You'll swap out with him."

Pietro nodded to let his grandfather know he'd heard the instruction. Nonno squeezed his shoulder, then moved on to check in with Alfredo, who was warming up by blowing a tempo onto the mouthpiece of his trumpet.

At the end of the colonnade, the wooden doors of the church rasped open.

Nonno dropped back off the bandstand to direct a last-minute delivery of rabbit stew and to hurry the servers putting out jugs of water. He came back just as the tide of Sunday shoes seeped into the piazza and around the tables set for the communal meal.

A drumbeat called the crowd to attention and, after the mayor's animated promise that this year, the ample crops grown in the rich soil of the land around San Damiano d'Asti were blessed by the weather and the dedication of the people of this proud town, Nonno waved his hand for the music to begin.

Pietro's part on the clarinet was as natural as harvesting grapes from a vine. He listened for the band to settle into the opening notes and for the song to unite people under a singular purpose. The first couple got up to dance. The man held the woman's hand too high and guided her, a wide grin fixed on his face.

More joined in, and on the third song, Pietro's cousin edged through the dancers and waited expectantly at the edge of the bandstand steps, ready for his first performance in front of the entire town. Pietro clung to his clarinet and briefly considered ignoring his cousin, pretending he didn't see him there. Not only did he want to be worthy of a full evening of performance, he also did not want to walk past the gaggle of girls standing near the steps. *Dash you, Giacomo.* Knowing how important the night was to his cousin, Pietro set his instrument on a chair and felt his feet carry him past Nonno and down the steps.

He turned and listened for his cousin's clarinet, keeping good time with the music, until one of the girls slid herself between him and the edge of the bandstand.

"Want to dance?" He never danced—he played music. He wanted to tell the girl this, but he couldn't think how to say it. At twenty-two, he supposed it was about time a girl presented herself to him. Many friends his age had started families. He'd like that—being a father to children, that is. He'd given little thought to a wife.

"Come on!" Her words scampered above the hum of the piazza.

Pietro felt her hand on his shoulder, another on his side. She squeezed, guiding his movements. His feet had grown to the size of cellos, but somehow he was following her lead.

"I was afraid you'd play all night." She smelled of Marseilles soap, and her words tickled his cheek then echoed inside of his chest. The world began to jumble into a blur of limbs and noises—laughter, percussion, glasses clinking, and trombones until her hands gripped tighter. He tried to move anyway, show her that he was getting the hang of it, but she held firm.

"The song's over," she said, her voice breathy and smooth, reminding him of a honeybee. He turned left then right, trying to orient himself to the bandstand—he saw it, tall and important above the crowd, and he pushed his way through, forgetting to say anything to the girl. Not a goodbye, thank you for the dance, wait for me later, nothing. He almost fell up the stairs; it took him two tries to pick up his clarinet, then Nonno called the polka. Pietro lifted his clarinet to his lips. He missed an E flat and hoped Nonno didn't notice. He played the next few notes too quickly, then overshot as he slowed down. Eyes clamped against the chance of seeing the girl, which would distract him further, he tried to feel for the music to steady himself. He gave it one more try to find the pace, but it was as though he had never spent those hours and days and weeks practicing. His mouthpiece still firm between his lips and his eyes still closed against the crowd's reaction to the incomplete song, he stopped playing altogether.

♫♩♪

She dissipated like a shooting star after their dance. Pietro didn't know whether she had witnessed his broken polka. She was the first thing he thought of when he woke the next morning, her honeybee voice playing in his head as he made his way downstairs.

"Sit. The milk is on." Nonna greeted him in the kitchen. Pietro knew better—before he sat, he dipped his hands in the wash bucket and splashed his face. His grandmother whipped crumbs from a towel and handed it to him to dry. He sat next to his niece, Ida, at the long table that took up most of the room.

Ida had recently turned two and never hid her adoration for her *zio*. She stood up on the bench and handed him a half loaf of fresh bread. Pietro held it to his ear and tore off a chunk, a bliss of slight crackles, air pockets bursting, faint, but audible. He dipped it, squishing and swirling into the bowl of milk and coffee Nonna set in front of him.

Nonno sat at the head of the table, staring straight at Pietro. Hat pushed back, fingers crossed, his thumbs bristled his generous mustache. Stern was not a mood that often afflicted Nonno.

Auff! Nonno could douse his happiness later. Yes, Pietro had made a mess of the polka, but everything had sounded more melodious since he'd danced with the girl, and he was not ready to give it up. He tore off another piece of bread and swooped it into the bowl, recreating the dance. Another few twists, then he put it in his mouth and smiled at Nonno.

Nonno didn't smile back. Instead, he tapped his finger on the cover of his leather-bound music book. "Because sometimes things are etched so clearly as part of our lives, we forget younger people don't know how things are. We presume they'll find their path to what matters in life," he said.

The honeybee. *She* was the problem. *She* was the reason Pietro had messed up the song.

His finger no longer tapping, Nonno spread his hand flat on the book like he was about to swear on a bible in court. No doubt to declare that Pietro would not have music *and* the distraction of a girl.

Nonno probably had Pietro's destiny written in that book. Instead of music, it probably had pages and pages of plans—what Pietro should and should not do because ever since the day he'd declared Pietro would study music, Nonno had had a plan, turn for turn, and he'd never once mentioned a girl.

Pa walked in and sat without washing his hands. He launched into an assessment of what they still needed to do before returning to the vineyard in the morning. Nonno gave Pietro one last glare, then withdrew his hand from his book and turned his attention to Pa.

Pietro dipped his bread again, this time without rhythm. His grandmother grated the iron pan against the stove. Voices echoed, separate in tone and word, then merged in a distorted mess. Caterina began to drone on about the imminent arrival of her next child.

Pietro scraped a solid note on the tile floor with his boots. A moment ago, determined not to let his joy be shaken, now he wished Nonno would just get it over and done with and say what he was thinking. He stood, rustled his niece's hair, and left the room.

The entire family would spend the coming week in the brick house that housed just three or four of them in the growing season. They had begun early to pile the cart with the extra belongings, pots, and tools, leaving little room for Nonna and Caterina to sit for the five-kilometer exodus to the family vineyard. Pietro eagerly took the lead rope attached to the donkey's harness. It would distance him and Nonno, who would walk behind the cart with the rest of the family. Nonno had still said nothing to Pietro about his polka disaster.

When they arrived, tired but eager to prepare for the work ahead, Pietro helped unload, fed, and watered the donkey, then he collected his clarinet from the cart and walked back to where he'd left the upturned basket, the place where he'd found the ending to his song a week earlier. He wasn't so much avoiding Nonno as being diligent with his practice. Besides, if anything could deflect Nonno's sternness, it was Pietro's first-ever composition.

Like before, he played softly so the sound wouldn't carry. His thoughts began to sink away to let the music take their place when somewhere off to his right, the screech of an overworked engine interrupted his flow. If Pietro hadn't been up here on the hill, he'd have said the noise came from the engine of an automobile, but an automobile had no reason to come this way.

Last spring, a man from Asti had driven one of them to San Damiano. Pietro had turned out with the rest of them to gape at the new machine, but he hadn't shared in the communal awe for long. The way it suggested a dependable tempo then sputtered and whined in a mechanical frenzy disturbed him. When the thing made an almighty bang that sent people scuttling, Pietro made up his mind —it was certain not to travel far.

All that was up here were more vineyards like Pietro's and the occasional hazelnut farm. People relied on carts and donkeys to get here—a donkey was strong enough to cope with the constant slope, up or down, of the Piedmont hills, versatile enough to get around impossible corners.

Whatever the noise came from, the screech settled into a tense hum. It faded to the edge of earshot, allowing the chatters of swallows swooping in the sapphire sky to come back into focus and the sounds of unhurried preparations to tumble down from the courtyard.

Pietro picked the song back up from where he'd left off. If Nonno liked it, he might not only forget about Pietro's polka, he might even walk differently, the way he did after a particularly good performance. Not his normal steady pace that would not be rushed by anyone, but lighter, excited, and anticipatory.

He might skip routine, leave baskets unmended, stomping vats unscrubbed. He might summon the rest of the family, tell them not to rally the neighbors for the grape stomp, call Ma and Nonna from the kitchen where they were preparing the evening feast. He might sit them down and have them listen to Pietro's music, his hand outstretched in front of them so they'd know not to make a sound but to listen only to the song about the chores they should have been doing.

Pietro kept his eyes closed after the last note hung on the warmth of the late summer air, but instead of the peaceful thrill of his music, he heard the whine and sputter of that darn engine again. There was no doubt now. It *was* an automobile, and it had rounded the hill and was coming up the road. It was sure to pass his family's house, and from the hollering and excitement happening up there, people were abandoning work to run to the road to see it.

Why such a fuss? Didn't they hear how it struggled? Pietro lay his clarinet across his knees and waited for it to go by. But it didn't go by. It stopped and idled, right outside the gate if he had to guess. He heard creaking, then footsteps—someone had got out.

Pietro kept still so he could listen. He heard another set of footsteps, then voices in halting conversation that quickly rose to dispute—his father's voice angry—then the footsteps resumed, another creak as the people got back into the vehicle, and the thing choked on its way.

Pietro left the basket in the middle of the row. He hugged the instrument to his side and walked up the hill. Whatever the visitors had come for, they'd caused a commotion. Pa was shouting, Nonno too—Nonno never shouted. Pietro started to run, trying to hear the turmoil in the courtyard over the dash of his own footsteps.

He stopped at the top, waiting for his lungs to loosen their grip and stop whistling so he could make sense of the words his father was throwing at his grandfather—*can't*—*must*—*money*.

"*Basta*! Enough!" Nonno's voice was deeper when he shouted, powerful. Like a singer's, only Pietro had never heard him sing.

"Give us a day and a half. We can harvest by Wednesday." Pa held his palms out to emphasize his words, which didn't make sense because the harvest didn't start until Friday.

"We've seen the warnings. We knew this day might come," Nonno said.

Pa threw his hands up above his head. "Not right before harvest, we didn't."

"The disease stops here." Nonno's voice was adamant.

The disease? The one they'd read about in the newspapers, and the one they'd talked about at Cooperative meetings? The one that came on the backs of lice so tiny you could barely see them, yet they were big enough to devour the roots of vineyard after vineyard in France?

The experts from the government ministry had long warned that Piedmont could be the entry point to Italy. The local growers had vowed it would be the endpoint, too. In their endless meetings and over countless glasses of Barbera and Amaro at the bar, they had decided they would pull all vines at the first sign of disease, choke it before it had a chance to march on to Lombardy or Liguria.

They had discussed it, clinked glasses over it, but none had never believed it'd happen. It was just theoretical, like planning to cope with a flood when you live on top of the hill or having a backup song to get people dancing if they didn't dance to the polka, but hilltops couldn't flood, and people couldn't *not* dance to the polka.

"We can't do without the income," Pa should not be pleading. Nonno was right if it was the disease they were talking about. They had no choice.

"What if the grapes are diseased?" Nonno stood firm. "What if the delay gives it time to spread to the next hill and the next? No. However, as much as this pains us, we must do what is right. We must burn the vines. Cleanse and begin again." There was no doubt in Nonno's tone. He always stood on the side of what was right; Pa had no business questioning him. "We'll round up all the hands we can find and begin pulling right away."

♫ 𝄐 ♪

Pietro took his clarinet apart and wiped each piece with the grey cloth he kept in the case before setting the pieces in their slots. He put the lid down and slid the stiff latch closed, knowing it would be harder to open than it ever was to close. Then he joined the group forming by the old pear tree, making sure he kept his back to the vines because, for the time being, he didn't want to see them.

His brother Nunzio and Pa were already stacking shovels, pitchforks, a hoe, and pickax—any tool they could muster against the old tree where Pietro might have played his music, right after the harvest.

The Sacco family from the hazelnut farm across the lane joined the group, answering Nonno's summons for help. Their son's name was also Pietro. He was the same age, taller than Pietro—though most people were, with darker hair, also like most people. At primary school, they'd called him by his last name, Sacco, and the name had stuck.

Nonno set his boot on the wooden bench and nodded in approval at the group that had gathered.

"The disease is coming. Phylloxera, they call it," he explained, as though they hadn't heard the term a thousand times. There'd be no grapes this year. No stomp, no reason to scrub the vats.

Nonno pushed his hat back on his head and outlined his plan. Most of the men were to dig the plants; runners would drag them up the hill to the fire—Nonno spoke in the same calm way he did if he was talking to the band before a performance, running through the order of scores, a waltz before a mazurka. The same warmth he'd exude to encourage tubas to bellow, trumpets to care.

As he spoke about the fire that would mark the end of the disease, he pointed to the open area between the vats and the courtyard entrance, as far away from trees as possible. Pa was already there, layering kindling and straw in the shape of a giant bird's nest. As angry as he had seemed, he was building a fire too big to fathom.

From the vantage point of the courtyard, the hills rolled like the rise and fall of a tempo, but the rows of vines didn't look quite straight like they had minutes ago when Pietro had sat on the basket.

Two songs, one jolly, one ominous, jarred in his head. One led back to the moment before the automobile strained up the hill when the harvest was certain to happen, and Pietro would play his song, the other to a place where it was all a big mistake. They'd got it wrong. Nothing felt right. Pietro tried to quell one of the tunes or at least pull their discordance together, but they didn't fit.

Nunzio dashed a shovel against the hard-packed ground. Figures, he'd chosen the strongest shovel. He turned it up and over, inspecting it, then walked away, humming a tune so off-key Pietro neither knew what it was intended to be nor did he want to listen long enough to find out.

"Pietro," Nonno said. "Were you listening? Pick a row, start from the bottom, and work your way up."

Nonno held a fork out to him.

"But are we sure?" Pietro asked before he realized he intended to ask.

"Sure of what? To start from the bottom? Yes. By the time we're tired, we'll already be at the top of the hill," Nonno said.

"I mean, who were those men? How can we be sure they spoke the truth?"

"They were from the Ministry, Pietro. They brought a letter with an official seal."

"What if they weren't from the Ministry at all?"

Nonno shook his head. "Doing the right thing isn't always the same as doing what we want. That's the way it is." He said it as a statement, allowing no room for further discussion.

Pietro took the fork and walked down the row where he'd been sitting on his basket. He passed Nunzio straining in the next row over. "Graaaagh!" His brother had hold of a vine and was shaking it furiously.

"We're supposed to start at the bottom," Pietro said.

"What difference does it make? You think this plant wouldn't get pulled in the end?"

Nunzio jumped onto the back of the shovel, trying to drive it into the earth. All he managed was another gash in the ground, then another, flicking the dirt like dust that mattered to nobody. After a few gouges, he grabbed the vine again with both hands, mid-stem, and yanked. The leaves and grapes shook in a rift more frenzied than Pietro had ever heard, even in the fiercest winds. Not a sound vines were supposed to make.

Next, he tried digging and pulling at the same time, limbs uncoordinated but determined in his attack, yet still, the vine remained upright, its arms stretched and holding fast to its neighbor.

"Trim the branches first," Pietro said.

"I'll get the bugger out," his brother stated.

From the courtyard, Pietro heard a match being struck. He wasn't near enough to hear the flare as it devoured its sulfur head, but he did hear a hum as the straw breathed in the heat, then the first crackles as the new fire began to feast on the kindling.

"He can't be lighting a fire already!" It just wasn't right.

"It'll take a strong one to burn fresh vines," Nunzio said, his tone smug. He seemed to be enjoying himself.

Despite the fact he was now building a fire, Pa didn't want to be doing this. Yet Nonno said it was right to do it. Pietro couldn't think of another time he'd known Nonno to be wrong. But whatever the decision or who wanted what, nobody was starting in the right place.

Pietro walked to where he'd played his song not an hour ago, leaving his brother to fight the ill-fated vine. The basket was still there. He ought to move it in case anyone else came down this way to rip the plants from the soil. Since before Pietro was born, their roots swathed by the same substance in the summer heat and winter chill year after year after year. Pietro sat down.

He'd left his clarinet in its case on the bench in the courtyard. He held his fingers in the air where the keys should be and pretended to play a silent run-through of his song, and of the harvest it should be singing. He got to the part where the grapes dripped from baskets, where the women plucked fruit nimbly from stems and rained them into the stomping vats, a circle of mothers and grandmothers around them, urging the children on their laps—poorly, weakened by ailments of the chest—to inhale the once-a-year chance for the healing grape-must release into the air and into their lungs to heal all.

But today was not a day of healing.

Pietro wanted to stop the song that played only in his head—what was the point now? But this part of the score might bring him solace, inspired as it was by his niece, Ida, as the first child lifted into a vat. He would lift her himself—swing her in the air, and she'd chuckle in excitement and a little fear, then he'd lean his ear to the rim of the vat and listen as her tiny feet popped the fruit. This part of the song signified hope, it was about handing the torch forward, and that hope carried him through to the grand finale.

The end.

The bit where people were supposed to clap—nobody clapped. Of course, they didn't. He had played the music in his head, not out loud for anyone to hear. It hadn't made him feel any better about what was going on. Whether he liked it or not, he needed to do what Nonno had told him to do. He *always* did what Nonno told him to do, *maledizione*.

At least before he began digging, he would separate the plants from each other, cut through their firm grip.

He left his fork there and went up to look for some shears. He found Nonno talking to Sacco's father.

"But what's going to happen next? No grapes, no harvest?" Pietro interrupted.

"We plant over," Nonno said as though it were obvious.

"In the same place? The plants will get sick again."

"Yes, the same place. Only this time, we graft. The sickness came from America, yet the cure is to graft new plants onto American roots. They gave us the disease, then they sold us a cure. It might sound like a bad business deal, *ragazzo*, but if you think about the science, it's quite something."

Sure, what Nonno said would be impressive, if only it didn't apply to their vines.

"There'll be no *vendemmia*, no celebration either."

"There's always something to celebrate in this life."

Nonno would not change his mind. Pietro took the shears Nonno had wiped clean and set out on the table earlier when everyone was preparing for the harvest, not destruction. He headed back down the hill.

♪♫♪

Nunzio had managed to pull the vine over, but not entirely out. It lay at an awkward angle, a shoot hanging down to the ground, partly held by its neighbors on either side.

"I got it," he announced, as though Pietro hadn't noticed.

Pietro said nothing and carried on walking.

"Start at the bottom, then, shall we, no?" Nunzio left the defeated vine and trailed after Pietro.

As if this wasn't hard enough, Pietro would have to work where he could see and hear his brother's every huff and strain as he laid claim to the plants' demise.

He picked up the fork he'd left near the basket and carried on to the end. He began on the right side, so, at least, his back was to Nunzio. He opened the shears and set them so a shoot fitted snuggly in the V of the blades. The grapes hung there trustingly.

A row over, Nunzio launched a new attack, making guttural noises as he thrust the shovel against the hard soil.

Pietro closed the shears' blades, and the shoot fell, the grapes hitting the ground with a soft thud.

Pietro could hear the ferocity of the new fire. A satisfied whistle and cackle as it bit into a chunk of fresh wood. The sound did not merit applause.

[11]

A bell tolled. *For death*, Pietro thought, even though he knew it signified lunchtime. The women would carry baskets of bread, cheese, and salami, jugs of last year's wine to the workers, even though they were destroying instead of gathering.

He could not do this. He dropped the shears on the ground and jumped over the fence at the end of the vineyard, into next door's hazelnut grove.

As kids, he and Sacco had a favorite spot where, because of the curve of the hill, they could hear sounds from opposite hillsides, but not from Pietro's family's vineyard. They'd meet there to escape when the chores were scarce, and big brothers found distraction by picking on smaller ones.

Pietro found the spot and sat against the tree. Sounds began to reach him from across the valley, from other vineyards. Burning. Voices—not the satisfied banter he should be hearing of pickers and stompers, but the nervous, determined voices of people collectively facing an unprecedented, dreaded situation. The situation that was never supposed to actually happen, and Pietro could think of nothing he could do to stop it.

♫𝄞♪

He lay with arms around his head, muffling his ears. He'd been sitting here a different afternoon—the first time he remembered talk of America, the country that had now sent death.

He'd been just a boy then, alone, conjuring happy make-believe of playing the clarinet to the grapes to make them grow, holding an invisible instrument to his mouth and nodding his head in time with the imaginary tune, years before he'd written a real one.

He hadn't heard Sacco coming until he was almost beside him. He hadn't been sure right away that Sacco had noticed him pretending like he was still five years old because instead of poking fun at him, Sacco announced in an important tone that he had something to show. "It's from the New World," he said.

Pietro fixated on the ground to see if it looked old, and Sacco sensed his confusion. "The New World is a place called America. It's a massive country where everyone's rich. Only fools don't know that." Pietro knew about America but remembered no word about it being new.

Sacco then produced his prize—a letter from his big brother, who had left home almost a year earlier. He smoothed the crumpled sheet that had been torn from a book.

"Dear Mamma and Pa," he began, his tone mechanical, flattened by the strain of reading. "I am in good health. I work at the docks. I rent a bed from a family from Veneto, but the food is good enough. Not as good as yours, Ma. I hope you are all well. Your son, Alessandro."

"That's it?" Pietro asked. It didn't seem like much of a letter.

Sacco yanked the letter to his chest. "He sent a photograph, too. Ever seen one of those?" he asked.

Pietro slapped a mosquito on his arm instead of answering. He made a big show of scraping up the squashed insect with a leaf and rubbing a dot of blood into his skin rather than admitting he'd never seen one.

"I didn't think so. You can have a quick look. Don't look for too long, though. It fades if you do," Sacco said. He crossed his legs in the dusty soil, set the envelope on his knee reverently. He pulled out the photograph like he was picking up a rare butterfly by its wing, turned it around, and gently set it on his other knee, leaning over so he could see it, too.

Pietro stared, mouth agape, at the group of men perfectly reproduced in miniature grays and blacks. A perfect image, like real people, only on a tiny piece of paper.

"It's a band!"

"Not just *a* band, it's *his* band."

"In the letter—he didn't say."

"That's him. He plays the drum."

Pietro recognized Sacco's brother standing to the right of what looked like the bandmaster, his rank suggested by his unbuttoned jacket. Each of the other men wore a uniform and flat hat with a short front rim topped by some kind of medallion. They had to be important. Sacco's brother looked stern, his hands clasped behind his back, at attention, and his drum on the ground in front of him, its harness still over his jacket. He looked a lot younger than the others, perhaps because he didn't have a mustache.

"You've looked at it long enough. I'm going now." Sacco put the photograph back into the envelope with the same amount of care he had used to take it out and scrambled to his feet.

"What were you doing when I got here, anyway?" he asked.

"Nothing!"

"You were pretending to be a musician. Look at me! I'm pretending to fly!" Sacco flapped his arms and zig-zagged between the trees. As he turned, the photograph fell from the envelope. It fluttered down to land in the dirt. Pietro leaped to pick it up.

"Sacco, come back!" he shouted.

"I'm flying!" Sacco shouted back.

He had not come back, and Pietro had not run after him. He'd sat there, looking at the photograph for a long time. He remembered Sacco's brother as quite ordinary, but after he moved away, his father spoke of him as though he was some kind of hero, his mother lamented his absence to Ma and Nonna.

Pietro had never given the photograph back, not even knowing the hours Sacco had spent looking for it. It was the only thing he'd ever taken; he'd soon learned better. His life of low morals had ended at age eight. Or perhaps it hadn't. Right now, he was skipping out on helping, and that was far from admirable.

So deep in the memory, it startled him when someone tugged at his arm. Of course, it was Sacco.

"I knew I'd find you here. You need to come quick."

"What? Why?" Sacco's clothes smelled of smoke.

"Come! It's your Nonno."

"Is he upset I'm not helping?" Even as he said the words, he knew from Sacco's tone that it was more than this.

"Just come."

Pietro followed Sacco through the hazelnut trees then across into the vineyard.

When they reached the courtyard, nobody was working. They stood in a huddle outside the kitchen door to the family home. Pietro stopped to stand with them, but one of the men pushed him forward.

"You need to go in."

He did as he was told. Inside, Nonno was lying on the bench beneath the kitchen window. Pa sat on a chair pulled up beside him, Nonna stood behind Pa chanting a prayer, Ma's hand clasped in hers. Pietro's sister Caterina noticed Pietro and pulled him forward.

"Here he is," she said, as though everyone had been waiting for him.

They jostled Pietro through. Pa stood and shoved him into the chair.

Nonno looked odd. One side of his face pulled down like wax too near the flame.

"Tell your grandfather you're here," Pa said.

Pietro didn't tell him—he didn't want to be here, but Nonno must have heard because he lifted his right hand.

"Go on, take it," Pa said.

Pietro put his palm to Nonno's palm, felt Nonno's fingers curl around his. His mouth, lopsided, began to move.

"Till the vines grow back, you travel. Find a new band, be an apprentice." His voice stretched from its normal soft but staunch linen to a net of sorts that let tones slip through and disappear. His words sounded like a finale.

"Where's the doctor? Why isn't the doctor here?" Pietro demanded. He could run for him—someone should—Nonno needed help *now*.

"He's on his way," Pa said.

'On his way' wasn't good enough—they should have found him help sooner. They should have done something. "Why isn't anyone helping him?" Pietro's voice cracked.

"Travel, learn." It took Nonno good effort to speak. "Heed the lessons I taught you, but I made a mistake, a lesson I failed to share." A tremble in his voice, "You can . . ."

Pietro waited for Nonno to finish saying his sentence. Nobody around them moved either. A full minute passed. A minute of willpower—*you'll sit up, Nonno. It's just a turn. A migraine—Ma had one once. This is all it is. You'll be fine. You have to be.*

Out loud, Pietro said, "I wrote a song."

There was a shuffling at the door. The doctor was here at last.

Pietro stood up to make way and edged his way to the bottom of the bed. They should have called the doctor sooner. They shouldn't have let this happen.

He turned and pushed his way past his brother and out of the room. He ignored the people still lingering in the courtyard.

The darn clarinet case wouldn't open. He tried to force it, but his hands were shaking. He dropped the case, knelt on the ground, and tried to open it again, forcing his breath to calm. He had to play. Nonno had to hear it.

At last, the latch clicked. Pietro dropped the lower joint twice and the mouthpiece once, then he had it together. He marched back to the kitchen. The doctor was talking. Something about it being too hard to get Nonno to town. Everyone in the room focused on the doctor. The only person who seemed to notice Pietro was Nonno. Over his breathing, which had changed, staccato almost, Pietro heard Nonno whisper the words, "Play it."

He lifted the clarinet to his mouth. Grains of dust picked up from where he dropped the clarinet scratched his lips. He rubbed them off, then prepared once more to play.

"Listen! Everyone listen, Pietro's going to play," Ma shushed everyone.

"But doctor, we can harness up the cart. We can make it."

"Shush." Ma said again.

Murmurs, words, shuffling—Pietro couldn't play. This wasn't how he'd intended to do it. He'd meant to play it for Nonno alone before anyone else. He'd come back later when they stopped gawking and left poor Nonno alone, when he could pull himself together and stop his hands from shaking.

Someone had left a shovel on the ground. They had probably dropped it when Nonno collapsed. Pietro picked it up, went straight to the nearest vine, and thrust its blade into the ground.

He did not count the vines he dug up. Soon Sacco and his father joined him and started to help without saying a word. Every so often, one of them set his shovel down to drag two plants at a time to the pyre.

Pietro didn't acknowledge their presence, and he did not slow when Pa came up beside him.

"*Figlio*, stop digging." Pietro carried on without pause. "He's gone. Stop now."

Pietro stopped, held his sleeve against his brow, then a moment later, he thrust the blade of the shovel harder still into the ground.

"It can wait, given what's happened. Come inside." Pietro paid no attention. Pa raised his voice, "Why are you doing this?"

Pietro pushed the handle hard until he was bent at the waist. "If I'd been doing it earlier, Nonno wouldn't have had to. He could've rested. I could have done his share. He didn't have to do it."

"Your grandfather was a proud man. You think he'd have sat this one out?"

"He might've."

"It's not your fault," Pa said.

Pietro tugged at the plant. He snapped the limbs that clasped those of the next plant and ripped fresh leaves from their stalks.

Pa stood watching for a few moments, then he, too, picked up a shovel and began to dig.

THREE

Bussolengo, Italy

Assunta had reconciled her heart to the fact that Nandy had married another woman in America. Mary, her name was. She'd even borne his child—may they both rest in peace. She would not remain bitter about it. He'd been far from home, alone, and he'd already paid the worst price by losing them both.

What she was having a harder time accepting was how he'd let Beatrice dig her seductive claws into him when he had returned to Italy.

"I would have come straight to you," he'd said. "But I was too embarrassed. I didn't know how to tell you about Mary."

They could put this all behind them soon. By the end of the day, she and Nandy would be married as they'd intended eight years earlier, and they would travel a world away from the clutches of Beatrice.

Assunta's wedding dress was an elegant yellow, not bright like a sunflower, more like a rose that grew on a balcony overlooking the piazza in Verona.

Mamma had surprised her with the fabric the same day Nandy had shown up to propose. "Pretty, isn't it?" she'd asked. "I came across it at the market one time when your father was still alive. It's been tucked hidden away all this time."

Mamma had spent the ensuing weeks industriously planning and incessantly cleaning, appearing wholly confident that Assunta's life had always meant to take this direction, despite Papà's decree. Mamma even had the style of Assunta's dress decided, and being so sure of her plan, she had very nearly forgotten to take Assunta to the dressmakers with her.

"You always look out for me," Assunta had told her. "I don't know what I'll do without you."

"You'll do just fine, that's how you'll do" Mamma had taken the fabric from the dressmaker's hands and adjusted the folds. "Wider pleats, this wide, all the way down the front to the hem."

Assunta would be eternally grateful to her mother, but for all the love in the world—and she'd never break her mother's heart by telling her this—it was high time she started to make decisions for herself.

She planned to start small. She might decide to have morning coffee *before* making the beds and sweeping the floor. It'd be up to her whether they had pasta or rice or minestra on what day of the week. And to think, no more mornings spent kneading the dough to make gnocchi for her brother, Vito, to sell in his shop. Perhaps she'd make them to sell elsewhere, and if she did, it would not be when and how her brother decided. She'd make sure her gnocchi looked as good as they tasted, and she wouldn't use the plain tubs her brother used. She'd choose wooden or copper bowls, oval like the gnocchi themselves, and worthy in their own right of being on show.

She'd sell her homemade tagliatelle, and once a week, she'd make pasta *al forno* and serve it hot mid-morning, none of which Vito had agreed to do. Then again, she barely made a lira on the work she did for him, so it was probably just as well.

Yes, this marriage and the journey ahead of them was the launch of a new and everlasting chapter, one where she would run the home, care for her husband, for their children. The final piece of the puzzle that was this life.

"Here, they're real silk," Mamma held up a garland of white flowers. "To pin to your veil. They can't blemish. That's my wish for you, a marriage with no blemish."

Mamma's intention might have been to ward off troubles. Still, the only blemish—the enormous blemish that everyone had so far avoided talking about these past weeks would be the wife and the girlfriend Nandy had had since he'd first proposed to Assunta.

"I couldn't be happier." Even to Assunta, her words sounded forced. "With the flowers, I mean, not—" Not what? His women? She wouldn't say that out loud.

"Crying shame, your father, not being here." Mamma had either taken Assunta's hesitation as a moment of sorrow or was deliberately redirecting the subject.

Assunta resisted the urge to set her straight and point out that if Papà *had* been here, she wouldn't be marrying Nandy at all, but there was little point opening that old wound today.

Despite her intention, Assunta spent the entire walk to church thinking about how, if Papà had let them marry eight years ago, Nandy would never have ended up with another wife and girlfriend in the first place. And following on from that thought, she reminded herself that she had forgiven him, and therefore those two women had no business being on her mind today. And yet they were.

Vito was waiting for them outside the church door, looking dashing though a little uncomfortable in a silk topper.

"Papà would have been proud to walk you down the aisle," Mamma said.

"He wouldn't be walking me to Nandy, though, would he?" Assunta said without thinking. There, she'd blown it. "Sorry," she murmured.

If Mamma reacted to the paltry apology, Assunta didn't see because her brother pulled her in for a swift kiss on both cheeks.

"You look beautiful." Vito let go of Assunta just in time for her to glimpse Mamma pressing her handkerchief to her nose with uncharacteristic drama and disappear into the church.

"She's taking this hard," Vito said, tilting his chin after Mamma.

Assunta lifted her veil, careful not to dislodge the silk flowers.

"Is Nandy here?" Assunta asked.

"I can't see around corners, but as he's the groom, I would presume so. Another thing I can't see around the corner is your future. It bothers me."

"I can tell you the future—we're getting married, and we're going to live happily ever after." Vito had chosen a fine time to cast his doubts. Well, if everyone intended to focus on what would hinder rather than nurture this marriage, she might as well not hold back. "Did Beatrice show up? Is she in there?"

"She wouldn't dare, and you shouldn't think of her. Not today, not ever again. As for your future, I have no doubt you'll make a perfect home and a happy husband. It's where you're going that worries us all."

America had always been the worry. Papà hadn't doubted Nandy's character so much as his destination. "We're not the first to go. Besides, Nandy can provide well for us in America."

"I'm sure he can. Things will work out for you, I know it."

Far from helping, her brother's sudden change in tone and certainty unsettled her. Now *she* felt uncertain again. She should send Vito inside the church, have him explain that she needed a bit more time to think about this marriage, not pulling out necessarily, just needing a bit of time alone. But knowing her brother, he would do it his way. He'd call out their other siblings, Mamma too, and make everyone else wait in the pews while they decided her fate as a family.

No, she'd got herself into this. Nandy couldn't be blamed for straying; he'd been a free man. Now Assunta needed to focus on how this was *her* time, and Nandy had always been the right man for her.

The organist switched to play the Wedding March. Assunta did not move.

"Our home will be joyous with the sound of children," she told Vito.

"We are supposed to walk, not talk when the music starts," Vito said.

Assunta felt the tug of his arm on hers but held still. This *was* meant to be. It was time to take her place at Nandy's side, the conclusion of a long path to a fulfilled adulthood.

"You want to leave?" Vito asked.

"I'm okay," she said, wishing she meant it.

She didn't look up to see if Nandy was there, nor to either side and into the faces of the congregation.

At the top of the aisle, she kept her eyes firmly on the stone floor. If Mamma was crying, Assunta would cry, too. If Mamma were stoic, Assunta would cry anyway because Mamma would be putting a brave face on the fact that this marriage meant a ticket to a life a world away.

She saw Nandy's feet first. They were big. She should have checked them.

She was grateful for the veil that hid her smile at the memory of just a few months ago after Nandy had turned back up, but before he drummed up the courage to speak to her, Assunta had asked Mamma to find her another man to marry. One who hadn't returned from his world travels, a widower to boot, and proceeded to walk out with another—Beatrice of all people—with not so much as a courtesy call to Assunta. She'd specified that the new version of husband Mamma was to find should not have smelly feet, nor a brood of ready-made children like the man her aunt had married.

Assunta kept her eyes down as Vito kissed her cheek. She clung tighter to his arm, but he pulled her fingers away from his sleeve. There was a moment of shuffling and silence, then Assunta let her brother go.

She knelt next to Nandy, and without greeting or welcome, the priest began his ritual. Someone in the congregation coughed, Assunta stiffened. Was this someone clearing their throat to speak, to call out that she couldn't, after all, have him? Nobody spoke. The priest carried on.

Someone sneezed. A sneeze didn't mean the start of an objection, but still, it made Assunta want to turn and look. She wouldn't put it past Beatrice to show up. Or for someone else to say it was all a big mistake, that he was still married, that his other wife had not died after all. Assunta clasped her hands tight through the liturgies and rites, her white gloves bunching around the fingers. Then the priest asked if anyone knew any reason why the two people standing before him should not be joined in holy matrimony—Assunta was surely going to choke—but the priest was talking again. Did that mean nobody had spoken? He was talking about man and wife—they were truly married.

She turned to look at Nandy for the first time today. Kneeling, they were equal height, the extra few inches he had on her must be in the length of his legs. His profile was important, his brown-black mustache freshly oiled, chin jutting forward slightly, clearly focused on the solemnity of the service. If she thought hard enough, perhaps she could make him turn and look at her, but he kept his gaze firmly on the altar. He was taking this so seriously, reverent in the face of their future—a comforting sign.

They stood up and were permitted to kiss. At last, Nandy turned, his eyes like something that would melt solid bronze. He took her in his arms, turned her, and bent her backward so she'd have toppled to the ground if he hadn't held her so tightly, and he kissed her like there was nobody watching.

FOUR

San Damiano d'Asti

After a paltry excuse for a night's sleep, Pietro walked past the bowl of milk Ma held out to him in the kitchen and past his grandfather's feet, covered by a brown blanket, waiting to be loaded onto the cart outside and taken to town.

After dusk last night, when the ground became a blackened mat of shadows, they had gone indoors where Pa announced that the women would take Nonno's body back to town at dawn and make arrangements. They should ask the priest to hold off on the funeral until the men got back. They were all to stay and finish digging and burning the vines—Nonno would have wanted it.

Pietro carried as many tools as he could out of the storage room, only briefly wondering who had thought to put them away last night. At the end of a partially dug trellis, he drove the shovel into the ground with all his weight then pulled it back out. He did the same further around the plant to cut through all the roots, a technique they'd perfected the night before. It didn't matter what it sounded like. He just had to get the job done.

He didn't look up when the cart took Nonno away.

The other men came to help dig, and by mid-morning, they'd finished. Pa locked up the house, Nunzio piled the rest of the belongings in the handcart, Pietro collected the hens in a cage without talking to them to quell their screeched protests.

The fire still crackled contentedly as they set off, satiated by its feast.

The town's band, Nonno's band, was already milling in the courtyard when they got to the family home. They had probably been there all day. They tossed condolences and shoulder pats to Pietro and the others.

Pietro wanted them gone. He wanted to find Nonno at the door, waiting for him. He would apologize and tell him he'd never question a decision again. He would listen because surely, Nonno would remind him why it was essential to know the difference between right and wrong. *Just be alive.*

He stopped at the doorway. They had dressed Nonno in his finest suit, the same one he wore for all special performances. His hands were crossed on his chest, clutching an emerald rosary.

Whispers of conversation tapered off. Only Nonna's cries continued, the air loaded with anticipation. People clustered around Pietro. He spent every waking day with Nonno. Everyone knew that. At the vineyard, with the livestock. If Nonno came down to help Pa with the land share, Pietro came with him. Most importantly, they were together for every rehearsal, performance, preparation, and discussion that had anything to do with the band. Nonno had taught Pietro everything he knew about music.

Were they waiting to see what he'd do? He didn't know what to do. He didn't even know what he felt. It didn't look like Nonno. Nonno had bold cheeks, full of breath to power his clarinet. And what had happened to his nostrils?

Pietro found no tears to match Ma, no wail to match Nonna. The world sounded like a dull, flat, empty drone. The body laid out a poor imitation of his grandfather.

The funeral director appeared in the kitchen doorway, chewing something. "I see we're all here now." He brushed off his hands, swallowed whatever food he'd helped himself to in the kitchen, and called the rest of his men and the priest.

The band members inched their way around Pietro into the room and stood, heads dipped, their backs to the walls. The priest began reciting.

Nonna jangled a rosary over her husband's colorless face and wailed, *"Pace eterno! Pace eterno!"*

The lid was placed, nails hammered sharply. Nonno's last song. The band hoisted the casket onto their shoulders, giving the impression they did this every day.

In the church, Pietro sat apart from the other men, envying the women who sat at the rear in their own section. Veiled. Nobody had to see if they cried or if they did not. The priest's deep voice filtered through thin wisps of incense smoke.

After the service, light filtered through the stained-glass windows dousing heads in red-orange-yellow benediction as the church emptied for the second time in less than a week, their mood this time in total contrast to the harvest blessing. Pietro wondered if Cosimo and Damiano could hear the depth of his pain, the loss he felt.

What could life possibly sound like when Nonno was not going to be part of it? Even footsteps sounded foreign on the ancient cobbles. Slow and theatrical. Pa and his brother flanked the diminutive figure of Nonna, propping her up. The rest of the family moved as a group behind them, pulling each other close. Nunzio firmly in the huddle.

Nearly the entire town followed down the main street, watched by empty windows and plastered buildings. They were waved on by the flags of Piedmont and Italy outside the local municipal building. Past the bar where Pietro had spied on the band's rehearsal plans. Across the piazza, past the cooperative where Pietro had often delivered their grapes, months later collected wine.

The priest finished his delivery of rites at the graveside, and the congregation trickled away, leaving colorful flowers standing in for love. Workers sealed the tomb.

It was not over. It could not be over. Pietro wasn't ready.

Alfredo, the band's trumpeter, hadn't followed the departing group. He stood in private mourning, then he joined Pietro and Sacco, who stood stubbornly behind Pietro's left shoulder. Alfredo handed Pietro Nonno's clarinet. "He said you were to have it."

It felt like a contagion, not a legacy in a black leather case.

"I can't take it," Pietro held his palms up to reinforce his words.

"It was what he wanted. Yours has seen better days. He wanted to pass it on to you."

Alfredo patted Pietro's hand, which now held the case, then he left.

"So sorry, *amico*," Sacco said.

"I should have been helping," Pietro's voice was barely louder than a whisper.

"It wouldn't have changed things. He was going to dig whether you were or not."

Pietro didn't want to hear logic right now. All he wanted to hear was that there had been a terrible mistake, that this wasn't happening at all. And yet the swallows carried on snatching their supper of mosquitoes. People were leaving, Sacco was trying to comfort him. "I should have told him to wait it out. I should have done his work for him."

"He would have listened?" Sacco asked.

Pietro turned to face him. "You have new boots. Going far?"

"Sure am. I was going to tell you. Remember my brother? I'm going out to join him. I'm going to America."

"I've heard that before." Sacco threatened to leave twice, if not three times a year.

"I'm going this time. I have a ticket. Come with me. What is there for you here?"

They turned to watch the rear end of the funeral procession rounding the corner toward the exit, the people at the back taking the event less seriously. Someone said something that sent laughter into the air. Pietro picked up a stone and threw it, hoping to hit someone, but it fell short.

Pietro thought about the photograph of Sacco's brother in his band uniform. "What is there for me in America?"

"Fame. Fortune. Whatever you want."

"Then that is what I wish you, my friend."

Back in the courtyard, the band was getting their instruments ready to entertain the mourners. Ma was herding women to place offerings of food on the table. Pietro's sisters were pulling up chairs and setting places. Some children kicked a football; the men poured wine.

The chatter of people reminded Pietro of the mothers and grandmothers gathered around the stomping vats. As though something was being created, not lost.

Pietro still clutched Nonno's clarinet. Should he play or join the rest of the family on the side of the mourners? Nonno would have told him what to do. Nonno always told him what to do.

Matches were struck to light candles against the dusk. Lanterns murmured. A goat was getting a late milking in the stable, the hens hummed and clucked, venturing as near as they dared to the table. Life was going to carry on, even without Nonno.

Pietro joined neither family nor the band. He crossed the courtyard, past the door to the room where the casket had been just hours ago, went halfway up the stone staircase, and sat, clarinet on his knees.

He'd sat on this same staircase so many years ago, just a boy. It was where it had all started. The day he'd followed Nonno from church to the bar in the piazza, slapping each column along the way, the day he'd heard the news, the band was going to rehearse at their house. At school the next day, too excited to sit still, he'd slipped through the gate at recess, half ran across the piazza, and he'd come here, halfway up on the cold, worn step.

A dumb kid he'd been, he'd thought there could be nothing wrong with sitting here instead of going to school. He went willingly to school each day, and therefore he could willingly *not* stay in school just this once. Only the nuns hadn't seen it his way, and Pa had been livid. The gravity of his mistake had hummed in Pietro's ears as Nonno and Pa spoke angrily about his misdemeanor. It was not unlike how they had argued about whether to follow orders and pull the vines, fragments of charged sentences between Pa and Nonno curling around the wall, ushering up to him like a gelid breeze.

Now, the snap of words, the confusion, death—it was all too much. Pietro clutched his arms across his chest and dug his fingers into his sides. *Stop!* He willed. *Stop. Stop stopstopstop!* He wanted to be a boy again. He wanted things to sound the way they did before.

The band was nearly ready, despite missing Nonno and Pietro's clarinets. The performance would be imbalanced. Pietro went down to the bottom of the staircase, still held the clarinet case in his hand. He could watch and listen; it promised to be a moving tribute. The courtyard thrummed peacefully.

A small hand slipped into his—his niece, Ida. They stood, hands holding. Ma and Nonna fussed around the table. Nunzio set out jugs of wine. Pa carried hay into the barn, children played. Of course, the livestock would still need to be fed; the children would want to be children.

"*Zio*, what are we doing?" Ida asked.

"I don't know. I really don't know." Ida let go of his hand and ran to join the other children.

Alfredo came over. "Can you play? We need a clarinet."

Obediently, Pietro took his place and slipped his finger beneath the clasp. It opened effortlessly with a tck sound. This was Nonno's case, not his. He should go and get his own. Nonno should have Nonno's case. Nonno should be in charge.

"Almost ready," Alfredo said.

The flair of the bell was smooth against his hand, the bumps of the keys cool. He wanted to go and get his clarinet, but his hands pulled the parts of the instrument together against his will. Lower joint to bell, upper joint to lower joint, barrel, and mouthpiece.

Pietro had grown up with this band. He knew them so well he could identify every musician by their preparations without looking. Carlo should be in a dither as though only seconds remained till they played. Alfredo should be blowing into his trumpet. Davide should be clonking his trombone against the ground, himself, and others, Stefano sighing and tapping a finger against his drum.

Some, now, were silent. Others fiddled with scores or instruments. They were pretending to be getting ready when Pietro knew they already were. They were appeasing him—pitying him. His fingers began to shake. The band in the photograph he'd never given back to Sacco wouldn't have pretended. They were serious, professional. They wore uniforms with shiny buttons and flat hats. They all looked at the camera.

None were distracted.

He swallowed hard. Nonno would've wanted him to play—Alfredo said so. It was the least Pietro could do.

He gave a little nod to indicate he was ready and brought the clarinet to his lips. Nonno's absence hit him like a clap of thunder. He stared at the page Alfredo had opened in front of him. *La Forza del Destino*. Melancholy, celebratory—a perfect choice.

You can, Nonno had told him. You can what? Play for the dead?

Just yesterday, he'd been sitting in a vineyard that today did not exist, preparing a piece of music to play for his grandfather, who today was not alive. What was the point of anything, now he'd never know whether his music would make Nonno walk taller or speak with awe in his voice?

The clarinet weighed in his hands. He needed to play it better than he'd ever played it in his life. This was the last time he would play for Nonno.

He closed his eyes and imagined Nonno right there in front of the band. Sitting on a chair, he'd pulled over from the table, hat pushed back on his head, listening intently. Every note, every breath, Pietro needed to make it count so Nonno would know how much he cared. He'd know how sorry he was for not digging, for not playing his song, and how much he would, from now on, always do the right thing.

Surely Nonno would send a sign—a swallow that will stop its feasting to listen, or a child in awe, a next-generation prodigy, but even Ida paid no attention to the music.

And the more Pietro imagined Nonno sitting there, the more mundane the music sounded.

Nonno couldn't hear. Pietro was a fool. What had he been thinking? That an angel would descend onto the roof? A star would shoot through the sky?

He heard the music from a distance, not playing it as his last tribute. Nonno's last words played in his head. *You can*—words that had to be the key to unlocking all his fears and doubts, in music and as a man, because he felt lost and adrift in a world where everyone else knew their place.

The music splintered from a melody and turned into a barrage of notes blown through the instruments of strangers—the magic and meaning nothing without Nonno.

♪ 𝄢 ♪

The next morning, Pietro came downstairs exhausted from the second night of barely any sleep. After Nonno's last celebration had ended, he'd lain in bed for what seemed like hours.

Nonna had his milk on. Dear Nonna. Yesterday she'd laid her husband to rest. This morning, she'd made breakfast as usual.

A loaf of fresh bread sat on the table.

"Did someone bring this?" Pietro asked.

"I couldn't sleep so I baked," Nonna said and set a bowl of milk and coffee in front of him.

Ma and Pietro's sister, Caterina, were also in the kitchen, but nobody spoke. Nonna moved as though weighted down by an invisible force. Ma sat with that same weight on her shoulders, darning socks. Nobody touched the bread.

Nonno's spot at the head of the table emanated the cold of silence. If he were sitting there now, he'd be complimenting Nonna on the bread, questioning where Pa was, making plans for the day. He'd sing a ditty to Ida and flourish compliments on Ma and Caterina.

Pietro tore a chunk of bread off and handed it to Ida.

"*Grazie, zio!*" Her tinkerbell-voice momentarily bringing joy into the room. Ma and Nonna both looked at her, and for an instant, their faces brightened.

Then the moment was gone, the silence heavy once more.

Sometimes when the rain made Nonna's arthritis flare, and when Ma's hands bled after milking, Pietro would play for them, here in the kitchen, and both their ailments appeared to lesson. He'd played when Caterina was so pregnant she could barely waddle, and he'd made her stand up and dance, of all things.

Last night he'd failed to play for Nonno one last time, but perhaps, just perhaps, he could break through this silence this morning. Maybe he could lift the living, just as Ida had done for a fleeting moment.

He went back upstairs for his clarinet and fumbled to put its pieces together. His hands were shaking, his breath heavy through his nose. He needed to do this; he needed to lift them. Music was the only good he could do.

The mood was still somber silence in the kitchen. Pietro chose the chair in the corner, the one set back from the table. He was inconspicuous there, and he wanted them to hear his music not to look at him.

He pushed the notes out and around the room, imagined them wrapping themselves around Nonna, around Ma, then his sister. Ida was the only one who appeared to be listening. She swung her legs back and forth and bobbed her head to a beat much faster than the one Pietro was playing.

They'd notice. They had to. Their faces would soften, their actions would become lighter, any minute now, his music would reach them.

He reached the end of the score. Ma didn't look up from her darning; Nonna grated the iron pan against the stove. Caterina put a protective hand on her belly and lamented how the poor lamb would never know his or her great grandfather. Ma still didn't look up. Nonna blew her nose on her handkerchief.

Pietro had not lifted them at all. They were as somber as the moment he'd walked in.

Pa appeared, and Pietro waited for him to fill the void. He took a chunk of bread and dipped it in the milk and coffee Nonna gave him.

After a few mouthfuls, he looked up at Pietro. "Work will be short for a time. Nonno wanted you to travel."

"I don't want to go anywhere."

"It was his wish. He told me to give you some money to get started, but wherever you go, you'll still need to work."

"Did he say where I should go?"

Pa shook his head, no. "He wanted you to study with someone outside this town. That's all I know."

♫ 𝄞 ♪

Pietro had been a fool to imagine he'd been the one to alleviate Nonna and Ma's pains in the past. They never said his music had helped. He'd merely presumed. Maybe Ma had used a salve for her hands, or maybe Nonna had been making healing tea for her arthritis. And when Caterina danced? Maybe Ida was dancing in her belly, kicking in time like she'd been kicking in time on the bench this morning when Pietro played.

He couldn't touch people through music any more than the next musician. He'd only thought he could because Nonno had made him believe that. Nobody else in the world had, and now Nonno was gone. Pietro was just an ordinary musician, not to mention a man without work. And to think he could write music. He could barely even sway people with *real* music.

But Nonno wanted him to travel. He'd done Nonno enough injustice by not digging the vines, letting him carry too heavy a load. He could at least honor this wish; it was his moral duty. If he found another band, it would feel no less foreign than the local band without Nonno.

He left his bowl on the table, went upstairs, and pulled a box out from under his bed. In it were extra scores he'd written out over and over for the band so everyone would have their copy. He dug through them until he found what he was looking for—Sacco's photograph of his brother's band.

The American roots were the solution for the vineyard. Musicians were important in America. What if Nonno meant for him to make his own path there, in America, where bands wore uniforms and got photos taken, and had never had Nonno in them?

America was a long way away, but Nonno hadn't told him how long to stay away except while the new vines grew. He could go for a year. America was a huge place, everyone knew that. It was certain to have plenty of bands like the one in the photograph. And it'd be far, far away from this place where the band felt like a misstep, where he could do nothing to lift his family.

Pietro slid the photograph back into a score and slid the box beneath the bed.

FIVE

Bussolengo

The last week of their lives in Italy had passed as quickly as a chestnut falls from a tree. At least Assunta had managed to avoid Beatrice the whole week. She wouldn't have put it past her to dig her claws in Nandy again, even after they were married.

Assunta walked briskly to Mamma's house so they could spend some last precious moments together before Nandy arrived with the cart that would begin their long voyage.

Some mountain buttercups waved in the breeze near the roadside—perfect to turn into ball gowns for fairies to wear at night. Then again, she should probably stop her childish daydreams now she was a married woman. But there was no reason not to pick something to take to Mamma. A mark of the fact they would never again walk past here to go to market, a seven-mile trek that Mamma believed to be much shorter if you talked your way there and back.

The buttercups were pretty enough, but Assunta had learned from experience that they didn't last in a vase. She chose instead flowers of Madonna's grass, which were more resilient. Their little pink clusters could be miniature dresses for ordinary fairies, not the grandiose fairies that wore the puffed skirts of buttercups, but ones who nestled in the hearts of people of more humble beginnings, like herself.

She chose only perfect petals and shook off a little bug. Mamma got upset if bugs came into the house on her flowers. She flattened them without a second thought, which, in turn, upset Assunta.

When she turned the corner onto their road, she expected to see Mamma leaning out of the window, watching for her, just like she did when Assunta delivered gnocchi to Vito or ran an errand around town. She must be busy with something because the window was bare. Not even a cleaning cloth hung from the washline.

Assunta stopped at the bottom of the stairs leading up to the apartment. She needed to savor this moment. She knew every crack on every step, every dip in the worn tread where industrious feet had walked up and down. On the landing, she knew where the breeze tucked away the dust behind her pots of rosemary, bay, basil, and parsley—would Mamma keep them once she was gone?

On the landing, she pulled three bay leaves off the plant and heard Mamma open the door above her.

"Will you water my pots when I'm gone?" Assunta asked, handing her the bay leaves. "Will you take care of your hands?"

"I'll have to manage," Mamma said.

Assunta went inside and put the Madonna's grass in a vase next to a picture of Saint Therese she kept for Papà. He used to say all saints had to be female because women were so much better at taking care of others. Assunta would add that some were not good at taking care of themselves. Mamma, for example, would she take the time to steep the bay leaves to soothe the lumps in her fingers?

"I might not see you for a while." Assunta lit a candle for Papà.

Never having been much further than Verona in one direction, Lake Garda in the other, it was impossible to imagine what it would feel like to travel halfway around the world.

"I'll be making a shrine for you when you're gone," Mamma said.

How could she say such a thing? "I won't be dead!"

"You'll be as good as. I'll never see you again."

"Don't say that!" This was not the way Assunta had planned to say goodbye. "That's not fair, Mamma!"

"It's just fact, and there's no harm to be had by it. See these?" Mamma took a jar of peaches from the shelf. "Peaches. Signor Trevi dropped them off. He's grown an orchard of them, says the climate for peaches is perfect here. Have you ever seen peaches grown here before? Things change, whether we like it or not. Who's to say, for all we know, we might see the entire area planted with orchards before we know it. Maybe it'll be a good change. The mills, they closed, can't say I see any benefit to that, nor all these factories being built all over."

"We could stay and grow peaches!" Assunta said. Why hadn't they thought of that before? Why had they presumed the only place Nandy could make a decent living was America?

"That's not what I meant. Where would your husband get the money to keep you while the peaches grow?"

Well, Nandy had spent nearly everything he had on their voyage, and even then, Mamma had had to come up with something toward the tickets.

"Your bag is packed, now don't go giving me a turn." Mamma sat down. In the middle of the table sat a little lace sachet of sugar-coated almonds they'd handed out as favors at the wedding. Assunta pulled out another chair to sit down, and Mamma continued, "Bide my words, don't be in such a hurry to live the next moment, the next step. Before you know it, your life will be behind you instead of in front of you where you thought it was, and it'll be too late to do anything about it," Mamma smiled and took Assunta's hand in hers. "I'm just an old lady. There'll come a time I won't be here for you to worry about. In the meantime, I have plenty of other children and grandchildren besides. Assunta, *figlia mia*, you go and make a good life, however far away your husband has seen fit to lay down his hat and earn the clothes on his back."

"What am I going to do without you?" Sure, they were going where they could be sure of a meal on the table every day, they'd be going far from Beatrice, but how could those be reasons enough to lose Mamma?

"Whenever you feel the need, think of me and what I might have to say to you if I was there."

Assunta's throat tightened. She hadn't meant to cry.

Mamma lifted her finger toward the window and the sound of hooves and a cart, and her brother's voice *whoa* through the open window. "They're here."

They both leaned out the kitchen window, elbows touching. Assunta could happily stay just right here.

"Where did you find that poor donkey, Vito?" she called.

"Oh, *signor!*" Mamma said.

Belongings were already loaded in the back of the farmer's cart harnessed to the donkey, Vito and Nandy sat on the front seat, and someone had tied a ribbon to the donkey's headpiece.

"I had a horse and carriage lined up," Vito said. "Honestly, it was going to be a fine ride. I can't help that the horse went lame. This was the very best second choice I could find."

Assunta pulled herself back inside from the window ledge. "Come on, Mamma, let's go down."

"Off you go. I'll put the peaches away. Then, I'll be down."

Mamma turned her back and began to rearrange the shelf, gathering herself, no doubt. Assunta took one of the silk flowers she'd cut from her wedding garland and laid it on the table by the sugar almonds, something for Mamma to keep, then she started downstairs.

"Steady on," Nandy met her at the halfway landing. He clung to her elbows and kissed her, his mustache itchy and urgent on her top lip.

So many times, when he was gone, and eligible man after eligible man left for work in the city or abroad, Assunta had fantasized over Nandy coming back for her, and, before their darn donkey had kicked Papà in the head and sent him to an early grave, she wondered a thousand times whether Papà would relent. For all her focus on Nandy's absence and the pain he'd left, time had obliterated the memory of just how exhilarating it felt when Nandy kissed her.

The exhilaration was no less now, but this was not the time. She wanted to ask him about peaches, suggest they could stay here and grow them, but she couldn't speak with his lips on hers. On the stairs, too, hardly the place for such a display of affection. She pushed against him harder.

"Someone will see us!" She managed to break free.

"Let them see how I feel about you," he smiled. His eyes meant what he said, but he didn't try to kiss her again.

"What if we stay? Or at least delay our departure. I'm not sure I've given America enough thought," she said.

"Our bags are packed, and our tickets are paid for. Don't you worry yourself with second thoughts." Nandy marched down the stairs and through the gateway to where a farewell party had gathered.

People hung in small groups around the cart. On it sat just two trunks, their entire belongings. Linens, a few kitchen utensils, clothes—they'd need to purchase everything else once they got there. The one thing Nandy had insisted Assunta have was a woolen overcoat. It'd be cold in Pennsylvania in winter, though Assunta didn't think it could be much colder than Bussolengo.

Nandy's parents stood watching, very still, apart from anyone else. Mamma appeared solemnly, sobbing more loudly into a handkerchief than she had at Papà's funeral. Everyone here, confident that she and Nandy were doing this. Perhaps on the train ride, she could persuade him to delay, sway him before they boarded the ship.

Even as she thanked each person that bid her good fortune, she wanted to tell them it wasn't real, she wasn't leaving, it was just a train ride, that's all, but instead, all she said was goodbye.

Without a hint of a breeze as a warning, a cold wind tore down the road.

"Assunta, *tesoro*, time to go," Nandy said.

Mamma wailed. Assunta enveloped her in her arms. "Be happy for me, Mamma. Please." She pulled out a handkerchief from her sleeve and dried Mamma's face. "When you go to the market, will you stop on the way back and pick flowers to remember me by?"

Mamma buried her face in Assunta's handkerchief, and Vito pulled her away.

Nandy guided Assunta onto the cart. She couldn't cry, mustn't cry. But no longer would she wander the streets, making up stories about the flowers growing by the path, making and delivering gnocchi for Vito to sell—she had to squash these thoughts. She couldn't think of doom now—she was to live happily ever after in a land of promise.

She was losing Mamma, her family, her home. She could not leave!

She stood up from where Nandy had sat her at the front of the cart, grasping for a handle hold but finding none. Nandy tugged her arm sharply, pulling her off balance with one hand, flicking the reins with the other. The blasted donkey began to walk.

"I can't!" Assunta cried. "Mamma!"

Nandy did not let go of her arm. "It'll be all right, you'll see. I'll take care of you."

Half standing, half sitting, Assunta struggled from Nandy's grip just in time to see Mamma swallowed by the group of waving arms. The cart leaned precariously as the donkey pulled them around the corner and out of sight of the farewell party.

"You're making a spectacle of yourself. *Che brutta figura!*" Nandy said.

"I don't care. They can't see me," Assunta's words jumbled with sobs.

"*They* are watching."

Assunta looked up—what 'they' could be watching when everyone was behind them? Through the smudge of tears, on the right side of the road a little way ahead, she saw Vecchia Carlotta, hunched, not much taller than when she sat. By her side, wearing a green bonnet stuck with a pink flower, stood Beatrice.

Nandy had told her enough times to convince her their relationship had meant nothing—Beatrice had thrown herself at his feet. Yet here she was, with Vecchia Carlotta, no less. An old and toothless woman from the scariest of fairy tales who rarely moved from her observation point outside the dim and grimy door to her home.

Everyone in town knew the tale, though most only believed part of it. Carlotta's parents, too poor to rub two pennies together, had abandoned her as an infant in the woods. Overcome by regret, they went back for her the next day. She looked no different from when they'd left her. Although Carlotta had been too young to remember the episode, the town's common belief was that she'd never forgiven them and had been responsible for her parents' long-suffering illnesses and painful deaths.

Of course, it was just a story, though it gave Assunta an odd and slightly spiteful sense of satisfaction that Beatrice's only companionship should come from such a woman.

She wiped the tears from her face with her hands, realizing Mamma still had her handkerchief. This, at least, would be the last time she had to look at Beatrice or look over her shoulder for her.

The two women did not move as the cart drew closer. Beatrice stared, a piercing gaze, waiting for them. Waiting. Until they were almost level. Then Vecchia Carlotta looked up, too, and for a moment, Assunta felt a physical pang in her chest, and Beatrice spewed, "You may have him now, but I swear you won't have him long! I curse you, Assunta Biscardo!".

SIX

Le Havre, France

Pietro pulled out the photograph that he'd slipped into the front of his new notebook. It seemed like the right time to give it back to Sacco, here on this immense vessel, before they sailed to the country where the photograph had been taken. Sacco had never guessed he had it. He set it next to him on his bunk and turned to the last page of the notebook.

His sister had given him the notebook. Just one of many surprises between the time he'd announced his decision to travel and his departure. Ma had handed him a pair of new socks and two new handkerchiefs. Pa had accompanied him to the Municipal building, paid the stamp duty, and waited while the official wrote the details of his passport, then he'd handed over the fare for Pietro's ticket. Nunzio had awkwardly wished him good luck.

But it was Nonna who had surprised him the most. She'd waited until he'd finished his dinner of *bagna cauda* and chard and wiped the table in front of him. Ma watched expectantly. She must have known what was happening. Nonna had put a bundle wrapped in tea towels in front of him. She'd paused then, and when she saw he didn't do anything, she urged, "*Avanti*, open it."

He'd turned the corners of the towels back one at a time. Inside was Nonno's leather-bound music book.

"This will be yours," she said.

The music book that Nonno carried everywhere. He had carried it since Pietro was a boy, as long as he could remember. Crackled black leather, gold border, a dented corner, a scratch Nonno used to buff his thumb over to no avail. At every performance, Nonno would be the last to walk onto the stage, and he would find somewhere to set the book. He never opened it on stage. Pietro couldn't remember him ever opening it. It was just a part of Nonno, omnipresent. Pietro had never given much thought to what was in it until recently. And now it belonged to him, and he didn't want to open it. At least not yet. He would open it when the time felt right. In the meantime, it was wrapped safely in a shirt inside his luggage.

He would only use the notebook his sister had given him for now. He took his pencil and wrote, in the best handwriting he could with the ship's gentle roll, *You can*—or should he have written *I can*? He held the pencil there some more, deciding whether to correct it or not, and either way, how he could finish the sentence.

Somehow he doubted Nonno had intended him to finish the sentence with *follow Sacco halfway around the world* or *sail on a ship that made the worst racket ever.*

The hum of the ship and murmurs of hundreds of voices reverberated and created a single pitch like percussion. Only he didn't hear it as percussion. He heard it as the ship's hum and hundreds of voices reverberating. No music. No melody. No instruments to compare. Sound devoid of meaning. These, like the fire that consumed the vines, were not the sounds he wanted to turn into music.

There hadn't been a moment of respite for his ears since he had boarded. Aside from the dismal murmurs and occasional groans of people suffering from the sea, the clangs of doorways and mops and buckets of poor attempts at cleaning, the wind whistling, the ship's engine roared endlessly. It was small consolation that it sounded more reliable than the engine of an automobile, relentlessly drowning out any music he might have in his head.

But he shouldn't be thinking about sounds to turn into music anymore. Nonno had given him his task to learn from others. He'd said nothing about taking matters into his own hands and writing his own music.

You can confess your crime, beg Sacco, ask for forgiveness.

He slipped the photograph back into the front of the notebook. He could not give it back, not right now. He needed it. It was the only physical proof Pietro had that he should be making this journey. He crossed out the line about confessing his crime and started again on the next line—*You can learn all the music there is to know in America.*

Loss had wrenched Assunta's heart since the familiar rolling hills had flattened to the plain. The majesty of Alpine peaks had given some distraction, then they, too, were behind them. Towns through the train window looked not quite real, as unreal as this journey.

"The first stage of our journey is over. You are now in France, *tesoro. La Francia!*" He'd told her she was in France three times already. It was sweet of him, though it didn't compensate for the fact that she had just left her entire life, her family, everything she knew behind.

"Are you thinking of that woman again? She's past praying for."

She hadn't been thinking of Beatrice, not before he mentioned her, that is.

"Don't fall for what she said, the *malocchio*, the curse, it's just words."

Assunta agreed the whole thing was ridiculous. Beatrice was a petty, spoiled child. It had only rattled her the slightest bit because that Vecchia Carlotta had been with her, but the tales were all just that—tales.

Nandy should have known she'd been thinking of the sight of Mamma's hunched shoulders, shaking with grief. Her Mamma, who would, if she were here, probably tell her right now that she was scowling. That she shouldn't be revealing her bitter thoughts to her husband, that she should be keeping her composure.

If only Assunta had Mamma's strength.

"I'm a little uncomfortable with the swaying of the train, that's all." Assunta forced her voice to sound calm and forced a smile she hoped Nandy would think sincere.

♪ ♮ ♪

At the port of Le Havre, foreignness was apparent from all directions. Not France exactly, at least not the France she'd seen from the train, but a mixture of skin colors—brown, tanned and milk-white, people wearing tweeds and silks, large hats and coarse scarves. Accents and words in languages so strange they had to be invented. Adults shouted and cried. Children, immune to the poignancy of lives about to change, chanted rhymes and skipped ropes. Seagulls screeched and frolicked in the air, laughing at the absurdity of the travelers leaving everything behind.

Until now, the move had been about her and Nandy. Now in this crowd, she felt more like a minuscule drop of something much larger than she'd imagined.

A man with a tufted mustache dangled brown bottles shrunken to the size of a finger in front of them. "A cure. Buy your cure before you board."

"Do I look like a fool?" Nandy said, pushing past him.

"What cure? Are you sure we might not need it?" Assunta pictured boils and vomiting—disease flourishing on the ship.

"They'll fool you into thinking it'll heal eye disease. It's just water tainted with herbs and coloring. Besides, eyes as beautiful as yours could never have anything wrong," Nandy said.

Next, a monk pushed a picture in front of her. "Our Lady of the Sea. She'll save you when the ship goes down. Special price."

"Come," Nandy pulled her away.

"Have some respect! He's a man of religion," Assunta said.

"He's no more of a monk than I am a king. We could spend a fortune and still not give to each of the phonies here."

He pulled her into a crowded room in the processing building. They found a seat amid the smell of too many people on a hot day at various stages of their journey, squashed into the inadequate space.

Nandy seemed restless. Things would be better when they got there, and they would finally be together without an audience. He would set about earning a living; she would set about making their home worthy. He would be able to push aside the uncertainties she was sure were troubling him, and then the cheerful, playful, spirited Nandy she used to know would surely return.

At last, their turn came for processing. An official peered at them and prodded them with instruments. A physician turned them around and made them bend over to touch their toes. Then, an official showed them to another interminable room before another officer in uniform questioned them. The way he perched his glasses on his nose suggested he took his job quite seriously. He wrote each answer with intense concentration in his large register, transcribing each word like treasured information.

"Family name?" he prompted.

"Vassanelli."

"Your wife?" he pointed to Assunta with his chin.

"Yes." His soft tone contrasted with the officer's, and he turned and smiled at her.

"What did he ask?" she said in Italian.

"If you're *la mia sposa*. It's a good thing for you to learn in English! It starts with 'W,' a letter they use in English. It's like a 'V' but you put your lips like this." He showed her what to do with her lips. "Wife, say it *vaief*."

"Your job?" the officer interrupted loudly.

"Miner." Assunta slipped behind Nandy to the shelter of his back. She surmised the officer was French. So odd to hear Nandy speaking a language she could not understand. He and the officer spoke deliberately, both outlining the words not native to them, watching each other closely, she an outsider to this language.

Finally, papers clutched proudly in hand, Nandy led her once more through the crowds toward a boat to carry them out to a ship, one of several towering righteously in the bay like an impossible gaggle of geese. The ships looked smug, floating effortlessly on the water, defying their enormity, almost daring the passengers to come aboard and challenge their buoyancy.

"What else did you have to tell him?" Assunta asked.

"Just information, nothing to concern yourself with. They'll ask the same things at the other end. You'll pick the language up soon enough."

She was doubly sure now she would not. There weren't only words she had to contend with, but new letters in the alphabet, too.

"When we get home, you'll take care of household business, like any of the wives."

"Home?" Weren't they just *leaving* home?

"Don't be concerned. The ones who've been there longest will show you the ropes."

The finality of his tone left no room for doubt.

She looked around the space, a little bigger than the width of the bunk beds, divided from other married couples by a hanging canvas. They would spend the coming week and a half here. Eleven days crammed into the space that had to accommodate them and their belongings, on a ship as large as a floating city, carrying the population of two cities on an ocean as large as—well, nothing was as large as the ocean. Sounds of other passengers coasted through and over flimsy partition walls delineating the small space they were allotted, reminding Assunta of the sighs and fidgeting of faceless priests in the confession box.

All she wanted was to be alone with Nandy. Truly alone. Not like their first week of married life at his parents' home where they were alone only in the bedroom, his parents sleeping in the next room, his brothers waiting for him in the kitchen while he bid her goodnight. He would take care of his marital duty, careful not to make a sound, then go back out to his brothers to drink. She'd lie there, a little in awe and wondering if it was okay to feel how she felt, and listening to their talk and laughter, telling herself it was important for him to spend time with them. Once they got to America, she'd have all the time in the world alone with him.

Even the times they'd managed to spend alone, when he'd kissed her, melting her into the floor, she felt the same tickling inside she used to get before he'd left for America. Silly, she'd thought it must have been the way only teenagers felt. She'd always thought there was a time when people changed, became serious and duty-bound, when they stopped minding chores and hard work, so much so, they stopped caring how their hands cracking after hours of laundry. When the sacks of flour they'd carried home from the market to make gnocchi became light to carry. She had no idea she'd still have tingles that started in her tummy and spread outward like a pan of golden polenta being poured on the tabletop.

If she'd been on this ship a mere two weeks ago, she would have qualified to stay in the single women's quarters at one end of the belly of the vessel, separated from the men's quarters by the married couple's quarters in between, located with the intent of maintaining decorum. Being married felt special. Staying in these quarters was like an acknowledgment, an announcement to the rest of the world.

She arranged her washcloth, soap, and towel on the small desktop, then refolded what she could in the trunk. Their clothes would fare better if she could hang them. Nandy lay on the bottom bunk, his eyes closed.

"Ei, are you awake?" she asked. "We're in the married quarters. We're married, can you believe it?"

"Hmm. I was asleep. A few minutes more."

"But we're married!" Surely he could share her excitement.

"We are. And my beautiful wife will take pity on her poor husband, who just needs a little nap."

"I can't help but be excited. I finally have you to myself. To be your vaief."

"My wife," he said, correcting her pronunciation.

Assunta sat on the wooden bench provided as their only seating. Of course, he didn't share her excitement. Why should he? It wasn't his first time around.

Fine, she'd lie down, too. She slung her foot onto the bunk where he lay and hoisted herself up on the top bunk.

"What are you doing? You shouldn't get up there, here take the bottom," Nandy said, jumping to his feet.

"It's where you were napping, my darling. I won't disturb you without good reason. I'm your wife now. I intend to do all I can to make you happy."

There. She'd said it out loud. She was going to make sure there was no question.

He sat back down on the bottom bunk and smiled a partial smile. He was probably looking forward, like she was, to arriving in America and getting started. America, where they would be on dry land, and the world wouldn't sway.

He stood back up, and she propped herself, which was an enormous effort because the bunk sagged terribly. She expected him to say something kind to her about her declared intentions. Instead, he put his hat on his head. "If you're quite comfortable, then I'll be going for a walk. To get my bearings, you know."

SEVEN

aboard *La Provence*

The air was putrid before they even pulled anchor, then it got worse. Assunta held a handkerchief to her nose before it, too, acquired the stench. The movement of the ship went from a rolling sway to sway and shudder.

Everywhere she looked, there were people. Every time she closed her eyes, she heard people, yet she had never felt so alone. Nandy had come back with the smell of liquor on his breath last night. She'd lain on the bunk with her eyes closed, picturing flowers falling from the balconies of Verona, coming to life as fairies in their colorful gowns, dancing on the moonlit cobbles of the piazza. This often helped her get to sleep, but this time one of the fairies turned into a wife, another a girlfriend.

When she eventually fell asleep, it wasn't for long. When the sway pulled hard enough, it pinched her in the sagging bunk.

Still tired from the poor night's sleep, the day dragged long until the aroma from the kitchens sent out a false tease. She objected to how they were made to dine separately in the women's and men's dining halls, but the powers that be were determined for there to be no disreputable liaisons on board. It deprived her of the chance to laugh with Nandy at how they thought the watery broth with a few cursory grains of rice could be called food. Mercifully, he'd known to bring bread, pickles, and salami. Also, mercifully, he came back to their bunks right after dinner.

"Can I offer you dessert?" Nandy held out a chunk of bread with a pickle stuffed in the doughy part. "It's the last bit of the loaf."

"We'd surely starve on what they give us," she said, but what she wanted to say was, don't leave me again tonight. Not with the murmurings of strangers, the smells, the dismal, bleak enclosure where no flower could ever blossom. "Tell me, are we going to meet the family you stayed with? The family whose daughter you—you know, married." Her choice of words even sounded wrong to her, but she couldn't bring herself to say his wife if it related to another woman.

"And if we did? They're good people."

"I was wondering, that's all."

The bread was hard and stale. No matter how carefully she ate, it left her with a front full of crumbs. She brushed them off.

"Here, let me help," Nandy said.

"Stop it!" she said in an urgent whisper, pushing away his hand.

"Why? Nobody can see us." He leaned toward her and kissed her neck. "We just need to be quiet, that's all."

Surely he could not stand her, not having got much use out of her washcloth in days, yet she let him put one hand on the small of her back, turn her face toward him with the other.

The ship rolled more sharply than before. They heard the thud of something that had fallen nearby. Nandy missed her mouth and ended up with his cheek to hers. His skin was tacky, the lack of air, the shuddering and rolling— "I don't feel so good," she told him.

He pulled back to look at her face. "My green bride. I'll take you up on deck." He wrapped the gray blanket from the bed around her and led her along the corridor and up the stairs. The crisp, fresh air hit their faces, for a moment blissful, only to be obliterated by gray smoke from the stack that swirled directly into the area cordoned off for third-class passengers. Despite the smoke, the air felt glorious on her cheeks, cleansing.

They held the railing, the air whipping their fingers, and watched the sun surrender to the horizon, gripping the far edge of the sea with its magnificent cloak of oranges, reds, and yellows. The waves played with the colors. Perhaps it wasn't the waves, perhaps it was dragons and pirates and sea monsters reaching up to grab the colors to paint their undersea worlds. She could add a score of mermaids and undersea gods to save the day.

"Better?" Nandy asked.

She nodded. She almost told him about the dragons and sea monsters, but even if he understood, which she doubted he would, she had a sudden urge to keep something of her own from this new existence. He had memories and knowledge of the place they were heading. He also had family there.

"Listen to the seagulls," she needed to push aside thoughts of a woman he'd touched the same way he now touched her, remind herself she'd forgiven him. "It's like they're laughing at the absurdity of leaving everything behind."

"They are seagulls, infuriating pests. They have no idea where we are going or what we are leaving."

If he saw no poetry in the seagulls, there was little chance he'd find any worth in the imaginings of sea dragons and monsters from the underworld.

She pulled the grey blanket up and over her hat, following the example of the other women. A bleak uniform that made them look the same. She could no longer tell an Italian woman from a Serb, a French woman from a Pole.

"Look at those children. Do you think they speak the same language or if being a child is enough to understand each other without words?"

"You like children, don't you?" Nandy asked.

She smiled. She couldn't be more confident in her answer. "I hope to have many." She waited for him to say he did too. Instead, he looked concerned.

Didn't *he* want them to be blessed with children? Children had always been part of Assunta's vision.

"I'm sorry, your daughter. It must have been hard." She had spent so much time focused on Nandy's other women; she hadn't considered the pain he'd gone through.

The strum of a guitar rose from somewhere behind them. A man wearing a brown vest and tweed jacket stood below one of the few yellow gaslights on the third-class deck. He had one foot on a coil of rope, guitar resting on his knee. People began to shuffle towards him. Bit by bit, a wall of three or four people formed, a jumpy audience lured from the gloom. The man struck up the tune of a traveling song.

He paused, and a man Assunta hadn't noticed at first played the same rift on the clarinet.

"Let's go and watch," Nandy said, pushing her forward. "You deserve the front row."

Sacco had come up with the idea to come on deck.

"I found a man who plays the guitar. Bring your clarinet," he said, pulling on his overcoat.

"I'd rather stay right here," Pietro answered.

"Most are struggling with the ship. They'll appreciate it."

So now Sacco was insinuating his music could help change the way people feel. Then again, this place was that dismal that even a tambourine would offer relief.

"Come on. Come!" Sacco slapped his shoulder with his hat.

"Does it mean that much to you?"

"To me and a deck load of people stuck on this ship."

Pietro followed Sacco up the stairway. Sounds changed from entrapped murmurs in the ship's bowel to voices swept and lost to the indecisive wind that blustered in one direction then another. Passengers stood still, few spoke. The man Sacco had spoken to had his guitar out to tune. Pietro stood next to him.

"My friend tells me you want to play some," Pietro said.

"It can't hurt," the man replied. "Shall we play Cento Lire?"

"We could do something more cheerful."

"Any Italians here will know it. Let's start with it. You sing?"

Pietro shook his head, no, and held up the clarinet in explanation.

"Ready when you are," the man with the guitar said. He strummed the intro. Pietro nodded, then he began to play. The guitarist had a point. All the people who shuffled closer to form a circle around them looked Italian.

Another Italian man came up to them and pulled a harmonica out of his pocket. The first man stopped strumming and held up his hand. "Let's start again with the harmonica this time."

The other man rubbed his harmonica on his pant leg, then blew on his fingers. The guitarist fiddled with his strings.

Pietro noticed a man to his left, making a fuss about pushing his wife forward. "You deserve the front row," he told her loud enough so everyone would know.

"But do you? Do you want children?" she said. All these people could hear, Pietro wanted to tell her, quiet for now. Not that there was an inch of private space on the ship, though truth be told, he was as curious as any to know the man's answer.

The man hesitated a moment, like he had something important to say, then seeming to notice the passengers waiting for his reply, he said, "You'll listen to the music now."

Her cheeks blushed visibly red even in the dim light.

"The color of the sunset, so beautiful, don't you think?" she asked a woman standing next to her, probably deflecting the embarrassment of her husband's reproach. She had the type of voice that embraced people, that intended only good toward others. He'd have to write that down in his notebook.

The guitarist stopped fiddling with his strings and nodded, and they began to play.

Someone near them started to sing in a cautious, quiet voice.
Mamma mia dammi cento lire
Che in America voglio andar;

Mother, give me a hundred lire
Because to America, I want to go.

Hundred lire I will give you
But to America, no no no . . .

Assunta felt as though she had a rope tied around her waist, the other end of it tethered to home. As they traveled further away, it crushed tighter until she thought she couldn't go any further.

She glimpsed through the people to the colors of the sunset over the prow of the ship. The direction they were going in, the color of promise. She hoped the color was true.

The musicians ended their dreary song about a girl drowning on the voyage to America. They began another, a jolly one this time. The man with the clarinet moved as he played. She really shouldn't stare. People might notice—Nandy might notice. Yet her eyes kept drawing back to him. He was short, a head shorter than her, the tufts of hair spilling beneath his cap were neither dark nor light, but a mousy in-between. His features, his mustache quite ordinary, she doubted she could pick him out from a crowd if he weren't holding his clarinet as a marker. Yet there was something authentic in his movements, fluid, as though he couldn't separate his body from the music he played.

"Are you warm enough?" Nandy spoke loudly, tugging her attention back to him.

"Thank you, yes."

"In any case, I'm ready to go back down. I've arranged to meet a few men, a card game," he said.

♪ $ ♪

During the night, Pietro woke suddenly and completely. He'd been dreaming the song. His song, the one he'd not had the courage to play for Nonno. In the dream, musicians hadn't played it. Rather the vines had, still gloriously rooted and laden with grapes, or were they clefs at the start of new lines? The branches of the old pear tree conducted fruit dancing from the sleeves of its arms. Leaves were notes, swallows were, too.

But when it came time for the harvest to begin, nobody arrived with shears and baskets. And in the courtyard, the vats stood empty and dirty. He'd taken the beat for his music from Ma and Nonna cleaning the vats in preparation for the harvest—slap of water, scrub of brushes stripping the grime of disuse, notes, and percussion from the whack and wrench of barrel repair, now that beat began to falter.

There was no rumble of neighbors come to pitch a hand, no orchestra of boots, steady bees, the wisdom of butterflies on the cusp of being heard.

The music stopped. Even the vines just hung, drooped, and forlorn.

The silence woke him.

He was sweating. He knew his breath was loud, others in the single men's quarters would hear him, but still, it took him a moment to get control.

For a moment there, the music had been beautiful, the silence dreadful.

♪ $ ♪

Before supper the next day, some people formed a line outside the dining hall. Pietro and Sacco joined the gathering crowd, ready to waltz in when the doors opened. Why would people wait like that? Surely it'd take longer to get inside. A man shunted through the group of mainly Italians, also ignoring the line and placing himself between Pietro and Sacco. It was the man whose wife had a beautiful voice.

"I'm glad I found you. You play the clarinet well. The name's Nandy," he held his hand out to shake.

"Pietro. This is my friend—"

"Nice to meet you, Pietro," Nandy made no attempt to acknowledge Sacco.

"Where are you going in La 'Merica?"

"New York, I suppose."

"To do what?"

"They say there's work to be found."

"I don't see a man like you making it in New York. Have you heard of the *prominenti*? They'll rip every last penny from your soul." The dining room doors opened, and the Italians pushed inside. Nandy followed Pietro and Sacco to a table.

"The *prominenti* are crooks. They exploit their fellow countrymen through painted grins. Promises of steady pay, of lodgings and real Italian neighborhoods, but all they'll get you are tenements and poverty. Travel right on through. That's my advice. You'd be better off in a small town. I have just the place. You'll find work in the mines, not the best job but it's the best pay. A friend of mine, a good man, he'll take you into the town band. You'll play weddings, festivals, events like that." Pietro and Sacco looked at each other, not sure what to do with this information. "You have some paper?" Nandy pointed at the notebook Pietro had put on the table in front of his plate.

Pietro didn't want to take any paper from it.

"I'll bring some next meal," he said.

"Just take a bit from there. I might not see you again. Lots of people on board."

Reluctantly, Pietro tore a leaf from the book. Nandy wrote out a name and address.

"You can't go wrong here. Board with this family. They'll feed you right. Good people, northerners.

EIGHT

Bracken

An interminable ten days later, a crew member passed around the word that they would be arriving in New York first thing in the morning. Nandy and Assunta readied their belongings and claimed a precious spot on the small deck well before sunlight. Many had the same idea, and every inch was packed.

Finally, her legs weary and head clouded from lack of sleep, Assunta saw their new land for the first time. So that was America. They headed for an inlet and into a bay where a flurry of boats and ships vied for a path through the murky water. The Statue of Liberty appeared like magic through the morning mist, tall in her welcome. Assunta pulled her woolen coat tight. Perhaps it'd be warmer on land, although from here, it looked like there was no room for people. Just building upon building, rising vertically from the harbor water to carve the skyline, as though the city had exploded into being overnight in a vertical quest to fill the sky with as many floors as possible.

Nandy leaned forward and over the edge. Assunta's insides screamed not to let him fall. She dropped her bag and pulled him back by his jacket tail.

"I'm getting a better view, don't fuss."

She picked up her bag and wiped the bottom of it with her gloved hand. The grime and dirt and salt of these eleven days at sea were now on her glove. She let the bag hang by her side and looked away from Nandy. Another time he'd toyed with dangerous water. She'd admired him for it then. It had been one of the fondest memories of her life.

Before he'd left for America the first time, they'd been at the river, in the days of their clandestine meetings, enabled by her brother. Nandy had begun to show off, wobbling on the low branch of a tree, balancing one arm out to the side with great drama, holding onto the trunk with the other.

"I'm going to risk my life for you, Assunta. I'm going to walk right out to the end." He pointed to the branch that stuck out over the water, reaching hopefully toward the other side. The current rushed below, uninterested.

That was back before the mills had closed, the days Mamma missed so much. Assunta always thought the mills looked like gigantic crabs, like the real ones Papà had brought home to eat once, only much, much bigger, standing guard over the churning water wheels, held captive to the bank by rickety walkways. So thin and fragile, they looked like they might snap at any moment, leaving them to be swept away and bombard the bridge downstream, cutting the town off from the other bank in revenge for captivity.

"If I live," Nandy said, "promise me you will give me your heart. I will love you each day." He let go of the trunk, teetering, waving his hands as if the branch was thin as a rope. "See what I'll do for you? Do you see? If I die, tell my mother I love her!"

"I'll tell her you were a fool, that's what I'll tell her! And to go looking for you at your cousin's mill. Because that's as far as you'll get swept."

She didn't know how he made it back without falling, but he did, because all of a sudden, he was kneeling in front of her. He kissed her hand then looked up so solemnly, "Will you be my wife?"

Nandy pushed himself off the ship's railing and took a step back to stand by her side. He hadn't knelt the second time he'd asked her to marry him. He hadn't kissed her hand, either.

"It's big," she told him, nodding toward the New York skyline as though he could not see the city for himself.

"It is." His tone was gentle, happy. "But it's nothing like that where we are heading."

She could not picture a place that was nothing like where they were heading. How could she imagine something she'd never seen, a void? The place where they'd build their new life. A house where she'd make her own decisions and make a home. Nandy had told her she might have a garden, too. She'd already decided she'd grow flowers by the side of vegetables, beautiful and practical. A nice life, she'd make sure of it.

♫𝄞♪

The ship, *La Provence*, jostled for position among the rush of ocean liners delivering the influx of immigrants. Huddled on the deck in pockets of people and possessions, all eager to disembark, they looked on quietly as the first and second-class passengers filed off the ship to continue their lives without further checks or scrutiny.

Hours passed before the third-class passengers were at last herded off the ship and onto a pier, and there they got to wait again.

Nandy looked anxious, shuffling from side to side. If he had more room, he'd be pacing. Assunta longed to lean on him, rest her head on his shoulder, but decorum didn't allow that kind of affection in public, not that others seemed to care. One family near them were all touching, husband's arm around wife, wife hugging children in front of her. Not Italians, clearly.

A second ferry boat pulled up to the dock. Nandy pushed through, carrying both their cases. Assunta put her hand on his arm, nervous she might get left behind. They managed to get on this one. It rocked to the rhythm of the waves much more violently than the larger ship. Hardly a passenger spoke. They simply clustered, gripping their meager bundles and each other's coat sleeves, holding everything they now owned.

They'd all heard the stories that the processing center at Ellis Island could be the most challenging stint of their journey. Assunta had heard of tales during the trip. Stories of despair, families forced to separate. Children sent back to their country of origin alone. These stories—untamed by the perspective of numbers, unchecked by reports of the millions who entered the country without a hitch—fueled the nickname of the Island of Tears.

"Do you think we'll have problems getting through, you know—?" She didn't say the name of the island, in case it brought bad luck.

"We'll be fine." Nandy didn't look as though he was convinced they'd be fine. He still seemed anxious.

"I'm ready to be alone with you," she said, speaking softly and close to his ear.

"Stay here. I'll be right back."

The ferry was cramped and carried a cacophony of sounds. Pietro thought he'd been separated from Sacco, for a moment fearing he'd never see him again, but then he caught a glimpse of him over the heads of the other passengers.

There was a shuffle to Pietro's left that nearly knocked him over. The cause of it was Nandy, pushing his way through. Behind him, near the window, was his wife.

"I'm glad I caught you," Nandy said. "You have to do something for me; you mustn't mention my name when you get to the Conatis, okay, my friend?"

"Who?" Pietro asked.

"The address I gave you. Just do it for me—you will, won't you?"

"You're not going to Ernest yourself?"

"Change of plans. But there's no need to worry. You'll make it all right without me. You'll be fine."

That he'd be fine hadn't been so much of a concern. It hadn't crossed his mind that he'd need Nandy to be fine. The only shame was that he'd not get another chance to hear the man's wife's voice again, but he bet there were plenty of women with beautiful voices. Some of them might not yet be married.

The ferry was nearing the dock, and a man yelled directions to the crew throwing ropes and tying them to wooden posts. The ferry's side scraped against the concrete, and water slapped furiously, as though objecting to the vessel's presence.

"Where are you going? Are you staying in New York?" Pietro called after him, but Nandy was already making his way back through the crowd.

When Pietro climbed off the boat, Nandy and his wife were ahead of him. The line shuffled slowly forward, and three children from the same family cried shamelessly. Pietro tried to listen past them for her voice, to hear it one last time. He listened for it near the door of the building where the passengers were herded, but it was no use. She was too far away.

The red brick building in front of them looked much friendlier than the stories circulating on the ship would have them believe. By the time Pietro reached the set of doors opening onto a large hall where uniformed men who did not smile—but neither did they shout or strike—he'd lost all sight of Nandy.

Inside, Sacco reappeared by Pietro's side, having somehow managed to shuffle through the crowd packed even tighter together now to make their way up a staircase.

"They're watching everyone," Sacco said, just loud enough for others in the immediate vicinity to hear. "They look for limping or the feeble-minded."

A few men holding thick sticks of chalk at the top of the stairs looked them up and down and let them inch forward into another large room. Herded into a sectioned area to wait in what seemed like a sea of thousands, they settled in to wait for their papers to be checked.

Hours later, their stomachs past the point of hunger, throats dry, it was Sacco's turn to be processed. Pietro watched his friend step forward to the wooden desk and tried to listen to the questions, but the murmur of so many people in the tall-ceilinged hall swallowed his friend's voice. When Sacco was released to join a steady flow of families on the other side of the row of desks, Pietro took his place in front of the officer, who scrolled through the ship's log. Pietro looked anxiously for Sacco and managed to glimpse him walking backward, caught up in the motion of a large family, his arm stretched up in the air waving.

Pietro raised his hand, too, more to stop his friend from leaving than in farewell.

"Port of departure?" the officer asked in Italian.

"Le Havre," Pietro answered.

"Occupation?"

"Musician," Pietro said.

"You're from Piemonte? My family is from Turin." The officer kept his eyes on the log on his desk, but his tone of voice was friendly. "What employment do you have in the United States of America? They forgot to write it here, but you have a job lined up, don't you?"

"No," Pietro said.

"No?" The officer drew out the word as an exaggerated question. Pietro had clearly said the wrong answer, but what was he to say?

"You will be joining family then, yes. Listen, *compatriota*, you need a destination, a job, a family. We need to be sure you don't become a ward of the state. You understand me, yes?"

"Yes," Pietro said, taking the answer the officer fed him. Two no's in a row might get him thrown right back on the ship.

"Their address?" The officer held his hand poised, ready to write the address in the log.

Pietro looked toward the place he'd last seen Sacco. All he could see now were the backs of heads.

"Sacco, Pietro Sacco. He's a musician, too. I'm joining his band," Pietro offered and wondered if they ever checked on this information.

"Now we're getting somewhere. Tell me his address." The officer held his pen ready once more to write the information.

"New York." Sacco had given him the address, but it was deep inside his case, in the back of the notebook, wrapped in his Sunday clothes with Nonno's book. The last thing he wanted to do was open his case and sift through his belongings.

"I need a full address. New York is a big place. *Ehi*, I didn't make these rules. They're just rules I have to enforce. You give me a name that goes with an address, or I'll have to send you to a different room with a different officer of the law who might not have family from Piedmont. You understand what I'm saying?"

Pietro didn't want to open his case, and he didn't want to be sent back to San Damiano, not least because he'd have to get right back on the ship with all its awful creaking and droning.

He felt inside his jacket pocket. Nothing there. He shifted his case to his other hand and checked in his other jacket pocket. Nothing there either. He slipped his hand inside his pants pocket—yes, that was where he'd put it. He pulled out the ball of paper Nandy had written on and uncrumpled it on the desk so the officer could see.

"Conati? Your uncle, perhaps?" The officer didn't wait for confirmation before he began copying the name and address in his log.

Satisfied now, the officer waved him through. Pietro followed the crowd along to the end of the hallway and down a staircase with brass rails. At the bottom of the staircase, he looked around for Sacco, but all around him were groups of people, all louder than in the sorting room upstairs, all heading in different directions. Sacco was nowhere to be seen.

Pietro looked at the paper in his hand. Famiglia Conati, Ernest, Pennsylvania. It sounded like as good a destination as any.

NINE

Pennsylvania

P ietro's first step in Ernest was chaotic with the hissing train and train guard's whistle, then the steaming of an engine pulled out of the station to reveal a peaceful town.

Pietro hadn't seen a flat stretch of land from the train window on the interminable train ride, but the hills were carpeted in thick forest between clearings dotted with farmland and towns, not crossed with grapevines like home.

He'd write to Sacco when he reached Ernest. If nothing else, it had been the name that convinced him to change his plans.

The train now pulled away. Pietro asked the train guard if he spoke Italian. He presumed the man's reply in English meant he did not. Pietro handed him the address Nandy had written for him. The man gave a lengthy explanation, luckily also indicating each turn with his hand. Pietro had not given thought to how, on earth, he was to learn from a band in a different language.

He set off in the direction the guard had pointed. A group of children he'd seen watching the train had resumed their game of hopscotch. The road wasn't paved or cobbled. The ground was packed and dry, sounding almost hollow beneath his boots. Birds sang from perches he couldn't see. He quite liked their patterns and repetitions.

From somewhere behind him, a church bell rang.

He turned down the first road on the right just as a boy threw a ball to another who swung a thick stick he was using as a bat. The impact made a dull thwack, followed by a rustle as the ball landed in a bush in front of a row of identical houses. Another boy rummaged in the bush, found the ball, and threw it back to the cheers of the other children.

This was no Piedmont, for sure, but the town sounded quite fine. He could get used to the sound of children playing, of church bells, and birds. This might have been a good place to discover new music if that had still been his intention. At least he could cope with these pleasant sounds, which was important because he might be here for as long as a year.

The town seemed to end right at the end of the short street, just a block down from the station. He turned left. The house should be here.

He set the case down and looked at the piece of paper. One of the boys playing ball came over, looked at it with him, and pointed to a house across the road.

The house was covered with the same grey slats as the other houses. Pietro went up the steps onto the porch to knock. A woman with two small children on either side of her holding onto her long skirt, answered.

"Buongiorno, signora," he began, then stopped —should he have prepared an introduction in English?

"Buongiorno," she answered.

Good, she was Italian. He slipped the piece of paper into his pocket and explained that he was looking for lodgings, having just arrived from Italy.

"We have a bed available. I'll show you."

She showed him inside and told him the house rules, her Italian accent odd and interspersed with some words in dialect. It wasn't too far off from Piemontese, and he caught the drift, nonetheless. It was, at least, more familiar than the English he'd heard with all its edges and rolling together, all at some mysterious rhythm.

She showed him through a sitting room decorated in fine wooden furniture. A large red rug on the floor muffled their footsteps, even seemed to flatten down the lady's voice. Next, there was a dining room with ample chairs, all pulled neatly in. The kitchen was at the back of the house. Spacious, though not filled with a large table like at home, just a smaller utility table with four chairs. A pot of sauce was cooking on the stove, the aroma reminding Pietro that he hadn't eaten for a long time.

Unlike the concrete stairs from the family courtyard, the stairs in this house were indoors and made of wood, and most of their width was covered in carpet. The woman walked ahead of him, the two boys behind. She opened a door at the end of the short corridor. There were three beds in the room. "Your bed," the lady pointed at the one in the middle. "You pay weekly."

He would like to know how the other two men, lodgers he presumed, slept at night. If either were snorers, he didn't want to be in the middle or the same room even, but he had little choice for now. This was the only place he knew about to look for a bed. Besides, if he accepted this right away, he might get a plate of the dinner that smelled so good.

"I'll take it," he said.

"Mrs. Conati," she held out her hand, and they shook.

"Pietro Maccagno, it's a pleasure to meet you."

Assunta had followed Nandy trustingly and had no idea how they had ended up standing outside of what looked like a flimsy stable, in the middle of a row of identical flimsy structures in a clearing that seemed to have been cut hastily into the splendid green forests like the gaping belly of a freshly slaughtered animal, spilling out the cheerless rows of identical shanties like guts, the trees not daring to reach too near the streets, as though they, too, feared contamination.

"You'd described things a bit differently." She intended it as a joke because surely they weren't going inside, let alone stay here.

"I heard there's good work in Bracken. I'll be on the crew by the end of the week."

"What happened to where you worked before?"

"Let me worry about putting food on our table. Don't you worry about the details," he said.

Only she was worried about the details. Why were they here?

"Let's go in," he said.

"What even is this?" She wasn't quite sure what question she should be asking.

"Some might call it a shanty more than a house, but it'll suit us for now. Let's see how quickly you can give this a woman's touch, eh?"

She stepped hesitantly after him onto a plank balanced on two rocks and up onto the wooden walkway against the front of the structure. She wouldn't honestly be surprised if she saw goats or even a horse inside.

Nandy opened the door with a large shining key. "There's a stove, see. And a table and things," he said.

In the dim light inside, she saw, indeed, that the inside had furniture meant for humans. It wasn't a stable.

She couldn't fault him. He'd told her the city was different from New York. Only instead of tall buildings, she'd envisaged elegant houses, with front and back gardens. If not like the villas by Lake Garda, at least like the homes she'd seen from the train this morning once it got light.

"We are staying here? How long for?" Surely it had to be temporary. A roof of sorts until they found a real place to stay.

"Come, let's get the linens out. It'll start to feel like home."

She very much doubted that but followed him anyway through a doorway. On the other side, in a room as small as the first was a timber cot, enough for two only if they slept touching. If it were only for a few days, she'd bear it.

When they had been released from the processing center at Ellis Island, she had been under the mistaken expectation that they were near their final destination, leaving her mentally unprepared to sit on a train for another night. She'd sleep on her feet if she had to, tired as she was. But first, she needed a bath.

"Where can I get clean?" She could see little opportunity for privacy here.

Nandy rummaged, looking for something not immediately visible in the tiny space. "I'll get you a bucket of water," he picked up an old wooden pail and headed outside.

A wooden pail? Even if the stove were lit, she could see no pans to warm the water. She'd been traveling for two weeks, snatching quick wipe-downs of herself with wash clothes on the ship.

She looked out the window to see where Nandy had gone, or at least she tried to, but the window was gray with dirt. She couldn't see the water pump, but she knew what direction it was because she could hear Nandy talking to someone.

When he reappeared, he was carrying a bucket, and a woman was following him—coming here? As filthy as Assunta was? She didn't want anyone to see her like this.

"A neighbor," Nandy tilted his head to indicate the woman who walked right inside without waiting for permission.

"I'm Anna. You can use my kettle. I'll have it back within the hour, mind."

"Assunta. Nice to meet you," she tried to sound welcoming.

"We'll help each other. It's the way we do things. On Wednesday, be ready early. We'll walk to the store."

The woman let herself out. Nandy didn't even turn back around. He stuffed some paper and kindling in the stove and lit it.

"What store is she talking about?"

"The company store. It's where you'll shop."

"Is there a market?"

"Not around here. You'll figure things out."

In the fog of profound fatigue a single night's sleep could not dispel, Assunta could barely comprehend what Nandy was saying to her. Already up and dressed, he was going somewhere. To get supplies and a job, he told her.

She picked up her shawl from where she'd laid it over the bed covers at her feet and wrapped it around her shoulders. Though it had been warm when they'd first arrived, the temperature had dropped after nightfall. The fire in the stove hadn't lasted the night.

"What time will you be back?"

"Whenever I'm done."

"What will I do till then?"

"I need to get set up for work. We can't live if I don't work," he said, which shed no light on the answer to her question.

Chill morning air blew in when he opened the door. He kissed his index finger and flicked the kiss in her direction; then he was gone.

She should have asked if he'd be looking for a proper place to stay. From the look on his face, he didn't seem to be bothered to be here, even though there wasn't a real house in sight, but fatigue likely had her mistaken.

The bleak wooden-planked interior still looked like a stable. The stiff bed made her muscles ache. The rough-hewn table with chairs that wobbled and the coal stove that had not been cleaned properly by the last user still did little to convince her this place was meant for humans, not livestock. Four glasses stood on a shelf next to a set of four ocher-colored plates and two matching teacups—a horrid color, but the only cups she had for her tea.

Alone in this strange place, Assunta had no idea what to do. And whatever was on the outside terrified her. After a while, she crept up to the grimy window, uneasy in case someone spotted her. A row of identical shanties stood across the street, virtually the same color as the mud road between them.

This place had no piazza, no church, no gardens. It had no history at all, and the way the shanties had been built with such flimsy materials, it seemed that nobody had intended them to last long enough to create one.

Assunta could not have felt more out of place if the sky itself had turned black. She sat on the very edge of the cot, watching the front door, waiting for it to return her husband to her. In the meantime, the coal dust settled noiselessly on every single surface, horizontal and otherwise.

After a while, her leg fell asleep, creating little blasts of sparkles inside her bones. She had to get a hold of herself. She stood up tentatively, pausing to make sure the thin walls would not collapse around her leaving her exposed to this strange place. She stretched and wiggled her foot to wake her leg. Think, she told herself. If she were home, she would help Mamma with the chores. The thought of Mamma jabbed cruelly, but it was also a comfort. Mamma would tell her not to sit there feeling lost and sorry for herself. There was work to do. There was always work to do.

Apart from tending the stove—thank heavens they'd got coal—all the useful things she could think of involved water. Nandy had brought in a bucket the night before, but the little water that was left smelled indistinguishable from the bucket. She had to brave the outdoors.

She pulled on her coat and looked both ways to make sure the street was empty before she went out, down the steps, and along the road to the well. She set her bucket beneath the spout and began to pump the rickety handle.

Bucket full, she turned back. Almost triumphant until she looked for her shanty. She had no idea which one was theirs. They each looked exactly alike. It was one on her left, that much she knew, but other than that, she could not tell one from the other. She hadn't seen which shanty her new neighbor Anna had come from either. She would be stuck out here all day. Her bones would freeze.

On the verge of panic, she recognized a pair of old boots outside a door. She had seen them from her window sitting on the step of the shanty opposite. She should not have been so worried. She was nearly there, unscathed if a little shaken, when the door the old boots were guarding swung open to reveal an abundant lady in a dress down to her ankles, a dirty apron tied around her waist and a scarf around her head.

"*Buongiorno!*" Assunta said, her voice shaking.

The woman glared at her, her expression harsh. Then the woman began what sounded like barking, a sound that projected to the end of the street and could quite possibly awaken hearing in the deaf. Assunta fought desperately to identify a word or even a syllable, anything. But no, the woman was talking gibberish. She slopped water over the edges of the bucket and rushed back to the shanty.

What mad place was this? Assunta wedged a chair against the door and was about to pull over the kitchen table when she remembered—this was a foreign country. Of course, people were going to speak a different language. She splashed water from the bucket against her burning cheeks. She didn't dry; she just let the water drop on the front of her dress. She wanted to go home.

♫ ♪

She had a fire going when Nandy came back, but the little coal left in the scuttle was almost gone.

"I'm glad you're home. Did you get something to eat? What took so long?"

"Getting set up, nicely," he said, setting a copper kettle stuffed with supplies on the table. He began pulling things out and putting them to one side–a small pan, a bag of dried pasta, a large brown bottle of wine, dried beans, onions, a loaf of bread, salt.

"Didn't you get anything else? We have nothing here."

"We'll have money for more soon. I start work tomorrow. Here's coffee." He put a tin on the table, then a pail she needed to fill in the morning with his lunch. "Put coffee in the bottom section, then onion, salami once we can afford it, bread on the top. And here's powder and squibs I'll need for shooting down the coal," he explained.

"Isn't that dangerous?" she asked.

"It's all dangerous down there. But don't you worry, nothing will happen to me. Look, a fine handle on this pick," he swung the pick to his side in a working stance. He didn't swing forward, or he'd have disintegrated the table, speared her, and probably knocked down a wall.

"Does that thing have to be in here? And that shovel?"

"I can hardly leave them outside where someone will pilfer them. These tools will put food on your table. They'll take care of our future."

"This place is not what I thought it'd be. You'll think me foolish, but I got lost on the way back from the water pump."

"You made it back again, I see." He turned back to the supplies. "This is carbide for the helmet. Used to be we'd wear Sunshine lamps, sounds nicer than it was. Sooty things that stank of paraffin."

She had perhaps thought her story interesting because it'd been the only thing that had happened to her. Nandy was right to carry on without paying any mind. It was only a trip to get water after all. Here he was, setting up for work to provide for them.

She picked through the things on the table. As absurd as this place was, as measly the rations he'd brought home, she had to make something to eat.

TEN

A shrill whistle woke Pietro from a deep sleep. It was the same whistle that had blasted yesterday afternoon.

"You'll hear it every day to call at the start of the shift, then at three," Mrs. Conati had explained. "It'll go off once if there's work tomorrow, three times if not. You'll mostly hear one."

The other two lodgers in the room got out of bed and began to get dressed without saying a word. They shuffled, one in front of the other, out of the room. They moved like men condemned.

Pietro waited until they left. No sense getting in the way when he didn't know the routine. When they'd gone, he went over to the window and cracked it open. Sounds of breakfast rose from the kitchen below, as did the booted footsteps of men heading to work, the clang of machinery, roar of engines. The town sounded sharp and jagged, not promising like it did yesterday. No sounds of children playing and church bells ringing.

Pietro took Nonno's music book from his case and went downstairs. Mrs. Conati was in the kitchen, dressed and well into her day.

"You can sit there," she pointed. He'd not washed his hands, but he didn't see a bucket, and this wasn't Nonna. "A cup of tea, okay for you?"

He put Nonno's book on the table in front of him and took a sip of the tea. Nonno liked tea in the afternoon, not for breakfast. The longer Pietro didn't know what was inside Nonno's book, the harder it'd be to open and find out at last. Old scores—Nonno's favorites? Music Nonno had written himself—now that would be something. What if it did set out plans for Pietro's life. There was no question, Nonno had plenty of them. Maybe it even finished the sentence that started *You can*.

"I normally serve oatmeal for breakfast in the week," Mrs. Conati went on, "but the hens'll not be laying soon. This might be the last egg we'll get out of them before spring."

"You don't light the coop?"

"Light it?"

"Keep a lamp out there long enough to make them think it's as long as a summer's day. They'll keep laying all winter."

"I've never heard of such a thing." Mrs. Conati set a plate with small cubes of potatoes, onions, and an egg. She went right on talking as he ate, about the chickens, about how her husband would be grateful to hear his advice, and she'd have him walk Pietro down to the mine office. It'd be as good as a written reference; he'd get hired on straight away.

Fancy him, working in a mine. Not outside in the sun or rain. It'd just be until he went home again, it couldn't be that bad, and he needed the income.

"I don't know English," he said.

"Not many do. You'll hear all sorts of languages. Plenty of men from Italy will help you out. We all stick together. Then there's Poles and Germans, Irish, any other language you can imagine."

The two boys that had followed Mrs. Conati yesterday when she'd shown Pietro around the house came running into the kitchen, trailed more slowly by three older children. They said good morning and sat at the table for their breakfast.

"You left family behind, no doubt," Mrs. Conati said as she set bowls of oatmeal out for the children. "Your parents will miss you, I'm sure. No doubt you'll think of having a family at some point, no funny business under my roof, mind. Once they start coming, they don't seem to stop—nine children, me. This is my youngest, and my last," she pointed at one of the smaller boys. "This here is Gino, my grandson, believe it or not. Same age as his uncle."

If Ma were here, she would approve of this lady. From what Pietro could see, she worked hard and took care of the children, lodgers, and household with no help from anyone else. She had a no-nonsense voice that rushed just a bit, mostly—he sensed, but could not be sure—to cover a background of sadness. She was a talker too. He'd barely had to say a word since he'd begun his breakfast but went about her business without that flustered way of moving some women have. When she ran out of things to say, he would ask her what she knew about the band.

In the meantime, he reached forward, fork still in hand, and pushed Nonno's book back a little bit. He'd not open it now. He'd do it in private, with the kind of reverence Nonno deserved.

♫ 𝄞 ♪

It had only taken a few days for Mr. Conati to secure a place for Pietro in the mine and take him to buy the supplies he'd need at the company store, the largest in the region, he'd explained proudly.

And here they were, dressed in jacket and pants and new leather boots that would be smudged with black by evening, a shining new food pail packed by Mrs. Conati in Pietro's hand.

The silence of the miners waiting to go into the earth emphasized the din of the coke ovens and the activity around the carts and tipple.

The gate dropped, metal scraped metal, and the men began to shuffle in the same condemned kind of way he'd seen in the other lodgers. Perhaps he would have been better to try his luck in New York, at least Sacco would have been a link of sorts to home, but there was no going back now. This was it. This was the work that would pay for his stay here. Without it, he didn't even have the return fare to Italy.

"Lucky this mine has an open face entrance," Mr. Conati said. "Before, I was in another mine where a lift jerked every fifty feet or so till it got way deep. As though the chance of cave-ins or explosion wasn't worrying enough for a day's work."

His voice and the noise of the men's boots became clipped almost as soon as they got into the tunnel.

Pietro couldn't fathom the distance they shuffled to get to the section where they'd work, except that it felt far too far to be going into the earth. Mr. Conati showed him how to nail his lunch pail to a post so the rats wouldn't get it, then explained he was going to set his charge and how Pietro was to hunker when he or any other man shouted three words in a row, "Fire, fire, fire!"

Mr. Conati's voice had an odd echo, as though bouncing from the solid walls of earth that let no sound get far, insulating any trace of sound from life above ground. When he stopped speaking, the only thing to be heard in the mine was work. Stark, jarring noises that lacked timing, the discordance of labor like physical blows.

Every thrust of the shovel's blade into the heap of coal pinched the pads of skin at the base of Pietro's fingers. The concentration of noise and absence of ordinary life drained him as the day went on, as though depriving him of the very oxygen he needed to breathe.

He dug into the memory of Nonno teaching one of his many lessons to help him pass the day. The lesson had been about patience and biding time, though it had taken years for Pietro to understand it fully.

It had come soon after Pietro had skipped school to hear the band rehearse. Nonno and Pa—Nonno mainly, had decided Pietro should study music. He could hardly believe his luck. He'd been so excited to start his lessons when they got to the summer house, but all Nonno had made him do was polish the clarinet over and over. And once he'd done that, he'd made him polish it over and over again, night after night. At the start of each of those nights, he'd put a candy on the table, its shiny red wrapper luring Pietro's eyes away from the polishing rag in his hand and to the candy that sat, waiting for someone to claim it. Pietro imagined the taste of it, but no matter how many times he'd ask, Nonno never let him have it. It'd stay on the table until it was time for Pietro to head to bed, then Nonno would make a great fuss and rustle over opening the wrapper.

One night, when Pietro was on the verge of never wanting to hear a clarinet again if it meant polishing one even one more time, he boldly demanded that Nonno play.

Almost as surprising as Pietro's own outburst, Nonno had agreed. He'd played, holding Pietro mesmerized in his tune.

That night, Pietro had forgotten to ask if he could have the candy. It had never reappeared, and Pietro had never had to clean the clarinet more than once at the beginning of the lesson, once at the end.

The lesson had been about hard work and focus–about what was important and not getting distracted by things that didn't matter. Yet, all Pietro could think of now was distractions to make him forget the ache in his back and the pinch of his sore fingers. He'd polish a clarinet a thousand times over if it meant never lifting another shovel-full of vineyard soil or coal.

But he had little choice, and little chance, too, of playing music any time soon. Blisters had already formed and begun to burst on his hands. He'd have to ask for something to put on them. Until the blisters turned to callouses and his hands got accustomed to the shovel, perhaps he should delay his visit to the town's band. It'd be a terrible shame to give a poor audition, particularly when joining the band was the whole point of being here.

♫ 𝄞 ♪

Assunta was surprised when Nandy said they'd been here for four days. Not that she thought they'd been here longer or shorter, it was more like she was surprised that something as familiar as time had carried on at all. America felt as foreign as the very first day. Foreign in the sense that every familiar thing in life had been somehow repainted, resized, and redrawn.

The air hung damp and stifling with the odor of industry. Bread and onions tasted different, perhaps poisoned by the mines. The sky, mostly a heavy blanket of cloud with an occasional blue, not quite so intense blue as back home, appeared bigger.

Today, at least, she would go through the forest, the barrier isolating the little town from the rest of the world, to shop for the very first time with Anna.

She woke early. She filled Nandy's pail, fearing the stale bread, onion, and apple fell short of providing a working man a just lunch, but soon she would be able to choose provisions that would stay with him longer.

She was ready with boots laced, watching from the window to see if Anna wore an overcoat. Hers was folded on the bench in case she should wear that instead of her shawl. Despite their awkward introduction, they were sure to become immediate friends.

Anna didn't step up onto the front walkway but leaned over to knock on the door and calling out, "You there?" She wore a thicker shawl than the thin one Assunta had and carried a basket, which Assunta did not have.

Assunta waited a moment, not wanting to look too eager. "Ciao, it's so nice to see you," she said.

Anna didn't smile. "We live in that one. No doubt you'll call for me when you need something." She pointed through a gap to the street that ran parallel to Assunta and Nandy's. "That's all there is—three streets and twenty houses." Anna led the way to the end of the street and down a path swallowed by thick woods.

"I've not spoken to a single person other than my husband since we arrived."

"You'll walk to town with me twice a week as a rule. Don't worry about walking in the woods," Assunta hadn't been worried until Anna mentioned it. "There are plenty of wild animals here, but they'll get you whether you're scared or not, so I've long learned not to be. You have to watch out for bears. They won't attack most of the time, but best get praying if you go near their babies. They say if one comes at you, it's no good running. They're much faster than you are. Just shout as loudly as you can. It's your only chance."

Assunta had never seen a bear, but her imagination painted a vivid picture of a massive, ferocious beast, roaring while saliva dripped in globules from its bared fangs, its paws tipped with knife-like claws slashing at the air in front of it.

"Snakes!" Anna announced. "Now you're much more likely to see snakes. Copperheads and rattlesnakes. Little garter snakes too, but they're harmless. It's not a bad idea to have a long stick with you. And listen for a rattle."

A train panted down the tracks beside the path they were following. A few passengers standing in the doorways tipped their hats to the two ladies.

"Sometimes I want to catch the train to the store, just as it's so much quicker. But you know it'd only mean more time at home doing the chores. Always try and walk with someone, mind. That way, if anything attacks, it's going to go for one of you, not both, and the other can raise the alarm. Not that it would do you much good."

The train passed, revealing the creek that flowed on the other side of the tracks.

"I've never seen orange water before." The sound of her own voice surprised Assunta, as little as she had spoken since the two women had met at the end of the street.

"It's the mines. That's what. Beats me why. Coal is black, but it makes the water orange."

"What about fishing?" Assunta's father and brother used to bring home such glorious catches.

"Don't waste your time. Whatever makes the water orange kills everything, too. If you want fish, you need to go further up to the north branch. It's still clean. People swim there in the summer."

Anna recited the chores expected of a miner's wife, from growing vegetables in the clay-mud out the back of the house to scrubbing and cleaning and canning the vegetables they managed to grow. "Not to mention the drink," she added. "Everyone makes something, shine, or wine. You need to set up some equipment. The men, they like their grog, much cheaper to make it than buy it. Some bars are only for the management, not the likes of our husbands. We're just immigrants."

Anna paused and put her hand to her forehead as though it would help her see in the distance. "Up there, on that hill," she said, "an old Indian man used to live there. He made belts and rings from snakeskin. I've seen some of the things he made, real pretty. Touched them too, the skin's so soft, and I'd much rather see it on a belt than on a snake, you know?"

"What happened to him?" Assunta asked.

"They made him leave when they were building the number six mine. His son came to get him, just in time. Ready to plow through the place where he lived, they were." Assunta looked at the spot in the woods with Anna in case they could glimpse the world that existed not only in legend. "Then there's a furnace a ways ahead. It hasn't worked for years, not since the boss's son fell in it and died. It's haunted, you know."

Anna appeared to be the authority on just about everything sinister. She gave Assunta the impression that the town was, from now on in, the entire reason for their existence, Assunta's previous life wholly irrelevant, the new one to be filled with doom and gloom.

She caught a glimpse of brick and smoke through the trees, then rounded a bend, and the town, Vintondale as Nandy had told her last night, lay before them. Despite the more intense smell of coke ovens, it looked to Assunta to be nice enough. Tidy rows of houses stretched out in front of her, and on the road to her left, she could see bigger ornate buildings.

The company store was built of stone, and it towered over the other buildings. Nandy had explained there was no outdoor market, no little shops crammed through tiny doorways, just the large and modern store that sold anything a mining family might want.

Inside, Anna told Assunta to tell a lady at a desk her name, then a contraption of wires and papers spun over the lady's head, and she announced how much they had to spend. "Three dollars," she drawled and dismissed Anna and Assunta, turning to ask the name of the person next in line.

"What is she saying?"

"You can spend *tre dollari*. You won't get far with that," Anna said.

"How much should I have? My husband worked a full week."

Anna said something in English to the lady, who sighed loudly and called something back to another lady behind her.

"Your husband spent the money already," Anna told Assunta the message that was relayed back.

"That's not a problem," Assunta said and walked over to the produce, picked a beet from the display.

A salesclerk flicked open a paper bag and took the beet from Assunta's hand. Anna spoke to the clerk in English—no doubt she told her about Assunta's lack of funds because instead of putting it in the bag, the clerk put the beet back on the pile. She rummaged through a heap of onions and held up two that looked the most beaten.

Anna directed the woman to weigh some rice, flour, and lard for the both of them, then glanced sharply at Assunta before moving onto the butcher's counter.

They headed back, Anna's basket full, Assunta struggling to think of how she'd use the provisions that half-filled a paper bag to make even one decent meal.

On the way back, instead of her dismal stories, Anna walked in silence, and it felt judgmental. Assunta tried not to care, even smiling a little as she admired the plants alongside the path.

"Look, Madonna's grass!" she said, leaning down to pick some.

"I'd forgotten that name. Here they call it witches moneybags," Anna said.

"That could hardly be more different."

"There's a lot that's different here; you have to adapt." Anna's tone sounded triumphant.

Assunta picked several stalks of Madonna's grass and set them on top of her groceries. Hopefully, Anna didn't have anything else to say because Assunta intended to start composing a letter in her head to Mamma. It was going to be about how complicated shopping was, about what a long walk they had to get anywhere through wild woods. Nothing about bears and snakes. She might mention Indians on hills and haunted furnaces, how much she missed everyone back home. Mamma, most of all. And she had until she got back to come up with something nice to say about her new home.

♪♬♪

"I see you found the store." Nandy wafted the aroma of the dinner toward his nose with his cupped hand.

"I didn't have much to spend."

"There'll be more next week." At least he hadn't told her she needed to adapt.

Nandy went to pick up the spoon from the dish Assunta had placed on the side of the stove. "Oh no, you don't! Get washed. You'll turn the soup black."

"Just a quick taste, I'm starving," he pleaded.

"No filthy hands near my food. But here," Assunta filled the spoon, blew gently on it, and fed it to Nandy.

"You know how to make a feast. Hmm."

She helped him unbutton his work shirt and let him take off his pants. She washed his neck and back first and worked her way down his arms to the elbows.

He didn't dip his hands but smiled at her and arched his eyebrow. She dropped the cloth into the water, took hold of his right hand and the soap, and massaged in the suds. Once she was done with both hands, she rang the cloth back out and wiped his chest, but he put his hand over hers and held it still.

"That tickles," he said.

"A big strong man, and it tickles?"

"Hey, you shouldn't mock me. You should comfort me. My lips are clean already."

"And so?"

"And so, you may kiss me." She did, and he tasted of soap.

When he was clean, they ate quickly without talking, looking at each other with intent. Nandy pushed his empty plate back and held out his glass. "Get me some more wine."

She stood to fill it. He took it, then pulled her by the hand into the bedroom.

She'd thought it awkward the first night of their marriage, when his brothers and friends made a point of hanging around outside their door, giggling like children. He'd told them to get lost, but they'd laughed and said things like, "It's only because we care. We need to make sure you make children to continue your legacy."

At least the bed had been comfortable and warm.

"Get your nightshirt on," he told her and returned to the other room to stoke the coals while she got ready. She heard him top his glass off.

"Ready," she said quietly. There was no sign of anyone outside, though Assunta didn't trust the thin walls to keep anything private.

The bed was narrow, stiff, the mattress full of pointy bits. But they were together. That's what mattered.

When he finished with his business, he rolled away, took a long swallow of wine from the glass he'd put on the floor, then fell asleep almost immediately. She pulled her nightgown back down over her legs and lay on her side where she could see him. The darn *malocchio* be cursed, the darn shanty be temporary, the darn pantry be stocked soon, and they'd have friends to laugh and to share food with. They *would* live happily. She'd make sure of it.

♫ 𝄞 ♪

It could have been the dampening sound of the mine, the way it kept hold of sounds, threatening to withhold them forever, but Pietro had made a decision. He would write down the composition he'd written for Nonno before it disappeared from his mind. If the past weeks were anything to go by, it could well turn out to be the only music he'd ever compose.

Once everyone had finished their breakfast, he got the paper he'd bought at the company store and went back to the kitchen where Mrs. Conati had already started on a sauce she'd simmer all day.

"Can I borrow the chopping board?"

"That would depend on what for."

"For lines."

"Now you've got me wondering, what do you need lines in pencil for?"

"I wanted to draw some lines. Straight ones."

"That's what I'd gather. And why would you need lines?"

"To write music. Nonna used to let me use her chop board."

"You write music?"

"Nonno made sure of it."

"A musician indeed. Of all the lodgers that could turn up here. I'll be darned. We've had farmers, once a blacksmith. There was one man who claimed to be a fiddler, but it turned out he was referring to the way he intended to pay his rent. Here, sit on this side, then you'll be out of my way."

She sat him on the side against the wall. This way, there was no hiding what he put on the paper, but he had little choice. He'd tried to work in the bedroom, but without a straight edge and a level surface, it was nigh on impossible. He glided the pencil along the board's edge.

"Then there was the lodger that became my son-in-law. Took a fancy to my daughter Mary, he did."

There, the sadness he'd thought he'd heard in her voice. Thicker now.

"Died. She and her little girl, the cutest little button she was."

"I'm sorry," Pietro said.

"It was the 'flu."

He didn't know what else to say. He had enough lines on the first page and started on another. He wouldn't want to stop once he began writing the music.

"There's some men that don't deal with that kind of pain. You're not that type, are you, Pietro?"

"I'm not sure what you mean," he said.

"My son-in-law, Nandy. He took to the drink for a few weeks when Mary died, then announced out of the blue he was heading back to Italy. Changed everything about his life, he did. There's others of us that go through the tasks of the day, but just carry on and hope we'll feel the sunshine in our hearts again one day."

"Nandy, you say?"

"He left some time ago. You wouldn't have met him here."

No, he wouldn't have met him *before* he left. But how many Nandys were there in the world that could direct him here?

"He never came back?" he asked.

"I'm not sure if he ever will. I'd read him wrong, that's for sure. I thought he'd lost interest in going back to the old country. I didn't expect him to grieve so much, so long, he had to leave town."

If it was the same Nandy from the ship, and Pietro would have bet his clarinet that it was, the man was not grieving that badly if he'd taken another wife so soon. The wife with the voice. Pietro felt an obligation to tell Mrs. Conati that her son-in-law might be back in town. But then he had given his word he'd not tell who'd sent him here.

"The youngest boy, Gino?" She phrased it as a question. Pietro nodded to say he knew which boy she was talking about. "That's Nandy's son. He couldn't even think clearly enough to figure the boy's future, though I'm grateful he left him in my care. Music, you say?" Her voice brightened. "That's a mighty fine thing. Would you play for me some time?"

Pietro had already promised Mr. Conati he'd help with the chicken coop this afternoon. He'd never cared for the way chickens demanded and strutted, but here it was, one of the few sounds that reminded him of home. Besides, it'd give him time to dwell on why a man would not come back for his son.

"I can play for you later." He'd need to come up with something quite moving to heal this poor woman's soul.

"Whenever you can. I appreciate a bit of music."

ELEVEN

A drip from the roof marked the passing minutes as time carried on, oblivious to the solitude that devoured Assunta every time Nandy left for his shift. Every day colder, and every day the odor of industry more stifling as it infiltrated clothes, bedding, and even her skin.

Not able to get by in English, Assunta endured Anna's company on the way to the store each week. Her drab accounts of how hard their lives should be here had recently changed slightly to how much worse they would be once the snow began to fly.

Assunta looked for Madonna's grass, but the flowers were wilted and defeated in the rain. She'd found nothing to pick, but then she'd kept finding herself looking upwards at the trees—their leaves had started to turn all sorts of yellows and oranges, some even vivid red, quite stunning after the rain when a patch of light broke through the clouds to make them glow.

Before Assunta put the supper on, she scrubbed the stove. She changed the washing water and decided to give the shelves an extra wipe, even though she'd done it yesterday. She set the dishes and the few belongings they were beginning to accumulate in a different order, then reshuffled them a second time.

She cleaned the table and the chairs and the chair legs. She usually waited until Nandy had bathed with kettle water before doing the floor, but it wouldn't hurt to give it an extra scrub.

Three-quarters of the way across, she sat back on her heels to rest a moment and admire the floor even though it didn't look close to decent, even when freshly scrubbed. The rain clouds made the light dim. The roof continued to drip, as it had done for days. Talking of days, it *was* Thursday, wasn't it? She put her hand on her tummy. She should have felt her woman's pains days ago. The laurel leaves she'd picked from someone's garden in town were still on the shelf. She knew that because she'd moved them from left to right and right to left when she'd been reshuffling.

She set her other hand on her belly, holding it like something that had just appeared there for the very first time.

Could she be—she laughed out loud. Every time her brother's wife got pregnant, she began to clean with frenzy. A Mamma. She was going to be a Mamma.

She couldn't wait to tell Nandy—but she surely *should* wait to tell him, just to be on the safe side. It was bad luck to make the announcement too soon, but she had nobody else to tell. Well, nobody except Anna, and she'd probably tell her that having babies was the way they did it around here. She'd have to adapt. Only now she thought about it, Anna didn't have children. Maybe that's why she was never happy.

Never happy. Because children bring happiness—why hadn't she stopped to think about what Nandy had gone through? He'd lost a little girl. A daughter. How in this cruel, bitter life, could anyone cope with that? To have a child to hold in your arms and love, only to have that child taken away, and there'd be nothing you could do about it, no matter how hard you willed them back to life. The knowledge, every day, that the child could have been there with you.

She let tears fall. The poor man had come with nobody; he didn't know a word. He'd lived with strangers. He'd found someone to care for him, and about him, they'd created life, and he had lost it all. She, at least, had him to look forward to. When he had first come here, he'd had nobody. Life in this country was harsh, not the instant comfort she'd expected, and she knew what it felt like to have no family nearby. She could hardly blame him for seeking to ease his loneliness with the landlord's daughter.

Why hadn't she cried before for the child he'd lost? She got up, her body racked with sobs, the guilt at not understanding before. Poor man, and being a man, hiding his emotions. But he had to be suffering inside, and that, right now, was breaking her heart.

Just when Pietro had scrubbed the last of Friday's coal dust from his skin, it was Monday. Time to start all over. Some mornings, before his mind began to wander, life hummed along as though he had always lodged with a family of strangers and memories of summer harvests belonged to someone else.

Pietro clocked in. *I can*, he thought, *spend every daylight moment in darkness broken only by the pitiful light of carbide.*

He'd lost track of how many days he'd spent in this place where there were no swallows swooping, no sunshine, no grapes to stomp. This place where men, Nandy to be precise, left and came back but didn't bother coming home or sending word. Men who left their children to grieving grandmothers while they frolicked with their new wives.

The whistle blew loudly—too loudly. The crew was all here. There was no need for it to be so shrill. One of the men coughed, suddenly and offensively. The gate dropped; metal scraped metal.

"You're on seam 43, a new crew," the supervisor told him as Pietro entered. He wasn't sure how he felt about working with strangers. Though he'd gladly eat in silence, he might miss Mr. Conati's attempt at small talk over lunch, and if the new crew weren't Italian, he'd be lost.

Below ground, the sky extinguished. Pietro found where he needed to work. Two other men had hung their lamps. One, a tall man who looked over-sized in this small space, was setting up to blast. Good, no wasting time. The bigger the load, the bigger the pay.

"The name's Guido," he said, stooped more than the others under the low roof. That was a relief—he was Italian.

When they'd got the first blast set up, Pietro and the other man bent over against the wall. No matter how tightly Pietro pressed his ears, he'd never get used to that sound that went right through the ribs in his chest. Guido used the pick to work the coal around the blast. Pietro and the other man moved in on the loose stuff the blast had tumbled. Kneeling, they shoveled the coal up at the right angle to bounce off the ceiling and into the cart. Only the other man shoveled at an irregular beat, as though each time he pondered what he was about to do, and the decision came to him at a different speed. Pietro should let it go, but the more he tried to ignore the bad timing, the worse it hurt his ears.

"How about in time?" he asked.

"In time to what?"

"You pick, I shovel, you shovel." Pietro pointed at Guido, himself, then the other man shoveling. "Tuck, shhhht, shhhht. Tuck, shhhht, shhhht." He illustrated the beat with his hand.

"You want rhythm? For coal? Hang on, I'll go get my violin," the man chuckled.

The tall man came close to look at his face, the light on their helmets only carrying so far. "You know music? D'you play?" he asked.

Today, Pietro was a miner. "I just prefer it in time. Let's work."

"No, it's okay. You know, it might make the day go a bit quicker. No harm in trying."

The other man made an irritated groan, but he watched for Pietro's shovel swing anyway. It took a few attempts to get it right, but then it came. Tuck, shhhht, shhhht. Pietro stole a glance over at them; neither looked back. The tools in their hands took their full focus. Tuck, shhhht, shhhht.

When they broke for lunch, the tall man pointed out the cart was loading more quickly now. "Let's keep the beat going this afternoon."

Sitting with his back against the cold mine face, Pietro opened his tin pail.

"Come on, confess, what's your instrument?" he asked.

"I never said I played."

"I'm in charge of the band," he said. "We're always looking for players."

Guido, the man had said his name was. Hadn't Nandy said the bandmaster's name was Guido? If Nandy knew this Guido, this Guido would know Nandy. "Do you know a man called Nandy?"

"Vassanelli?"

"I heard his wife and daughter died." Pietro offered the statement. If the

Nandy who married Mrs. Conati's daughter was the same Nandy who'd sent him here, Guido would confirm it. The thought of a man who'd not sent word to his son's carers bothered Pietro more than he'd realized.

"Tragic it was, losing them both like that."

So it was him. "You know where he is now?"

"Went back to Italy as far as I know. Listen, band practice is at seven, Tuesdays and Thursdays. You'll come along? I'll need to hear you play."

"I didn't say I played."

"You don't need to say it. You're the first miner I've met who wants the coal to hit the cart in time."

This was what he'd come to America for—this was what Nonno had wanted for him. Here was the opportunity. And his fingers curled at night from the pain.

"I've been using my time to help my landlord set up the chicken coop. When that's done, I'll see."

After a stint working on the chicken coop, Pietro took out the clarinet to play for Mrs. Conati.

His fingers hurt just putting the thing together, but it felt good to move them, and the blisters were hardening up. If he could work his fingers for a week or two, he might be okay to audition.

His chest a little tight, he anticipated a lack of breath and blew so hard the first note could have made a sleeping dog jump. The next was too quiet, but he persevered with the tune that came from his clarinet and into his ears as though someone else was playing it. It sounded fair, which would have had Nonno shaking his head and making circles in the air with a finger to let Pietro know he had to begin again from the beginning, playing like he meant it this time.

But it appeared to suffice for Mrs. Conati. She mixed the sauce and chopped herbs more deliberately, and with a lighter touch, she even stopped to listen a few times and swayed as though dancing with the stove.

He might have lifted her for a moment, yet something told him it'd take a genuine tune to stop the sorrow from coming through her voice. Sorrow that'd likely be back as soon as the boys came to the dinner table, reminding her of her daughter and granddaughter who'd never come to the dinner table again. All the while, Nandy was nearby with his new wife, not doing a thing to raise his son, not even letting Mrs. Conati know that he'd returned.

After Pietro had played, he gathered his things. Before he stood up to leave, he pulled the note where Nandy had written the Conatis' address, remembering how eager Nandy had seemed writing it in the dining hall, then the effort he'd made to get through the crowd on the ferry to tell him to keep quiet about who'd written it.

Mrs. Conati hummed at the stove, the happiness still with her. Pietro set the note on the table, then left the room.

He was past the dining room when he heard her call him back.

"You forgot something!"

He walked slowly back to the kitchen, giving her time to see it.

"Oh, that, your address. I don't need it anymore. I should have thrown it out."

She read it. "It is indeed, our address. Is this your writing?"

"No, ma'am. It's in the hand of the man who advised me to try here for lodgings."

"And who was that, then?"

"I can't rightly tell you the fella's name." That was no lie. He remembered the name but couldn't tell her because he'd said he wouldn't. "He was on the same ship as me, traveling with a new Italian wife."

"If you can't tell me his name, what did he look like? I'd like to place him, know who's handing out my address, you understand."

"A tall man. Dark hair, thick mustache. Likes his drink and his smokes."

"Apart from the bit about him being tall, that describes just about every Italian man in town."

Pietro thought about it a moment longer. "He has a timbered voice. He rushes through sentences, beginning the next word before he's even finished this one."

"Where is he now?" The resignation in Mrs. Conati's voice suggested she'd understood who he was describing.

"He got off the train before the town of Indiana. Long last name, began with a V. That's all I know."

♫ 𝄞 ♪

Assunta didn't turn around right away when Nandy got home, not wanting him to see her face blotched red from her emotions that had, like every one of the past several days, risen and fallen, up and down, the entire afternoon. She gave one final, futile wipe of her eyes and turned around. Nandy held out a bunch of flowers.

"You brought me flowers?" she burst into full-blown tears again.

"'Sunta, why does that make you sad?"

"I'm not sad, well I am, but I'm so happy. You remembered how much I love flowers!"

"You do?" He sounded surprised but then added, "Of course you do. I'm teasing. Don't cry."

Assunta filled a glass with water and put the flowers on the shelf next to the laurel leaves she'd not needed to use to calm her pains. She'd move them to the table once he'd washed, and she could put the kettle away. After all the pain and hurt he'd gone through, here he was, taking time out of his day to bring her flowers. No doubt she'd be short at the store again next week, but she'd manage. His gesture a sacrifice, she'd make one, too.

"You're still crying. Tell me what's wrong," Nandy said.

"I wasn't going to tell you yet, but I can't keep this news from you. I know your heart must be broken."

"What news, who died?"

"Nobody died. I'm going to have a baby."

"You are?"

She nodded, still crying.

"That is wonderful news." She let herself melt into his arms, her tears smudging into the shoulder of his shirt.

"You're happy?"

"Very. You'll give me a boy, now, won't you?"

But he'd lost a girl! She pulled away from him and wiped her cheeks with both hands.

"Now look at you," he said.

She looked at her hands—grey from his shirt. She looked down at her dress, smudged with coal, and laughed.

"All I've been doing is cleaning. Good thing I have this dress to take care of now, or I'll polish the shanty right off the square of mud it sits on."

Assunta had fallen asleep with a smile and woken this morning, still wearing that same smile, thankfully, without any more tears. Today she could manage the entire day without them and without yearning for home and Mamma.

A bit of patience was all she'd needed. She'd been naive to think they would arrive in the land of opportunity and everything would fall into place.

After yesterday's rain, the blazing sun intensified the color of everything it touched, nearly making the wretched little excuse for a town look attractive. Assunta welcomed it. The three straight rows of houses and muddy walkways were becoming familiar.

She had to get her dress washed. She'd been shocked to see the coal from Nandy's shirt rubbed all down the front, handprints on either side. He'd been rather proud to point out one that was lower than her back.

Nandy had filled the pail before he left for work, so she didn't need to go out to the well in her dirty dress. She had on her chemise, a pretty cotton one with embroidered flowers around the neckline that Mamma had given her as a gift before they came. Nobody could see her, and the first thing she'd do today was wash her dress, even if it wasn't Monday.

She hummed as she rubbed the cotton, smiling to herself as the incriminating handprint of coal dissipated into the suds.

When it was done, she would hang it over the chair by the stove, and wait, quite naughtily, in her underwear until it was dry.

There was a knock at the door. Nobody had knocked at her door before except Anna, but she'd call out, too. She couldn't open the door as undressed as she was. The only other garment she had clean was her Sunday dress.

Another knock.

"*Un momento*," she said, wondering even if the person outside spoke Italian.

She pulled on her Sunday dress but couldn't do up the buttons in a rush. Contorted to reach, she strained to button the top one and one in the middle. Whoever it was, she'd have to make sure she didn't turn her back to them.

She opened the door.

"Buon giorno." Italian, at least. The lady stood on the walkway, looking far too fine in her green tailored dress for this shantytown. Assunta's hand went defensively to her hair. She hadn't even brushed it. She'd worn it loose for Nandy last night.

"Good morning."

"Is this where Nandy lives? Vassanelli?" Her accent was from the same area of Italy as Assunta.

"Yes, it is. He's at the mine." Her intonation asked the question that Assunta could not find the words for—who are you?

"Forgive me. I should have introduced myself straight away. I'm Mrs. Conati. Mary's mother."

"Mary." Assunta felt her heart beat faster; blood rushed through her ears.

"Yes," she said, with no inflection of accusation or righteousness.

Manners would have Assunta welcome this lady into her home and offer her whatever she could, however little that may be. Her insides wanted this woman gone, never to come back.

Not only the mother of the woman who Nandy had started a life with, but a woman who was seeing the life Nandy had given *her*, clearly inferior in this shanty to whatever the woman was used to. From her clothing, this Mary had had for certain a more dignified life.

Manners. Think of Mamma. Remember your manners.

How unfair. A dress in the kettle on the table, and not even on laundry day.

"You must forgive me. Please, do come in! And please understand, I usually try and keep this place rightly gleaming, despite the coal, but I uh, I spilled something on my dress."

Could this woman's timing be any worse? And what did she want in any case? Assunta dug deep for the composure Mamma would demand.

"You must be lonely. How often do you talk to Italians here?" Mrs. Conati's tone was kind.

"Not often at all. There's Anna. Sometimes we walk to the Company Store."

"You poor dear. This is no place for someone like yourself. You must come and visit us. I insist. Life can be brutal. You need—well, I know it's hard without family." She hesitated, seeming to weigh her words, "Gino—we have him to consider."

Gino, Gino, Assunta tried to remember if she had heard the name before. "Of course. You must think us rude. Nandy has spoken highly of your family. I apologize. My husband is proud. Things have been quite difficult, the journey and setting up work and home. He's doing his best."

"I'm sure. But he can't overlook Gino. The boy should know his father."

Mrs. Conati's words echoed long after Assunta closed the door behind her. The boy should know his father. Nandy, father not just of a daughter, rest her soul in peace, but of a living boy. A boy he had never mentioned—slipped his mind perhaps.

Ah yes, that boy, the flesh and blood one.

Lists of words fit for the bar coursed through Assunta's head. She strained to clamp them tightly before they spilled into the air. *Be a lady. Do not lose your temper.*

She'd not yet moved. She'd just stayed there, by the door.

In any case, where could she go? How many steps could she take until she reached the stove on the wall opposite the front door, then turn right and about as many to the bed? Their marriage bed, where they slept, blissful, in their happily-ever-after, with all the joys of togetherness she'd wished for. But she *hadn't* wished for such an uncomfortable bed, nor this poor excuse for a house with no garden. She hadn't wished for this deception, for Nandy's expectation that they could live isolated with barely enough food to keep them alive.

She had only wished for Nandy and a life that only existed in her dreams.

Well, she had tried living with him. She had tried making dinner from scraps. She had tried to wait for the man she knew to reappear and make her laugh and fill her heart with joy. She had even felt pity for him, for having shared this same fate with her eight years ago and vowed to make his life as happy as she could because she had understood his pain. And all the while, while she'd been determined to be a good wife, he had kept his son, his flesh and blood, a secret from her.

So far, the only thing they appeared to have shared a vision for was getting married. But just how they would live together, how their marriage would work, the time they shared, and most drastically, the parts of their lives important enough to let the other know about appeared to be entirely different. And if they saw things so differently, Assunta had to decide whether she could let

Nandy make any decision for her—for them. Where would he lead if she sat back and waited for him to define their future? He'd shown no inclination to lead her anywhere near where she expected to be or hoped to arrive.

She took the steps now, to the stove, and then to the bed—five steps to the stove, then five to the bed.

It made sense now, why he hadn't come looking for her when he'd got back to Italy. He said he'd been embarrassed, which at the time she thought funny. But in reality, he hadn't come because he was a coward. Plain and simple. And he'd let that Beatrice get her grips into him. And Assunta had given up her family, her home, the town where she knew every person who lived or had business there because he had no courage.

She wiped at the damp tears on her face. Was she to spend the entire pregnancy in tears?

She went back to the dress in the kettle—three steps—and resumed the scrubbing she'd begun before the knock on the door.

Coward was a strong word. Not one that appeared in fairy tales, at least not referring to a knight in shining armor.

She missed Mamma; she missed home. She missed not being able to walk down the street and greet everyone because she'd known them her whole life. Even Verona, where she didn't know everyone, but she did know the market vendors and enough regular customers to at least wish them a good day. And they wished her a good day back, in the same language that she spoke.

She had got herself into this mess. She thought it would be her happily-ever-after. She thought she'd come here, and Nandy would be the Nandy she once knew, and they'd have a lovely home and a lovely family, and they'd build a new life, day by, sun-shining day. Just the two of them and their children.

She could go back to Italy. She could pack her case right now and leave. Go back to her simple life, without airs, without hopes of a more comfortable existence, but where she'd have Mamma, they'd make gnocchi for Vito to sell in his shop every day. Mamma would berate her for picking flowers; she'd tease Mamma about finding a man to marry with feet that didn't smell.

And Beatrice would glare and gloat. Her curse would have come true. Assunta hadn't paid much mind to how the *malocchio* would play out. Was this it? That she would leave him and go home? Is that why she wouldn't have him long?

How childlike she'd been, thinking Nandy's past would stay behind in Italy, that as soon as they got away from Beatrice, she'd be rid of it. She'd thought she wouldn't have to look over her shoulder here. Her rival in America had died, after all. But his past was here. His past would never be behind them.

But no, the curse could not break them this way. And nor was it anything more than words infused with ill intent. Assunta had no money to go home, and even if she did, how could she leave a second child without a father? Not to mention the scandal of the separation. If she went, it would be a defeat. No, she'd wanted this marriage. She'd brought it upon herself. What was the saying? Who marries for love by night has pleasure, by day has pain. And as upset as she was with him right now, she did not doubt the depth of her love.

She would just have to figure out a way to keep the pleasure and dull the pain.

When Nandy got home, fragrant minestrone with fresh vegetables, *fagioli*, and a small chunk of Parmesan rind simmered on the stove.

Assunta's dress hung over a string tied up by nails in the corner above the stove. She wore her chemise, the small, knitted blanket wrapped around her shoulders. The kettle was ready for his wash.

She handed him a mug of wine, clinging onto it a second longer than she needed to. He took a long swig, then unbuttoned his shirt.

"How was your day?" She rubbed his back with the cloth. "That feels good."

"Something you forgot to tell me was there?"

Nandy paused. "Got a good load today. Jimmy's missus had a baby. Not much else."

"A baby? Boy, was it?"

"Didn't ask."

She dipped the cloth in the water but didn't put it against his skin.

"My back's getting cold," he said.

"Gino's a fine name for a boy, don't you think?" She made sure she spoke slowly.

Nandy sat up, so water dripped to the floor. She'd already cleaned the floor after washing her dress; she'd be doing it again before bed. "What made you think of that name?"

"I think you know."

He bent back down again. "Not sure I do."

"Is that so?" Assunta stood up, the cloth clasped tight in her hand. "So, you don't know Mrs. Conati, who paid me a visit today?"

Nandy scooped water with his hands and smoothed it over his hair.

"I meant to tell you," he said.

"Pretty important thing to tell. Why didn't you?"

"Why didn't I what?"

"Tell me."

"I just . . . can I get clean?"

He leaned back over the kettle and waited for her to resume.

"What did you think I'd do when I found out you had a son?" She rubbed the cloth firmly on his back.

"How could I chance losing you again?"

"Losing me? You think you would have lost me because of a son born in wedlock but not because of that floozy Beatrice who only had to bat an eyelash to snare you?"

"Her again? Are you never going to forget?"

How could she ever forget? And *why* should she ever forget? Her anger threatened to take over, but that was not what she had decided. She wrung the cloth, dipped it once more, then scrubbed his lower back where the water had run rivulets through the dirt.

"Will the boy live here?" she asked.

"He doesn't need to be here, in this shanty. He's fine where he is. It's a nice home."

Oh good, a nice home. That was reassuring to her. She bit back the question that sprang to mind, the one about how this shanty was, then, good enough for *her* child.

She couldn't let this go. She couldn't let him dismiss her feelings any more than she'd let him ignore the boy.

"The lady, she said we should come one Sunday. I see no need to wait," Assunta said. "You'll get word to her that we'll come the Sunday after next." At least this decision she would make.

TWELVE

Nandy held her arm as she climbed up onto the train. They were really doing this. If Papà had let her marry him in the first place, there would be no reason to visit a child and the family of someone who had shared a bed with her husband. But she could not blame her father, and they would go. She'd not have Nandy getting any ideas in his head about seeing the boy in secret, and she had to see what Nandy's life had been.

"The Mountain Goat, that's what they call this one," Nandy said. The train chugged like a happy kid, and Nandy looked perfectly at home on it. Blatantly eager to return to his family. The train followed along the path of the river to avoid endless ups and downs of the hills and passed farms and a couple of villages. Everywhere looked nicer than the shanty.

Passengers were dressed in Sunday best, as she and Nandy were. The children, in particular, raised her spirits. Funny how kids seem to behave better dressed in bows and caps.

"After being stuck in that stable this long, I had begun to think the rest of the world had simply disappeared," Assunta said. There, it was an effort at least to make light of the fact she was about to meet the son Nandy hadn't bothered to mention.

"The world's still here, look!" He twisted his head so he could look out, as though that would help her see.

"I had no idea the colors of the trees could be quite so stunning. What's the red tree?"

"I wouldn't know."

"I shall have to find out. It's not one I remember seeing back home."

He nodded but looked uninterested by what she said. Such instant distractions. He was thinking about his son, these people that had been his family, and who she would now meet. He was going home, and, to him, she was simply a new appendage to drag along. But being dragged along didn't suit her.

"How old is he? Your son." She constrained her tone on those last two words.

"Three."

She tried to picture Gino seeing his father turn up with a stranger. Oh gosh, would he cry? And the family, Nandy's other wife's family, how would they treat her? Maybe she didn't have the strength for all this. Perhaps she should pray hard enough for the train tracks to be washed away or torn up by Indians. Then they could go back, and it wouldn't be her fault.

"Are there still Indians around here?"

"This isn't the Wild West." Now he seemed not only absentminded but also irritated.

The train drew into the station. Nandy pointed Mr. Conati out to her. Tall, buttoned brown jacket and black bowler hat. He spotted them getting off the train and bent down to Gino and pointed in their direction. The boy followed the finger, broke from his grasp, and ran determinedly towards them. His eyes locked on Nandy's, but at the very last moment, he swerved and flew himself into Assunta's arms. She threw her arms out in the nick of time to catch him and swung him up.

Mr. Conati laughed, "Someone likes you! How do you do?"

Nandy lifted Gino from Assunta's arms. "In your condition, careful! Look what a handsome young man we have here! My, my!"

"I was catching up on railroad news from a friend. How was your journey?" Mr. Conati asked.

"Can't complain. I want to introduce my wife, Assunta," Nandy said.

"It's a pleasure!"

Assunta's cheeks felt hot. Why did everyone have to be so nice here? Here she was, turning up with this man's son-in-law, and he was smiling like she was Queen Elena herself—smiling like an American.

"Nandy. You are looking just fine!"

Mr. Conati put his hand on Nandy's shoulder and steered him along the road. Gino took Assunta's hand, and they followed. He swung her hand playfully, and they must have looked like a real family out for a Sunday stroll.

With Gino jumping into her arms and the quick introductions that followed, she hadn't yet had a good look at the child's face. From this angle, all she could see was his nose and the shape of his face. His nose was like any child's, unlikely to reveal its adult self until later, but he already had defined forehead and cheekbones, like Nandy.

Many children were outside playing; some families and couples were out for a stroll. Houses here were big, set even further apart than Vintondale. Everything looked so new, shining with the hope that ordinary people could afford so much space.

Gino tugged her arm. "Are you going to come and live here? I used to have a mommy once."

"Which one is your house?" Assunta asked, counting on the roving mind and short attention span of a young boy to avoid answering.

"This one!" He ran up the three steps to the porch then turned to her. "You can live here if you want! My daddy too!"

"Gino! Sorry Assunta," Nandy shrugged in apology.

Mrs. Conati appeared in the doorway with a boy, not much older than Gino, hanging on to her skirt.

"Your daddy's working in a different mine, for the time being, in any case. Off and play with your uncle now." The other boy let go of her skirt and ran with Gino around the side of the house. "It's the last child I'm having, I swear! Look at you!" She kissed Assunta on both cheeks, then she kissed Nandy's cheeks and hung her hand on his arm.

"Come on, help me in the kitchen if you would."

Mrs. Conati led the way through the front door into the house that, Assunta reckoned, had to be four times bigger than their shanty. The aroma of meat and sauce she'd first smelled from the street was more potent inside. The front door opened directly into a living room with a tidy sitting area made up of a burgundy sofa draped with a knitted throw and two armchairs upholstered in a tapestry-like fabric, their wooden arms looking ready to welcome an occupant.

The living room led into a dining room with a large oak table, set for a host of people, a cluster of chairs on one side and two ends, a bench, and a fine wood cabinet of colored plates and dishes. Both rooms had woven red rugs arranged on the polished wooden floors. Assunta looked at walls, tabletops, and mantles, searching for anything she could attribute to Mary, realizing she was distracted and rude only when Mrs. Conati said, "The kitchen is here."

Assunta followed her through a door into a modern, ample space.

"Salt the water, if you would. We'll put the pasta on." Assunta held her breath as she carefully measured the salt in her palm, then poured it into the pot. The water rebelled, bubbling furiously. Assunta could almost feel Mrs. Conati's breath on her ear as she watched over her shoulder.

"I should have told you, a kilo and a half of pasta. There are twelve of us."

The breathing on Assunta's ear resumed. She poured again, the second mound smaller than the first, and slipped it in without comment.

"*Perfetto*! I see you can cook!"

"What else can I help with?" Assunta looked around, seemingly to look for chores, really looking for Mary. Everything in this kitchen would have been familiar to her; she would have touched everything. There had to be signs of her—pictures, mementos, memories of any kind— but none jumped out at her.

"It's mostly done—but what is all that fuss about?" Mrs. Conati opened the back door to see what the kerfuffle coming from the back of the house was all about.

"Two chickens are deaded!" Gino jumped up and down on the spot as he made this announcement.

Mr. Conati appeared behind Gino. "You threw pickles out?" he asked, looked visibly concerned.

"I did. The seal was broken. I thought they had gone bad." They shuffled out onto the back porch. Assunta could see a mess of drab debris on the ground off one end of the porch, a place to throw out vegetable trimmings and eggshells to be claimed by the chickens or deteriorated into compost.

"Look, another one's a goner." Another chicken fell, eyes shut, beak open, wings splayed in the dirt.

"It's like payday at the bar," Nandy said. He stood with a group of men, apparently fully at ease. He knew these people. Assunta knew nobody.

"Oh, but look at me, I'd forget my head if it weren't screwed on." Mrs. Conati held Assunta's arm as she spoke. "Ferdinando, meet our new lodger, Pietro. Pietro, this is Assunta."

The man called Pietro was short. He wore a felt bowler and had a bushy mustache, neither of which was remarkable, yet she felt like she'd seen him before.

"Ma'am," he said in greeting, she presumed to her though he was still looking solidly at Nandy.

"Fresh off the boat, eh? How do you like it here, the mine? A man can't complain when his pocket and belly are full," Nandy said. He seemed intent on not letting Pietro get a word in edgewise. He still kept on while Mrs. Conati told Assunta the other lodgers' names, and as they all watched the chickens fall, but even he fell silent when the last chicken went down.

"Guess those pickles were bad. Bad enough to kill the chickens." Mr. Conati shook his head. "Just when we'd fixed the coop, too."

"A disaster. We'll leave you men to sort this out," Mrs. Conati said.

"Mammam killed the chickens," Gino began to sing. "Made the pickles bad, and now the chickens are deaded."

"They won't be good eating. The feathers are probably about all we can save. Everyone, grab a chicken, and I'll get some buckets," Mr. Conati said.

Mrs. Conati tugged Assunta inside.

"I cannot apologize enough. This certainly was not what I'd planned for the day."

Assunta wiped her hands on her skirt. The chickens were unplanned, but the confusion they'd created had broken the awkwardness. Only now, it was just her and Mrs. Conati again. "What do we need to do?"

"Nothing, it's all done. But we don't want to serve dinner too soon," her tone that of a conspirator. "Can't have them come in before they've finished. Learn to guide your man wisely. Make life easy for him, and he won't even notice who's ruling the roost."

"The roost?" Assunta pointed to the back window, and her shoulders relaxed just a little as they laughed together.

♫ ♫ ♪

Mrs. Conati moved the saucepan for the spaghetti to the kitchen table so Mr. Conati could heat the large kettle to strip the chickens.

Assunta fiddled around the table, polishing silverware, adjusting and readjusting each plate until it was perfectly straight, playing Mrs. Conati's game of delaying dinner. It smelled good. She went back into the kitchen. Spaghetti sat stacked on the table, ready by the pot of salt. Assunta lifted the lid to smell the sauce.

"I thought this was sauce for the spaghetti, but you made *polpettini*?"

"Meatballs in Americano. They go on the spaghetti."

"On the spaghetti?"

"No, it's good. Wait till you try it."

Polpettini didn't go on spaghetti. They were a dish in their own right.

"Be a dear and see what they're up to, would you?" Mrs. Conati asked.

Assunta looked out.

"They found some wine to help them work," she reported. "This new lodger, the short one, is he from Verona?"

"You didn't hear the way he talked? No, he's from Piedmont."

"He didn't get a chance to say much."

"He's a gentle soul. Quiet. Knows his manners."

"You speak English, too, don't you?"

Mrs. Conati poured a scoop of salt into the salt bowl. "That I do."

"Did it take long to learn?"

"Not long, but then I was young. Hard to adjust it was, even as a child, not just to the language, but to the way everything looks, the way things are done. It must be harder at your age. But you seem bright. You can pick it up. The trick is to spend time with English speaking folks."

Assunta shrugged. The only English-speaking folks she reasonably had anything to do with were in the store and not at all inclined to talk. She looked around the room again, scouring for traces of Mary, and a picture on the wall caught her eye.

"Saint Theresa?"

"It is indeed," Mrs. Conati answered. "I like to pray to her for my sorrows."

"She'll send roses to let you know she hears you and to tell you everything will be just fine."

"*St. Theresa, the little flower, please pick me a rose from the heavenly garden and send it to me with a message of love. Ask God to grant me the favor I thee implore—,*"

"*—and tell Him I will love Him each day more and more.*" Assunta finished the prayer. "It was Papà's favorite."

Pietro had plucked three chickens already, snatching the feathers out in handfuls, which sounded like linen being torn into strips. They'd accumulated a good pile already. It should make Mrs. Conati at least one decent cushion. They would have enough for even more if they did the belly feathers, but they would have to pull them, and the tougher wing feathers wet. They'd only do it if Mr.

Conati decided to use the carcasses for food. He'd have to decide soon, they had a pile of several birds already dry plucked, and the kettle was heating. The question was, nobody could decide whether the poison that killed the birds could harm the people if they chose to eat them.

"Want a smoke?" Nandy held out a pack of Luckies, then landed, rather than sat on the bench, a splash of wine from the glass in his other hand spilling on the wooden slats. Pietro leaned into the match. He took a big breath, flexing his lungs before he inhaled, unsure why men, himself included, added smoke to the putrid taste of the air. Then again, the doctors said cigarettes were good for you.

He tapped his foot, listening for meaning in the sound. All he heard was the hollow of a wooden floor. They favored wood here instead of terracotta and colored paper on the walls instead of white paint. They even had flat ceilings, preferring texture as decoration over the arched ceilings they had back home. He wondered if any of this would make a clarinet sound different.

"The ladies in them new tulle ruffles ruffle my feathers!" Nandy held a poor chicken to his chest and fanned his face with the chicken's wing, pretending it was a tulle ruffle. He fluttered his eyelids, then he took the chicken by the head and flicked it in a somersault, the crack of its neck like a whip.

The two lodgers who shared the room with Pietro laughed. Gino and his same-age uncle had been trying, with little success, to pull feathers from one of the chickens, now Gino snatched it to his chest and flung it in a lackluster attempt to imitate his father.

"Have some respect!" Pietro told him.

"Respect for a chicken? Let the boy play," Nandy's tone whip-sharp, defensive of the boy. Then he smiled and said, "It won't get any *deader* than it is!" Again, the lodgers laughed.

Mr. Conati took hold of the bird from Gino. "Let me finish this one, lad. You know, it's probably not worth the risk to eat'em. Let's heap 'em back by the pen, burn 'em in a day or two."

Pietro ground the cigarette butt into the wood of the deck. A movement from the window caught his eye. It was the man's wife, the one with the voice, then she moved away and was gone from sight.

They'd spent all that time waiting for the chickens to be taken care of, then the men had decided not to go through with the wet pluck, and all of a sudden, dinner needed to be on the table.

Mrs. Conati called for her other children, two sons, three daughters. They were all between Gino's age and younger than Assunta. Assunta supposed Mary had been the eldest.

Mrs. Conati gave Assunta a rundown of where the grownups sat and left her to take care of getting people in their places and pouring water or wine. Assunta made sure to sit Gino across from her and Nandy on the bench.

"Mind you don't spill your water," she told him. He gripped the glass with both hands, sipped it, and grinned at her, all his cute little teeth on show. The lower part of the boy's face must be like his mother's. Then again, Nandy didn't seem one to smile anymore. She'd practically forgotten what he looked like when he did. Gino set the glass back down. Assunta kept looking at him while she carried on pouring for the others. He sat patiently, bopping up and down as though he was kicking his feet beneath the table. He seemed polite, contented.

♫ ♪

Memories were often generous in their retelling, but if anything, Pietro's memory of Nandy's wife's voice was an underestimation. Hers was a voice that wrapped itself around him, as though, instead of calling to him to sit in the chair, she was physically pointing, her arm on his shoulders, guiding him there. Back on the ship, he'd written about her voice in his notebook. He'd looked for other sounds the rest of the voyage, at first intending to make a list of nice sounds that defied the ship's reverberations. He didn't notice any, so he started searching for just one worthy of recording on the same page as her voice. Nothing else had come close.

He'd only caught a glimpse of her that night on the ship's deck. To his knowledge, she hadn't come on deck again. If she had, she hadn't spoken anywhere near him.

She'd appeared unsure of herself when she first arrived tonight, hesitant when she'd been introduced. He didn't think she recognized him at all. Now she was helping seat people as though she belonged. Or perhaps she was trying to usurp. Like she had not only taken the dead woman's husband, she was taking her place under this roof, too.

Mrs. Conati stood hands on hips in the doorway to the kitchen, watching people find their places. Pietro couldn't tell if she was happy or not.

"Pour me wine," Nandy told Assunta, then turned to Mr. Conati. "A good batch, is it? What grapes did you use?"

He seemed intent on speaking more than anyone today, which was fine. Pietro had nothing to say.

Assunta came around the table and poured wine for Nandy and then for Pietro, the sound of it soothing in any language. It marked the end of the workday, time to eat, then time, in the world that had Nonno in it, for music.

Pietro wiped his sleeve across the bridge of his nose. This was not home; there'd be no music after dinner. Nandy offered him another cigarette. They'd barely have time to smoke it before food, but Pietro took one in any case.

He stubbed it out half-smoked when Mrs. Conati asked her husband to say grace. He slipped in a word for the chickens. He was a quiet man, but you could still catch his sense of humor. Pietro listened for Assunta's amen in the chorus. It rang clear, like a single bell in a chorus of spoons on saucepans.

People began to eat. The satisfying sounds of many mouths being fed were one thing that changed little from Italy to here. It was no comfort. It only emphasized how far Pietro was from his own family and how absent Nonno would be from his own family's table.

Nandy ate rather like he spoke, with furor and haste, spilling chewing sounds as he did so. She ate softly, thoroughly. She didn't join in the conversation. Nandy stuck to talk of the wine and plans to clean up his equipment, which was in the Conati's basement. He'd have to get a batch started soon, he'd said at least three times.

Like any woman of the house, Mrs. Conati flittered and fussed, refusing to sit down until she was sure everyone had everything they needed, then she made doubly sure. Her tone a tad higher than normal, her intonation more concerned. She wanted people to think she was more at ease than she was.

Pietro hadn't meant to cause her distress, but even if he hadn't left the note, she would've found out Nandy was back sooner or later. When he'd left it on the table, he'd thought only of bringing Nandy to rights, not about how it would make Mrs. Conati feel. And he'd thought less still about Nandy's wife.

It was rude to look directly at her. She was another man's wife, a respectful *ma'am*, and *please* and *thank-you* were all he should allow himself. But he looked at her anyway. When she did look up from her plate, she was intent on watching the boy, Gino.

Her head turned suddenly. She was looking directly at him. He shouldn't have stared.

"Have we met before?" she asked.

She *didn't* remember him from the ship, which was no surprise. Pietro had spent his life being forgettable. He was unsure how he should answer her question, so he simply didn't. He twisted spaghetti around his fork without pause and put it in his mouth.

Gino, too, put a large forkful into his mouth.

"Here." Assunta's single word embodied motherhood. She reached across for Gino's plate as he sucked in the spaghetti that dangled from his mouth, then she cut the rest of his food into smaller lengths he wouldn't have to twist on the fork. Nandy was talking again. The moment for Pietro to answer her question had passed.

She shouldn't have asked. The question was blunt and out of place in the midst of so many people. She should have kept to herself, eating this odd concoction of *polpettini* on spaghetti. She might even call it delicious, but *polpettini* didn't go on spaghetti, and that was that. She should have left talk to the others, whatever the subject was. She'd lost track, distracted by Gino, the way he gallantly maneuvered his fork with such care and good intention. She wanted to reach out and use her napkin to wipe the orange-red trail of sauce streaked down his chin. All that effort, he deserved to get all the food inside his mouth.

The familiar-looking man looked shocked at her question, shocked at her manners. He didn't answer, not that he had much choice—Nandy was ranting again, something about where Mr. Conati kept his carboy and how well it reached a boil there. She knew enough about wine to know that a boil had nothing to do with heat being applied. Rather it was the natural process of grapes fermenting that made the juice bubble as though it were boiling.

"He's a musician, you know," Mrs. Conati said, raising her voice to be heard over Nandy. Assunta had never heard him talk so much, not even with his family in Italy.

That was it. Assunta remembered him now. The musician from the ship. How odd they'd ended up in the same place. And how off Nandy hadn't recognized him.

♫ 𝄞 ♪

"Why did the chicken fall in the ditch?" Nandy asked.

In the pause around the table, while everyone stopped to think of the answer to his joke, Pietro heard a scratch.

"Something outside," he said.

"No, the answer's because he'd eaten the pickles." Nandy laughed at himself.

"No, outside," Pietro said. "I hear a scratch in the dirt."

They heard a puck-puck of a chicken. It was tentative, not the typical, confident narration of a chicken serene and feeding.

The Conatis stood and went out the back door onto the deck, followed by Pietro, then the other lodgers and the Conatis' sons. Without a moon, their eyes adjusted to the light indoors. The backyard was a pattern of dark shadows.

Another scratch. "It's over there." Pietro pointed into the dark.

"How can you see?"

"I can't, I can hear." More shuffling and scratching. Not panicked or threatening, actually very much like normal. "It's the chickens."

"But they're dead."

Pietro walked down into the yard, certain of what he heard. He didn't need to see, he couldn't have seen less if he'd closed his eyes, but he found what he was listening for, swooped down, and grabbed a chicken.

Stripped, it's back and sides puckered with empty feather pores, its wings, tummy, and tail still in full plumage, its head jerked in utter confusion.

"I don't understand," Mr. Conati said. "They were dead."

"Dead drunk. The pickle juice must have turned to alcohol. It was more like payday at the bar than I thought." Of course, it had to be Nandy, who now stood with them on the deck, to figure it out.

Mr. Conati fetched a lantern from the kitchen and held it up high, then went to turn on the light Pietro had helped him install in the coop. Another soft carcass reappeared from the ditch, then another and another. Before long, the yard was crawling with yellow, goose-bumped, and oddly-feathered birds, startled by their nakedness.

"Come look!" Mr. Conati yelled to his daughters and Assunta, who peered to see the fuss through the window.

Before long, the noise drew neighbors to the porch. Neighbors drew other neighbors, who drew bottles of wine and cigarettes, an audience for the half-naked chicken party.

Pietro hung back in the yard, listening to the unplanned party unfold and helping the chickens to their feet when they woke. He took the lantern and searched the ditch to make sure all the dead chickens had resurrected. Only one still lay lifeless, its neck snapped. Of all the people on the porch, Nandy spoke the loudest, celebratory as though he'd gathered these people here, oblivious to the chicken he'd killed.

Pietro's song, the grapevine song, started to assail him first thing the next morning. It followed him to breakfast, repeated all day in the mine, and tormented him when he played for Mrs. Conati after dinner. It hadn't stopped since.

Nandy and Assunta had been to the house again the past Sunday. No chickens died, Nandy had not hogged the conversation, and his wife was clearly with child.

Hands still stiff and sore, Pietro was managing a tune here and there for Mrs. Conati. And if he couldn't stop the orchestra playing in his head, it could be time at least to find out what a band rehearsal in Ernest sounded like—the chicken coop was done, fitted with the light to encourage the chickens to lay in winter. He was running out of excuses.

Scrubbed free of coal, his belly contentedly full of Mrs. Conati's stew, he took the long way across town to the bar.

He slowed as he got near, feeling quite mischievous, like when he would skim the cream from his brother's milk if he was late for breakfast.

The door was closed. Pietro propped his back up against the dull gray building, crossed his feet, and stuck his hands in his pockets. A tall, gaunt-looking man carrying a tuba arrived and entered the building with no hesitation or mind for Pietro. He should, perhaps, have followed him in. Or he could carry on walking to the bar.

A flustered youth with slicked-down hair appeared next. He was carrying a clarinet case. Pietro peeled himself from the wall and followed him. The boy even held the door for him. It led straight into a large hall where surely the sound would clatter off the whitewashed walls and concrete floor. Chairs arranged in a horseshoe were being claimed by arriving musicians. Pietro hung back and tried to feel inconspicuous, listening to guitars being tuned, trombone bells fitting into slides, lips puckering in warm-up, cases sliding under chairs, and music stands being raised or lowered.

"How are you going to audition without an instrument?" Guido said, walking over.

"Not auditioning." Working alongside Guido in the mine, Pietro had never noticed how he stood, leaning slightly forward, a little out of proportion, off-balance even. Pietro wondered how he did not topple, mustache first, into the music stand in front of him. "I'll just listen. If that's all right?"

"Can't have everyone thinking this is some kind of public performance. You come again, you play."

Pietro found a chair out of the way to listen to the rehearsal, which was somewhat stilted, interrupted by Guido's instruction and repetitions. Despite his over-sized frame and gruff approach, he was a talented musician, demanding plenty from all the players. He was about Pietro's age, as far as he could tell. The young clarinet player who had held the door for him, though, hardly merited the title of musician. His pitiful rendition ground on Pietro's ears. He managed the most reprehensible squeak when he transitioned. Yet something in his manner and knitted forehead spoke of determination.

At the end of the session, the musicians began to pack up for the evening. Pietro introduced himself. The kid hesitated before shaking Pietro's hand. "Bolek."

Polish, Pietro supposed.

"Play a few notes, will you?" The boy looked over at Guido, who joined them. "I don't mean to intrude," Pietro added.

"Go right ahead. He doesn't know Italian. I'll translate." Guido pulled up a chair and sat on it backward, his arms crossed against its wooden back.

"Play a C? Okay. B. An A?" Bolek managed solid, even notes when he could concentrate on them one at a time. "You need to play the notes. Just the same note, over and over again. Every day, for weeks. Practice until you think you never want to hear that note ever again in your life. You're picking out the tie before the shirt, know what I mean?"

Guido translated, then told Pietro, "Here they say you're trying to run before you can walk."

"Yeah? In any case, he needs to master each note before he tries to string anything together."

Bolek nodded, his expression glum, then left.

"You know your stuff, but I need to hear you play before I can say there's a spot for you. You understand me?"

"I haven't picked up an instrument in a while, not seriously anyway."

"There's also room for someone around here to teach children. Plan for the future, you know? So, we can pick out the ones we want for the band when they grow older. You teach much?"

Pietro had just tried to help, and now he had Guido laying down grand plans for him. He shook his head no; he was no teacher.

Guido turned his attention to another musician. Pietro left and headed for the bar to calm his thoughts with a glass of red and quell this feeling of excitement that had crept up. He had never taught before. There was nothing to get excited about and no reason to think anyone could have anything to learn from him. But he hummed a tune in any case.

THIRTEEN

1912

Assunta fought the losing battle of providing a clean, functional home in the shanty. And with barely any room for her and Nandy to maneuver from door to table, table to cot, heaven knew how an infant could fit. Already the hats and booties Anna and other neighbors had knitted for her, and an afghan Mrs. Conati had crocheted, had to be stored in a grape crate on the dresser. Still, she found it hard to fathom she'd soon have a baby to fill these clothes, despite the way her belly had grown large enough to hinder every move.

Nandy was already gone for work when the first contraction came, with such violence it doubled Assunta over. She clutched her back with one hand and the table with the other, reeling in fear as to how she could endure even a minute more, let alone several hours of this. Is this as bad as everyone got it? Could she get word to Mrs. Conati? *Caspita*, what had made her think of *her*?

She filled the pail with fresh water from the well, dabbed at the surfaces, horizontal and vertical, with less fervor than usual, shook out the rug, and tugged half-heartedly to loosen dust from the curtains, though all she'd done the entire time she was expecting was clean.

Two more contractions deluged through her, about an hour apart. She cracked open the door to be sure to hear the doctor. Bracken was not big enough to warrant a physician, so Dr. MacFarlane walked from Vintondale late each morning, pacing the length of the two streets, calling out in case anyone needed him.

Assunta heard him loud and clear. She stood, hand on the small of her back, watching from the window, waiting for him to follow his usual path until he was near.

"Get on the bed." He put his hat and coat on one chair, his black bag on the other without invitation, and waved Assunta to lay on the cot in the bedroom as though once he walked in, anyone's home became his domain.

Luckily, he didn't go in for small talk. Assunta hadn't much opportunity yet to learn English. Once or twice a month, when they visited the Conatis, she'd have Mrs. Conati teach her words—salt, bread, table, and fork, not at all helpful for having a baby.

He felt her tummy. "You're fine! I'll send the ladies," he made a gesture to indicate people walking. "I'll check on the baby tomorrow."

She caught the words fine, ladies, baby, and tomorrow. "Baby?" she asked.

"That's what I'll wager," he nodded enthusiastically. "It's going to be a baby."

Whatever he'd said, he seemed pleased as he gathered his belongings and left.

♫ 𝄢 ♪

Anna broke into a rare smile when she appeared in Assunta's doorway. She took off her hat and shawl in silence and threw an extra bucket of coal on the furnace, then pushed her sleeves up and dipped her arms into the hot water on the stove.

"It's pretty hot. How long between contractions?"

"Less than an hour." Assunta clung to the table.

"We've got to wait, then. Here, I'll sit with you," Anna said, watching her charge with an air of amusement. Assunta was hesitant to be lulled into a serene mood. Surely Anna would know more scary stories about childbirth than any other subject.

"Delivered plenty of babies, I have. With none of my own, everyone thinks I'm the natural one they should call out day and night."

Anna went on to reminisce about times she'd helped, when the well had frozen over, about the time there were two babies instead of one, when they didn't get the word out to the father, and he'd walked in on full-on labor and fainted in the doorway. Surprisingly, in none of her stories did anything terrible happen to baby or mamma.

"I'm going to get others now. You hang tight a mo. I'll make sure the men know to gather somewhere else for their drink." Anna crunched a section of the sheet and pushed it into Assunta's hand. "Squeeze that when the contraction comes."

The women Anna gathered chattered as they washed their hands, acting as though they did this every day, and they settled into the routine duty of delivering a neighbor's baby.

"'Bout time the rain let up," one said.

"My potatoes rotted before they had time to grow."

Assunta grabbed the woman's arm, contorted her mouth in an attempted restraint, but the yell erupted from somewhere deep inside of her where she could not tame it.

"I'm so sorry," she said, as soon as she was able.

"Now you stop saying that. You're entitled to make a fuss. They all do it."

"There are no men to hear. Do what you have to do."

A tiny mess with a ferocious cry, the baby arrived at just about the time swollen drops of rain began to thump on the roof. Assunta wanted nothing more than for everyone to leave so she could sleep, but when Anna handed her

her baby, cleaned off, and swaddled, she traced the soft plumes of black hair and explored her miniature features. Like an onslaught of peace, love rushed through her. A love so strong, she began to cry. This was her baby, hers to keep—a girl.

The sun was coming up when Nandy was released to come home. He came in slowly, as though it was not his house. He shuffled his dripping hat in his hands.

"Come on in," Assunta welcomed him. "Come and see our daughter."

"A daughter, you say?" he pulled the blanket back with the tip of his finger to look at her face. "Hey, your big brother Gino can't wait to meet you."

That wouldn't happen for weeks. Assunta would stay here until she got her strength back from childbirth, and a newborn shouldn't be exposed to all the people on the train. It wasn't healthy. She pushed aside a twang of dread at being confined to this place with Anna for company. She'd likely revert to her frightening tales, though she'd seemed to enjoy helping with the birth. And Assunta had a healthy little girl—and that's what mattered.

"I've got to thinking," Nandy said. "I'd like it if we named her Mary."

At dinner, Mrs. Conati announced the news that Nandy's wife had delivered a girl.

"Let's raise our glasses. Here, you too," Mr. Conati said, pouring a splash of red wine into the children's water glasses. "Gino, you have a sister."

"What's she called?" Gino asked.

Everyone at the table looked at Mrs. Conati. She didn't seem able to speak for a moment, then when she did, her words were rushed. "They called her Mary."

The grapevine song came roaring back in Pietro's head if such a song could be said to roar.

Assunta was quite the lady to choose that name.

To think, a life that had not existed when they'd met on the voyage over now existed. It'd be a mighty thing to become a parent, something Pietro fully intended to do one day when he met a nice Italian girl who didn't mind if he played instead of danced.

It also meant that time was passing. A winter of callouses and cracked skin, of getting the swallow song on paper, and other excuses came to mind as to why he hadn't been back to try out for the band. If he didn't join soon, he'd be heading back to Italy without having fulfilled Nonno's wish for him.

He'd only got part of the song on paper. Now it threatened to change, to add new life. He'd get to and finish writing it. Then he'd see about the audition.

He walked into rehearsal the next Thursday. Guido acted like he had been expecting him all along, barely extending a greeting before flapping a hand at him to get set up.

Bolek was there, watching, his face sad, though no more pained than last time. Most of the other men ignored Pietro completely while they prepared their instruments. He put his clarinet together slowly, refusing to be rushed, and brought it to his lips only when he was good and ready.

Who knew if the baby would have the same voice as her mother?

Guido pulled up a chair backward and tipped his chin up to indicate he was ready.

Pietro wiped his face before lifting the clarinet to his lips. Only instead of the polka he'd meant to play, he found himself playing the grapevine song. It felt short, so he played it again without pause. When, finally, he lowered the clarinet, everyone was looking at him. The whole room was silent. All other practices and preparations had stopped.

"What piece was that? I didn't recognize it," Guido said.

Pietro could have choked. He should have stuck to the polka, what he knew best. Sharing this tune had probably cost him a place on the band, and now he was sure to return to Italy without learning a thing.

"I'm sorry, let me try something else." Even he could hear a near-beg in his voice. "I apologize for wasting time."

"I didn't say you were wasting my time. I just don't recognize it. Must be some Piedmont tune."

"Just something I came up with."

"You wrote that? Have you written anything else?"

"I don't write, not really." He pulled his shoulders back, stuck his chin forward. "Should I leave?"

"No, no. You're in. Come on, people, show's over. Are your instruments tuned? Hey, that piece. Did you give it a name?"

Pietro shook his head no.

Rehearsal sounded familiar, not wholly different from rehearsal with Nonno's band, yet foreign at the same time. It went quickly, almost as soon as it started.

Instead of packing up, Bolek came over and lifted his clarinet as though to ask whether he could play.

"Sure." Pietro set his cleaning cloth down, giving the boy his full attention.

Bolek ran through his scales. Still a squeak of sorts between notes, but not bad. A definite difference.

"Your notes are improving. Transitions too," Pietro said.

Guido came over to translate, though Pietro had learned some English from the men in the mine.

"Now you're more confident with the basic notes, you need to practice playing something simple. Here let's see." Pietro thought for a moment. "How about *Three Blind Mice*? I'm serious. Try it. Over and over like you did with the notes." Bolek nodded bleakly. Pietro wondered if he was disappointed, but then his face perked up for a moment, just long enough to say thank you.

"Good practice," Guido said.

Pietro nodded. "The boy, he looks so sad."

"Yep. Came out here alone. To America, I mean. No family. Nobody knows his story. I don't have the heart to get rid of him, you know?"

"Then don't. He works hard. I'll keep an eye on him. If you don't mind, that is?"

"Not at all. Have you really not written anything else?"

"Just that."

"I have a cousin in New York. Works in the theater, has connections, he does. Write some more, and I could get you an audition."

"That's not what I came for. If it's all right with you, I'll just play."

"Suit yourself. Though the offer will stand. Let me know when you change your mind."

Pietro closed the door gently and walked toward the bar. But then he carried on walking right past it. Guido had liked his piece. They all seemed to enjoy it. He could get an audition in New York. He didn't want to go to New York, but they thought him good enough to go.

His music. The music he'd feared might not get past Nonno's ears. How life could change. He walked to the top of the town, then looped around the longest way he could find before tracking back to the bar. There he ordered wine, and, to heck with the money, he bought the two men next to him one too. He didn't know where they were from, but a free drink was a free drink in any language, and they all knew the word for cheers.

When Pietro got home, he got out Nonno's book and sat on the back porch. There was a full moon. He'd be able to see quite clearly.

He'd played the song he'd meant for his grandfather, and who would have guessed, they'd said it was good enough.

Now he was ready to see Nonno's music.

He ran his thumb along the bottom edge of the front cover, left to right, then pulled it open, not realizing he was holding his breath. On the first page, nothing. He turned the page, still nothing. He paused, then, not so cautiously, turned another and another. Nothing, nothing, nothing. The book was empty. He closed it and turned it over in his hands. It couldn't be the same book.

He took it down to the chicken coop and held it beneath the light, shushing the fuss they were making, in case it woke someone.

Pietro would recognize the book anywhere. Crackled black leather, gold border. A dented corner, a scratch Nonno used to buff his thumb over. Completely empty.

FOURTEEN

1913

Boots shuffled, someone coughed, and another spat. A tall man wearing a supervisor's cap pushed his way through the crowd to face Pietro. "Hey, you. They say you've an ear for things."

Guido pushed through and helped with the English. By the look on his face, he knew something.

"I play," he shrugged, not knowing what this man wanted.

"Don't need no piano accompaniment. Need someone to check for widowmakers." Pietro had heard the word. Widowmakers were sections of loose ceiling rock that might collapse without warning, crushing whatever or whoever was below. When they contained gas build-up, they posed an even greater danger of explosion.

"Let's go in ahead of the crew. You'll tap. If you ask me, everything needs to be tapped before every shift. But it's hard to tell this to someone who thinks they know what they're doing. Them frickin' bosses."

Bent at the waist, he followed the supervisor into the blackness of the mine. The men's safety was no small thing.

"Start here," the supervisor said, leaning close to Pietro. His eyes not quite adjusted, Pietro could see little more than the man's light. But he needed no instructions. He lifted his pick and began to tap methodically from one side of the ceiling to the next. He held the pick in his right hand and held his left up instinctively, flat to the ceiling. He didn't need to look. The only thing that mattered was what he heard. *Thuckthuckthuck.* Any kind of *tingtingting* or *taptaptap* might be a hidden hollow, and that would mean danger.

Pietro worked quickly but missed no sections larger than a square foot. He stepped aside for an irregular stream of workers shuffling their way out from their shift and for carts squeaking protests at the weight of coal. Then the men from his shift entered in a shuffling stream, causing him to stop. He leaned against a damp tunnel wall until he could resume. More than one man tipped a finger to a cap.

He resumed, and the tapping took his complete focus. When the supervisor slapped his shoulder, he jumped. He had forgotten all about him.

"Good to go. Do this first, every day. The men'll thank you for it."

Pietro listened to crunching footsteps disappear back towards the light, then went to find his team. They slipped effortlessly into the beat, no longer needing his cue.

"You're Mary after Gino's sister," Assunta told her baby, mostly to convince herself. "And Mary after the Virgin Mother."

She longed to go out and parade her beautiful daughter to earn coos of admiration. This tiny shanty felt like a prison, an uncomfortable one at that. The interminable winter that all of Nandy's warnings had not prepared her for had been followed by a hot summer that cooked the shanty. The fall had been a stunning explosion of color, but it had not lasted nearly long enough. Now, a kitchen floorboard had fallen out, and through it, she could almost touch the snow of yet another winter that had come far too soon. Her days had become a new war of coal versus snow. Neither could win; the battle just kept ending in a pewter colored slushy tie.

No warm breeze from the lake here. This was no place for a baby. Mary was already sickly, so Assunta talked to her to calm her. Mary simply ignored her, or at best, she grumbled back.

Assunta should probably put her down to sleep while she scrubbed the place, but she loved the feeling of her tiny body in her arms, her total dependency. She did not want to miss a second. Besides, she seemed more settled now than she had all morning.

The last time Assunta had gone to the company store, she'd searched on the way back for herbs of any kind. Mary wasn't thriving. She needed some kind of pick me up.

"It's so quiet in here. Feel free to speak up from time to time," she said, but the baby just pulled faces back at her. "Italy is your homeland, my little one. That's why I speak Italian to you. Don't you listen to those who say you need to learn English and only English because you're going to be American. You need to know where you came from. The English will come. Just not from me. No point speaking with Mamma's broken words anyhow, is there? And Mamma wants you to learn, so she has to talk, but what can she talk to such a beautiful little creature about?" She paused, allowing Mary to reply, or at least soak in what she was saying as her hands bobbled in the air, not yet under her control. "I should tell you a story. How about I tell you about your family back in Italy? One day I'll take you there. You can meet your Nonna and all your aunts and uncles. You have so many who would adore you, I'm sure. I'd even let you meet your uncle Vito! Oh, but your Nonna, now she's quite the woman." Mary did not appear to mind waiting while Assunta thought about her Mamma, nor when she wiped a few tears away with the ball of her hand.

"I hope life is good for you here, little *marmocchia*, but it's a shame you can't grow up with Nonna. She was married to Nonno before he went to heaven.

Now let me tell you a story about them," Assunta began. One story after another popped into her mind. She carried on telling them even after Mary had fallen asleep.

But how was Mary to learn anything at all here? And how was she to thrive when they could see the snow through the floor. And since she'd been born, getting groceries had become a momentous task; Assunta was more reliant than ever on Nandy, which had not at all been her intention.

"It's too hard on me, on the baby, living in this place," she told Nandy after she'd scrubbed his back. She set a sparse bowl of minestra in front of him.

He took a swig of wine, a long drag on his cigarette, then stubbed it into the saucer he used as an ashtray.

"You should ask for a job in Ernest," she said, half expecting the words to get stuck in the back of her throat.

"You want to move there?" he looked surprised. Well, he ought to be. She'd been surprised herself to realize it was the best decision for them.

"It has the best company store around. We could be nearer Gino because we can't bring him here."

Nandy slurped two spoonful's of minestra before he responded. "I'll look into it."

"No need to infringe on the Conatis, though. The other side of town would suffice, as long as it has a garden of sorts. I could grow vegetables, plants for my teas, too, medicinal, you know."

He nodded and settled back into his dinner.

𝄞

On the morning of moving day, Mary was making a great effort to cry.

"Here," Nandy handed Assunta the bottle of whiskey. She wet her finger and rubbed the baby's gums. Her front bottom teeth had come in. By the way she fussed, it had to be hurting toward the back of her mouth.

Assunta upended the bottle again, this time spilling a trickle of whiskey on her skirt. She pushed her finger into the other side of Mary's mouth.

With Nandy's wine equipment, their possessions had grown to over a third of a load on the back of the oversized cart pulled by stocky, resigned horses.

Assunta had scrubbed the shanty clean, ignoring the urge to leave it in the state she had found it in. She even left a bunch of flowers for the next tenant. Mary had thankfully slept through much of the packing but started to fuss on the Mountain Goat. Nandy fiddled in his seat and looked the other way.

"Do something. People are staring," he said eventually. "Didn't you feed her before we left?"

Assunta renewed her efforts of comfort, laying Mary on her shoulder, then over her forearm, rubbing her back and humming to no avail.

Nandy led them to a house just two doors from the Conatis. The moving cart stood in front of the house, and the movers were carrying crates and carboys inside.

"Did you know it was this close?" Assunta asked.

"Not as such," Nandy said.

They walked up the short path to the front door to find Mrs. Conati standing with a mop in hand and making sure the movers stomped their boots on a cloth spread out on the wooden floorboards. "They gave me the key yesterday," she explained. "I gave it a good clean for you. It'll need another, I fear."

Why they would give the key to her, Assunta had no idea.

"Come and see." Mrs. Conati invited Assunta and Nandy into their own home for a tour.

The house offered double the room of Bracken. They could eat at a little table in the kitchen, but they had a sitting room also with a window onto the front porch overlooking a small garden that ended somewhere in the mud of the road. As Assunta looked out of the window in the second bedroom at the view of the town, Mary woke up and resumed her crying immediately.

"What's wrong with that little might?" Mrs. Conati asked.

"Something upset her on the train, I suppose." If anything, she was crying harder than before. Her face was red with the effort.

"She's been on the train before, poor lamb." Assunta pulled Mary tighter, sensing Mrs. Conati wanted to take her from her arms. She held on and turned her back to survey the bedroom. "Thank you for washing the place up. It looks spotless."

"I wanted you to have a nice welcome."

Assunta drew Mary to her lips, still just a low fever. She walked through to the kitchen. Someone had set a package tied with brown paper and a pink ribbon on the shelf above the stove. "What's that?"

"I thought you could use it," Mrs. Conati said.

Now Assunta had the dilemma of reaching for it and risking unsettling Mary again or handing her to Mrs. Conati. Manners, Mamma would say. Assunta placed Mary gently in Mrs. Conati's arms. She began to fuss, but Mrs. Conati knew just how to rock her to settle her back down.

Assunta pulled the ribbon from the package and opened the paper. An Italian-English dictionary. It was just what she needed.

"Thank you. That's very thoughtful of you."

Mary had calmed to a grumble, but now let out a long wail as though some mortal offense had been committed against her.

"Do you want me to take her to my house? I can rock her while you get settled," Mrs. Conati said.

"If it's no trouble." Assunta arranged the blanket to Mary's chin. "See you in a little while, *marmocchia*."

Assunta was making their new bed—a real bed with springs and a sturdy mattress—when somebody knocked at the door. She paused, half-made bed sheets in hand. They'd been here for a couple of hours. Who would be looking for them? It was unlikely to be Mrs. Conati because apparently, she just walked in uninvited. She heard a second knock. Nandy was in the tiny basement setting up his wine-making equipment and perhaps couldn't hear down there, so Assunta maneuvered around a case full of bedding and went down.

Pietro stood at the door, looking surprised to see her. "Good evening."

"Nandy's in the basement," she said.

"I came for you, ma'am. Mrs. Conati sent me. It's the baby." His voice trembled when he said the word baby.

"Please call my husband."

Assunta rushed past him and over to Mrs. Conati's house. She burst in without knocking, and Mrs. Conati delivered Mary straight to her outstretched arms. "I can't calm her. She won't eat. She feels hot."

"We need to cool her off," Assunta said. Why had she let Mrs. Conati take her? She took Mary in her arms and turned to leave. But to go where? She didn't even have a bed made at the new house.

"The unpacking—your house isn't ready yet. Stay here. We'll lay her on the sofa."

"She needs cold."

"Then we'll open the windows and not feed the fire."

Mrs. Conati lay the afghan receiving blanket she'd crocheted as a gift on the sofa, indicated for Assunta to set Mary there, and then she opened the front door wide. Assunta peeled open Mary's robe.

"I'll get a wet rag," Mrs. Conati said. Assunta could hear her in the kitchen, closing the grate on the stove, and opening the back door so the icy evening could sweep right through, front to back, and fill the house.

She reappeared with the rag, followed by Nandy. Thank goodness he had come.

"Will she be all right?" he asked.

"We'll have to wait and see." Mrs. Conati's words stung. Assunta fought her urge to pick Mary up. To hold her and protect her, but Mary needed to be cooled, not warmed by body heat.

"Did you look at her gum?" Mrs. Conati asked. "She has an abscess—I'll make a poultice. Some of this, for the meantime." She handed Assunta the whiskey bottle.

"A poultice is a good idea." Nandy backed away. "I'll get back. Call me if you need me."

Nandy slipped out, leaving Assunta staring at the door frame. "But—"

"Men don't like sickness. They can't control it," Mrs. Conati called from the kitchen.

"I'll be heading out then." Pietro had been so quiet, so inconspicuous in the corner that Assunta had forgotten he was there. "When we were sick, Ma used to sing to us," he said.

Mrs. Conati came out of the kitchen, rubbing her hands on a tea towel. "I have the poultice on the stove. It'll take a while. What a grand idea, Pietro, we'd love you to sing."

"I didn't mean me, I—"

"Then how about the clarinet? It might soothe the little thing."

Pietro pulled a stool into the corner by the stairs, staying as far away as he could on the other side of the room. He was intruding. Mrs. Conati shouldn't have asked him to play. He shouldn't have told her he would.

He rubbed each piece of his—of Nonno's—clarinet. Perhaps a second polish would not go amiss.

One more rub for each piece—Mrs. Conati came and stood over him, like a silent instruction for him to begin. He set the cloth on the case and slipped lower joint to bell, upper joint to lower joint, barrel, and mouthpiece. Mrs. Conati didn't move.

He hadn't tried to play a lullaby in years. It would be the right thing to try. He gathered air, held the clarinet to his lips, but couldn't find the courage to begin.

"The poultice? Is it ready?" Assunta's voice, hesitant.

Pietro's lungs released, notes rang. Hesitantly searching the room, then finding their place, whole, unified, yet gentle, content to remain in the background.

Mrs. Conati returned to care for the baby. Pietro barely dared to move a thing except for his hands and mouth in contact with the clarinet. He felt like he was standing on a precipice, listening to somebody else create the music, and if he shifted an inch, he'd break the spell and topple into oblivion.

He played, over and over. After a while, the baby stopped crying, and he dared a glance at Assunta. Her shoulders drooped in defeat, poor woman. She'd clearly been dragged to this country by her husband to fill his gap and now left to watch her baby's suffering.

Despite the way she must be feeling, Assunta had a kind tone saying goodnight to each member of the family who stopped to wish Mary well on their way upstairs. Warmth shone through in her voice, despite her distress.

A few times, Mrs. Conati smiled at him, just a brief smile, enough to keep him playing the same lullabies over and over without thinking too hard about what he was doing, without his fear returning. The baby's tiny rapid breaths reached him between notes–fitful sleep. She still had a fever.

The baby fussed but didn't quite wake when they reapplied the poultice. Mrs. Conati found blankets for both of them to wrap around their shoulders against the air that still chilled the house.

Mrs. Conati soon fell asleep in her chair. When Assunta began to sleep-breathe, Pietro put the clarinet down on his lap, holding it tight in his hand. It would probably be right for him to leave. Or perhaps he should find blankets, too. But the peace of the room held him here.

The still of the night allowed small sounds to grow. The house itself had things to say if only people listened. Pietro hadn't been listening until now. He sought the voices of the walls and rooms with his ears. Someone shifted in bed, a breeze rustled a tree outside, and walls sighed, relaxing for the night. Mrs. Conati stirred gently, as though busy in her dreams.

Assunta's head lifted; something had stirred her. She took baby Mary's hand in her own, and neither moved for what seemed like minutes. Then she set Mary's hand back down abruptly and set her head once again on the back of the sofa, as though asleep. She inhaled, long and trembling, a sharp, forced exhale. She was deeply troubled, yet she pretended to sleep.

The baby!

Pietro stood up. Assunta's breath was clamorous now, as though all the peace of a home at rest had been snatched and wrenched into the most despicable pain.

No rapid breaths.

Assunta knew! Her eyes clenched shut against the truth. He strode across the room and watched his hand, detached from the rest of him, rest on her shoulder in insufficient comfort. Trails of tears framed the coarse sound from her throat. His hand reached toward her face to wipe the tears away, but he caught it in time. He didn't trust himself to touch her. If he did, he might hold on so she could release her pain into him, so he could take it from her, shield her.

He stepped back, shocked at his feelings. He prodded Mrs. Conati's shoulder to wake her, then withdrew back to the corner.

Shrieks of piercing agony called the rest of the family down the stairs. Pietro stood as flat against the wall as he could, not wanting to be in the way, not escaping the noise bombarding him. *Nononononono.*

Nandy! He ran out of the door, up the street. The door was unlocked, ready for Assunta's return.

Nandy was slumped on a chair in the living room, surrounded by boxes.

"Wake up—the baby. They've called a doctor!"

Nandy sat up. He stared angrily at Pietro.

"Go—your wife—"

Nandy stood but said nothing. He shook his head no. No. What did he mean, no?

And yet Pietro couldn't force him. He took a step back toward the door, then changed his mind and walked over to the sofa. He watched Nandy pick up a glass half full of wine from where it sat on the floor and gulp it down in one go. Some spilled down the side of his chin.

"I can't go." Nandy stood, swayed so violently Pietro thought he'd fall. He staggered into the kitchen. He picked up the jug of wine from the table, then started to go up the stairs.

"Your wife!" Pietro's voice twisted in an attempt to contain his anger. Nandy just kept on walking.

Pietro leaned on the table. What to do? What could he do? The poor baby, poor Assunta with a scum of a husband. Her smile, her eyes. She was sincere, warm. In pain, her loss was inconceivable. A violin, her heart. Crying, breaking, yearning for her baby. A clarinet, embracing her, supporting her, holding her in her grief. Letting her pain happen, but not leaving her alone, the music building, telling a story, finding resolution.

Mannaggia! He wanted joy from music. He didn't want music from pain, from sadness.

Suddenly it was Nandy's fault. His fault for everything. Pietro would not stand for this. He would not allow Nandy to turn his back on Assunta tonight.

He stomped hard on each stair, letting Nandy know he was coming, that he meant business. The bedroom door was open, and Nandy sat on the bed.

"Go to your wife. Now," Pietro said.

Nandy closed his eyes for a moment. "You don't know what it's like." He wiped his sleeve across his face. "I don't know if I can deal with it again."

It?

His first wife and daughter. So, he did care. Not that Pietro had room for sympathy right now.

"They need you," Pietro insisted, his tone gentler now.

Nandy nodded. Yes. He'd go. He followed Pietro down the stairs and over to Mrs. Conati's house.

The sorrow from the living room was dulled slightly by the presence of the doctor, a final grasp at hope. Assunta cried out when she saw Nandy. Pietro watched them embrace, their sorrow shared. Nandy in the right place. Pietro had done the right thing by fetching him.

Pietro went to his room. Lying in bed, the music of earlier played on and on in his mind. Eventually, he took out his notebook. The other lodgers were gone, probably downstairs. His pencil needed a sharpen, but it would do for now. He drew a treble clef, perfectly rounded.

Musical notes spilled across the line after it. Music that may have come from pain, but he felt compelled to write it down, nonetheless.

FIFTEEN

S pring was fighting out winter. The snow had melted, and a warm breeze blew. It would be a good morning for drying diapers. The breeze would dry the laundry before it got too dusty. But there were no diapers, not until the next one. Let her be healthy and strong, Assunta willed, but she didn't put her hand on her belly. She wasn't ready to bond with her new baby yet.

She folded a bedsheet in half and hung it lengthwise, listlessly securing it with pegs. Her hands stung from scrubbing too long. Her soreness was poor reparation for a life lost.

As for Nandy, he appeared to cope best at the bar, which suited her just fine. She probably ought to begrudge his absence, but instead, she cherished it. She could take the cushion from the sofa Nandy'd had delivered. At first, she'd felt annoyed that he thought furniture a good substitute for a baby, but she found some comfort from hugging the cushion, cooing to her tummy, moments of love telling him or her the stories she had told Mary. Her Mary.

She shook out a pillowcase and pegged it to the line.

A movement caught her eye. It was Mrs. Conati waving from her back porch. Why did Nandy insist they live so close? If Assunta could make a list of people she did not want to see today, Mrs. Conati would be close behind Beatrice and all her empty curses. And yet here she was, no longer on the porch but marching right on over.

"Are you done hanging?" Mrs. Conati asked.

Assunta looked down at her basket and was disappointed to see it was empty.

"I bought you some Valerian root. You can make an infusion. And I thought we could plant some dahlias." She held out the box she was carrying in explanation. Assunta could only see scrunched up newspaper in it.

"I have some linens soaking." Assunta looked back at the house.

"Let them soak." Mrs. Conati set her box down and walked into the middle of the small stretch of yard. "The sun is probably best over there." She set the box next to the section of dirt she'd pointed to.

"I had not planned to plant anything today."

"There are many things you don't plan in this life. And yet." Mrs. Conati pulled out a wad of newspaper and unraveled it. She pulled out what appeared to be a shriveled potato.

How could she make this woman and her rotten box go away?

"These are called tubers. Funny looking things, aren't they?" Mrs. Conati took a trowel from the box, bent down, and began digging the dirt.

"I don't want—" Assunta began.

"They'll grow into nice bushy plants. Are you familiar with the flowers?" She paused and looked around. Assunta had just been caught in a blatant scowl, but Mrs. Conati's all-business tone did not falter. "The flowers are big. They are made up of the most delightful petals, not flat like some flowers, but like little tubes clustered in a circle. Lots of colors too. Here, I brought another trowel." She pushed the tool into Assunta's hand, then delved back into the box and pulled out a small rug. "Let's kneel on this. It'll be easier than bending over."

Mrs. Conati knelt and resumed digging. "Break up the soil. When the plant starts to grow, it shouldn't be too solid. We get a lot of clay around here. You're lucky. There's good soil mixed in your yard. I knew the people who lived here before. If you tend them, they grow year after year."

She went on and on while Assunta stood, trowel hanging from her hand, watching.

"Each fall, you dig these up. They don't last the winter in the ground. Store them, and next spring—"

For a lack of willpower to continue ignoring Mrs. Conati's instructions rather than for intention, Assunta sank to her knees and began to dig, sticking the trowel in tentatively at first, then attacking it with more conviction, turning a dull and barren patch of dirt into the bed where they'd plant life. The physical effort made her feel alive for the first time since Mary wasn't.

"We've all lost people we love." When had Mrs. Conati stopped talking about flowers and started talking about people and love? And who said Assunta wanted to hear it? She shook her head, but Mrs. Conati carried on. "They'll tell you time heals the pain. Poppycock. After a time, it might not be with you every second of the day, but the pain'll wrench you just as cruelly when it does come. They'll tell you other people have dealt with it, so should you." That's precisely what Assunta had tried to convince herself. "That doesn't help either. Or that the person who died is in heaven. Or that they'd want you to be happy. All these things together might help for a moment here, a moment there, but the pain still gets you. You ask me?" Assunta had not. "The best thing I find is to fill my day. Never let my hands rest. Fill it up with chores and people and preparations and clearing away. Grow plants, cook for the people around you."

Assunta struck her trowel harder and harder into the ground. What did they tell you about holding a slight against your baby? A tiny slight, but one nonetheless because the poor creature had shared the name of another woman. What did people say about having that slight and then having your baby taken from you? About every time she uttered the baby's name, the love was tinged. Ever so slightly, but tinged, nonetheless. How was she supposed to overcome not loving every single thing about her daughter with every bit of her heart and back? That she'd been a terrible mother?

The ground in front of her was all turned over now, she moved further along, still on her knees, off the rug, and onto the grass, and she attacked the next section.

"Help your neighbors and even the people you don't think deserve it. Just work and keep busy and don't give yourself time to think," Mrs. Conati went on.

Tears dropped onto Assunta's arm. It didn't matter. Nothing mattered. She just wanted her baby back.

She didn't want to hear what Mrs. Conati was saying, and yet it was just what she wanted to hear. She wanted someone to know her pain, but why did it have to be Mary's mother?

She kept on turning soil, strike-turn, strike-turn until the effort drained her arms. She could picture the flowers that would grow here, the colors she'd see from the kitchen window. A dream of flowers. Colorful tribute. This might just bump her heart to beat again.

Pietro hadn't seen Nandy since the funeral. He hadn't come by the house, and they had not crossed paths in the mine. On a Tuesday, Pietro was tapping when Nandy passed by. Nandy didn't acknowledge him. He might not have noticed him all dressed as they were in miner's garb.

Pietro noticed *him*.

He was complaining loudly about the same thing every man in the mine was complaining about—the switch from carbide to safety lamps. Pietro got it. He didn't want to wear a clunky helmet with a cord tying his head to his belt, a cumbersome, heavy battery at his hip. As if life underground weren't uncomfortable enough. But the tapping he was doing here was also a good reason to make the switch. They all knew the risks. They all knew how many men died each year. If a landslide or a detonation released a big enough pocket of air, the open flame of a carbide lamp could ignite it, causing an explosion that would maim or kill.

Mrs. Conati had told Pietro that Nandy himself had lost a brother. Perhaps Nandy thought his family had already paid the price of mining, or maybe he thought the same thing as every other man out there—bad things only happened to other people.

Yet Nandy had lost two children. Sure, he wasn't the first father to have lost, everyone knew childhood was a risk in itself, but it should make the man more cautious.

But in any case, Nandy should not be concerned about what *maledetto* helmet he had on his head when his baby had just died. His poor wife was home; her heart shattered into pieces.

If Pietro had a wife facing such grief, *his* heart would be broken for her. He'd covet her, play the clarinet while she laid her sweet head on his shoulder. He'd play the part of the song that was the breeze tumbling up the slope, swallows scampering a rhythm—and then a new part of the melody, a part where someone needed him, and he needed her.

This she, this woman he'd meet one day, she'd find him, put her hands around his waist, and lay her head, enveloping him in a safe place, where bad things could happen to neither of them—Pietro realized he hadn't been listening at all to the sound of his hammer on the wall and ceiling. He was tapping mindlessly, and the line of men had long finished passing.

He could back up and repeat it or go onto his shift.

He'd best go onto his shift and come back to cover this area tomorrow when he might better keep his focus.

As he shuffled through the tunnel, he relived the music of the imaginary woman embracing him.

Shoots of green had pierced through the surface of the soil this morning. Assunta knew because she checked them every morning after she'd made the bed and swept the floors and every afternoon before her three o'clock coffee. Afternoon coffee was a routine she'd begun in the new house where she had more than a square foot of surface. Every morning she set aside a cup from the percolator and later heated it to drink at the kitchen table, a few minutes of respite before she started on supper.

The shoots had already grown by this afternoon. If only her day could pass as quickly as they grew. For all the time she'd daydreamed about flowers, even collected them to make teas and remedies, she had never stopped to think about a plant's first miracle when it thrust a shoot from its seed or tuber, and that shoot found its way through the dirt to sunshine. All happening without a mother or anyone to guide it; it just knows how to find the sun. Babies for the princesses she imagined adorned the petals of flowers as gowns when nobody watched.

The turn of the back-door handle made her jump and knocked the table leg with her knee, though she held tight to the pillow.

"You're home," she greeted Nandy. She looked at the clock. "Oh," she said to its certainty that this was the time Nandy should come home if he didn't instead stumble into the bar on his way back.

"No smell of dinner to welcome me?" He hung his jacket on the hook he'd put up, a bit too right of center on the narrow strip of the wall for her liking.

"I'll put the water on right away," she said.

"It won't kill me to wash in cold."

He poured some water, ice-cold, from the pitcher, and rolled the soap slowly in his palms. He didn't look up at her. Was he angry? Who would know? It seemed like he didn't look at her at all anymore. They were two people living in the same house, exchanging information when they had to. Nandy announced he was working the second shift next week. Assunta said she needed a coal delivery. Goodbyes in the morning, a perfunctory inquiry about the day in the evening. At night, in bed, they didn't talk, but that's when Assunta absorbed him, drew his strength greedily into her. She didn't know how she'd survive without that.

She managed a minestra of sorts. The hunk of cheese rind she threw in didn't have time to infuse the sweet flavor Nandy liked so much, but it was supper, nonetheless.

"Get me another glass, 'Sunta." He pushed his plate away from him, his glass toward her.

"Not going out tonight?" If he wasn't at the bar, he was on the Conatis' back porch with that lodger, the musician.

Tonight, Nandy didn't leave, and he didn't talk, and she didn't mind. There was something healing about the way he just sat while she cleared up. When she was done, she sat next to him, and he took hold of her hand. Tenderly, like he was ready to start mending the sorrow they'd shared.

For all the darn roughness and manliness, he loved to show the world, this was the man she loved. Heart as tender as a buttercup when he let you see it.

"Come with me." He stood without letting go of her hand. She made a sound in the back of her throat that meant no. "I mean it, come," he insisted.

If he'd pulled her with more force, she might have resisted. But his tenderness was as unfamiliar as it was unexpected. She let him lead her to the back door and wrapped her shawl around her before he guided her outside. He said nothing, just led, his hand encompassing hers with even pressure, as though he'd considered how each finger and his thumb touched her.

They went down the road that led away from town and turned onto the trail into the woods. Clouds muffled the moonlight, yet there was just enough light to see where the path led. Parallel to the rail lines, the creek on the other side of it.

"This way." Nandy took her to the right, into the woods, then the trees stopped. They were on the edge of a clearing. There was nothing more than darkness to see, but then a magical light flashed in front of her. Then another and another. The entire area sparkled in a dance of dashing lights—hundreds of them.

Nandy pulled Assunta forward until the magical lights were all around them. "Fairies!" she said.

He held his open palms in front of him, patiently, then grasped them closed. He let Assunta look between his thumbs into his cupped hands.

"Some might think they're bugs. But you and I know better. For you, my lady, a fairy." Light flashed on and flashed off, illuminating his hands like a lantern.

"Queen of all fairies." Assunta blew her a kiss, and Nandy opened his hands like a book to let the fairy queen go.

He put his arm around her. "I'm no good, you know, to help you through what you've gone through. I can't take your sadness away. I wish I knew how."

Assunta felt tears well. She wanted her baby. She wanted to hold her and kiss her soft head. Nandy didn't say anything more; he just held on to her and let her cry.

When her head began to ache from the tears, she pulled away. He handed her his handkerchief to dry her face.

"This one's going to be healthy," she said and couldn't help but smile.

He touched her belly. "You mean? Another? What a woman you are, 'Sunta. This one, she'll be a fighter. I know it."

"She?" she asked.

"Hmm mm, you make beautiful girls."

"If it is a girl," a sob in her throat pinched the word girl. Assunta took a deep breath, and then she said, "We will call her Mary."

SIXTEEN

1915

Pietro set the teapot in the middle of the table with the contented sigh of steam escaping the lid. He set the sugar to one side, clinking the handle of the spoon toward him, and the jug of milk on the other. Everyone was gone. He should have an hour or more to himself.

An hour. Such a small fraction of a year, which had been the amount of time he'd meant to stay here.

He pulled his chair in and checked once more that he had everything he needed. The tea setting was arranged just as he liked it. Two sharpened pencils set to the right, his clarinet, still neatly snug in its case, to his left. He would only pull it out if he felt he needed to make sure the music sounded the same to his ear as it did in his mind.

He hadn't so much decided to write this, as it had come to him when he'd been sitting on the back porch watching Nandy and Assunta's little boy two yards over, chasing the chickens, belly forward, hands in the air, while their littlest one sat on a blanket, finding amusement in a flower. He'd watched Assunta bend over and hand the flower to her, a plush, full bloom, yellow as the sun. The little girl squealed with delight, then Assunta went back to tending the flower bushes. He couldn't hear over the sound of the chickens and little boy's laughter, but she was probably humming as she filled a basket with flowers.

The page on the table in front of him waited patiently, its lines suspended in eager anticipation of the tune they were about to be given. He closed his eyes and let the music return. It was a happy song. If Assunta's voice were a song, it'd be something like this. The way it made him feel like someone had hugged him, someone cared. Her laugh when the boy had fallen on his backside—the boy had laughed, too, and Pietro had yearned for something he could only imagine might be fatherhood.

It made him nostalgic for his own family. Ma had recently written to ask if Pietro had thought of returning home, that they expected the war to be over soon. She'd also insisted yet again that Nonno had never learned to read or write, and yes, she had checked again with Nonna as he'd asked.

He should write to Ma to say he was composing pieces Nonno might've approved of. He wouldn't tell her he could only write these pieces when his neighbor's wife was nearby. Of course, he wouldn't, though if he were to write that, he'd explain his admiration was purely platonic, not immoral, as it might sound.

He began to write. The pencil flowed lightly, fluently whispering the tune to the page as he drew each note carefully, each curl rounding off at just the right point, the next starting at an even distance away. He stopped only from time to time to close his eyes again and tap something on the table, and gently whistle.

Just as time these past years had flown, now all notion of time disappeared. When Pietro reached the bottom of the page, he remembered the tea, but the steam was long gone. He lifted the tea cozy and felt the pot—only a hint of warmth remained. He shouldn't be so careless. He turned the page—surely he could write another few lines and still manage to clean up before Mrs. Conati saw. She need never know he had let it go to waste.

A sharp rap at the door made him jump up from his chair. The tea cozy was still lying flat and accusingly on the table where he had left it.

Perhaps a little more hesitant this time, the knock came again, leaving a question mark in the air. He stood up reluctantly and prepared to excuse Mrs. Conati's absence to whoever it could be.

When he opened the door, Pietro recognized Walter from the mine and the girl who hung on his arm from town.

"Good morning to you, Mr. Maccagno." The couple looked at him expectantly.

"Mrs. Conati isn't back from her errands," Pietro said.

"We came to see you. This is Angela." Walter bobbed up on his tiptoes as he pointed to the girl. She was rocking on her feet eagerly. Both of them looked like they could burst from excitement at any moment.

"I see."

"May we come in?"

"Have a seat." Pietro waved his hand over the table, all too aware of the teapot, but all the young couple seemed to see was the music book.

Angela elbowed Walter. "See? He's a composer."

"Angela has kindly agreed to be my wife."

"Good. Yes."

"The bandmaster sent us. We were hoping you would write some music for us. You know, our own wedding score, just for the occasion."

"Would you? Please, say yes!" Angela piped up, as though an instant were plenty long enough to formulate an answer.

"The bandmaster, you say?"

"He said you'd do a fine job. You'd write us the most beautiful score in the whole county."

"I hate to disappoint. None of my music is much good."

Angela looked devastated. "But they said you'd do us proud."

"I think Guido's stuck on a single piece I wrote." Pietro hadn't yet decided what to do with the new pieces. Songs he thought might be worthy.

"So, what's that?" Walter pointed to the music on the table. Then he laid his arm around his bride to be. It was a simple, earnest gesture. Love was so admirable. It made Pietro think of a flurry of piano keys.

"You know what? I can't promise, but if you'll be patient with me, I'll try."

The sunny day had drawn many people out of town to enjoy the relatively smog-free air and one of the last stretches of crystal river. Pietro had been quite touched at the invitation to join Nandy and Assunta for a picnic. He often had a glass of wine with Nandy at the end of an evening, even now, the family had moved away from the Conatis and to the top side of town, but a picnic felt like a gesture of greater friendship.

Pietro and Nandy dropped the blanket and baskets of food for Assunta to sort, then the men headed straight for the water with Gino and little Max in tow. Pietro didn't mention he couldn't swim, but the water was shallow enough. Perhaps there was no need.

Nandy held Max in his arms, dipped him under cautiously, splashing him with handfuls of water to get him accustomed to the cool. Pietro kept his feet firmly on the ground, wading back and forth, watching Gino swim, and hoping he wouldn't get in trouble and expect Pietro to rescue him. It was hardly any time before he felt his chest tighten. It must be getting worse with age.

"I'll just watch from over here, catch my—" Pietro patted his chest at Nandy.

"Get a drink. My wife made fresh lemonade," Nandy offered.

Pietro wished he had taken his towel down to the river's edge. Now he had to walk up, his scrawny chest bare. He probably should wait on the rock, but he could do with the drink.

"Ma'am. If you don't mind, your husband told me to ask for some lemonade. I apologize." He unfolded his towel and wrapped it around his upper body, realizing his knees and legs were still exposed. Assunta cradled the baby in one arm and poured a glass from the pitcher.

"I'm glad to oblige. How's the water?" She could wrap her children up in that voice of hers if they needed comfort.

"It's a tad cold. They don't seem to mind, but it's a bit chilly for me. You have a fine family." Pietro wheezed the last word of his sentence, suddenly feeling lightheaded.

"Are you all right?"

"Fine."

"Why don't you sit for a moment? Rest."

He looked back at Nandy and the river. A moment wouldn't hurt.

He sat on the far edge of the blanket from Assunta and attempted to arrange his legs at an angle that wouldn't offend and sipped methodically.

Neither said anything; the baby gurgled.

A funny thing, water. It seems like the most innocuous and harmless substance, yet it could steal your breath, cut through mountains, and drown all other sounds around it. As for his breath, the doctor had told him it was asthma. He lit a cigarette. He still didn't like the feel or taste, but the doctor said it'd do his lungs good. He drew a few long drags, listening to the paper and tobacco burning. A clump of ash fell with a sound so soft, it might not have even happened.

Assunta began to hum softly to the baby. Since Walter and Angela's visit, not a single melody had come to him, but now her soft hum became the intro for a tune. He listened to it unfold, then Assunta said, "You're very talented with the clarinet. I enjoy hearing you play."

"You're too kind."

"We were at a dance recently—your band was there. It reminded me of summer festivals on Lago di Garda."

Her vision reminded him of festivals in the piazza, and summer evenings in the hills, playing to the stars, the grapevines an unseen audience in the dark. Pietro downed the rest of his lemonade. Instead of relaxing, his chest felt worse. For propriety's sake, he had to get back to Nandy in the water, but he did not trust himself to stand right away.

A hummingbird appeared over the rug, flitting back and forth to see if they'd brought any food for it, then it disappeared.

"I love the sound they make," Assunta said.

"You do?"

"It's not that far off an insect but nicer somehow. Like a gentle and overly busy bumblebee."

Pietro took a few deliberate breaths, then said, "All birds sound different. Their song obviously, but their wings too."

"I quite like the dove. I bet that's why it's the bird of peace—for the sound of its wings."

"There's one bird, black and white with a little red bib—"

"Grosbeak?" Assunta said.

"That one, yeah. Sings beautifully. More when it's sunny."

"I love birds, but they aren't that smart. One flew into the kitchen window the other day."

"It didn't die, did it?" Pietro said.

"No, it was just stunned, then it flew away. Your concern is touching."

"My grandma would say if it dies at the window, it means someone in the house is going to die. You've never heard that?"

"Don't suppose I have." The baby woke and gurgled at Assunta. He shouldn't stare, but she looked so radiant.

"Have you seen an oriole? Mostly bright orange, some black, too." She turned as she said it and had probably caught him watching her.

"They chatter like they're scolding all the others?" he asked.

"I never noticed." Assunta laughed. "The wives are scolding the husbands for staying out too late."

"The hummingbird—" Pietro was hesitant to go on.

"Yes?" her voice was encouraging.

"Like a water wheel, a minute wheel that belongs to little people, only take the visible sound of water away because air is invisible, it's like their sound is there but not there."

Assunta said nothing, but *her* breathing changed. He could hear that. Whatever had possessed him to talk this way, yet she hadn't laughed at him.

Max suddenly appeared, showering river drops. He planted himself on Pietro's lap.

"Oh, there you are!" Assunta said. "You're getting him all wet again!"

Max shook his head, so his hair flicked Pietro's chest with droplets. Pietro and Assunta laughed; Max laughed harder. Gino came next and sat between them.

As the family settled in around him, Pietro noticed the heady babble of the river. Steal his breath though it might, it certainly sang a happy song. Soothing.

"Sit down, darling!" Assunta beckoned Nandy to a spot next to her.

"I left my towel on that rock over there. Would you be so kind as to help my wife unpack the picnic?" he asked Pietro in a stern tone.

What had he been thinking, talking to her like that? So blatantly, so publicly. Assunta piled plates with watermelon, salami, cheese, and slices of cucumber freshly picked from her garden and handed them to him to distribute to the children.

Nandy stood near the water, rubbing a towel over his arms, his back to them, then rolled his towel lengthwise and hung it around his neck, still ignoring the family.

Max sucked on his watermelon, Assunta cooed to the baby. Nandy was stubborn and missing out on time with his family. He had no right to be angry at an innocent conversation, and by gosh, Pietro had no reason to feel ashamed. But just in case, he resolved to talk only when spoken to for the rest of the day.

♪ ♫ ♪

Mary fell fast asleep on the way home. Max stoically kept his eyes open, his head firmly on Nandy's shoulder as he carried him into the house.

"Let's get you settled, my sweet," Assunta whispered into Mary's ear, then louder, "Then we can find these men some wine."

"I don't want to go to bed," Max wriggled, trying to escape his father's arms.

"That's a shame because I had a little story about a naughty little piglet to tell you. I'll tell it to anyone under the covers in five minutes!"

From downstairs, Pietro smiled as he listened to the family's routine. He put the picnic basket and blanket down in the hall and sat at the kitchen table to wait for Nandy to reappear.

Perhaps he should let himself out, but that would surely be rude without first saying goodbye. It'd turned out to be a nice day. Especially the talk about the birds.

A refrain appeared in his head. It seemed to capture the movement of birds with a hymn-like reverence. He might have something quite special here. He'd love to play it for Assunta, see if she recognized the birds in it.

He fumbled behind his ear and in his pockets for his trusted pencil, but he hadn't brought one because he had been planning to swim. He closed his eyes and tried to secure the music in his memory. It hovered majestically, pulling his heart along on a ride through the air. It lifted like a bird on the wing, soaring, reveling in the magic of flight.

There were too many details to forget. He needed to write it down. He walked around the kitchen once, wondering whether to open a drawer on the dresser. Instead, he spotted a scrap of paper sticking out of a dictionary on the windowsill, a pen sitting nearby. He pulled the paper out. Good, it was blank. He scribbled the notes down as small as he could to fit as much in as possible. With his left hand, he tapped the beat on the tabletop. When that side was full, he turned the paper over.

It did have writing on—it was not blank. In neat handwriting, it said *My love, my soul. Anima mia. Forever.*

Why had he not checked both sides of the paper? Nandy's handwriting or Assunta's? *Sweet love.* He looked back at the dictionary. Could it have been stuck in a special spot like a bookmarker? Darn it. Footsteps creaked down the stairs. He crumpled the paper in his palm, then tucked it into the inner pocket of his jacket.

"I sent Assunta straight to bed," Nandy appeared at the door. "We'll pour our own."

Nandy set two glasses on the table, lit Pietro's cigarette for him, then disappeared into the basement, empty wine jug in hand.

He took his time. Pietro stubbed out the butt of his cigarette and felt the letter in his jacket pocket. He should have left earlier; it would be rude to go now before Nandy came back. From the sound of it, he was shifting things around down there. Pietro swirled the empty glass on the tabletop to make a constant roll of noise.

At last, he heard Nandy's footsteps coming up the stairs.

"Sorry it took me so long. Had to find a fishing hook in case I fancied going back to the river, you know?"

Pietro didn't know. He pulled another cigarette from the pack on the table.

"Let me," Nandy said. He picked up the matchbox in his left hand and poured them both a glass with his right.

Pietro hung the cigarette from his mouth, wishing he had left earlier when he had the chance.

"Assunta, she's giving me another kid. Churns them out, she does." He laughed. Pietro took the cigarette, still unlit, from his mouth and took a long sip of wine. It was a bit on the sweet side for his taste.

"Oh, here," Nandy took a match from the box but didn't strike it. "Mining's a damn dangerous business. A man with a wife and kids—four soon—he's gotta think of what will happen to his family, to his wife, who'll look after them if something happens down there."

Nandy struck the match. Pietro fumbled the cigarette back into his mouth and drew in the whisper of fire. He followed it with another long swig.

"I suppose you're lucky, not having a family of your own to worry about, eh? You don't have the concern. You can sit back and let the next man worry about what'll happen if he snuffs it."

Nandy raised his glass, Pietro copied.

"To your health," Pietro said.

"To my health," Nandy replied.

After the end of shift on Friday, it could have been any time at the bar, day or night, because there were no windows to remind patrons of life outside its walls. A cloud of smoke hovered above heads, muting the sounds of bar stools and boots scraping on the wooden floor. Voices harmonized in a chorus of conversation, all male with the sole exception of Lola, who flitted among the men and in and out of the worrying minds of the wives in town.

Pietro made his way through to a spot at the bar, stopping once for a man who spat tobacco juices on the sawdust. He listened through the discordance in the noise, fleetingly wondering when it had stopped upsetting him. Nandy should be here somewhere, and he'd had time to have a few drinks already. He shouldn't be too hard to locate. Pietro needed to find a way to let Nandy know the conversation at the river was innocent, reassure him he was a good fellow. He'd meant no disrespect.

Before he could listen for Nandy, Guido edged through to him.

"Nice piece you're working on for Walter's wedding," Guido said. "We should be ready to let them hear it soon."

Michael, a trumpeter, passed drinks to them, hard-won from the busy barman.

"I'm happy to know you, Pietro. You're a talented man." Guido slapped his shoulder. Pietro took a long slug from his glass, waiting to find out the point of the flattery. "My cousin's ready to set auditions up for you in the city."

"I told you, Guido—" Pietro began to protest.

"You tell me a lot of crap, Maestro. You just don't know how good you are.

See, nothing's gonna happen for you in this town. Nothing. Nobody's going to come and ask you to perform for hundreds, thousands of people. You're just going get the same weddings and festivals, the same frickin' coal miners and their hapless wives. Tiny town, you know what I'm saying. Over and over, the same thing, the same people. You got something special. The world needs to hear."

"I like the same people."

"You need to think of the masses. Don't deny all those people your music. If it was me, Pietro, I'd jump at this. You don't think I'd like my music played in the theater, on the wireless?"

"The wireless? Now hold on a minute—"

"Where do you think that music comes from? People write it. People with talent. Composers. You're letting the world down, my friend, by not sharing. You're letting my cousin down. I'll arrange everything. A few years, that's all. Try it. Earn some real money, something to live on."

"Why would I do that? I'm with the band. You even have me composing."

Guido laid a hand on Pietro's shoulder.

"Seriously, my friend. You have a room you share with two other men. You have a woman who cooks for you, but she's someone else's wife. You crouch down each day in the mine to get dirty. Let me see your hands. As I thought, calloused. Can you honestly tell me you have everything you need?"

"It's a good wage and honest work. The bed is clean, food decent. Besides, I'll be heading back to Italy soon."

"Last I heard, there's a war on."

"It won't last forever."

Guido bobbed his finger in front of Pietro. "What about when you play? Isn't that better than the mine?"

"Sure is. See, I play every week. For friends."

"Your prerogative. My cousin has a fine wife, though. Sophisticated. You could find yourself lucky, too."

"Here's to your cousin and his wife." Pietro raised his glass, then turned his back to the bandmaster.

Through clouds of smoke, he heard Nandy.

"Excuse me, Guido. Nandy!"

"Pietro. Dear Pietro." Nandy was already slurring.

"Been here a while, have you?"

"Suppose so."

"Want another?"

"Nother. A nother." Nandy held his almost empty glass at the barman for a refill but could not keep it still.

"Enough, my friend. Don't want any trouble." The barman said.

"I said just one more. Then I'm on my way."

"And I said no more. Beat it." The barman leaned forward threateningly, wiping the bar with a cloth that may once have been white.

"Come on. You know me. Can't a man get a drink 'round here?"

The barman didn't budge. Beer trickled to the front of Nandy's shirt as he drank. He took one step back, and without the bar to prop him, fell into the man behind him and knocked the glass in his hand.

"*Cretino!*" he slurred. "Out of my way, sakes alive."

The man whose pants were now wet with beer handed his glass off to another man and slung his arm in a punch. Pietro willed Nandy to dodge it, but he was too drunk. The punch landed deep in Nandy's stomach, doubling him over. The man followed up with a right hook under the chin. It made a popping sound as Nandy's teeth clapped together, and his head snapped back, a line of saliva flying and landing on Pietro's shoulder.

Pietro had to get him out of there. It was not wise because Pietro was the shortest, but men liked the entertainment of a fight. It took a friend to break one up. He stepped in between them. Nandy was now upright only thanks to his elbows on the bar behind him. His feet shuffled and slid on the sawdust to find a good connection with the ground.

"That's enough now. I'll get you home." Pietro pulled Nandy's arm around his shoulders and took his weight, forcing his way forward.

"That's it. Get lost." The man's tone smug.

Pietro made it to the door. He pulled Nandy through it, then let go. He took a few steps. He should leave and let Nandy make his own way home. He heard his friend stagger behind him, then decorate the snow with stomach contents.

"The police are going to find you!" Resigned, Pietro grabbed Nandy's sleeve and dragged him, still doubled over, into the alleyway beside the bar. Out of sight of the main road, Pietro used Nandy's sleeve to wipe the spit off his jacket, then let him fall to the ground. He listened for the tell-tale clopping of horses' hooves over Nandy panting, then, hearing none, he slid his back down the wall of the brick building.

"Come on. I need to get you home."

"Leave me. I'll just sit here for a bit. I don't need help from the likes of you."

"You don't know what you're saying."

"I said, leave me!"

"And I say we're friends, come on!"

"'S'pose you think you're better than me, don't you? You and your fancy clarinet."

"Stand up."

"I only sent you here in case. Dumb curse. But I am here, all right?"

"What are you talking about?"

"I'm not going anywhere, hear me?"

"You're going home, that's where."

"I see what you're up to. Fancy, high-perishing-fatutin clarinet," Nandy muttered.

"Now shut up and stand up."

Nandy gathered his uncoordinated limbs and swung a shot at Pietro from where he was sitting–a puny shot that missed its mark. Pietro grabbed Nandy's balled fist and pulled him to his feet and toward home.

Nandy let himself be led for a while, but then he stopped. Pietro tugged, but he could only steady him, not make him move. "Tell you what, musician, good man-fatutin. If anything happens to me—*when* it happens to me, you *should* be the one. Just as I decided back then on the ship."

"Walk. You need to get home before the police throw you in the slammer."

"No, no, no. Musician man. You'll do it—" His voice trailed off, so Pietro had no idea what 'it' he'd do.

"Just move." Pietro tugged.

Nandy began to sing. "Shhhhh! The police! I'll leave you here." Nandy sang louder and carried on singing the whole tug-and-drag way to his house. Pietro pushed him as far up the porch as he could, then collapsed him in a heap. He rapped three times sharply on the door, then turned, slapping his hands together to wash them of Nandy.

How dare that blasted man? He'd *sent* him here? He'd given him an address, that was all. And Pietro had only *talked* to his wife. He'd never touch her, never dare be inappropriate. He was an honest, moral man. Nobody would question that. It was simply and exclusively only about the music. Nothing else.

How could Nandy—a lug who wouldn't understand the meaning of music—possibly see his heart? His heart that he was in full control of.

Other than the day he'd not helped his grandfather, there was one immoral act he'd done in his life—he'd taken a photograph, and that was a wrong he *could* right.

Back at his lodgings, Pietro wrote Sig. P. Sacco on the front of an envelope from the new pack he'd bought at the company store. Or should he have said Mr.? It was written, anyhow, so there was little he could do about it without wasting an envelope. He finished the address, then wrote a letter of apology to go with the photograph. It felt like too little too late, he should never have kept it in the first place, but an apology is an apology, even this late. Surely Sacco would know he meant it sincerely.

He would not think of Assunta ever again when he composed.

He licked the back of the stamp and attached it to the envelope.

Whether Nandy's words were in jest or heartfelt, the man had been drunk, so this, Pietro hoped, would be the end of it. Sacco would have his photograph back, Pietro would be above accusation, and Nandy, the buffoon, would see just how innocent Pietro was. As soon as the wedding piece was done, he'd not look to Assunta for inspiration ever again.

SEVENTEEN

How another Friday had come so soon, he'd never know. Tonight, they had an extra rehearsal to do a last run-through for the wedding. Pietro had struggled with the score. He'd channeled the melody he'd heard at the river; it had sounded so full of promise, so close to something he could be proud of. But the night he'd dumped Nandy drunk on the doorstep had hung heavily each time he'd tried to develop the piece. He couldn't feel its joy without the shadow of that night intruding on his mind.

Pietro *had* to tell Guido that it had been a big mistake, that they needed to revert to their routine wedding line-up. What had he been thinking, risking such an important event for a pleasant young couple? An amateur arrangement would set their marriage off to a bad start. He would not forgive himself for subjecting them to such a disaster. Best go with what the band knew.

He would get to practice early, let Guido know before everybody got there—he was a coal miner, not a composer, and he had better remember his station. It felt better now he remembered it. The miserable, black coat of grime on him was proof. He just happened to be a miner who, once in a while, heard a song in his head—a song best kept to himself.

He peeled off his jacket, shirt, and under-vest with purpose and picked up the soap Mrs. Conati left out for him. It amazed him how the coal worked its way beneath his clothes. Not as thick as the exposed parts of him, but there, nonetheless. Mrs. Conati had overheated the water again, but better too hot than cold. He began with his hands. No point washing your back with dirty hands. He lathered on the soap, then swapped the soap for a scrubbing brush and began the laborious process of wrist, palm, back of the hand, each finger—front, back, and in between. The tune of his daily wash. His bane as a coal miner. That was all he was.

The dull and repetitive scratch of the brush, the squelch of soap, the flap of clothes peeled away. Splash, a crescendo of optimism, layer after layer of defeat cleaned off. Rinse and shine, fingers, then arms, chest, and back.

A coal miner. Like Nandy.

He stopped, ignoring the voice in his head that was saying he was dripping everywhere. He could see his reflection in the only tiny mirror Mrs. Conati allowed, just big enough to shave. His face, still various shades of coal, his hair pressed into the shape of his hard hat, only partially dirty from the neck down.

Nandy couldn't impact everyone in that room in a month of Sundays unless it were by spiking their drink. He couldn't lift their spirits, make them feel special inside.

Pietro looked again in the mirror. His face stared back, a face that didn't look a bit like Nandy. He should not compare himself because he could, quite possibly, lift that entire room. He *could* be a composer. No reason why not. Even if he lifted one person with his music, it was better than none at all.

Pietro hummed the start of the wedding piece. His fingers and toes tickled like swallows chattering in his bones. He resumed his scrubbing. He could do it—he had done it. Good thing the water was hot. He would be ready sooner. He had a rehearsal to attend.

♫♩♪

Father Farri joined Walter and his bride in Holy Matrimony under the all-knowing gaze of the Madonna and the scaffolding of the new church, which was in mid-construction, a replacement for its predecessor that had burned down a few years earlier. His voice echoed in the nave, so much smaller and the roof so much lower than the church in Pietro's hometown.

Pietro wiped the sweat from his palms with the tips of his fingers. He had no idea how he would play, as nervous as he was about his music being heard. He wanted to fidget like one of the children resisting their parents' commands to sit still. To squirm and slide below the pew and not come back up until the band was well into their routine medley, his composition forgotten. Instead, he made himself sit stock still and repeated inside his head—*you can be a composer. They asked you to write the score. The piece isn't terrible.*

His mind didn't settle a bit, but somehow he managed not to move another muscle, not even to wipe his palms. He didn't need to look around to see faces, many familiar or known, others foreign. A congregation of nations, but Italians mostly.

Straight after the service, the men headed for the reception, and the women laid out the food they chipped in to provide. Pietro, like Guido and the rest of the band, had worn his uniform to church. Unlike the others, he didn't go up to get a drink before the performance. He sat to wait on the edge of the stage. He didn't look but listened to the dishes being put on the table, lids removed, cutlery clinking.

As focused as he was on the food being set up, he didn't notice the sound of a woman approaching, leather heels a delicate tit-tat, until she said his name. Assunta. He turned to face her and was relieved to see that Nandy was not with her.

"Nandy asked me to bring you this," she held out a glass of wine. When he took the glass, his finger touched hers. He didn't take a sip, and she didn't leave. "Nice service, wasn't it?"

He needed to talk, to say something. His finger burned where it had touched hers—not burned as in pain, but rather in warmth. "Nice service," he agreed.

"Let's get ready," Guido said, striding toward the stage trailed by Bolek and followed by the other musicians. Assunta walked away. To Pietro's dismay, she didn't walk far, just to one of the nearest tables. Nandy wasn't there, not yet, but then it wasn't his style to rush away from the bar.

Pietro set the glass Assunta had brought him on a table, resisting the urge to run his thumb over the spot where she'd held it.

People fidgeted and waited for the bride and groom. The band members had all taken their places now and held their instruments ready. Focus, he had to focus. He had to remember the first note at least of his song, darn, what was it? Guido gave the signal, and the band struck up Pietro's song just as the newly-weds entered the hall to cheers, rice, and laughter. Pietro was going to be fine—he hadn't forgotten the music, his hands did not let him down.

People gathered around the bride and groom, their first dance as husband and wife. Pietro did his best to hear the music and half-see the dance floor like a sea before him but glanced three times at the table where Assunta sat. The third time, Nandy was there, sitting with his back to the band, a waft of cigarette smoke rising as though from his shoulder. He was looking the other way, at least.

The whole room clapped at the end of the piece. Pietro kept head down, pulled apart, and reattached his mouthpiece to the clarinet. They began a string of soft instrumentals as people settled to eat.

When there was more chatter than eating, the band stopped, and the groom's father stood up to make a speech. Pietro paid little attention. He took a long sip of the wine. When applause broke out, he looked up. The whole room was looking in his direction.

"Pietro," Walter's father said when the clapping died down, "You have made this a special day for us. Such beautiful music. Please, all of you join me in raising a glass to Pietro, to *Il Maestro*!"

A cheer of *il Maestro* reverberated around the room.

Pietro did not know which way to turn. He knew he was blushing. Maestro? He shook his head and held his palms up, defending himself against unmerited compliments. Then to his good fortune, the attention turned back to the speeches.

The music they'd played for the bride and groom was mesmerizing. It sounded like yearning, like love, like something Assunta wanted to feel blossom inside of her. It sounded like her happily-ever-after. She almost wished she could get married again just to have music like that bless her ceremony.

When it was done, she looked around at Nandy. If he'd felt it too, he'd have to brighten up. But if anything, he looked grimmer. His eyes downcast, jaw— still bruised and swollen—held firm.

He'd seemed gruff since the night someone had dumped him on the front step. She'd been hoping a wedding would cheer him. So far, the only sign of anything remotely resembling pleasant had been when he asked her to take a glass of wine to Pietro. But he'd looked sour and not said a word after.

Look at me, she willed. *Look at me like you love me with a fraction of the love that music had.*

He didn't look. Without thinking, she got up and walked back across the hall to Pietro. She should have walked right on by or turned back, but she didn't do what she should have. Instead, she leaned down and spoke directly into Pietro's ear.

This time he recognized the sound of her approach. He wished she hadn't come back. He already felt giddy and ready to be home.

He looked in the opposite direction, doing his best to portray the image of innocence, as though her voice wasn't already coursing through his veins. He couldn't trust the expression on his face if he looked at her right now.

He felt her hand on his shoulder. The finger touch before had been accidental. This was intentional—this was not the way things were done. Wind swirled through his ears, his heart raced, but he dared not move. Her lips near his ear—he could feel their heat.

"The music, it was *bellissimo*, Pietro!"

She breathed his name as nobody had done before. Then she was gone.

Guido called the polka. Polka. He knew how to play that, didn't he? Surely he did, but right now, his mind was blank. It came back to him as soon as he lifted his clarinet to his lips.

Polka. He closed his eyes. It was just him, the clarinet, her voice in his ear. He felt light in the music—not in it; he *was* the music. It was coming from inside of him, whooshing beneath his skin. He hovered on thin air, the polka solid in the sky with him. It was clarity. It was bigger than the piazza, higher than the town, not to be confined by even the blackest of skies. It was holding the notes up and mixing them like confetti thrown at a bride and groom.

The last refrain lowered him gently to the ground with an odd sense of loss because it had ended, then he opened his eyes. Everyone was quiet and looking at him. He'd played the polka, and nobody had danced. None of the other musicians had been playing. The band was looking at him.

Somebody began to clap, and others followed suit. Some whistled, and some shouted bravo *Maestro*, or *encore*. So much for blending. He looked at Guido— he would not look in the direction of where he knew Nandy sat, willing the signal for the next song.

When it was time to take a break, Pietro stepped down from the stage and picked up the glass Assunta had brought him. This day could not end soon enough. He'd done his thing; he'd written the music, the rest—her touch, her voice, his whatever had happened in the polka—he just wanted to be home.

Yet here, Nandy appeared another drink in hand. "Not done with that one yet? But I've brought another."

Assunta stood by his side. Pietro turned, so she stood to his back left, out of his line of sight.

"Beautiful music, Pietro. Beautiful!" Nandy said.

"Listen, about the other night—" Pietro began.

"I didn't get wrathy, did I? Don't remember a thing, and I hope you don't either. It's past, right?" Nandy downed half the contents of his glass. "Pietro, my dear friend," his voice faltered on those words, "If anything ever happened to us, I couldn't think of anyone I'd rather take care of my children. Of Assunta, too. What do you say, my friend? You'd do that for me, wouldn't you, Pietro. Or do we *all* have to call you *Maestro* now?"

"I—?" What should he say? Should *she* say something? She made an odd noise like her throat was in a tangle. Her dress rustled. Had she shaken her head?

"Aw, come now. You'll promise me."

Pietro listened elsewhere. The rest of the band eating, some fiddling with papers or instruments. Tables of guests laughing and talking. Assunta made an indistinguishable noise, then, "Nandy, please, let it go," her voice urgent, pleading.

What must she think of him? He had to say something.

"What a man! See everyone, a musician and a man." Nandy's tone was sharp now, straining to sound pleased. The other band members turned to look at them. "He's going to take care of my wife if I hang up my fiddle!"

Could the man shut up? Could he make more of a scene? Couldn't he just leave? Assunta made that funny noise again. She sounded like she'd rather be farther away than he did.

"Tell you what, you'll be godfather to the next one. You'll do that for me, won't you? You'll think of a name, as well. 'Specially if it's a girl, the only name we can figure for our girls is Mary. Nice name, but can't have too many of them, can we?"

"What are you saying?" Pietro asked.

"I think you understood me. You will promise, right?"

"Sure," Pietro said because that was the only way the dullard would shut up and lead Assunta away. "I promise."

Nandy had never been anything but a fool. And now, he had become an even greater fool. Nothing about the promise was good. The only thing to count on was a long life for Nandy. Pietro would start drinking to his health every mealtime.

He marched in the back door, hesitating momentarily when he saw the kitchen lamp alight, Mrs. Conati sitting near it. He didn't notice what she was doing, and he didn't stop to speak with her. He didn't want to hear her opinion on his music, and he certainly didn't want to remember his debut as a composer on a day overshadowed by Nandy's ravings.

He strode up the stairs, ignoring the creaks and ignoring the way his jacket flapped. He'd undone the buttons as soon as they'd finished playing, annoyed at how constricting they felt.

The darn lodgers were already in bed, one doing that pathetic half snore— he couldn't make up his mind even in sleep. Pietro could not stay in there with them. The music in his head would not allow him to stay still right now. He went back down and left the house, ignoring Mrs. Conati again on his way though nothing was her fault. He strode purposefully toward the trail.

How dare Nandy ask this of him! He had not sought this. He had not sought anything from Assunta except the simple, harmless, arm's length presence to give him a little boost to coming up with the music.

Never could he mean anything to a beautiful woman like her. A less attractive woman, perhaps. Someone plain. Assunta was different. She was gentle, warm. The way she seemed so at ease, so immune to the shortfalls of her husband, so kind to those around her, loving to children, as though she could embrace them each individually, make them feel like they were the most important creatures in the world.

He'd been innocent. He'd never meant harm done to anyone. He would never be disrespectful. Yet what Nandy had asked of him insinuated he *had* done wrong. Like he had been seeking this.

Pietro carried on walking in the moonlight, the cymbals and bass in his head covering the crackle of his careless footsteps on the trail path. He hadn't had an intended destination. He'd just drifted because he had no place in this land. He'd been a fool to come. Yes, he had a uniform. Yes, he'd learned from a band that didn't belong to Nonno. But there'd been no need to come this far away from home. No need to come here where the woman who made his music flow belonged to another man and where he had no place he could call his own. He couldn't even sleep in a room of his own.

The river flowed near the trail. He turned toward it and followed its course until he reached the opening where he'd sat with Assunta—where they'd talked of hummingbirds. Where, according to Nandy, Pietro had committed the crime of seducing another man's wife.

It was innocent. It wasn't hurting anyone. At least that was his intention. He would never overstep the boundaries of another's marriage. Ever. A decent fellow would understand this—a decent man with morals.

Yet, damn him, Nandy, of all people. A man who could not possibly understand a thing about the language of music. Nandy had no morals. And yet, Nandy recognized himself in Pietro.

EIGHTEEN

1916

Assunta looked at the kitchen cupboards she had just rearranged and wondered when she had begun to like the ochre color of the plates and why she had just spent so much time shuffling things about. There had been nothing wrong with how she'd arranged them before. This urge to clean and organize more than her regular routine, plus the hunger that had been nipping at her stomach these past few days, could only add up to one thing. She set her hand on her belly—another baby on the way already. She would wait until she was sure to mention it to Nandy.

Max came down the stairs, up from his nap already, bouncing his backside down one step at a time.

"*Ciao*, Mamma." He held his arms up for her. He reminded his parents at almost four, he was a big boy now, but when his sisters were not around, he always stole a cuddle.

"Are the girls still sleeping?" She sat him on her lap and wrapped her left arm tightly around him.

Max stuck his thumb in his mouth, laid his head on his mother's chest, and nodded. She hugged him tighter, her little boy. She wondered if the new baby would be a boy or a girl. If a girl, that would be three girls in a row. Nandy would appreciate another boy. Whatever it was, just the thought of another made her tired. Mary was walking, getting into anything she could. Baby Ida now six months old, always wanting to know what was going on, and she was learning to crawl but couldn't keep up with her brother and sister, so was often left on her belly, screaming at the top of her lungs.

Hard work, but three blessings.

"It's about time to start dinner. Run off and play now." She sat Max down.

Max pulled out the box of tin soldiers his daddy had bought him from the big store in Indiana and began to set up a fort under the table. Assunta kept her feet to the side to give him room to play and started shucking the peas from their pods and into a bowl on her lap. She had been distracted. She should have been working on dinner while the kids were napping. Nobody cared whether the cups or the glasses were on the left. Would she spend the whole nine months nesting again?

A thump at the window shattered her thoughts and made her jump. It was just enough of a jump to upset the bowl of peas on her lap and send them flying, a thousand tiny pops as the peas landed and bounced like a cascade of bullets around Max and his soldiers. A bird! She set the bowl on the table and went to the window to look, but Max thought a bowl of spilled peas was the funniest thing ever and exploded in a kind of tummy laugh only young children are capable of. It was infectious. Assunta laughed, too, and they crawled on their knees, giggling and picking up peas until every last one had been picked up.

Pietro had avoided the bar, kept his head low on Sunday dinners when Nandy and Assunta came over to the Conatis, excusing himself on the pretext that he had to write a score right after dinner. It was an outright lie—he hadn't written a line since the wedding.

After Nandy's outburst, Pietro had asked Guido to go ahead and set up an audition. He had never intended to stay here this long. A year he'd predicted, two at most, certainly not five, yet the war meant no ships could sail. Besides, Ma had written that the vines were still not producing enough to support all the mouths of the family, and Caterina was certainly doing her best to add to the number of mouths that needed to be fed. All this made it difficult for Pietro to get home to Italy, but he could get away from here.

He ought to leave without saying goodbye to Nandy. Just let the man find out through the grapevine that he was gone. That he'd have to find someone else to take care of his wife and children if Nandy happened to find a way to check out. Better still, he ought to find a way to stick around and take care of them.

And yet Pietro found himself walking to the bar to say goodbye. At least Assunta wouldn't be at the bar. He preferred it that way.

As Pietro had expected, Nandy stood propped at the end nearest the door.

"I've been waiting for you," he said without the hint of a slur.

"I'm getting ready to leave town." Pietro didn't veil the challenge in his tone.

"I heard. All the more reason for you to come to my home. A last *cin cin.*" Nandy made the signal of drinking to good health with his hand.

"Let's have one here."

"Let's go to my house," Nandy insisted.

"I'd rather not." What if he couldn't hold it together when he saw Assunta?

"I'd rather you did."

Well, if he did make a fool of himself when he saw her, could it get any worse than it was already? It'd be the last time he'd have to see her. The last time he heard her voice.

They didn't talk along the way, their silence amplifying the splash-scrunch of melting snow underfoot.

When they got to the house, Nandy marched up the porch steps, opened the door, and called for Assunta to bring wine and a box of matches, then he turned back and watched Pietro walk up the steps. He didn't want Nandy to notice his trepidation and certainly didn't want him to think he was nervous at the thought of being in his wife's presence for what might be the very last time.

"It's not too cold. Snow's melting. We'll have a drink outside."

Nandy pulled over a low stool and set it near the bench. He sat on the bench and indicated to Pietro to sit down on the stool. Pietro couldn't have felt more vulnerable if he'd been performing a solo in a dramatic opera to a bunch of hungry, thirsty miners who had just got off shift. He could feel Nandy's gaze, watching for him to do something. Nandy could be quick with a punch. Pietro turned to look at the space between him and the steps off the porch, wondering if he could cover it before Nandy knocked him out.

His head was turned when she came out of the door. He heard her pause, then say, "Here," he turned to take the glass she held but didn't look up past her feet.

She went back indoors.

Pietro shouldn't have come. He shouldn't have gone to the bar and definitely shouldn't have done Nandy's bidding and come here. This was some kind of sick test. He didn't deserve this.

They sat in silent challenge. Rightful husband, wrongful admirer. One man who had no idea of how special his wife was, another man who saw her beauty on every level.

Nandy broke the silence when, Pietro supposed, he was good and ready. He raised his glass. "*Cin cin.* To long life."

They clinked and drank, both taking long swigs. Then as though that moment of challenge had never happened, Nandy shook the box of matches in the air, then handed them to Pietro and pulled out a pack of Luckies.

Pietro set his wine on the porch deck and lit a match, its sulfur flare bringing back memories of outdoor dinners. Some chance of eating underneath the stars in New York.

"So, you make me a promise, then you leave town." As Nandy spoke, his cigarette bobbed, the flame Pietro held for him went out. "Light another." His voice was cold. Damn him!

Pietro had never lifted a finger–never done a*nything* wrong. He looked directly in Nandy's face. Be damned if the man could hear Pietro's soul through his music. Yet something in Nandy's face said he could.

"Go on, light another, I said."

Pietro did so, willing his hand not to shake.

"I like to hold on to what matters to me, you understand?"

Pietro nodded but didn't trust himself to speak and hold the match steady at the same time.

"I also like to have a plan, see, if I'm not around to hold on to what matters." He sucked on the cigarette, the red whisper as it caught oddly reassuring. "No need to look so worried. I only meant it, see, if anything ever happens to me. But don't be counting the days, my friend. I'm hearty stock. I'm holding tight."

♫♩♪

Assunta wasn't surprised when the men came inside. She hadn't imagined they'd last long on the porch, a cold winter's night like this. She shoved an ashtray on the table and brushed some crumbs from the tablecloth.

Pietro, or Maestro as everyone was calling him nowadays, hadn't been around in a while. She'd missed him, in a vague sort of way. The shining buttons on his band uniform, hair neatly parted, looking everywhere but at her. But tonight, when he came through the door behind Nandy, he did look at her. Just for a moment.

She turned to the stove, took out a cloth from her apron pocket, and rubbed at a non-existent food stain on the stove.

"Pour us wine," Nandy told her. He didn't say please, didn't soften his order, as though he was intentionally coarse and rude in front of Pietro. She'd noticed it before but never wondered much about it until that silly business at the wedding, whether he did it to assert his ownership over her. As though he'd long considered Pietro his rival.

She poured the wine.

Ida sat on a blanket on the floor, where Max and Mary were building towers with wooden blocks. She started to make *look-at-me* sounds like she was berating Pietro for not paying her any mind.

Bless him, Pietro's face softened, and he bent beneath the table to pull cute faces at Ida. His goddaughter, he'd chosen to name after his niece, he'd said. She wanted to tell him Ida had crawled up three stairs today, that in the blink of an eye, she'd be walking, but Nandy sat tense in his chair, watching hawk-like.

"I helped Mamma with dinner today!" Max piped up.

"Oh yeah?" Pietro said.

"She dropped the peas, and I helped pick them all up!"

"How could I forget? A bird hit the window today!" As she said it, she looked pointedly at Pietro. She had to know what he thought of the bird—he had been the one to tell her what a bird at the window meant. "Do you think it's an omen?" she asked.

Pietro sat back upright but didn't look at her. *Answer me, will you?* He didn't. He took a swig of his wine.

"Why would he think it was an omen?" Nandy interjected. "You know what it was? It was a bird hitting the window, that's all."

She looked again at Pietro, who again ignored her. His face looked troubled. She gave up hope of an answer and leaned against the glass, trying to see below, dreading seeing a tiny carcass frozen in snow and death, but she couldn't see directly below. She could call Pietro out, tell Nandy to stop behaving like that nonsense at the wedding meant something, but she'd rather not taunt his temper. He'd get over it soon enough.

Max stood up from the rug where they were building towers with blocks and bumped his head on the table's edge. He began to wail, followed by Ida, then by Mary, for no other apparent reason than solidarity. Assunta wiped her hands on her apron and scooped the three of them up into her lap, their arms draped around her like blankets, and rocked them as she sang.

Manina bela, to sorela, n'do seto sta? da la mamma? dal papà? cosa t'hai dato? pan e late?

Cate cate cate!

Pretty little hand, your sister, where have you gone? To mother? To father? What did they give you? Bread and milk?

Tickle tickle tickle!

"I'll miss them," Pietro said.

Assunta set Max down to hug daddy, then dropped the girls in his lap so he could kiss them goodnight.

"Pietro is moving to New York." Nandy mouthed the words slowly. Was he accusatory? She didn't deserve that.

Nandy had been so ridiculous recently. It was probably best that mild-mannered Pietro was off to the bustling city of New York. Perhaps it didn't snow so much there. She paused to look at a tiny white feather smudged to the window. She tugged the kitchen curtain closed and went back to collect the children from Nandy, daring one last meaningful look at Pietro. He might have the decency to say something.

He didn't speak, but he did look up. Perhaps for a second, long enough to convey a lifetime of meaning. Not about the bird at all. She saw in his gaze the reason for Nandy's jealousy. It wasn't anything *she* had done—it was him. If she hadn't been sure of it before, she was now. He *did* have feelings for her.

♫♪♪

Assunta lay waiting for the bell to call the men from their beds, her mind still honey-thick from sleep. Strange, it seemed lighter outside than it usually did when the bell chimed. Her mind snapped alert. The bell was not going to chime because it already had.

"*Tesoro*, wake up. It's late." She reached over and claimed Nandy's chest in her hand, ran her fingers through his hair. "On second thought, why don't you stay here?"

"What day is it? Did I sleep in?" He almost fell out of bed and scrambled into the clothes Assunta had set out the night before.

"Don't go. A day won't hurt. Come back to bed." She would show him he was the only man for her.

"You catch no fish when you're asleep."

Reluctantly, she pulled on her housecoat, a long yellow cotton one she'd ordered from the Sears catalog and headed downstairs to put lunch in his pail.

She wrapped a hunk of bread in a damp handkerchief to stay moist, and a chunk of homemade salami. Her head began to throb. She shook it gently, slightly, then an invisible wind that existed only between her ears swirled frantically, blocking even the clonking sound of the knife she dropped into the metal pail.

Make it with love. It's his last meal.

The words flashed across her mind. A random voice in her head that made utterly no sense. None whatsoever.

"*Che c'è?* What's the matter?" He took her shoulders and turned her square toward him. "You look like you've seen a ghost!"

"That bird at the window yesterday!"

"It's just a bird, I told you. Is my lunch ready?"

"Nandy, the bird might have died. It's a premonition."

"Who says?" She couldn't answer that question. It'd start the whole tirade all over again. "Get hold of yourself. I'll be home for dinner."

She slipped her arms around his waist and kissed him. "Stay home, my darling. Just today."

"I can still make it. I'll be fine. I have to provide for my lovely wife and all these children you keep bringing me."

That cleaning she was doing yesterday—the nesting, should she tell him now that she might be expecting another child? She searched his face, and the wind in her head swirled faster; his voice sounded like it was coming from a different room. "Please! Go and see if you can find a dead bird—if you do, stay home!"

"It snowed last night. Even if it's there, we won't find it." He hugged her briefly and took the pail from her and turned to go out the door.

"Nandy?" If she told him about the new baby on the way, he might stay.

His head reappeared from behind the door, accompanied by a blast of frigid February air. "You're the best, Assunta." He blew her a kiss with the theatrics of a circus magician. Before she could say anything further, the door pulled shut. She felt dazed and dizzy for a moment, then her head cleared.

It's in your head. It's all superstition, she told herself. She took a cloth from the bucket at the top of the basement stairs and began scrubbing every surface she could find. She scrubbed until the children woke up to distract her.

She fed and dressed them, then felt much better. Nandy was right. What on earth had she been thinking? She had probably been disoriented because she got up in such a rush. Her mind just had not woken up straight.

She lay a hand on her belly. This was also why she was not thinking straight. She should tell Nandy tonight. He was going to be happy. A boy this time, she felt sure.

♪𝄞♪

Pietro clicked the latch closed on his leather suitcase. He slid a box with the rest of his belongings beneath the bed. Mrs. Conati would allow him to keep them there—either until he had a working chance in New York or, better still, a ticket home to Italy, in which case he would send for them, his music unheard in New York. Feeling somewhat nostalgic about this town he'd called home these past years, he might be inclined to favor the latter option, but that would be letting Guido down after he had worked so hard to line up the auditions. And Pietro could not stand a single painful evening with Nandy ever again.

The door creaked goodbye when he closed it. Mr. Conati sat on the bottom stair, overcoat over his arm, tossing his hat in his hand.

"I'll walk you to the station."

Pietro nodded. He should say goodbye to Mrs. Conati. He raised his finger, pointing towards the kitchen.

"You don't think she'd let you slip out while she was in the kitchen, do you? Come on. She's on the porch."

A handful of children clutched around Mrs. Conati. "You'll let me know when you find boarding with an Italian woman to take care of you? Not sure as to how you'd do without."

"First, I need someone foolish enough to give me a job."

"You go and play your clarinet like you do round here. Show them all that fancy writing of yours, too. There's no need for you to come back. The mine'll manage without you. Now come and say goodbye." She puckered a loud kiss on each cheek. "Be off with you. I don't want to see you any time soon."

♪𝄞♪

The children noticed nothing amiss in Assunta's frenzied cleaning. She was collected, as a mother should be, only zealous in her pursuit of cleanliness. When they got up drowsily from their afternoon nap, they sat on the rug in the kitchen, playing quietly. Assunta poured the coffee she'd left herself this morning from the percolator into the small saucepan. An odd shudder ran through her. Violent enough to make her spill the coffee all over the stovetop. This would set her back. She glanced at the time. 3:20. A bit late to make fresh.

With most people kept firmly inside by the cold, the next shift of miners had headed to work almost unnoticed, but the movement caught Assunta's attention. Nandy should be home in the next hour. Then again, it was Friday, so there was a good chance the barman would see him before she did.

Someone—not a miner—ran past the window toward the mine. Assunta recognized Anna. She'd moved here from Bracken just a year ago and had still not changed her doom and gloom ways. Her feet flapped as she ran, most ungainly. She half-slipped on some ice but caught herself without falling, and then she carried on running. Why on earth would she run? And her hair untied. Why would she go out like that? It looked like she had just washed it.

Someone else ran by. And another. But there was no alarm. The bird last night—

Assunta threw the forks down, grabbed the children's coats, and pulled Max and Mary's little arms through the sleeves.

"I'm taking the train, Mamma," Max chattered. He held up his wooden caboose. "Look. We're going on a train ride, just like Maestro."

"Yes, take it. Hold your sister's hand, too, mind." Assunta pulled Ida from the perambulator and wrapped her snug in the afghan, as deliberately as her nerves could manage.

"My sweet, Mamma's got you." Her voice shook.

Assunta grabbed a spare hat for Anna, hoisted Mary onto her free arm, and stepped out into the cold, Max trailing behind.

People were making their way to the mine entrance like iron filings to a magnet. Some were risking a run on the ice, others more cautious. All shared a sense of urgency.

The two policemen from the town already stood by the bridge that led to the mine entrance. They were not letting anyone across. So, something *had* happened.

"Leave room. Rescue might need to get through."

"What happened?"

"Are any of the men hurt?"

"I heard Jimmy Moody found a body."

The malocchio. An icy chill ran through Assunta.

Questions and snippets of news hopped in voices so quiet they were little more than whispers as the crowd grew. There were other languages, too. Assunta listened hard in case someone—anyone—had news.

The people who'd arrived before the police were being herded back across the bridge, Anna included. Assunta pushed her way through to her and handed her the hat. Anna accepted it, a look of fear her only thanks. Assunta should say something, comfort her, and reassure her that everything would be fine; her husband would appear unscathed at any moment. But everyone knew there was no rhyme or reason; mine accidents claimed the strong as greedily as the old, no matter how much their wives loved them or if they were young bachelors with seemingly no one to mourn.

But Nandy had to be saved. He had to be. His foolishness recently meant nothing. Deep down, Assunta knew he had dwelled on the curse. Perhaps he'd never stopped worrying about it. But *she* knew Beatrice's words were empty, nothing other than spitefulness.

She wanted to reach out and hold Anna's hand but could not without putting Mary or Ida down. Instead, she began "Our Father." Anna clasped her hands in front of her, and the two women prayed.

The engine sighed up slopes, screeched around the Horseshoe Curve to the passengers' murmured admiration, then settled into a resigned chug as it took Pietro further and further from Assunta. Perhaps he might find some enthusiasm for this new adventure once he got to New York, but that was unlikely unless they'd found a way to get the stench from the air. He looked forward to the chance to see Sacco. America had just swallowed them up into their separate lives.

At some point, lulled by the train's repetitive song, Pietro fell asleep, only to be woken by screaming brakes. *Panic, something wrong?* Then calm, *just slowing for a station*. He settled back into his chair to anxious voices directing baggage to be pulled into the aisle. He wiped his chin and straightened his back—still a way to go. The train finally at a standstill, passengers pushed toward the doors, eager to alight, but instead, a man in a tweed suit stepped up, blocking their way.

"Big accident out west. Mine explosion. Numerous dead."

Then he hopped down and hustled down to the next door. The odd things people enjoy doing. A bearer of bad tidings.

"Poor buggers," the man sitting next to Pietro said, referring, he presumed, to the dead.

Pietro tipped his chin up in agreement. How many men, he wondered? Killed because they went to work. How far out west? West was a big place. Nothing he could do for the *disgraziati* from here. He settled back in his seat, woozy. He would let sleep retake him as soon as the train pulled out and as soon as the agitated whispers around him tired of disastrous news.

"Hundreds dead."

"Italians mostly. Not that the bosses care."

"Ernest, Pennsylvania. Near Indiana."

He sat bolt upright. "Ernest? They said west."

"It's west of here. Yea. Ernest, they're saying. You know someone there?"

Pietro stood up. He needed to get off.

"Hey, mister. Are you all right?"

"I need to go back. Please, my bag." He pointed to his case, wedged in behind a black leather bag.

"Why don't you sit back down? There's no train back the other way until tomorrow. Have family back there, then?" The man next to him said.

Pietro shook his head.

"Someone important, though? Had to be if you were to head back without even finding out if something happened to them first."

Right. What was he thinking? It could've been any crew. It could've been any mine or any section of mine. It could've been strangers.

The engine drew breath, preparing to pull away. He really should think this through. What good would he do back there? What would he be giving up? Especially if nobody he knew was hurt or worse.

His first audition beckoned. Tomorrow night, he had a meeting in a New York theater. It was a once in a lifetime opportunity, Guido had said. Pietro tried to picture the theater in his mind, hear the orchestra that might, one day, play his music. He had imagined it before when Guido was first trying to convince him, and the vision of hundreds of unfamiliar faces listening to him had almost made him sick.

He tried now to imagine the theater empty. The orchestra pit would be between the stage where he'd be—with many other musicians, sure, but when the people swarmed in to fill the rows of red velvet chairs, they would notice how he didn't belong. They would know he had been a simple farmer from a small town in Italy, who had become a simple coal miner in La 'Merica.

He pushed aside the thought of an audience and pictured the stage, but it morphed into a dark and empty space. Then it turned black and into the mine where dynamite, not percussion, set the pace. Where men panted with the exertion of yet another day without daylight, scraping shovels, squeaking trolleys, tapping picks. The train picked up motion, teasing him.

Tappingtappingtapping pickspickspicks.

Pietro covered his face with his hands. He could not think that. There were causes of explosions other than widowmakers, surely. And surely he was not the only one who would have tapped. Somebody was bound to have taken his place. And they would have done it just as thoroughly. He closed his eyes. Listened through the compartment for a noise to distract him, but people were still talking about the disaster, *a hundred dead, ten dead, a couple of dozen.* They did not know. Listen elsewhere. *Tappingpickstappingpickstappingpicks.* Elsewhere still, he heard a squeak, almost inaudible over the rest of the noise, coming from the pin connecting one compartment with another. That would do.

A tiny squeak, a tiny chance, that she might be needing him.

As newcomers joined the waiting crowd, murmurs were handed back through the ranks to share what little was known so far. Jimmy had indeed found a body. There might be more. A few men, some said three, some said four, were being pulled out alive. Burned, but alive.

"Stand back, stand back!" a voice commanded, and everyone shuffled back as one. Voices from the front of the crowd called out the names of the men who shuffled their way out of the mine. Apart from the names passed backward, nobody spoke, as though their collective silence could will more men out of the mine and into safety.

Anna's husband's name was one of the few passed back. She looked at Assunta and folded her lips inwards, in a gesture that Assunta took to indicate sympathy for not yet knowing Nandy's fate, and a good luck wish, then she worked her way out of the crowd, still wearing Assunta's hat.

Once the handful of wives whose husbands were alive had left, the crowd found a new stillness. More people arrived, but fresh news did not. Dark began to settle, and with it, Mrs. Conati arrived, weaving her way through the crowd.

"I'll take the kids," she said. "I take it you're going to wait here?"

Assunta nodded and kissed her children one by one. "Daddy and I will be home soon."

Mrs. Conati left. Assunta absentmindedly rubbed her arms that were sore from holding the girls.

A fresh ripple of concern spread through the crowd. Assunta craned to see what had caused it. A rescue crew in uniform was getting out of an automobile. The local rescue team could have pulled one dead body out of the mine. A second vehicle pulled up and out got men carrying doctors' cases.

"What's going on? Any dead?" People shouted. "We need to know."

The new arrivals were ushered through the crowd and across the bridge.

"Calm, everyone calm," a policeman urged.

Again, they obliged but huddled closer as the bitter chill took advantage of the arrival of night to sink deeper.

It was dawn the next day when they began to pull the bodies up. They'd fallen three miles in, someone had said. *Nandy would be one of them.* No! Assunta scolded herself for that thought. She told herself instead that he would join her any minute. He was down there helping or trapped maybe—but not gone.

Men in uniform started to pick women out of the crowd. Eventually, someone came to tap her shoulder and lead her aside before saying something about being sorry for her loss.

NINETEEN

T he train took him to an enormous, new station named after the state of Pennsylvania. No ferry from Jersey City like when he first arrived. With its cathedral-like roof and columns, the station felt like a city in itself. Conductors shouted over whistles, engines, steam, trolleys piled with luggage. Shoe shiners calling for customers, people talking and laughing, some saying goodbye—dissonance of modern life.

The city itself was even louder than Pietro remembered if that was possible. Automobiles everywhere, horns blasting, horses pulling carts, vendors shouting. He passed a construction site, teeming with hammers and barrows and urgency. Soon after, a bar blasted music. Trumpet, double-bass, clarinet, saxophone—banjo? What species of music did they have in New York? Reminiscent of ragtime, but not ragtime. An energetic composition of seemingly unrelated pieces in a medley that somehow worked, so vibrant he could feel it jumping up and down.

He peered through the bar window but couldn't see the band—patrons, tables, and waiters in black bow ties and vests blocked his view.

A kid knocked into him. "What are ya just standing there for, Mister?"

He wanted to know more about this music. To listen until he knew what he thought of it. That would have to be for another time. For now, he needed to find the hotel. He glanced at the paper in his hand with the directions. He should be nearly there.

"Sir." The doorman's smooth British accent welcomed him to the hotel. He opened the door in one hand, holding the other out for a tip.

"Is there a phone I can use?" Pietro asked.

"At the desk," he said, now in coarse Brooklyn, holding his hand higher.

Pietro dug around for a coin and shuffled inside.

"The name's Maccagno," he announced at the desk.

"Welcome. I'll have someone show you up." The man dinged a bell.

"I need to make a phone call. To Ernest."

"Does Ernest have a last name?" The man's tone was haughty. Irritated.

"It's a place." Pietro tried to think. Who had a phone? The Company offices. The company store. Nobody would answer either, not this late. "On second thought, I'll call in the morning."

Time moved on, unconcerned at Assunta's sorrow. She followed along, doing whatever Mrs. Conati and the Company told her to do, drawing together every ounce of strength not to crumple to the floor.

The Company arranged three stores in nearby Indiana to display the bodies, saving each family the trouble of holding their own wake. Some of the men had yet to be identified. Some had no family here. Twenty-six men, gone. Her man, gone. No privacy to mourn.

Nandy lay in a coffin and had nothing to say. They'd set him at the end of a row of nine of the dead miners in the store where Nandy had bought tin soldiers for Max. Only a handful of family members could stand between the dead and the store counter behind them. The cash register sat chest-high behind Assunta, waiting for this inconvenience to be done with so it could resume its daily tally.

Mrs. Conati stayed with Assunta, Mary clinging to her dress, Max and Ida played with a couple of empty boxes beneath the table that bore their father's coffin.

Doors opened for people to pay their respects at four sharp. A stream of total strangers and an occasional familiar face entered the other end of the store. By the time they got to Nandy, they were starting to lose interest. He was the ninth dead body in a row. There was nothing spectacular about him in death.

Some filing past forgot to pause or even look sorrowful. Assunta tried to look over their heads. She tried not to overhear their curiosity about whether any of the bodies were burned or mangled in the explosion, their plans for which of the two other stores they would go to next.

None stopped for long. She wanted to look these sightseers in the eye, challenge them to be sincere. Instead, she sat down, defeated—a wilted sunflower.

"Assunta?"

Pietro! He looked haggard, circles beneath his eyes. He bowed his head over Nandy's body. If she wasn't mistaken, his shoulders shook. When he lifted his head, she looked away. She didn't want to see if he had cried.

"I got back as soon as possible."

She took a half step towards him, her balance faltering. So tired. She felt his hand on her arm, propping her. It felt solid. She could lean on him. It was his loss also.

Pietro opened his mouth to say something, commiserate perhaps? But nothing came out. *Why can't this man speak up?*

She filled his silence. "These people, they don't know him. They're just here to gawk."

"Did anyone tap?" Pietro asked.

"I can't wait to be gone from here," she carried on as though he hadn't spoken.

"The tapping, explosion . . . I shouldn't have left—"

"The children. They need to be home. I need to find a way to feed them. They need to play. They need their father."

"I'll take care of that."

Take care? Of that, of her? The children? What else had he said? She hadn't listened. He said something about having left. Left for where? "New York? You were in New York?" she remembered.

"I'd forgotten how awful the air was."

"The air?" Incredulous.

"It's all right. I wouldn't have wanted to stay."

"You're not going back." She said it as a realization, not a question or a request. She remembered the look he'd given her the last time he'd been at their home.

Did he think—what Nandy had said—that promise? He thought he could dash back and cash in on her loss?

"The funeral is tomorrow," her tone suddenly cold. "I trust we will see you there. Thank you for stopping by."

"But—"

"Thank you. Goodbye, Pietro."

The rain beat its message to Pietro on black umbrellas and a regiment of coffins—*youdidn'tstopit youdidn'tstopit*. The rain filled the freshly dug graves before the coffins could.

At the service, official after official—people who surely had never spoken to any of the dead—had droned on about this being Ernest's worst mining disaster ever. Another man had been found only this morning, his body sent to the embalmers but not ready in time for the burial.

It also had to be the biggest congregation the town had ever seen.

They lowered the coffins in the mass grave first, slowly, negotiating with the deluge. One by one, the coffins disappeared. Orange and yellow leaves left over from fall fluttered into the muddy rivulets that overflowed like tears of the land. It could have been snow, people kept saying over and over until it sounded like part of a ritual.

Mr. and Mrs. Conati looked smaller than normal, crumpled in black. Assunta, so frail, so vulnerable, stood a little apart. The children looked confused.

Youdidn'tstopit youdidn'tstopit.
Itcouldhavebeenyou itcouldhavebeenyou.

Pietro had barely been able to look at himself in the mirror since it happened. These men's lives the price for a paycheck. Many burned, some, like Nandy, seemingly unburned, but missing helmet and a boot, as though they'd disintegrated in the blast that sucked the last air from their lungs.

He'd called Nandy his friend, despite the troubles they'd had between them. He once thought Nandy only did wrong, but in this end, Pietro had wronged him plenty. Then wronged him even more with that fleeting moment when he had wondered on the train whether Nandy was among the men, whether Assunta would be free.

Youdidn'tstopit youevenwantedit.

Just a fleeting moment, a fleeting thought. Yet he hated himself for it. He should never, ever, have thought it.

Men shoveled mud into the hole in a vain attempt to dispel the water. The mourners turned to leave en masse. At last, they lowered the casket into Nandy's hole, dug some twenty feet from the mass grave. Assunta and the Conatis made a cluster of sorrowful noises; the rain slopped and slurped as the land claimed Nandy for the final time.

Nandy was sunken into a rectangle of dirty water. His death was final. More real now than when Mrs. Conati had placed pen and paper in front of Assunta and made her write to his family and her own. The only consolation was the knowledge she would not witness their grief as they read her harsh words. She told them he had not suffered, about how she and the children were to miss such an admirable husband and father. The words she didn't write were that another baby was on the way. She could not bring herself to tell them because she had not had the chance to tell Nandy.

Bills still arrived. The coal man made his delivery with an odd look on his face: could she pay? She had always paid. Why should he presume? Assunta was no longer a trustworthy customer. She was a new entity—a woman without a husband, a liability. Women eyed her suspiciously. Men watched her carefully—some with interest, others with a protective hand on their wallets.

The only thing she was grateful for was the chasm that appeared to have formed around her, keeping most people at bay. She needed to mourn and to be left in peace.

Her grief had almost strangled her when she had walked head high, purse clutched tightly to tell the stone smith what to carve. It would be placed sometime in the next month. Right there at the end of the dirt, they were shoveling into her husband's grave. For now, she simply put a rose in its place.

She had written the wording over and over, finding herself angry at Nandy for not being there to help her, but in the end, she had gone back to the first draft she had written.

*Qui riposa Ferdinando Vassanelli nato addì 29 Aprile 1880 morto il 11 febbraio 1916
la sposa Assunta ed i figli vinti dal dolore questo marmo piangendo deposero*
Here lies Ferdinando Vassanelli born 29 April 1880 died 11th February 1916
his wife Assunta and children overcome by grief lay this marble in tears.

Unable to repeat the words out loud, she handed them neatly scribed on a
piece of paper ripped from the pad in the kitchen drawer, the one she used for
a shopping list. The stone smith read each word slowly; someone might have
thought nervously checking for spelling, but Assunta had no reason to think he
understood Italian.

"Just making sure I understand the lettering, ma'am. I am sorry for your
loss," he added as he directed her towards the door. "I will make a tombstone
worthy of your husband." He slipped an envelope into her hand with one
gloved hand and opened the door with the other. Assunta did not look at it. She
knew it was the bill. She walked home with stiff poise, the envelope burning in
her hand, clasping it so tightly her thumb was numb by the time she got home.

♪♭♪

Pietro ate breakfast while listening to Mrs. Conati's account of the family
down the street, packing up and moving out. Of little Edward, Bobby, and
Louise in Gino's class who had also lost their fathers.

"I should have been here to tap," he told her.

"I'll have none of that talk. Nobody could tap the entire mine, and even if
they did, they still couldn't be certain to stop an explosion from happening."

He did not add how he'd had bad thoughts, nor about the promise he'd made
to Nandy. How quick Assunta had been to brush him aside. Or how life would
be clouded forever by his fall from morals, by his admiration for Assunta that
Nandy had seen, clear as day.

He could go back to New York. To a place that could drown his thoughts.
People with no notion of keeping sound to themselves. And cars, cars
everywhere. What destination warranted such a contraption over a tram or good
old-fashioned feet? He could beg for another chance at the audition he'd not
shown up for, beg as though he yearned for the stage in front of a crowd of
strangers. The commotion of the city, the anonymity of his audience, would
disguise the memory of Assunta, drown out his guilt over how he'd wronged
Nandy.

Or he could stay, look out for her from a distance—respectfully, of course.
And he could resume his task of tapping the mine, appease the men who'd died
when he hadn't.

FROM ASHES TO SONG

He lit a cigarette and waited for his chest to settle and his thoughts to stop skipping backward and forth like pages of a music book that had been thrown and scattered, then pieced back together in no particular order.

"I'll be on the first train out tomorrow," he told Mrs. Conati.

TWENTY

Assunta named the baby Ferdinando after the daddy he'd never know. She didn't sleep the night he was born. She just held him, stared at him, searching his face for Nandy.

She had started to take in other people's laundry before he was born and resumed a mere week after. If she wasn't carrying the kettle to heat on the stove, she was scrubbing clothes on the washboard in the sink. If she wasn't feeding the baby, she was putting supper on the table for the other three.

She hung the last pair of socks from the line she'd rigged near the kitchen stove. Pants were so rarely mentioned in polite company, it'd been a long while before she learned the word in English. Now her entire kitchen hung with them and shirts and undergarments. They looked like *contrada* flags in an insane asylum.

She picked up the baby even though he was still sleeping peacefully. He stirred but settled back to a contented sleep in the crook of her arm.

Her brother's letter glared from the only corner of the table untouched by laundry. Why had it taken someone else to write and suggest she move home to Italy as soon as the war ended? Assunta hadn't thought of it herself. Mamma wasn't getting around as well as she once did; she could do with the help. And life was harder than ever with the war. They all had to band together and help each other.

She pictured herself with the children at Mamma's. The five of them in one room.

She'd have no luck in Italy finding a husband even if she wanted one, which she didn't. A lifetime of spinsterhood stretched ahead, her only certainty—an old woman at thirty. If only she were shorter, she would be able to borrow Mamma's black clothes.

If she moved back, she could take the children to market, show them around town. Walk the piazza, even buy them ice cream—they'd like that. Yet when she tried to picture it, the actual streets eluded. Colors, dimmed by years of absence, distances between things compressed to next door or extended too far to walk, the walls and street where she had spent so long watching for Nandy when he'd returned. The church where they married—she could see that perfectly, steps up from the piazza, then red brick rising from there up to higher importance. The market, the little patch where she gathered flowers for Papà, the way the fields stretched across the plain to be brought to a sudden halt in the distance by the mountain range. Yet she could not remember the details of the house next to Mamma's, nor how many houses there were to the end of the street. It felt like the memories belonged to someone else.

Here, she had her dahlias. She'd be unlikely to have her own garden in Italy. She had her own little home and a job taking in laundry. A staircase indoors, not outside, shared with the other people who lived stuck up against each other. The parish that relied on them all to pitch in, Mrs. Conati and Sunday lunches, heck even meatballs on spaghetti and a world covered in coal dust. It felt like home. A home Nandy had brought her to and then left her in to fend for herself.

She had no choice but to struggle on for her family with the pittance of an apology the union man had delivered as Nandy's death benefit. It could hardly be called a fit sum after he had given his life for some grubby black coal that would be burned in any case. She had their diligent savings and the cash she could earn from other people's bloomers.

Her children got stuck in the front room to play on rainy or snowy days. Her saucepans were hidden behind long johns the color of faded piano keys; garlic was out-fragranced by starch for shirts, warmth not from the stove but the iron. Socks to darn, barely an inch of her kitchen left to cook supper.

Yet it was a home untouched by war.

She pulled her writing pad from the drawer, sat near the only square of space at the table. What she wouldn't do to see Mamma, to hug her, make gnocchi, walk to market with her. Worth the entire horrid journey. But she couldn't face such a journey with the children. And it was impractical right now. Perhaps she would reconsider when the war was indeed over.

♪♪♪

Pietro knew he'd been right to think Guido's New York hopes for him were too lofty. It was a miracle in itself they'd given him a second chance at an audition a week after he'd dashed back to Ernest. He played them the wedding score for Walter and Angela. He tried to conjure Assunta whispering in his ear, but the only memory his mind conceded was the way she'd dismissed him over Nandy's body laid out in wake. How sad she'd looked, how he had caused her grief and the grief of twenty-five other families. He'd not been able to bring himself to play his harvest song.

The men auditioning him in their sharply tailored suits and fedoras did not hide their annoyance at their time being wasted. They cut him short with a clipped thank you and started to talk among themselves, leaving him to find his way off stage and out of the theater that was far above his station.

Instead, he played in a club, waiting for another opening for an audition, waiting for inspiration, waiting for the chance to go back to Italy. Occasionally, he'd halfheartedly listen to the women's voices in the clubs—none came close to Assunta's.

Tonight, the giggles and flirtatious drawls from a table of women were particularly loud. The only effect the music seemed to have on them was to make them act brazenly, openly flirting with the group of men who'd joined them. A woman forced a laugh, and a man showered compliments, his voice as fake as they come.

Pietro would never find love among the giggling city girls. They began the next score, and Pietro thought, as he did at least once a night, how lucky he was to play the clarinet, so he didn't have to smile like the other poor beggars in the band.

On his walk home between the dizzy-tall buildings, some asleep for the night, others still exuding party life, he spotted a coin on the ground, glinting under one of the many streetlamps that never let it fully be night. He picked it up and stuck it greedily into his pocket. A stroke of fortune on the dreary walk in the wee hours of the morning when good men slept, and only drunks and lowlifes walked the streets.

Now what to do with an unexpected penny?

He took the penny back out of his pocket and threw it on the ground in disgust. Was this what his life had become? He was making plans for a penny he picked from the dirt in the street. His existence was so pitiful playing the same songs over and over, night after night, a small wage and tips that barely kept him in rent for a lousy cot, a lumpy metal excuse for a bed in a room jammed with lousy metal cots. He'd thought sharing with two others was an imposition in Ernest, here there were six men to a room. And beds were in high demand—he wouldn't be surprised to find himself turned out mid-sleep if someone came along offering more for his space.

New York was a dreadful place. Noisy, jumbled chaos. Full of people dressed for the high life. Even he wore a tux and bow tie for work then like, he imagined, all the other high-life dressers, he returned to his dismal sleeping place. If people lived in nice apartments or nice houses, he'd not seen them.

He had to go home—home to Italy.

The war had to end one day.

I can return home to my family, to my homeland, he should write in his notebook, the notebook he hadn't opened in a long time. *Only I can't because even if the war ended today, I am a poor man.*

If he could go home, he'd go out of his way to look for a girl. A simple Italian girl. Hopefully, she'd inspire a song or two in him, definitely make him a father. But he was never going to get there if he couldn't afford a ticket. The only way he knew how to earn a decent wage in this country was in Ernest.

But *she* was in Ernest.

He couldn't face the tone of her indignation again, her rejection. Only he couldn't face life like this either.

He walked back to where he'd thrown the penny, scoured the street until he found it. He'd use it toward train fare.

He had no other choice. He had to go back to the mine and earn his fare back to Italy. A winter would do it. He'd write to Mrs. Conati.

It didn't take long to pack—he'd added nothing to his possessions since he got here. He returned the tux and bow tie to the top honcho in the band and the key to the grubby landlord, who'd no doubt raise the rent before handing it onto the next guy.

Pietro tried to sleep on the train, but when he closed his eyes, he heard her voice, singing to the children in the kitchen, whispering *bravissimo* in his ear. Then he heard music—his music. The grapevine song he'd hadn't played for Nonno.

It'd not come to him in a long time, now it felt like an old friend, celebrating his return home.

Not home, he had to remind himself. Italy was home. Just a steppingstone.

"You'll go to the dance. The children will be fine with me," Mrs. Conati said. "There's no reason you shouldn't stay with Mammam Conati, *fantolino*." Mrs. Conati reached her hands out to the baby.

"I can manage," Assunta said.

Mrs. Conati shunted the perambulator a few inches forward to catch the rays of sun coming through the window. "Then at least put him in here to get a bit of sunshine. It's not good for him if you're always holding him."

Assunta kissed Ferdinando's head, and with her free hand, spooned the chicken from the pan to a serving plate. She had done plenty Mrs. Conati had told her since Nandy died. But if she wanted to hold her baby, she would, and she had no interest in dancing.

"I'm staying home," Assunta said bluntly.

"I'll pick the children up," Mrs. Conati said anyway.

She was being unreasonable. Dances were for young people looking for love or for couples who knew where they stood. Assunta's chance at happily-ever-after had turned its last page the day she lost Nandy. Maybe that was what really happened in fairy tales. They stopped the story when they could fool you into thinking life would be wonderful.

"Maestro, Pietro, he's back in town for a few days. You know he'll be there to play. I'm sure he'd like to see you."

That was no incentive to go. Just because he was Nandy's friend, she had no connection other than that. Though if she went, it'd be a sort of gesture, a nod to Nandy. "Fine," she said, kissing Ferdinando's soft forehead before handing him over.

In her best dress, still rigorously black, Assunta went to the community hall with Mrs. Conati's daughter and her unmarried friends. The others kept shooting glances in the direction of the throng of single men. Assunta sat, unsmiling, stiff. She might have conceded to come. She hadn't said anything about dancing or enjoying herself.

Just as Mrs. Conati had said, Pietro was there, but he was more interested in his clarinet than her. He could at least have the decency to walk over and say hello. There were breaks in the music, after all.

The band struck a polka. What else? People still talked about Pietro's polka, how he stopped the dance with his magical clarinet.

Couples exuded energy from the dance floor; the band's music and the laughter came together to momentarily make her wish for happiness and for all this grief to be over and out of her life. She looked over at Pietro. He didn't seem happy either—if anything, he looked glum.

Someone put a glass of wine in Assunta's hand. She took it. She had not touched a drop from a batch that Nandy had not made. Well, everyone kept insisting she should have fun, so she took a large sip.

"Signora, may I?"

She didn't recognize the man holding his hand in an invitation to dance. From his accent, he was from the north of Italy. He didn't ask why she was wearing black. Perhaps he didn't know; maybe he didn't care.

She looked again at Pietro. This time he was looking back, right at her. Then he looked away, showing no sign of acknowledgment, as though he'd never been Nandy's friend, or he'd no longer know her now he'd spent some time in the big city.

"Signora?" The man said again. Fine. She was not going to crumble into dust with just one dance. Tomorrow she would get back to her children, to her sorrow.

His hand firm on the small of her back felt so wrong and so good at the same time. It didn't feel the same as dancing with Nandy, but good, nonetheless. Grief let her be for just a while. He didn't let go of her, and she didn't pull away.

She lost count of the songs. Eventually, the music stopped, and the lights went on. Many people had left, including Mrs. Conati's daughter and friends, Assunta's supposed companions for the evening.

"I'll walk you home," the man said. She didn't even know his name. She looked in the direction of the band.

Pietro was staring at her. He had no right. It was *her* life, and he was not a part of it. And this stranger would not be a part of it either.

"There's no need," she said firmly and took her leave.

♩♪ $ ♪

Warmth still tinged the night air. It felt good on her skin. But she never went out alone at night. She should go back to the hall, swallow her pride, and ask Pietro to walk her home. Then again, he should have offered, not glared at her in judgment. The moon lit her way, but it also cast shadows. The breeze rustled a branch and conjured a bear. Attackers lurked behind bushes. Snakes, ghosts, even dragons readied to pounce. She froze for a moment. She could not go on. She needed to go back, no— she needed to get home or have somebody by her side. What if someone was behind her?

In a panic, she began to run. The sound of her footsteps scared her even more. On her porch, the keys jangled in her hand like a bell announcing her helplessness. She dared not look behind. She mastered the key and opened the door. She slammed it behind her and fumbled for the lamp. She should have closed the curtains earlier. She did it now.

The house felt lost without the children to protect. It had been a bad idea to go out and a bad idea to allow the children to stay with Mrs. Conati. Every move echoed between the empty walls. She needed to relax. She was safe, even though she had been vulnerable tonight. But that was nothing new. She had been vulnerable since Nandy had died.

She poured a glass of water and went to bed. Sleep, thankfully, came quickly, dreams also. She dreamed about a whole family, one that knew laughter and kept fear at bay. Children playing, a husband to hug her. She wanted to see this husband's face, knowing that it was not Nandy, but he wouldn't let her see. He wouldn't tell her who he was. He made her feel safe, nonetheless, despite that awful noise at the window. He should take care of that—she told him so in her dream. Still, he didn't show his face. And still, the window rattled.

Assunta opened her eyes. This was no dream. The window *was* rattling. Scraping. Her throat tightened—she might choke. Whoever it was, an intruder with bad intentions, he would come in and do things to her, maybe even kill her. Thank goodness the children weren't here. They were safe. But if this intruder killed *her*, what would happen to her children? *Think*, she almost said out loud. She needed to protect herself—for the children's sake. She climbed slowly out of bed, trying not to make a sound. She set her ear against the bedroom door. It sounded like it was coming from the kitchen window at the back of the house.

She must not leave the room. If he heard her, he might try harder. She gently but sturdily jammed a chair under the handle to the bedroom door. Fumbling in the dark, she took her clothes from her wardrobe, set them on the bed, and pulled out the rod that had held them up. Not too heavy, but long. It was the only weapon she could think of in the room. She pulled a blanket around her shoulders and sat on the floor behind the door.

Any minute, she'd hear glass breaking or a door or window creaking open. The scratching noises continued. Her mind played scenarios, flitting from brave defense to the despicable things an intruder would do to a woman alone. She was breathing heavily. She had to stay calm. Saint Theresa! She should pray.

After an interminable time, the scratching stopped—no crash or thud. Assunta waited to see if footsteps replaced it in the house but heard nothing. She should go back to bed, but what if he came back? Just in case, she took a pillow from the bed, curled on the floor behind the door, and waited for sleep, for morning or the intruder.

Pietro sat at his old spot in the kitchen, the sounds of breakfast preparation giving him a feeling of comfort, much like an old scarf might. His old bed upstairs had long been rented, but Mrs. Conati was letting him sleep on the sofa on the condition that he was last to bed and first up.

"Tell me about the dance," Mrs. Conati said.

"Assunta danced with an absolute stranger." Pietro hadn't meant to say that. He hadn't meant to say anything about her. But what had become of her? A floozie, only in Ernest, not Manhattan.

Mrs. Conati placed a cup of tea on the table. "Drink this. Was it a problem she was dancing? That finally she was enjoying herself? If it bothers you so much, Maestro, why weren't you the one dancing with her?"

"I was playing."

"They've done without you for more than a year." Mrs. Conati stood, cloth over her shoulder, hand on hip, ignoring whatever was sizzling on the stove.

Pietro heard music in his mind at the vision of dancing with Assunta, but it was a haunting beat, anger on the verge of exploding. He lifted the cup of tea to drink but changed his mind. He couldn't stomach it.

"So, Nandy told you what he made me promise him?"

"No. What was that?"

"He didn't tell you he made me promise to take care of her?"

"He did not."

He shouldn't have brought it up now. Saying it out loud pained him. Now Mrs. Conati knew the shallowness of his moral fiber. "Then why would you suggest I should be dancing with her?"

Mrs. Conati took the cloth from her shoulder and began to dry her hands that weren't wet. She turned around, mumbling, "*O Signor!*" Then she turned back. "I would think that was obvious, isn't it, maestro?"

"Not at all."

"I think you ought to pay her a visit. Do it now. I took the children back this morning. She had quite the night."

His entire world out of tune. What did Mrs. Conati mean that he should have danced? Was she, too, insinuating he lacked morals? And what did she mean, quite the night?

He went upstairs to the box of belongings he'd left here. The bed didn't belong to him anymore, but he sat on it in any case. He opened the box, untied a brown length of string holding his sheets of music, and leafed through them.

Scores of other people's music he'd copied to play for special occasions, the music he'd written for Walter and Angela's wedding, the song he'd written for Nonno—song of grapevines, song of Italy.

He didn't need to read it to remember every note, and the images of the vines, the women gathered around the vat, the men beneath the old pear tree. How he wanted to be back there. See how the new vines had flourished, hug Ma, Nonna, his brothers and sisters. His niece Ida would be as tall as him by now.

Yet, there was something flat about the music. Something missing.

He dropped the music back in the box, not bothering to tie it. He pushed the box beneath the bed and strode downstairs and out of the house.

When he got to Assunta's, he walked straight in through the back door without knocking. The children looked up at him from the blanket on the floor, a few toys scattered between them, just as he had seen them so many times before. Assunta was at the stove, the baby in the perambulator crying. What he'd never seen before was this much laundry.

Assunta walked right over to him, dodging long johns and dress shirts as though she'd been expecting him. She took his hand, taking any words he may have had from his mouth.

"You heard?"

"Heard—?"

"The robbers! I was so scared. Thank heavens the children weren't here. If they'd have hurt them!"

His head swirled at her closeness, a rolling and complex spin—he couldn't fathom what her words meant. What robbers was she talking about?

"It's all right. I'm here now." And he wanted to stay. Right here.

"I don't know what they would have done with me. I took the rod from the wardrobe, but I was so scared."

She was a spring day, a concerto of wind, the thrill of her nearness obliterating any anger he should have had at the intruders. *Don't let go.*

"I made a promise." His words sounded like they were coming from someone else. They couldn't be his because he had not a dime to his name. As soon as he had a dime, he'd be out of this country, and yet he found himself saying, "I want to take care of you, of the children."

Just months ago, his words would have repelled her across the room and physically away from him. Back then, when Nandy had been for certain the only man she would ever allow to touch her.

"That's not the kind of help we need." She dropped his hand but didn't back away.

"I didn't think it would happen—I didn't want it to happen."

"You didn't want what?"

"For Nandy to—for you to be left alone."

"Neither of us did. But it's still not the kind of help we need. I tell you how you can help—you can buy his wine equipment. I won't be needing it again."

She couldn't tell if his hesitation meant disappointment at her not wanting him to barge in here and impose himself as her husband or if he didn't want the equipment. "You'll tell me your price for it," he said.

"I'll let you know. Now, if you'll excuse me, you're a man in my house—the neighbors will talk."

"Tell me before I go, have you thought about going back to Italy?"

She'd thought about it plenty. The war had meant she didn't have to think too hard. There was no chance to get there. But deep down, she knew her decision. "This is all my children know. Besides, I couldn't leave *no*body to tend the graves. We stay here."

What use could the wine equipment be to him? He couldn't take it on the ship; he didn't even have a home here where he could store it. Worse still, he didn't have the money for it.

He got to the rehearsal hall early, knowing Guido would already be there.

"Hey, if it isn't *Il Maestro!* I can't say I'm not disappointed with how things worked out in New York, but I'm happy to have you back. You're here to rehearse, I see." Guido pointed to Pietro's clarinet case.

"I'm thinking of taking a break from music. While I figure things out, you know."

"No, I don't know. Enlighten me." Guido crossed his arms.

"I need to sell this. How much will you give me for it?" He willed his hands to stay steady as he held Nonno's clarinet case out to Guido.

Guido took his cigarettes from his pocket, tapped one on the back of his hand, and put it in his mouth without lighting it.

"You want to sell your clarinet?" he asked.

"How much'll you give me?"

"How much are you asking?"

"As much as you'll give me."

Guido took a match from his box and flicked it between his fingers. "Here's what I'll do. Can't say I have much use for your clarinet right now. Maybe another time. But I do have use for someone to compose me a score for a wedding."

"You don't need to pay for that."

"Nah, figure if it's free or if I'm undercharged I won't get the best quality, know what I mean? Then I have these kids who need lessons. Pays a fair bit an hour. I'll give you two weeks upfront. Can you take them on?"

"I would if I could, but I don't have a place they can come to."

"A bed just came free at my house. First month of rent is free to any man who can fix up my chicken coop. The missus has been at me to get it done, but I'm always busy with the band."

"I don't need a handout," Pietro said.

"And I don't give handouts. But I pay for what's right to pay for. Now most men, I'd give an advance, pay the balance when the job's done. But if there's anyone I can trust, it's you. You bring your things tomorrow after work, settle in. I'll have the cash for you. I expect you to start work on the coop at the weekend, or the missus'll have my hide.

Pietro took the money to Assunta ahead of rehearsal. This time he knocked on the front door and waited for her to answer. She took her time, and it looked like she'd freshly pinned her hair once she did answer. She was carrying the new baby, and he could hear the other children playing inside.

"Sit," she indicated the stool on the porch where he'd sat with Nandy.

He handed her the envelope of money, and she put it straight into her apron pocket.

He wanted to ask how she was, how she was coping. Tell her he missed the way things were.

"You'll be wanting to see the equipment. I wasn't expecting you today. I haven't had time to clean it."

"You don't need to clean it for me."

"I'll wait here. You go and look at it yourself. The neighbors," she flicked her head, and he understood her reference to the way people liked to gossip. "It's in the basement."

He knew where the stairs were—the stairs she used to go down to fix him and Nandy a fresh jug. The press, carboy, all the pieces Nandy used—everything was covered in dust. Shelves in disarray, an empty box had been discarded on its side, newspaper was strewn on the floor. Pietro had never seen the house or basement anything but immaculate. He righted the box, folded the newspaper as best he could, and stuck it on the shelf. It'd be a trick to get the glass carboy clean enough to use. He checked the barrel. Not bad, wine still in it. He'd pour some now, but there was nothing clean to decant it into.

He heard the front door click, footsteps coming down. Assunta still held the baby despite the rickety stairs.

"I just remembered how bad I had left it here. It's not the normal way I keep things."

"I know," he said.

"You must think me awful, the mess. It's hard to leave the baby upstairs, not good air for him. I should clean."

Her voice rose in distress. She was shaking her head as she spoke, jiggling the baby too quickly.

"Hey, it's all right," he didn't like to see her troubled. He put his hand on her shoulder. She didn't pull away.

"I should leave him with the other children, just for the time it takes to clean." Her anxiety was like a violin off tune. He put his hand on her cheek, rubbed it with his thumb to soothe her. "I wouldn't be far—" her voice even higher. He had to stop her talking, calm her. He couldn't help himself, and he couldn't hesitate because somehow, if he didn't kiss her now, he would never have the courage ever again.

Her lips stopped moving when his lips touched hers. She didn't kiss back, but she didn't pull away.

"I promised," he said. "Let me take care of you. I'll ask nothing in return except a good supper."

She pursed her lips—did she taste his? She nodded, yes.

"I need to take the baby upstairs," she said.

He heard another click of the front door. He'd just kissed her. She'd just said yes. A tune came to him, distant, faint, neither joyous nor somber. Life was about to change. His duty would be to take care of her and the children, as promised. He had no idea if he'd prove up to the task.

TWENTY-ONE

The church sounded hollow without a congregation. Mr. and Mrs. Conati stood next to Pietro, ready to act as witnesses. One of Mrs. Conati's older daughters sat with Max, Mary, and Ida, scrubbed and tidy in their Sunday best even though it was Tuesday. The baby's perambulator was in the aisle. Guido and Bolek slipped in uninvited and unobtrusive. Every rustle and fidget sounded like an announcement that Assunta had changed her mind and would not come.

She had insisted she didn't want the fuss of congregation or a dance, so Father Farri had agreed to this simple midweek ceremony. This was all a formality. It was a way for Pietro to protect her, look after her, extract her from the weight of other people's laundry. He hadn't kissed her again, and for all he knew, he never would.

Father waited with Pietro, bible in hand. The organist sat on his bench, waiting for the bride before he played. Pietro had wanted to write a special piece, only Assunta had said now they'd decided to marry, she saw little point in delaying. Pietro had hardly been able to object to the rush. Hadn't she been what he'd wanted all along?

When the organist began to play, it took him a moment to comprehend that Assunta had arrived. He couldn't force himself to turn and look; he simply listened to everyone else's movements and to the generic music that could have played for any bride for any man, in America or Italy.

She stood beside him, her breath as sweet as a grosbeak's song. A short sermon, no hymns, vows that echoed in the rafters. They told each other promises of forever-after resolutely in English, resolutely in America. He may never see Italy again. He wasn't too sure how he felt about that, even if, on the bright side, he would be under the same roof as her every day. If this was platonic, if she never loved him back, he couldn't decide if that would be heaven or if it would be hell.

Then they were done. Married. Man and wife.

A photographer, the only concession Assunta would allow, waited for them in the entryway. "For the children to remember it by one day," she explained.

Pietro sat for the picture; she stood behind his chair. He guessed the idea behind that was so nobody would see just how much taller she was.

They had supper at the Conati house, spaghetti and meatballs, a midweek luxury even the lodgers benefited from, then Assunta pushed the perambulator up the hill, Pietro carried the travel case that had almost marked his new life in New York, the children ran with the excitement of a change in routine.

Assunta hung Pietro's overcoat and hat by the back door. He set his box at the foot of the stairs, his clarinet in its case on top of it. He tucked his music composition books, all three of them, none full, underneath his arm, wondering what he might do with them.

"You can lay more claim to the house than a lodger, you know. I'm going to put the children to bed."

He set the books in a spare corner of a cupboard in the dining room. The children were scrubbing faces and brushing teeth in the kitchen. He sat still, wanting to stay out of their way. He heard them go upstairs and did not want to follow. Was there a spare bedroom? Would he sleep with the children? Perhaps he should sleep on the sofa. Then if the robbers came, he would be ready.

A tune came to him. The protector, guarding a flock of innocent women and children, the music revolving around the outside, a delicate core inside. He thought about writing it down, but he hardly felt like a protector. His wife was taller than he was. His wife, *la moglie*. It sounded strange. He'd have to write home with the news.

He hoped Assunta would tell him what she expected about the arrangements. He'd hate to be disrespectful and upset her, get off on the wrong foot. Up the stairs, he heard her laugh and one of the children being silly. Her crystal laughter. He had now, if he wanted, the right to hold her, to kiss her. Her lips on his. He jumped up from the table and went into the kitchen—the water was still warm, he needed cold. He went outside and stuck his head under the well pump. He shouldn't be having such thoughts. She only took him in as a protector. Not a lover. *Not a lover not alovernotalover.*

When she came down, he was standing in the middle of the kitchen. Hair wet, sticking at angles, looking like he didn't know where he was allowed to sit.

"The children are asleep. I tell them stories," she said. He nodded.

She had wondered about this moment. About the moments before bed every night for the rest of their lives. Pietro, reliable, loyal companion. She could not even begin to think of him as a lover. But in front of her, vulnerable, terrified, she could not help but move closer.

She had not contemplated making love to Pietro. Even when she'd agreed to marry, she had never intended to make love again. Her womanhood had died with Nandy. This was a marriage of convenience. Only now, the thought of human touch—someone to hold her and tell her it would all be set right, that he would take care of her, that she was loved—didn't seem like such a bad thought after all.

"I sleep—um—the sofa?" He backed away from her. She should let him go—if that's what he wanted, she should want it also. Of course, he shouldn't find her attractive. He was only here because Nandy had asked him. But that look the night before Nandy was killed—she'd misread him?

"I'll get you a pillow." She made it up two stairs, then went back down. He *had* looked at her that way that night. He *had* kissed her in the basement. She walked right over to him and kissed him. Only their mouths met. A kiss delicate at first, then harder. Making up for time lost, for nights alone, love snatched. He may or may not have kissed back, then she pulled back a little, took hold of his hand, and turned to lead him upstairs.

In the bedroom, Pietro stood statue stiff as she unbuttoned his shirt. She pushed the shirt back off his shoulders, letting her hands run against his skin. She felt him tremble. He moved his arm like a tin soldier. She felt his hand like a rolling pin on her waist. His lips were stiff like the rim of a glass. Like he wanted her but didn't want to intrude. But she wanted—she needed him to intrude. She brushed her chest against his, blew gently on his neck, inched her way up and, breathing heavily, and she took his ear lobe between her lips.

If he'd been rigid before now, he was like rock.

His hands clenched into fists held air, no longer on her. His eyes clamped shut, his mouth drawn down—distraught?

"Hey?" she whispered.

He shook his head.

"Not your ears?" A nod of the head told her she had understood.

She ran her fingertips gently on one of his balled fists, touched her lips to his knuckles then did the same on the other side.

"Think of me as a clarinet." His arms slipped around her waist, less mechanical now. "I am music," she whispered.

He hesitated a moment then his entire body seemed to deflate. He touched her hesitantly with fingertips.

He lifted the bed covers back, and they lay down. She felt his fingers running slowly on her right side, then on the left. He put his head on her, and she had the odd sensation that he was listening to her, learning her. This man, so familiar and yet so foreign and unknown, would take care of her. She'd not decided whether she'd take him into her bed before now, and now all she wanted was to take hold of him, pull him closer to her, but this slowness, this exploration, it was like nothing she'd ever known.

His attention on her, like a celebration of her actual being, not focusing on how to satisfy his own fulfillment, as Nandy did.

She clutched the bed sheet so her hands could not slow him or urge propriety. To heck with propriety, she'd let him play her music in his own time. She couldn't help herself. She pulled her nightdress over her head and let it drop to the floor. She didn't care that she'd never taken it off for Nandy.

TWENTY-TWO

1918

Even now, after half a year, Pietro turned down the road toward Mrs. Conati's on his way home. How could he forget he lived in his friend's home with his wife and children? No, once again, he needed to correct himself. He lived with *his* wife and her children.

Assunta seemed quite content to talk to him when it pleased her. Otherwise, they both kept a respectful distance. She needed time to get on with her home-keeping and dealing with the children without him under her feet. She showed him the same courtesy when he was working on his music.

The only times she allowed him to be a husband, the nights she reached for his hand under the covers and pulled it to her, those nights dulled his guilt for stepping into the void he had created in her and her children's life because he had not tapped the day her real love died.

He even had a score of sorts started. Not the flow of writing he'd have imagined if he'd truly dared to imagine what it might be like living with Assunta, but something, nonetheless.

The key slid into the keyhole with the reassuring sound of home—his home.

Assunta, no doubt busy with the children, called out from the living room. "There's a letter on the table for you."

"Hi, Petro!" Ida, who still couldn't pronounce his name, skipped into the kitchen and held her arms up for a hug.

One day, not too far off now, it would be his own child skipping to the door to greet him. The thought conjured that hesitation of taut silence between the moment the conductor lifted his hands, baton poised, and the instant he asks the orchestra to begin. Such big responsibility ahead. Once his baby was born, would the others feel inclined to call him daddy?

"I'm coal dusty. Go back with Mamma. I'll be quick." Ida went back to the living room with a disappointed *oh*.

In the kitchen, Pietro hummed to the splash of soap. If only Nonno could see him now. What would he think about him becoming a dad for real? A baby Pietro—or Pietra. He had a new idea for a lullaby to write. If the child had half a voice, he'd write songs and verses. Maybe they'd have a dozen children, make their own choir—as long as Assunta wanted that. How would one go about asking, or did it just happen? He'd best wait and see.

After dinner, instead of opening the letter from Ma, Pietro drew a piece of paper from his pocket and shook it from habit that came from everything being dusty from the mine. He needed paper with him because a tune could turn up unexpectedly, like a butterfly that from nowhere flicks in front of you. He hummed a snippet he'd thought of this afternoon.

He half-listened to Assunta, herding the children up to bed. He knew the routine. She'd get the children dressed, and they'd curled up in one bed or another, a tangle of arms and legs listening to Mamma's stories. All cozy and together. Close enough to feel each other fidget. A togetherness and a world under the covers that he belonged only on the fringe of, but the fringe was plenty.

"Hey, Pietro, *vieni*!" Assunta called from the top of the stairs.

Him? Go up? "Something wrong?"

"No, just come!"

He went up, pausing twice to see if she changed her mind and told him she wouldn't need him after all. Ida appeared in the bedroom doorway. She took hold of his shirt sleeve and dragged him in with all the might of a mouse and sat him at the foot of the bed. Assunta sat at the head of the bed with the children, telling a story.

"If only you could see, flowers dripping from villas like jewels from the neck of a countess, the sun sparkling off the tufts of water playing pat-a-cake with the boats glinting like fairies out to enjoy the hot summer day." She certainly had a way with words. Pietro could hear the day she was depicting. "Birds circling far over our heads, crying messages to each other in a language only they know. Maybe they were plotting to swoop down and steal the picnic Nonna had made for us!"

Pietro could hear the breeze, the lake lapping.

"Mamma?" Max asked. "If you liked Italy so much, why did you come here?"

"I came a long time ago."

"Yes, but why?"

"Did you like Italy too?" Ida asked Pietro.

"I did."

"Now it's your turn to tell us a story," Mary said to Pietro.

"I wouldn't know how. Your mother has that talent."

Just for a moment, Assunta looked at him. He could barely think, let alone string a sentence together.

"I could sing a song?"

"Pleeeeeaaaaase!" three children cried in unison.

Pietro cleared his throat, straightened his shoulders. He would never sing in public, but to children, where was the harm? He began, his voice gentle.

Ninna nanna mamma
Insalata non ce n'è
Sette le scodelle
Sulla tavola del re
Ninna nanna mamma
Ce n'è una anche per me
Dentro cosa c'è
Solo un chicco di caffè.

Quando sarò grande
Comprerò per te
Tante cose belle
Come fai per me.
Chiudi gli occhi e sogna
Quello che non hai,
I tuoi sogni poi
Mi racconterai.

A Lullaby Mamma
There is no salad
Seven bowls are set out
On the table of the King
A Lullaby Mamma
There is even one for me
In it what is there
Just a bean, a coffee bean

When I am a big girl
I will buy for you
A lot of pretty things
Like you do for me.
Close your eyes and dream now
Of what you do not have
Then after you tell me
The dreams that you dreamed

Max began to fidget. Pietro paused, looking at him, "Did you want to sing with me?" He shook his head.

"You know you got the verses mixed up?" Max said.

"I suppose you're right. It's been a while."

"And it's a song for babies. Don't you have anything a bit more grown-up?"

"I like it," Ida said.

"Well," Pietro thought a moment. "I know one you'll all like."

Gentle and sweet and ever kind,
Ready to serve and bear,
There is no richer gift to earth
Than woman's patient care.
Aminist'ring angel, though
To work, to watch, to pray,
The troubled spirit prompt to calm
And smile its grief away.
Gentle and sweet and ever kind,
Instant to meet each call,
Thine to soothe the bed of pain
With tender thought for all.
Thy presence, like a sunny beam
That's cast upon the night,
O'er stricken men still softly shines
In purity and light.

This song was now part of the band's repertoire. Each time they played it, Pietro thought of Assunta. "Like a sunny beam," Pietro said to the children, but he looked at Assunta. Her light shined upon them all, a lucky family.

A short while later, she climbed into bed after him. As always, he lay still, half expecting her to oust him from the bed where he did not belong.

"The flowers I told the children about?" She said, her voice radiant, contented. "I used to imagine them coming to life, becoming beautiful maidens from a fairy tale, dancing with their splendid petal-color gowns." Her words tickled the side of his face. "Sometimes, the music you play reminds me of the flowers. But it didn't strike me until recently, listening to you play, I realized for the first time I never imagined my flower maidens singing. I wonder why that was. They could've sung in happiness."

She reached for his hand and pulled it to her belly. He felt a fidget in her skin. "Is that our child?" he asked.

"It is."

He moved his head closer to her, "May I?"

She laughed. "You want to listen? You may."

He rested his ear gently in the place where she'd guided his hand. He wasn't quite sure what he was hearing, except that it was their baby making the noise.

After she fell asleep, Pietro came down and opened his notebook to write the song that had come to him for his new child. A song barely touching on the immensity of his joy, there may not have been song enough in the whole world to capture such joy.

When Pietro got home the next day, the letter he had forgotten to open lay waiting for him on the little table. He slit open the envelope. A letter from home was a rare treat.

Caro Pietro,

Such wonderful news you shared, yet how's a mother supposed to sleep at night not knowing the woman who shares a home with her son? Do you think you can learn to love, and she you?

It's gallant of you to take in your friend's wife and another man's children. I shouldn't be surprised. Nonno used to say if there's one person in the world we could rely on to do the right thing, it was you. Your sense of morals always put everyone else to shame.

The letter trembled in his hands, a soft fluttering of delicate wings. The next sentence was something about the weather and the grapes. He read it a few times but still didn't know what it said. He folded the letter and slipped it into his pant pocket. From the other room, Assunta was clearing the dishes. Her routine. She knew the order of her life. He wished he did.

"I am—" I am what, he thought. "I'll be back," he called instead.

"I didn't think you had rehearsal tonight," Assunta called.

Pietro did not answer. He stuck a pencil behind his ear and left.

He went straight to the bar. He sipped his wine too fast and wondered if Nandy ever felt any guilt leaving Assunta alone. He toasted the glass to Nonna and his own impeccable morals.

Rely on him to do the right thing. *I can always do the right thing,* he should write. Or better still, *I can rest assured Nonno went to his grave believing I can do the right thing.*

Did he even know that's what they thought of him? He couldn't recall a single instance when morals were discussed.

Guido appeared at the bar, tugging Pietro away from his memories, and ordered them both a drink.

"When I was a kid, I spent half the summer once worrying some swallows who'd built a nest outside my window would starve when we went up to the vineyard, and I couldn't put polenta out for them," Pietro said.

"Didn't anyone tell you swallows eat insects?"

"Years later. I felt like a fool. Nothing new. Can I ask you something?"

"Fire away Maestro," Guido said.

"Would you say I'm a moral man?"

Guido squinted. "Surprised you don't know the answer to that one. You can't help but be a moral man when you have the passion you do. Don't think I've ever seen any man more passionate about a clarinet or any other instrument. Or, for that matter, any rehearsal or performance. Why the heck would you ask such a thing?"

"What if it wasn't true? What if I'd just managed to make people think that of me?"

"D'ya rob a bank or something?"

"Nothing like that, course not. I should repay you the money you gave me. I would if I was a moral man."

"I told you I wanted music for that money. And if you hadn't been the most moral man I've ever met, I wouldn't have given it to you. Or I would have wanted to know what trouble you'd got yourself into to need it. And I was right. Look at you, taking care of another man's children. You keep on keeping them, stop being too hard on yourself, and have another drink. Things'll look better in the morning."

♪ 𝄞 ♪

Pietro went in the mine ahead of shift change as usual. He worked methodically. He would allow no undetected hollows today. Men nodded on their way in and out. Here, at least, he knew his place, one that carried a high price when he left. He was a part of the whole, not only after dark when the lights went out.

When he'd apologized to Assunta in the morning for going to the bar, her answer had made him all the smaller. "Don't you worry about that. A man has to spend time doing what he has to do. Come on, drink your tea. And here," she cracked an egg into a cup for him. "It'll clear your head."

Today he didn't even care to work in time with the beat.

Merda, he should have done things differently. He should have proposed like a man coming to her to take care of her because he knew that was the right thing to do and because he loved her. Not in turmoil because someone had made him promise—someone whose death he'd had a hand in.

It didn't have to be too late. He could make a fresh start. He could make things happen differently from now on, especially with the baby coming. It was worth a shot. He was the only one to blame for feeling like a protector. He *could* change things. A moral man loved his wife—there was no shame in that. He *could* declare his love for her. The jewelry store in Indiana would be a good place to start.

He'd get the prettiest ring he could afford. He'd get down on one knee after the kids had gone to bed, and he'd let her know that, from now on, he wanted it to be their marriage. Pietro and Assunta, husband and wife. A marriage of love, morals, and passion. A marriage for the right reasons.

"Come on, men, in time," he yelled.

♪ 𝄞 ♪

Max appeared from his afternoon nap. He was often the first up; the others would follow shortly. Max would be starting school soon. One less to worry about in the day. It was so exhausting running after them all and getting her chores done.

Assunta missed Nandy. Every day. She would be married to him again in a heartbeat if it was possible. But being married to Pietro was not such a bad life if she was honest with herself. To think she had felt nauseated at the wedding, the thought of living with this man had petrified her. But it gave her purpose to have someone besides the children to look after. And he was good to them too. She had no complaints there. No thrashings. A little hesitant, perhaps, but he would find his confidence when he became a daddy himself. Just a few more months and he would be. She touched her belly.

A familiar stab of guilt pierced, followed immediately by anger. Nandy had told Pietro to take care of her, leaving her no choice.

Pietro was, as Nandy had told her countless times, a good man. He demanded very little. He still felt like a stranger—an endearing one, though.

She had never met anyone who recounted stories in sounds. He'd described his family's house in the hills, long summers tending the vines and, at last, harvesting and crushing. He gave the most extraordinary detail to the sound of grapes underfoot, the laughter, and merriness that went with it all.

Ida and Mary burst into the kitchen together, giggling and jostling each other.

"Where's your little brother? Isn't he awake yet?" They shook their heads, then climbed up on chairs to watch Max, who was lining his soldiers up on the table.

Her little Ferdinando. The very last gift Nandy had given her, a small piece of himself for her to keep. She went upstairs and lifted him gently, held him to her before laying him on the bed to change.

♫ 𝄞 ♪

Pietro returned triumphant from Indiana, a gold ring with a cameo inset, a promise in his pocket.

He patted Max, Mary, and Ida on the head, then Assunta on the shoulder in greeting. He wanted to kiss her cheek, but he still had not decided if this was appropriate in front of the children.

"Ferdinando has a cough. I'm going to make him a poultice," Assunta said, tucking in a corner of his afghan. "He woke up from his nap with a fever. He's not himself."

Pietro nodded. Mamma knew what to do. "There's a lot of anti-alcohol talk down the mines. Damn dries. They're likening drink to the Germans, saying Americans should have nothing to do with it. Beer mostly, but wine will be next.

We'll need to think about a double batch as soon as we can get grapes."

Ferdinando let out a pitiful moan, not quite a cry. Assunta stroked his little face. "Pietro, you have a good ear. I often think you could hear a flower sigh. Would you have a listen to the child's chest? Make sure he's not congested."

Pietro leaned in, but he could hear her breath more than the little boy's. The breath he heard at night, the breath he set to the gentle breeze of the song of love and played on pace with his heart. His cheeks flushed. He wanted to kiss her. He didn't move for a moment.

"Here, let me hold him." Pietro took Ferdinando from her arms, the only way to hear without the distraction of her. When had this little man grown so big? He should pick him up more often. He could get some practice for when the new baby arrived.

He held his ear close to the little chest, listening intently for nothing because nothing is what he wanted to hear. Instead, he heard a minute rattle.

"You'll have him see the doctor tomorrow."

The doctor praised Assunta for bringing Ferdinando to him so soon. "Most wait, then the pneumonia is harder to treat."

Stop mocking me. She had been around long enough. She knew how hard pneumonia was to cure at any stage. She tried hard to focus on the directions he gave her. He could not be sick, not her little Ferdinando.

"You were right for us to see the doctor." She told Pietro slowly, articulating each word to avoid breaking down in tears. "You heard it early. You gave him his best chance."

He nodded, then continued his supper. *How can you eat?* She thought.

She chopped pasta for the children with a fork in one hand and with the other spooned homemade broth to Ferdinando, who sat on her lap. Pietro dabbed his mouth with his napkin then bent over the infant. She could smell the garlic on Pietro's breath, all the more pungent because she had not eaten.

"Be strong little man," Pietro said, then moved to the little table in the front room and, as he usually did when there was no rehearsal to go to or wine to make, he spread out his things in an order known only to him and disappeared into his music.

Part of her wanted to talk to him, wanted him to speak to her. He could at least leave his music alone, just tonight. She wanted him to reassure her everything would be fine. Another part wanted to scream at him—*Nothing can happen to Ferdinando. Nothing!*

"Mary, help Mamma with the dishes. Max, tidy the toys. Ida, wipe your mouth." She put a saucepan of vinegar on the stove to heat and sat back down with Ferdinando, rocking him gently. When the pan was hot, she set him on a blanket on the floor, bared his chest ready for cloths dipped in the hot vinegar.

The stringent aroma of vinegar was enough to make the notes in Pietro's head scramble and refuse to stick to the page. He'd be smelling it until the kid was cured or—the alternative did not bear thinking about. Assunta often sang when she did anything with the children. She didn't tonight. His music out of reach, he listened to her breathing through her nostrils slowly and fiercely. She must be so worried about the poor cherub. He'd hold onto the ring for now.

Her movements a little brusque, she said nothing as she gathered the cloths from the boy's chest, rubbed in some oil, then wrapped him in the blanket and ushered the others to get ready for bed. The thought nagged at Pietro that he should be saying something when she returned, only he wasn't sure what.

Max and Mary reached up for a kiss goodnight; Ida clambered onto his lap for hers.

"You coming to sing a song?" she said.

He'd rather not. Assunta had sounded bitter with him since she'd relayed the doctor's diagnosis. "I need to finish. Tomorrow perhaps."

He listened as they went upstairs and heard bedsprings. The rascals must be jumping while Assunta took care of Ferdinando. Then instead of the muffled recounting of a bedtime story, he heard the bedroom door close, and Assunta came back down.

She always gave him the room and the time to do his own thing. *Not tonight.* She wanted to stride over and snatch the paper from in front of him. Break his pencil in two with her two hands—yell into his face. He had to make everything better. He had *promised* Nandy he would take care of her. He needed to take care of Ferdinando, too. She would not be able to stand it if something happened to him. Pietro *had* to do something.

Mamma, think about Mamma—in control, composed. She could be better than this. She could cope.

The lead on Pietro's pencil suddenly snapped, leaving a jagged line from the last note he'd written. The sound snapped her back to reality. What had she been thinking? Poor mild-mannered Pietro. Here to protect her but couldn't say boo to a ghost. It was she who needed to take care of him, not him, of her.

Assunta prayed to St. Theresa, dutifully changed Ferdinando's vinegar cloths, and spent hours rocking him. Pietro wondered if it was healthy for the new baby she was carrying but dared not ask.

He thought about playing the clarinet, but the last time he'd done that, the baby had died.

Ferdinando may have been one of five children Nandy left in this world, but he was the one who kept his father alive. He already looked like him, though he was showing none of his father's resilience. Every day weaker, he appeared to be sapping the strength from Assunta at the same pace. She had barely uttered a word. She hardly even spoke to the children. When she did speak, her voice was monotone.

On Tuesday after work, Pietro found Mrs. Conati with the doctor on the front porch. The doctor tipped his hat and left. Mrs. Conati's face was red, streaked with tears. She shook her head.

"He's gone."

What could she mean? The doctor's gone? She had to mean the doctor—she couldn't mean Ferdinando. Pietro's feet made hollow echoes on the steps. He opened the front door, the hinge creaked. Mrs. Conati was sobbing. Stoic, strong as a pillar Mrs. Conati. Of course, she wasn't crying because the doctor had gone.

Little Ferdinando. The cheeky little mite only got a chance to hint at inheriting his father's character.

The way Assunta cared for Ferdinando like he was the most precious thing in the world—how could he wilt, unmoved to survive despite the love she enveloped him in? And where was he, Pietro, stuck underground, rehearsal on his mind instead of by his wife's side. Not present to take a little of her pain on himself.

"How is she?" he asked.

Mrs. Conati shook her head again, then disappeared up the stairs.

A violin, mournful, played in Pietro's head. He went back out through the front door that creaked the same creak, whether he walked in or walked out. He sat down on the stool on the porch. He'd sat on this stool when Nandy had been alive, drinking wine with his friend. It was still Nandy's seat. It was still Nandy's wife inside the house, and she had just lost Nandy's child.

If it had been Nandy out here avoiding his wife, Pietro would have sent him packing inside to comfort her. Nandy was the real husband; Pietro was just a stand-in. He'd go in soon. Come up with something to say. Hold her, comfort her. He tried to think of words of encouragement. He'd have to say something. Instead, all that came to him was a solo for a violin.

A sudden scream curdled from upstairs. It was like a physical slap to Pietro, swamping his ears.

Assunta!

More footsteps banged down the stairs. This time the front door screeched in protest as Mrs. Conati slung it open. "Call the doctor back!"

♫ 𝄢 ♪

Pietro found the doctor outside the company office chatting to one of the bosses like it was an ordinary day, as though he hadn't just pronounced an infant dead.

He came right away. Not jogging like Pietro, but using a long stride, practiced in reaching emergencies without losing composure.

Pietro followed him up the stairs. Mrs. Conati had the bedroom door open, waiting. Pietro could see Ferdinando's crib near the window, covered with a sheet. He could hear Assunta, in bed, gasping and moaning, not crying, not anything he recognized.

"She's in labor." Mrs. Conati's words a cymbal that stopped him. A husband didn't go into the room of a woman in labor. He turned and went back to Nandy's stool on the porch and wondered if Nandy ever sat here when Assunta was in labor. Unlikely, he'd be at the bar or someone's house drinking their wine. Celebrating early or drinking away the thought that things may go wrong.

Pietro should get a glass if it'd ward off things that may go wrong. But what could go right? It was too early for labor—way, way too early.

♫ 𝄢 ♪

The doctor had never stayed with her the whole time until delivery before. Not that the labor lasted that long. Brought on by the grief of losing the other one, he told her.

This baby was small, not ready for the world. Mrs. Conati set him, swaddled, on her chest.

"He'll not be with you long," the doctor said and left.

The baby felt tiny, his face minuscule. He hadn't cried. His breathing was shallow, miraculous, and improbable.

She barely noticed Mrs. Conati had left the room, nor when she came back in with Pietro. This day, the very worst of her life, she'd not thought of Pietro. Mrs. Conati had been her shadow the entire day. She had visited Ferdinando every day he had the sickness, helped with the vinegar cloths, called the doctor, and held Assunta strong in her arms when the realization slammed her. She'd held her hand during labor, dampened her forehead, given instructions firmly but gently.

Now Pietro was here, and Assunta needed him to hold her. To climb into bed with her and hold her. Touch her, at least. Somewhere, anywhere. To look at this tiny angel's face so they would remember it.

He came closer to the bed, to the side where she lay. She willed him to the other side where he could climb in with her but didn't find the strength to tell him so out loud.

If he touched her, her body might remember it needed to function. It might remember there was hope, someone to share the burden. It would know the searing pain was not going to last forever.

Way too early, the doctor had said.

Pietro bent over and looked at the baby's face. He said nothing. He didn't reach so much as a finger in her direction.

Touch! Let me know I will feel again. Let me know that tomorrow will be worth living!

He didn't hear the voice in her head. How could he? But how could he not know!

But he didn't know, or if he knew, he didn't care. He turned around and left the room. He was gone, she was alone.

He couldn't go back in there. He was no better than Nandy the night their daughter died. If he couldn't go in there, the only thing he could do was play the clarinet. A part of him knew he shouldn't, but it was his only hope. His son, hearing the magic of the music, might find strength, might hear the only language Pietro knew how to use to give him that strength. If ever there was a time to change the world's course with song, it was now.

He held the clarinet to his lips for more than a minute before he drew air from his heart and began to play. As he played, he pictured a beating heart, lungs full of air. *Breathe, little one, live.*

Something thudded right by him. Not something falling, something had hit the door. Then something else—this time glass shattered! She was throwing things at the door. She was throwing things at him, at his music. The third thing was a clatter, even though he'd already stopped playing. She didn't want him. She didn't want his music for her son.

He stumbled down the stairs, went out of the door, and ran.

The music orchestra of joy, clamoring brass of death. Every instrument he could think of, each playing its own tune—intense pain, intense joy, nothing that could exist together, a mighty cacophony, drowning him in music. His head felt on the brink of imploding.

He knew he had to go back, but the music. He couldn't. He had to run.

Assunta didn't cry at the funeral for the two babies. She took flowers to the graves of Nandy's Mary, of their Mary, and now Ferdinando and Dino. She'd chosen the name Dino. It sounded like Gino and seemed somehow appropriate for such a little might. His little body, his little life.

She dug some valerian root. She took it into the kitchen and should have washed it and chopped it to make an infusion to help her grief. But she stopped there, looked at it, the mud from it dirtying her tabletop. She would not use it. If she did, it might bring solace. Even if it were fleeting, it would not do. Solace would take away the pain, it would take away the value of the lives of those two little creatures. Two little boys, two lives she'd created, then watched slip away.

No, there'd be no solace. They deserved her mourning. Her pain was all she could give them now.

Except for one thing, one strand of slim hope that she could grasp, a thin tenuous thread.

He came into the kitchen—her thread—the man she was supposed to call husband. He needed to walk right over to her, take her in his arms, and stop her from falling further into the abyss. Stop her from curling into a ball right here on the floor—no, she couldn't do that. The children. She couldn't let them see. But when they couldn't see, she would fall. Only he could stop her.

He stood, as he'd stood these past days, on the other side of the room. The very thing she needed the most, to feel his skin against hers, was the one thing he would not give her.

"I'll be going to rehearsal, then," he said. Not how sorry he was, how he'd pull her through, but that he was going to rehearsal.

"You do as you see fit. You're only here because Nandy told you to be here. That's all." She willed him to defy her. To march across the room and take her in his arms. Be strong. Be the one to hold her up. But all he did was turn and walk away.

TWENTY-THREE

1920

The bar looked uninviting without lights. Pietro, Guido, and some other band members loitered outside, instruments dangling from their hands in defeat. If buildings could have souls, this one had lost its the moment it became against the law to drink wine. All that remained was a sign in the window that said CLOSED.

"We came to this country for what?" Guido said.

"Apparently not an honest drink," Pietro shook his head. Someone spat at the window; another punched the wall.

"We mind our own business, follow the rules. This is just plain wrong."

"Makes you wanna leave town," Pietro pulled a pencil from his pocket and rubbed his thumb up and down it.

"New York still could be a possibility, you know."

Guido still had a dream, heck Pietro had once had a dream of sorts, too, but now he had a family. Not like his family back in Italy, that spoke and conferred and banded together to achieve a common cause, but one that drifted day after day. Where the children were taken care of, washed, dressed, and fed, but the attentions stopped there in a home where no music played.

"City's dry too. Besides, I'm a married man." Pietro hung his head as he spoke.

"Take her with you, get out of this place. You'll make it this time around."

"You overestimate me." He overestimated the fact that Pietro had a say. That Assunta noticed he existed. She fed him, sure, got his clothes ready, sharpened his pencils even. She even spoke to him when necessary. Rarely when the children weren't there. And in bed, she turned, a frozen block, her back to him.

"Aren't you the boss? Shouldn't it be up to you where you live? You'd give the kids a better life too."

"Who's to say anyone but you will ever appreciate what I do?"

"You have no idea, do you?" Silence hung for a while. Then Guido raised his head, suddenly enthusiastic. "Don't you have a barrel going at your house, Pietro?"

He had. He'd managed to get Nebbiolo grapes, too. The trouble was, he had a wife at home. A sullen shell of a wife. A wife, who once upon a time inspired music he shouldn't have written, and who now, when the music was permitted, gave him only the most solemn of songs—nothing he'd ever want to share at a wedding or party.

"I ought to be getting home. 'Nother time." Pietro walked away.

"Don't get in trouble with your old lady!" Guido teased.

Pietro held up his hand in place of goodbye and wandered toward his silent home. What did Guido know? It might have been different if the baby had survived. Then he dismissed the idea as he had done time and time before. It was Ferdinando Assunta had wanted. Nandy's baby.

Since that day, there'd remained no hint of their initial complicity. In hindsight, in any case, it hadn't been romance, more like greed for solace, an attempt to overcome the past and start afresh. Funny though, for a time, they had almost felt like a real family. The children had even stopped asking about their dad. Life had been better than he deserved. But little Ferdinando had torn their imperfect world apart.

Ida danced around the room in her new dress on her first day at school.

"Now I'm big like you." She beamed at Mary.

"Walk together now. No leaving your sister behind." Assunta kissed each one on the cheek, straightened a collar, a button, a hat. "Off you all go now. Don't be late. Listen to the teacher and speak English."

Finally, all three children could go to school. She watched them walk down the path to the street, waved, and closed the door. Relief, aloneness. Quiet. The first time she had been alone since—well, just since.

She had longed for this moment for weeks, longer probably. For a pause in the endless trail of children's existence, of toys, of forgotten coloring pencils, of dropped socks. No baby toys. No perambulator, no burping cloths. Max's tin soldiers set at strategic guard posts on window ledges and curtain rails. Mary's hair ribbons tied on the kitchen table leg to practice her bows. Ida's dolls tucked up for bed on the armchair.

The three wonders in her life. The three that made her get out of bed in the morning and function through the day. The three she lived for, and yet, how she had longed for them to be gone, at school, and she could rest.

She turned the lock on the door. She needed to look around the kitchen, start some chores, but her eyes lost focus. Her shoulders dipped; her body begged to let go. No responsibility until the children returned—no reason to live until then.

She almost let her back slide down the door to sit right there. *Who cares if I move? If I sit here?* A tiny, deep down voice told her no. Mamma? *Move your legs. Walk out of the kitchen.* Her legs obeyed. Slumped, she couldn't even feel a trace of emotion. It wasn't like a weight on her shoulders, more like someone had taken her insides out.

She made it to the bottom of the stairs and held onto the handrail. She willed her legs to carry her up—she did it all the time with the children, didn't she? She couldn't care less if she sat here until they returned, yet she forced her feet to move one step at a time. She got to the top and shuffled along to her room where she half fell, half lay on her bed. She didn't adjust to a better position or get under the covers for warmth. It didn't matter. All that mattered was that she did not have to function. She could lie there and let the rest of the world carry on. That world outside that still had hopes and dreams. The world that was no longer hers.

♪ 𝄞 ♪

Pietro watched Assunta wrap her dahlia tubers in newspaper and place them in a box to store them for the winter. He'd brought home two new paper bags of dahlias for her in the spring—for the children, he explained. She'd not acknowledged him. The flowers and the children were all that kept her going.

She carried the dahlia box to the bottom of the basement stairs and left them there. She'd kept the basement tidied and sorted for a while, but it reminded her of when she'd been overwhelmed with laundry, a new baby, and a widow's paltry pension, so now she couldn't bear to be down there. He'd have to rearrange the shelf to make a space. He needed the room to get a second batch of wine going in any case. His homemade wine was more precious than ever now it was forbidden. Not that he could invite people over to share, not with her silence.

He shuffled some items on the second shelf up, then picked up a box from the bottom shelf. He pulled open the lid sections that were slotted together. Inside was Nandy's mining equipment. This find underscored the sunken feeling weighing on Pietro that this was still Nandy's house.

He pulled out the jacket folded on the top. It had dust on it, but he could tell Assunta had washed it before putting it into storage—she actually might have earned a few dollars for it if she'd sold it. Under the jacket was his helmet. It was his safety helmet, the cord still attached to the battery that would have attached to his belt.

He covered the helmet back in the box and put it on the second shelf. Then he pulled it back off and took the helmet back out again, the battery, too. It was the safety helmet.

He carried the helmet up the stairs and held it out to Assunta in the kitchen. "What's this?"

"Nandy's helmet." Her voice cold, stating the obvious.

"I can see that. But what's it doing here?"

"It's here because you brought it up." Everything about her voice conveyed a weary sense of resignation.

"You told me they never found his helmet. That it, along with one of his boots, had been lost in the blast."

"You all had two helmets."

"This is his safety helmet. Which means he was wearing his carbide lamp that day."

"He didn't like the battery."

"There's a reason they're called safety helmets. Explosions don't just happen without an open flame."

She made a sound of non-committal. Did he need to spell out the implications of the helmet to her? That gas required a flame to explode—that Nandy had gone to work with a flame. Didn't she see that maybe just maybe, the explosion might not have happened if there'd not been an open flame?

She turned away, and he didn't bother with another word. He carried the helmet, its revelation heavy in his hands, down into the basement. He didn't put it in the box where he'd found it but set it in full view on the shelf as visible proof that the blame did not weigh entirely on *his* shoulders.

It was darker than usual outside, the nighttime held in by the rain. It made Pietro wish he could go back to bed. He would rather that. He would rather a lot of things—top of the list being an ordinary marriage or no marriage at all.

He caught the early streetcar into Indiana, picturing Assunta waking up and finding him gone. Let her.

He went into St. Bernard Church. The door was unlocked, and nobody appeared to be inside. Pietro made himself at home at the organ and filled the altar and nave with *Abide With Us*. He let the music be the hymn but sang aloud the line 'Ills have no weight and tears no bitterness'.

Ever since he had found the helmet, he could not rid himself of the fact that he might not be entirely to blame for Nandy's death.

It was a short walk to the cemetery. Pietro kept his head low, not wanting to notice any of the headstones around him or the too many familiar names on them. It was not far to Nandy's grave; his wife's love etched eternally in stone for him. Pietro could still recall Nandy's voice clearly, his serious tone when he demanded the promise of him. Perhaps he knew already what price it would carry.

He crouched, hands knitted between his knees. "Nothing to say now, have you?" Pietro sat listening to the wind speak through leaves. "Why didn't you wear the safety helmet?"

Pietro kept as still as a rock and waited—for something, an idea, an answer, the path forward—anything.

Nothing came to mind, so he contemplated the sounds around him—bird song, distant footsteps, a shovel biting into the earth, everyday sounds belonging to a life that continued purposefully, sweeping around the empty void shaped like the outline of his body. His empty, silent body didn't feel like it belonged to anything at all.

He broke off a piece of grass and stuck it in his mouth. He smoked a cigarette and coughed. He heard women in the street, going about their business. Silently, he pleaded with Nandy or Nonno or someone to give him a path forward so he might know what to do with the realization that he wasn't the only one to blame for twenty-six lost lives. To know how to stop feeling the guilt that weighed upon him, even knowing Nandy's helmet could have caused the explosion.

"Why did I ever talk to you, Nandy Vassanelli? I should've stayed away. I needed a drinking partner like I needed a cymbal in the dead of night. Darn you!"

He wished like he'd not wished for a long time, that Nonno's book *had* had instructions in it. That it *had* spelled out his future, measure by measure. That it *had* contained the moral to all his stories, like the phylloxera story. Despite the efforts of his family and the rest of Piedmont, the disease had gone on to obliterate vineyards throughout Italy. Not a single vine remained that didn't grow on American roots. And yet, they had acted upon the only hope they had at the time, which was to cut down their vines that looked perfectly healthy, burn them, and use new roots.

Pietro could think of no other hope he might cling to. He couldn't live in silence any longer, biding his time, going through the motions of the day. The mine, rehearsals, and performances, *porca miseria*, without even the pleasure of a drink with the men. He stuck his hand in his pocket and turned the box carrying the ring in it in his fingers.

When their children grew up—he might as well resign himself to the fact he would never have children of his own—when *her* children grew up, she would likely stop feeding him altogether.

He had a vision of himself as an old man, alone, ignored in a corner, watching other people's grandchildren from a window. The vision felt like physical pain in his gut.

The old man by the window had waited for someone else to do something.

Where had he been all this time? Sitting waiting for Assunta to stop hurting, that was where. For *her* to fix what was broken. All the while, he'd done wrong. He, Pietro, had fallen short. *He'd* been the fool.

And yet, he was the only fool Assunta could count on right now.

The only fool who had a chance to remind her of the light she once shone.

He strode over to the gravestone marking the mass grave for many of the men who died with Nandy. "Nobody," there was a quiver in his voice, "Nobody could've tapped the whole mine."

FROM ASHES TO SONG

When Assunta took the children up to bed, Pietro opened his notebook.
I can stop feeling guilty for loving my wife.
I can be a true husband to her.
I can see the children happy again.
I can make HER happy again.
This time, he didn't cross out any of the sentences.

TWENTY-FOUR

A month after visiting Nandy's grave, Pietro helped Ida cut up her dinner and waited for Assunta to sit. She did, without a single glance in his direction.

"They're starting a town band in Colver. We will move there," he said.

"All right." Still not looking at him, not even a pause before she spoke.

"All right? That's all?"

"I'll do as you say." She said it with flat intonation.

"They say it's a nice town. A good place to bring the children up."

She pushed her food around her plate. Eat a bite, at least. Do something! For an instant, Pietro wanted to yell through the invisible wall she'd erected, grab her shoulders, and make her listen.

But no, he was in charge of himself and of their future. A fool in charge was better than *nobody* in charge.

"I would like to go."

"It's settled then." No discussion. Most men yearned for a woman who did what they said, not only in public but behind closed doors, too. But Pietro would have welcomed a fight. At least it would have been some kind of reaction.

But things did not change overnight. He reminded himself that he needed to be patient.

♫ 𝄞 ♪

Neat boxes and empty space surrounded the table and cabinet where he kept his music and pencils. Assunta had packed his clothes and belongings but left his music alone as he'd asked.

Beneath the surface of the earth, Pietro had gone over his plan in his head as he chipped a rhythm into the coal face. He would go through with it. He might well throw up, but it was the only way. As Nonno had taught him, doing the right thing isn't always the same as doing the thing we want.

He looked through each sheet of paper and each book, trying to ignore how the papers trembled in his hand. He separated the music he had written that

Assunta had inspired in him when Nandy was still alive—music he'd written when baby Mary died and on the night of the picnic. Pieces he'd written when he'd seen a light in the living room, knowing she was sitting up waiting for Nandy to come home from the bar. When she'd talked about the beauty in the way birds sounded, sang to her children, danced with Nandy, laughed, poured wine for him, when he saw her tending the dahlias, when she'd blushed at his promise to Nandy.

That music went in one box. His grapevine song and the scant scores he'd written since they'd been married barely covered the bottom of a different box.

Outside, the moving men were strapping the last of the belongings to the cart. Assunta had taken the children to say goodbye to the Conatis. Pietro had told her he would do one last check of the house.

His footsteps echoed on the floorboards of the empty rooms. He glanced around, making sure nothing was left except memories and the box containing the music he'd written because of her. He went into his and Assunta's bedroom. He would not be sorry never to set foot in it again.

Even after all this time, it still felt like Nandy's room. Pietro, the impostor. Only now, he was ready to be a husband, and he was leading Assunta right out of town. Nandy could stay, left behind to cast his invisible shadow over the next occupants. Ones who would not know his name, ones who had never declared eternal love for him.

"*Amici*, eh?" he said out loud. He walked around the full circumference of the room, tracing the wall with his finger. From now on, he would be the only man in this marriage. "You did wrong, too. I'm the only one left that can do anything about it. Now do me a favor and rest in peace."

Out of the window, he could see the cart pulling away. He was all alone in the house, and he was ready to rid his heart of guilt.

He picked up the box of music, Assunta's music. He took it into the kitchen, added a few logs to the stove, and stoked the fire. He allowed himself to hold onto the memory of Nonno for a moment. In the courtyard, his last night on earth, holding the men entranced in his story about strong, healthy-looking roots threatening to ruin the future. The fire a clean start, the past cleansed.

Pietro took the first page of his music from the pile. The notes jumped off the page into song. He put the corner to the flame and heard the fire's excitement as it devoured the paper and yearned for more. Page after page. Each one erased, leading him closer to a new start. He picked up what was left of the pile and put it unceremoniously into the stove. He closed his eyes and observed crackles and sighs as notes turned quickly to ashes.

It was final. There was no going back now. No matter what, the future had to be rewritten.

TWENTY-FIVE

ssunta had let herself believe for just a moment that the move might be a new start for her. A town where nobody knew her pain, where she could allow herself the indulgence of being judged for who she was rather than the things that had happened to her—a life without her story.

But then she closed the door on that, too. Starting again suggested happiness, and she knew all too well how quickly happiness could be taken from her. Better not to feel at all.

Boxes were stacked in every room of the new house. There was so much more than when she had come to America with her scant belongings and naive heart. The number of things she owned had grown as much as her hope had diminished. She gripped the handles of the copper kettle, the first thing she would need. She pulled out the kitchen utensils that had been wrapped in tea towels and packed inside of it, not a bit of space wasted in packing. She could almost feel the memories stored in its metal. The kettle had come with her from Ernest, but she had meant to leave the memories behind.

Pietro didn't expect the Assunta of before to reappear in the new house magically but couldn't help himself for hoping. With a little amazement and envy, he listened to her calmly unpacking their things and settling into the new house, transforming it from empty walls to their home in just weeks, without, it seemed, even noticing he'd moved with her.

Not that any of her administrations made the house feel welcoming. It just felt resigned, like Assunta. As though the house and she intended merely to survive the motions of the day and wait for nighttime.

The mood in the house did not seem to fit in this town. It was a new Company town, modern. It even had its own hospital. Its rigid straight streets looked similar to Ernest, only bigger, and it perched on the top of a hill overlooking the tipple.

Pietro went to the mine office to sign the papers and get assigned to a shift.

On his way back, he passed the bosses' houses, grouped for solidarity, but the miner's homes weren't so bad. Girls chanted rope skipping songs, boys smacked baseballs, and dinner sounds escaped from open windows. The mooing of cows carried up from the dairy farm in the valley.

He got home to find the children still playing outside. Nice, they'd made friends already. Assunta was in the front yard, shovel in hand, a half-empty box of dahlias on the grass near her feet.

He had watched her dig up the dahlias in fall, wrap them in newspaper and store them, ready to replant next spring.

Back in the early days, when they still spoke, she had told him how she loved the pattern of the flowers. She thought they were like real life, the petals an arrangement of episodes and little stories coming together to form a perfect whole. She had forgotten that petals droop, brown, and fall—that the whole was rarely perfect.

She seemed almost content out there. Comfortable with her space. He went upstairs and watched her from the bedroom window. He wanted to open it, to hear what she could hear, but that would draw attention now her barriers were down.

He tried, as he had done so many times, to remember what she had been like once. He remembered her laughter, lively and sincere. He remembered her singing to the children, a sweet voice, and he remembered her not talking at all while she poured wine for him and Nandy. Her smile, though, eluded him. All he knew was that she did smile back then.

The sun broke through the clouds and illuminated her like a spotlight on a stage. A new tune, the song he'd been yearning for sounded its first notes. The song was delicate, tentative, holding back intentionally before it dared quicken to a pace that might tread on the path of contentedness. It was melodic, a great depth emerging from its simplicity, camouflaging the hurt encased layers below— buried hurt, encapsulated in notes with the potential to burst out with joy. There, he'd been right to cleanse himself. Rid himself of the music of guilt.

That was it. Exactly the right rhythm, melancholy, and joy he'd been looking for—cyclical, changing, and progressing and returning to what she was before. He longed for that to happen, to hear the color back in her voice.

Even if she never loved him, he would show her his love, untainted by Nandy's memory. Heal her if he could. He pulled himself away from the window and went downstairs to the dining room. He opened the cupboard, pulled out Nonno's leather-bound music book, and set it on the table. He wrote his name on the front page, turned the leaf, and drew a clef.

After the shift at the end of his first week, Pietro fell into step with a man who had good rhythm underground. "Nowhere for a man to get a drink 'round here, then?" he asked.

The man spat on the street and looked around as though contemplating an important question. Satisfied, perhaps, no policemen were within earshot, he said, "In Jewtown, there's a man with a wine sweet enough to gag. But it's wine. Can't be picky these days."

"How much?"

"Fifty cents a jug. Quarter for a half."

"Ever been busted?"

"The police, the Pussyfoots, got a still in the woods a few weeks ago. Otherwise, they've left us alone. Tough walk home, though. Uphill."

When they had loaded the moving cart to come to Colver from Ernest, Pietro had hidden a barrel ready to spigot amongst the rest of their belongings. The moving men had seen, he couldn't help that, but they had said nothing. It could have been over when they were stopped by one of the two Pussyfoots on their way into Colver.

"Big John, they call me," he informed them. A solid man, all the more intimidating because he was on horseback. He asked Pietro their names, what business they had in town, and which house they were heading for, asking the next question before he barely had time to respond, the way people do when they are sure they know the answer but are obliged to ask the question in any case.

Pietro did the math. Selling his barrel of wine by the glass and jug for the same price would bring nice returns. It could also help his plan to involve Assunta with people. As far as he knew, she hadn't gone farther than the yard, not even to church. If she wouldn't go out to see people, what was to stop him from bringing people to her? He wouldn't even tell her. Let her get angry. Let her react. She hadn't even blinked an eye when the policeman had stopped them. *Let* her feel something.

♫ 𝄞 ♪

"It was a monster, Mamma. It was black, covered in coal, and it burned me." Ida said.

"It was just a dream," Assunta said.

"Can we sing a song, so it doesn't come back?" she asked.

Mary clambered over from her bed and pushed her sister over to get in. Max sat up but did not get out of his bed.

"You're supposed to be getting to sleep. Come now," Assunta said.

"Oh, Mamma, sing. Please! I'll just sleep here, right, Ida?" Ida nodded in agreement.

"Maybe tomorrow. So, where did this monster burn you, dear?"

"Here, on my hand. It hurt so bad!"

"Now, now. Settle." Assunta took the precious little hand, but she didn't sing.

They heard the thud of the kitchen door closing below them. Assunta expected to hear Pietro's footsteps. Instead, she heard extra shuffling, extra boots.

"Sleep now. No more noise," Assunta told them.

She went downstairs to find three strangers sat at the table with Pietro, but none of them looked directly at her. They all murmured a good evening of sorts. He never brought people over. She didn't know what to do. If this had been Nandy, she'd have set glasses in front of them. These were strangers. They could be Pussyfoots. It could be a test. If Pietro had ever brought anyone home before, she might know what to do. She looked at him for guidance.

"Red. Full jug," Pietro said.

Assunta pulled on an apron, making a point of tying the bow slowly. He should realize he needed to give her more instruction. But fine. She'd do as he'd told her, consequences be darned. She went down into the basement to fill the jug.

She hesitated again before she came up. Men were in the house—she'd had no warning, and she had to serve them illegal drink.

The basement smelled yeasty. Pietro had not mentioned how he still got grapes, what with the Prohibition, though it was probably best she did not know.

She went back up and set the jug on the table. The men settled into conversation washed down by wine, paying little mind to her. She went into the front room to sit and wait until they needed something. She glanced several times at the door and adjusted the curtains, making sure nobody from outside could see in.

Quiet Pietro. Who made not so much as a squeak. He demanded nothing of her. Whatever she offered, he took but never asked for anything more. He just went about his day. Thank goodness, too. It took all her energy to cope with the children.

Bringing people home was something that Nandy did. All this talking and laughing, she found herself thinking of the old days. She had hoped to forget Nandy here. She was supposed to have left her past and memories behind, to have wiped the slate clean and started over. The heart was cruel.

She heard a fit of giggles from the stairway. The children! She didn't so much as glance at the men as she crossed the kitchen and ushered the children quickly back upstairs. To make sure they did not escape again, she sat guard at the top of the stairs.

She did not go back down—let them pour their own. She paused for a moment outside the children's bedroom to make sure she heard no wriggling or plotting. Then she went to bed. It was cold and empty, just like her soul.

The rich smell as she brewed the coffee lifted her spirits a little, though a little from the depths of gloom wasn't much to speak of. She didn't mind mornings so much when the household still slept, and she had a moment all her own. But then not minding implied happiness, and she had none of that left.

Pietro came down early. The interruption bothered her a little, but she poured him some coffee in any case.

"There was money on the table this morning." She handed him the sugar bowl.

"The boys. For our trouble."

There were implications to them paying. "Are they friends?"

"They are, but what with the risk of sharing a drink nowadays, they want to come back."

She didn't want an interruption to her lonely solace, but the effort to tell Pietro this felt unattainable. "I have the money here," was all she said.

"Perfect. Collect it if it happens again."

"People know that if the flowerpot is on the left side of the front porch, we're closed for business. And if our patrons miss that, you hitch the curtain over the glass to the back door open. If they see in, it means we're closed. If we have customers, the curtain stays closed to block the view."

Pietro looked at Assunta, waiting for a response. She had just hung a crucifix and a picture of the Blessed Mother on the kitchen wall to keep everybody in check, now her arms ached, and her head felt heavy.

"You hear me?" Pietro asked. "I'm closing the curtain, right?"

Assunta forced a single nod to acknowledge him, hoping nobody would come, and she could go straight to bed.

Muffled voices outside told her she was not to get her wish. The thought of strangers coming into her kitchen and seeing her stand idle was incentive enough to go into the front room.

Pietro had set up tables here, too. She'd not asked where he'd come by them. Against the wall dividing the room from the kitchen stood a buffet she had picked out in her old life when Nandy had still been her husband. She had polished it weekly and set things inside reverently until the final payment had been made, and it truly belonged to them. After that, she also allowed herself to place a vase on a crocheted doily on the top. She'd found things to keep in that vase year-round—small branches clipped from the maple tree in fall, hydrangea stems in winter, daffodils in spring, and dahlias in summer.

Pietro had set out two glass bowls next to the vase that had been empty since she had lost her babies. This afternoon he had filled one of the bowls with shelled walnuts, the other with grapes.

Pietro had let the men into the kitchen. She could hear the sound of someone wiping his feet and stilted conversation. They were Italian and spoke a Northern dialect she could understand.

If they came right through to this room, they would catch her standing idle, so she took out a stack of small bowls from the cabinet and tipped some walnuts and grapes into one of them.

Pietro led the men through to the room and sat them at the first table. "A jug for my friends," he said, and Assunta forced herself down into the basement to get one.

When she got back, there were two more men in the room—Poles by the sound of it. She went back down to fetch a jug of wine for them but did not give them walnuts and grapes.

There was another knock at the back door. The money from this venture might well be welcome, but the effort they would have to go through felt too large.

This time, Pietro led in a tall man with round-rimmed glasses carrying a doctor's case.

"Assunta, this is Dr. Martin. He is new to the area, new to the hospital," Pietro said. Fancy, a doctor coming to their humble home.

"Very nice to meet you, ma'am," he said and took his hat off. She murmured a greeting and was relieved to see he sat at the table of Italians. She only needed to get an extra glass and not an extra jug.

Pietro collected the coins from the tables—a quarter for half a pint jug, two quarters for a full one. He slipped them into Assunta's hand and might as well have handed her lead weights.

When there was yet another knock at the door, she just could not make one more ounce of effort. She walked back through the kitchen and, not even bothering to look in the direction of the latest arrival and walked upstairs to bed.

♫♪♪

Pietro worked on the piece after his guests left at night. He tapped what he had written the time before, in his mind trying to picture Assunta in the garden. The song she would feel as she tended her flowers.

He pushed aside the painful memory of flickering pages and burning notes, of the flames consuming his music. That music was passed, gone.

He whistled a rift. In some ways, this song was melancholy; in other ways, it was searching for joy. It was Assunta. Like a dahlia, withered and fallen. But with love and care, dahlias came back. Assunta could come back—she had to.

He tapped and tapped again on the table, gently, to himself, still unsure how the music would sound once it told a complete story.

The rest of the household slept; he knew no other time to write. He closed his eyes and tapped some more. The piece inside of him, inside of his heart, was there, just waiting to be brought to life. He closed his eyes and listened. He wrote the music down as fast as his pencil would allow. It was birth, beginnings, growth, heartache and grief, the icy grip of loss. It was like Nonno's words—it was the reason for living, an endless cycle.

This piece he was shaping and creating needed to be something more than the music he usually wrote. This would be no ordinary piece. It should be a symphony, except he did not know how to write for an orchestra. He knew something of the violin, but little of the viola. Trumpets and horns posed little in the way of challenge; cellos were entirely foreign to him.

He simply could not do it. Yet, the thought of a symphony for Assunta would not leave his head. Mozart had an orchestra to work with, Pietro had a brass band. Nonno had an empty book because he couldn't read or write, yet he could play any tune and lead the best band San Damiano had ever known.

He would write a symphony for a brass band. Nonno would approve.

Pietro locked the door after the last person left. They'd been operating for three weeks now. Every evening, Assunta would begin serving the men, delivering jugs and half jugs of wine, walnuts, and grapes randomly if she remembered, then, at a time when only she would decide, she would disappear up the stairs.

He put the coins he collected into a Mason jar and set it by Assunta's coffee percolator. In the morning, she would pour the coins on the table, make piles of nickels, dimes, and quarters, and then enter the amount in a ledger she kept hidden behind the dinner plates. Not once had he seen so much as a flicker of enthusiasm when she did this.

His back was sore from a day in the mine and an evening on his feet, but he still had work to do. He pulled out a pencil and paper.

Whether Assunta liked it or not, she was going to see how much she meant to others. And she was going to hear the symphony written just for her.

Dear Guido,

As we discussed, I'm sending you the scores for the musicians.

He'd composed the letter in his head. Which musicians he wanted Guido to pull together to play his symphony. Bolek on the clarinet with him—he liked writing that. The kid had improved immensely. Not only did he merit the title musician, he even deserved to be called a good musician.

Pietro finished his list, signed the letter, slipped it inside the envelope, and inside the box of scores he'd written out. If everything was coming together, it was in part thanks to Mrs. Conati. She had been the one who suggested performing the symphony at her house, surrounded by all the people who cared. She'd even come up with the suggestion of telling Assunta they were coming for the christening of her latest grandchild so the grand performance would be a surprise.

This was a culmination. It pulled together everything Pietro had ever feared and everything he had dared to hope for. Perhaps he did have a gift, and perhaps it was all right for him to use it. When he let love in, there was a power, a beauty that had always hung just on the brink of being within his grasp. Perhaps.

Pietro had moved the flowerpot and opened the curtain last night to give them time to work on the new batch of wine. The barrel of good wine was low, less than a week left, he'd figured. Another batch was fermenting in the children's wardrobe, the back of which they'd hollowed out.

Assunta went down to the basement where the new barrel stood. They'd wanted this one too in a bedroom but had had little time to figure out a second hiding place. Pietro had declared they should be able to alternate one barrel down here, one upstairs.

Between the mine, his guests, and the time he spent composing his symphony, Pietro barely slept. The area below his eyes had turned an odd shade of gray, which was all the more reason not to go to Ernest to the christening. Why on earth wasn't he too tired to go, too?

Last night she had helped him for a time, working in silence until the grapes she had washed earlier in the day were through the crusher and into the press. She'd handed Pietro the weights to put on the press, watched him turn the contraption at the top, then transfer the jugs of juice into the new barrel. She'd been grateful at least that all the while, he had nothing to say.

At some point, sleep had begun to weigh too heavily, her head nodding as she sat on the stool, jug in hand, ready to hand to him.

"I'll finish," he said, and she had let him.

Now he had left for the mine, and she had to deal with half-dried grape innards stuck at angles from the crusher. The rim of the press a streaked, sludgy mess. She gathered up wooden spoons, a long stirrer, and the crusher, and headed upstairs to clean them. She would get this done, then she'd see about forcing herself to make the beds. Some days she managed it; some days she didn't. Luckily there was little cleaning to do in the front room or kitchen because they had not had guests the night before. But the upstairs windows needed to be washed, everything up there dusted, and the floors mopped. She'd rather get out into the garden. The dahlias were doing beautifully; they seemed to like the soil around here. Not that she had the energy to care, but if she did, the mass of colors created the best front yard in the street.

Utensils still in hand, she looked out of the front room window to admire her flowers. Except all she saw was green. Green lawn, green stalks—no flowers, no color. That couldn't be. She swung the door open and marched out.

Every stem had been cut.

Fury raged in her throat—she grew her flowers in honor of her children, and someone had taken them away. She stomped out of the yard, looking up and down the street like a tea kettle about to whistle.

Three houses down, she saw something that had not been there before. Each step nearer brought her flowers clearer and clearer into focus. There they were, plain as day—stuck, stalk only, into the ground, heads dipping over into the mud. Someone had replanted them! Only they hadn't taken the roots—the part that gave them life.

She looked around. Could anyone else see this? Was the person who had done this to her here? A woman was looking at her. Another, then another stopped and stared. Assunta gritted her teeth, stopped the accusation that whoever lived in that house had stolen her flowers. She wanted to yell it; she wanted to let everything go. Collapse right there in a heap. To heck with anyone who saw her.

A woman rushed from the house whose yard had acquired her flowers.

"They're mine," Assunta shouted.

"I'm so sorry," the woman said. "It was my son! Be sure I'll be telling his father when he gets home. He said he just wanted our yard to look as beautiful as yours. How can I make it up to you?"

Assunta didn't want it made up to her. She didn't want to be seeing her flowers stuck, drooping as the life drained from them, like melted sewing needles. She pulled one with her free hand. It came up easily. She plucked another and another.

"I'm sorry, truly." The woman said again.

Assunta gathered as many as she could in one hand then walked away.

People were staring, and she did not care one bit.

"Ma'am," a man ahead of her said. She looked up. What man was bold enough to talk to her in the street? "What do you have in your hands?"

She gritted her teeth harder. She went to step around him. She need not answer, this town be damned.

But he did not let her step around.

"I'll ask you again, ma'am. What do you have in your hands?"

Dahlias are not illegal. I have nothing to say, she thought. She stepped wider to go around him, but his hand gripped her arm. The pain was sharp. Then he blew his whistle behind her ear. What was wrong with this man? How dare he? She pulled, her arm stung harder with his grip, and he blew his whistle again.

Now he was marching her to her house. He better leave her in peace when they reached her house, but not before apologizing for hurting her arm. She wanted to be inside, to lock everyone out. To draw the curtains and crawl into bed.

He steered her along her path, through the front door she'd left open. There was a clattering of horses' hooves—the fuss over a few flowers that were hers to begin with, this was as absurd as making drink against the law.

"Ma'am, stay in the kitchen, please."

"What right have you?" she demanded.

"I'm a policeman. That's what right I have. Sit at the table. Stay there, and do not move."

How dare he? He let go of her, and she had little choice but to sit on the kitchen chair. It was only then that she looked at what she held in her hands. Dahlias in one—wooden spoons, stirrers, wine-making tools in the other. All splattered purple.

"But someone stole my flowers!" she said.

Another policeman stomped through her kitchen, muddy boots and all, and followed the first into the basement.

"But my flowers," she said to nobody.

They brought the almost empty barrel up first. The second one, just filled, took them longer. It was heavy, but they were large and strong. They set the barrels in the street outside. Assunta heard the ax falling on wood. Her and Pietro's income was running down the street, past the garden with her dahlias.

Assunta didn't look at the men when they came back into the room. They shuffled nervously for a moment. One sighed as though he didn't want to be there.

"Ma'am," he said. His voice was not mean; if anything, it conveyed a trace of sympathy. "We're obliged to arrest you."

The whir of the pulley told Pietro they were nearly at the top of the man lift. What relief, there'd be no shift now until Monday. Tomorrow was the big day. Guido and Mrs. Conati had both sent word that all the arrangements had been finalized, the performance was all set to happen. Bolek would drive over and pick them up. Assunta would hear the symphony he'd written for her, and she would start to heal.

The machinery clonked to a whine and then a halt. The gate grated open, and men spilled out. Pietro heard voices tight, concerned. Not the normal relief for the end of a day, a hot shower—in this more modern facility, the steam from the generation room that ran the man lift also heated water for showers. Something must have happened. Whatever it was, he had no time for chatter tonight. He pushed through towards the shower room.

"Hey, Maestro!"

They could follow him into the shower if they wanted to talk. They'd understand, especially if they knew he had a business to run.

"Eh," he said, letting them know he heard and pulling off his jacket.

"You need to come. Now."

Dirty? No way. He started unbuttoning his shirt.

"Now! There's been a raid."

Pietro sat at the kitchen table. Pencil in his hand but tapping nothing. The house was quiet—the children in bed. Assunta sat across from him. At least they'd let her stay home tonight. It was hard, even for the Pussyfoots, to put a woman in jail.

She'd said nothing. Not a word. Not to him, not to the children. She was not even a shell. A shell held the promise that it could, if it wanted, hold something. She sat crumpled at the table—a discarded sheet of music.

Men had come in droves to find out what had happened, to sift through the bits of the barrel looking for anything to salvage. Someone found a bowl to put on the kitchen table. One by one, men dropped coins in it. They had spoken in hushed tones and downed glasses of wine. Pietro wondered which one of them had tapped the barrel in the bedroom or who had gone up and down stairs, keeping the jugs filled. At least that barrel had been saved. Lord knew he needed a drink but hadn't anybody else seen the irony at how they'd spent the evening drinking, commiserating about the lost wine and avoiding the subject of Assunta's arrest.

While his house had been full of people raising glasses to each other in sympathy, Pietro had gone up to the offices and put a call through to Ernest to let the Conatis know that the symphony performance was off.

Now the men were gone, and Assunta had not spoken or moved.

"Can I get you anything?" he asked.

She looked at him, as though for the first time. Her gaze pierced him deeper than the deepest silence. Then she stood and went upstairs.

Pietro was left alone to contemplate what he had done, how he had finally stepped beyond his shadow and dared to take their lives into his hands. But his hands were meant only to play the clarinet. He was a musician, not a magician that could save a person from their grief. His tool was a simple, physical instrument, not something he could use to wield a miracle that could change the course of someone's life. It was just a simple, black, and silver tube that anyone could play.

He refilled his jug one extra time and took out the cameo ring he'd intended to give her from his pocket, looking at it like someone looking at a penny tip.

Some husband he had turned out to be—a husband who'd sentenced his wife to jail.

Per carita, what would happen to the children? Motherless, all because he'd had lofty ideas. He poured another glass. Who cared if he'd reached his normal fill? Tonight, he'd make it all disappear. Tonight, he didn't want to be able to think, to acknowledge what he had done. He downed the glass and reached again for the jug.

TWENTY-SIX

Assunta was supposed to drop off the children with the lady across the street. That had been the plan agreed the previous night, before people started slurring their words too badly. She walked down the path to the neighbor's door but couldn't make herself knock.

Pietro's friend Bolek pulled up in a motor car. "I'll take you," he said. She didn't ask how he knew.

The children knelt on the back seat, watching the world disappear behind them. Assunta stared at the dashboard until they pulled up in front of the courthouse in Ebensburg, a regal red building that looked like it belonged somewhere else.

"Why are we here, Mamma?" Ida asked as they walked up the steps to the door.

"It won't take long," Assunta said, for lack of anything better to say.

Max said nothing. He knew Mamma was in trouble, and he may very well be the one leading his sisters out of there.

The clerk's face showed pity as he gently ushered Assunta up the stairs and to a wooden bench.

"Wait here until you're called," he said. There was a small crowd of men already waiting. She was the only woman, and hers were the only children. The center of the courthouse was domed with a round, stain-glass ceiling, allowing light to shine down into a central foyer, ringed by a balcony that on a typical day would have been a certain lure to the children.

Assunta did not look at anyone else. She shuttered the people out as effectively as she shuttered her emotions in. Once, she might have cared about people staring at her. Once, when it still mattered.

The clerk called her name, stretching it out to sound American. Max stood tall, eyebrows knitted. Assunta locked the girls' hands in hers. She arranged her invisible wall of composure around herself like a neatly buttoned coat. The aisle on the other side of the door looked long, lined on either side with chairs dotted by the backs of heads. She let go of hands and reached an arm around the girls—Mary on the right, Ida on the left—and hugged them to her skirt. They were rigid for a moment; then they hugged back. Ida whispered, "Mamma, I'm scared!"

"It's all right." It was not reassuring enough. Ida reached her arms up. At seven, she was too big to be carried. But what did it matter? Assunta gathered her up on her hip. She felt her wrap her arms around her neck and push her cheek against her bony shoulder.

That feeling of arms around her neck reminded Assunta of a time long gone, shorter, fatter little arms. Her baby boy, she dared not say his name even inside her head. She chided herself for not concentrating, for letting herself get distracted. She could not think of him now. She was about to walk in front of a judge. She was about to go to jail.

But Ferdinando's face, serene in death, already the face of an angel, flashed in her mind, tearing at her layers of resolve. She would not cry—she had not cried for five long years.

Mary pulled closer, almost hanging from her arm. Max held the back of her coat. Each step closer to the front of the courtroom added more weight to her heart.

All eyes were on them. Eyes that were condemning, boring into Assunta to measure the depth of her guilt. She was sure they could see every moment of her life, every word she had ever uttered, every time she had been impatient or short. Every time she had wished she was in her true love's arms, instead of with the man she now called husband.

Each step chipped away at her resolve to never be vulnerable again. The judge's gaze pierced her, stripping away her armor. The judge knew—with all his power, he had to know that her feelings were not gone, just hidden. Risking at any moment to creep up and devour her with grief. To rise and clench her heart and twist it until she cried with no hope of regaining control. She pulled the children closer still. Ida began to cry.

They were almost at the bench. She was a law-abiding citizen——a good person. God-fearing. Yet here she was, about to be sentenced for following the wishes of her husband, for doing her duty. She would be thrown into a cold, damp, and dark cell by this giant man in a black robe, who stared at her with nothing but contempt. She was about to lose her freedom, here, the country that claimed to be the land of the free—a land where she'd not been free enough to raise her family with the man she loved.

A tide threatened to rear. She could not hide her face and pinch her arm until it passed like she sometimes did. She could not close her bedroom door and double over, clutching the pain that wrenched her stomach until she regained control.

Mary began to cry. Assunta did not acknowledge her any more than she had Ida.

People were watching. Assunta had nowhere to hide, and she could hold it no longer. Tears began to claw their way from her eyes and down her face. Max joined in, and when they reached the judge, they were gripping each other in a sobbing quartet. He began to speak, his words of law like chisels on the wall of a dam, scratching away.

Assunta had lost all threads of control, and she did not hear the accusation against her. Whatever was said, it was said in fret, and then an officer was by her side, trying to peel her children away. She cried harder. She was not ready to say goodbye.

The silence woke Pietro. Nobody was moving about the house. There were no sounds from the street and no whistle from the mine. His back ached, his temples pounded. He forced his eyes open and saw he was in the basement, a glass still in his hand. He had a vague recollection of coming down to toast the end of a wine-making era.

He pulled himself up, head pounding like the roar of thunder with the slightest movement. The light of day streamed confidently through the window into the empty house. The clock told him he'd slept past nine. Assunta must be at the courthouse already.

She'd left him an egg on the table for the hangover she knew he'd have.

He picked it up and weighed it in his hand. He almost cracked it to swallow but then thought better of it. He didn't deserve her tending him. He threw the egg at the window and left it to rot.

He moved through the motions of getting ready to leave, but in no particular hurry. She did not need him at court though he'd go in any case. He wished today was not happening.

He walked up the hill to the main street. Jack's car was parked outside the post office. Darn contraptions were cropping up all over, but they sure came in handy sometimes. A bell jangled when Pietro opened the door and asked, "Weren't you supposed to be taking us to court? Assunta—hasn't she gone?"

"Some Pole from Indiana told me he would take her. He asked where you were. Guess he must think quite something of you. He told me he'd drive you and your family to California if you needed a ride to California."

"Bolek?"

"Yeah, that was his name, I think. Come on. I'll run you up there."

Jack dropped Pietro outside the courthouse. He got there just in time to see Assunta start towards the judge with the children. What was she thinking, bringing them here? For an instant, he thought the neighbor had been unable to look after the children, but something told him Assunta had not been able to let them go.

She was holding Ida, Mary hanging on the other side, Max clinging tight also. Her face firm. A mask. Everything about her demeanor was controlled. She was going to be defiant to the judge. Stand tall. Indifferent even to him and what he was about to inflict. Pietro slid his hands in his pockets. Maybe he should leave.

He lost sight of her over the backs of heads, unable to do anything, forced to leave the fate of his wife in the hands of a stranger. Someone far more important than him. Pietro had put on his best suit, though he still felt shabby— less of a man than the judge, for sure. Every inch of the courtroom was decorated. The ornate domed ceiling culminated in the magnificent stained-glass coat of arms of Pennsylvania. When Pietro went to work, his ceiling was made of coal.

It was despicable how the onlookers in the courtroom became an audience, glancing surreptitiously at Assunta, their curiosity almost reluctant. They did not look back at him, to see who she belonged to. Many were defendants themselves, and most had kin waiting. Yet some of the men started to crane, to watch Assunta. How cruel. Because she was a woman, Pietro supposed. But there was quite a stir now, shuffling boots too as more and more of them strained to see her.

Pietro moved along the row, apologizing to people as he pushed through to the next aisle, where he again caught sight of her. Her shoulders were shaking. She was crying. The children, too. Even Max, his arms gripped around her waist for dear life.

Pietro fought the urge to run over and embrace them, to tell them that he loved them—as if he ever could. Assunta's sobs bounced off the walls, rippled through the crowd. He looked back at the faces watching his wife and children, half expecting to see sneers and laughter. Instead, he saw pity and something else. Camaraderie? Assunta could have been anyone's wife standing there.

"Dismissed." The judge's hammer rapped. Did he say dismissed? There was a murmur of approval from the onlookers. Officers were trying to manhandle Assunta and the children, they gestured for her to leave, but she was rooted. Pietro strode down the aisle toward her, momentarily forgetting he had caused this whole scenario and was not, therefore, to be trusted.

Pietro steered Assunta and the children, all still crying, to the foyer and out the door.

Mrs. Conati was waiting outside the courthouse, the brim of her hat fluttering in the breeze. Pietro never expected to see her in Ebensburg, but he had never been so glad to see anybody. At the curb, Mr. Conati sat in the driver's seat of what had been one of the first cars in Ernest.

"The judge took pity." Pietro pointed at Assunta as though Mrs. Conati didn't know who he was talking about.

"I thought I might need to take the children if—well, you know." Mrs. Conati dug in her purse for a fresh handkerchief and handed it to Assunta. Assunta held it to the center of her forehead, tears still streaming.

Pietro thought about guiding Assunta off to the side of the steps, out of the way of those leaving the courthouse, but then decided against it. Let them walk around.

"What now?" Pietro asked.

"What do you mean, what now? You go home and you carry on." Even Mrs. Conati could not hide the resignation from her voice.

"The musicians—?"

"I left word that it was off," she answered.

Well, that was that then. Everything taken care of. He heard his own footsteps backing away before he realized he was moving. Assunta still sobbed. The children crowded around her. She deserved better.

"Take her with you," he told Mrs. Conati.

A trickle of people walked in the gap between Pietro and the others. The distance felt reassuring. "Just for a few days," Mrs. Conati said when the people had passed.

Assunta let Mrs. Conati lead her away. Pietro heard the quiet rustle of clothes, the familiar way Assunta walked with minimum effort, arms hanging, chin tipped forward. Her movements bereft of joy, despite the court's reprieve.

"Just for a few days," Mrs. Conati said.

Like notes erased from a music sheet, he was lost. As though standing in the center of an orchestra, everyone playing, but he didn't know how. He'd already tried the only thing he knew. He'd yearned to heal this woman he loved, and all it had got was an arrest and a hangover. *Fine*. The word meant *end* in Italian, *just dandy* in English. The end was about as dandy as he deserved.

Bolek was parked down the hill. He waved, and Pietro walked toward him. He didn't want to look back, but despite himself, his ears reached out to his— no, to Nandy's family. He heard scrambling on leather seats, the creak of the vehicle's frame as Max, Mary, and Ida clambered and bounced inside, pitched engines never got old for them. He heard Assunta's foot on the edge. He knew she would get into the car in one fluid movement, quick, as though she feared the movement of getting in the most. But she didn't. She hesitated. Her sobbing paused—a sigh, faint as a flower. As surely as Bolek was right in front of him, Pietro was sure Assunta was looking at him.

What did her hesitation mean? Suddenly he had to find out. "A minute." He raised an index finger to Bolek and marched toward the Conatis' car.

"Assunta, come home with me."

Without a word, she withdrew her foot from the rim of the car door and followed Pietro back to Bolek's car. There, her tears resumed and no longer faltered. Kept in for years, they might take a lifetime to shed.

Mr. and Mrs. Conati's car, children and all, drove up the street and made a left towards Indiana.

What had he done?

They shut the car doors as though they knew what they were doing, and the tires screeched to action. Bolek did not say a word, and Pietro sensed he didn't once look at them in the rear-view mirror. Respectful. Always a good kid. Not a great driver. Even looking forward, he almost sailed off into the field at the hairpin bends. Assunta's sobbing didn't falter.

"Here you are," Bolek said, pulling up in front of their house.

Pietro considered inviting him in for a drink. They could sit and talk and wait for Assunta to stop crying. But deep down, he knew he had to do it alone.

"Much obliged. I owe you." He patted Bolek on the shoulder.

"You owe me nothing. It's a pleasure to help." They got out, and Bolek pulled away in gasping spurts. Assunta stood still, appearing to have no inclination to walk up the path or stop crying, even though the neighbors could see. Pietro took her hand, held it like they were children, and walked her to the door.

He unlocked the kitchen door, then took hold of Assunta's hand again as they stepped inside.

At least through the tears, she might not notice the egg on the window. He contemplated calling Dr. Martin, but there was probably nothing he could do either. Pietro pulled off her coat, led her to the living room and onto the sofa, sat her down, and pulled off her shoes. He went upstairs to get a fresh handkerchief, then into the kitchen to pour a glass of water. He got a dining room chair and sat down in front of her.

The only thing a musician could do was play. He took his clarinet from the cabinet. He polished it and slipped the pieces together. Music would be better than this silence, and heaven knew that words were the thing he failed at the most miserably.

He brought the clarinet to his lips. What to play? Music that captured the pain and the hurt of a lifetime, wrapped and embraced it, comforted until the pain could abate—until it could heal.

He set the clarinet back on his lap. He'd written the symphony especially. He'd written it for her, and he'd written it for a brass band. A performance to surround her with music and the people who cared about her: to play it without the ensemble would take away the power of the people who could heal her, leaving only the music.

But it was his last chance.

He nodded the count in his head and began to play. Not too loudly. Just *sotto voce*, the same way he lived his life.

A few movements in, his eyes closed. He slipped away from the room, stopped knowing where he was. He reached inside to his heart and across to Assunta's.

He did not know whether Assunta reacted in any way. He just played, eyes closed, his heart aching yet healing at the same time. Him, his clarinet, love. If his music had ever had the power to heal, now was the time to wield it for this woman he loved, who tolerated him by her side.

Pietro's clarinet circled and tugged at her, nudged her shoulder. Her tears paused to listen. She had never heard anything like the music he played tonight. It was the most beautiful piece she had ever heard.

She swallowed—her throat burned. She had an ache behind her eyes, and her head throbbed. Her back jabbed, urging her to move, but she'd let it hurt just a moment longer. She'd been numb so long.

Pietro carried on playing, never once opening his eyes. His eyebrows moved with the notes. His mustache danced above his lips that caressed the clarinet as they had, for a time, caressed her. They coaxed a song that slipped itself around her waist and held her firm. She let it embrace her. The music felt like going home.

She felt her lips twitch, not a smile, but the beginning of one. After years of emptiness, the tears she had shed had released the dam that had been clogging her sadness.

She set her water glass on the side table and picked up a dahlia from the bunch someone had put in a vase. It was wilted from its escapade in the neighbor's garden. The wilted part felt crisper yet still soft to her finger—a different kind of beauty. Despite the part that had died, the flower was still complete. The rest of it had not shriveled in grief.

She cupped it in both hands and held it to her chin. She watched Pietro as he played, illuminated by the music or illuminating it; she wasn't sure.

The music felt her, nudged her, gently pinched the skin on her forearm. It soothed her. A firm blanket wrapped around her just tightly enough, not constricting but rather strengthening, empowering her to take back her life. Overthrow the darkness, turn a light on in her soul.

Her husband playing to her.

She could think of no better reason to wake up from this misery.

She reached out and touched Pietro's knee. He opened his eyes. Like the puff of a dandelion in a sudden gush, she was engulfed by a feeling of loneliness. He carried on playing a few minutes more, something very much like love shining in the way he looked at her.

He set the clarinet on the little table. She put the dahlia right next to it.

She pulled herself to the edge of the sofa, tugged his hand toward her, and set it on her knee. She didn't want words. She wanted touch—to not be lonely anymore. Eyes still open, following a desire she could neither control nor understand, she leaned forward and brushed her top lip against his.

He felt stiff. She'd seen the way he looked, heard the way he played. She kissed the corner of his mouth. Another moment's pause, then he returned her kiss, hesitantly, making sure this was real, then with more conviction. She pulled his hand to her waist, where he held it rigid, then squeezed her and held firm.

She whispered against his lips. "Pietro, I was blind. I was—" her throat twisted, trying to stop the words that might make her crumble once more. "Your patience, all this time—will you forgive me?" She rushed the question and kissed his reply before he had time to say it.

She felt him push her gently away and fumbled for something in his pocket with his shirt half tucked, his hair ruffled.

He pulled her left hand toward him.

"Assunta, will you let me be a true husband to you?"

He held something to the tip of her finger—she looked down to see he'd plucked a ring from thin air and slipped it onto her finger. A gold band topped with a blue background and ivory cameo—a flower. Not just any flower. Pietro had given her a rose.

The magnitude of her words felt like clarity. "I will."

Pietro pulled her close. His movements were deliberate, expert—like she was his clarinet.

She'd forgotten how the top of his head came up to her chin. She no longer minded. She bent her head forward and kissed his ear, a tender kiss. He did not recoil, but realizing her mistake, she did. "Sorry, I—"

"Kiss it again," he said. "Everything's going to be all right."

She ran her thumb against the ring on her finger. "I know," she said.

TWENTY-SEVEN

1952

Pietro ran a finger along a page of the symphony. Despite the insistent passing of time, it still sounded ready for a stage debut he would never hear. He rested his thumb on a smudge of prints he'd not noticed before in the bottom right corner of the page, a remnant of miner's fingers shuffling through the music, checking and crafting melody with the purpose of someone who dared to believe.

He closed the book, placed it between wedding arrangements and children's songs in the semblance of a pile he'd built on the bedside table. He gathered the rest of the books spread across the flowers of the bedspread and stacked their bindings in order of size, the memory of what had driven him to each one flitting through his mind like another might see photographs. He wrapped the lot with brown paper and tied the brown paper with string.

A pipe rapped from the new bathroom across the hall. He had to stop calling it new. It'd been fourteen years since they'd petitioned the coal company to install it. He needed to get the hang of how time seemed intent on rushing these days.

Whenever he heard water, it reminded him of the night that, in his mind, his marriage to Assunta really began. Water was not so unlike love. A normal part of any day, changing in intensity from the trickle of a faucet to the desperation of a swollen creek after a mighty thaw. The gentle yet infinitely powerful swish of waves. The gentle power that had swept them to stand, from then on, as one. Doubts and sorrow erased like a message drawn in the sand on an incoming tide. Water could make a flower grow. He'd written songs about it.

Until yesterday, or at least until not that long ago, with Assunta by his side, it had taken no effort to pull a sound from his day. Entwine it with a moment of joy to tell a contented story or pit it solidly against an annoyance in dramatic conflict. Now his cough drowned out the song, clenched his tired muscles, echoed a hollow bark in his ear. Nothing begged to be taken up by a clarinet. Blank pages of music no longer excited or lured. They were just blank pages. Pencils might as well be for adding numbers. He had nothing to write, no scores to compose.

He stood and shook his head at nobody but himself for sitting here with misplaced pity. He'd had a good run. He certainly wasn't the first to have breath chipped away a little more each day. The best thing he could do was tidy his belongings to save others the bother. A simple courtesy—his family needn't be distracted from their busy lives and plans for tomorrow. They had enough to think about. They hadn't even noticed the broken nib of his pencil, nor the absence of music books that he had collected and carried up one at a time over a period of weeks, willing his breath not to fail him. Last time, he had almost been caught and had found himself scurrying and panting along the hallway to his bedroom. He wasn't doing anything wrong. Only if anyone saw him, he didn't want them to feel obliged to help.

He picked up the package, the last of his work, and paused to listen for a moment. The house was still empty. He put his foot on the bottom rung of the attic ladder, preparing for the hardest part, and gripped the rail to compensate for shaky footing. At the top, dank air sucked his strength. His head throbbed and his body hurt.

He put the package in the corner opposite the nativity scene, behind boxes of sheet music from home. Anyone poking around might stop to leaf through these treasures from another lifetime and probably never notice his music in their shadow.

One day, if life conceded any reason, somebody *would* stumble upon the pile. Sift through books of his music. They would pull out the symphony, marvel at why it had been stowed away. They would find it when it was time, when they needed it most, as he had.

Perhaps, when they found it, the symphony would launch a new beginning. He had thought for a long time that a day would come that the symphony would be performed. That he would dust off the sheets of music and host rehearsals for a grand debut performance. Then, finally, a whole town could hear his heart, his love for Assunta.

But he'd never played it after the night everything changed. The symphony sang of something broken, while life had become happy. Assunta was happy. She spread that feeling to everyone she encountered. Every time she entered a room, the air would ignite like a million tiny bells, lifting the spirits of anyone who happened to be there. People became, for the time they shared with her, the most important people in the world.

On an exceptionally warm day one March, Bolek, and Gino had come to help with yard clean-up. They decided to build a fire to burn the winter debris and had accidentally used Assunta's box of dahlia tubers as kindling, mistaking it for a box of old newspapers. Her precious dahlias, nurtured year after year, gone. Not only had she *not* crumbled, but she'd also gone as far as to laugh at their mistake. She had to sit them down with a cup of tea and a generous slice of cake to stop their stream of apologies. A week later, she asked Pietro to drive her to the nursery and had happily picked out new varieties.

He'd never seen fit reason to bring up a solemn song that might remind her of her sadness and remind him of time when he'd lived in the background.

He closed the attic door and made his way slowly back down. The song, however elusive it had become, fell silent. Clicked shut with the attic door like a period at the end of a sentence. Years of work relegated to darkness, where no instrument would find it.

He could hear nothing. A black, tangible nothing. He had packed the music up at the right time. Air had found its way less and less frequently into his lungs. A slab pressing tighter and tighter on his chest, whistling and wheezing filled his ears, drowning out the music.

He nudged aside the flat key of regret, reminding himself that he was no longer able to play. Let somebody discover it. One day—next week, next month, next year. Somebody who needed some healing. Wouldn't that be something?

He pursed his lips, searching for air that had found reason to avoid him, but then he relaxed. What was the point? He gave in to the grip on his chest. At least the pain was more forgiving than the silence. It would almost be a just reward if his breath ceased soon after the song.

He started downstairs to the kitchen but stopped, halfway, and lowered himself stiffly to sit for a moment. A burden, that's all. He had to remember that. He had removed the burden of his music from the shoulders of others. He had tidied up, left little of himself strewn around the house.

The heavy quiet around him stabbed more acutely than his miner's lungs.

The music was gone, packed away. The world was quiet.

A realization clamped his throat. What would they have to say about him without the music? There was nothing left to say about his life. Nothing at all.

The grip on his chest tightened, snaked up to his throat. The cough he desperately needed would not come. This was it. He'd be gone with the music. Despite the quiet, he would be at peace, knowing Assunta had loved him back.

But then there were hands tugging at him, pulling him up, not letting him die here on the steps. Quite right, he'd block the way where he sat. He tried to find his feet to help them move him, up; they wanted him up, where had the air gone? They set him on his bed. Relief.

♫♭♪

"Bravo Maestro!" the crowd shouted. They had mistaken him for another, but Pietro bowed anyway, gripping his clarinet behind his back. Only it was no longer a clarinet. He waved his hands at them to stop—any moment they'd see, the only thing he held was a pencil.

The scamper of a piccolo teased him like a boy with a revelation to share. He'd best follow, see what adventure the dream led him to next. The missing clarinet reappeared beside them. It insisted nothing. It simply was. It had no pretensions of its worth.

He heard the creak of a floorboard, then a voice, melodic with the certainty that life was going to treat her well, told him to wake up. *Accidenti*, reality got so easily blurred these days. He ought to pull himself to do the voice's bidding, but he just plain liked the melody. He'd pause in the hollow of confusion a moment longer.

The cornet struck in to join the fun, enthusiastic to be with its new friends. But the clarinet became sorrowful, commiserate, informing the cornet that there was reason for mourning. Understanding needed before healing.

What wise instruments and wise people playing them also—skilled musicians. Of course, it was Nonno's band, not a dream. Why would they be playing this early? But then why hadn't the rooster said so? He listened for breakfast sounds from the kitchen, bleats, and stomped demands from the goats in the stable. He found neither.

He tilted his head to search for other sounds of the day and found his neck was stiff like he'd been in bed too long. *Open*, he told his eyes, but they ignored him.

Outside, the dependable whistle of shift change rose above the steam room's hiss and clank, pulling him to wakefulness.

There was no rooster because this was not Italy. This was America, and he was a silly old fool.

The man-lift hissed with its mechanical chore, spilling one weary crew and swallowing the next. Boots stomped down the hill through the slush of new weather. He wasn't supposed to be on shift today, was he? *Wake up!* He didn't go down the mines anymore. His old mind was so daft it was still letting the music part of the dream carry on—in it, the clarinet squeaked a transition. It sounded deliberate. He knew someone who could squeak as awfully as that. He was the type of person too who'd do it as an apology for beginning this performance right about the time the mine whistle was going to go off.

The baritone swept into the melody and enveloped Pietro's heart with reassurance. The music was still playing. Not in his dream, not on the gramophone or wireless, but really. Pietro tried again to lift his head, but a spasm wracked his chest, hiding air in secret pockets of his lungs. A hand–Irene's?— held his. When his breath calmed, she held a water glass to his lips. The water was warm from being by his bed all night, but it did not matter. It was soothing, like the music.

He had certainly never heard this piece before, but he knew it—that made no sense, and yet it did. A song worthy of the finest celebration of life. Mozart-like. Grief yet redemption, played by a brass band.

He rubbed his eyes into assent. Irene picked up his spectacles from the bedside table and held them to his face. He took them from her before the tips touched his ears. She sat on the edge of the bed and smiled. A tune nudged through the music and through the silence that had surrounded him for the past month—the first tune his mind had offered since the day the attic door shut—then it was gone.

"Do you hear that?" Irene asked. So, it was real. She stood back up and looked out of the window, the cardigan buttoned above her belly, framing her unborn child like a stage curtain. "They said it was about time they got around to playing it. They said you couldn't say no this time."

"Who—?" the rest of the sentence lodged in his throat.

"The Ernest men."

"They're playing outside? In the snow?"

"Isn't it wonderful? They're doing it for you, dad."

He shook his head, although she wasn't looking at him. She must have it all wrong.

A weight constricted his chest. He couldn't be expected to breathe with it that taut. He scrunched the sheet in his fists.

Let go or let me go!

He sensed Irene back at the bed, her palms soft against his cheeks. Through splotches of black, some red, he saw her lips moving all-fired, but he heard only sections of words. This might be his time. The sound was getting fainter. No words at all now—only the song. His eyes closed, this time pushing out tears.

Of course, he knew the song!

The pressure subsided as a harmony carried off the pain. The symphony was more beautiful than he'd ever imagined.

Irene was still there when he awoke,

"Dad!" His Irene, why did she sound scared? In her condition, too. After all these years, fancy, still hard to believe he had a daughter of his own, and his little girl was going to be a mother.

"You gave me a scare."

"I heard music."

"Yes, you did. Remember, the Ernest men are here. They're playing in the snow for you."

"I heard it. They're—" still here, he wanted to finish, but the words got trapped in his throat. Irene wiped a drop of water from his bottom lip. Her fingers scraped. His bristles were past the point of stubble. He would have to shave. If he had counted the days rightly, he had been in bed a whole week. Perhaps Irene would bring a bowl and towels and help him.

"Mom's cooking spaghetti meatballs for everyone." Just yesterday, he was writing songs for Irene, playing guitar as she sang. She'd even won a talent contest, Colver's Shirley Temple, they called her. A clarinet rose and swirled, plucking joy from his heart and tossing it up into the air, nudging each note with a hint of mischief to create an ensemble. He gripped hold of the tune, exerting such an effort to snare it and hold on, a task that once was as automatic as breathing. Now that too was a trick. But it was a good tune, worth saving.

"Help me up." Perhaps he would even write this new tune, set this music to paper before the silence returned. He hoped he still had some blank sheets in the drawer downstairs.

Irene helped him into the bathroom and propped him against the sink while she went to fetch a washcloth. An old man stared back at him, his eyes unforgiving. Did she have to leave him here, propped against the sink, this new-fangled contraption, where the only thing he could see was the mirror? Those eyes, berating him for thinking he still had plenty of years tucked away for tomorrow. There was no practice for the rest of your life. There was just one shot.

She came back and gently cleaned his face with the washcloth, then dabbed him dry.

"What has happened to me, Irene? Look what a mess I am." He inhaled. The effort of speaking was making him wheeze. "Just like a baby. I was young once, just like you."

Irene gathered his clothes that had been set out days ago, clean and pressed, waiting for him to get back to life, her arms reaching wide around her belly. How strange that his little girl would soon be a parent. He clung desperately to the tune in his head, willing it not to disappear. He heard it over and over. He was, he knew, ready to write it down. It was a song of starting over from the beginning—the next generation, his grandchild.

A girl. He was sure it was from the pimples on Irene's forehead—a girl always borrowed her mother's beauty. She'd get it back after the baby was born; there'd be plenty of beauty for the both of them. What a shame he would never be able to play for her. Perhaps someone would think to tell her about her grandfather.

His footsteps on the way down were slow, shuffly. His hand slid an unreliable percussion down the rail.

"Come and sit down, dear." Assunta held his shoulders as he sat. She kissed his temple—such a satisfying sound.

"Did you hear the music?"

"Weren't they something?"

"They're in the front room waiting for you. But first, I have something for you."

He held onto the beauty of her voice for a moment, then took the package she handed him. It was tied with brown paper from the same roll he had used to package his music; only it was topped with a blue bow, not held by string.

Irene sat next to him, fidgeting with excitement. "Go on, Dad, open it!"

Pietro's chest gripped tight. He waited until it released him before he tore off the paper.

Inside was a brand-new sharpener and a box of five pencils.

"Oh," Irene said, her disappointment clear. "Doesn't dad have a ton of pencils already?"

"I was hoping you didn't notice when you weren't well, but the sharpener broke. Now you're up, I'm sure you'll be wanting to write again." He did not need to look at Assunta to hear she was smiling.

"As for you, Irene, take note," Assunta said, turning to her daughter. "Just because your John brings you every treasure he can, he won't always adore you as he does now if you're not dedicated to him and to your marriage. Love takes effort."

"He loves me to pieces. He adores me!" Irene squealed.

"Yes, we see that. Poor man can hardly talk straight when you walk in the room," Assunta laughed.

"Thank you, *cara*," Pietro said. "I remember the first pencil Nonno gave me. Did you know, he taught me to write music but never knew how to write a word himself?"

"You've mentioned it, Dad."

Assunta's hand rubbed over his, whispering affection.

"Ahem." Bolek cleared his throat from the living room doorway. He was old too. Gray, his skin a size too big, but he still sounded like a kid to Pietro.

"Guido too?"

"Sure thing." Guido's voice still shook the room. He still stooped forward, but no more than he did when he was young.

"I brought you something." Guido held up a bag—one of the thin paper ones they put candy in at the store. He showed Pietro what was inside. Acorns.

"I used to think you needed to go to the city to be someone. That this place was too small for your talents. Don't think I'm going soft in my old age," Guido's voice shook a little, "but these little acorns remind me of you. One of these tiny things that grew into a great big tree, it didn't matter if it was in a small yard. It gave a lot of joy and a lot of acorns to a lot of people."

Pietro tried to stand, but Bolek stopped him. "No! Sit."

"You played the music," Pietro said. "But how, I'd packed it away?"

"We copied scores years ago, to perform, remember? We kept ahold of them."

"They told me about the symphony," Assunta said. "All I ever wanted was for you to write some music for me. A little piece would've done. But you were always so busy doing for others. I didn't want to jump the line. Why did you never tell me?"

It was all for you, Assunta. All of it.

The rest of the band piled into the kitchen. Each shook Pietro's hand, told a quick story of a time they'd shared. Somehow, chairs were set around the table, the table set. Gino, Max, Mary, and Ida came in, too.

"What is this, a family reunion?" Pietro asked.

"Something like that. You know I never turn down Mom's cooking, Dad! Have I ever thanked you for teaching me to play the piano?" Max said.

"You were always a friend, but yet a Dad, too." Gino shook his hand.

"I'm proud you walked me down the aisle," Ida said. "At least I invited you to my wedding." She prodded Mary.

"It's been almost twenty years since we eloped. Drop it, will you? Dad, I want to thank you for playing to me when I fell down the stairs and burned myself. I was in such miserable pain, but you cheered me up."

"Is it my birthday?" he asked.

Assunta handed him a glass of wine and set a bread roll on the table. "Today's just an ordinary day when a few people decided they wanted to celebrate you, that's all."

He shook his head. They were all getting sentimental. He'd barely done a thing. But a celebration was a celebration, and he was sure happy to see all these faces. His friends, his family. He raised his glass with the rest of them. "*Alla salute!*"

It tasted pretty good. Well-aged. He picked up the bread—ah, fresh from the oven—held it to his ear and tore. Such an ordinary, satisfying sound, bless his lucky stars his hearing hadn't faded like his sight and every other part of him.

"Eat, please." He waved his bread at them.

Assunta and Irene filled bowls and glasses. Outside, a shovel fought the day's snow. Somewhere, a dog barked. Irene chattered about the imminent arrival of her baby, her words stringing together so hastily. Pietro listened to her tone, letting her actual words slip away. Assunta was saying something about Mrs. Conati—they didn't make many like her, may her soul rest in peace. Guido and Bolek were trying to plan a performance on stage for his symphony.

All this excitement, perhaps they should have played it sooner. And from the bit he'd heard those fools play out there in the cold, it didn't sound half bad. He'd asked them if they could play it again. He'd dedicate it properly to Assunta this time. He'd tell her she gave him all the love in the world, while all he ever had to give her was a song.

It had been quite a feat getting everyone together like this. Assunta was glad things had come together. Pietro'd had her worried this week. She missed his music. She couldn't imagine her life without it.

Ever since she'd put her sadness behind her, so long ago, it almost seemed like it belonged in someone else's life. Whenever she felt a little melancholy, she'd ask Pietro to tap out a tune on the piano or serenade her with his clarinet.

Sometimes she simply listened in on one of the music lessons he gave half the kids in town. That's all it took to bring her spirits round.

Even if he got distracted once in a while, gave his music or students his focus, and didn't notice if she put on a new blouse or put her hair up a different way, other times his thoughtfulness was as pleasant as a warm glass of milk from Mamma on a stormy night. Like if they were going on a trip—Pietro had never learned to drive, but they never lacked a ride to wherever they needed to go—he'd always have an orange, a napkin, and a knife ready for her. She couldn't even remember when the ritual began. All she knew was his gesture of love never failed to brighten her day.

The sauce looked about ready. She gave it a last stir. Behind her, someone opened the back door. Dr. Martin's large frame appeared.

"Just in time, come on in, Dr. Martin. We just sat down." Assunta pulled out the chair she'd saved for him.

The doctor pulled off his overcoat and stomped his feet on the mat.

"So, how are you today, Maestro? Mmm, it smells good, Assunta!" Dr. Martin washed his hands at the sink, sat down, and took a healthy swig of wine before he set in on one of his stories. "I had to get out to the Mackenzie farm on Saturday night. That snow came so fast the car got stuck. I had to traipse all the way on snowshoes. Just think, the kindness of people. Word spread, and each house had something for me. Hot cocoa, newspapers to stuff in my coat to keep me warm. I didn't get back till this morning. Glad to see you up and about Pietro. I've been getting used to Lido's wine."

Pietro did not answer. From the stove, Assunta turned to look, expecting a comeback.

It looked like the words were stuck in Pietro's mouth. His face was a hue of red, his eyes glazed.

Dr. Martin dropped his fork and clambered over the many people at the table, calling his friend's name firmly, a hint of a friend's despair in his voice. He pulled Pietro from the chair and dragged him into the living room where he laid him on the floor, knelt by him, and pulled at the clothes Irene had just helped him put on.

Irene cried out. Assunta reached out to her just in time to stop her collapsing, her left hand cupping her by the elbow. It pressed on the ring Pietro had given her.

The crowd that had gathered to celebrate this day with Pietro bottlenecked at the door, watched with breath held. Dr. Martin bent down to hold his ear above his mouth, then sat back on his heels and shook his head.

Assunta's heart heavy, the rose ring pushed into her finger felt firm and oddly reassuring, telling her she wasn't to crumble this time. She could hold strong, hold her daughter when she needed it the most. Then she heard the most extraordinary silence.

THE END

AUTHOR'S NOTE

I am so grateful you chose to read From Ashes the Song, thank you!

While some of the characters and settings were inspired by real life, this is ultimately a reimagining of events, places, and people. I hope I have not caused offence by straying from fact. Instead, it is my sincere hope that this fictional portrayal pays due tribute to the extraordinary passion, dedication, and talents of the people who ventured from their home countries and built the coal communities in Pennsylvania.

Note that phylloxera swept across Europe in the 19th and 20th centuries, leaving only a handful of parcels of vines intact. To my knowledge, accurate records on when and where it impacted Italian vineyards were not kept or have been lost. However, it is likely that phylloxera impacted the region of Piemonte earlier than depicted in this novel.

For the sake of fluidity, I've made mention of Pietro having a different accent from the characters from Verona. In truth, at that time, Italians spoke regional dialects which are truly different languages. They would have been able to communicate only—and with some difficulty—using the Italian language they learned at elementary school.

To find out more about the people and settings that inspired this story, and access special material for book clubs, please visit me at www.hilaryhauck.com. Also, please tag along with me on my quest to discover the extraordinary in the ordinary by subscribing to #storyeverywhere.

And, if I may ask for a few minutes more of your time, to help other readers discover this book out of the one million books published each year, please consider leaving a review on your favorite book review site, or wherever you buy your books. You would be doing me a wonderful service!

ACKNOWLEDGEMENTS

I may have been the one typing and retyping the words to this novel, but the story would not exist without a multitude of people who have impacted its coming to life. I am grateful to you all.

First and foremost, endless gratitude to my dear late friend Irene Smylnycky who shared with me the story of her parents, Pietro and Assunta, and who allowed me the creative freedom to shape the story as fiction. I treasure the friendship we found, field trips to Ernest, Indiana, and our epic trip to Italy.

Endless gratitude and appreciation also to Susan Datsko, who continues to embody Assunta and Irene's spirit of togetherness and good food. You have become a treasured friend, I've so enjoyed sharing every step of this journey with you.

Immense thanks to the Smylnycky, Datsko, Maccagno, Vassanelli, and Biscardo families. A special mention to Jenna Palmerini. I'll never forget that surreal moment in Pittsburgh when you told me that Nandy was your great grandfather.

Immense thanks also to Italian cousins from Verona, Gilberto and Laura, and from San Damiano d'Asti, Teresina and Maggiolino, Sr. Marvi, Fabio, and Paolo.

Thanks also to Johnny Tortella, for a historical tour of Ernest; Evalyn Martin, for sharing stories of her father, the much-revered Dr. Martin; and Eileen Mountjoy for her accounts of the Ernest mine disaster of 1916, and life in a mining town; Lido and Marge Sisti, for stories of growing up in Colver; and Bill Smith, for coal mine facts and stories; Tami Kubat, for always believing, and for our friendship.

I'm grateful also to the people of Colver, who welcomed me into their community and whose pride in their heritage inspired me to write this story.

Immense thanks to the team at Sunbury Press, especially Chris Fenwick, for believing in the story and bringing it to life.

Many thanks to passionate, fierce, and talented developmental editor with a reverent sense of story, Kathryn Craft. You pushed me far beyond my comfort zone and landed me in a much better place.

Immense thanks to JD Dunbar, wordsmith, pure joy, friend – for the best title, for RULE, and for knowing it was inside of me all along. Arriba! And to Larry Rock'n'Roll Schardt, for positivity always, being the bearer and beacon of gratitude, and, in everything you do, exuding success that rocks—as in rocks!

My dear friend Denise Weaver, thank you for your unwavering support, for reading several novels-worth of pages, and for bringing food and comfort in my most challenging moments.

My eternal gratitude to the late Ramona Long for sitting me at my desk every morning to sprint, for her wisdom, support, and friendship. And to the Writing Champs, for the comradery of beginning each day doing our favorite thing together.

Kim Gray, rescuer of Katydids, sharer of tables, my twin and banter buddy, thank you for feedback, support, and friendship.

Kathleen Shoop, endless thanks for the incredible Mindful Writer Retreats, endless luminance, and gifts – tangible and otherwise.

Madhu Bazaz Wangu, thank you for Mindful Writers daily practice, wisdom, friendship, and for inspiring me to keep a skull as a reminder that today is a gift. Thanks also to artist Lacey Kreutzberger, for painting the skull.

Thank you Hank Phillippi Ryan, for your feedback, advice, and for being a shining beacon of inspiration.

Grazie infinite Jean Jenkins, my first reader, Italian history pal, and bringer of wine.

Timons Esaias, my first writing teacher. You've been an endless source of knowledge, support, friendship, and guidance ever since. I truly would not be here without you.

I would also not be here without the knowledge and support of Pennwriters, my first writing family, and the generosity of its members in paying it forward.

My gratitude to the Inkwellodians, for monthly inspiration and sharing, and to Tanya Schleiden, Jenn Diamond and Shirley Stuby for your energy, support, and friendship.

Immense thanks also to the State College Poets, whose skill with words I aspire to, and who inspire me always – Sarah Russell, Steve Deutsch, Teresa Danter, Lisa Mcmonagle, Mark Shirey, John Ziegler.

My lifelong gratitude to my RULE family. Special thanks to Genna Kasun and Danielle Rhubart, for carrying on the spirit and support; to Dave Popp, for your dedication to the Festival of Books in the Alleghenies; Cassandra Gunkel, artist and inspiration; Tara Homan, for tireless support, always.

My thanks to the following people for sharing their special knowledge and expertise with me – any errors in the story are mine, not theirs: Robin Malloy, musical expert and pianist extraordinaire, I've so enjoyed our cultural and retail travel adventures; Dr. Mike Warner, for your knowledge of medicine in history; Claudia Baldoli, for your knowledge of Italian history and story feedback; Rose Jachimczuk, for your wine-making stories; to Stefano Trevisan, for Italian linguistic guidance.

Nonna Emilia, grazie infinite per avermi insegnato a cucinare, e per aver sempre creduto in me.

Thank you Pat and Dale Hauck, for your constant support.

Mum, I'm so grateful for your love of gardens and all the family stories. Dad, I wish you could see me now! Thank you for telling me you were proud. Mum and Dad both, I'll never be able to thank you enough for your endless belief in me, and for instilling in me a love of travel and curiosity about the world.

Kyle, thank you for always knowing how to make me smile, and for sharing your passion for your hometown.

Lacey, thank you for your beautiful, sparkling spirit, and for brightening our lives with grandorables, Melody, Porter, and Autumn.

Jess, thank you for sharing this journey with me, and for unwavering confidence. For analyzing every character, celebrating every success, and pulling me up from every setback.

To my husband, my rock, Darryl. I could not have done it without you. Thank you for your boundless support and patience, for giving me the time to write, for reading pages out loud, and for bringing me coffee to start each morning knowing that I am loved.

ABOUT THE AUTHOR

Hilary Hauck is a writer and translator whose work has appeared in the Mindful Writers Retreat Series anthologies, the Ekphrastic Review, Balloons Lit. Journal, and the Telepoem Booth. She moved to Italy from her native UK as a young adult, where she mastered the language, learned how to cook food she can no longer eat, and won a karate championship. After meeting her husband, Hilary came to the US and drew inspiration from Pennsylvania coal history, which soon became the setting for her debut novel.

Hilary is Chair of the Festival of Books in the Alleghenies, past president of Pennwriters, and a graduate of RULE. Hilary lives on a small patch of woods in rural Pennsylvania with her husband, one of their three adult children, a cat with a passion for laundry, and an oversized German Shepherd called Hobbes—of the Calvin variety. Follow her at www.hilaryhauck.com.

ORGANIZED CRIME

ORGANIZED CRIME
Concepts and Controls

Second Edition

DENNY F. PACE

Public Services Department

Long Beach City College

JIMMIE C. STYLES

Vice Chancellor

Tarrant County Junior College

Prentice-Hall, Inc., Englewood Cliffs, N.J. 07632

Library of Congress Cataloging in Publication Data

Pace, Denny F.
  Organized Crime.

  Bibliography: p.
  Includes index.
  1. Organized crime—United States.
2. Law enforcement—United States. I. Styles,
Jimmie C. II. Title.
HV6791.P3   1982   364.1'06'073   82–13128
ISBN 0–13–640946–6

Editorial/production supervision and interior design by Pam Price and Alice Erdman
Cover design by Ray Lundgren
Manufacturing buyer: Ed O'Dougherty

Prentice-Hall Series in Criminal Justice

Printed in the United States of America

10 9 8 7 6 5 4 3 2 1

ISBN   0-13-640946-6

Prentice-Hall International, Inc., *London*
Prentice-Hall of Australia Pty. Limited, *Sydney*
Editora Prentice-Hall do Brasil, Ltda., *Rio de Janeiro*
Prentice-Hall Canada Inc., *Toronto*
Prentice-Hall of India Private Limited, *New Delhi*
Prentice-Hall of Japan, Inc., *Tokyo*
Prentice-Hall of Southeast Asia Pte. Ltd., *Singapore*
Whitehall Books Limited, *Wellington, New Zealand*

To

ELLIE and JIMMIE

and to our children

who make life worthwhile

CONTENTS

Part II

Vice Crimes of an Organized Nature   47

Part IV

Internal Agency Operation   167

Part V

Education and Training   221

PREFACE

How can organized crime be controlled? This is a question frequently asked by the citizen and a problem that has long been beyond the reach of local enforcement agencies. To bring some semblance of control to organized crime, the system itself must improve and increased public support and help must be sought.

The citizen's role in suppressing organized crime has always been thought of as a matter of abstinence rather than one of active participation in enforcement. Rather, the citizen should be viewed as a potential aide in organized crime control. While oriented toward the police segment of the criminal justice system, this text is structured so that both the citizen and members of enforcement agencies can view the interaction of the many social variables that create organized crime and allow it to exist as a part of society. In so doing, they may then follow a common path in the eradication of organized crime.

Organized crime control is the responsibility of both the citizen and the law enforcement officer. If a democratic form of government is to prevail and operate under "people control," it is time the citizen provides active support to the criminal justice system in the control of organized crime. The role of the citizen in effective organized crime control is stressed throughout this book. There is hope that concerned citizen support will be generated for the criminal justice system and the effort will minimize the influence of organized crime in any community.

Several key concepts should be reviewed so that both citizen and an enforcement agent will acquire sufficient knowledge to contribute toward controlling organized crime. These concepts are: (1) the interrelation of organized crime to the social structure; (2) symptoms of organized crime in the community; (3) political influence in organized criminal activities; (4) the role of the legal system in organized crime control; (5) specific vice violations; (6) business operations infiltrated and controlled by criminal interests; (7) administrative structures and procedures in agencies for crime control; and (8) the citizen-officer role for organized crime control.

Organized crime is defined in a number of ways. It is viewed by the authors as being a prohibited criminal activity between two or more persons which may consist of a conglomerate arrangement or a monolithic system. The term as used in this text implies a more diversified organization than that which describes the activities of the Mafia or La Cosa Nostra. The basis for a more expanded definition were the descriptions that originated from the Oyster Bay Conference of 1965, in which it was indicated that organized crime is the product of a self-perpetuating criminal conspiracy to wring exorbitant profits from our society by any means. The full operational definition is cited in Chapter 4, but this definition in itself freed the authors from thinking of organized crime as being a few select crimes committed by a group of henchmen with a common boss. Whether a violation of a penal statute may be construed as organized crime will depend upon the scheme or plan used to commit the crime. Thus, no particular crime is excluded from the definition of organized crime.

The importance of organized crime control in the United States is cited in the Organized Crime Control Act of 1970. This act begins as follows and gives a capsulized view of the problem of organized crime:

> Organized crime in the United States is a highly sophisticated, diversified, and widespread activity that annually drains billions of dollars from America's economy by unlawful conduct and illegal use of force, fraud, and corruption; organized crime derives a major portion of its power through money obtained from such illegal endeavors as syndicated gambling, loan sharking, the theft and fencing of property, the importation and distribution of narcotics and other dangerous drugs, and other forms of social exploitation; this money and power are increasingly used to infiltrate and corrupt our democratic processes; organized crime activities in the United States weaken the stability of the Nation's economic system, harm innocent investors and competing organizations, interfere with free competition, seriously burden interstate and foreign commerce, threaten the domestic security and undermine the general welfare of the nation and its citizens.

Because of the diversification and variety of criminal activities engaged in by organized groups, there can be no true ranking of priority for the criminal activity. Until such a time as there are clearer guidelines to identify what organized crime is and the extent of the confederations' involvement in the social order, the true nature of their relationships cannot be shown. There has been an attempt to limit references to the terms Mafia and La Cosa Nostra. These terms reflect an ethnic heritage of some criminal confederations, and tend to distort the true ethnic variety of many different organized criminal groups.

This text addresses organized crime so that law enforcement officers and lay citizens can see data brought together to support allegations of the existence of organized criminal groups. By studying how organized criminals

ply their trade, the reader will be able to understand the complexity of administering agency enforcement policies.

In the decade of the 1970s there has been some new research. In 1976 the Justice Department published *Basic Elements of Intelligence* and in 1977, *The Investigation of White Collar Crime.* These two publications were designed as manuals for use in law enforcement agencies. In 1978 a report entitled *Racket Bureaus: Investigation and Protection of Organized Crime* was published by the Cornell Institute on Organized Crime. The U.S. Government Printing Office came out with a program model titled *Prevention, Detection and Correction of Corruption in Local Government.* Changes in policy and procedures for organized crime will require reference to these and other sources.

There have been some positive movements in the fight against organized crime. These movements include the training of officers for organized crime units, the training of intelligence officers for the collection and analysis of intelligence data, a firming-up of task forces in some key cities, and the increased use of the 1970 Racketeer Influenced and Corruption Organizations (RICO) statutes. But the few positive movements have been overshadowed by the strengthened growth of organized crime activities in most of the cities and states throughout these United States.

Denny F. Pace
Jimmie C. Styles

ORGANIZED CRIME

PART I

THE SOCIAL RAMIFICATIONS OF ORGANIZED CRIME

America grows with stories of organized criminals. The stories present a variety of ideologies about how criminal groups organize and operate. The criminals are a product of our social system and are often held in professional esteem. They are intricately woven into our economic system because they thrive in our free market economy. And they perform in a conspiratorial fashion which draws a variety of responses from law enforcement.

The stories reflect latent patterns of ethnic criminal activities, of corruption in the public workplace, and of mob-influenced corporate structures controlling legal and political systems. The stories tell us how they operate and who their victims are. But seldom are the criminals identified with any kind of specific activity.

This part of the text (Chapters 1 through 4) looks at the issue of organized crime and attempts to examine its influences, gauge its subtle behaviors, and finally assess how this systematic criminality creates a dynamic influence that has a direct impact on the moral and economic fiber of a community.

1

THE RELATIONSHIP OF ORGANIZED CRIME TO THE COMMUNITY

LEARNING OUTCOMES

1. Develop an operating definition of organized crime.
2. Be able to identify some of the social and political influences that allow organized crime to exist.
3. Determine the sources of power in a community that can affect organized crime.
4. Know the different cultural patterns of a community and see how these patterns influence the control of organized crime.
5. Be able to discuss the pitfalls and the merits of legalizing or decriminalizing certain prohibited activities that support organized crime.

Within our social structure, many forces establish standards for social conduct. These forces are powerful influences on how society organizes to protect itself against the natural and man-made trends of disorganization that prevail in modern urban cultures. Very brief and perhaps oversimplified concepts about how society adjusts to these disorganizing concepts are presented so that both the citizen and the law enforcement officer may realize their proper role in the control of organized crime.

The amount of organized crime a nation or community has depends upon a large number of social, political, and administrative variables. The interchange of these variables dictates how organized criminal violations will be identified and enforced. The basic causes of organized crime allegedly stem primarily from social and individual weaknesses. Thus, the most effective suppression of organized criminal activities will arise from the cultural pressures exerted by citizens, individually and collectively, in a community. It is when these community pressures fail to satisfactorily subdue violations that it will be necessary for governmental enforcement units to intervene.

Formal groups such as legislative bodies, the judicial system, and law

enforcement agencies are the administrative units basically responsible for implementing legal controls. Often these controls do not function adequately to protect society. Should this occur, the controls that are then necessary will evolve from informal pressure groups such as political parties, churches, social organizations, civic organizations, vested interest groups, or other informal organizations. The interaction among these different organizations in providing just laws, reasonable enforcement, and consistent court processes often determines how organized crime can or will be controlled.

Organized crime control is not solely a law enforcement problem. The solution to the problem of control, if there is one, lies in the application of many control factors. The factors or elements for organized crime control may be conceptualized as being composed of both organizational and individual dynamics that control human behavior within our social structure.

By examining the processes involved in community and agency interaction, the law enforcement officers and citizens involved in social control will be better able to understand community desires, to develop patterns of enforcement, and finally to determine the degree of control necessary to guarantee society reasonable and equitable management of prohibited criminal behavior.

The most acceptable restraints for organized crime control are no longer vested in a policing agency. The roots of effective control are centered in many social entities and are influenced by many forces, one of which is public awareness. Another is the social dynamics of the community. Let us take a closer look at both.

THE IMPORTANCE OF PUBLIC AWARENESS

The ultimate solution to organized crime will not be achieved through enforcement alone. All efforts must be directed toward reducing society's desire to indulge in and sanction these types of criminal activity. Because this is not likely to occur soon, approaches emphasizing control will remain until new behavioral patterns are established. An ideal approach would be the changing of human weaknesses in our social structure, recognizing the fallacy of social acceptability of activities that create organized crime, and developing the ability to establish a consistent public attitude toward the suppression of these crimes. By revealing some of the weaknesses in present control systems, perhaps a more acceptable plan for control may be presented to both the police and the public.

One premise for the suppression of organized criminal activities is to recognize that lack of awareness and concern by the public is organized crime's greatest ally. The efforts of any branch of society directed toward controlling organized crime activities will be largely unsuccessful unless the public is made aware of criminal methodology and the magnitude of

organized crime. Publicity and honest exposure of illegal activities is one of the surest ways to dry up sources of revenue for an organization engaged in criminal activities.

The U.S. Chamber of Commerce identified the problem of controlling crime in this statement:

> A formidable problem faced by the nation's Criminal Justice System is insufficient citizen involvement. Indeed, why not leave the crime problem to the professionals who are paid to cope with it? Perhaps the most pragmatic answer is that the professionals themselves are keenly aware and readily admit that without citizen assistance they do not command sufficient manpower or funds to shoulder the monumental burden of combating crime in America.[1]

For example, the President's Commission on Law Enforcement and the Administration of Justice, the National Commission on the Causes and Prevention of Violence, and the National Advisory Committee on Criminal Justice Standards and Goals have all taken the stand that if society is to have a tolerable degree of crime, the citizen must be involved. Active citizen involvement in the control of organized crime is an absolute must.

FACTORS OF SOCIAL DYNAMICS

Basic social factors for understanding and controlling organized criminal activities include cultural mores, social acceptance of criminal behavior, the entropic processes in society, and the permissive attitude present in society.

Cultural Mores

There is a wide divergence in what society purports to believe and what it does. As a result, there are many who, although espousing morality, are inclined to engage in illegal activities and "look away" from a workable enforcement of the law. Cultural mores should serve the purpose in our society that a newel does for a circular stairway.

Before any agency can exert more than a "hit-or-miss" policy of crime control, a new national image of what our society is going to be will have to emerge. If institutions of enormous power that are "quasi" or "in fact" illegal can exercise control in our society without being legitimized, we shall have to be satisfied with a gangster-dominated environment. Should society hold to

---

[1]Chamber of Commerce of the United States, *Marshaling Citizen Power against Crime* (Washington, D.C., 1970), p. 3. Organized crime is a part of society. See S.L. Hills, "Organized Crime and American Society," *Midwest Quarterly,* 9, 2 (January 1968), 171–82.

the image that social, political, and economic power may be derived from "any source," the Christian ethic of morality as presently perceived will wither and vanish.

Social Acceptance and Organized Crime

Although nothing is inherently immune from some degree of measurement, organized crime and related activities are about as close as one can come. The reluctance of victims to prosecute and the cloak of secrecy in criminal operations have caused organized crime to thrive. Because of this reluctance and secrecy, there has never been a wholly objective viewpoint published on organized criminal activities. A number of attempts have been made, but no adequate explanation has been made to the public and/or to law enforcement outlining what must be done to expose organized crime so that legal sanctions may be imposed.

In the task force report from the National Commission on the Causes and Prevention of Violence, the commission has this to say about the informed citizen:

> The single most important ingredient of improved citizen participation in the law enforcement process is improved understanding of the law and its enforcers, the police....[2]

The only logical way to let citizens know about organized crime is for each individual to receive the information that is of public record and that is often buried in police files. This information requires intensive research to assimilate or be put in a format and presented through newspapers, television, and community programs that are understandable to the average citizen. When citizens can understand some of the realities of organized criminal activities, the lack of punitive actions by the police, and the covert political protection given organized crime, they will demand action.

Entropy in Social Control

By applying a liberal social interpretation of Weiner's concept of entropy, we may identify forces that tend to corrupt and disorganize the social norms of society.[3] The disorganizing forces are those that advocate and implement moral misbehavior. In the realm of organized crime control, the disorganizing elements would be people who engage in bookmaking, loan sharking, racketeering, and other assorted violations.

---

[2]James S. Campbell, Joseph R. Sahid, and David P. Strang, *Law and Order Reconsidered* (New York: Bantam, 1970), p. 440.

[3]Norbert Weiner, *The Human Use of Human Beings* (Boston: Houghton Mifflin, 1954).

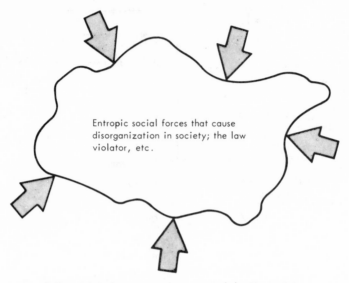

Figure 1–1 Entropy and social control devices.

Thus, the anti-entropic forces are those forces operating within society to keep social norms in check. Of this group, legislatures, courts, and law enforcement agencies are the primary preventive forces. An illustration of this concept is shown in Figure 1–1.

In the entropic/anti-entropic concept there is no firmly identifiable focal point for intelligent decision making. This lack of decision-making authority makes it nearly impossible for an enforcement organization to meet the goals for a perfect crime control system. Thus, organized crime control cannot be just an effective intelligence squad, an infallible court system, or an enlightened public. It must be a combination of all the desirable elements, such as citizen concern, self-discipline, and a desire for freedom from organized crime dominance, that make up our social system.

This is further illustrated in the conceptualizations made by Stokes in his study of vice in our social order. Stokes cited another closely related social theory in Parson's concept of polity.[4] He uses polity as a conceptual term to discuss the specialized process that handles the input of expectations, reasons, and so on, and the allocation of costs, values, and so on, in our society. These processes are shown in Figure 1–2.

In organized crime, and especially with those to do with vice, the powers exercised by pressure groups become an important decision-influencing

[4]Harold R. Stokes, "Vice Enforcement and Its Dynamic Relationship in Administration of Criminal Justice" (University of Southern California, 1965), pp. 6–12.

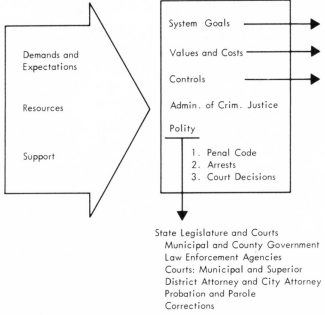

Figure 1-2 Inputs and outputs within the polity indicating forces that influence organized crime control.

factor for law enforcement. Stokes illustrated the interaction problems of the administration and the social group pressures when he said:

> The administration of criminal justice becomes a sounding board and a feedback system for groups that try to change the course of events or policies that affect the social system at large, and in particular, their own areas of concern.[5]

This idea is logical in conceptualizing goal attainment for criminal justice and in describing the framework of goal attainment processes for the control of organized crime.

As Stokes points out, the job of our criminal justice system is to transform the inputs into effective decisions or actions on the output side.[6] Identifying how these processes take place requires subjective research techniques. The structural-functional technique of gathering research data has no single dependent variable. Thus, observations made in identifying the problems of organized crime are not comprehensive or empirically validated. There has been no attempt to quantify data in this text.

[5]Stokes, "Vice Enforcement," p. 5.

[6]Stokes, "Vice Enforcement," p. 6, cited in William C. Mitchell, *The American Polity,* New York: Free Press, 1962.

The Permissive Society

There has been a trend in the United States and throughout the world to reduce what violations we now classify as crimes to harmless deviations that carry little or no punitive action. For example, the manipulation of securities becomes an acceptable business practice. Labor union racketeering is looked upon as a nuisance business must live with, and political corruption is swept under the rug by the party in power. Volumes are devoted to the issues of public morals, habits, and how much latitude there should be in human behavior. Conversely, there is also a reverse process by which harmless deviations become crimes.

Most police thinking today coincides with the following pattern of reasoning. An attempt to dictate the sociological and psychological arguments for or against the legalization of certain crimes is not a legitimate role for law enforcement officers. If the legislature determines a particular act to be illegal, then the statute prohibiting it should be rigidly enforced. If it is decreed to be legal, the police will then abide by the will of the people and abstain from enforcement activity. The enforcement officer and lower court judges cannot be moralists, but they are commanded to enforce the legal statutes of the nation, state, county, and city. If statutes prohibit and provide punishment when certain acts are committed, the court should see that the crimes are prosecuted within the framework of the law.

The issue of individual morality permeates the whole of our society. It is interesting to note that the same people who speak out vehemently against certain crimes are frequently the ones who ask the local enforcement group for exceptions to the law. For example, lotteries are favorite fund-raising techniques for church bazaars, school carnivals, and so forth.

Many people rationalize that gambling, for example, is all right as long as "gangsters" are not running the show. They contend that gambling is all right if it is conducted in a private home or among friends. If this is the intent of those who create the law, then it should be so stated.

Whatever society determines is prohibited should be set forth in explicit statute form so that those enforcing the law are not burdened with the decision of illegal or unethical enforcement. In spite of allegations that law is a hocus-pocus science, laws can be written that convey the intent of society.

The whole issue of social permissiveness should be of utmost importance to state legislatures. While the federal government is busy enacting statutes to prohibit the interstate transportation of lottery tickets, racing information, and gambling paraphernalia, some states are creating loopholes in legalizing certain types of lotteries,[7] in creating lax securities laws, and other laws that create a lack of uniformity of enforcement.

---

[7]Two states have casinos, 15 states have lotteries, 31 states have horse racing, and 14 states have dog racing. Exemptions exist in federal laws for state-sponsored gaming activities.

Should a state have the right to pass laws that create national problems? With few exceptions, state-supported gambling has not been as lucrative as anticipated. Some 1300 gambling schemes have gone down the road to corruption and bankruptcy in the history of the United States. A close look at most schemes has shown they were ill-conceived by private groups, poorly supervised by the states, and ultimately run by the syndicates.

Americans are not known for strict adherence to the rule of law, nor are they known for their strict morality. The mixed cultures of free-thinking individuals have been famous for initiating rigid rules of self-conduct, then winking and looking the other way as rules and regulations are violated. Prohibition was a grand example of this indulgence. As a result, in recent U.S. history, there have been double operating standards for law enforcement personnel. Each state has adequate laws for the effective control of organized crime. Yet, nearly every major city in the United States has all the organized crime conditions that are common to the other cities. Whereas there are few valid statistics of a local nature to support such criminal activity, the attorney general's First Annual Report and the unpublished and covert meetings held by various intelligence officers throughout the United States support the commonality of organized crime conditions as they exist in the major cities. The attorney general's report merely alludes to the problem and goes on to list isolated activities, such as six gambling rings in New Jersey and adjoining states resulting in the arrest of 65 persons. The Postal Service has expanded its efforts in investigating organized crime involvement in postal related offenses—there is without question data that support these operations; yet, the public are not privy to such data because enforcement and political administrators do not view the disclosure of such information as important to crime control.

SUMMARY

Control of organized crime is not such a simple task that enforcement agencies can just go out and eliminate it. Through the influence of formal and informal pressure groups, the criminal organizations will persist in spite of the enforcement effort. By identifying a few of the basic social and cultural influences, the complexity of the control dynamics for organized crime has been shown. Public awareness can strip powerful protection from criminal confederations. There has been an attempt to point out that public action groups, both formal and informal, can influence the degree of pressure exerted against organized criminals. The issue of permissiveness is raised as an important concept in determining if punitive enforcement is a viable alternative for the control of many types of organized crimes.

QUESTIONS FOR DISCUSSION

1. Why is it not feasible at the present time to establish a taxonomy for organized crime?
2. Identify and discuss the different objectives of the *formal* and *informal* pressure groups.
3. In addition to those listed, identify major processes that influence the control of organized crime.
4. Identify ways in which the public is made aware of organized criminal activities. How are they concealed?
5. Point up specific ways in which different cultural patterns influence organized crime in your community.
6. How does the entropic/anti-entropic theory illustrate the complex factors that go to create social control?
7. Does the interaction described by Stokes indicate that informal and formal group action can change the course of social control in our society?
8. Poll the class on the question of legalized vice. Should certain types of vice be legalized? What is the police role in these crimes?
9. What is the prevailing police attitude toward identifying acts that are illegal?
10. Should the police be active in lobbying activities?

2

SYMPTOMS OF ORGANIZED CRIME

LEARNING OUTCOMES

1. Gain insight into the workings of organized criminals in a community.
2. Understand the need to keep the activities of organized criminals before the public.
3. Recognize the businesses and other activities in the community that are related to organized crime.
4. Determine what is "myth" and what is "fact" about organized crime.
5. Gain knowledge about how organized crime groups have become entrenched in society.

Citizens tolerate so much organized crime because they are not actually aware of its form or magnitude, and when they are aware of its existence, they are not concerned because they do not know how it affects them. The direct link of criminal activity to organized crime is difficult to show and almost impossible to prove.[1] In order to show the symptoms of organized crime, it is necessary to (1) identify the need for exposure, (2) determine if organized crime is a myth or a reality, and (3) show how the evolution of the criminal syndicates has caused them to be entrenched in our society.

THE NEED FOR EXPOSÉS

A major factor in the growth of the crimes that are controlled by the confederation[2] is the lack of knowledge on the part of the citizen and the local

[1]Denny F. Pace, *Handbook on Vice Control* (Englewood Cliffs, N.J.: Prentice-Hall, 1971), p. 27.

[2]The term "confederation" is a more accurate term to describe the organization of criminals. This term will be used throughout this book to replace the term "syndicate," which is normally used.

12

police officer that criminal activity exists in their community. Activities of the confederations are so covert it is impossible to detect them in casual inquiry or in a normal police investigation. In many cases this information becomes known only years after an investigation has ended, and in such devious ways that it would be impossible to prosecute the criminal. Some of the most effective ways for a citizen to know about specific criminal activity is through the exposés of crusading newspapers, television, or other methods such as the Kefauver Committee publicity, federal grand jury investigations, and open public inquiries such as the Valachi hearings. Frequently, these are carried out only to the extent that they do not expose clients, friends of clients, and so-called responsible members of the community. Obviously there is need for an informed public, and some effort should be made to see that crime commissions, crime prevention committees, and other citizen groups organize and operate effectively to make the crime picture known. The crime commission and other citizen groups will probably not bring about a concerted effort against organized crime, so the most effective device may be the news and television exposés.

There is danger in the exposé because a city in which the exposé is made is cited as the bad example. Citizens of other cities fail to realize the same situation exists within the confines of their metropolitan area. There are law enforcement agencies that are satisfied in letting the public believe that an individual under investigation is the only culprit. Most city officials think it is better for a community if the exposé is made in a far removed city.

Even though exposés emanate from local informers, local grand jury hearings, or from investigations developed from within the police department, it is safe to say that organized crime of any nature is not a local matter. An exposé in New York, Chicago, or Miami would find its equal in Los Angeles, Seattle, or Las Vegas. The only difference in the cities would be the degree of infiltration, the political temperament at the moment, the vested interests of those making the exposés, and geographic location.

It is amazing how many citizens, judges, police chiefs, and other public officials are surprised when an exposé is made in their community. It is even more ironic when the criminal justice administration of a major local city states that its city does not have an organized crime problem.[3] Prostitutes do not have to be walking the streets, nor does each back room of the local taverns need a "bookmaker's layout" for a city to have organized crime. The degree of coordination between courts and enforcement agencies and the corruptive influences of the local political parties are ways in which the presence of organized crime may be shown to exist.

---

[3]See Theodore R. Lyman, Thomas W. Fletcher, and John A. Gardiner, *Prevention, Detection, and Correction of Corruption in Local Government: A Presentation of Potential Models* (Washington, D.C.: U.S. Government Printing Office, November 1978).

ORGANIZED CRIME: MYTH OR REALITY

Some men of high stature in law enforcement still maintain that organized criminal activity per se is a myth. Findings of the 1930, 1951, and 1967 Crime Commission Reports, however, show a common pattern that must be termed "organized." The structure of the organization is not a formal hierarchy as we normally picture our giant corporation, but it is an offshoot of about 24 main families in the United States, plus other groups. Some of these better known families are shown in Figure 2–1.

During the 1970s other organized criminal groups gained power. These groups consist of lucrative drug distribution systems, ethnic gangs, and political splinter groups. For example, in California, Mexican gangs alone accounted for 300 murders during the 1970s. Chinese, Japanese, Vietnamese, and Korean organized groups have taken up the extortion and blackmail activities similar to those of the Italians and Irish of the eary 1900s. Even the Dixie Mafia continues to operate with success.[4] In black neighborhoods, black criminals control the rackets through affiliation with confederation-controlled services. During that decade, Eastern gangsters continued to purge one another's gangs. Most of the murders and well-planned crimes were not solved and prosecuted.

Organized crime extends far beyond the boundaries of traditional criminal activities, so the cases cited here may be considered only a sample of the overall activities of confederated criminal groups. In organized crime a dramatic transition is taking place because crime leaders are attempting to move the organizations from activities in illegal enterprises such as narcotic smuggling to lucrative areas of the legitimate business sector.

The 1976 *Task Force Report on Organized Crime* showed the extent of organized crime penetration into all regions of the United States. The report showed that there were about 1900 personnel in 96 funded projects which resulted in a $1.5 billion loss to organized crime. While this may be an impressive statistic, another report estimated that organized crime was ripping Californians off for $6.3 billion annually.[5] Obviously, the present efforts must be bolstered by massive state and local efforts.

In reality, the very nature of the confederations makes most known methods of control difficult. Most of the criminals who are in control of organized crime activities in the large cities take great care to conceal evidence of their connections. Public officials and businessmen are frequently

---

[4]The "Dixie Mafia" is a loose-knit group dealing in stolen merchandise, fencing, and other types of organized crime. This group operates throughout the southern states. It apparently has few ties with national confederations.

[5]*Report of the Task Force on Organized Crime* (Washington, D.C.: U.S. Government Printing Office, 1976), and "The Mob's Plot to 'Buy' California," *Reader's Digest,* December 1979.

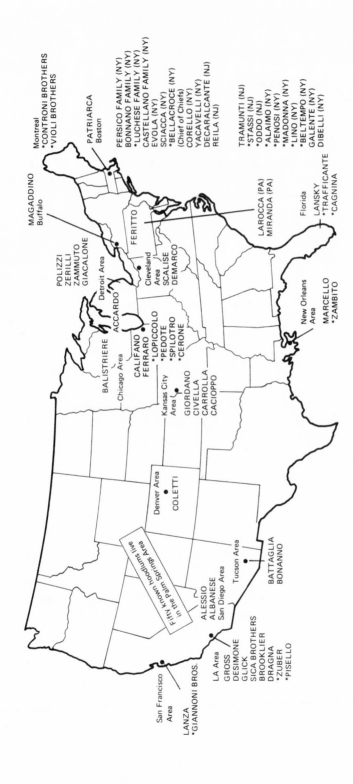

Figure 2–1 Identified Mafia leaders and associates in the United States (List is from contemporary sources such as magazines and newspapers; because of deaths, this list may be inaccurate. It is offered for information only.)

*Indicates Major Drug Distributors

15

involved with confederation activities without any knowledge of their affiliation.

If organized crime is going to be effectively suppressed, efforts must be directed toward the upper echelons of the organization. The very nature of the structure makes it almost impossible for the local officer to be successful in gathering evidence for more than petty prosecutions. For example, the "handbook" is the only one who has to worry in a bookmaking ring. The "pimp" or "madam" of a house, if they do not become too overt in their operation, need have little fear of prosecution from local sources. Labor racketeering or government corruption have little to fear from local prosecution.

There are a number of reasons why local control is likely to be ineffective in the control of organized crime.

The procedures for investigation are unlike those for a regular crime. The police operator is frequently the only effective technique through which a crime can be solved. This is dangerous and too expensive for local units of government.

The investigations into organized crime activities are frequently conducted over longer periods of time than other investigations. Local cities cannot afford to sustain these investigations.

Undercover operators need funds for extensive investigations. At the local level, these funds are not usually adequate.

Leaders of the syndicates tend to split operations between cities and states, so a complete picture of the operation is unknown to the local officer.

Participating criminals will frequently transfer personnel, thus causing local officers to lose contact with both the violator and the informer.

There is a great overlapping into legitimate businesses, and local laws are not adequate to cover borderline cases.

The crime leaders are so closely affiliated with local politicians that the local officer, if he becomes overly ambitious, finds himself transferred to assignments where he does not come in contact with organized crime.

The lack of wide jurisdiction for local police agencies brings about limitations. Investigation cannot in many cases extend beyond the city limits.

The failure to impose available sanctions through licensing and permits at state and local levels results in less crime control.

Failure of the legislature to make adequate laws limits enforcement action.

Failure of the courts to rigidly enforce existing laws encourages crime.

The dismal lack of public concern toward such crimes is one of the most significant of these reasons.

In order to better understand the clandestine operation of organized crime groups, a few brief statements about the history of the Mafia indicate how one of the most powerful criminal groups in America today has sprung from groups organized to protect themselves against encroachment of other ethnic and business groups that extorted and blackmailed the new immigrants to this country.

THE EVOLUTION OF THE CRIMINAL CONFEDERATIONS

In the past, law enforcement agencies were able to recognize participants in the so-called rackets. Because those participants identified with socially unacceptable behavior, by choice, they were alienated from the mainstream of American society. Gradually, the social acceptability of such activities as bootlegging, bookmaking, and legalized gambling has brought about a new attitude toward the racketeers and has made them a part of community life.

Social acceptability of quasi-legal activities and the desire to expand the economic base of the organization have brought the confederations into legitimate enterprises. The dispersion of the criminal element into legitimate enterprises has created covert confederations so powerful that no law enforcement agency can cope with them.

Nonconfrontation Policies of Organized Criminal Groups

Organized crime has the unique distinction of being unlike any other criminal activity. There is no question of impulse or insanity, nor of ignorance of law or negligence. In organized enterprises each activity is planned and carefully prepared to avoid direct confrontation with law enforcement. Because of this nonconfrontation policy, the public is not reminded of the millions of dollars that change hands as a part of illegal activities. Confederations would like the public to believe that activities such as prostitution or bookmaking are nothing more than the isolated deviate behavior of an individual. Thus, the conditions emanating from organized criminal activity do not bring pressure to bear on either the police or the public.

No one actually knows the extent of crime that results from these illegal activities. There is no barometer to measure the corruption, legal inconsistencies, and political deceptions that result from the covert activities of organized criminal action.

The history of organized crime in the United States is of importance only to show the interrelationships and the evolution of the families. It is more important to show contemporary problems of society.[6] These studies illustrate why law enforcement officers cannot "just go out and put the hoodlums in jail." The complexity of the organizations dictates a more comprehensive view.

At the mention of organized crime, people immediately say "the Mafia" or "La Cosa Nostra." This is, of course, the most notorious and probably the most powerful syndicate in America. There are, however, thousands of smaller independently organized groups. Until they become a threat to the "big group," they are permitted to exist and continue to grow. For example,

---

[6]The reader is referred to updated references in popular magazines—for example: "Tieri, the Most Powerful Mafia Chieftain," *New York Magazine,* August 21, 1978; "The Mob's Plot to 'Buy' California," *Reader's Digest,* December 1979; and a series by James Cook, "The Invisible Enterprise," *Forbes,* September 29–November 24, 1980.

this is illustrated by the conduct of organized groups in Southern California in the early 1950s. In that era Mickey Cohen became powerful enough to challenge the group headed by Jack Dragna to see who would control the lucrative vice activities in Los Angeles and Orange County and other areas of the Southwestern United States. After slugging it out with no less than 14 gangland killings, many beatings, and much publicity, both groups retreated. After the publicity, police harassment, and finally federal prosecutions, the gangs called a truce, with Dragna retaining the more powerful hand. Today there appears to be a workable coexistence with a live-and-let-live attitude as both factions quietly rebuild and expand.

Across America "bigness" has become a virtue. Giant cities enlarged from villages of three decades ago dot the landscape. Small businesses have mushroomed into giants or have been absorbed in corporate mergers with complex ownership structures. Into these industries has seeped the money from illegal drug transactions, prostitution, and gambling.

With the investments have come ownership, partnerships, or controlling shareholders who dictate policy for the giant companies. To the companies have come friends, relatives, and gangster partners who seek profitable respectability. They do this without having to relinquish control of lucrative illegal enterprises. Trusted old friends from bygone days become fixtures in the new legitimate environment. By careful planning, company representatives then move into politics, labor unions, or other community service organizations. Thus, the net is woven. Lines of communication from every community endeavor are established. The organization and infiltration process has been completed. New and advanced techniques of modern management make it function.

As with any commercial organization, groups involved in criminal activities must find a product of profit. The organization, which in the past was engaged solely in illegal enterprises, now finds that much money can be made in legitimate businesses. However, there can be no inference that an organized group, which has moved into a legal enterprise, will forsake the riches of the illegal rackets. It is merely expanding its spheres of operation to include legitimate business enterprises.

In Fred J. Cook's *Mafia* a complete history of the origin of organized crime is shown.[7] His study supports the findings of several special Senate subcommittee investigations regarding the existence of a Mafia.

These hearings concluded that there is an organized criminal syndicate known as the Mafia (Cosa Nostra) operating throughout the United States and foreign countries. This group has its roots in the Sicilian Mafia. Its revenue is from gambling, prostitution, and almost all other forms of legal and illegal enterprises. The power of the organization emanates from the ruthless enforcement of its edicts, violent vengeance, and intense loyalty of its criminal soldiers.

---

[7]In Fred J. Cook, *Mafia* (New York: Fawcett, 1973), the documented research on the Mafia has been brought together in one source reference.

The Mafia is a semiformal organization. It is ruled by unwritten codes, but its activities are cloaked in a covert organizational structure. It apparently has no allegiance to any legally constituted government, but places the family as the center of allegiance. The following citation shows how the loyalty to the family grew and how the early operation of the Mafia evolved in the United States. While the legend is historically accurate, it has been questioned.

> The Mafia had its origin in Palermo, Italy, in 1282 as a political and patriotic organization devoted to freeing Sicily from foreign domination, and to accomplish this purpose it decreed that persons of French descent must be killed.
>
> Its motto was "Morte alla Francia Italia anela." (Death to the French is Italy's cry.) The initial letters of the motto, MAFIA, were used as a secret password for purposes of identification, and it's from this password that the organization derived its name.
>
> In the early 15th century the Mafia branched out in criminal activities. Intimidation and murder were adopted as weapons. It was an organization of outlaws dedicated to the complete defiance of the law.
>
> After 1860, the organization expanded enormously in Sicily with smuggling, cattle rustling, and extortion as the principal sources of revenue. Administration of justice was openly defied in ineffective drives, but continued pressures against the Mafia caused many members to migrate to the United States. As early as 1860, large numbers of escaped Italian criminals settled in New Orleans....
>
> There is no reliable data on the extent of the operation of the Mafia and its international ramifications. The leaders are in control of the most lucrative rackets. The leadership in the United States is in a group of board of directors. It has infiltrated political offices and some law enforcement agencies, the extent of such infiltration not being known. Its members are not necessarily of Sicilian descent, but include others of Italian extraction.[8]

Family ties created by specialization are no longer feasible in all important posts of the organization. The placing of specialists from outside the family over long-time blood brothers has made it increasingly difficult to maintain discipline and authority, as evidenced in the ability of enforcement agencies to make inroads into the organization. The organizations as identified by the many researchers probably derive their power from an organization structure similar to the one shown in Figure 2–2.

Elements and Purpose of the Confederation

Confederated criminal activities extend into many areas other than vice-type activities.[9] A confederation implies an organization conducting activities under a coordinated plan of action. By setting aside melodramatic adjectives

[8]John Drzazga, *Wheels of Fortune* (Springfield, Ill.: Charles C. Thomas, 1963), pp. 16–17. Later information has the board consisting of twelve members.

[9]Office of the Counsel to the Governor, *Combating Organized Crime* (Albany, New York, 1966), pp. 18–22. The James Fratiano investigations of 1979–80 showed the diverse interests of organized crime.

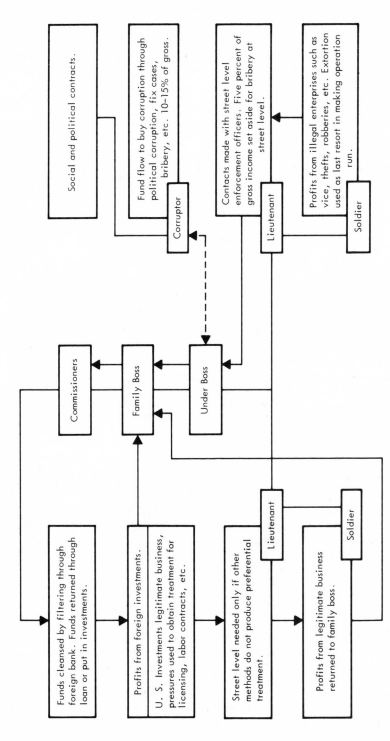

Figure 2-2 Source of power for organized crime members.

that are frequently used in the descriptions of "organized crime," we can identify some of the major common elements and activities of the so-called syndicate groups.

There is an unlawful conspiracy between two or more persons.

The agreement may be actual or implied.

There is a semipermanency in its form much like the modern corporation.

The organizational structures are in a continuous fluid transition to compensate for political and criminal misfortunes of its members.

The regional organizations are heteronomous; thus, the fear, corruption, totalitarian influences, and the insulation of leadership have a common pattern throughout the United States and even in many other parts of the world.

The type of organizational control varies with the charismatic personalities of individual leaders. Control can be authoritarian or a loose-knit laissez faire structure. Either may be equally effective.

Activities may frequently be contrary to good public policy, yet they may not constitute a crime. An example is the donation of funds to a political campaign by a criminal confederation.

Failure to understand the basis or organization in the criminal confederation causes many persons to doubt its existence. The documentation in Cook's *Mafia* establishes a model for the New York area families that could be related to any area in the nation. The patterns of organized crime are difficult to distinguish because there are few overt individual criminal activities that can be traced to an organization; consequently, how the groups can be controlled cannot be precisely nor simply stated, nor can the control attempts presently being made be accurately or objectively evaluated.

Purpose of the Organization

Organized criminal groups are simply business organizations operating under many different management structures and dealing in illegal products. A requisite of the organization has been the establishment of illegal enterprises to produce large profits, then convert those profits into channels of influence and legitimate enterprises.

How an organized group generates illegal profits is generally known to the chief of police but he is unable to maintain a sustained enforcement effort against the confederation. Because of the organization's policy of "insulating" the higher-ups in the organization, it is unlikely a local agency will prosecute more than street agents at the lowest echelon in the criminal hierarchy. The organized groups are structured to accommodate the loss of a large number of street agents because of arrests and intergang violence. Thus, organization is vital to the survival of these confederated groups. The confederations are active in all phases of American life; they have a grip on real estate involving hundreds of millions of dollars; control of numerous

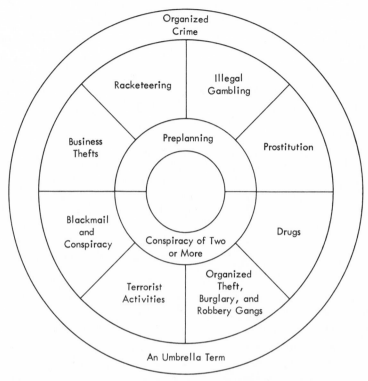

Figure 2–3 DEFINING THE SCOPE OF ORGANIZED CRIME.

banks, loan firms, and financial institutions; control of prostitution, gambling, narcotics, and other vice activities. As early as 1964, for example, *U.S. News and World Report* stated that the Mafia was deeply involved in the garment industry. The U.S. Senate's Permanent Subcommittee on Investigation listed two hundred trades or types of business with which organized crime has become involved.[10] And the degree of involvement is still being expanded at a rapid rate.

Organized crime is somewhat synonymous with principal types of underworld criminal activity. One expert explained organized crime in the way shown in Figure 2–3.[11]

The presence of organized elements in a city may be influenced by

[10]"How Criminals Solve Their Investment Problems," *U.S. News and World Report,* March 30, 1964, pp. 74–76. In a 1979 article, it was alleged that at least 200 companies are owned or controlled by organized crime in California.

[11]National Conference on Organized Crime, *A National Strategy for the 1980s,* University of Southern California, November 8–9, 1979.

geographical location, ethnic group population, historical heritages, and many other physical, cultural, and social traits.

The location of a city such as a seaport, a transportation and convention center, or a boomtown will be a natural to attract organized elements. Frequently these settings create the "open city" atmosphere with liberal attitudes toward organized crime enforcement. Pressures from business favor laxness in law enforcement. Businesspeople believe that overlooking certain violations will enhance the attractiveness of the city. Conversely, however, the closed city may be a greater attraction to the syndicates. For example, the so-called dry areas, with reference to liquor availability, have always been spawning grounds for organized criminal activity and governmental corruption.

Whether civic leaders adopt an open or closed city attitude does not deter the influences of the syndicates. It is the highly industrialized, the tourist spas, and the prosperous cities that attract commercialized crime, which then infiltrates into local legitimate businesses. Once these inroads are made, pressures from illegal business and informal pressure groups exert just enough influence to see that their vested interests are allowed to operate.

Ethnic group composition of a city tends to promote the growth of organized crime. These groups have different values, cultural mores, and ethics, and as such do not readily adapt to white middle-class standards. These ethnic groups, frequently of lower economic status, find hope in promises of a big lottery win or a long-shot win with the street corner bookie. Perhaps, because of intense social frustration, these groups find emotional outlets in gambling and prostitution. Through necessity they patronize the loan shark, and because of ignorance they become victims of organized frauds and swindles.

Historically, gambling has been the financial foundation of organized crime. Funds gained from gambling have been used to underwrite all the other types of criminal activities, such as the financing of drug purchases and the purchase of protection from corrupt officials. While gambling may still be a big source of organized crime income, the 1970s brought a transition to drugs as the major source of revenue. In a special edition of the *Arizona Republic*, July 22, 1979, it was estimated that 450,000 drug addicts in the United States spend more than $22 million per day for heroin. According to the article, most of the people involved in drug sales and distribution are members of national confederations in Mexico and South America.[12]

Since 1967 the government, through the strike force concept, has endeavored to check the growth of the power of the national confederations. By bringing the combined expertise of the federal government into strike force operating units, there has been a reasonably successful effort against the confederations in many major cities. Such operations have in the past ten

---

[12]In the Southwest there are the Banditos and the Dixie Mafia. In California, most of the ethnic gangs have no known ties to the national confederations.

years caused substantial changes in the operation of the five New York families. The five families, which are estimated to number about 2500, have been forced to tighten security in internal operations, to make business connections more covert, and to contend with rebellion among the ranks of the young.

There appears to be little question of the existence of organized crime. How it will be ferreted out and prosecuted remains the prime problem.

SUMMARY

The existence of organized crime does not indicate massive societal dishonesty. A more logical reason for its pervasiveness is because citizens are not actually aware that organized crime as such exists. Because of the covert nature of organized crime, there is a need for exposés as a method of enforcement. The organizational structure of the present families derives from Mafia history. The elements of the national confederation have a loose formal organizational structure. Because the organization's business moves through the informal or family-based structure, organization members are practically impossible to arrest and prosecute successfully. Factors that are present in a community with a high degree of infiltration by organized crime have been shown. These factors are so subtle, however, that most citizens accept and tolerate acts such as lottery, bookmaking, and others under the mistaken belief that they are individual violations.

QUESTIONS FOR DISCUSSION

1. Identify possible sources of organized crime related to government functions. Can it be eliminated?
2. Discuss the "nonconfrontation" policies of major organized criminal confederation.
3. Why is "confederation" a more descriptive term than "syndicate"?
4. In the history of the Mafia, how have family ties been instrumental in the evolution of the organized crime structure?
5. Draw a sociogram on the blackboard and indicate how communications move through the entire class. Note that certain members can be insulated from the feedback by having spokesmen.
6. Identify the so-called business activities indulged in by organized crime.
7. What are the legitimate enterprises that are subject to pressure from organized elements? How are the pressures exerted?
8. With reference to organized crime, does a "closed city" necessarily indicate a "clean city"?
9. Explain how minority neighborhoods affect syndicate operations.

10. Why are local efforts at enforcing organized criminal activities basically ineffective?
11. Show the difference between traditional and organized crime.

	Traditional	**Organized**
Structure		
Law		
Enforcement policies		
Enforcement procedures		
Personality of criminal		
Other differences		

3

POLITICAL INFLUENCES IN ORGANIZED CRIME ENFORCEMENT

LEARNING OUTCOMES

1. Become aware of the risks and benefits of a democratic society with reference to organized crime suppression.
2. Be able to understand the dynamics of political campaign financing, and how favors are paid off by the political candidate.
3. Understand why citizens or police cannot go out and eradicate organized crime because of political influence.
4. Become aware of political pressure groups and how these groups influence the passage of laws.
5. Recognize that the party in power sets the enforcement policy of the enforcement units in government.

Our democratic republic is viewed as the utopia of political organization. The preservation of an organization that provides for individual liberty has been the basis for its strength. What happens to that system when organized criminal elements move in? In recent years it has been possible in some instances for organized elements to allocate sufficient financial resources and exert enough influence at the local level to dictate who will or will not be elected. At the state level, organized criminals subvert the processes of government sufficiently to kill or enact a legislative bill. At the national level organized criminal lobbies exert an untold amount of political pressure on our lawmaking bodies.

Political contacts with organized crime flow from the apex of the criminal hierarchy. The political representatives of the crime confederations, however, are not linked to the operating processes of the criminal conspiracy. Those in politics who deal with representatives of criminal combines do so in complete freedom from the stigma of known hoodlum association and may be totally unaware of confederation connections.

There is a good deal of guesswork involved in identifying the political links that bind elements of the legitimate society to organized crime; some links exist in almost every phase of social and business interaction. The stronger ties, however, come through the political and legal systems. It is natural for the attorney, who must represent a criminal client, to also become that client's advisor. While it is easy to be hypercritical of certain legal practices, it must be remembered that allegations of an attorney's criminal links come to the investigators in bits and pieces. Conclusions derived from these bits of information lead to certain unsubstantiated assumptions regarding political and criminal ties. Therefore, many criminal-attorney relationships may border on unethical rather than illegal collusion.[1]

How to identify patterns and trends indicating political corruption is shown in Figure 3-1. The cases cited in this chapter are from intelligence files and other documented events. The problems of political influence are divided into three major categories: (1) politics and the complex factors in organized crime control, (2) the evolution of the political leader, and (3) political influence by the party in power.

POLITICS AND THE COMPLEX FACTORS IN ORGANIZED CRIME CONTROL

The political influence in the growth of organized crime should not be underestimated. There should be new legal ways or means developed to minimize the deleterious effects of political corruption both in law enforcement and with the political decision makers. What law enforcement does is going to be ineffective unless there is the honest cooperation from all political leaders of a community. For example, in the early 1960s there was a concerted effort to clean up Youngstown, Ohio. Federal agents moved in and gambling closed down. Within a short period of time the federal agents left, and the gambling activity resumed.

This story could be played out in nearly every major city in the country. In the report by the Chamber of Commerce, the writers acknowledged that it is the local groups who must supply the impetus for crime control.[2] This the cities did not have and, in spite of the efforts by a few individuals, the wide support necessary to eliminate organized crime could not be identified and activated.

Because there are few valid statistics about organized crime, the political leaders of a community can dictate the degree of enforcement merely by the allocation of money and manpower for the investigations of organized crime.

---

[1]The ties between the legal and political corruptors were clearly established in the 1972–73 Watergate conspiracies.

[2]Chamber of Commerce of the United States, *Marshaling Citizen Power Against Crime*, p. 77.

Participants	How Obligations Are Incurred	How Debts Are Paid
Elected Officials (Federal)	Support in political campaigns Trips, vacations on company expense accounts, cash through foundations, and cash bribes through lobbyists, etc.	Political appointments Contracts Personal favors Paroles, pardons
Appointed staff	Campaign workers Liaison with revenue sources Cash payoffs	Hired as staff worker Retains contact with revenue sources Conducts business for elected officials
The elected official	*State* Campaign contributions Trips on private accounts Cash through lobbyists Tips on investments, i.e., public franchises and licensees	Contracts Allocations of franchises Granting licenses such as liquor Contracts for local service—garbage, ambulance, towing, etc. Abstain from enforcing certain type of laws
	Local Campaign contributions Promise to self-interest groups—gamblers, etc. Money to citizens' committees during preelection campaign Cash payoffs through lobbyists	

Figure 3–1 A typology of organized crime payoffs.

Participants	How Obligations Are Incurred	How Debts Are Paid
The judge	*All Levels* Campaign contributions Cash payoffs	Favorable decisions Probation, parole, and select court assignment
The lawyer	Client contacts and referrals Campaign workers Liaison with business and criminal clientele Cash payoffs (fees)	Appointments to positions to keep contacts with proper clients Consultants on contracts, crime commissions, etc.
The police	*All Levels* Political patronage Campaign contributions to elected offices Budget manipulation Cash payoffs	Select enforcement methods Preferential treatment in degree of enforcement Lack of enforcement

Figure 3–1   continued

How corruption infiltrates the social structure is shown in this program model.[3]

The contrast between honest administration and corrupt practices is, of course, not exclusively directed to the elected politician. The citizen who overcharges customers, cheats on repair bills, and misrepresents a product is as guilty as the criminals who are being indicted. The citizen, in cases where fraud and collusion are "a way of doing business," may not class himself as a member of the criminal confederation, but he is equally effective in subverting good government.

Once the life pattern of "dealing under the table" is established, it is only a very short distance to the total seduction of honest government. Many situations that put political figures in compromising situations are not created with criminal or even malicious intent. The political compromises are a part of the system that must be changed if political honesty is to become a reality. These situations are cited as examples:

Ever since Lincoln Steffens charged in *The Shame of Our Cities* that "the

[3]Theodore R. Lyman, Thomas W. Fletcher, and John A. Gardiner, *Prevention, Detection, and Correction of Corruption in Local Government* (Washington, D.C.: U.S. Government Printing Office, November 1978).

spirit of graft and lawlessness is the American spirit" we have almost tacitly accepted the role of corruption in the politics of the American city.[4]

The "third legislature" (lobbyists) in a state may exert enough power to keep out state regulation of certain rates. Whether state-regulated rates are desirable is questionable, since many states have decided it necessary to protect consumer interests. The very fact that this type of influence may be exerted over a political body is cause for concern. The second example where poor political policy subverts the processes of justice is the provision that allows a legislator to be retained as an attorney for a criminal client. This means the case will be continued until the expiration of the current legislative session. The abuse of this provision is obvious when a legislator allows himself to be identified with a case on a retainer basis even though the legislator knows he will not be a part of the defense for the client.

These are only examples of what can happen. However, similar abuses are not unusual. In time of "pressing manpower needs" most cities accept the philosophy that the less heard about the problem of organized crime, the less of a problem it will be. This is exactly what the confederations desire and strive for.

The institution of politics as revealed through the many exposés of yesteryear may be summarized in the lessons learned in Ohio, New Jersey, and dozens of other localities where corruption is being exposed. From these investigations and others, there is little question that the confederation can control any given area in which it desires to exercise influence.

The corruption of American politics is summarized in this statement:

> In the estimation of the [Pennsylvania] Crime Commission, the most harmful effect of the crime syndicates is what they do to government. To ensure the smooth and continuous operation of their rackets, they finance political campaigns or bribe and corrupt political leaders and criminal justice personnel—either the policeman, prosecution, court clerk or judge depending on the type of protection desired and also on who is the weakest link in the criminal justice chain.[5]

The big fixes are replaced by thousands of "little fixes." For example, during 1977 these two stories appeared in local news sources.[6] One reported the Orange County California grand jury continued its investigation into reported links between a supervisor and a man with county contracts to salvage scrap from county refuse dumps. Before sealed bids were opened, the

---

[4]Francis A.J. Ianni and Elizabeth Reuss Ianni, "Organized Crime: A Social and Economic Perspective," paper prepared for The Academy of Criminal Justice Sciences, March 1980. See also Fletcher, and Gardiner, *Prevention,* p. 1. A survey of 250 newspapers from 1970 to 1976 showed 372 incidents of corruption in 103 cities.

[5]Pennsylvania Crime Commission, *Report on Organized Crime,* Scranton, July 7, 1970, p. 2.

[6]Los Angeles *Times,* March 22, 1977. The second example was also carried in the *Times.*

contractor had contributed $2500 to the supervisor's campaign. Two days after the supervisor was elected, the contractor contributed another $2500 to the campaign fund. In another story, a businessman and political fund raiser was indicted on charges of bilking various companies of $1.5 million through the operation of a bogus pension fund program. Fifty thousand of these dollars were then used to finance the campaign of another Orange County supervisor. What must the citizen think when graft such as this is found in the power structure?

As the complexity of government increases, so do the policy-making processes. As the number of governmental processes increase, the pressures of special interest groups prevail and the merry-go-round of politics opens a way to lay a firm foundation for unethical and illegal activities. The first goal of a crime commission must be to lessen the influence of organized crime where it affects the agencies of criminal justice.[7]

THE EVOLUTION OF THE POLITICAL LEADER

In the interaction of politics a political leader will rise partly because of a charismatic personality and partly because of an ability to raise money. Typically, this latter activity is done through legitimate contributions. Money from illegal sources, however, has a way of creeping in.

Historically, political manipulation by organized confederations is not new. Some criminal figures were made powerful by support from organized conspiracies, and many were famous for riding the crest of political fortunes. The important point is that money from the confederations seldom backs a loser. In part, this is due to clever planning. Several public relations firms have announced that with a "proper candidate" and an "adequate" amount of campaign money, they will produce a winner, and they have.

American states and cities are often called political museums. Within the museums are the tribal customs that stem from a membership of private interest groups, social organizations, and precinct-level political parties. Organized crime interests create inroads into each of these organizations. Thus, corrupt influences are inevitable.

Our political system creates "bedfellows of organized criminals" engaged in many types of crimes. Many people well placed in business and politics deny that such collusion exists. Their denial must be respected because not all business or political figures are a part of the conspiracy, nor even a majority of them. Only a few select areas, assignments, and persons are needed to tip the balance of power at the local, state, or federal level. The very fact that this balance of power exists should create a desire to examine the techniques used by political manipulators.

[7]Pennsylvania Crime Commission, *Report on Organized Crime*, p. 2.

Means of political control are pointed out by Tyler, who shows the workings of the organized gangs:

> Organized crime deprives many individuals of their inalienable rights, not by turning the overwhelming power of the state against the citizen, but by exercising the power of private government against the nonconformist. Strikers lose their right to picket; businessmen lose their right to buy, manufacture and sell as they please and are forced to accept unwanted junior or senior partners; citizens lose the right to testify and others are forced to bear false witness. Even the right to honest and free election is repeatedly jeopardized.[8]

Next to having a well-informed public that can scrutinize the total election operation, it is important to have a branch of the local political clubs analyze "the man" and "his money." Frequently, well-meaning political groups at the local level are victims of too much syndicate money being put on a candidate they do not know or cannot support from available funds. This concept is illustrated in Figure 3–1.

Frequently there will be a candidate who is "ready made" for the party. He will come to the party trained in showmanship and possessing his own campaign funds. Through the "campaign money," "friends" are made in local businesses. Many of the "friends" have a vested interest in the candidate. An honest candidate operating through campaign managers may not have recognized the encumbrances to donors. For example, in a recent California election a major candidate's representative was openly entertained and given financial support by a known West Coast mobster leader. This social connection could have far-reaching consequence with respect to power centers, political appointees, and sources of campaign expenditures.

This type of activity may appear petty and, when viewed as an individual donation to the political party, insignificant. However, when a syndicate leader and hundreds of wealthy friends donate to their "favorite candidate," the sum can be staggering. The intelligence files covering this type of activity are impressive.

The "ward heeler," or, more politely "field office representative," has an increased need for massive amounts of money for campaign funds, thus putting the power structure directly into the hands of the corruptible. It is a matter of survival for the local politicians to follow the person with the money. To have politically appointed department heads, judges, and people in lesser positions who are well connected with money, from whatever source, may become necessary.

---

[8]Gus Tyler, "An Interdisciplinary Attack on Organized Crime," *The Annals*, 347 (May 1963), 109. The reader is referred to this and other publications by Tyler for a comprehensive documentation of political influence.

Yes, Race Track Gambling will bring "Tourists" to Texas...

| 564·7432 | 348·3210 | 215·4213 |

Unless you are a friend or relative of one of the fellows above...

Vote Against Race Track Gambling and Organized Crime in May 4 Primary.

a·c·t THE ANTI-CRIME COUNCIL OF TEXAS
SUITE 1300 • 511 N. AKARD • DALLAS, TEXAS 75201 • AC 214 RI 2-9487
ABNER McCALL • WILL WILSON, Chairmen

Figure 3–2   The citizen and the struggle against organized crime.

Organized Crime Funds Eliminate Competition

Tyler alleges that corruption can almost be assumed.[9] There seems to be no reason to disagree. Strangely enough, not all money spent by the mob is spent to create corruption. Some years ago a vested gambling interest in Nevada was reported to have spent several million dollars in Mexico to dry up "illegal gambling" in Rosarita Beach. It took them two nights to wipe this operation out and close other operations that would keep customers from the tables in Las Vegas.

The same Nevada gambling interest finds it expedient to keep anti-gambling laws rigidly enforced in surrounding states. Whenever there is illegal activity that tends to draw action away from the tables of Nevada, quick work by local police vice squads eliminates the threat. It is no accident that information on gambling games in the adjoining states is funneled into the police departments in an almost hour-by-hour account. The political policy makers cannot be criticized for rigidly enforcing the laws. For example, Figure 3–2 might imply that no organized crime exists within the state;[10]

[9]Tyler, *The Annals*, n.n.
[10]*The Fort Worth Telegram.*

because there is no legalized horse racing in the state, there is no organized crime activity. This type of strict enforcement is no reflection on the agencies enforcing the laws, because only a select number of "political ambassadors" benefit financially from this type of activity. The fact that this control exists gives the political manipulators an "in" for any other type of pressure they desire to exert.

POLITICAL INFLUENCES BY THE PARTY IN POWER

The history of political exposés indicates that the party in power feels it is entitled to certain benefits.[11] The political pressures are felt even in the lowest echelons of law enforcement. Whether the selection system of a department is political or whether it is "merit" makes little difference. There has been no selection system devised that can eliminate politics from personnel policies.[12]

Political pressures may be illustrated in a different way. In a recent state election where power shifted from one party to another, a political appointee who handles more money than all but two other persons in the state government was retained by the incoming party. This appointment came after a grand jury investigation strongly suggested the appointee had solid connections with organized criminal elements who were doing legitimate business with the state.

How do the organized gangs manage to operate so covertly? The public assumes there must be no criminal activity of an organized nature because they do not hear about it. Nothing could be further from the truth. Organized crime flourishes in peace and calm. With few exceptions, most major cities have been fairly free of open warfare in recent years. There were nearly eight years of peace between the Gallo-Profaci feud and the Colombo shooting of 1971. There have been more than 20 years of gangland peace in Los Angeles. Other cities have had exposés that resulted in the prosecution of members from small theft and burglary gangs of semiprofessionals. Most of the major confederations, however, have learned to live in harmony. Areas of dispute are now settled by arbitration. Merely because a city does not hear of widespread organized criminal activity does not mean crime is not present. The corrupt politician cannot afford to be without these violators. The honest politician who is either uninformed or lacks the courage to challenge them must suffer in silence.

The professional politician should begin to look to organized crime as a

[11]This attitude was evidenced in the ABSCAM investigations and in recent national elections where known organized crime figures were actively engaged in overt election activities.

[12]John A. Gardiner and David J. Olson, "Wincanton: The Politics of Corruption," *Task Force Report, Organized Crime* (Washington, D.C.: U.S. Government Printing Office, 1967), pp. 62–64.

real problem in our society. He should realize organized elements are creating a subculture that is out of step with the rest of society. For example, in the ghettos of American cities, ineffective vice control is one of law enforcement's most critical problems. In a minority neighborhood vice-type crimes serve as a catalyst for political unrest. No other crimes cause so much conflict, bitterness, and lack of confidence between police and the minority community as do these violations. The basic problem in the ghetto is not more police but a better system of operation so the police can take impartial and consistent action on law violations. When a "policy runner" or a "bookie" roams the same neighborhood for years without an arrest, the citizens can rightfully assume corruption. When prostitutes and narcotic users stand on the same corner year after year, the honest minority will lose confidence in any type of enforcement activity. There is not much incentive for this social group to be law-abiding.

SUMMARY

Organized crime is not simply the result of lax or corrupt police practices. These practices may contribute to the growth of organized crime, but the unseen manipulations in the political and legal arenas share a major responsibility. Several sociologists have made statements implying organized crime could not exist without the connivance of law enforcement agencies. To be more precise, organized crime cannot exist without the connivance of the participating public, and corrupt politics at all levels of government. No government agency can do more than attempt to control the most obvious forms of crime. The very complexity of the organized criminal organizations indicates they operate in many fairly large cities without the actual operations being known to the police. This may be due to a lack of police expertise, a lack of money and manpower to sustain investigations, or a lack of interest by political officials.

The nature of the democratic process offers a breeding ground for all types of organized crime. The fine line between individual freedom and social chaos is of prime concern in the area of organized crime. For a person to understand why organized crime cannot be easily controlled, the link to political influences must be shown. Through the illustrations of political influence one must be made aware of the tenacious grip that corrupt politics has upon the entire community. Through a brief insight into some of the more common techniques of corruption, a person will be more aware of the magnitude of criminal organizations.

Closely related to the political governing element is the legal system. An understanding of the legal system's role in organized crime control is important for the well-informed citizen and enforcement agency representative.

QUESTIONS FOR DISCUSSION

1. Why do the so-called democratic processes encourage the growth of organized criminal influence?

2. How does the "use of cash" assist the confederation's influence in the community?

3. Are people involved in supporting the goals of organized criminals without being aware of it?

4. Can methods be devised to shield local political parties from the criminal-influence peddler?

5. How do the appointive processes in our system of government tend to shield criminal inroads into the system of justice?

6. May the rigid control of vice assume a form of corruption?

7. What are the ramifications of organized crimes in the city ghettos?

8. Is the "closed town" necessarily the "clean town"?

9. What do the police statistics indicate in describing the number of organized crimes in a community?

10. Discuss the political ramifications of such issues as statewide utility regulation and local franchises such as those for taxi, bus, and other business enterprises.

4

ROLE OF THE LEGAL SYSTEM IN ORGANIZED CRIME CONTROL

LEARNING OUTCOMES

1. Understand the importance of the legal (judicial) system in organized crime control.
2. Recognize how the activities of attorneys who defend organized crime figures tend to be insulated.
3. Gain knowledge about the failure to discipline members of the legal system whose activities are illegal or unethical.
4. Recognize how inconsistency in law creates natural loopholes for organized crime.
5. Gain an overview of the functions of crime commissions and other investigative agencies emanating from the legal system.

Without diligent development and maintenance of an honest legal system, no efforts by citizens or enforcement agencies will be effective against most types of organized crime.[1] The legal system personnel (the defense lawyer, the prosecutor, and the judge) are the keystones to the control of organized crime. There are a number of important areas over which the legal system exercises almost exclusive domain. The following areas are selected as being representative: (1) the defense lawyer and the criminal client, (2) providing adequate law for enforcement, and (3) legal agents and the governmental crime commission.

THE DEFENSE LAWYER AND THE CRIMINAL CLIENT

The moral and legal question as to where legal advice stops and criminal conspiracy begins is critical to the control of organized crime. Without the collusion, and frequently outright conspiracy, on the part of a lawyer,

[1]The authors are unable to locate a definitive research study which has identified the defense attorney as being a major problem in organized crime enforcement.

organized crime would wither away by sheer pressure. The involvement of a defense counsel in an organized crime operation raises the following interesting theoretical social questions:

1. Who are the groups that support organized crime legislation? Does this legislation support vested interest groups, or social norms established by the majority of society?
2. Is so-called white collar crime, so closely allied with organized crime operations, really a crime or merely nonconformity with accepted business practices?
3. Are laws governing organized crime mere social conventions and thus subject to case by case interpretation in courts of law before acts can be adjudged crimes?

When the issue of defense counsel involvement rises above the pragmatic level it becomes easier to understand why a lawyer acting beyond his or her "legal charge" might be willing to lend active and constructive support to many organized criminal activities.

For example, in 32 states legal or enabling legislation has been passed that makes the state overseer of the gambling enterprises in that state. Thus, it is not difficult to defend a man against felony bookmaking charges in three-fourths of the states where it is illegal.

It is easy to see how a lawyer becomes involved with an organization dealing in criminal enterprises. Schwartz illustrated this in his study of lawyer involvement in organized crime.[2] He indicated that the lawyer, merely by agreeing in advance to represent or counsel members of a confederation at a criminal trial, would raise questions of proper involvement. Until there is some reconciliation of this question, law enforcement has very little opportunity to exert effective control over organized crime.

The Syndicate Attorney

There are lawyers who are well known for their defense of persons deeply involved in organized crime. They are not, however, exclusive representatives of the organized element. They will also represent many local individual violators as a front for their major clients. A close scrutiny of their clientele could show the major portion of their income is derived from the confederations. While those individuals who are clients are entitled to legal counsel, the public should be aware that there are lawyers who serve on retainer for the confederated groups.

A person, merely because he or she is a lawyer, has no legal right to compound a crime. If an attorney becomes an integral part of the planning and development of legal subterfuges for organized criminal activities, then it

---

[2]Murray L. Schwartz, "The Lawyer's Professional Responsibility and Interstate Organized Crime," *Notre Dame Lawyer*, 38, 6 (1963), 711–26.

is time to reappraise the delicate distinction between what is unethical and what is illegal. The ethical relationship of lawyer and client is a matter that should be rigidly enforced by punitive sanctions if necessary. The American Bar Association and the different state associations have the authority to take such action. As a matter of practice, such action is rarely taken, and it is even more unusual to find very many actual sanctions. While there is no attempt to vilify the good job done by most members of the legal profession, when an attorney assumes the role of "middleman and fixer," the problem of ethical standards exists.

Internal Discipline for the Legal System

There is a double standard that our society accepts in apprehending criminals. If the thief is without the protective cloak of professional societies, he or she becomes a subject of prompt police action and prosecution. If the person belongs to certain state and national associations, he or she has a strong cushion of judicial protection. For example, in California the state constitution does not permit the Commission on Judicial Qualifications to make public the names of the judges who quit or are dismissed for illegal or unethical conduct. There is no such protection for the criminal, for police officers who are dishonest, and for many others who do belong to the cloistered organizations. Although it is recognized that the legal system (lawyers and judges) may require some protection from the public, there is certainly no reason for letting their own peers decide what illegal or immoral acts the public should know about. Until such practices are ended, there is little hope for expecting effective cooperation from organizations that are outside the coveted protection of the professional associations. Organized criminal confederations have built-in security for their representatives in the legal system.

A crucial area for maintaining internal discipline within the legal system is the division of function and authority between law enforcement and prosecution. The Cornell Institute on Organized Crime published a comprehensive report on these units and their relationships and came to the conclusion there is no common pattern of operation between these critical units.[3] The legal (judicial) system, it appears, has tended to extend its jurisdiction into the functional areas of organized criminal investigation. The "task forces" have tended to be dominated by the prosecutor's office, the determination of who to investigate and the mode of investigation being more frequently made by this arm of the legal system.

---

[3]G. Robert Blakely, Ronald Goldstock, and Charles H. Rogovin, *Rackets Bureaus: Investigation and Prosecution of Organized Crime* (Washington, D.C.: U.S. Government Printing Office, March 1978). Also Robert M. Morgenthau, "Police and Prosecutors: A Professional Partnership," *FBI Law Enforcement Bulletin,* March 1981, pp. 6–7.

[4]Ibid., pp. 4–5.

In outlining how each unit was organized, the Cornell Institute identified four functional patterns of operation.

These patterns of operations are:

(1) The functional unity between a rackets unit, (2) interaction with police departments within its jurisdiction, (3) relations with other prospective agencies will be as varied as the personalities and (4) the quality of the interactions and relations will vary with the experience of the unit's director.[4]

The precise organization is not important. The failure to have checks and balances between the executive and the judicial branches of government will result in a long-term, self-defeating effort to control organized crime.

PROVIDING ADEQUATE LAWS FOR ENFORCEMENT

No other segment of society has more responsibility than the legal system for the control of organized crime. No segment, unless it is law enforcement, has been more thwarted in its performance. The legal system is responsible for initiating and conducting research and recommendations for the legislative and administrative branches of government. Semiprivate legal organizations, such as the State Bar Associations and American Bar Association should be staffed with personnel of allied disciplines (sociologists, psychologists, and criminologists) to formulate realistic and workable laws. The fact that a law is technically sound from a mechanistic point of view does not mean that it serves the public. Many of the laws that support vice and other organized crime are of this category. Many of these statutes are not realistic in an enlightened society. For example, within the environs of the city of Los Angeles, three different applications of the law prevail for the control of gambling:[5]

1. It is illegal to bet on a horse unless you wager the bet at a state-licensed track.
2. It is illegal to wager on any game of chance (except draw poker, which the legislature of the 1870s decided was a game of skill).
3. Draw poker may be played only if authorized by local ordinance.

In Texas the local option law for distributing over-the-bar alcohol is equally absurd. A person cannot attach a very strong feeling of wrongness to laws based on abstract whims. These inconsistencies of law create a multi-million-dollar morally acceptable racket in illegal betting activities, in racketeering, and in abuses of liquor laws. Realistic laws in these and other

[5]California Penal Code section 330 and Los Angeles Municipal Code.

organized crime areas would minimize the opportunity for corruption and profit for the confederations. Under the federal 1970 Organized Crime Control Act, realistic statutes have been designed. The states should bring their own laws into a consistent pattern with this law.

Consistency in the Law

The legal profession, while defending the need for more lawyers, is not expected to enact statutes that would not be liable to a legal challenge. But in legal practice changes should be sought for statutes and procedures that follow a doctrine of consistency. A doctrine of consistency is mandatory for any acceptable degree of legal control, but is rarely found. For example, in California and many other states it is a felony by statute to engage in bookmaking. Yet, statistics will bear out that bookmakers seldom go to prison. Even long-time recidivists who are punished with summary probation can, if arrested within the probationary period, have the case transferred to another court. Thus, the terms of the summary probation are nullified. The reason is simple: money and legal talent to see that the case gets to the right court. With this lack of consistency in conforming to the code, a few judges and lawyers have acted as effectively in perpetuating organized crime as has any of the syndicate bet takers.

It is interesting to note that a few attorneys who are mentioned in the 1950 Crime Commission Hearings in California and the Kefauver hearings are still the legal representatives of the same bookmakers who were being arrested from 1945 to 1950. This is no coincidence. The same allegations could be cited for New York or Illinois.

Because of the need for consistency, the application of law should not be a part of a "drive" or a "war on crime" by politically ambitious crusaders. This type of activity is likely to pose a threat to a normal legal protection of the accused. In crusaders there is a tendency to abuse immunity from prosecution provisions so that quick information is available at exactly the right time for news releases. This technique is regularly overworked when there is an overlapping of state and federal statutes under which the suspect may be tried.

One of the most maligned uses of the legal system by confederation criminals has been the use of the Fifth Amendment protection guarantee. Rufus King, a Washington, D.C. attorney, identified the problem this way:

The Fifth Amendment privilege of silence combines three disparate elements: (1) the privilege of the accused, formally charged with crime, to remain silent at his own trial; (2) the privilege of a suspect to be free of sanctions applied to make him confess and, (3) the privilege of unsuspected persons to conceal guilt known only to themselves. It is felt that the Fifth Amendment privilege should have been confined narrowly to the protec-

tion of persons accused of crime when they appear as defendants in their own trials; it has been intended to protect two other classes: persons merely suspected and under investigation, and unsuspected persons who have, in fact, some guilt to conceal. This extension has worked harmfully to limit the interrogator and to prevent the public's right to everyman's evidence from being carried out. The immunity device is suggested as a valid palliative for this situation, but no new enactment of immunity legislation should confer immunity automatically as some of the immunity provisions of the federal regulatory agencies do. Any law should exclude the offenses of contempt and perjury from the scope of their immunization, and, perhaps, all should require the concurrency of the Attorney General or of a federal judge before their provision could come into play.[6]

State vs. Local Laws

Local communities jealously guard the historical concept of local option. With communication and transportation systems drawing the communities of a state closer and closer together, the need for a "model of adequacy" appears to be more important than laws of doubtful legality in every "incorporated crossroads" of the state.

Technology in police service has made it desirable to have similar laws that extend across city and county lines. The state should give law enforcement an adequate system of laws to regulate those crimes that confront the people of the state. There are no situations, especially in the field of organized crime, that the state cannot adequately legislate for local protection. The state legislatures should preempt areas of vice law and other local ordinances that furnish organized criminals an opportunity to "beat the system."

LEGAL AGENTS AND THE GOVERNMENTAL CRIME COMMISSION

It is impossible to determine how extensive the corruption of the public and/or public officials by organized crime has been. We do know that there must be better identifying and reporting of corruption. There must be better ways for the public to communicate information about corruption to appropriate governmental personnel.[7] One of the ways in which information may come to appropriate authorities is through established crime commissions. The placement of the investigative commissions, although a responsi-

[6]Rufus King. "The Fifth Amendment Privilege and Immunity Legislation," *Notre Dame Lawyer*, 38, 6 (1963), 641–54. Also see G.R. Blakely, *Investigation and Prosecution of Organized Crime and Corrupt Activities* (Washington, D.C.: U.S. Department of Justice, 1977).

[7]John A. Gardiner and David J. Olson, "Wincanton: The Politics of Corruption," *Task Force Report, Organized Crime* (Washington, D.C.: U.S. Government Printing Office, 1967), pp. 22–23.

bility of the executive branch of government, is nevertheless subject to control through judicial appointments and acquaintances. Whether a governmental crime commission functions will depend greatly upon the cooperation offered by prosecuting agencies, courts, and defense attorneys. The very fact that the judicial branch of government exercises such great power over a legitimate executive function offers perhaps the weakest link in the reporting and prosecution of organized crime violations.

Crime commissions can come in many forms. The ones most prominent in the organized crime field have been the Senate Permanent Subcommittee on Investigations and the Senate Select Committee on Improper Activities in the Labor and Management Field. These two subcommittees, which are serving in place of specified crime commissions, have been responsible for substantial investigations. A great deal of information about organized crime has been revealed. These two committees and dozens of lesser committees are charged with the investigation of hundreds of criminal violations involving organized crime. These committees have many shortcomings. For example, there is little preinvestigation, so certain types of criminal activity may be excluded from the hearings. The autonomy of past crime commissions has also revealed problems of whitewash, favoritism, and conspiracy simply because selected representatives of important interest groups—"sixty-year old smiling public men" or "eager, pink-cheeked, name-seeking friends of the fraternity"—constitute the typical investigative subcommittees. Their participation, it is alleged, is essential to make funds available from other congressional subcommittees. A new selection process for commission members is desirable.

In order to have effective organization in governmental commissions or subcommittees, they should be set up according to the recommendations of the President's Crime Commission, which recommended the following:

> A permanent joint congressional committee on organized crime. States that have organized crime groups in operation should create and finance organized crime investigation commissions with independent permanent status, with an adequate staff of investigators, and with subpoena power. Such commissions should hold hearings and furnish periodic reports to the legislature, governor, and law enforcement officials.[8]

The Law Enforcement Assistance Administration of the Justice Department provides for such units in its programs of financial support. In the past, few local units of government have provided such support simply because there was no coordination between units engaged in the organized crime control effort.

Because many states are in fact politically controlled by attorneys and

---

[8]*Task Force Report: Organized Crime,* pp. 22–23. This recommendation was also supported by speakers at the National Conference on Organized Crime, Los Angeles, November 8–9, 1979.

judges, they are the ones who must be made aware of the potential of the crime commissions for the control of organized crime. The legal segment of the criminal justice system is the one that can ensure that crime commissions are composed of qualified representatives rather than of cronies who may bargain away favors for appointments.

Governmental investigative committees exist for the purpose of putting before a lay audience clear and credible information taken from immensely complex and detailed accounts. Intelligence information must not only be gathered, it must also be analyzed by experts who are in the business of crime control. The issues raised and identified by an investigative commission must be documented, thoroughly investigated, and followed by prosecution if necessary. Sufficient time and money must be allocated for ongoing studies and analyses of local crime conditions as revealed by the crime commissions.

By singling out the legal system for criticism there has been no intent to take blame for the existence of organized crime from either the legislative or administrative branches of government. The position of the legal system is so critical that any effort at organized crime control must thread its way through and use this system.

SUMMARY

The importance of a noncorruptible legal system cannot be overstressed. It is not enough that most attorneys and judges be honest. A small minority allowed to omit ethics, and frequently legality, can defeat the efforts of the entire system of criminal justice. The relationship of the lawyer to a criminal client should be subject to research, and more stringent rules of conduct should be imposed. The issue of honesty also includes the enforcement of realistic laws and consistency in the courts. The legal system is the catalyst for crime commissions as a means of investigating organized crime. Appointments to these commissions as presently structured are almost exclusively in the hands of the legal power structure. The system of selection can be self-defeating. It is no longer the local police agency that can dictate whether organized crime will exist. It is the total criminal justice system with the power centered in the legal subunits that dictates how much organized crime will and does exist.

QUESTIONS FOR DISCUSSION

1. Why is the legal system termed the "keystone" to the control of organized crime?
2. Where should legal advice stop in advising a criminal client of methods to subvert the law?

3. Do the operating patterns of "syndicate lawyers" show a consistency over the past two decades?

4. What steps should the legal system impose for better internal ethics?

5. Identify the local and federal laws most commonly used in your community. Are there wide variations in content and enforcement application?

6. Why don't people attach much "wrongness" to organized crime?

7. Do the crime commissions, as presently constituted, offer a solution to the identification of organized criminal enterprises?

8. How can liaison among the various levels of organized crime control agencies be improved?

9. How can the legal system be utilized to increase the efficiency of organized crime control?

10. Identify provisions in the federal 1970 Omnibus Crime Bill for providing crime commissions made up of lay citizens.

PART II
VICE CRIMES OF AN ORGANIZED NATURE

The financial keystones for organized confederations have been the crimes commonly classified as vice. With vice being defined as a moral failing, evil or wicked conduct, corruption and depravity,[1] there are a great number of crimes that fall into this category. For all practical purposes vice crimes, as they relate to organized groups, are gambling (Chapter 5), prostitution (Chapter 6), narcotics trafficking (Chapter 7), and obscenity and pornography (Chapter 8).

Generally, vice crimes are viewed by the public as an act of individual moral weakness and the decision to engage in such acts as one that should be left to the decision of the individual. Many allege that legislation against this type of moral behavior is fundamentally wrong. This concept may be right and if such control were to be removed, perhaps vice crimes might be less susceptible to control by organized confederations. But because of the right of society to impose sanctions that it believes are necessary for the regulation of human behavior, the right of self-determination, while being increasingly liberalized, is not apt to soon become general in our culture.

The relationship of vice to organized groups has had much publicity. However, many people refuse to believe that the prostitute in the local bar may work for a national confederation or that the bookie in the local barbershop may have the same boss as the prostitute. The direct link between vice activity and organized criminal groups is frequently difficult to show and almost impossible to prove. Activities of vice confederations are so covert that it is impossible to detect them through normal investigative methods. By their very nature, vice crimes are a catalyst for criminal activity.

The evolution of organized crime has been synonymous with the expansion of these vice crimes. The growth of vice crimes has remained fairly constant in relation to increased population and trends toward

---

[1]*Webster's New World Dictionary*, College Edition. Copyright © 1968 by The World Publishing Co., New York & Cleveland.

urbanization in spite of campaigns to clear out the bawdy houses and eliminate the red light districts.

A double standard exists for sanctions against vice crimes. The citizens who pressure for the elimination of vice crimes are the same ones who patronize and engage in these illegal activities. This double standard has caused the confederations to gain public support while the criminal coffers grow rich from vice profits.

The trend in vice crimes today is toward bigger and more lucrative crimes. In spite of increased enforcement, the monetary take from gambling, narcotics, and pornography continues to spiral upward. Television sports coverage has contributed to gambling on events that in the past were ignored. This trend is supported by the federal government, which in 1978 passed legislation that enabled newpapers, radio, and television to report the results of state-run lotteries without running afoul of federal laws. At that time 13 states ran their own lotteries, while 25 other states have authorized lotteries which are conducted by some other organization. Some states have both forms of organized lotteries.

It is difficult for the citizens to psychologically distinguish between gambling conducted by organized crime and that conducted by government. Because the citizen fails to make this distinction, the illegal activities of organized crime continue to supply the ever-increasing citizen demand.

5

GAMBLING

LEARNING OUTCOMES

1. Know the ways in which organized crime perpetuates gambling empires.
2. Understand the structure of confederation gambling operations and realize why local enforcement agencies cannot eleminate organized gambling.
3. Gain knowledge about the ways in which gambling operations are conducted.
4. Recognize that society has a dual standard for enforcing gambling laws.
5. Associate community activities that pertain to gambling with a common scheme or plan designed by syndicate members.

This chapter will cover three important types of vice crimes. These are the traditional crimes commonly associated with the confederations: (1) gambling; (2) bookmaking, betting on sporting events, and gambling devices, such as cards, dice, and slot machines; and (3) miscellaneous lotteries that are partially or completely dominated by the confederations.

Confederation domination and operation are identified with many major gambling activities. For example, there are no bookies who do not owe allegiance to the confederations. Gambling activities are the direct link to street crimes.

The evolution of gambling may be described in this manner. Gambling begins as entertainment for the family and a small circle of friends. It is perpetuated by fraternal groups and social gatherings, where it is still looked upon as entertainment. There is little danger of antisocial behavior in this type of activity as long as it is a form of social entertainment. The next step, however, is the identifying and bringing together of mutual groups whose only interest is gambling for profit. When this occurs, friendships vanish and what was formerly social entertainment becomes a lucrative commercial enterprise.

Municipal governments, although obligated to enforce the gambling ordinances, frequently find it expedient to encourage or turn their backs on illegal gambling operations in order to placate vested interest groups.

Newspaper accounts document gambling operations throughout the nation that apparently have public sanction and political collusion enabling them to survive. For example, Little Rock, Arkansas, long renowned for its vacation spas and gambling, closed the doors of its "locally favored" commercial operations. Other cities of major size have condoned gambling for a time due in part to the indifference of citizens. Active local citizen support is what makes gambling flourish. There seems to be a feeling in America that life itself is a gamble, so risking money in a game of chance is just another acceptable part of our social system. This is exactly what the confederations want the public to think.

THE MORAL ISSUES OF GAMBLING

Sociologists, psychologists, and theologians universally promote and expound on the issue of legalized gambling. Most studies indicate no empirical basis for the adverse influence of gambling in a society where it is legalized.

Fred Cook believed, however, that when gamblers are sheltered by the law, as they are in Nevada, the morals and ethics of the gamblers become a part of the accepted pattern of life. Virgil Peterson, a leading investigator of gambling influences, set this stage for the gambling controversy. He states:

> Whenever the light of public attention has been focused on the unsavory gambling racket, when gangland killings arouse some measure of public indignation and when corruption arising out of alliance between hoodlums, politicians, and law enforcement officers is exposed, there recurs agitation for the licensing of gambling. Whether gambling should be licensed or not is a highly controversial question.[1]

An honest difference of opinion exists among many who are strong advocates of licensing and those who are in opposition. The position to be taken is that as long as the activity is prohibited by statute, it should have no positive recognition in our society.

Some of the more common comments for and against gambling illustrate how behavior patterns tend to form around mysticisms. Gambling is a belief in the supernatural. However, the *Encyclopaedia Britannica* states "In no society has the rise of rationalism brought about a decrease in the incidence or volume of gambling."[2]

---

[1]Virgil W. Peterson, *The Problem, Gambling—Should It Be Legalized?* (Springfield, Ill.: Charles C Thomas, 1951), pp. 3–7. The position of this author is updated and supported by Seth Kupferberg in "The State as Bookie," *The Washington Monthly*, July–August, 1979, p. 57.

[2]*Encyclopaedia Britannica* (1971), IX, 1115.

Gambling is a natural law because life itself is a gamble. This is accepted by many groups in society. Yet, most religions maintain that there is a spiritual design in every life that may preclude a commitment to the concept of gambling.

Gambling is nonproductive and immoral. Jewish, Muslim, and most Christian faiths have held gambling to be immoral. Oriental religions and modern Roman Catholics have held that gambling for amusement does not offend a deity.

Gambling should be legalized and taxed to provide revenue for the governing functions. Several states have chosen this alternative and most have had only moderate success in terms of raising operating revenues. The late Los Angeles Chief of Police, William Parker, had this to say on the subject of gambling as a source of revenue: "Any society that bases its financial structure on the weakness of its people doesn't deserve to survive."

Gambling is justified for the financial support of churches and private charities. History indicates that in many societies scholars connected with religion conducted gambling. Priests with divinatory devices and occult activities sustained gambling. In modern society it is very questionable whether such enterprises contribute to the public welfare. In England, many private clubs have been the benefactors of the 1968 Gambling Act and now serve under license as public betting parlors.

Thus, with this reasoning, the ethic against gambling is established. In order to see how this ethic has applied to gambling throughout history, a brief review follows.

History of Gambling

The history of gambling has been fairly well documented through the centuries. From artifacts found by archeologists, there are indications that people, rich and poor, have always been gamblers. There is little question that most people at some time in their lives will gamble. The great social problem to be resolved is this: *How can society regulate gambling so that human beings may afford the luxury of indulgence?* Whatever the argument, for or against gambling, one can look to documented history and see that gambling in most of its forms has been with humans since the beginning of recorded history. Because of that long history, organized crime has attached itself to a reliable profit maker.

Many authorities document the evolution of gambling. The ancient Greeks considered gambling on athletic games a quasi-religious observance. Yet most philosophers, including Aristotle, grouped gamblers with nonproductive thieves. Following the Greeks, the Romans imposed strict regulations against

gambling except during the December holiday called Saturnalia. The opposition to gambling was in only rare instances repulsive to the religious deities, but the waste of resources was a severe drain on the economy. In the early Middle East cultures, chess was the one game of skill that was not forbidden.

Card playing is not mentioned as one of the prohibited games, and historians believe cards were first used in Europe around the early fourteenth century. English and French laws were enacted at this time for the purpose of keeping the common person away from the card and dice tables in order to divert his talents to archery, which would be of benefit to the state. Penalties for gambling were minor.

For at least 300 years there has been control over licensing and state control of gambling. "Nevertheless, the need for tax revenue from indirect—hence not unpopular—sources has persuaded nearly every sovereign entity, including more than thirty states of the United States, to license some form of gambling...."[3]

National History

In the United States in colonial days, there was widespread difference in public reaction toward various forms of gambling. It is quite possible that cards came to this country soon after the Pilgrims, or possibly with them. As early as the seventeenth century, the law, influenced by New England Puritans, established a fine of $5 for one or more individuals who brought cards into the colony. About 1645, the Massachusetts General Court prohibited all gambling and gaming and included in the category bowling and shuffleboard. In spite of the sanctions against gambling, there was a steady increase in the activity. Each of the thirteen original colonies conducted public lotteries as a source of revenue. As public sentiment changed, card playing was punished by the stocks in many areas of New England. In other parts of the colonies, it was looked on with some degree of tolerance.

THE STATE AND GAMBLING

To what extent is the guilt of the casual participant distinguished from the gambling house proprietor's or the horse bettor distinguished from the bookmaker? As would be expected, the answer fluctuates from state to state. The laws prohibiting gambling are enforced in various ways throughout the United States, usually quite inadequately. Large segments of our population feel that such laws are proper and necessary, but they reserve for themselves the privilege of deciding whether or not the laws apply in their own particular

[3]*Encyclopaedia Britannica*, IX, 1115A.

case. This rationalization complicates the enforcement of laws and creates a haven for organized criminals.

In the 1970s many states decided that gambling was going to be a "something for nothing" bonanza for financially troubled states. The number of state lotteries increased from 2 to 15. Four states went for jai alai, and New Jersey legalized the first casinos outside Nevada. State lotteries have suffered only minor scandals. However, New Jersey's casinos figured heavily in the Justice Department's ABSCAM probe of bribery of congressmen and state and local government leaders in 1981.

The history of legalized gambling in the United States would indicate it is only a matter of time before most of the gambling ventures will be counterproductive because of the drain on law enforcement resources and the corruption that surrounds gambling enterprises. The present trend in this country is mixed and confused; the federal government is attempting to crack down on professional gambling in general, and on bookmaking activities of an interstate nature in particular. Although there are occasional proposals for a nationally sponsored lottery, they have generally met with public disapproval. In many states, the movement is in the other direction. The game of Bingo, which is a form of lottery, is now legal in many states and others are considering legalizing other forms of lottery.

Those states that now allow horse betting (31) are adding extra tracks and expanding racing days. Fourteen states permit dog racing. In addition, there are trotting races and other sporting events to stimulate the bettor. In the encouragement of new race tracks some states take a very realistic view. Laws usually provide that a specific total be taken from the bettor's dollar but permit state officials some latitude as to how much of the total various track operators will be permitted to retain.

Gambling and Corruption

Whether corruption is a result of gambling or gambling is a result of corruption is a matter of individual decision. The Pennsylvania Crime Commission identifies the problem this way:

A U.S. Senate subcommittee, studying organized gambling in depth, concluded that "organized crime in the United States is primarily dependent upon illicit gambling, a multi-billion dollar racket for the necessary funds required to operate other criminal and illegal activities or enterprises." Illegal gambling provides a steady source of lucrative profits which organized crime syndicates then invest in either more profitable or high risk ventures.[4]

Today organized criminal groups are "pyramiding" their wealth. They are able to flaunt this wealth because they service their customers by promoting

[4]Pennsylvania Crime Commission, *Report on Organized Crime*, Scranton, July 7, 1970, p. 25.

illegal enterprises alongside the state-run gaming enterprises. It is estimated that 8 to 10 percent of the total gambling take in Nevada is from an unlicensed and illegal source.[5] Other state lotteries are playing second fiddle to the organized crime enterprises. State-run lotteries tend to run for the convenience of the state, while crime-run enterprises are designed for the convenience of the gambler. Until legislators recognize this is a competitive enterprise, no state will be free from the influence of the corruption of gambling billions.

The Function of the Federal Government.

The United States has federal laws prohibiting lotteries and wagering across state lines.[6] In the past two decades, many new laws, such as the Omnibus Crime Bill, have been passed to combat the syndicate operation. These laws have, to some extent, discouraged the movement of persons and information in interstate travel for racketeering purposes. For example, it is a felony to transmit bets and wagers between states by any means.[7] This law has caused changes in techniques for transmitting information. The information today, however, moves more rapidly and as freely as it has ever done.

THE BETTING SYNDICATE

Some of the largest segments of the organized crime groups and allegedly the most profitable are those that handle horse and sports betting. The very nature of this operation dictates a highly sophisticated communications network. Through the wire services, instantaneous information is available for the bookmaker's "business office." Figure 5–1 illustrates this system.

The recordkeeping function of the business offices closely parallels the information flow. As each bet, taken by a "handbook," is recorded in the business office, a flow of information on new races and events is transmitted back to the "handbook."

The Handbook

The handbook is the member of the organization who must contact the bettor and relay bets into the organization's recordkeeping service. The handbook's operation depends solely upon the imagination he exhibits. Most

[5]Information from a member of the Organized Crime Strike Force Los Angeles and partially confirmed in an article by Frank Fortunato, *Betting with Bookies*, Reference Unknown, October 1980.

[6]The U.S. Code has several sections on carrying, knowingly taking or receiving chance, share, interest, etc. In a lottery a gift, enterprise, or similar scheme is in violation. You are referred to the following sections: 18 USC 1301, 1302, 1303, 1304.

[7]U.S. Code 1084.

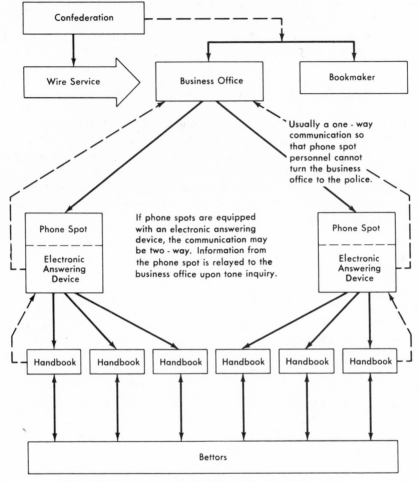

Figure 5-1 The bookmaking empire. New techniques employ a programmed minicomputer in the business office; this gives on-line access to the wire services.

frequently he will have an established pattern of operation. Thus, the investigator must observe and study his mode of operation until he can detect a weakness in the handbook's system. A number of clever techniques by the bookmaker will create problems for the enforcement officer.

The Wire Service

Without this service, confederation-operated bookmaking operations would be forced to fold. Or at best, the syndicate would be able to take bets only on local tracks and events. If information that eventually gets to the

bookmaker were curtailed, so would information used to keep the public informed. In some instances, reporting of this type can be one and the same. Computerized wire service, in code, is now available to the subscribing bookmaking office.[8]

BOOKMAKING, SPORTING EVENTS, GAMBLING DEVICES

A two-dollar bet, multiplied by thousands, gives organized syndicates throughout the United States a prime source of revenue. Each state regulates its own horse racing and pari-mutuel betting. For the customer who cannot make it to the track, there are many obliging bookies. From the local barbershop to the largest missile manufacturing complexes, the handbook finds a niche to ply his trade. (The handbook is the agent who actually takes the wager from a bettor.)

The Bookmaking System

As part of a large organization, the bookmaker does not actually risk his own money in bookmaking activities. He is merely an instrument of the confederation, which has agents take the bets and make payoffs to the winning bettors when necessary. For a fee, the local bookmaker can "lay off" bets with the syndicate. To "lay off" a bet is similar to the underwriting techniques used by insurance companies as a guard against large losses. This technique enables an individual to share the loss, if there is one, with a larger organization or combination of medium to small organizations. Thus, the losses are spread over a large number of bettors, bookmakers, and race tracks. The law of probability dictates odds in favor of the larger bookmaking organizations.

In Figure 5–1, the sequence of betting information has been shown. To maintain this information sequence, the bookmaker, with new developments in electronic communications systems, is now able to eliminate the "phone spot" person. Now a small, inexpensive instrument can receive the bets from the handbook and store this information until queried by the business office with a simple "tone inquire" device.[8] This system eliminates a weak link in the bookmaking enterprise. Under present search and seizure laws, there are few legal techniques by which the local vice operator can apprehend anyone higher in the organization than the "handbook."

The memory system. Perhaps the most difficult handbook to apprehend and prosecute is the one who takes bets solely from established clientele, commits these bets to memory, and calls the business office only after every

---

[8]In 1979, two separate cases were prosecuted in which programmed computer systems were used to record bets.

30 or 40 bets. Many handbooks have phenomenal memories and never write down bets, nor will they accept a bet written on a piece of paper. All business is committed to memory until the handbook is called by the business office, or contacts the phone spot or an electronic answering device.

The employee bookie. Another difficult handbook to apprehend is a messenger, toolman, or representative in large plants who contacts the same people daily on business matters. He will come to know those who are sports minded and through his contacts may operate so covertly the worker on the next bench will not be aware of his activities. The wins and losses are frequently handled at payday. If the handbook keeps records in codes that cannot be interpreted,[9] his longevity is practically guaranteed. Plant owners frequently do not wish to cooperate with police investigators because every employee is a member of some employee group. To have him removed from his job can be done only for cause. Usually, to have one handbook removed is only to have him replaced by another. The plant owner's attitude is usually live and let live rather than incur the wrath of organized employee associations.

The traveling bar "bookie." One of the most common operations is to have a "bookie" cover several bars or cafes in a given area. He will drop in, pick up his action, and move on to the next establishment. If the patrons of a bar, for example, sit and study a scratch sheet or racing section of the newspaper, chances are good the "bookie" will be around at intervals preceding every two or three races.

Frequently, a bar patron will study the races, then go in search of the bookie. By following, the police investigator can frequently be led directly to the transaction between bookie and bettor. Once consummated, these betting transactions are then relayed to the bookie's office from phone booths along his route.

An establishment that caters to the traveling bookie or one that has its own bookie will usually be receiving rent from the confederation as part of normal business.

The fixed spot. From sophisticated "horse rooms" to telephone spots, the bookie must take his chances in order to meet the bettors. The spot where a bookie can come and socialize with his betting friends is very popular. The front of the spot may be a small grocery, a book and record shop, or any other small business that should have a high incidence of pedestrian traffic.

A popular fixed spot is a newsstand on a busy metropolitan corner. The operator is a natural because of his multiple contacts with people, especially

---

[9]The court requires that an expert in bookmaking be able to interpret what is written in code. A coded message on a tool room requisition may appear to be a legitimate tool request yet be a handbook's record.

employees of department stores or offices who cannot afford the time to visit the race track. It is virtually impossible to detect a betting transaction during the sale of a newspaper. However, if the operator leaves the stand to make frequent telephone calls, he may be calling out bets.

A good news location that has betting action will frequently sell for $20,000 to $40,000. The news vendor is usually an independent contractor and is not usually an employee of the newspaper publisher. This type of fixed spot is often "wired politically" and can survive only where corruption exists.

Fixed "phone spots."   The technique for placing an off-track bet by phone is quite simple. If a person is well recommended, he or she may contact a bookmaker and place the bet by telephone. (From time to time the bookmaker will change phone numbers as a precaution.) All betting transactions are handled over the telephone. At predetermined times, the bookie will send a runner to the bettor to collect for the losses or pay the wins. Appointments with the runner are sometimes unscheduled, private, and secretive. Only cash is involved, and there is no exchange of receipts or written memorandums.

Phone spots will frequently have the added protection of a "drop line," "a black box," or "a wire out" so that the bookie sitting on the phone spot will have time to destroy the evidence in case of a police raid. This technique is shown in Figure 5–2.

Numerous types of equipment are used by bookmakers to avoid detection. One type is the "blue box," which enables the user to simulate a touch-tone signal and use toll-free 800 WATS telephone numbers. Used in this manner, there is no charge for the call and no toll record.

The betting marker.   One of the most desirable pieces of evidence to come into the vice operator's possession is the betting marker. The betting marker may be a piece of paper with the race, the horse's name, and the amount to be wagered (2nd, Rose Red, 2.2.2). It may also be a stick of gum, a piece of ceramic tile, or an intricate group of numbers on an adding machine tape. The variations for recording bets are limitless. The notations made by the bettor on a slip of paper and handed to the bookie along with cash for the bet is still the most common technique in bookmaking. Figures 5–3 and 5–4 illustrate the various types of betting markers.

Sporting Events

Gambling confederations usually are not content with accepting wagers just on horses. They also give odds on contests, such as football games, basketball games, prize fights, political elections, and so on. Usually the bookmaker does this by "handicapping." For example, if through careful analysis competitor A is thought to have a better chance than competitor B, a

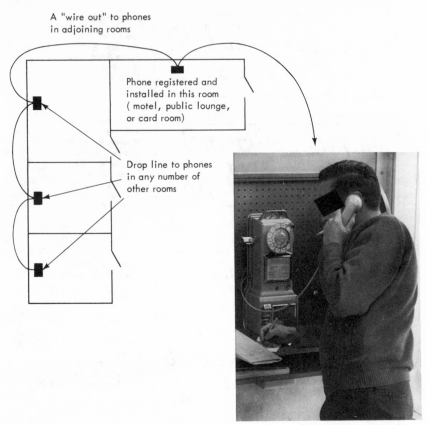

A "wire out" to phones in adjoining rooms

Phone registered and installed in this room (motel, public lounge, or card room)

Drop line to phones in any number of other rooms

Figure 5–2 A phone spot with a "wire out" to phones installed in adjoining rooms. (This technique is often called a cheesebox.)

handicap given in money odds or a point spread is given to equalize their chances. The customer may choose either competitor on the basis of the handicap. Thus, a weak team may be given points to compensate for a superior rival. Those betting on the stronger team can win if that team wins by a larger margin than the handicap. This system can also work for betting on elections, with the underdog given a handicap of so many votes.

It would be unusual for horsebets to be taken in regular working offices, but sporting pools are widely accepted by some businesses on the grounds that they promote office morale. The office baseball or football pool, although not usually of an organized criminal variety, will find its criminal counterpart in the bars and betting parlors that are confederation-sponsored.

As for the sports bookmaker, there is little gambling involved in the operation. He is simply the middleman, charging a commission for services rendered. He seldom bets against the bettors; they actually bet against themselves. If his books balance, his percentage will vary from 4 percent to 8 percent, depending on the price line he quotes the bettor.

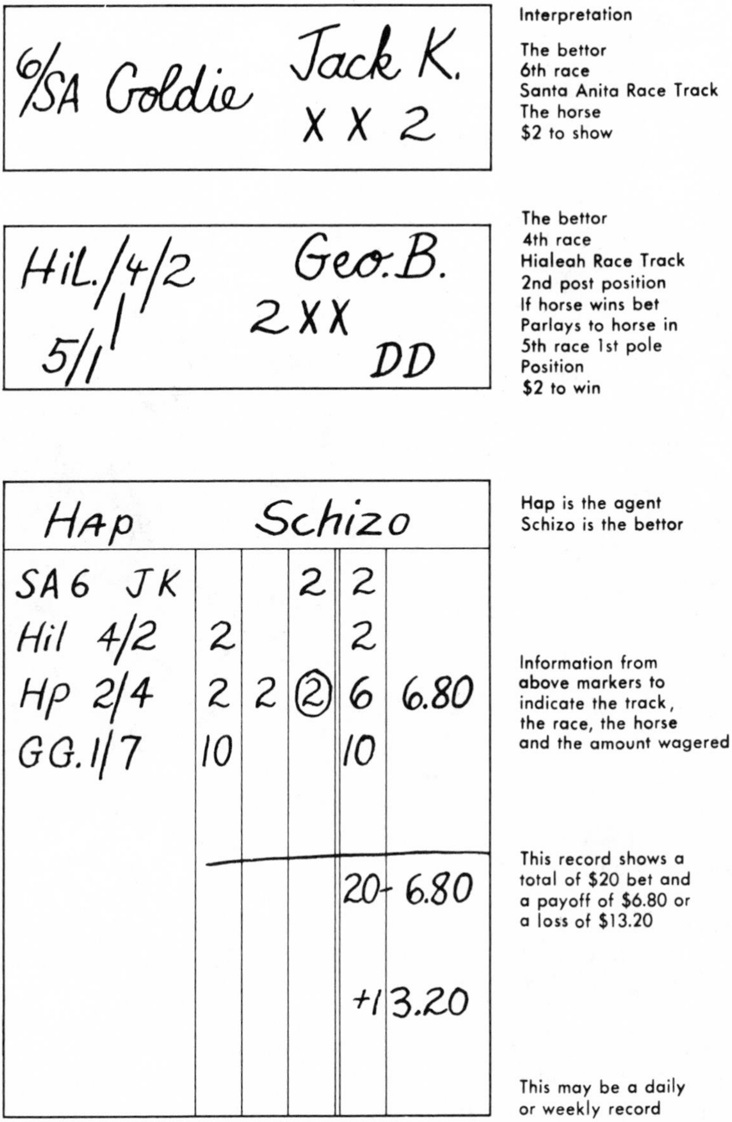

Interpretation	
6/SA Goldie Jack K. X X 2	The bettor 6th race Santa Anita Race Track The horse $2 to show
HiL./4/2 5/1 Geo.B. 2 X X DD	The bettor 4th race Hialeah Race Track 2nd post position If horse wins bet Parlays to horse in 5th race 1st pole Position $2 to win

Hap is the agent
Schizo is the bettor

Hap				Schizo		
SA 6 JK			2	2		
Hil 4/2	2			2		
Hp 2/4	2	2	②	6	6.80	
GG.1/7	10			10		
				20-	6.80	
				+1	3.20	

Information from above markers to indicate the track, the race, the horse and the amount wagered

This record shows a total of $20 bet and a payoff of $6.80 or a loss of $13.20

This may be a daily or weekly record

Figure 5–3 Typical betting markers with interpretation and the professional betting marker found at phone spots and offices to record action.

Like the "morning line" in horse racing, the "opening sports line" is made up of handicappers who sell their services to bookmakers in the United States, Canada, and some of the Caribbean Islands. The opening sports line is believed to originate in four places: Houston, Las Vegas, Chicago, and Seattle. The basic research for this information requires scores of daily newspapers, college publications, and sports releases. From these, vital

NATIONAL DAILY REPORTER

Pimlico

— OFFICIAL JOCKEYS AND POST POSITIONS —
Percentage of winning favorites corresponding meeting
1965, .36; current meeting, .30. Percentage of favorites
in the money, .59. Daily double on first and second races.
United starting gate. Confirmation camera.

★ Indicates beaten favorite last time out.
Horses listed in order as handicapped by EL RIO REY

WEATHER CLEAR—TRACK FAST

FIRST—Purse, $3,300   Probable POST 10:00 A. M.
1 1-8 Miles. 4-Year-Olds and Up. Claiming
Colts and Geldings

Hcp.		Last Finish	Wt.	P.P.	Odds	Jockey
1	§Red Erik		113	11	3-1	R.Adams
2	Beech Time	3	116	14	7-2	G.Patterson
3	News Wire	4	116	*18	4-1	C.Baltazar
6	Keb	5	122	6	5-1	J.Brocklebank
8	Friendly Cat	9	116	1	8-1	W.J.Passmore
9	Milrutho	3	116	7	8-1	J.Block
10	Even Swap	7	116	10	12-1	C.F.Riston
11	Sterling Prince		116	12	15-1	R.J.Bright
12	*Mr. Songster	9	107	15	20-1	E.Belville
13	‡Jambar	9	109	*8	30-1	N.Reagan
16	‡Spider Spread	5	109	9	30-1	A.Garcia
17	Billy Giampa	12	116	4	30-1	R.McCurdy
4	Congratulations	1	122	17	——	SCRATCHED
5	Dumelle ★	5	119	16	——	SCRATCHED
7	Fast Answer	3	116	5	——	SCRATCHED
14	Regal Lover	6	116	3	——	SCRATCHED
15	Little Rib	10	116	13	——	SCRATCHED
18	Graf Smil	11	116	×2	——	SCRATCHED

SECOND—Purse, $3,300   Probable POST 10:26 A. M.
6 Furlongs. 3-Year-Olds. Claiming

		Last Finish	Wt.	P.P.	Odds	Jockey
1	Broken Needle	2	111	×1	2-1	G.Patterson
2	Woodlake Witch		111	5	4-1	P.Kallai
3	Lady Macbeth	11	117	7	5-1	F.Lovato
4	‡Mink Boy	6	109	8	6-1	R.Nolan
5	Craig's Fault	8	116	9	8-1	B.Phelps
6	Fast Lass		116	*10	8-1	C.Baltazar
7	Tora Tora	10	116	11	8-1	P.I.Grimm
8	Hawkins	7	116	*3	10-1	T.Lee
13	*Carole A.		116	6	12-1	N.Reagan
14	Its a Star	9	116	4	15-1	T.Guyton
16	Mr. Cricket	11	116	12	30-1	R.Kimball
17	*Marv's Joy	10	111	2	30-1	J.Taylor
9	‡Blocker	—	109	14	——	SCRATCHED
10	Yokel	—	116	15	——	SCRATCHED
11	Drag Pit	—	116	16	——	SCRATCHED
12	Little Nancy	—	111	18	——	SCRATCHED
15.	Ginnygem	8	111	13	——	SCRATCHED
18	Jovial Lady	12	111	17	——	SCRATCHED

THIRD—Purse, $3,300   Probable POST 10:52 A. M.
6 Furlongs. 3-Year-Olds. Claiming

Figure 5–4 The *National Daily Reporter*, a publication, annotated as a betting marker.

statistics are obtained on past performances of players and teams. For last-minute and more detailed reporting, they employ scouting systems composed of sportswriters, bookies, assistant coaches, players, students, and professional tipsters. The goal of handicapping is to make the underdog team as attractive as the favored team. In order to do this, the underdog is given a point or spot handicap. The initial line is based on the relative ability of the

teams; the final line is adjusted to the national betting trends. The line is frequently juggled to protect the profit margin of the confederations.

Each succeeding sporting season reaps a richer gambling harvest than the previous one in terms of dollars bet. For example, college and professional football, which is the leading sport for gambling, may have as much as $20 billion bet annually on the outcome of games. The televising of championship games and the New Year's bowl games may cause the betting action to double. In horse racing the Kentucky Derby brings out the bettors. The championship series in basketball and the world series are the bookmakers' delight.

The Crime Commission report indicated the take by organized crime in profits to be approximately $6 to $7 billion per year.[10] Sports betting is the leading contributor.

Gambling Devices

Each state has its own laws prohibiting certain games of chance. Many states and cities have laws that follow no pattern or reason. In such areas there are few consistent enforcement activities. This creates an environment in which the confederations thrive.

Cards are a popular gambling device that is well suited to house-run games. House-run games, however, have no common method of operation. Some professional houses, such as those in England, charge a membership fee to enter the club, and play at the table is free. In Nevada, where all forms of card playing are legal, and in Gardenia, California, where draw poker is legal under local option, the gambler may enter without paying a club fee. The house collects periodically from individual tables, and amounts collected from each player usually depend upon the size of the game.

A broad general rule that seems to apply in most states is that any card game based on chance, not skill, is illegal unless specifically permitted by law. Any wager made on the turn of a card in such a game completes the elements of the offense. The amount wagered does not increase the severity of the crime (exception to this rule is made in the 1970 Omnibus Crime Bill). Court decisions have held that the intrinsic value of the thing bet is sufficient for prosecution.[11]

A police investigator, if he is to testify in court as an expert, should be well versed in rules of the game. It is not necessary to identify a suspected gambling game by name.[12] If a suspected illegal game is being conducted and money or an item of value is being wagered, an arrest will usually be made.

[10]*Organized Crime: Task Force Report* (Washington, D.C.: U.S. Government Printing Office, 1967), p. 6. Some sources report $20 to $25 billion per year.

[11]This will vary from one locality to another. You are referred to the state laws and local ordinances applicable in a specific geographical location.

[12]In California, where draw poker only is allowed by local option, it would be necessary to prove the suspected game was not legal under local ordinance.

Common card games. A few of the more common games are cited for illustrative purposes:

Poker. Draw, stud, and low ball games are so common that the average teenager knows how to play. Note: In an illegal professional house game the house will frequently sell poker chips to the players so that no money is on the table.[13] In an investigation there should be an initial attempt to locate the bank. Money seized, if it can be related to the game, should be booked as evidence. The Internal Revenue Service will be interested in larger games.

Black Jack or 21. Play is against the dealer, each player is dealt two cards. The object of the game is to get 21 or closer to 21 than the dealer. The odds in this game favor the dealer because the players must make their hand before the dealer. In this game aces count as 1 or 11, numbered cards are counted as their numerical value, and face cards count 10. The bank or the house has approximately a 6 percent advantage.

In England laws require that games do not have odds favoring the house; thus, to satisfy the law, house dealers offer the deal to a player when he has black jack. In reality, most customers cannot afford to bank against the table and refuse the deck.

Pique. Frequently referred to as the "Chinese game," pique is played with cards or blocks similar in shape and appearance to dominos. Combinations of red and black dots are used to denote winners. As many as eight players may participate. Side bets may be made by any number of players. In the investigation of pique the investigator may distinguish the game by the sound of fast clicks of the blocks. In Mahjong and dominos, the clicks will be slower.

There are an unlimited number of card games that lend themselves to gambling operations. Games that are well known with *fast action* are the most desirable.

Dice. Dice in various forms are the oldest gaming implements known. Innumerable game variations are and have been played with them. Dice is probably the most prevalent and fastest way for the gambler to invest money. From the plush layouts of London and Las Vegas to the back rooms of many towns and cities, gamblers gather in small and large groups to try their luck at the crap tables.

Archeologists claim the forefather of the modern "die" was the astragalus bone in the foot. Six-sided cubes resembling our present dice have been found in ruins of the Egyptian tombs of 2000 B.C., the diggings at Pompeii, and Greek burial vaults from the year 1244 B.C. The dice found were made of stone, ivory, porcelain, and bone. There is evidence that many of the dice were crooked. Recent artifacts from Britain and France indicate that "Roman crap shooters" lived there from 55 B.C. to A.D. 410.

In the past two decades explorations under the London financial district have revealed artifacts proving that dice games are not new. "Shaved dice"

---

[13]Frequently equipment supply houses will furnish equipment to private clubs. A donation to enter the room is collected and free chips are supplied to the donor. If more chips are desired, a new donation must be made. These types of transactions are legal under the laws of some states.

and "loaded dice" were fairly common. Many of the dice found under London were made from the knuckle bones of sheep or goats. Thus, today, dice are frequently referred to as bones.[14]

The evolution of dice indicates that they were probably used primarily for religious purposes. Each society evidently chose a dice form and retained it through several centuries. For example, cubical dice were used by both Egyptians and the Chinese. The American Indians used waferlike dice having only two effective faces.[15] Various other forms of dice have been found in the different societies.

Dice as a modern gambling device is perhaps the most prevalent illegal game operating. It is easy to conduct, any number of persons may play, and the action is fast. In ghetto areas of the cities dice games are a way of life. It is not uncommon to find games that operate around the clock. These games may operate in a fixed location, or they may "float" from location to location. When a game operates at the same location for a period of time, it is reasonably safe to assume that payoffs are going to local officials.

Games played with dice.   Early in the twentieth century, *craps* became the principal gambling game of the United States. This game is popular because any number of people may play and betting is fast. The shooter bets as much as he likes, and his bet may be covered by one bettor or split among a group. Side bets, wagers between bettors, may involve any amount of money and any number of bettors. The game has much fascination for gamblers because money is being exchanged on nearly each roll of the dice. Confederations are active in this type of gambling.

Poker dice.   Five standard dice may be used, but there are also special dice with six faces marked as playing cards with ace, king, queen, knave (jack), ten, and nine. The dice are normally thrown from a dice cup. By following the regular rules of poker, the winner may be determined. This game is frequently found in bars where the house will roll the customer for drinks and money. Depending on local and state laws, this technique may not only be a gambling violation, but may also be prohibited by liquor laws.

Barbudi or barbooth.   This is a two-dice game of Balkan and Levantine origin. It is played in the United States chiefly by persons of Greek, Armenian, and Italian ancestry. Alone among popular dice games, it provides no mathematical advantage for any player or for the gambling house. Two persons play against each other.

Crooked dice operations.   Dice are popular for house games and portable outfits that may be set up easily. Floating games are common and

---

[14]*Encyclopaedia Britannica* (1966), p. 373.

[15]Robert Charles Bell, *Board and Table Games* (New York: Oxford Press, 1960), Chap. 5.

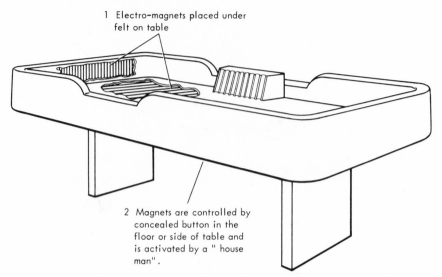

Figure 5–5 Typical dice table with electromagnets.

lend themselves to loaded dice activities or to electromagnets under the table, or in the wall, that can control the roll of the dice.

It is important for an investigator to recognize the more common forms of crooked dice operators. The presence of crooked dice in a game may supply the elements for a grand theft (bunco) charge against their owner. Figures 5–5 and 5–6 illustrate some of the more common types of crooked gambling devices.

Slot machines. Two decades ago, nearly every diner along the transcontinental highways had some form of slot machine action either as part of the dining room attraction or to lure customers to the back room. Most states now prohibit slot machine operation, either statewide or via local option. Federal law prohibits their interstate transportation.[16] The law also, in certain instances, prohibits transportation to a place where gambling is being conducted (gambling ships). Many states make it a misdemeanor to possess a slot machine. These statutes are frequently loosely enforced. Some states, such as California, make it a felony to possess a slot machine, and the statute is rigorously enforced.

Slot machines have a unique role in American gambling habits. No other form of gambling appeals so strongly to the woman gambler. A study conducted in Las Vegas, Nevada, indicated that the average woman gambler

[16]It shall be unlawful knowingly to transport a gambling device to any place in a state—from any place outside of such state—, 15 U.S.C. 1172.

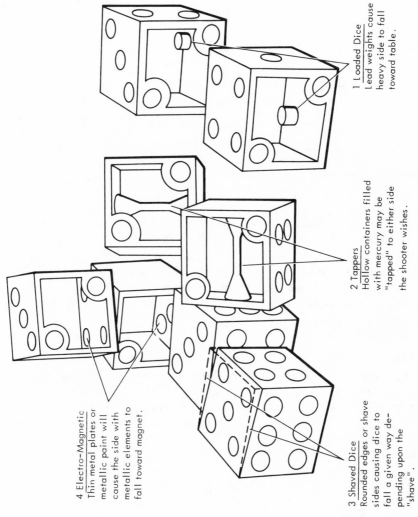

1 Loaded Dice
Lead weights cause heavy side to fall toward table.

2 Tappers
Hollow containers filled with mercury may be "tapped" to either side the shooter wishes.

4 Electro-Magnetic
Thin metal plates or metallic paint will cause the side with metallic elements to fall toward magnet.

3 Shaved Dice
Rounded edges or shave sides causing dice to fall a given way depending upon the "shave".

Figure 5-6 Cheater dice.

spent $17 per day on slots. The reasons for their preferences were summarized by Zimmerman.[17]

Receive a lot for their money in terms of action.
Lack knowledge of other games.
Requires small investment.
Feel sexual excitement while gambling.

The average woman would hesitate to play if she knew that large jackpots pay off at about 1 in 2700 times. The house will keep at least 5 percent and frequently up to 50 percent of every dollar played.

LOTTERIES: THE NUMBERS OR POLICY GAMES

Whereas cards, dice, and horse betting may satisfy the professional gambler, there are millions of people from every echelon of society who like to participate in a "little game" of chance. Number games are popular because they are simple and may be played inexpensively. Ten cents to a dollar per chance is the usual price, and all a player must do is draw a number or bet a hunch. For the numbers bettor, there is very little chance to win. For the numbers operator, there is absolutely no risk of loss.

To participate in the numbers game, for example, a bettor will draw a number between a preset number limit (1 to 1000). The operator will have regular drawings. These drawings may be by chance or they may be associated with race results, policy wheels, stock market figures, or other attention-getting gimmicks.

The term "policy" is frequently used to identify the numbers game. This derivation comes from the early days, when poor people set aside nickels, dimes, and quarters to pay on insurance policies. Frequently, they invested the money in numbers for quick profit, only to find that the odds of 1 in 1000 did not pay off very often. In the southern part of the United States, it is called "bolita" or "the bug."

The numbers game is usually an integral part of a poor neighborhood. The chances for quick riches make it attractive to those who cannot afford the luxuries of race tracks and gambling casinos. The "quick profit" or "big winner" atmosphere overshadows the fact that at least 25 percent of all money bet will go into the coffers of the confederations. Figure 5–7 is a hypothetical model of the numbers organization. A numbers ticket is usually nothing more than a simple form in triplicate. Frequently, only a simple plain number is used. Colors, number style, and special codes to avoid forgery will change daily.

[17]Gereon Zimmerman, "Gambling," *Look,* March 12, 1963, pp. 21–35. Also, Diane Weathers, etal, "Gamblers Who Can't Quit," *Newsweek,* March 3, 1980, p. 70.

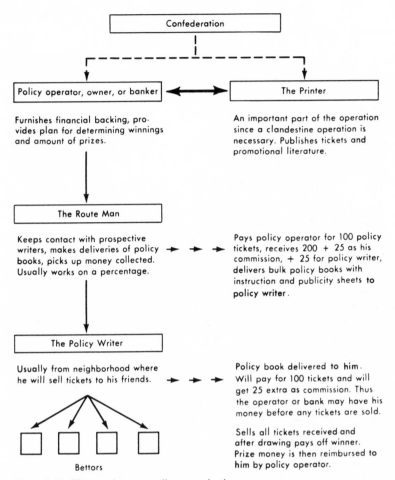

Figure 5-7 The numbers or policy organization.

In the past, drawing of the numbers was dramatic enough to bring out a crowd. For example, a Chinese numbers game was conducted in Los Angeles each morning. Bright and early the numbers writers would make their morning rounds, sell their tickets, and inform the bettor of the location of the noon drawing. At noon, at the prearranged place, a truck would pull up to the gathered crowd and park. There would be a rapid drawing of numbers from a washtub and the winners would be announced. The truck would then speed away before police arrived to take violators into custody.

In one Eastern city more than 1500 "number writers" collected in excess of $90,000 daily. There was a well-established "banking system" where the employees received full fringe benefits. Enforcement against this type of operation is nearly impossible because of public participation and apathy. Lottery or policy is becoming more a part of everyday activities and receives a high degree of public acceptance.

It is of interest that a legal lottery system will not interfere with the illegal lotteries now found in major United States cities. The twenty-five cent to one dollar lottery player likes action. He will buy his ticket and expect a payoff within hours. Most gamblers will not be happy with weekly or monthly payoffs based on just a few drawings per year, as used in the state systems.

Some of the most prevalent lottery schemes in use are shown in Figure 5–8. These illegal lotteries are in violation of federal and state law. They are the object of continuous enforcement action.

Lotteries may be chain letter schemes, raffles, bingo, football pools, baseball pools, and hundreds of similar schemes. Most lotteries are controlled by federal statutes as well as by state and local law. Basically, federal lottery regulations state it is a violation to:[18]

> Bring into the United States, for the purpose of disposing of the same, or
> Knowingly deposit with any express company, or
> Carry in interstate or foreign commerce, or
> Knowingly take or receive (when so carried) any paper, certificate or instrument:
> purporting to be or to represent a ticket, chance, share or interest in or dependent upon the event of
> a lottery, gift enterprise or similar scheme, offering prizes dependent in whole or in part upon lot or chance, or
> Any advertisement of or list of prizes drawn or awarded by means of such a lottery, etc. (Title 18 U.S. Code, Sec. 1301).

Federal law also prohibits the use of the United States Postal Service to send any offer, ticket, money, money order, etc., for tickets or any newspapers or publication advertising lotteries or containing any list of any part or all of the prizes. In spite of these prohibitions millions of Irish Sweepstakes tickets are sold in the United States annually.

SKIMMING AND BRIBERY

Gambling is more of a problem for others than those directly involved in losing to the system. The following problems will be present where gambling exists.

Skimming

One of the profitable gimmicks for organized gambling has been the skimming of money from legal casinos. A 1960s investigation in Las Vegas,

[18]U.S. Code 1301–1304 prohibits the carrying, knowingly taking, or receiving of chances, shares, interest, etc., in a gambling scheme. In 18 U.S. Code 1084, there is prohibition against the transportation of wagers across state lines.

Figure 5–8 Typical Football Pool Ticket

Nevada, indicated that the government had evidence that chunks of $100,000 had been going untaxed from the counting tables to private investments. Those involved were gamblers and syndicate representatives from all over America. While "skimming" has little interest for local enforcement, the investment of this money is bound to show up in the liquor business, the financing of prostitution activity, and other enterprises. Skimming rackets in Las Vegas and the group that is engaged in them read like a chapter from the "blue book" on organized crime.

Some of the money skimmed off the top will leave the country for foreign

deposit; some will go to special funds to insure that nearby states do not have gambling. Much of it may go into legitimate business.

In spite of adverse publicity, federal investigations are still being conducted and offenders are being prosecuted with evidence obtained from "listening devices." These cases in the next years will establish legal guides on how prosecutors must handle future cases of skimming. The Omnibus Crime Bill of 1970 contains provisions for utilization of listening devices, and Justice Department policy has made them operational. Most state laws, however, prohibit the use of listening devices such as phone taps.

Bribery

Some professional gamblers who concentrate on sporting events resort to bribery to make their bet a "sure thing." They bribe or attempt to bribe participants who can shave points to lose the even margin or cut down the winning margin. These are characteristics of the types of third-party criminality that become by-products of certain forms of gambling.

By implication, the relationship between sports and big business investments will probably always border on ethics rather than law.

Major organized sporting groups have kept investigators on their payroll to protect the player from this influence. Only in isolated instances have the major sports been tainted by bribery. However, those who know the business report bribery as a constant and continuing problem.

SUMMARY

Gambling, of all the vice type crimes, is the most lucrative and the most difficult to regulate. Individuals and communities sanction organized gambling operations, in an unconscious manner, merely by participating.

There are many viewpoints regarding the issue of punitive police sanctions imposed upon select types of gambling operations. Many well-informed citizens believe gambling will always be with our society; thus, it should be regulated and taxed as a normal business. On the other hand, there are those who believe it is morally wrong to sanction an activity that preys upon the weaknesses of human nature.

Throughout the history of civilization there is evidence of the human propensity to gamble. There are also indicators that laws regulating gambling have been token gestures of societies that are divided on "how much" gambling can be tolerated.

Statistics, gathered for decades, indicate that society as a whole does not attach great moral or legal wrong to gambling. As a result of the diverse attitudes about gambling, law enforcement officers and administrators are placed in the position of interpreting social attitudes in the application of the

legal statutes. These facts lead to the breakdown of legal sanctions and superimpose a criminal confederation upon every community.

The criminal confederations are not represented by overt gamblers hustling bets from strangers on the street. The confederation representatives are the neighborhood bookies, the football pool sellers, and club friends who just happen to always have lottery tickets of some variety. The gambling empires are built around the twenty-five cent to two dollar bets. Only with massive public participation can they exist.

Law enforcement cannot presume to make much of an impact upon gambling organizations. The organizations are "wired into" every level of government. Only through legal collusion and, frequently, corruption can professional gamblers exist.

This chapter illustrated a few of the more common gambling schemes. These schemes are not unusual; they are known by nearly every teenager and adult in the United States. The popularity of gambling creates vice enforcement problems that make acceptable regulation extremely difficult.

QUESTIONS FOR DISCUSSION

1. Discuss what is meant when the term "malum prohibita" is used in referring to gambling.
2. What proof do we have that there are degrees of disagreement on the issue of legalized gambling? Poll the class and discuss the different viewpoints.
3. Is there a double standard in many church and civic organizations with regard to gambling?
4. There tends to be a cycle in the dynamics of gambling—as amount of gambling increases, prohibitory legislation increases, legislation becomes poorly administered, which prompts repeal of local laws for revenue purposes, causing increased gambling and the cycle to repeat. Explain.
5. The federal and state governments may impose sanctions against gambling, but the problem must ultimately be resolved in the community. Explain.
6. The organizational structure of the betting syndicates makes them nearly immune to legal arrests. Why?
7. There are five specific booking activities cited in this text. Explain why the number could be ten or fifteen.
8. The betting marker is perhaps one of the best bits of evidence for prosecution purposes. Why?
9. Sports bookies are generally said to work on a commission. Why?
10. Why are there differences among the "morning line," the "opening line," and the "initial line"?
11. Why are cards and dice such popular gambling instruments?
12. What are the paradoxes of lotteries that make them so difficult to control?

6
PROSTITUTION

LEARNING OUTCOMES

1. Learn why law enforcement is involved in the control of prostitution.
2. Understand how the organized confederations gain control of prostitution activities.
3. Recognize the common modes of operation of the prostitute and the relationship to ancillary crimes.
4. Realize that control of prostitution has always created a social, ethical, and legal problem.

Law enforcement interest in the control of prostitution is based upon a number of criteria. First is the crime itself: Society finds it repugnant to have the prostitute barter sex for favors without an emotional attachment between partners. Second, society has become a moral moderator of activities it will sanction. Prostitution, as an occupation, does not meet the approval of society as a whole. Third is the necessity to eliminate ancillary crimes that cluster around the profession of prostitution. Fourth, enforcement activity limits the number of contacts between prostitute and client, thus discouraging the transmission of veneral disease through random sexual contacts. These reasons may be subject to debate, but they are the rationale that supports the suppression activities directed toward prostitution.

The profession of prostitution is a sad occupation for the male and female prostitutes. The hope of riches soon gives way to fear, exploitation, and guilt. The prostitute acquires criminal friends, venereal diseases, and eventually the easy way out becomes drug addiction. Drugs and thieves gravitate to the high earnings of the prostitute.

Prostitution, like other vice crimes, is not controlled in a consistent way. The sporadic control exerted by law enforcement will usually be prompted by

political cleanup campaigns or as a result of protesting citizen groups. This is frequently done in a manner that proves unreliable and ineffective. Proponents of legalization do not understand the dynamics of this problem, an observation noted in *Organized Crime Task Force Report.*[1]

States and localities should exercise caution in considering the legalization or decriminalization of so-called victimless crimes such as gambling, drug use, prostitution, and pornography. These are known to provide income to organized crime. There is insufficient evidence that legalization or decriminalization of such crimes will materially reduce the income of organized crime. On the contrary, evidence does exist that the elimination or reduction of legal restraints can encourage the expansion of organized activities.

The reasons why legalization or decriminalization may not work with prostitution depend on the underlying reasons for the prostitutes becoming involved in the business. Here are some general reasons:[2]

1. There is a high unemployment rate among young unskilled men and women.
2. The exchange of money and the sex act is a manifestation of social rejection.
3. The prostitute retains differing roles in society, lending credence to the accusation that he or she will in many instances be schizophrenic.
4. The prostitute is usually a social isolate in terms of friends, couples, and normal social life; therefore, many become heavy drug users.
5. The prostitute has a paranoidal distrust of the opposite sex, possibly because of parental deprivation in childhood.
6. The prostitute has little self-concept so far as lying, loyalties, or violating a trust.

Prostitution, as the term is generally employed by sociologists, social workers, and the courts, refers to the promiscuous bartering of sex favors for monetary consideration, either gifts or cash, without any emotional attachment between the partners.

Prostitution is the practice of offering one's body for indiscriminate intercourse, usually in exchange for something of monetary value. The word "prostitute" is not a technical one, and it has no common law meaning. A woman or man who indulges in illicit sexual intercourse with only one person is not a prostitute. Prostitution is not synonymous with sexual intercourse.[3]

---

[1]National Advisory Committee on Criminal Justice Standards and Goals, *Organized Crime: Report of the Task Force on Organized Crime* (Washington, D.C.: U.S. Government Printing Office, December 1976), p. 65.

[2]The conclusions drawn here were taken from law enforcement officer observations over an extended period of years. These observations have no documented basis.

[3]*Corpus Juris Secundum* 224, "Prostitution" Section 1 (St. Paul, Minn: West Publishing Company, 1951).

HISTORY OF PROSTITUTION

Prostitutes, honored, scorned, and crucified, have had a tormented background in their struggle to escape the controlling efforts of society. Sociologists, psychologists, and law enforcement agents all have different theories as to why someone becomes a prostitute. Whatever the causal factor, history indicates that any single control measure will eventually prove ineffective. As society has changed, so have the laws governing prostitution. As the laws have changed, so have the prostitutes' methods of operation.

Prostitution is as old as civilization and appears to be closely related to urban life and mobile populations. Prostitution was recognized and respected in many ancient societies. Parents sold daughters, husbands compromised wives, and religious practitioners engaged in prostitution. The Semites of the Eastern Mediterranean were notorious for their practices. Jewish fathers were, however, forbidden to turn their daughters into prostitutes,[4] and the daughters of Israel were forbidden to become prostitutes.[5] From the biblical teachings, our modern moral code and habits have evolved.

The naturalistic attitudes of the Greeks and Romans were in direct contrast with the teachings of the Hebrews and Christians. In the classical period of ancient Greece, marriage did not attain the same dignity as it did among the Hebrews and the Christians. Women from prominent families and high society often became the playmates of affluent Greek men. As conquests spread, slaves seized as the prisoners of war become their conquerors' prostitutes.

The Romans adopted the Greek attitude on prostitution. The excessive supply of prostitutes from the wars lowered their social position and led to compulsory distinction of their dress, loss of civil rights, and registration of those in houses of ill repute. Eventually, women became shielded because of tainted blood in marriages with prostitutes. Rigid laws were passed and heavy taxes levied on the occupation of prostitution.

During the reign of the Anglo-Saxon kings in England, antiprostitution laws were severe. Violation meant banishment or death. Later, prostitution was legalized in the London area, and strife over church or civil control brought disrepute and corruption to both the church and the municipalities. As in England, all of Western Europe was in moral turmoil over prostitution control and enforcement. The control was inconsistent, and corruption prevailed. Frequent reform movements were unable to cope with the well-established profession. In the Middle Ages, prostitution was tolerated, the caprice of passions being recognized as a necessary evil. Efforts were taken to control it or at least to keep it within reasonable bounds.

[4]Leviticus 19:29.
[5]Deuteronomy 23:17.

During the Reformation, moral attitudes shifted due to medical necessity. Syphilitic epidemics swept over Europe in the fifteenth and sixteenth centuries and wiped out nearly a third of the population. Fear and disease had done what moral attitudes had failed to do. Major European cities vigorously punished those engaged in prostitution. In the seventeenth century, major cities instituted medical treatment for prostitutes and reverted to the Greek-Roman system of licensing houses of prostitution and punishing private entrepreneurs. The basic form of control remained a common practice through the eighteenth and up to the end of the nineteenth centuries.

At the end of the nineteenth century, British reformers organized antivice organizations. As a result, the Criminal Law Amendment Act of 1885 was developed in Great Britain. In the United States, vice commissions became the popular pastime of civic groups, and the Mann Act of 1910 emerged.[6] Most of the states followed with laws that prohibited third-party profit from the activities of prostitutes.

International control was implemented with the Paris Agreement of 1904. In 1921, the League of Nations established a commission to study the problem of prostitution. Although the League of Nations had little direct effect, it caused the countries of modern Europe to abandon the houses of prostitution and in many instances to offer free medical treatment for venereal diseases.[7]

COMMON METHODS OF PROSTITUTION AND ORGANIZED CRIME AFFILIATION

The problem of prostitution has been studied primarily from the emotional rather than the more objective statistical method. These studies have assisted the sociologist and the psychologist, but have been of little help in identifying the importance of punitive control as a regulatory process. Few studies have been conducted that identify prostitution with organized crime.

Prostitution is identified as an antisocial behavior manifested to meet the psychological needs of the individual prostitute and customer. There is considerable doubt whether enforcement, as it is conducted in Western cultures, has much impact upon the professional prostitute's activity. Many psychiatrists and psychoanalysts see prostitution as a more complex problem than do the legislators and law enforcement officials, who often allege that money and unsavory associates are causal factors. Social scientists trace the roots of prostitution to emotional factors. It is therefore generally conceded today that a wide variety of economic, sociological, and psychological factors

---

[6]Title 18, U.S. Code, Section 2421, 2422, 2423, commonly referred to as the White Slave Traffic Act.

[7]*The Encyclopedia Americana* (1970), XXII, 674.

is involved in the profession of prostitution. Thus, the crime of prostitution awaits control by logical, clear-thinking legislators.

Sociological studies tend to suggest that most postitutes come from areas with high delinquency and crime rates. In such social subcultures the potential prostitute identifies with members of society who are alienated from the ethical standards of a larger society. Thus, these subcultures live with, tend to accept, and adhere to many of the mores of the underworld.

Drug addiction has been cited as a growing factor in the recruitment of prostitutes and in keeping them in the trade. The majority of drug addicts are young adults from the underprivileged areas of large cities. They are mainly unemployed and uninterested in employment other than to maintain their drug supply, largely by crimes against property and by prostitution.[8]

Types of Prostitute

A prostitute at some time in her or his career may work within each of many classifications of prostitution. One need only look at the Yellow Pages of the telephone directory to discover the innovative methods employed by independent and organized prostitutes. Some of the more common methods are explained here.

The streetwalker. Streetwalking is perhaps the most common form of prostitution in which the amateur can become involved. This method is also least apt to have confederations sharing in the profits. In poor neighborhoods, the streets are full of young people who are in the business full time or use streetwalking as a means to supplement other income. In the age of the automobile, the streetwalker is an instant business success. Old professional streetwalkers are on the prowl to find new prostitutes to refer to their customers for a small fee. The old streetwalker in fact becomes a madam. These madams can usually show fairly solid business associations with local organized criminals. Young women who become street hustlers often begin their careers by raising a few dollars to make financial ends meet. Their intention is to turn a few "tricks" and then seek other avenues of employment. However, once in the business and under the direction of a pimp, it is difficult for them to return to the work-a-day world.

The call girl/boy. The telephone offers the prostitute a degree of sophistication in contacting clients. It also offers large organized operations clandestine protection from discovery. The telephone serves to maintain a

[8]*Encyclopedia Britannica* (1966), XVIII, 648.

wide circle of contacts for the prostitute. If discreetly used, the telephone gives a certain degree of security from enforcement. Call girls are frequently a part of organized crime because of referrals and protection offered by pimps.

The working prostitute maintains a "black book" of customers. When the prostitute wants to work, she uses the phone to contact listed prospects. If the prostitute is a part of a stable, working for a confederation, customers will be referred in a variety of ways. A good black book contains more than the name and phone number of the client. For example, identifying notations may contain a prospective trick's social security number, the wife's first name, the wife's maiden name, the names of children, a physical description, and facts about his business that only a particular client would know. From a black book the prostitute can quickly reestablish a business. Thus, the black book has a high monetary value and frequently is sold by the prostitute before she leaves town or is jailed for any length of time because of illegal activities. Through male partners in the confederations, the black book may pass from one prostitute to another within the organization.

The electronic call girl/boy.   A popular new technique for the prostitute is the installation of an electronic answering device. The communication between prostitute and clientele is then screened through the medium of a recording device. This device protects the prostitute if he or she is cautious in accepting customers. This answering instrument also eliminates the possibility of an information leak to the police. Frequently, the phone is installed in a vacant room and the prostitute then takes messages from another location via a tone or automatic response from the electronic device. Willing pimps gladly supply maintenance.

The lonely hearts hustler.   Enterprising prostitutes, with the assistance of confederation members, have always found clever ways in which to obtain new clients. The pages of pulp magazines are full of cases where boy meets girl through the lonely hearts club. The numerous contacts made by a prostitute in this manner are seldom reported, and they very seldom come to the attention of the police. The only control law enforcement has over this type of operation is to purchase lists of girls and boys and endeavor to screen professional prostitutes from the legitimate clients. Most departments, however, simply ignore the problem because the apprehension of this type of hustler is tedious, slow, and expensive. Because of the difficulty of apprehension, the organized criminal element may often operate lonely hearts clubs.

The computer-selected date.   Computerized dating firms are in the business of introducing couples. Illicit operators can take advantage of the situation and contact cash customers through this medium. Prostitutes pay the nominal fee, submit a questionnaire, and let the computer select the customers. This automatic matchmaker not only selects congenial prospects,

but categorizes as to financial endorsement. In this setting of cybernetic bliss, the hustler is able to choose a $10,000 or a $50,000 per year client. As of this date, the prostitute still has to make the deals and consummate the transactions.

Computerized dating bureaus are interested in protecting their clients, especially women, from unethical males. They compare the variables on the questionnaire and then make the men's names and qualifications available to qualified women members. For the smart hustler, what better and cheaper way is there to have clients screened? Law enforcement has only one alternative, and that is to begin the slow process of joining the club, getting referred to women with the right personality coefficients, and discovering the professional hustler.

The public relations gimmick. The line between legitimate and illegitimate enterprises is frequently so fine it is not a matter of law, but one of morality. The public relations "action" is so covert and the mating of the male and female so shrewd the customer frequently believes the romance is for love. The sponsoring company paying the public relations firm must have a satisfied client, so the amount of money spent is not a factor.

Some years ago a member of a California hoodlum group spent his entire time locating "nice girls" for public relations firms. His title was respectable and the women were hired as secretaries (if they could type) or as product demonstrators (if they had no business talents). The company would send the women out of town to business meetings or conventions to conduct ethical business. During the evenings the women were entertained in the best places, drank the best drinks, and slept in the softest beds. What they did not know was that the hiring agent knew of their every activity. Photographs and tape recordings were used to blackmail both the woman and client. Once the women were in no position to refuse, they became full-time call girls for the hiring agent.

Call girls were then available for weekend trips with clients referred from the public relations firm and others of financial means. When these trips were made full documentation was made of the trip. Generally, the women were able to keep their salaries and tips received from the client. Later, the hiring agent would offer to sell photographs and recordings of the weekend to the prostitute's client. Known victims of this shakedown paid sums of $14,000, $10,000, $8,000 and so on. Although this activity was known to police sources, victims refused to prosecute because of adverse publicity. Every city has, in addition to the legitimate public relations firms, a group that is for hire.

The photo studio. Photo studios operate in areas that are liberal in certain types of conduct. In areas around Hollywood, California, the small entrepreneur rents an old house and puts up colorful oversized signs

advertising nude models to photograph. He then waits for lonely males to beat a path to the door. In many instances the models may be legitimate and the photographer may actually take pictures. In many cases the model uses the posing session to make contact with a photographer who never bothers to put film in the rented camera.

The secretarial service.   Wherever a profession is predominately female there are bound to be a few professional prostitutes who join the ranks to make contact with male customers. Most secretarial services are legal, well supervised, and render a vital service. Occasionally, however, illicit operators will have business connections and begin contracting secretarial services to unethical clients.

The Jeleke case in New York showed this operation. The secretarial service received fees for the girl's service as a secretary. The secretary and the male customer were then able to work their own deals. From the select list of thirty-seven secretaries in one secretarial service, it was found that only three could type.

The housewife.   It is not unusual among the ranks of prostitutes to find housewives who supplement the family income. This is fairly common among impoverished minorities who must either assist or entirely support a family. A few years ago a national magazine article revealed that a group of housewives from middle- and upper-income families of Long Island and New Jersey were merchandising their favors for $25 to $100.

The favorite spots for the hustlers were the race tracks and bars. When this amateur activity threatened the professionals, the professionals immediately informed the police, who quickly jailed the trespassers.

The massage parlor.   The most obvious inroad of organized crime into prostitution during the past two decades has been through the massage parlor. Wherever a corrupt government agency can be found, there will shortly follow a colony of fixed massage parlors or the more "mobile variety," each catering to prostitute-client relationships. The massage parlors are mutli-million-dollar businesses that point a direct finger at corrupt public agencies.[9] The parlors are often referred to as the poor man's country club and with honest law enforcement cannot survive.

Social Habits and Federal Law

Kinsey report.   Kinsey and his associates found that about 69 percent of the male white population in the United States had some experiences with

---

[9]New Mexico—Governor's Organized Crime Prevention Commission, *Annual Report,* Albuquerque, 1979.

prostitutes, ranging from those who only visited a prostitute once or twice to those who paid regular visits. Kinsey found, however, that the percentage of men who visited prostitutes varied with educational achievement. By the time that they were twenty-five years old, 74 percent of the 5300 men studied, who had not gone beyond grade school, had visited prostitutes; in contrast, 54 percent of those who had gone to high school, and 28 percent with college or university training, had visited prostitutes. Many of the married men had some illicit relations, but only 1.7 percent of their total sex outlet was with prostitution.[10]

Rigid sex standards are obviously not accepted by males in the United States, and this complicates any program for eliminating prostitution.

Federal laws. In 1910, the Mann Act became a major deterrent to interstate transportation of prostitutes. This federal act, known as the White Slave Traffic Act, prohibits and penalizes as a felony the act of any person who transports, causes to be transported, or aids or assists in transporting any woman or girl in interstate or foreign commerce for the purpose of prostitution, debauchery, or any other immoral purpose. The White Slave Traffic Act covers a broad field. In defining the purpose for which interstate transportation of a girl or woman must not be furnished, the language of the act is broad enough to include practically every form of sexual immorality. The previous character or reputation of the woman or girl transported in interstate commerce for immoral purposes is entirely immaterial. The statute is violated where the defendant has transported, procured, or aided in procuring the transportation of a woman or girl from one state to another for the purpose of inducing or enabling her to engage in the business of prostitution.[11]

Statutes regulating public morals, including the regulation and punishment of prostitution and pandering, fall within the police power of the state.[12] There is no attempt to regulate private immorality. There are limits to the degree in which criminal law can regulate the profession of prostitution. The law does not attempt to dictate private morals or ethical sanctions, but only to regulate offenses that are injurious to another's rights.

The law enforcement officer cannot compromise the law. Every case, however, has to be approached with care and caution. What may appear to be a clandestine case of prostitution could be a legally married couple. The

---

[10]Alfred C. Kinsey, Wardell B. Pomeroy, and Clyde E. Martin, *Sexual Behavior in the Human Male* (Philadelphia: Saunders, 1948).

[11]*American Jurisprudence* 268–271, "Prostitution," Section 11, Bancroft-Whitney, San Francisco, California.

[12]In Nevada prostitution operates openly in all but two counties. Local residents favor this type of control and do not choose to abate the activity as a nuisance. It is said that direct airline service from Las Vegas delivers passengers to at least a dozen different established houses of prostitutes.

officer may be the subject of a civil suit if a prearrest investigation is improperly or inadequately conducted.

With prostitution, as with many moral problems, there seems to be no definite or final solution because the problem is a recurring one for each individual and for each generation.

Perhaps the strongest argument for the control of prostitution is not from a moral approach, but from one of protection from venereal disease.

VENEREAL DISEASE AND PROSTITUTION

A law enforcement officer, in order to understand the basic philosophy for enacting laws prohibiting prostitution, must be aware of related venereal diseases. Although the control of venereal disease is primarily a medical problem, the courts and law enforcement are an integral part of the total process. Most states, as part of their sentencing procedures in prostitution cases, require the prostitute to pass a physical test or be sentenced to jail where he or she will be treated.

There is much disagreement among the experts on how to control venereal disease (VD). It is uncertain whether rigid enforcement drives the illegal activity underground where contacts are not reported, or whether "open houses" under close medical inspection, with more contacts, is better for control of the disease.

Few human maladies have influenced the course of history more strongly. The destinies of empires have been decided upon the ravages of venereal disease epidemics.

Gonorrhea. Egyptian writings refer to and describe the miseries of gonorrhea. Ancient philosophers have referred to the cases of gonorrhea as pleasure excesses, urinary tract ulcerations, and the burning fires of the devil. There are references in writings that in Egypt relief was gained from extracts of certain plants. In Arabia it was not uncommon to resolve the problem through surgery.

Syphilis. In the history of medicine, no infectious disease has ever been eradicated or completely controlled merely by treating infected persons. Improved transportation methods encourage travel and migration, and a disease may be erased in one country only to flourish in another.[13] Travel and war seem to have been the companions of the venereal disease called syphilis, since it is alleged Columbus brought the disease back from the New World. Also, around 1495 in military campaigns against Naples by Charles VIII of France, the scourge of syphilis is reported to have hit his armies and caused

[13]*Encyclopedia Americana* (1970), XXVI, 177.

retreats back into France. The disease spread to all of Europe, and by 1500 every major country was victimized. The rise and fall of social sanctions against prostitution can be traced to reactions against outbreaks of syphilis.

For more than 400 years after syphilis first became a problem, progress in knowledge of the disease was slow, halting, and wholly clinical.[14] Thus, the social aspects of prevention and education did not really begin until the twentieth century.

Because there were not adequate facilities and knowledge available, the prevalence of syphilis was related to the contact with the prostitute, which in many cases was accurate. The social struggle to stamp out prostitution and thus the disease has been one of society's long wars. Perhaps the profit factor alone has kept prostitution and its companion, syphilis, much a part of the political struggle between the rights of the individual and the rights of society to sanction certain personal behavior. Civil and ecclesiastical authorities have met in conflict time and again. This disagreement between the two most powerful bodies of society has created a vacuum in which organized crime has found it most convenient to move in and control.

After the initial shock of the great syphilitic pandemic of the fifteenth and sixteenth centuries, reformation of the citizen became the order of the day. Out of fear of the disease, prostitution control spread throughout Europe. Medical treatment, and the isolation of houses of prostitution, both under the control of the police, became the standard for the progressive European countries by the beginning of the twentieth century.

The medical inspection of houses of prostitution was never very successful. First, the prostitute in multiple contacts could spread the disease before it was detected. Second, there was a tendency for unethical doctors and police officers to engage in bribery to overlook inspections, so the sanctions were useless. Third, the enterprising prostitute was always ready to bootleg the illicit merchandise. The Criminal Law Amendment Act of 1885 was initiated to curb the international trade in white slavery and served to restrict some of the international trade between countries so that control of the prostitute would be reflected in a reduction of syphilis.

While the authors do not hold that the control of syphilis is directly related to the rigid control of prostitution, there is evidence that the reduction of prostitute-client contacts must have an impact on the venereal disease rate. The cities that are noted for tight control of prostitutes generally have substantially lower rates of venereal disease. Obviously if organized crime controls a city, there can be no effective enforcement.

It is of interest to law enforcement to note the trends in VD. Figure 6–1 shows indications that once the state begins reporting the incidence of venereal disease and the military disease incidence is removed, the incidence of syphilis dropped sharply and remained constant at that lower level. The

[14]*Encyclopedia Americana* (1970), XXVI, 180.

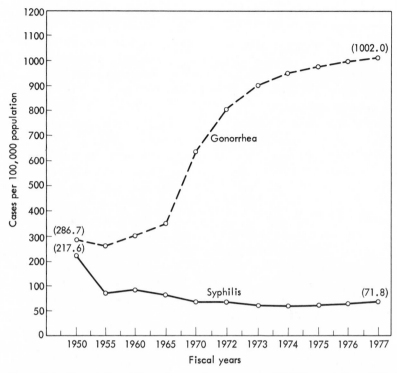

Figure 6–1 Reported syphilis and gonorrhea cases per 100,000 population, United States, 1950–1977.[15]

incidence of gonorrhea cases has not shown that trend. These data have been broken down by regions. Region IV (Colorado, Montana, the Dakotas, Utah, and Wyoming) has a syphilis rate of 464 and a gonorrhea rate of 18,754 per 100,000 population. This compares to Region III, consisting of the Southern states, with a syphilis rate of 14,679 and a gonorrhea rate of 24,819 per 100,000 population. The Western states have a rate of 13,267 for syphilis and 13,792 for gonorrhea. These trends may show an attitude toward the enforcement of prostitution, but, without more comprehensive data, there is no positive correlation between lax enforcement and VD rates. Maxwell makes these observations:

> Adolescents contract venereal disease, (syphilis or gonorrhea) at the rate of 1300 or more each day. Youth 15 to 20 years of age contribute to 56 percent of this daily infection rate. Also, 1300 adults per day fall victim to venereal

[15]U.S. National Center for Health Statistics, *Vital Statistics—Special Reports*, Vol. 37, No., 8, and U.S. Center for Disease Control, Atlanta, *Morbidity and Mortality Weekly Report* (annual supplements).

disease. Unfortunately they seem to be as misinformed about this subject as the teenagers.[16]

Government venereal disease experts contend that even these totals fail to represent the true number of cases because many private doctors do not report the diseases as they should, and because many people who can pass on the diseases go untreated because they do not know they have VD.

In the opinion of Dr. William Brown, chief of the venereal disease branch of the Communicable Disease Center in Atlanta, only one in ten VD cases treated by physicians is reported, and he believes that the actual number of Americans being treated each year is more than a million. Dr. Brown rates VD as a major threat to the nation's health.

The objective symptoms of VD. Law enforcement officers will have occasions to associate with suspected or active cases of VD. Both for understanding the problem and as a medical precaution, the officer should be familiar with the symptoms.

The primary stage is the most infectious stage in syphilis. These germs do not float around in the body as commonly believed, but settle in body tissue. Their favorite locations are the brain, heart, and liver. In this primary stage the germ enters the body. Their presence can be noted in the blood from ten days to three weeks. This stage is painless to the infected individual.

The secondary stage still produces no pain. Often the victim will break out in a rash. During this stage the carrier is infectious.

The latent or dormant stage occurs about two years after the initial infection, and no signs are usually present. This stage may last from ten to twenty years. It is during this time that infection from syphilis sets in.

In the terminal stage the vital organs are so badly deteriorated that death results.

Although law enforcement does not hold the answer to the control of VD, if the vice officer is aware of medical ramifications, it is easier for him or her to understand the reasons behind rigid laws for the control of prostitution.

SUMMARY

There are many reasons for law enforcement to be involved in control of prostitution. Society views the crime itself to be wrong; society also views itself as a regulator of morality. Ancillary crimes need controlling, and legal sanctions curb venereal contacts.

Although these reasons are logical and unemotional, it is believed that the

[16]Edward Maxwell, "Why the Rise in Teenage Venereal Disease?" *Today's Health*, 1965, pp. 18–23, 87–91. These data are still valid; today, the problem of herpes would be added.

enforcement officer needs a strong rationale for enforcement policies. With a more thorough understanding of the prostitutes' historical role in the different cultures, an officer can better appreciate the need for some form of restriction on the prostitutes' activities.

Causal factors range from emotional to economic. Perhaps prostitution, more than crimes of property and crimes of violence, supports the "multiple cause" theory of the social sciences. There are very few empirical studies on the "why" of prostitution; therefore, many observations made about prostitution are purely emotional. Alienation from established values by various subcultures tends to perpetuate this antisocial behavior.

An attempt has been made to identify the role of law enforcement as a possible deterrent to venereal diseases by imposing sanctions that minimize contact between prostitute and client.

Police control of prostitution fluctuates along a continuum from no control to fairly rigid control. The degree of control exerted depends upon the legislation of proper statutes, the attitude of the community toward suppressing overt prostitution, and the effectiveness of the enforcement agencies in initiating and maintaining control measures.

Most frequently, a city will have areas that attract certain categories of prostitutes. Poorer areas will have streetwalkers and doorway hustlers, while the better apartment house areas will attract bar hustlers as well as call girls working through cabbies and bellboys. The prostitutes who are most overt in their actions will receive a greater share of police attention.

QUESTIONS FOR DISCUSSION

1. Identify and discuss the prime rationale for police involvement in the enforcement of antiprostitution measures.
2. Because of the controversial role of the police in prostitution control it is important for the police to have a knowledge of the history of prostitution. Why is this so important?
3. Identify at least five ways in which organized criminal groups are involved in prostitution activities.
4. How does the practice of prostitution relate to such crimes as drug abuse, burglary, thefts, and so on?
5. Would you normally expect organized criminals to be involved in more sophisticated prostitution activities than the streetwalker? If so, what kind?
6. What are some of the advantages in using the Mann Act for the prosecution of interstate prostitution rings?
7. If the law is wrong with regard to the enforcement of prostitution, why is it important to change the law rather than have police make a lax enforcement of the law?
8. Does the evidence presented about venereal disease offer a logical rationale for some type of control over prostitution?

7

ORGANIZED CRIME AND DRUG TRAFFIC

LEARNING OUTCOMES

1. Have an overview of how politics affects international drug enforcement.
2. Develop an awareness of the difficulties in enforcing drug laws at the local level.
3. Understand how drugs flow in international trade and how the money moves from consumer to peddler.
4. Be able to identify the importance of metropolitan enforcement groups.
5. Know the influence of new laws and the applications of civil sanctions against known drug dealers.
6. Connect known peddlers with established confederated groups.

In order to address effective drug control, whether it be an instrument of organized crime or a private business enterprise, we must deal with the issues of federal political negotiations, of federal activity in law enforcement efforts, and of determining the extent of organized crime involvement in drug trafficking. Organized crime involvement deals only with the securing, transporting, and selling of various drugs. The pathologies of the drug user and the impact of drugs on society are the highly emotional and visible elements of the drug problem. But there has been little public concern about the key to the solution of the drug abuse problem, which is to stop the peddlers who make an occupation of dealing in drugs.

The peddlers involved in drug distribution are members of the confederations as well as groups of people who are not dependent on a central authority. These groups depend on mutual trust based on profit interests and an agreed-upon division of labor. Because of the diverse groups involved in drug distribution, all contingencies cannot be covered. This chapter will attempt to show that the involvement of confederations in drug traffic is real. During the past decade, known members of established Mafia families have

been identified as drug dealers, and some have been convicted on drug charges. The involvement of confederations in drug distribution and sale is addressed in these areas: (1) a political overview of drug traffic history and organized crime involvement; (2) the role of federal, state, and local government units against confederated drug trafficking; and (3) the state and local role in future drug traffic enforcement.

DRUG TRAFFIC: HISTORY AND ORGANIZED CRIME INVOLVEMENT

The involvement of organized crime in drug traffic is, by the nature of the transaction, a national and international problem. International political alliances, carried on by the Department of State, are keystones to the success of drug traffic suppression. When it becomes apparent that political agreements and treaties are unable to curb the flow of drugs, trafficking problems then become of national, state, and local concern. In the past decade there has been increased federal activity in both political relations and enforcement activities. The primary effort of the State Department has been through the secretary of state's chairmanship of the Cabinet Committee for International Narcotics Control. There have been a number of bilateral negotiations to encourage the United Nations to move actively against drug abuse.[1]

The recent history of drug negotiations has little meaning unless the early history is put into perspective. There is little question that organized gangs were involved in drug transactions prior to the ninth century. In the seventeenth century, Western European traders were reportedly prime culprits in the illegal movement of drugs across borders. In the eighteenth century, when opium became the common tonic for pain relief, it also became a prime commodity of tradesmen who traveled from the Orient to Western Europe. When morphine was developed and became a cure for opium addiction, the processing laboratories of Europe became the middlemen controlling drug flows from the poppy fields to retail merchants in Europe, the United States, and throughout the world. The legitimacy of merchants was not questioned, for they were looked upon as providing a necessary service. In 1874 the German chemist Dresser found the cure for both opium and morphine addiction in a drug called heroin.

In the United States the distribution of heroin was regulated by the Harrison Act of 1914. The result was a disastrous rise in heroin addiction. Reportedly the merchandising was done through established drug outlets. A few years later foreign production, sale, and distribution were banned by the Narcotic Import and Export Act of 1922. (The domestic manufacture of

---

[1]For a comprehensive review of drug trafficking problems, see James D. Stinchcomb, *Trafficking in Drugs and Narcotics* (Richmond: Virginia Commonwealth University, 1979).

heroin was outlawed in 1924.) Since that time there have been various updates of the laws:

Marihuana Tax Act of 1937
Opium Poppy Control Act of 1942
Boggs Act of 1951
Narcotics Control Act of 1956
The Drug Abuse Office and Treatment Act of 1972
Currency and Foreign Transactions Act of 1978 (deters the use of international financial transactions and secret foreign bank accounts)

It is since the 1920s that organized gangs have controlled the major flow of drugs into the United States. Basically, the statutes covering drugs are adequate, but they have had no appreciable and lasting impact on drug distribution in the past 50 years.

Recognizing the deficiency of enforcement efforts, the federal government has not been idle in attempting to negotiate accords among nations. The Cabinet Committee for International Narcotic Control has negotiated mutual assistance arrangements with Mexico, Turkey, and France in cooperative efforts against illegal drug traffic.[2] This negotiation was brought about by the United Nations' Commission on Narcotic Drugs, which includes 24 member nations. Through a special fund for drug abuse control, a comprehensive UN plan for action against drug abuse was developed. The objectives of the plan are these:

To expand the United Nations' research and information facilities.
To limit the supply of drugs to legitimate requirements by ending illegal production and substituting other economic opportunities.
To enlarge the capabilities and extend the operations of existing United Nations drug control bodies.
To promote facilities for treatment, rehabilitation, and social reintegration of drug addicts.
To develop educational material and programs against drug abuse in high-risk populations.

The first effort under this program was in December 1971 when the United States, Thailand, and the United Nations agreed to coordinate their efforts in drug control projects. This was preceded by a March 1971 Single Convention on Narcotic Drugs, in which 90 nations adopted the basic international regulation to control the flow of narcotic drugs such as opium and heroin. In 1972 a 97-nation United Nations Plenipotentiary Conference in Geneva adopted a protocol amending the Single Convention treaty of the previous

[2]*Attorney General's First Annual Report* (Washington, D.C.: U.S. Government Printing Office, 1972), p. 266.

year. This treaty commits 97 nations of the world to a resolution of the drug abuse problem.

The protocol empowered the International Narcotics Control Board to:

Exercise new authority to curb illicit cultivation, production, manufacture, trafficking, and consumption of opium, heroin, and other narcotics.

Require reduction of production of opium poppy cultivation and opium production in countries shown to be sources of illicit traffic.

Extradite and thus prosecute narcotic traffickers who have taken refuge in other nations.

The Convention on Psychotropic Substances imposed the same constraints on nations producing "mind-bending" hallucinogenic substances such as LSD, mescaline, amphetamines, barbiturates, and tranquilizers.

With these accords, law enforcement agencies are for the first time in a position to make a lasting corrective impact on drug trafficking. The major problems remain how to tie organized confederations into the distribution complex and secure prosecutions against top level dealers.

RESULTS OF THE 1971 CONVENTIONS

We are now viewing the results of a decade of United States involvement in active efforts to curb drug importation. These enforcement efforts are based on two philosophies:[3] (1) to seal the borders of the United States against drug imports and (2) to move into the producing countries and attempt to curb the growth and production of narcotics and other illegal drugs.

Sealing the Borders of the United States

The political decision makers who sealed United States borders immediately found there were massive problems. First, the borders, open on four sides, could not be sealed with the manpower available. Second, because of the reduction in the flow of drugs from Turkey, Mexico became the major supplier to the United States. For at least three decades organized crime had been making Mexican contacts. Almost overnight, the dealers who had been furnishing modest, low-visibility amounts to American distributors were inundated with volume orders. By 1977 there were over 100 well-established Mexican organizations handling the transportation of narcotics going north. Where ounces had once been the standard, kilos became the new measure. Mobility and flexibility became the byword of the organizations and the bain of the enforcement agencies.

---

[3]*ABC Nightline*, news interview with DEA administrator, Thailand, May 15, 1981.

Curbing Growth and Production in Foreign Countries

When a foreign power moves into a country to regulate any facet of that country's sovereign rights, there is a great risk of offending the host country. Relationships established to control drug growth and production in several countries have apparently met with some resistance. For example, Mexico is glad to take money and equipment to assist in its efforts to curb drug production, but it does not want the United States to tell Mexicans how to run their enforcement machinery.

The two-faceted philosophy, while theoretically sound, has many deficiencies when pragmatically applied. With open borders on all sides, this country has become a veritable sieve for drugs of all varieties.[4] A review of some of the drug import problems and the American effort in each of the major drug-supplying countries may offer some insight as to why our policies are not working better.

The Mexican connection.. When a people cannot earn a living legitimately, they will resort to any means to survive. So it is that Mexico, an agrarian culture, without a market for its products, must find a product with a market. Mexicans have found this product in the tons of marijuana and the kilos of "brown heroin" that are shipped north to the United States.

It is unrealistic to believe that the Mexican farmers are ethically tied to stemming the growth of their only cash crop. They are practical people; if they can sell the "gum," they can eat. These farmers sell their products to a wholesaler, who most probably is a relative or a long-time friend. The drug is then channeled into the distribution pipeline.

In attempting to curb the growth and production of narcotics in Mexico, the United States has spent about $75 million. U.S. bureaucrats agree that the amount of drugs coming into the country has been curbed by this effort. They are also optimistic about further inroads to cut drug growth.[5] The drug problem with Mexico is political. If Mexico cooperates, the program is marginally successful. If it does not cooperate, it will be a dismal failure.

The South American problem. Over the decades most countries in the southern hemispheres have had some involvement in narcotic traffic. The major contributors to the problem at this time appear to be Colombia and Peru. These two countries have tended to hold the spotlight on drug activity for the past decade.

Colombia is estimated to furnish about 70 percent of the marijuana that supplies 16 million American users. It is estimated that about 225,000 acres of marijuana are under cultivation. An acre of cultivated marijuana produces

---

[4]"The Mexican Connection," *Arizona Republic,* July 22, 1979.

[5]"Drug Investigation Led to Intrigue, High Living, Murder, Arms Deal," *Los Angeles Times,* August 5, 1978, p. 14.

about two tons of merchandise per year. A farmer growing marijuana can obtain $3 to $8 per pound for the product, compared to 10 cents per pound for coffee. The economic benefits to the grower and the nation are obvious. It is estimated that 43 percent of the GNP of Colombia is generated through the sale of marijuana. Modern communications systems furnish orders for ship lines and fleets of aircraft that operate all over the world. The Colombian government's concern is that the products escape taxation. This drug problem for the United States will probably not be settled through negotiation.

Peru has, throughout history, been the cocaine connection for the world. In recent history it has been so for the United States. The coca plant is grown in the "eyebrow of the jungle," described as the foothills that extend along the eastern slopes of the Peruvian Andes. Here the natives harvest the coca leaf that has grown wild in this area throughout history. It is estimated that the area produces about 80 percent of the cocaine imported into the United States. Because the initial production of leaves furnishes a cash crop for hungry people, there is little possibility that the problem will be solved through diplomatic negotiation or punitive enforcement.

Of the 30,000 tons produced yearly, only a small amount is used in the legal manufacture of medicinal cocaine and flavoring agents. It has been alleged by some intelligence sources that the government has vast stores of cocaine stored in vaults and that the government is able to control the export supply and thus the price. Because of the impact of the cocaine trade on the Peruvian GNP, it is unlikely that negotiations is going to affect the amount of cocaine exported.

The Middle East.   Politics has brought new "connections" in the Middle East. It is reported that Pakistan and Afghanistan are replacing the "golden triangle" of Southeast Asia. The proximity of the Middle East to Europe makes it a much more desirable source of supply. Also, as the supply from Mexico is under pressure, new sources, through Europe, are desirable.

Because of the insurgency and political turmoil in these two countries, international efforts for internal control of narcotics has failed. The amount of drugs reportedly moving from this area rivals the days of the "French connection."

Southeast Asia.   The "golden triangle" will not change as long as there is a market for the farmer's opium crops. When a nation, or a tribe, depends upon narcotics as a money crop and there is a user somewhere in the world, there will always be accommodating peddlers to help the distribution along.

United States efforts are limited to the governments of friendly countries. These countries border on hostile nations, so the flexibility of grower and peddler is always being tested. For example, in Thailand drug peddlers have their own armies for protection. When the armies are overpowered, they

merely move their operations to a neighboring country, where they are unmolested. Any political agreement on drug control is just an agreement. Agreements that cannot be enforced have the same impact as no agreement at all.

Asian opium, in spite of agreements, will still flow into the drug pipelines of the world. How these drugs move in international and national trade is basically the same once they reach the hands of the major drug peddlers.

Organized Crime Patterns for Drug Distribution

Through various publications it has become general public knowledge that there must be organized elements involved in order to make a complex business operation like that shown in Figure 7–1 function.

Drug traffic patterns illustrated in Figures 7–2, 7–3, and 7–4, while authenticated only by intelligence reports, do indicate planning and implementation of intricate procedures, which can be done only by a cohesive confederation.

The evidence of organized crime control is shown in the shifting patterns of drug distribution. In the 1950s most American heroin flowed from the Middle East through France. After enforcement pressure was applied, Mexico and Southeast Asia became the major drug sources. When the war ended in Vietnam and control of the drug source was lost, Mexico again became the big supplier. By 1975, with a highly concentrated enforcement effort against the Mexican sources, the supply routes were reestablished into South America. With European sources moving back to the Middle East, it becomes apparent that much sophisticated planning and organization has gone into these major shifts.

While we give too much credit to the organization of the drug smuggling groups, the major problem is the lack of organization in the American drug control effort. Following the reorganization of drug enforcement agencies in 1973, there has been little coordinated effort among the big federal enforcement units. The information contacts that had been built upon over time in the Customs Service Agency suddenly disappeared.

Psychotropic and Dangerous Drugs

The 1971 conventions also covered the psychotropic substances, and they became a part of the agreements between governments. While dangerous drugs such as amphetamines and barbiturates are not necessarily an international problem, they are included in the agreements. Most of these drugs tend to be local and national problems, since they can be manufactured in the bathtub or in small laboratories.

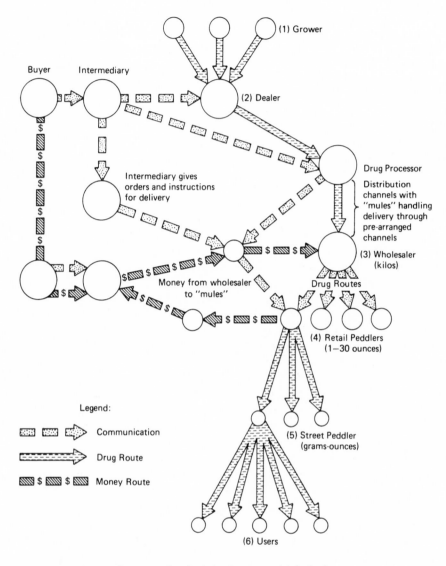

Legend:

▨▨▨ ▨▨ ▨▷ Communication

⊏⊏⊏⊏⊏⊏⇢ Drug Route

▧▧ $ ▧▧ $ ▧▧ Money Route

1. Commercial and small growers sell to the dealers in raw materials (opium)

2. Buyer uses intermediary to contact dealer who arranges for processing and distribution.
   A token payment may change hands.

3. Intermediary carries orders and instructions for deliveries. Wholesaler has "mule" deliver to
   pre-arranged location. Sample is tested and buyer has "mule" make payoff to pre-arranged location.

4. Retail peddlers are contacted by the wholesaler with "mules" making all deliveries and contacts.
   Communications downward. Retailer sends money by "mule" to intermediary.

5. Street peddler is contacted by the retail peddlers. Street peddler then deals with the user.
   Communications both upward and downward.

Figure 7–1 Drug sale procedures from grower to user.

94

Figure 7–2 Distribution routes to the United States.

FEDERAL, STATE, AND LOCAL GOVERNMENT UNITS AND CONFEDERATION DRUG TRAFFICKING

Four agencies form the nucleus of the drug control effort by the United States on an international basis. The International Police Organization (INTER-POL)serves as an intelligence and records source. The Bureau of Customs uses intensive searches at ports of entry as part of its enforcement effort.[6] The Department of Defense is a potent deterrent to drug importation in conducting investigations, furnishing intelligence, and maintaining records for drug activity on military posts. The last federal agency in international drug control is the Federal Bureau of Investigation of the United States Justice Department. This agency, in the reorganization of 1982, has been assigned all intelligence, investigative, and law enforcement responsibility dealing with national and international drug control.

With the collaboration of foreign nations these agencies have conducted operations which confirm that large volumes of narcotic drugs are being financed and imported to the United States, where they are then distributed to major cities. For example, seizures of 180, 380, and 248 pounds of heroin in different international operations indicate that large bankrolls are being risked to promote the entry of drugs into this country.[7]

---

[6]The Drug Enforcement Administration was dismantled and agents were transferred to the FBI.

[7]*Attorney General's First Annual Report*, p. 63, and the *Los Angeles Times*, August 5, 1978.

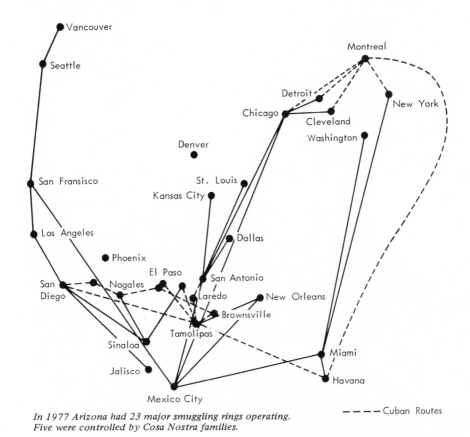

In 1977 Arizona had 23 major smuggling rings operating.
Five were controlled by Cosa Nostra families.

— — — — Cuban Routes

Figure 7-3 Distribution route for Mexican and Cuban marihuana.

Although the United States maintains no regular law enforcement liaison with foreign powers, a number of agencies retain contact sources. For example, the Federal Bureau of Investigation, the Internal Revenue Service, and the Bureau of Customs all have intelligence resources that contribute to the enforcement effort. International enforcement efforts to date have not been able to successfully penetrate the tightly woven mesh that organized crime has established abroad because the right of sovereignty is highly respected and jealously guarded.

The next step has been to organize internally so that federal resources can be quickly deployed where needed. Although the "strike force" concept was not designed for drug enforcement per se, the Federal Bureau of Investigation is a participating member in the units now operating. The strike force seems to offer advantages in all types of specialized investigations, and the success of this concept has brought major reorganization to federal law enforcement efforts.

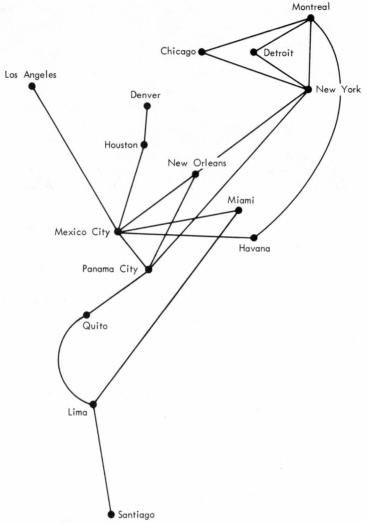

Largest siezure—In October 1977 the Colombian Government siezed 950 pounds of cocaine base worth about $250 million.

Figure 7-4 Distribution routes for cocaine.

National Drug Control Efforts

The latest published strategies for drug control are the policies formulated by the Strategy Council on Drug Abuse. These strategies are not much different than those formulated in times past. The formulation of policies has been an evolutionary process, one that has changed to fit the ideology of whatever party is in power.

The current three-part strategy is designed around these major efforts:[8] (1) treatment, rehabilitation and prevention; (2) domestic drug law enforcement; and (3) international narcotics control.

The treatment and prevention effort will give priority to those drugs that are pharmacologically most dangerous and, because of their nature, cause the most harm. The programs will focus on the drug taker rather than on the drug. This strategy follows that practiced by the Bureau of Prisons for many years. It would appear these program planners are treating heroin addicts in much the same manner as they have been treated in the past. Ironically, these treatment programs have not been effective in the long term. Until the hardline or justice model treatment of the heroin addict is followed, the sale of hard narcotics will defy control. Kill the demand and the market will dry up.

The strategy for enforcement within the United States suggests exclusive authority for the Drug Enforcement Administration. It also stresses increased activity on the financial aspects of drug trafficking. If prosecutors at the federal level used all the financial information obtained about major drug dealers, every prosecution could come under the RICO statute, which is section ix of the Organized Crime Control Act of 1970 (1978). The Internal Revenue Service could have been decisive in the fight against drug trafficking, but it has refused to be involved in prosecutions. Solid application of RICO (The Racketeering Influences Corrupt Organization), as long as the courts will back it, seems to be the surest way to eradicate drug distribution cartels.

The international program is directed to the gaining of international cooperation. If this strategy works, it could be the best thing that ever happened, or it could result in adverse world opinion. Mexico is a classic example; while there may be accolades from a particular government diplomat, the United States is still viewed as a meddler in the internal affairs of the Mexican government.

International programs are designed to: (1) reduce illicit narcotic supplies at the source; (2) enhance participation in international drug control organizations; (3) foster cooperation with foreign narcotics enforcement agencies; and (4) develop international drug abuse treatment and prevention programs.[9]

The strategies set forth in the federal programs are designed to make maximum use of intelligence. There is a need to develop financial intelligence so that any international carrier may be prosecuted under RICO. There is a need to automate information programs on peddlers so they are more readily traced and accounted for. Only when this kind of intelligence is refined will the RICO statutes be effective.

[8]The Strategy Council on Drug Abuse, *Federal Strategy for Drug Abuse and Drug Traffic Prevention* (Washington, D.C.: U.S. Government Printing Office, 1979).

[9]Ibid., p. 34.

The domestic drug law enforcement effort has not changed. The objectives are to reduce the supply of illegal drugs; to control the supply of legally manufactured drugs to avoid illegal diversion; and to achieve the highest possible risk for drug trafficking. This latter objective will lead to prison terms for the violator and the forfeiture of all assets gained from racketeering practices.

The domestic enforcement strategy includes the consolidation of some of the border service agencies, such as Customs and Immigration and Naturalization, into a Border Management Agency. According to the new organization within the Justice Department, it would appear that all internal enforcement agencies will be under an associate attorney general. But this type of goal setting and manipulation of agencies is primarily a political ploy; as long as these agencies are staffed with attorneys whose claim to fame is their faithful work for the party, the domestic enforcement effort is in trouble.

Border interdiction, to be passably effective, would take all the personnel of the armed services. As long as the movement of people and products across an open border remains subject to politics, there will be no stemming of the drug tide. The chaotic situation in Florida has been created by bad political decisions, and the cure for the massive drug traffic and the laundering of funds will cease only when civil and administrative sanctions are strictly applied. The new legislation amending the Bank Security Act makes it illegal to transport unreported money outside the United States. If this law is not enforced, the situation will not improve.

These problems will remain until an aroused public gets fed up with bureaucratic double talk and demands action. Until this is done, the drug import problem will continue to get worse, not better.

Federal, State and Local Cooperation

One major weakness of the national drug effort has been the lack of consistent and effective cooperation: the failure of the federal government to assign specific lead agency responsibility; the lack of a plan to bring state and local agencies together in enforcement groups; and failure to integrate intelligence sources.

Assignment of lead agency.   The Drug Assistance Administration has now been assigned the lead agency role. If properly executed, this coordinating role should eliminate many of the problems caused when represenatives of two or three federal agencies and of two or three state and local agencies all show up on the same case. With this change, and the reorganization in the Justice Department, it is possible this problem may be solved.

A second difficulty was the proliferation of task forces, each working independently of the other. DEA should now assume control over all task

forces, and the legal specialists furnish technical staff assistance. Task forces should have the benefit of a legal staff specialist, but an assistant U.S. attorney cannot run a strike force simply because no one in the strike force has a commitment to answer to him. Field operations should be under the line supervision of experienced investigative personnel with the assigned responsibility for that function.

Plan to bring enforcement groups together.   In the past, individual and agency jealousies have been a disaster for cooperative efforts with local agencies. With the RICO statute to serve as a catalyst, a task force can now operate with a realistic law applicable to the racketeering activities of the suspects. The lead federal agency now has more than just money to lend to an investigation. If local agencies can see the advantages of prosecution under the RICO statute, working cooperation can almost be assured.

At this point, some observations should be made regarding the feasibility of using the RICO statute in narcotic convictions. Despite the fact that defense attorneys are slicing at this broad criminal statute, it has withstood several appeals.[10] It would appear that the RICO statute could be easily applied in most drug cases. For example, based upon Stofsky guidelines, the racketeering acts must be connected by a common scheme, plan, or motive. The term "enterprise" might need a clearer definition, but cases are being successfully prosecuted under the present wording. The criminal forfeiture procedure will eventually encounter sentimental problems in the courts. In the meantime, RICO is a powerful law that could pull task forces together against middle and upper echelon drug dealers.

There is a need to file several hundred or perhaps thousands of RICO cases so that the full impact of 25-year sentences and the seizure of property gained from the racketeering may be shown. To file many cases will require the coordinated efforts by federal, state, and local agents.

Failure to integrate intelligence sources.   Until information flows up and down the investigative ladder, good cases will not occur. If information gained by federal and local agencies is forced into one system, the "need to know" doctrine can be more clearly determined.

The Drug Enforcement Administration has been a prime mover in antinarcotic squads called Metropolitan Enforcement Groups (MEGS). These units have successfully used computer-based data to zero in on street level peddlers. There is reason to believe they can bring some sensible structure to the enforcement plan for the United States.

Another program begun on a pilot basis has been the Drug Diversion Units based on the strike force concept of bringing together federal, state, and local efforts to obtain prosecutions, revocation of licenses, and other sanctions against those who are exceeding the authority granted by law to get legal drugs into the illicit market. Results from these units indicate gross abuses by

[10]An abstract of the 1970 Crime Control Act is given in Appendix B.

legitimate drug manufacturers, druggists, doctors, and private dealers who use various unethical and illegal means to secure otherwise legitimate drugs. These Drug Diversion Units are uncovering evidence that gangs of criminals are in the business of forged prescriptions, obtaining drugs by false representation as well as by burglary and hijacking of drug supply sources.

For the professional druggist and doctor, the abuses uncovered have revealed lucrative profits in the drug dispensing business. The fact that a doctor may often become suspect when administering drugs such as methadone to an addict has caused many legitimate physicians to refuse to maintain drug users as patients. Because of this, a few unethical members of the medical and pharmacological guilds are reaping tremendous profits at the expense of society as well as individual users.

State and Local Roles in the Future of Drug Traffic Enforcement

Local and state agencies will always exert the major effort in drug abuse enforcement. By virtue of numbers, jurisdiction, and physical presence, these agencies are committed to the suppression of drug distribution. The apprehension of middlemen at the state level and the street peddler locally may ultimately offer the surest road to street control.

Because the confederations are not involved locally, we believe that narcotics intelligence and enforcement must move nationally and internationally if there is to be any reasonable control on a large scale. These types of programs are being brought about through federally funded efforts and should have top fiscal priority for a number of years to come. But the idea that national control is ultimately going to prevail if enforcement is effective does not detract from the thousands of cases being made at the local and state level.

Organized criminal groups are being arrested daily. Most of these groups do not owe allegiance to the large drug financiers, but are agents for the men who front with the big money. From a local perspective, the border cities in Texas, Louisiana, Arizona, and California can hardly justify organized confederation involvement. There are so many amateurs and semi-professionals who rush to the border for a few ounces of heroin, a kilo or two of marijuana, or a barrel or two of pills that the professional cannot compete. In major cities inland the story is different, for there the organized group becomes involved simply because a tight distribution network is a necessity.

The nature of a large transaction shows why locals rarely deal with top-echelon peddlers. The financing is always in cash; the plans are made prior to the transaction, so no one knows who sent the shipment; and no one knows who is to receive it. From initial handling through processing to delivery in the United States, "mules" or "couriers" are hired to carry the merchandise. If a shipment is lost, the void in the pipeline can be filled within twenty-four

hours. The profit margin is structured to accommodate the losses. Once the drug shipment reaches the point for consignment to the street, local agents can respond. The response at this level is too late. For example, from one kilo (2.2 pounds) of pure heroin purchased for about $70,000 overseas, the heroin is "cut" until there may be 90,000 fixes or more. It becomes an unsurmountable task when local officers must make seizures of grams. At that level, it is impossible to dry up the pipeline.

SUMMARY

Twenty-three states are now considering the legalization of marijuana on a controlled basis for easement of cancer pain. The decriminalization of marijuana has made it a big-money crop. With further easement of restrictions, it is anticipated marijuana will be organized crime's new moneymaker in the next decade.

In the past five years, specific connections have been revealed between organized crime and drug distribution organizations. International intelligence files link these criminal organizations. The link to the money flow through these operations has not been easy to find or police, but new procedures may cure this enforcement weakness. The message about the adverse impact of drugs has finally reached the political leaders of this country and of the world. Pressure to control drugs has resulted in new laws regulating international money movement and secret bank accounts, and the move to tax and secure civil recovery of properties acquired from the sale of drugs. Cooperation at various levels of government and new technologies have resulted in the seizure of massive amounts of drugs. Whether this mode of enforcement proves to be effective, however, remains to be seen.

QUESTIONS FOR DISCUSSION

1. Discuss the difference in enforcing general drug abuse laws and conspiracy laws that relate to confederation participation in drug traffic.
2. Why is it so difficult to gain public support for action against the large drug distributors?
3. Has politics been instrumental in creating a drug trafficking problem? Explain.
4. Discuss in detail the importance of the involvement of international agencies and national governmental agencies in the drug sale problem.
5. Review the political mandates that now make international enforcement efforts a possibility.
6. Discuss the difference between the old drug control laws and the comprehensive Drug Abuse Office and Treatment Act of 1972.
7. Discuss the UN plan of action against drug abuse. How does this affect enforcement efforts?

8. Identify the significant role of the International Narcotics Control Board.
9. Dišcuss the two important political accords dealing with narcotics and psychotropic substances.
10. Examine drug distribution and analyze why it is difficult for enforcement officers to secure evidence against important dealers.
11. What are the prime advantages of having a massive federal cooperative effort? disadvantages?
12. Would the seizure of large amounts of drugs overseas indicate that past efforts were successes or failures?
13. Discuss the merits of the strike force concept in both narcotics enforcement and in organized crime enforcement activity.
14. The Drug Enforcement Division has identified ten major systems dealing in drugs. Do you know of any evidence that would indicate organized crime involvement?
15. Discuss new national programs and how these will influence the drug control effort.
16. Will the legalization of drugs eliminate peddler profit?
17. What areas of agreement and disagreement with the authors do you have regarding the local role in drug enforcement?

8

OBSCENITY AND PORNOGRAPHY

LEARNING OUTCOMES

1. Have an understanding of the complexities of enforcing obscenity and pornography statutes.
2. Recognize that organized crime is deeply entrenched in the distribution of obscene materials.
3. Know court decisions affecting the distribution of obscene materials.
4. Be able to apply the four court standards to obscene materials.
5. Know the ways in which action may be taken against peddlers of obscene materials.

Obscenity and pornography are distributed all over the world. In spite of the worldwide scope of this operation, there has been little investigation and research done on who actually controls the markets that distribute these materials. When these investigations are made, the public will find that most of the obscenity and pornography markets will reflect direct control by established, nationally known confederations. At the local level, an investigation will show that many local newsstands dealing in hard core pornography will also be fronting for bookmaking activities. The wholesale pornographic movie and stag show distributors will all relate to the total distribution network established by confederations. See Figure 8-1.

In recent years, there has been an increase in the publication of literary and pictorial pornography. While the problem of obscenity is not new, it is a continuing and critical problem for law enforcement and citizens who are interested in seeing that community morality standards are not established by organized crime. The police role in enforcement of obscenity statutes is akin to walking a tightrope. Each alleged violation is a direct challenge to the

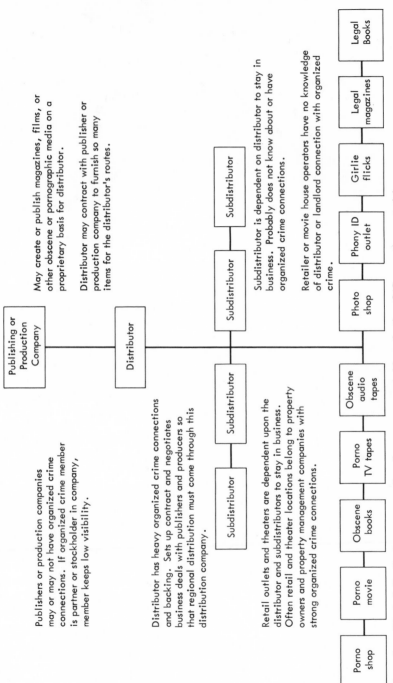

Figure 8–1 Typical distribution structure for obscene, pornographic and other O/C operating materials.

Publishers or production companies may or may not have organized crime connections. If organized crime member is partner or stockholder in company, member keeps low visibility.

Distributor has heavy organized crime connections and backing. Sets up contract and negotiates business deals with publishers and producers so that regional distribution must come through this distribution company.

Retail outlets and theaters are dependent upon the distributor and subdistributors to stay in business. Often retail and theater locations belong to property owners and property management companies with strong organized crime connections.

May create or publish magazines, films, or other obscene or pornographic media on a proprietary basis for distributor.

Distributor may contract with publisher or production company to furnish so many items for the distributor's routes.

Subdistributor is dependent on distributor to stay in business. Probably does not know about or have organized crime connections.

Retailer or movie house operators have no knowledge of distributor or landlord connection with organized crime.

Publishing or Production Company

Distributor

Subdistributor · Subdistributor · Subdistributor · Subdistributor

Porno shop · Porno movie · Obscene books · Porno TV tapes · Obscene audio tapes · Photo shop · Phony ID outlet · Girlie flicks · Legal magazines · Legal Books

rights guaranteed by the First Amendment to the Constitution.[1] This chapter examines the complexities of the obscenity and pornography issue so that a philosophy for enforcement may be developed by each person concerned with community standards of morality.

Obscenity, according to a dictionary definition, is "something offensive to modesty or decency; lewd, disgusting; filthy, repulsive, as language, conduct, an expression, an act." Pornography is defined as "originally a description of prostitutes and their trades; hence, writings, pictures, and other materials intended to arouse sexual desire." Although these definitions are oversimplified, they are adequate for most purposes.

Obscenity, in general, refers to conduct offensive to the public sense of decency. From the point of view of law, it is essentially concerned with publication of indecent written, graphic, or pictorial materials.

In most states, the possession, exhibition, or dissemination of obscene and pornographic material is prohibited.[2] On the federal level, interstate transportation or mailing is a criminal offense. In spite of its widespread prohibition, no other area of enforcement has so many constitutional ramifications. In this chapter, we will look at these aspects of the problems, (1) a moral and political viewpoint, (2) history, and (3) law enforcement.

A LEGAL AND MORAL VIEWPOINT

What ultimately results from the analysis of facts pertaining to pornography and obscene writings is that a person's preconceptions about right and wrong are reinforced by logical arguments presented on several sides of the issue. The main viewpoints are legal and moral.

The Legal Viewpoint

The legal view is split between the absolutists and the conservatives. The absolutist position is this: "Congress shall make *no* law...." It is simple. No law can be passed that would abridge the freedom of speech or press.[3] Another logical argument for the absolutist position is that the Supreme Court has merely assumed "obscenity" was never meant to be protected

[1]The Supreme Court has held that the state cannot pass laws which violate First Amendment rights.

[2]In the case of *Stanley* v. *United States,* 393 U.S. 819 (1968), the Supreme Court ruled that possession of obscene materials in one's home is not a violation of the law.

[3]Alan F. Westin, *The Supreme Court: Views from Inside* (New York: Norton, 1961), pp. 173–90. Reprinted from the James Madison Lecture, "The Bill of Rights," New York University School of Law, February 17, 1970. In 35 *New York University Law Review* 865 (1960). Reprinted by permission of Mr. Hugo L. Black and the publisher.

constitutionally. Conversely, the Court has also created categories of "free speech" by completely disregarding all previous standards established and treating "obscenity" entirely differently—as if it were not really speech.[4]

In trying to define the position to be taken by the power structure regarding the establishment of guidelines for courts and law enforcement, the Supreme Court has left a legal void. This legal void has put the burden of determining what is obscene upon the community.

This chapter offers arguments from each ideology. Bass, a researcher in this field, offers arguments for the absolutist position. He cites the following reasoning:

> The Supreme Court of the United States has assumed that one of the most basic of all liberties known to man, the freedom to read, write and think what he wants, is not protected by the First Amendment.[5]

This may appear to be a harsh statement, but it is true. The Court has said:

> ...expressions found in numerous opinions indicate that this Court has always assumed that obscenity is not protected by freedoms of speech and press.[6]

Among the cases cited to justify such a conclusion, Judge Brennan, speaking for the Court, quotes *Chaplinski* v. *New Hampshire,* in which it was said that:

> ...there are certain well defined and narrowly limited classes of speech, the prevention of which have never been thought to raise any Constitutional problems. These include the lewd and obscene...[7]

[4]Larry R. Bass, "Free Speech v. Obscenity: The Only Alternative Is the Absolutists Approach." (Unpublished research report, Kent State University, March 12, 1969.)

[5]Larry R. Bass, "Free Speech v. Obscenity."

[6]*Roth* v. *U.S.,* 354 U.S. 476 (1957). Obscene material is not protected by the First Amendment, which was reaffirmed in the 1973 obscenity case of *Miller* v. *California.* In the case of *Miller* v. *California* the Court does not change the right of determining what is obscene. It only prescribes that the facts of a case shall be based upon community rather than national standards.

[7]The cases cited for this were: *Ex Parte Jackson,* 96 U.S. 727, *U.S.* v. *Chase* 135 U.S. 255, *Robertson* v. *Baldwin,* 165 U.S. 275, *Public Clearing House* v. *Coynes* 194 U.S. 497, *Hoke* v. *U.S.* 227 U.S. 308, *Near* v. *Minnesota* 283 U.S. 687, *Hannegan* v. *Esquire* 327 U.S. 146, *Winters* v. *New York* 333 U.S. 507, and *Beubarnais* v. *Illinois* 343 U.S. 250. Brennan is correct; the Court has always just assumed that obscenity is not protected. Among the other reasons discussed was an international agreement that "obscenity should not be restrained." It is interesting to note that at the convention where this was decided, the people spent almost three days attempting to define obscenity. They finally agreed that obscenity could not be defined and then proceeded to outlaw something—even though they did not know what "it" was. Albert B. Gerber, *Sex Pornography and Justice* (New York: Lyle Stuart, 1965), p. 15.

Based on these assumptions and nothing more, the Supreme Court has concluded that "obscenity is not Constitutionally protected."[8] As a result of this, the Court has legalized censorship of both writers and readers.

Also, by assumption, the Court has created categories of speech and has concluded that some speech categories have a "preferred position" and other categories do not. The Court has always held that the First Amendment allows "...the widest possible dissemination of information from diverse and antagonistic sources,"[9] and that "...Constitutional rights may not be denied simply because of hostility to their assertion or exercise."[10] Also, the Court has said "the idea of imposing upon any medium of communication the burden of justifying its presence is contrary to where...the presumption must lie in the area of First Amendment freedoms."[11] The Court has further held that picketing "may not be enjoined...merely because it may provoke violence in others,"[12] and that speech may include "vehement" and "caustic" language.[13] However, obscenity is different and enjoys none of the usual protections, because it has always been assumed that it does not have these or other protections.

The Moral Viewpoint

The absolutist position is opposed by moralist factions, such as church and community groups who believe there is a moral view that should be heard. Obscenity issues from a moral viewpoint are much more important to these people than legal technicalities. Members of the Supreme Court in their 1963 decisions as well as in subsequent cases have been very careful not to alienate the community. They have allowed community standards to prevail to regulate the sale of obscene and pornographic materials, yet prosecution is practically impossible because of the vagueness of the law. Only those persons who dare challenge the constitutionality of the law are engaged in the business. The great number of X-rated movies and newsstand publications is evidence the absolutists are gaining ground. Into this confusion has moved the power of organized crime. The public sits oblivious to the millions being made while legal actions are stalled in the appeals process.

The public attitude toward sex-oriented businesses and laws controlling these businesses are classic examples of why organized crime is doing so well

---

[8]*Roth* v. *U.S.*, 354 U.S. 476 (1957).

[9]*Associated Press* v. *U.S.*, 326 U.S. 1 at 20.

[10]*Watson* v. *Memphis* 373 U.S. 251.

[11]*Estes* v. *Texas* 381 U.S. 532 (1965). In Stewart's dissent (joined by Black, Brennan, and White), it is interesting to note that with the exception of Black, the others here have actually put the burden on the "medium of communication" to justify its presence in the obscenity area.

[12]*Milk Wagon Drivers Union* v. *Meadownoor Dairies, Inc.* 312 U.S. 287.

[13]*Rosenblatt* v. *Baer* 383 U.S. 75.

financially. The National Advisory Committee on Criminal Justice as late as 1976 was unable to connect organized crime to the pornography industry.[14] An example of the ties that should have been made by the Task Force was published in the Los Angeles *Times*. In 1975, the Los Angeles Federal Organized Crime Strike Force arrested four persons for attempting to shake down a dummy pornography shop set up by undercover FBI agents. In 1976, this extortionist, who was well known in organized crime circles, was finally sentenced to prison. After two years of appeals, the bond was finally revoked and the person remanded to prison when his appeal failed. In the meantime, this suspect had been indicted on mutliple charges relating to interfering with commerce by threat and conspiracy. And this is only one case in one city.

In order to understand why we are so reluctant to come to a firm decision on the complexities of dealing with obscenity, a brief review of its history should help.

HISTORY

Plato predicted that democracy, of all forms of government, would produce the greatest variety of individual differences. To him this seemed the fairest of organizational concepts for all people. Yet he suggests that it is a state in which liberty can grow without limit at the expense of justice and order. This tends to set the stage for the evolution of obscenity. As freedom has expanded, so have the individual differences of morality with regard to human behavior.

One of the first recorded cases of obscenity in Anglo-American legal annals was that of the drunken driving companion of Charles II of England. His combination of filthy oratory and urination on the street brought him a conviction for gross indecency. A similar action today would probably produce the same result.

In the early eighteenth century several books were charged as being obscene. In at least one instance the court ruled the offense was spiritual rather than criminal, so the case should rightfully be tried in an ecclesiastical court. Later in the century this thinking was overruled, and publication of obscenity was punished as a common law misdemeanor.

In the early American colonies, the common attitude toward obscenity was that it should not necessarily be permitted, but that each man should be held responsible for his own discretions in writing, pictures, or prints.

In 1875 in England, Lord Chief Justice John Campbell secured the passage of the Obscene Publications Act, that provided for the destruction of obscene books by a justice of the peace. The statute was widely and successfully employed. In 1869 in the United States, the case of *Regina* v. *Hicklin* gave the

---

[14]*Report of the Task Force on Organized Crime* (Washington, D.C.: U.S. Government Printing Office, 1976), p. 66.

law its most enduring definition of obscenity. Chief Justice Cockburn enunciated the famous test in that case:

> I think the test for obscenity is this, whether the tendency of the matter charged is to deprave and corrupt those whose minds are open to such immoral influences and into whose hands it may fall.

From 1869 to 1957, Cockburn's test dominated the law. Regulation of obscenity in the United States had, of course, predated the Hicklin decision. Indeed, the earliest reported case dealing with a book, *Commonwealth* v. *Holmes,* decided in Massachusetts in 1821, was a prosecution for selling Cleland's *Fanny Hill.* Most early prosecutions were, however, based on the common law. The Tariff Act of 1843, the first piece of federal legislation dealing with obscenity, was not passed until the second generation of the American Republic. Even so, it was enacted without any challenge on the score that it was inconsistent with the First Amendment guarantee of free speech. The second major statute became law during the administration of Abraham Lincoln. This statute was directed against New York pornographers exploiting the loneliness of Union soldiers by authorizing criminal prosecutions for mailing obscene material and by empowering the Post Office to seize it.

In 1955–56 the Kefauver Committee investigations revealed some lucrative business enterprises based upon pornography and controlled by organized crime. This subcommittee's findings brought about a series of changes in the laws in order to combat what had become a racket of gigantic proportions. The laws that evolved covered these areas: the transmittal of obscene material through the United States mail,[15] importation of immoral articles, and importation of merchandise contrary to law,[16] and transporting obscene matter in interstate or foreign commerce (by means other than by mail).[17]

In June 1973 the Supreme Court handed down three new decisions: *Miller* v. *California, Paris Adult Theatre I* v. *Slaton,* and *Kaplan* v. *California.* These cases raised further doubts about establishing consistency between the law of obscenity and constitutional doctrines regarding freedom of speech and expression. The fundamental constitutionality of obscene legislation was again thrown into chaos when the tougher guidelines were laid down and the determination of what is obscene was returned to a form of "local option." The Court, however, in restating the basic definition of obscenity, held that a work is obscene if:

> Sexual conduct is portrayed in a patently offensive way.
>
> Taken as a whole, the material does not have serious literary, artistic, political or scientific value.

[15]18 U.S.C.A., 1461, 1463 (Supp. 1963).
[16]18 U.S.C.A., 545 (Supp. 1963).
[17]18 U.S.C.A., 1462, 1465 (Supp. 1963).

Taken as a whole, the material appeals to the prurient interest in sex. Whether the material meets this standard will be determined by the community rather than by national standards.[18]

This restatement, which the Court now adheres to, is an important change in the law. Yet the rationale for the decision given by the Justices is not substantially different from those cited in the 1957 Roth decision. Thus, the arguments presented in the Roth case are substantially the same as those of the June 1973 decisions.

Not only did the Roth case make it unquestionable that the relevant audience is the average reasonable adult and that the work must be considered as a whole, but it strongly intimates that any more restrictive test would violate the United States Constitution.[19] The new cases are more explicit as to the political and social value of the material.

Justice Douglas indicated that the 1973 decisions are making new definitions of obscenity. He indicated the difficulty is that we do not deal with constitutional terms because "obscenity" is not mentioned in the Constitution or Bill of Rights. He further contended that until a civil proceeding has placed a tract beyond the pale, no criminal prosecution should be sustained. No more vivid illustration of vague and uncertain criteria could be designed than those we have fashioned.[20] Justice Harlan, in dissenting, indicated that to give the power to the censor as we do today is to make a sharp and radical break with free society. He maintains that conduct which annoys one may not bother another. In all of this we find that no sound legal ground has been assured.

LAW ENFORCEMENT: CENSORS WITHOUT LAWS

The enforcement of laws governing obscenity and pornography is generally a duty of the vice division of a police department. There is a wide area of controversy for certain materials, and there will generally be two major community groups in conflict. One group, made up of church leaders and representatives of other community organizations, will lead those who want to draw the dividing line near one extreme. Another group, equally vocal, will have a more diverse membership. It will include people sincerely interested in protecting the right of free speech and the accompanying right of

---

[18]*Miller* v.*California*, 93 S.ct.2607, (1973), Supreme Court of the United States, No. 71–1422, Decided June 21, 1973.

[19]*Encyclopaedia Britannica* (1966), XVI, 828. This rationale would still apply after the June 1973 decisions.

[20]*Miller* v. *California*. As the law now stands, every single book, magazine, or film must be proved to be obscene, in a separate judicial proceeding, before it can be enjoined. This makes it almost impossible to take any general action against businesses that regularly deal in pornography.

a free press.[21] There will be authors and artists with a sound interest in all work. Some participants will come from groups interested only in the sale of the material in question. This latter group will again be divided, with one part made up of respectable publishers with a fear of excessive and unwarranted censorship and control of their publishing activity. The other group of publishers are those that publish the questionable materials, that make up magazines from press agents' releases, never name authors, and frequently change the name and often the place of publication.

Development of pornography cases is a highly technical and often frustrating experience for those officers involved in enforcement activities.[22] The June 1973 case of *Paris Adult Theatre I* v. *Slaton* illustrates how a civil action causes the filing of the civil complaint. With the judgmental criteria in the *Miller* v. *California* case where national standards are no longer needed to judge obscenity there will be a rash of local actions against obscenity. If a police department is not careful in its approach to enforcement procedures, lawsuits against the enforcing agents will nullify many of the present laws.

An honest accommodation between the requirements of free speech, the hope of legitimate artistic expression, and the simple demands of common decency has been and is being worked out, though it is not yet perfectly realized.

In the three 1973 cases there has still not been a resolution of the constitutional issue. Until that issue is firmly settled, every obscenity case will still end up in the federal courts. Thus, local departmental procedures in pursuing the investigation of obscenity cases need to be perfected.

One case the Supreme Court ruled upon concerned a record peddler. The records in question were in themselves adjudged to be "not obscene." The Court decision affirming conviction was not based upon the content of the record but upon suggestive advertising and the printing of lewd mailing labels.[23] This case appears not to be on the content of the material but on the business of smut peddling. The conduct of the person in this case makes it easier for the Court to arrive at a more practical approach in determining "contemporary community standards" or the "prurient interest" of the "average person."

In a 1968 decision, *Stanley* v. *State*, 393 U.S. 819, the Supreme Court ruled that the possession of pornographic materials in one's home is not in violation of the law because of guarantees granted by the First Amendment. In *U.S.* v. *Orita*, June 1973, privacy encompassing the possession of obscenity in one's home does not extend to transportation that is prohibited by 18 U.S.C. 1462.

[21]In 1977 publisher Larry Flynt was convicted of conspiracy under the Ohio organized crime law. This case is still on appeal.

[22]Alternatives for direct arrest are frequently used. Thus, state laws that do not provide for the civil process should be passed by the respective legislatures.

[23]U.S. Code Title 18, Section 1461 in substance says, "it is punishable by fine and imprisonment to *knowingly cause the mails to be used to transport obscenity.*" This section is used by the Postal Service and has proven to be a fairly reliable statute.

The Sociological Reasoning behind Obscenity Enforcement

It is a common assumption that reading affects behavior. This substantiates something that everybody has known for years. Would anyone doubt that reading the Bible has affected the behavior of the people of the Western world? However, people usually avoid the real issue. Is there a connection between reading "pornography" and illegal conduct? Whatever the connection, if found, it should be beyond a "reasonable doubt." Most studies do not show this. Sheldon and Eleanor Glueck, authorities on juvenile delinquency, did not mention reading among factors that they found to be correlated to youth and delinquent behavior.[24]

Studies have been unable to provide a definite causal link. For every study that shows a connection, other studies are brought forth to disprove them.[25] However, recent and more rigorous studies do point to the conclusion that there may be causal relationships between reading of obscene material and sexual crimes.

In light of new findings by Feshbach and Malamath using improved research methodology, it might be logical to conclude that depiction of violence in erotica and pornography could be harmful. Feshbach says:

> The erotic presentation sometimes even approximates a how-to-do-it instructional film....Further, the juxtaposition of violence with sexual excitement and satisfaction provides an unusual opportunity for conditioning of violent responses to erotic stimuli.[26]

The Kinsey study, however, had this to say about pornography and illegal conduct:

> When one reads in a newspaper that obscene or pornographic materials were found in an individual's possession one should interpret this information to mean that (1) the individual was probably a male of an age between puberty and senility, and (2) that he probably derived pleasure from thinking about sex. No further inferences are warranted.[27]

For those who are also convinced that the reading of "pornography" causes an abnormal deviant reaction, Dr. Gebhard states that "Sex offenses

---

[24]Charles H. Rogers, "Police Control of Obscene Literature," *Journal of Criminal Law*, LVII (1966), p. 431.

[25]Paul Cairns, "Sex Censorship: The Assumptions of Anti-Obscenity Laws and the Empirical Evidence," *Minnesota Law Review*, XLVI (1962), p. 1009.

[26]Seymour Feshbach and Neal Malamath, "Sex and Aggression: Proving the Link," *Psychology Today*, November 1978, pp. 111–22.

[27]Gebhard, Gagnon, Pomeroy, Christenson, *Sex Offenders* (New York: Harper & Row, 1965), p. 404.

do not correlate with the possession of pornography or with the degree of response to viewing pornography...."[28]

Thus, there is considerable evidence to show a causal link between "pornography" and illegal conduct. This conduct is not known to the courts, or the researchers, so we must go to the agency that can best evaluate the impact or pornography on society.

The Police Position

The basic police function in relation to obscene or pornographic material is to receive complaints, as in the case of other offenses, and discover the presence of such material as a part of their regular duties. The next step, thought to be most desirable, is to assemble evidence rather than make physical arrests. If there appears to be a violation of the law, evidence should be presented to the proper prosecuting authorities.

The police position, as viewed by Frank Dyson, chief of police in Austin, Texas, can be drawn from a speech he gave in 1971:[29]

> A police officer has always been the man in the middle—the umpire in the game of life. He does his best to make judgment calls according to the rules. But, there are times when the rules of the game are not clearly defined...and the police are caught between the rock and the hard place. Let me cite an example. We have received many calls from citizens asking why we don't do something about the showing of so-called skin flicks in Dallas...why we don't do something about the dirty books that are being sold?
>
> We answer calls of this type with requests for as much information as the caller can provide and then conduct follow-up investigations. If we have what we consider to be a solid case—based on city and state statutes—we ask the City Attorney or the District Attorney to accept a case. Then, it's up to the jury and the courts.
>
> In recent years, two members of the U.S. Supreme Court (Justice Douglas and the late Justice Black) consistently adhered to the view that a State is utterly without power to suppress, control or punish the distribution of any writings or pictures upon the ground of their "obscenity."
>
> A third jurist has held to the opinion that a State's power in this area is narrowly limited to a distinct and clearly identifiable class of material....
>
> One jurist was moved to make this comment about a pornography case: "My conclusion is that certainly after the fourteen separate opinions handed down in these three cases today, no person—not even the most

[28]Paul H. Gebhard, Director, Institute for Sex Research, Bloomington, Indiana (personal citation, October 16, 1972).

[29]Speech given by Frank Dyson, former chief of police, Dallas Texas, on television, 1971. These general rules are still applicable.

learned judge, much less a layman—is capable of knowing, in advance of an ultimate decision in his particular case by this court, whether certain material comes within the area of 'obscenity' as that term is confused by the court today."

To say that the issue is still somewhat clouded is an understatement. This should give you some idea of how difficult it has been for police agencies, the District Attorney's office and the courts to deal with the pornography problem.

Pornography *is* a problem in Dallas. A report from our Special Investigations Bureau states there are fourteen pornographic bookstores in Dallas. It further states that there are nineteen pornographic theatres and six pornographic lounges, some of which have "live" pornographic stage shows. Fifteen producers and distributors of movies and reading material are located in Dallas or in the immediate metropolitan area.

According to the report, the Dallas-based pornography industry has distribution outlets in cities all over the United States. Several of the Dallas-based pornographic industry distributors and producers have financial backing and direct business connections with larger out-of-state pornography dealers.

The pornography business in Dallas has all of the earmarks of an organized crime operation. We have learned that the organizations in Dallas are linked to an organization which owns and controls the production, printing, distribution and retail sale outlets for pornographic material. This enables the organization to receive profits from all levels of production and sale.

Pornography is a very lucrative business! Figures from *The Report of the Commission on Obscenity and Pornography* state that the cost for production of paperback pornographic books is ten to twenty cents. . . and that the cost for production of magazines of pornographic nature is forty-five to sixty cents. These periodicals sell anywhere from eight dollars to twenty dollars for each copy.

Exploitation films, according to the commission report, gross 70 million dollars annually! An "X" film produced in Dallas—actually filmed in the office of a dealer—grossed over 2 million dollars!

"Mob" tactics have been employed by members of the industry in Texas to achieve their ends. These include thirteen bombings and fires.

The gangland-style murder of Kenneth Hanna—found shot to death in the trunk of a car in Atlanta, Georgia—has been linked to the pornography business. It has been learned that Hanna met with a man known as the "Pornography King" just prior to the murder. At the time that Hanna was killed, he was under federal indictment for interstate shipment of pornographic materials.

Even more alarming to the police department in Dallas are the deaths of two persons in Texas—under very suspicious circumstances—persons who were linked with the pornography industry in the state. Furthermore, we are aware that a Dallas-based pornographic enterprise has—on several occasions—used strong-arm tactics to further their business interests in the state.

As I stated earlier, the pornography business in Dallas is *organized*.We are well aware that the affluent heads of the organization hire others to run their business outlets. And...that is why we intend to arrest and prosecute not only the managers, ticket sellers, projectionists and salesmen, but the leaders of the pornography industry in Dallas as well. The heads of these organizations are operating their business outlets and *they* are going to be held to account.[30]

METHODS OF ENFORCEMENT

The police in their enforcement activity should work in close liaison with the prosecuting attorney in any of the following methods.

Action Against Material

The first method is, in legal parlance, an action *in rem*. In other words, an action against the material itself.[31] This method is a statutory action that provides for the seizure of the obscene material upon court order; for notice and hearing; and for disposition of the material involved by ordering its destruction or ordering it returned to the owner. This type of proceeding is heard before a court without a jury. Applying the community standard, the court sits as the conscience of the community and rules upon each piece of evidence suspected of being obscene.

Besides the foregoing advantage, the *in rem* action normally allows more expeditious determinations than are obtained in a trial by jury through criminal proceedings against an individual. It should be noted, too, that once the determination of the obscene character of the suspected material is made by the court through an *in rem* action, there is no bar to further criminal proceedings against the individuals involved in the sale, circulation, and distribution of the obscene material.

Injunction

A second form of proceeding that has been used with success, particularly in the State of New York, is an injunction against defendants enjoining them from the sale, circulation, or distribution of obscene material. The injunction

[30]In March 1973, this enforcement policy lead to the seizure of the film "Deep Throat" on three separate occasions. Convictions resulting from the showing of this film are on appeal in three states. In the next decade this will be a landmark case for obscenity. These cases were not upheld; this film is still playing in theaters around the country.

[31]See Vernon's Annotated Missouri Statutes, Vol. 38, Sect. 542, 380 to 542, 420. In re. Search Warrant of Property at 5 W. 12th Street, Kansas City, Missouri v. Marcus, et al., 3344 S.W. 2d 119. Broad civil injunctive relief against pornography-related businesses is barred by the prohibition of prior restraints, regardless of the number of underlying obscenity convictions.

proceedings provide for the seizure of the material, for notice, hearing, and disposition of the material by the court. The U.S. Supreme Court has upheld the legality of the proceeding.[32] A similar purpose may be served through injunction as by the *in rem* procedure. The injunction is an expeditious method of handling a given case where there are several defendants. Here again, criminal prosecution can be instituted after the court has adjudicated the character of the questioned material.

Prosecution

The third and most common method of handling suspected obscenity is by direct criminal prosecution against the purveyors for the sale, circulation, and distribution of the material. With the crowded criminal court dockets of today, this method is time-consuming and necessitates, somewhere in the proceeding, an adjudication of what is or is not obscene or salacious material. Prosecution does not necessarily achieve the ultimate purpose of removing such material from public availability, particularly while waiting for a case to be tried.

SUMMARY

Police receive many complaints concerning the sale or possession of certain magazines, books (particularly paperbacks), photographs, picture playing cards, motion picture films, comic book-type drawings, and various items with an objectionable theme. The police administrator should be aware of the social ramifications and the legal implications that follow these complaints.

There are known groups of organized criminals engaged in the distribution of pornography in all forms. Independent dealers may operate only at the convenience of confederated criminal organizations. This association may be unknown to an independent dealer because the tribute to pay bribes, provide for lobbyists, and other necessary expenses are included in the base price of a document or film. This is paid for by the publisher or producer as a cost of doing business.

There is a wide area of controversy for suspected obscene materials. Generally, two major groups are in conflict. One group, made up of church leaders and representatives of other community organizations, will lead those who want to impose rigid legal interpretations. Other groups will be more liberal in their attitudes. People who are sincerely interested in protecting the right of a free press will favor self-censorship. There will be authors, artists, and teachers with a sound interest in working with no limitations placed on their creativity.

[32]*Kinglsey Books* v. *Brown*, 354 U.S. 436, 77 Supreme Court 1325.

Respectable publishers with a fear of excessive and unwarranted censorship and control of their publishing activity are going to be critical of all censorship. Other groups of publishers will not be so vocal but will utilize arguments of all groups for their benefit. This will be the organized group that publishes the trash, that makes up magazines from press releases, never names authors, and frequently changes the name and often the place of publication. Their only investment is in the pair of scissors and bottle of paste needed to make up the copy for the magazine. Their resourses for distribution have been carefully selected and managed by the confederation.

In the interpretation of obscenity such as the Miller case of 1973, Justice Douglas indicated that obscene material now must meet the three-pronged test: (1) "whether the average person, applying contemporary community standards would find that the work, taken as a whole, appeals to the prurient interest, (2) whether the work depicts or describes, in a patently offensive way, sexual conduct specifically defined by the applicable state law, and (3) whether the work, taken as a whole, lacks serious literary, artistic, political, or scientific value."[33] In 1982, the supreme court ruled that the interpretation of child pornography was not required, according to state law, to meet the three-pronged test outlined above.

In the final analysis, in order to keep the police from becoming censors, a number of ways have been suggested to provide for case preparation and presentation of evidence to the prosecuting agencies who then must make the decision on specific material alleged to be obscene. Many police agencies do not concern themselves with the enforcement of obscenity laws simply because the case histories are so vague.

QUESTIONS FOR DISCUSSION

1. Discuss the dilemma for local enforcement agencies when "acting on statute law" and "honoring case decisions."
2. What are some of the merits of the *absolutist* position on obscenity?
3. Why are obscenity and pornography frequently dissociated from protected speech?
4. Identify the three general rules for establishing what is obscene as outlined in the *Miller* v. *California* decision of 1973.
5. What impact does the phrase "whether the work taken as a whole lacks serious literary, artistic, political, or scientific value" have upon the publication of obscene materials?
6. In the case of *U.S.* v. *Orita* the Court held that the possession of obscene

[33]*Miller* v. *California.* In a follow-up case involving Illinois law, the Supreme Court in 1977 held that a state may prosecute persons for obscenity even though the kinds of materials describing sexual conduct might not be specifically prohibited. This decision appears to expand the *Miller* definition of what is a patently offensive way to display material.

materials in one's home does not extend to the transportation of such material. Discuss.

7. Why will the police position on obscenity enforcement usually split community attitudes that are otherwise quite cohesive?

8. Should there be "national standards" on sexual expression?

9. Should content of the material as well as the "business" of peddling smut be considered in obscenity cases?

10. Does the reading of obscene materials show a causal relationship to sexual crimes?

11. There are several ways in which the police may proceed against obscene materials. Discuss the merits and weaknesses of *in rem,* injunction, and direct criminal prosecution.

12. How does the community disagreement on matters of obscenity benefit organized confederations in the distribution business?

13. Why are obscenity and pornography cited as classic examples of the "double standard" of law enforcement in the United States?

PART III

OTHER CRIMES RELATED TO ORGANIZED METHODS

This part of the text focuses on business crimes and ideologically motivated crimes. The crimes described in Chapters 9, 10, and 11 are subject to control by organized groups, although many of them are not committed by the traditional confederations.

White collar crimes (Chapter 9) are of four basic types which range from individual indulgence in crime to highly organized groups that own and operate conglomerate empires. Chapter 10 covers the business transactions affected by organized criminal groups. There is a shopping list of criminal activities and a typology about how organized crime rips off the commercial interests in a community.

The last chapter in this part discusses a different kind of organized crime, the crime committed because of ideological commitment to a cause and an emotional commitment to the group. These are the reactionaries of the world, organized to meet a common need. In a sense they are dedicated to a criminal activity that requires organization to function. Because of the increased prevalence of militant group crimes and their impact upon enforcement activities, they are included here.

9

ORGANIZED WHITE COLLAR CRIME

LEARNING OUTCOMES

1. Develop an awareness for the great number of commercial actions that are susceptible to organized white collar crime control.
2. Identify the ways in which white collar crime penetrates a business.
3. Recognize the social ramifications for a business community controlled by organized white collar crime operations.
4. Determine the impact of white collar crime on the economic stability of a community.
5. Know the general investigative techniques for controlling white collar crime.

Because of the number of violations that concern business enterprises, a large number of crimes have been classified as white collar crimes (see Appendix A). Crimes of a white collar nature may be described as (1) *intent* to commit a wrongful act or to achieve a purpose inconsistent with law or public policy; (2) *disguise* (of purpose); (3) *reliance* on the ignorance or carelessness of the victim; (4) *voluntary victim action* to assist the offender; and (5) *concealment* of the violation.[1]

In one of the best documents published at the state level on organized crime, the Pennsylvania Crime Commission identified what is commonly referred to as white collar crime affiliation in this manner: "A roster of our 375 legitimate businesses that were involved in the following ways with criminal syndicates: (a) total ownership, (b) partial ownership, (c) hidden interest, (d) use of business for some illicit purpose."[2]

[1]Herbert Edelhertz, et al., *Investigation of White Collar Crime: A Manual for Law Enforcement Agencies* (Washington, D.C.: U.S. Government Printing Office, April 1977), pp. 21–22.

[2]Pennsylvania Crime Commission, *Report on Organized Crime,* Harrisburg, Pa.: Office of the Attorney General, Department of Justice, 1980, p. 40.

Whether these crimes are organized will depend upon how they are perpetrated. For example, credit card frauds, which are normally a one-person operation, become a type of organized crime if two or more persons get together and develop a scheme to further the criminal conspiracy. The same may be true of any of the categorized crimes in Appendix A.

In order to delimit and systematize the discussion of white collar crimes, those crimes that most frequently incur physical violence and thus come to the attention of the police have priority here. In order to orient both the officer and the citizen, the following concepts are considered important: (1) the impact of white collar crime upon the social structure, (2) typology of the crimes and techniques of the criminal, and (3) techniques and rationale for investigating white collar crimes.

THE IMPACT OF WHITE COLLAR CRIMES ON THE SOCIAL STRUCTURE

Due to complexity of identifying the deleterious effects of organized crime, we will focus here on (1) general implications on the social impact of organized crime, (2) the economic impact of white collar organized crime, and (3) how business enterprises are penetrated by organized crime.

Social Impact

Solerno and Tompkins most accurately describe the social impact of organized crime and specifically crimes of a white collar nature in the statement that crime is so well integrated into our lives that we often do not notice it moving in or recognize its face when it arrives. The book and the movie *The Godfather* and dozens of other documents have all attempted to point out how the criminal enterprise exists without police awareness, how the operations of an illegal enterprise naturally lead to influence and finally to domination of the legitimate business sector of society.[3] The evolution into legitimate enterprise may be illustrated in this manner:

A partner embezzles money from his firm to pay for the bets wagered with a bookie, who, in turn, converts much of this cash to wire services, the distribution of which is controlled by a highly sophisticated organization. Then, in order to cover his expenditure of company funds, the partner secures a loan from a loan shark suggested by the bookie. When usurious

[3]Ralph Salerno, *The Crime Confederation* (Garden City, N.Y.: Doubleday, 1969), preface. This is supported by former FBI Director Webster in a speech, January 8, 1981, when he said that a study by the American Management Association indicated losses of $44 billion annually. This translates to a 15 percent surcharge on all consumer prices.

interest rates cannot be paid, the loan shark becomes a silent partner in the operation and shares in the profits of the company.

Through the permissive attitude toward the crime of betting, society has sanctioned at least three other types of major criminal activity. Even veteran police officers still do not see the value of enforcing vice statutes. Unless the citizen and the field officer can visualize the connection between the single offender and the crimes of an organized nature, there is little hope of eradicating criminal organizations. Organized crime must be attacked at the street level as well as at the apex of the organization. Criminal confederations cannot be eradicated from the top, simply because authority and responsibility flow through too many insulating layers.

The importance of white collar crime in the social structure has been further described by Edelhertz:

> White collar crime is covert, and not immediate in impact. It is, therefore, difficult to move to the forefront of issues calling for public attention and a place in the priorities for allocation of law enforcement resources. Common crimes always appear more pressing, and no white collar victim clamors for attention. Yet, white collar crimes are serious, and must be investigated and prosecuted promptly. To ignore white collar crime is to undercut the integrity of our society, just as we ignore the safety of society when we fail to cope with common crime. To delay or postpone action is an abdication of enforcement responsibility and not an ordering of priorities.[4]

The difficulty of apprehension and the near impossibility of prosecution make white collar crime a strong ally for regular organized crime activities. A local officer must take the lead in preventing, detecting, and investigating crimes of this nature. These crimes frequently come to light in the investigation of traditional crimes and are presented here for the purpose of making the citizen and the field officer aware of white collar crime. Edelhertz further states:

> The important point to keep in mind is that some wrongful activity, or some aspects of a wrongful pattern of activity are committed by the use of guile and deception, and that there are statutes, methods of analysis, and techniques of investigation which will be particularly appropriate and effective in dealing with them.[5]

[4]Herbert Edelhertz, *The Nature, Impact and Prosecution of White Collar Crime* (National Institute of Law Enforcement and Criminal Justice, LEAA, U.S. Department of Justice, May 1970), p. 1. To update the methods of organized crime operations and to show techniques of business infiltration, see James Cook, "The Invisible Empire," *FORBES*, September 29–November 10, 1980.

[5]Edelhertz, *The Nature, Impact and Prosecution of White Collar Crime*.

In many instances, the so-called white collar crimes will characterize violators rather than violation. Thus, we may be dealing with a person who, singly or with others, derives a living from these activities. More important, in relation to the discussion of organized crime, is the fact that individual crimes of a white collar nature are committed to cover losses incurred through affiliation or transaction with the traditional organized crime groups— embezzlement to cover losses on bookmaking activity, the purchase of inferior merchandise forced into a store through illegal pressure tactics, and the purchase of bad stocks and bonds not within the normal channels of government control.

Legitimate businesses must be concerned. Historically, during the more militant phases of labor-management conflict, both sides recruited goons from the organized underworld. As partial payment, a few businessmen turned over certain commercial enterprises to criminal elements, while some labor officials forfeited union locals. Racketeering infestation intensified in ensuing years.[6] Many businesses have been taken over through factoring (the lending of money against accounts receivable or other asset collateral). This is done most frequently at a high interest rate (30 to 40 percent), and failure to repay in time may result in a partnership with a confederation.

Another illustration of the social impact of organized criminal groups was a 1971 case in which a suspect testified that he was the main worker in a 100 million dollar airport theft ring. Thefts included such items as mail, diamonds, and securities that were fenced throughout the country. The securities were also used as loan collateral and security in illicit business deals. The illustrations are endless and increasing at such a rapid pace that local police action is almost totally ineffective (see Figure 9–1).

Economic Impact

There are a number of techniques used by organized confederations that have a substantial economic impact upon society. These are, to mention only a few:

> The acquisition of massive amounts of money through illegal enterprises, and reinvestment of those funds back into the legitimate business market.
>
> The ability of the labor union to "squeeze" a business through corrupt and illegal tactics thus driving the cost of certain types of labor inordinately high. Therefore, prices are selectively out of proportion to the prevailing economic condition of society.
>
> Prices and interest rates are controlled through anticompetitive pricing.

[6]Chamber of Commerce of the U.S., *Deskbook on Organized Crime* (Washington, D.C., 1969), p. 9. For an update, see A.N. King, *Emerging Areas—The Federal View* (Raleigh, N.C.: National Association of Attorneys General, 1978).

Type of Business	How Obligations Are Incurred	How Debts Are Paid	Results
Bank, loan or investment company use laundered funds that come through "ghost"	Business experiences cash flow, needs funds for capital improvements, expansion	Company signs for personal or corporate loan, stock; secures options stock	Full or partial ownership in company; blind partnership; may put company in bankruptcy
Land development, real estate, builders	Use of pension funds, use of laundered funds invested back through foreign banks and loan companies, sweetheart labor contracts.	Outright ownership of property; ownership through trusts or relatives, property management companies, or silent partnership	Full or partial ownership of major properties; no strike assurance in construction
Casino gambling	Favorable licensing laws secured through political contacts, assurance of monopoly	Hidden control through stock, monopoly on supplies and equipment, and favors rendered	Hidden control of casinos, buildings, supplies, and equipment; corruption of government officials
Clothing	Money invested through loans; equipment furnished, raw materials supplied, labor contracts arranged or private contractors secured	Distributorships awarded both wholesale and retail; awarding of sewing and supply contracts to "private contractor"	Control of distribution; control of outside job contracts; setting of prices; no quality control; use of slave labor
Entertainment	Money invested through independent producers; "up-front" operators in places of entertainment	Silent partnerships, options on distributorships, retail outlets; use of nightclub talent provided by O/C	Control of distributorship and retail outlets; use of outlets as fronts for bookmaking and prostitution

Figure 9–1. How business and organized crime relate.

127

The use of strong-arm tactics to force legitimate businesses to sell out or come under the domination of confederation management.

The losses to business through organized theft of stocks, securities, merchandise, counterfeiture, and trade secrets espionage.

Bankruptcy fraud, where a company is forced into receivership through various guises.

The retention of lobbyists to assure that proper legislation is passed.

The documentation of white collar crime has been steadily improving for the past decade; at least two major government grants have addressed this problem.

How Business Enterprises Are Penetrated by Organized Crime

The Chicago Crime Commission made this observation:

We recognize the right of a person to choose his associates, but when a business opens its doors to the public, it must accept the correlary right of the public to know with whom it is doing business....

When a business open to the public is owned or operated by known members of the crime syndicate, keeps among its officers, directors and employees persons who have direct relationship with the syndicate or countenance open meetings of hoodlums on its premises, then we believe that the consumer is entitled to know these facts.[7]

Both the public and the police are entitled to know who these businesses are and how they operate. Although there is no simple way to illustrate how businesses are penetrated by organized crime, these illustrations from the study by Bers may establish some orientation. The reasons for penetration other than pure profit motive are these:

The quest for a safe haven for profits for illicit enterprises.

A desire for legitimacy.

Holdings in business may be viewed as a second base of power.[8]

Types of penetration are described by a number of authors. For example, Cressey cites these two basic forms:

Businesses legitimately purchased "with the fruits of crime" and operated—
Legitimately
Illegitimately.

---

[7]*Computerworld,* December 6, 1970–January 6, 1971.

[8]Melvin Bers, *The Penetration of Legitimate Business by Organized Crime: An Analysis* (National Institute LEAA, U.S. Department of Justice, 1970), p. 12.

Businesses illegitimately acquired and operated—
Legitimately
Illegitimately.[9]

The scope of these operations would include but not be limited to the activities described by Bers.[10]

Legal holding, legally operated. In addition to profit, this constitutes a base of power and influence for organized crime. For example, liquid assets such as cash hoards, domestic bank deposits, stocks and other securities, foreign bank deposits and other foreign assets, holdings in real estate and other normal business functions shield organized criminal activity.

Predatory or parasitic exploitations. For example, coercion and extortion such as sweetheart contracts, threat of labor difficulties, loan shark connections and forced purchase of supplies and services. Bankruptcy fraud adds a threat to these techniques.

Monopoly. The limitation of entry into a business by the destruction of competitors and threats of new entrants. Illegal price fixing such as voluntary or forced collusion.

Unfair advantage. For example, discrimination in wage and other standards by control and manipulation of labor organizations and pressures from labor organizations. Kickbacks in trade associations. Guaranteed market shares by the intimidation of customers and suppliers securing government contract through corruption. Other means such as the adulteration of goods and failure to observe minimum standards as set by law.

Businesses supporting illicit enterprise and receiving reciprocal support. For example, business providing outlets for illicit services such as gambling, narcotics, prostitution, and loan sharking. Businesses supportive to organized crime by covering as "legitimate income," through normal profits and through "strong-arm" retainers whose contributions to a business are fictional. Business facilities for hijacking, robbery, burglary; providing outlets for stolen property.

Through the processes just described, there is little chance that any business showing a profit is not going to be penetrated to some degree by elements of organized crime. The ease and magnitude of this fertile field of endeavor is shown in the Bers study. In an economic analysis of figures cited by authorities, about two-thirds of the national elite, in terms of national income, consists of associates of organized crime.[11] If, in fact, these figures are true, $30 billion per year in profits are siphoned off by organized criminal elements. Investments, as cited by the Internal Revenue Service, indicated

[9]Donald R. Cressey, *Theft of the Nation* (New York: Harper & Row, 1969).

[10]Bers, *The Penetration of Legitimate Business by Organized Crime,* p. 12.

[11]Ibid., p. 13, updated at $63 billion from narcotics, $22 billion from gambling, $8 billion from other crimes, $50 billion from white collar crimes, for a total of about $150 billion.

some 98 percent of 113 major organized crime figures were found to be involved in 159 individual businesses.[12]

Bers further stated:

> The total value of industrial and business assets for the national economy is approximately $3 trillion. If organized crime associates control as much as $30 billion, their share is 1 percent. Such a share is far from "takeover," but it is impressive nevertheless. And it would be cause for grave concern on several counts even if the share were half this size, as may well be the case, given the volume of funds thought to be simply hoarded or held abroad, and even if all holdings were in companies currently operated without resort to illegal methods.[13]

Perhaps of equal social impact would be the predatory and parasitic activities normally associated with organized criminal activity. For example, Walsh, in his investigation of corruption at the nation's airports, says:

> The other half of vice on air freight is the teamsters. If the union can get a single master contract with the air freight industry, it could back up future negotiatory demands by shifting down the whole business at will. A nationwide contract would also be a boost to the teamsters' campaign to organize thousands of other non-cargo airline employees with the control of the air cargo industry alone; however, the teamsters would be in a position to close an entire airport, or perhaps all major airports. If that happens, the public can expect to pay more to fly.[14]

This method of operation works well in every industry. For the confederation there is no violation in gaining power, and once power is secured, there is no one in a position to furnish sustained information in order to gain a conviction and unseat those in power.

The A&P case is another example of the coercive methods used by organized criminals. In this case, a member of the syndicate attempted to force A&P to stock an inferior grade of soap. When the store refused, there was retaliation against both the employee and the store. By not yielding to this pressure and seeking police protection, the store was saved from buying into a partnership with hoodlums.

Still, if A&P represents the scale of enterprise that is necessary to resist such predations, there is little solace in the fact that approximately 55 percent

---

[12]Ibid., pp. 14–15.

[13]Ibid., p. 16.

[14]Denny Walsh, "The 'Second Business' at our Airports: Theft," *Life*, 1971. Later case examples are presented in R.C. Thomas, "Organized Crime in the Construction Industry," *Crime and Delinquency*, 23, 3 (July 1977), 304–11. See also a compendium of cases: National Association of Attorneys General, *Intergovernmental Cooperation in Organized Crime Control— Examples of States Activities*, Raleigh, N.C., 1979.

of all industrial and business activity is conducted by firms that are in manufacturing, have less than 250 employees, and make less than $5 million annually. (Thus, they are classed as small businesses.) Approximately 95 percent of all business firms in this country meet these criteria.

Monopolies are so numerous and the schemes so diversified that we can identify only basic schemes (see Appendix A). Thirty-six different frauds are identified in the Battelle study completed in 1977.[15]

TYPOLOGY OF WHITE COLLAR CRIMES AND TECHNIQUES

To identify criminal activity by function is to oversimplify the interrelationship of one activity to another in the highly sophisticated organizations. The activities described in this chapter are closely interwoven with vice and drugs. In the section discussing loan sharking, we are talking about the manipulation of money and thus the catalyst that holds all organized criminals together in their struggle for power.

These major functional areas are arbitrarily chosen as those white collar crimes with which the police most frequently deal: (1) racketeering, (2) the loan shark business, and (3) black markets.

Racketeering

Gangsterism or racketeering, as it relates to white collar crimes, furnishes the means by which the confederations establish a monopoly or through extortion cause legitimate firms to pay tribute in order to operate.

Racketeering is one of the most pervasive forms of organized crime. Its use against businesses has been an American innovation that is now receiving added attention. Under 18 USC Section 1961–68, the Racketeer Influenced and Corrupt Organizations (RICO) law says that racketeering activity is committed by an individual committing any two of a variety of crimes (24 separate types of federal crimes and 8 types of state felonies) and is subject to severe penalties. The two key elements for prosecution under RICO are these: (1) a pattern of racketeering activity and (2) the existence of an "enterprise" with which the individual has some connection. This definition has broadened the scope of federal prosecutions. While all has not gone well for this law, there have been notable prosecutions and the courts have tended to uphold questions raised about the act.[16]

---

[15]Edelhertz, et al., *The Investigation of White Collar Crime,* Appendix C.

[16]J. Atkinson, "Racketeer Influenced and Corrupt Organizations—18 USC Section 1961–68—Broadest of the Criminal Statutes," *Journal of Criminal Law and Criminology,* 69, 1 (spring 1978), 1–18. See also G.R. Blakely, "On the Waterfront—RICO (Racketeer Influenced and Corrupt Organizations) and Labor Racketeering," *American Criminal Law Review,* 17, 3 (winter 1980), 341–65.

Major racketeering operations have been traced to regional crime families. Their operations, although varying from state to state, accommodate to weakness in local laws, but still show common patterns. For example, in Illinois acceptance agencies can deal in stocks, bonds, warehouse receipts, bills of lading, and other commercial paper. These companies can serve as a cover for disposing of stolen merchandise, the transfer of money between illegal organizations, the manipulation of political bribery, the coverup of loan sharks, and the cooling-off of hot or counterfeit money. "Skimming" from Nevada's gambling casinos proved to be a lucrative sideline for organized elements.

The basic factor of success in racketeering is the exertion of the proper amount of pressure so there is no alternative for the victim. Once racketeers are in a position to exercise pressure and force, they are able to extort levy and tribute. Reckless identified two types of racketeering: the *simon-pure* and the *collusive agreement*. An example of the simon-pure involves one individual who can levy power with a minimum of organization and affiliation. The collusive agreement, however, is an interlocking conspiracy. This type of racketeering operates like wheels within wheels, which makes it difficult to expose.[17]

Rackets are further reduced to two fundamental subtypes, monopoly and associations. The monopoly is the simplest type that employs the aid of politicians. In this example, the racketeer places himself as a necessary middleman. The association type approximates the collusive agreement among businessmen, labor leaders, and racketeers for the purpose of fixing prices and preventing undercutting. In this fundamental type, the racket is one in which tradespeople or shopkeepers are forced to join and pay dues for protection against violence to their persons and property. Furthermore, the criminal enterprise is able to dictate terms of doing business and the control of prices of commodities. In discussing the rackets, functions frequently overlap these classifications, and many criminal enterprises may be identified as belonging to both classifications.

The monopoly. Criminal monopoly is the use of criminal means to destroy competition.[18] It may be by the levy power with little affiliation or the collusive association bordering on extortion. The curtailing of competition by threat or by force has been a common method of operation that may take in both definitions by Reckless. Weston and Wells describe how the confederations have gained and retained their power:

> The object of the syndicate (confederation) is to get protection from competition when the law will not allow it or legal techniques cannot be

---

[17]Walter C. Reckless, *The Crime Problem* (New York: Appleton-Century-Crofts, 1961), chap. 15.

[18]Paul B. Weston and Kenneth M. Wells, *Criminal Investigation: Basic Perspectives* (Englewood Cliffs, N.J.: Prentice-Hall, 1980), p. 431.

used to achieve it. The syndicate (confederation) members learned the technique of curtailing competition in their black market areas of prostitution, gambling and narcotics through strong-arm methods that originated in the beer and whiskey-selling days of Prohibition. Strong-arm tactics are also used to bulwark the operation of one of the syndicate's (confederation's) firms to buy solely from syndicate suppliers. Linen and laundry services, sale of food products, and placement of vending machines are businesses in which this tactic has been used. A legal business, illegally operated by strong-arm methods, can be a profitable enterprise under organized crime.[19]

The association. As identified by Reckless, the association is probably organized crime's most potent ally for gaining control of activities that will eventually lead the confederations into legitimate businesses. These associations include such organizations as trade and labor unions, and other organizations in which access to business is through a third party. Activities may include the price-fixing of merchandise. For example, a criminal cartel may exist if the garment trade eliminates cut-throat competition by an agreement on prices and wages, hiring thugs to enforce the agreement.[20] This may or may not violate a federal regulation or statute, except that coercion to enforce such agreement may lead to a crime.

The associations serve as a clearing house to get organized criminals into a trade where cheating may be more easily conducted. For example, in the bar business, who knows how many drinks are served, how many are given away as business favors and bribes, how much liquor is brought in the back door (not invoiced from the regular sources), and how many employees are hired thugs not related to the conduct of the business?

Labor racketeering. Organized labor's control of the work force through hiring hall practices has been a sad exploitation of human dignity. Both overt and subtle abuses involving the hiring halls have included but are not limited to the following abuses:

> Unethical local union officials cause blackmailing of contractors through the withholding of labor forces unless certain special conditions are met such as overtime, attachment of wages to payoff, hiring hall bookies and gamblers who are kicking back to union leaders.
>
> Loan sharks, with the cooperation of crooked union management, maintained officers at the hiring hall, and the hiring was not done unless loans were paid up, usually at a bonus rate in addition to the already usurious rate.
>
> Raises, acquired through pressure tactics of the hiring hall, may be siphoned off into flower funds and other special projects not in the regular union dues.
>
> Concessionaires, peddling lottery tickets, stolen merchandise, and other side

[19]Ibid., p. 432.

[20]Thomas C. Shelling, "Economics Analysis and Organized Crime," *President's Commission on Organized Crime*, p. 117. This is updated by Blakely.

businesses, find a mecca about the hiring halls. All pay a fee for the right to service the workers.

Arrests made by local officers in the vicinity of the hiring halls are compromised and settled out of court through union pressure tactics. Lower fines negotiated through the hiring hall representatives never show on court documents. The loyalty of union managers pays well.

A most obvious example of labor union racketeering centers around the murder of Joseph Yablonski in 1969 in Pennsylvania. In a power struggle for leadership, Yablonski split the solid support for leadership and incurred the wrath of that leadership. Subsequent investigations have indicated there were paid murderers recruited by union leadership to avert an overthrow of the group in power. As trials were held, there were indications that the killings were most effectively planned. If it were not for the alertness of the victim, the crime would probably have gone unsolved.

The Loan Shark Business

Loan sharking may be defined as a financial transaction at usurious or exorbitant rates of interest, usually without collateral and with the fear of physical force to guarantee payment.

Shylocking, or money lending outside the regulation of government, has persisted throughout history. Ancient Rome had its money lenders and English history identified many famous shylocks. Not until the past two decades, however, has organized crime moved in to make it a lucrative nationwide business. Many major cities rank loan sharking as the number one moneymaker for the confederations. The dollar amounts are estimated nationally at $350 million to over $1 billion.[21]

The economic impact of loan sharking and the ultimate cost to the general public are undoubtedly substantial. Through loan sharking, professional criminals siphon off significant resources from the legitimate economy to finance additional illegal activity. Loan sharking is the fifth-ranking crime in terms of financial cost to the public; adding the cost of government efforts to combat the problem, the total price to the public becomes a matter of concern to every person, whether a victimized borrower or not.[22]

Loan sharks depend upon the comfort of the confederation affiliation when force is necessary in collecting payments. It is also natural that loan sharking be affiliated with the organized groups, because many of the loans

---

[21]President's Commission on Law Enforcement and Administration of Justice, *Task Force Report: Crime and Its Impact: An Assessment* (Washington, D.C.: U.S. Government Printing Office, 1967), p. 53.

[22]"Loan Sharking: The Untouched Domain of Organized Crime," *Columbia Journal of Law and Social Problems*, p. 92. An update on contemporary loan sharking can be found in R. Goldstock, "Controlling the Contemporary Loanshark—The Law of Illicit Lending and the Problem of Witness Fear," *Cornell Law Review*, 65, 2 (January 1980), 127–289.

are made to cover confederation-sponsored gambling losses. Loan sharking, of all organized criminal activities, is the linchpin that controls every other segment of organized crime.[23] Through proper manipulation, the shylocks are in a position to encourage business takeovers, to cover gambling losses, to encourage burglaries by giving loans against merchandise that will go through a "fence" for stolen goods, and keep loan recipients obligated through usurious rates and through loan contracts that cannot be paid off. When a person is in control of money, his influence is enhanced. The flow of illegally acquired money through loan sharks destroys the continuity for tracing such funds. Because of transactions through loan sharks, economists' and accountants' estimates on the amount of money involved in organized crime are a combination of guess and speculation.

In his research into the shylock business, John Seidl defines three common elements for loan sharking:

> The lending of cash at a high interest rate.
>
> The borrower-lender agreement which rests on the borrower's willingness to pledge his and his family's physical well-being as collateral against a loan with its obvious collection implications.
>
> ...a belief by the borrower that the lender has connections with ruthless criminal organizations.[24]

Based upon these elements, a multimillion-dollar industry has evolved. Actual field operations do not necessarily dictate violence as a means of collection, nor are all debts collected. *Often a bad debtor will be pressured by threats and intimidation; when these methods fail to work, the debt is forgotten.* This type of settlement, however, is not the type of image that is good for organized crime confederations. If the citizen has an honest police department, district attorney, and court to depend upon, there is usually little to fear from the loan sharks of organized crime. The *fear* of reprisal is organized crime's greatest collection tool.

Unfortunately, it is not always an individual who must do business with loan shark operations. Business firms borrow funds from "money lenders." Companies that finance a product in production and prior to sale are often controlled by questionable groups who lend at usurious rates. A business that must borrow this kind of money may find itself with perpetual high interest rates. The detailed operation of business lenders has been described by the Institute of Defense Analysis. In another study, shylocking was described as a multi-billion-dollar guaranteed annual income for the confederation.[25]

---

[23]Much of the loan shark industry is conducted by individuals not allied with any organization. This book is concerned with the organized segment.

[24]John Michael Seidl, "'Upon the Hip'—A Study of the Criminal Loan Shark Industry." (Ph.D. Dissertation, Harvard University, December, 1968), p. 30.

[25]Institute of Defense Analysis, LEAA, *Task Force Report: The Courts* (Washington, D.C.: U.S. Government Printing Office, 1967), p. 3.

The flow of money through the illegal operators is practically impossible to trace, as shown in Figure 9–2, which is taken from a government study. The method of operation of the individual engaged in the business will vary according to geographic location and the clientele.

How the loan shark operates.   Money coming into the confederation will be pushed into circulation through the hierarchy and ultimately through the street loan shark. The street shark usually pays from 3 to 4 percent interest per week for syndicate money. He, in turn, will loan it to "street friends" for 5 percent per week (approximately 260 percent per year). Deals generally occur through acquaintances who become known to the street loan shark, or referral through friends. Because of the nature of the business, a loan shark may be involved as a receiver of stolen property. Furs and diamonds at 10 percent actual value can often cancel a debt.

Loan activities are basically of two types: (1) "vigorish," which provides for weekly payments of interest only, payments on principal being made when "convenient" to the borrower; and (2) "pay down," which provides for weekly payments of interest and principal for eventual liquidation of the entire debt. The first is most harmful to borrowers because it commonly results in their having paid much more than the initial loan, while still owing at least that entire principal amount.[26]

Black Markets

There are basically two forms of black market operations in which organized criminals are involved: (1) the black market commodity, and (2) the black market monopoly. Activities such as narcotic sales will cover both categories because it is the monopolizing of an illegal commodity.

The black market commodity includes a vast number of consumer goods and services. Illegal transactions, pornography, and all contraband are prohibited by law, as are reselling tickets above purchase price (scalping) and wartime control on restricted items. The second party to these transactions will usually be aware of their illegality.[27]

The black market monopoly occurs when the marketeer enjoys a protected market in the same way that a domestic industry is protected by a tariff. The black marketeer gets automatic protection through the law itself from all competition unwilling to pursue a criminal career.[28] For example, a labor racket is a local monopoly. A second party is frequently unaware the transaction is illegal until it is too late.

These classifications are important only in that they clearly illustrate the complexity of prosecutions at the apex of an organization. Frequently, it is the crime itself that must be attacked if organized groups are to be eradicated.

[26]"Loan Sharking: The Untouched Domain of Organized Crime," pp. 94–95.
[27]Commission Report, *Organized Crime*, p. 116.
[28]Ibid., p. 117.

SOURCE OF FUNDS		RECIPIENT OF FUNDS
ILLEGAL ENTERPRISES		**ILLEGAL ACTIVITIES**
Gambling	The loan shark may be a one person unit or a 100 person organization.	Individual contracts (bar rooms, country clubs, etc.)
Burglary (fencing stolen property)		
Skimming from profits (coin machines, etc.) (prior to paying of taxes)		Employment agency or labor union lending, banks and loan companies with questionable ownership.
Forgery or counterfeiting		
Lending agencies which receive under the table kickbacks		Financing of merchandise through individual companies (used autos, furniture, etc.)
LEGAL BUSINESSES		**LEGAL INVESTMENTS**
Legitimate lending agencies		Foreign bank deposits and investments
Liquor (bootleg-retail)		Investment through holding companies, minority shareholders in any legitimate business
Coin-operated machines		
Franchise operations i.e., laundries, restaurants		
Estates in trust		Factoring companies
Employee pension funds		

Figure 9–2 Flow of money into and through the loan shark industry.

TECHNIQUES AND RATIONALE FOR INVESTIGATING WHITE COLLAR CRIME

The suggestions offered here are for the orientations of the field officers who will have an opportunity to investigate white collar crimes. What does the field officer look for in detecting and seeking out criminals and criminal activity that may be affiliated with organized crime of a white collar nature?[29]

The officer should review crime reports and study newspaper stories of stock market manipulations and "suspect business transactions" for names and locations of persons living in the district who are involved in activities that may be unethical, although not necessarily illegal. A loose surveillance by the district officer on suspected persons frequently reveals good intelligence information on many varieties of white collar crimes.

Frequently, in the investigation of business burglaries, robberies, and other crimes, there will be attempts to cover shortages of partners and associates.

> For example, at a burglary scene, where checks were taken, an officer investigating the check ledger for missing checks was notified by a secretary that a loan company received checks from the business at weekly intervals in round number amounts. Subsequent intelligence and investigation work revealed the loan company was a collection agency for a syndicate bookmaking operation.

> In a second case, the discovery by an employee of a large number of stock certificates in a business safe that had been burglarized led to the solution of an interstate burglary and embezzlement gang. Both the field officer and the citizen, if properly trained and reasonably alert, can be effective contributors to the intelligence process.

The patrol officer and the businessperson in street contacts should listen for hints that embezzlement, corruption in government, extortion, labor racketeering, and dozens of other crimes may be occurring. Prostitutes, cab drivers, and bartenders are notorious for knowing what goes on. The field officer is in daily contact with these people and should be encouraged to submit simple intelligence information reports as part of daily reporting activity.

> For example, a prostitute in one case was able to identify the "torch men" for a maverick labor union effort to unionize restaurants. This information came to a uniform field officer from the informer because he made his patrol work a challenge rather than just routine patrol.

[29]Weston and Wells, *Criminal Investigation*, p. 425. The concept of "wraparound" is important to the investigation of confederation operations. This means organized criminals trade off in every business of organized crime until the operation is wrapped around every possible means of making money.

The uniformed officer is frequently a liaison between specialized units in large city departments and departments in rural areas. He or she deals with field situations that may cross specialized lines such as narcotics, homicides, burglaries. If proper procedures are not established to debrief this officer, valuable information will not be gathered, compared, and evaluated. Roll call training sessions, when conducted regularly and properly, may bring this type of information to light.

The field officer should know his or her district and the knowledge should be put to work for a department. Investigators who desire information on a particular person or place over a long period of time should be forced to sit down and review cases that might be generated from some intelligence collection. Investigators, who are conducting an investigation, if the investigation will not be compromised or endangered, should be required to sit down with officers who are assigned to a district. All too often, investigations are ineffective simply because "secrecy" preempts logical investigative procedures. All too often, the "need to know policy" imposed by investigators at all levels of government is detrimental to an investigation. Uniformed patrol officers should be trained to render such aid, and liberal use should be made of their knowledge and contacts in a district or precinct.

In gaining an overview on white collar crime, the field officer must see how governmental processes are subverted through corruption, how business enterprises are penetrated, and how prosecutions are thwarted.

SUMMARY

In this chapter it has been pointed out that organized criminals are deeply involved in business ventures. This involvement may come about through a number of monopolistic and coercive practices. These practices are highly refined techniques designed to avoid the publicity that may associate a business venture with confederated crime organizations. Because publicity is avoided, the public will frequently be active participants in street level crimes that support the organized criminal hierarchy. In citing the elements of white collar crime it has been shown how easily business enterprises are penetrated, why this association is desirable for the organized group, and how each criminal enterprise operates within these classifications: (1) legal holding, legally operated, (2) predatory or parasitic exploitation, (3) monopoly, (4) unfair advantage, and (5) businesses supporting illicit enterprise and receiving reciprocal support.

Three major subcategories of white collar crimes have been identified. Racketeering has been discussed first because through monopoly or association, the confederations are able to exert control over any business. In labor racketeering the coercive forces of an unethical or illegal act by a union can spell life or death for a business. The loan shark has been shown to be a vital

and dynamic part of organized criminal power. Money manipulators through the loan shark make the confederations cohesive and powerful. Black markets, although normally associated with wartime shortages, also include products that are illegal or in short supply. Many organized criminal groups receive protection from the law while holding exclusive control over a business franchise such as city bus lines or ambulances.

Because of the variety of violations, how a crime is investigated will depend upon the criminal methodology of an individual or group.

QUESTIONS FOR DISCUSSION

1. Identify and discuss those businesses in a community that may be subject to organized criminal influences.
2. Do the citizens of a community support an activity such as bookmaking? How may this relate to subversion of business?
3. Do city political figures know who hold their franchises? Are there past histories of criminal records that show a common pattern?
4. Are the public services, such as airports, bus, and train stations, subject to large theft losses?
5. Do the crime rates of theft and burglary indicate that merchandise is being fenced?
6. Are businesses controlled by permit or some other form of regulation? Are complaints against firms that fleece the public thoroughly investigated?
7. Who owns the coin-operated machines?
8. Who may control local labor unions, and is coercion through strikes and stoppages a common method of operation?
9. Are there an unusual number of harassment activities against businesses in the community?
10. Are bids let by public agencies to questionable contractors for poor work?

10

ORGANIZED CRIME AND BUSINESS TRANSACTIONS

LEARNING OUTCOMES

1. Know how the confederations actually control and manipulate different businesses in the community.
2. Develop an awareness that some businesses in the community are more susceptible to organized crime control than others.
3. Understand in some detail how securities, including credit cards, are used to defraud.
4. Identify key elements of special frauds, including use and abuse of computers.
5. Recognize how political contributions from businesses affect organized crime.

There are more than 100 identified crimes closely affiliated with organized groups. It is fair to say that any transaction or any activity that requires trust may be subject to dishonest manipulation by an individual or by an organized group. In addition to the three categories, in Chapter 9, there are these: (1) business acquisitions by racketeering, (2) manipulation and embezzlement of stocks, bonds, and credit cards, and (3) special frauds, swindles, and thefts.

BUSINESS ACQUISITIONS BY RACKETEERING

Officers at every level of the enforcement hierarchy will see business maneuvers, exchanges, and transactions for which there is no apparent reason. Officers will see organized crime figures engaged in almost every legitimate business enterprise. Businesses, such as the bars and restaurants, offer quick turnover and accounting methods that are easily manipulated. Thus, confederations are attracted to these businesses. Legitimate businesses

are particularly susceptible to manipulation and coercion by organized criminal groups. Activities such as the following are only illustrations of events that are occurring in hundreds of locations each day of the year. Gangster infiltration of legitimate business through racketeering methods may be done in many ways.

The Coercive Contract with Public Agencies

A subtle but effective way to gain government contracts, for example, can be found in a San Diego County, California case where an organized crime member, with union assistance, moved in to force independent hauling contractors into joining the union or losing the right to work on a multi-million-dollar state highway project. When the independent operators were squeezed out, the organized crime member moved in as a prime subcontractor and with leased equipment did millions of dollars worth of contract hauling simply because he was able to eliminate the independent contractor as a competitor.

Strong-Arm Tactics

This method is still in popular use. It can bring a business into a cooperative arrangement in a swift fashion. For example, if a confederation decides a particular business location would be desirable for a bookie spot, lottery office, or pornography shop and the owner refuses to cooperate, a number of techniques are used.

Usually, the confederation will first try to "buy off" the business. They make the initial offer so attractive that it is difficult for the owner not to cooperate. If a cooperative agreement fails to materialize, a few threats against the owner's family may bring concessions.

If the owner will still not cooperate, mob-controlled distribution monopolies will not deliver services. For example, a restaurant is dependent upon food supplies, garbage services, and miscellaneous services such as waiters, dishwashers, linens, glassware. The loss of any of these services will bankrupt a business. As a last resort the business may be picketed, burned out, bombed, or other strong-arm tactics such as beatings or kidnappings may take place.

Often these actions take place without police knowledge. Even when brought to the attention of the police, nothing is usually done to protect the citizen. There is a very fine line in determining whether we are dealing with methods that may border on competitive business practices rather than criminal activities.

Legitimate business takeovers through racketeering tactics in such areas as coin-operated machines, loan and other fiscal operations, and the deceptive expenditure of public funds through public official and gangster association are but a few of the methods of business acquisition by outright acquisition,

by corporate control, or by the corrupt use of employees already in the organization. The infiltration by whatever means includes "mom and pop" stores as well as stockholder influence in many of the nation's conglomerates.

MANIPULATION AND EMBEZZLEMENT OF STOCKS, BONDS, AND CREDIT CARDS

This section concentrates on some financial manipulations that constitute less than complete control of a business. These manipulations of the financial strength of an organization can have a disastrous impact on the operation of a business. When organized crime, through fiscal manipulation such as manipulation and embezzlement of stocks or bonds, can control the operation of that organization, it is then easy to maintain a cover for other illegal operations.

When asked about organized crime involvement in the theft and counterfeiting of stocks and bonds, the late FBI Director Hoover made this reply:

> I would not credit La Cosa Nostra or the other elements of organized crime with all the thefts on Wall Street, but quite frequently either members of La Cosa Nostra or their close associates turn up in our investigations.
>
> One...case involves eight separate thefts totaling about $17 million in which we have made a number of arrests and recovered many of the stolen securities. One of the persons we arrested is known to us as a member of La Cosa Nostra and additional arrests are pending. Before we were called into the case, the subjects were able to realize in the neighborhood of $1.8 million.[1]

In other multi-million-dollar cases spurious covers were developed for laundering stolen and counterfeit securities. Brokerage firms had agents prepare phony documents to show prior ownership of stolen securities. This laundering process, when completed, filtered clean documents back through various corporate structures, and the monies were then fed into legitimate businesses.

Other common crimes perpetrated against businesses, but not further discussed in this text, include bankruptcy fraud, including the scam of planned bankruptcy and fraudulent concealment, where assets are concealed in anticipation of insolvency. Another popular fraud scheme is the *boiler room,* which involves the use of telephone solicitors to sell securities, solicit donations, and so on.[2]

---

[1] J. Edgar Hoover, "The Bull Market in Stock and Bond Thefts," *Nation's Business,* March 1970, p. 30. Updated in James Cook, "The Invisible Enterprise," *Forbes,* September 29–November 4, 1980.

[2] Herbert Edelhertz, *The Investigation of White Collar Crime: A Manual for Law Enforcement Agencies* (Washington, D.C.: U.S. Government Printing Office, April, 1977), pp. 298–99.

Securities Manipulation and Theft

The illegal use of securities, such as stocks and bonds, has come of age since the President's Crime Commission failed to address the problem in depth.[3] The massive movement of "hot paper," which has been the subject of theft or counterfeiting, has been operating without adequate sanctions to protect the public. Several reports suggest that multi-million-dollar corporations can be set up instantly through the use of paper to be counterfeited or not yet stolen. Either of which alternatives gives certificates that are sufficient for brokerage to the public. Some estimates by government officials in the Securities and Exchange Commission indicate that these types of fraudulent transactions may be as many as 300 million per year.

The U.S. Chamber of Commerce states that a majority of the securities that find their way into organized crime can be used in these ways:[4]

1. Sold to a bargain-hungry investor for 30 cents on the dollar.
2. Offered to banks as collateral for loans to finance underworld enterprises.
3. Rented to dishonest businessmen, who will include the securities as assets that will appear on certified balance sheets.
4. Dummy companies sell Financial Guarantee Payment Bonds to those in need of bank loans. When the loan is granted and the borrower defaults, the bank is left with worthless paper.
5. Dummy corporations issue notes or other paper to purchase assets of other corporations.

A major problem in any of the areas listed is that no federal agency has either sole jurisdiction or the people to cope with the massive amounts of paper securities that are accumulating. Several subcommittees are attempting to work out new, more secure methods of handling stocks. Under the present system an unethical stockbroker can use the same securities for any number of transactions without an owner being aware of illegal manipulations.

There are any number of ways for confederation members to manipulate stocks. For example, it is not unusual to find a marginal business organization with stolen or counterfeit stocks and bonds in its portfolio. It is not uncommon to use these documents as a basis for credit for inventory buildup, for expansion of facilities, or as a basis for floating legitimate stock on the open market.

In businesses owned by the confederations, it is easy to hold hot documents until they cool or through intercorporation transfer get the hot stocks out of

[3]The 1972–73 Equity Funding case in New York is an example of fraudulent manipulation to benefit the stock exchange at the expense of the public. In this case an analyst released information detrimental to a corporation about adverse conditions within a listed agency (Equity Funding) that was not being released to stock purchasers.

[4]Chamber of Commerce of the United States, *Deskbook on Organized Crime* (Washington, D.C.: An Urban Affairs Publication, 1969), p. 51.

the country so they can be traded or negotiated for new money that may then be returned to this country without taint.

It is not unusual for a case of stock theft on the West Coast to be consummated on the East Coast within a week. Again, the speed of transmitting stolen documents exceeds that with which the police are able to transmit information that will curb such practices.

In the bond business there are a number of ways in which organized criminals have been involved. There are two common methods of operation. (1) Forgery of an owner's name on a registered bond is a common activity of the confederations. (2) Some big operations have involved unregistered bonds. These thieves simply add a name and the bond is cashed through normal channels. By the time the theft of the bonds is discovered, the salesperson has vanished. Women are often used as passers in this type of activity.

The manipulation of stocks and/or bonds within a company has become an important moneymaker for the confederations. They purchase an old defunct corporation and through loans secured by using stolen stocks or bonds as collateral, members of the confederations are able to form new corporations and eventually put company stock on the public market. Once the public has subscribed to the legal limit, the confederation drains off all the liquid assets and declares bankruptcy.

There is serious need for new and better methods to control the paper transactions of a company. There are a few states where practically no binding law exists for the control of corporations. In such states the "fly by night" operators are busily fleecing stockholders from throughout the world. Some of the best illustrations of how intricate business operations are open to unethical and illegal manipulation are in the great salad oil swindle and in the Billie Sol Estes case. These cases are supplemented in police files by those of hundreds of victims who have been fleeced by unethical and/or illegal operators.

The Futures Market

Another phase of stock market operation that is highly susceptible to manipulation by both confederation and unethical business groups is the investment in futures stock. The quick turn-around in this high-profit (or loss) operation makes it attractive to professionals who may need a tax shelter for their income. Although one would expect the fluctuation in prices to be responsive to economic and other conditions, frequently it is the manipulation of large amounts of money that makes the investment in futures desirable.

Because most speculators never see the commodities in which they are investing, their participation is the buying and selling of papers. Thus, these investments are subject to many abuses.

Many companies, and especially those owned by the confederations, "lay off" by purchasing futures on their own products. This type of hedging opens doors for many types of deceit and fraud. For example, a business with a large inventory of marketable products can negate its loss on its cash stock value by investing an equal amount of the product in the futures market. Many questionable companies are "selling short" in such schemes. In such instances it is the consumer who ultimately pays.

This type of maneuver can work in reverse. For example, a farm coop may have orders that exceed its stock on hand. It will buy futures contracts equal to the extent of its orders. If the price of the commodity goes up, the price of the futures contract will also increase by a similar amount. Even though the coop may have to purchase a quantity of a commodity and sell at a loss, the rise in the futures contract will still generate a profit. If this type of practice is the order of business, a consumer must eventually be the economic victim.

Credit Card Frauds

Organized groups are a natural for this crime. Through thefts, burglaries, and the manufacture of illegal cards, organized groups thrive on volumes of business and weak verification of credit card holders.

Many petty thieves and professional burglars steal credit cards in the normal course of their work, and these they pass through fences. In turn, the fences sell the cards to shoppers who make fraudulent identification to match the card and present the card for the purchase of merchandise. The merchandise in turn is peddled back through the fence for about 10 percent of its original value. Other credit card abuses include false statements in gaining cards and in securing cards under false names with no intention to pay. Prosecutions of these crimes may be had under state theft, forgery, or federal mail fraud statutes.[5]

SPECIAL FRAUDS, SWINDLES, AND THEFTS

Fraud of the Elderly

One of the big swindles of modern America has been with elderly victims. They are susceptible to hard-sell gimmicks on radio and television. Pharmaceutical dispensers, auto repair operators, and dozens of businesses patronized by the elderly are first to swindle the elderly. In 1968, the Subcommittee on Consumer Interests of the Elderly identified schemes that were swindling the elderly of billions of dollars. Devices for cosmic ray treatments, new cures for old age illnesses, and fad diet foods are all sold to the elderly. Health insurance, cemetery lots, and inflated burial contracts are

---

[5]Edelhertz, *The Investigation of White Collar Crime,* p. 287.

all part of the swindlers' game. Whereas all these crimes may not be the forte of the better-known organized confederations, there are enough in these businesses to classify them as organized operations.

Although most crimes of an organized nature that directly affect the elderly cannot be identified separately, they are important to mention. For example, the garage operations probably fleece more elderly victims of more money than all the commonly recognized crimes such as burglary and robbery. Being fleeced by the unethical and frequently confederation-owned garage operator is so common that most persons accept the gouging without complaint. The poor and the elderly are prime victims for such ads as "complete motor overhaul $89.95," with "if engine condition permits" in very small print. Once in the garage the vehicle owner must sign to have the vehicle worked on. If the vehicle owner is not careful, he has signed an open-ended contract that permits the garage to do the work it deems necessary. In any event, after a vehicle is dismantled, the "engine condition" rarely allows a $89.95 overhaul. The garage will then contact the vehicle owner and advise him that his engine is in such poor shape that it will require a $539 overhaul job. When the victim says he does not have that kind of money, the friendly garage indicates it will accept the $89.95 as down payment and float a loan, frequently at a usurious rate of interest. An alternative to going along with the garage is to pay a reassembly fee. This fee is generally from $35 to $50. If both offers are refused by the victim, the garage dumps the parts in the vehicle and stores the vehicle, usually for a high fee, until an independent tow truck can retrieve it. The nature of the small garage operation makes such businesses attractive to the confederations. For example, stolen vehicles can easily be converted to spare parts, and control over garage mechanics can be exercised.

Welfare Swindles

Swindles in the welfare programs are basically one- or two-person operations and would not normally be classed as organized crime. However, when a number of persons conspire to steal welfare, pension and other checks from mail boxes and to engage in a concerted effort toward other crimes, the organized crime title is appropriate. For example, a news release from New York City indicated how such crimes are perpetrated. Obviously, New York is not unique in these types of swindles:[6]

Four men were accused of donning a variety of disguises and faking credentials to bilk the state of $300,000 in unemployment insurance over a five-year period.

"At a time of unemployment so high and a tax burden so great, the crimes

---

[6]Investigators for Health and Human Services in 1980 arrested a welfare recipient who had defrauded the government of $265,000.

committed by these men are particularly insidious," Brooklyn District Attorney Eugene Gold told newsmen.

"This is the most expensive fraud perpetrated on the agency in its thirty-three years of existence."

Gold said the men, working together, employed wigs, dark glasses, other means of disguise, and used bogus identification, names of employers, and other data required by the State Division of Employment.

Thus prepared, the prosecutor went on, the ring went from one unemployment insurance office to another, obtaining in all more than 5,000 checks averaging $60 each and made out to more than 100 different identities.

Eventually, Gold went on, a Brooklyn agency became suspicious when one name appeared three years in a row on a claim for unemployment benefits.

The ringleader of the operation, Gold said, was Joseph Shotland, forty-six, father of two. He faced a variety of charges, including grand larceny and forgery.

Similar charges were made against Max Nice, sixty, William Schaefer, thirty-four, and John Dermody, thirty-six.

Political Contributions

How corruption pervades the political picture may be shown in this news release:

A federal grand jury today indicted President W.A. "Tony" Boyle of the United Mine Workers union on charges of embezzlement, conspiracy, and unlawfully contributing $49,250 in union funds to political campaigns.

A special panel investigating tangled affairs of the miners' union charged that Boyle, in conspiracy with other UMW officials, embezzled $5,000 in union funds and gave, among other contributions, $30,000 to the presidential campaign of Democratic nominee Hubert H. Humphrey in 1968.

Charged with the sixty-six-year-old Boyle in the indictment were John Owens, secretary-treasurer of the union, and James Kmetz, director of the Labor's Non-Partisan League (LNPL), a political arm of the UMW. If convicted, Boyle could receive up to two years in prison and a $10,000 fine on each of 11 counts of violating the federal Corrupt Practices Act, and 5 years and $10,000 on each of the conspiracy and embezzlement counts.

The indictment noted that the union's LNPL has made political donations of approximately $1.5 million since 1943. This is one of the purposes for which it was established, since federal laws permit political donations from nonpartisan organizations established by unions for this and lobbying purposes....

The $5,000 Boyle was charged with embezzling in the one count was included in the contribution to the campaign fund of Humphrey and to other fund-raising functions by both the Democratic and Republican parties.

The Regulatory Commissions

Partisan politics and political favoritism are the two major factors that allow organized crime to retain a controlling interest in the vital regulatory functions of federal, state, and local government.

In recent years, commissions have become increasingly important in the conduct of government as they relate to the regulation of businesses. The efforts of government commissions, although active in revealing some symptoms of organized crime, have not had the resources or the expertise to adequately perform their assigned responsibilities; thus, guilty parties have been allowed to shrug off allegations and continue as before. The failure of the commissions to generate interest in acting against these crimes is reflected in this example. In fiscal year 1971 the Federal Trade Commission referred only one case to the Department of Justice for prosecution, and this was for failure to respond to a subpoena. Three cases were referred to the Department of Justice for violation of the truth-in-lending provision of the Consumer Credit Protection Act. Twenty cases of antitrust violations were sent to the Justice Department in the past two years for criminal prosecution.[7]

This failure of the regulatory agency to perform points up a lack of interest in prosecuting certain regulatory violations. In order to offset this disinterest, consumer protection committees have been established in many cities throughout the United States. These committees function as a coordinating body between federal, state, and local governmental organizations involved in consumer protection. These committees include members of the Federal Trade Commission.

Another important commission that deals with the control of organized crime in the areas of fraud and theft is the Federal Communications Commission, which under the authority of statutes 18 U.S.C. 1302 (broadcasting lottery information), 18 U.S.C. 1343 (fraud by wire or radio), and 18 U.S.C. 1464 (broadcasting obscene language) has the opportunity to regulate organized crime's use of the communications system. In addition, this commission investigates unauthorized interception and divulgence of law enforcement radio communication (Section 605 of the Communications Act). The entire spectrum of communications, as it supports organized crime, needs more research.

The Civil Aeronautics Board is important to the control of thefts involving organized crime. By the nature of its law enforcement activities, the CAB regulates such activities as unauthorized air transportation (tour groups). Under the Fair Credit Reporting Act, credit terms offered to airline consumers must be fully disclosed. Although about two dozen criminal violations were alleged in fiscal year 1971, no prosecutions were reported.

---

[7]*Attorney General's First Annual Report* (Washington, D.C.: U.S. Government Printing Office, 1972), pp. 502–3.

This is an area that in the future will receive increased attention as airlines diversify into other business activities.

The Federal Deposit Insurance Corporation is a vital link in controlling organized crime manipulation involving internal bank operations and the character of bank officers. Special types of organized criminal activities, by necessity, must be housed in a bank or savings and loan organization. A bank can lend vast amounts on securities, and can negotiate for and cover for stolen securities. Exposés around the country have shown that internal control of the banking industry is necessary.

Oil Pricing Frauds

Some of the best-paid thieves of the 1970s have been manipulators in the oil industry. Ironically, the federal government's ill-conceived energy laws were the prime culprits. In 1973, the government set up a two-tier price structure for crude oil, $5.34 per barrel for old oil and $11.87 for new oil.[8] Since all oil looks the same, the switch from old to new was but a matter of paperwork to hide the origin of the oil. The oil itself in most instances never left the original storage tank.

In 1978 a Miami-based oil strike force indicated that over 100 companies (70 of which were newly formed) were under investigation. The investigations, however, were soon tied up in politics; there were few prosecutions and even fewer prison terms. For example, in a Houston, Texas, case, an 84-count indictment charged two companies and five individuals with participating in a scheme to make about $3.8 million in excess profits by violating federal oil-pricing regulations. The judge set bail at $200,000 and released all defendants on their own recognizance. Obviously, the justice system does not view this type of white collar crime seriously.

Burglary

Although many professional burglars operate as independent agents, they are tied to organized crime through the sale of merchandise to fences or receivers. Frequently, stolen goods, such as automobiles, will be fenced directly to a drug dealer, who in turn will make a profit on the sale of the drugs. Professional burglars dealing with organized groups are most apt to be in the business of stealing jewelry, furs, small business machines, and securities.

The life blood of the professional burglar is to have a fence. There would be no commercial jewel thieves if there were no fences. The burglars are

---

[8]These cases have been described in several magazines (including *Time,* July 24, 1978, p. 51), and in daily newspapers.

interested only in the cash, not the jewelry. Thus, the fence or receiver of the stolen property is an integral part of the organized groups who engage in burglary.

COMPUTER CRIMES

Many crime experts predict that one of the big white collar type crimes of the future will be that involving computer technology. This technology has begun to regulate our movements and direct our lives. Computer systems control the flow of $35 trillion per year between member banking and financial institutions. Thus, most major businesses are dependent upon the communications and information networks that make up the computer industry.

Because of the rapid growth of machine technology, the application of the system has not been subject to tight administrative control in the installation or operation of the systems. The weaknesses of the systems are attracting criminals, who usually work in a position of trust and often with an accomplice. As the complexity of the computer systems grows and the scope of the operations increase, the next logical step would be to see organized crime move into computer frauds.

In a December 1979 *Reader's Digest* article, author Nathan Adams, writing about California, indicated that the confederations have major investments in the banking industry, the garment industry, and electronics. From these combined investments, about $6.3 billion per year is being stolen from the citizens of California. Many of the industries mentioned in this article are heavily computerized. Obviously, many of the operating and controlled industries of organized crime are already computerized.

There are many areas of interest for the law enforcement officer in the computer field.[9] Several new books deal only with computer fraud investigation. For the purposes of this text, we will look at three areas: (1) laws that control computer abuse; (2) computer uses by organized crime; and (3) the potential for future use of the computer network by organized crime.

Laws That Control Computer Abuses

Computer networks span the world, so in order to maintain integrity in the security of the system there will have to be international standards of construction and operation. It would appear that the American enforcement agency in international operations will be the Federal Bureau of Investigation. In 1977 a bill was proposed to give the FBI jurisdiction, but without

---

[9]In a 40-hour training course held in computer fraud and countermeasures sessions at Long Beach (CA) City College, 21 areas of training were presented. In the six-week course offered by the Federal Bureau of Investigation, dozens of different areas are included.

success. In 1979 another bill was introduced; again, there is still no agreement in Congress regarding the bill, called The Federal Computer Protection Act. This bill is still pending before Congress in 1981. The major parts of the act have been published in the *Congressional Record* and in *Computer World,* a trade magazine. *Computer World* identifies the major effects the law, if enacted, will have upon enforcement agencies.[10]

> When federal jurisdiction "exists concurrently with state or local jurisdiction," federal law enforcement officers, in determining whether to exercise jurisdiction, should consider among other things,
> 1. The relative gravity of the federal offense and the state or local offenses.
> 2. The relative interest in federal investigation or prosecution.
> 3. The resources available to the federal authorities and the state or local authorities.
> The bill defines the computer as a device that performs logic, arithmetic, and storage functions by electronic manipulation and includes any property and communication facility directly related to or operating in conjunction with such a device. Misuse of home computers, automated typewriters, and hand-held calculators is a matter for state jurisdiction.
> State laws to control computer fraud are being modeled after the federal statute. On January 1, 1980, California became the fourth state to have such a law.
> Penalties under the federal statute call for fines of two times the amount of loss or $50,000, whichever is higher, and/or five years in jail.

Until the political question of making adequate laws is settled, those involved in computer type crimes are being prosecuted under the different theft and fraud statutes of state and federal governments.

Computers and Organized Crime

Computer crimes may be described as computer abuse, computer fraud, computer-related crime, and automatic data processing crime. By whatever title, there are are a great number of ways to use the computer in committing criminal acts.

Perhaps the most important computer fraud, and a different kind of crime than we would normally contemplate, but of great value to organized crime, would be the case cited in one congressman's *Newsletter.* In this letter the congressman said: "The day after my motion to expell Charles Diggs from the Congress failed by just eight votes, I found out that one of those listed as voting against my resolution was in Chicago, Ill., at the time of the vote." Despite his absence from Washington, D.C., the offending member of Congress was recorded by the House Computerized Voting System as having voted not once but *six* times that day. *Members of Congress are not allowed to*

[10]"The Federal Computer System Protection Act," *Computerworld,* November 19, 1979, p. 2.

vote by proxy. Now, some months later, this problem has yet to be resolved. The culprit, however, is a member of the House Ethics Committee.

The billion-dollar Equity Funding case of several years ago has faded from memory as the biggest corporate swindle of all times. False corporate assets were manipulated to create one of the decade's fastest growing conglomerates. After Security and Exchange Commission investigators finished their investigation, it was said the only thing straight in the corporation were the shafts driving the computers. The next big swindle was the Los Angeles Security-Pacific Bank theft of $10 million. This crime was committed by a systems analyst who knew how to manipulate the system and transfer funds to other banks. The culprit was subsequently sent to jail and Security-Pacific stands to lose $1 million from the theft. While this was not a typical organized type crime, it certainly sets the pattern for future schemes.

In November 1979, in Tulsa, Oklahoma, the Organized Crime Task Force spent nine hours deciphering a minicomputer code to crack a bookmaking ring making $181,000 per week, on a $15,000 machine. If the programming had been slightly more sophisticated, law enforcement would not have broken the code. This is probably a forerunner of the future for numbers and bookmaking outfits.

Parker reports on two cases of organized crime being directly involved with a computer operation.[11] In one case, a janitor associated with the Mafia was running embossing machines during the operators' lunch break with blank credit cards and authentic names and account numbers; these produced duplicate cards that would avoid computerized rejections when used for purchases. The criminal was caught and agreed to help authorities catch others in the organization. He went the way of all good Mafia informants.

In another case in the Midwest dealing directly with organized crime, during raids on football betting establishments FBI agents discovered computer printouts listing scheduled and betting odds. The name of the paper company and the page serial numbers were printed on each page. The paper was traced back to the central computer center and a case was made for prosecution. It would appear that with proper programming and coding, this type of crime would not be solvable.

There are indications that many forms of organized crime have already sought the shelter of the computer. Coded messages, impervious to police penetration, can move nationally and internationally via telecommunication systems. If we extrapolate from the cases cited here, we can see that confederations may succeed in a crime while individuals fail.

The Potential for Future Crime

Approximately 50 percent of the GNP is related to data processing and communications. In 1975, there were about 71,000 large-scale computers and

---

[11]Donn B. Parker, *Crime by Computer* (New York: Scribner's, 1976), pp. 269–70.

200,000 minisystems. It has been projected that there will be about 600,000 systems by 1982. It is predicted that by 1984 there will be 4 million terminals in government, business, education, and the home.

Very few law enforcement agencies are even partially trained or equipped to recognize, process, and prosecute computer crime cases. Systems analysis, accounting, and auditing operations are not normally areas of study for local, state, or federal criminal law enforcement investigators. Thus, most known crimes involving computer technology are neither investigated nor prosecuted, as one Senate subcommittee noted.

1. Only 1 percent of all computer crimes are detected.
2. Of the 1 percent, only 15 percent are reported.
3. Of the 15 percent, only 3 percent are convicted.
4. One computer criminal in every 22,000 is detected and convicted.

The attraction for organized crime must be obvious. The areas of susceptibility of a system are shown in Figure 10–1.[12]

According to Colvin, the data entry specialist is the least skilled person and the area with the greatest number of people assigned, while the systems analyst is the most skilled, with the fewest personnel assigned. The culprit may operate internally or externally. Because of the nature of the systems, it is rare that a crime is committed against a computer system without inside assistance.

Identification of the suspect is in part dependent upon a study of the processes of the organization. One investigator has established a formula for factoring key positions in an organization that may be susceptible to computer fraud. While it is only a guideline, it enables an investigator to zero in on

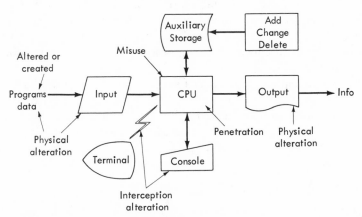

Figure 10–1 Vulnerability of computer systems.

[12]Bill Colvin, "Computer Crime Investigators: A New Training Field," *FBI Law Enforcement Journal,* July 1979, pp. 9–12.

certain critical areas. For example, a simplified approach to suspect identification is included in this formula.

CF_p = Probability of being a computer fraud victim (Rating 0.0–1.0)

D = Honesty factor (0–10 rating)

O = Opportunity factor (0–10 rating)

M = Motive factor (0–10 rating)

$$CF_p = \frac{D \times O \times M}{1000}$$

$$CF_p = \frac{10 \times 10 \times 10}{1000} = 1.0 \text{ (probability of 100\%)}$$

This is an interesting approach; it shows that "to catch a crook requires a basic understanding of systems and systems operations."

Computer crimes have varied from box cars to gambling, and it is not likely that organized crime will pass up an opportunity to make an easy dollar. It would appear that computers are beginning to appear in many areas where organized crime has been active in the past. The situation can only be worsened because there are serious problems of gathering and presenting evidence. The complexity of computer crime can tie up a court for months or perhaps years.

SUMMARY

Business acquisition by racketeering may occur through coercive agreement or by force. Both types of acquisition may be so subtle that control of an organization may move from legitimate to illegitimate without the principal administrators of a business being aware of the transaction.

Many business schemes today may be merely unethical and some may be illegal; yet they are so numerous and covert that they seldom come to the attention of law enforcement agencies. In many cases, local enforcement agencies do not have the geographical authority to deal with such crimes, and federal participation is limited because of the vastness of the problems.

Special frauds and influence in criminal activities such as those against the elderly, people on welfare, use of political contributions, oil and computer frauds and others illustrate the fine line between fraud and honest participation.

QUESTIONS FOR DISCUSSION

1. From your own experience, cite businesses in your community that are subject to control by organized crime elements.
2. What areas of the public domain are most susceptible to inroads by confederation members?

3. Control of many crimes such as the embezzlement or theft of stocks, bonds, or credit cards must be vested in the business domain, not in law enforcement. Explain.

4. The use of stolen documents as collateral against legitimate loans is a direct link to the establishment of fixed interest rates. Explain.

5. Why are present regulations inadequate for persons dealing in market futures and how can the manipulation by "money interest" crime confederations affect small investors?

6. What are some of the dangers of filtering law through administrative regulations to be administered by regulatory commissions?

7. Describe how organized fencing operations provide employment for street-level burglars.

8. Describe ways organized crime can use computers to aid in circumventing the law.

9. Are computer crimes easy to identify? Are they easy to control? Why or why not?

11

MILITANT GROUPS: A FORCE IN ORGANIZED CRIME

LEARNING OUTCOMES

1. Relate the problem of militant group objectives to confederation activities.
2. Have knowledge about the groups and how they relate to functional organized crime control.
3. Identify select groups and observe reported actions of these groups.
4. Determine what enforcement tactics are best suited to counter tactics used by covert militant groups.
5. Be able to help develop strategies that counter the political manipulations of militant groups.

In reflecting over the past decade of group violence in the United States and all over the world, there is little question that many of these radical activities fall within the definition of organized criminal acts. Many of these acts have been addressed by local, state, and national law enforcement as an organized crime problem. The militant groups cited in this chapter are criminal activists, political radicals, social reactionaries, and plain criminals who just happen to have organized into groups. All pose a severe problem for law enforcement. The basic differences between these groups and traditional confederations are their motives and methods of attack. But even these motives and methods are often similar to those of traditional confederations. Mass demonstrations and bombings have given way to kidnapping, murder to maintain control, and direct assault upon society.

Sheriff Peter Pitchess of Los Angeles County indicated that ethnic gang members, in and out of prison, have been responsible for 300 murders in the decade of the 1970s.[1] The conditions that nurture militant causes have been

---

[1]National Conference on Organized Crime, *Bringing Those Engaged in Organized Crime to Justice* (Los Angeles: University of Southern California, November 8–9, 1979).

EXTREME SITUATIONS	APPROACHES	ENDEMIC CONDITIONS
Total institutions	Biologism	Deviance
Mass terror	Economism	Discrimination
Genocide	Psychologism	Rationalization
Thermonuclear war	Social psychologism	Alienation
	Sociologism	

Figure 11–1 Social problems and pathologies that assist in identifying the causes of militant behavior.

documented by social scientists. In the broadest perspectives, Rosenberg, Gerver and Howton identified the major problems in the classifications shown in Figure 11–1.[2]

Few other kinds of crime have so many ramifications or so little hope for control by punitive means. Thus, this text identifies the problem but offers few solutions. Traditional police methods are not going to be the solution; however, the police are charged with intelligence gathering and controlling these groups. If criminal activities by militant groups are to be curbed or controlled, local police are going to need national resources such as military intelligence. Whether one likes to admit it or not, local police forces are inadequate to deal with the necessary gathering of intelligence and the deployment of forces in the face of major confrontations with organized militant groups.

Many of the groups discussed in this chapter are dedicated revolutionaries whose ultimate goal is the overthrow of our present form of government by force. Some groups may be merely idealists. These organized groups and their objectives are known through intelligence information; therefore, a police agency cannot ignore them in the hope that they will go away. No methods in current police literature have been developed to minimize their deleterious impact upon society. Basically, these groups consist of (1) international conspiracies, (2) national conspiracies, and (3) splinter groups. All of these groups' objectives are to disrupt and destroy the established social system.

INTERNATIONAL CONSPIRACIES

Terrorism is the ultimate weapon of international revolutionaries. In terrorism revolutionaries have found a coercive weapon that meets their specific needs. Coercive terrorism by organized crime has been used in the United

[2]Bernard Rosenberg, Israel Gerver, and F. William Howton, *Mass Society in Crisis* (New York: Macmillan, 1971).

158

1. Communist Party, USA (CP-USA) and its youth group, the W. E. B. DuBois Clubs
2. Cuban National Liberation Front, FLNC (Cuba)
3. Irish Republican Army, IRA (Northern Ireland)
4. IRA Provisional Army (Northern Ireland)
5. Basque Homeland and Liberation Movement Army (Spain)
6. South Moluccan Extremists (The Netherlands)
7. Turkish People's Liberation Army (Turkey)
8. Eritrean Liberation Front Factions (Ethiopia)
9. Armed Proletariat Nucleus (Italy)
10. Tupamoros (Uruguay)
11. Montoneros (Argentina)
12. People's Revolutionary Army, ERP (Argentina)
13. Black Panther Party (United States)
14. April 19 Movement (M 19) (Cuba, South America)

Figure 11-2 Some international militant groups.

States for the past century. It has been used for decades in urban guerrilla warfare in Latin America. Reactionaries in Northern Ireland and the Quebec Province of Canada have kept the spark of "patriotism" alive for many years. The tactics used by these reactionaries range from kidnapping, hijackings, and bank robberies to bombings. The domestic problem with these crimes has been addressed in a 1976 report by The Private Security Advisory Council.[3] Organizations such as the International Communist Party and Weather Underground factions are examples of the national and international groups dedicated to the overthrow of the current system and the instalment of governments that follow their ideologies. Some of the major groups are shown in Figures 11-2, 11-3, and 11-4.[4]

The reactionaries discussed in this book may or may not be associated with any international apparatus. It should be made clear that there are two distinct kinds of international groups in operation. One is ideologically tied to Marxism, the other is ideologically tied to a utopian concept of government where human values replace the traditional machine orientation of capitalism. Frequently, the two will merge in common interests.[5]

[3]U.S. Department of Justice, *Prevention of Terrorists Crimes: Security Guidelines for Business Industry and Other Organizations* (Washington, D.C.: U.S. Government Printing Office, May 1976).

[4]"Communism and the New Left," *U.S. News & World Report,* 1970, Chapter 1, Editorial Research Reports, Dec. 2, 1979 and various daily newspapers.

[5]This text is not about international conspirators, but they are discussed to show how relationships may be established with national militant groups. For example, three days after Pope John was shot in Rome by a Turkish militant, a New York airport terminal was bombed by an empathetic national group.

Position: U.S. branch of the international Communist Party. Policy comes directly from Moscow.

Leadership: May vary from year to year.

Location: Headquarters, New York City; membership estimated at between 12,000 and 13,000.

Character: Predominantly white adults.

Brief History: Founded in Chicago, Illinois, September 1, 1919. Poverty and the U.S. depression helped strengthen party during the 1930s. It polled 100,000 votes for its presidential candidate in 1932. Hitler-Stalin Pact of World War II, preceding the German invasion of Russia, caused many U.S. members to drop out of the party. After the war, CP-USA went underground to escape the 1940 Smith Act, which made it a crime to conspire, advocate, or teach the violent overthrow of the government; and the 1950 McCarran Act, which required registration of members. By mid-'50s, Senator Joseph McCarthy had died; the Smith Act was "gutted"; the McCarran Act registration requirement was ruled unconstitutional. The party returned to its open activities.

Although the Moscow brand of communism is considered reactionary by much of the New Left, party membership has increased about 25% since 1960. In 1968, the party had an official presidential candidate on the national ballot for the first time in 28 years. July 1968, Zagarell reported that "the student unrest on the college campuses and the anti-draft demonstrations have been helped along by the Communist Party." The party's youth group, the W.E.B. DuBois Clubs, had less than 100 members in March 1969, but party officials claim much of their own new membership consists of young people. At the May 1969 national convention, Hall cautioned that "it is not yet time to organize armed struggle;" but the party's Commission on Black Liberation approves "cooperation" with BPP.

Figure 11–3 Communist Party—U.S.A. (CP-USA) Published with permission of *U.S. News and World Report. U.S. News and World Report,* Chapter 1.

Communist Party in the United States

The Communist Party holds a unique position among subversive groups which requires extensive intelligence and police type investigations at the national level. Few local agencies have the expertise to maintain extensive intelligence activities against this group.

At the local level, however, intelligence officers of major cities are charged with assimilation of data on suspected Communists. This information becomes a part of the intelligence file and is made available to federal agencies. The role of the local officer in Communist Party subversion basically ends at that point.

Whether these international terrorists are freedom fighters or criminal terrorists depends upon who is doing the interpretation. After years of siege, many nations are now willing to class these groups as international criminals. The acts of violence they commit have become common crimes rather than a form of political expression.

Palestine Liberation Organization (PLO). Viewed by many as Third World shock troops. This group has organized political factions throughout Central Europe and engages in coordinated efforts in hijackings and bombings.

Popular Front for the Liberation of Palestine. This group maintains liaison with the PLO and is also active in Western Europe. Both groups have become famous for their commando raids and their willingness to die for a cause.

United Red Army (URA), in Japan, *The Italian Red Army,* and The Spanish group known as *GRAPO* are all active throughout the world and are all identified with the Marxist philosophy.

The Black September Group of North Africa. This group gained notoriety by killing three Western diplomats when Western governments refused to negotiate for the release of other groups. It includes the *Baader-Meinhof Gang* of West Germany and the *FLN Armies of Liberation from Algeria.*

Figure 11–4 International terrorist groups.

Other International Groups

Acts of terrorism have dominated the headlines in the past few decades. Aerial hijackings have necessitated an entirely new intelligence and security system for United States law enforcement. Bombings, skyjackings, kidnappings, and other forms of political terrorism have become the way to gain media attention for terrorist groups.

The acts of international terrorism are a means to an end, the end being the destruction of a free society. Thus, the terrorists have always tried to provoke repression in order to hasten the collapse of authority. The media may have been their greatest aid in this endeavor. Poor intelligence and underreaction by the civil police may have been the terrorists' greatest ally.

NATIONAL CONSPIRACIES

In the past decade, many hard-core militants emerged from campus demonstrations of the 1960s (see Figure 11–5). Others emerged from ethnic frustrations regarding equal rights, and still others developed from prison populations. Many of the militant groups are dropouts from the competitive economic system and find satisfaction in forceful retaliation against what they

National incidents common to terrorist activities are reflected in data from a 1969 Bureau of Alcohol, Tobacco, and Firearms report. Many bombings indicated the presence of militant factions. In the past decade some 21 terrorist groups, with 5000 members, were identified, among them these:

The Weather Underground. A splinter group from the campus disturbances of the 1960s, this group is said to be very active. It was infiltrated by the FBI, which gathered information for approximately two years. Many of the conspirators were jailed when they conspired to bomb a senator's Washington, D.C., office. Factions from this group were trapped in a Brink's robbery hold up in New York in 1981 and nine members were killed or captured.

The Weathermen. This group is said to operate on a transnational basis. The group evolved from the Students for a Democratic Society (SDS). In 1976 SDS voted to accept "local insurgency" as the organization purpose. Guerrilla warfare and arson are their major objectives.

World Community of Al-Islam in the West. There are about 2 million native and immigrant members in the United States whose allegiance is to the Islamic religion. In addition to their Islamic beliefs, they also consider themselves citizens of the United States. At this time they are fairly passive.

Other national groups include *The Student National Coordinating Committee (SNCC), National Lawyers,* and *FLAN-Urban.*

Figure 11–5 Contemporary national groups.

see as an alien society. Whether Americans want to recognize the facts or not, they have created armies of militants who will struggle for the downfall of the system simply because they believe the present system is not responsive to their needs. Every police agency in this generation will feel the impact of the militant groups. The acts perpetrated by the extremists are going to be criminal activities and will be subject to the same police investigations as other types of traditional and organized crime.

SPLINTER GROUPS

In addition to the political radicals and other militants, there are many groups who identify with neither cause (Figure 11–6). Groups of ideological believers have taken up practices that are in conflict with laws of the nation and the individual states. One example would be the religious cults, where violence and torture frequently become part of the code of conduct. For example, in *The Bible of the Church of Satan* nine points of the cult's

In the early 1970s the Symbionese Liberation Army (SLA), the Black Panther Party, and the Black Liberation Army split from the original group, called the Venceremos Organization.[6] Since that time, the SLA has lost most of its leaders. The Black Panthers have had a change in philosophy, and since the highly emotional marches of the late 1960s, not much has been heard from the Black Liberation Army.

Prison-related groups such as LA EME, Nuestra Familia, the Aryan Brotherhood, and the Black Guerrilla group have evolved in California, and some of these groups have filtered into other states. LA EME, the Mexican Mafia spawned in metropolitan centers, is the largest of the four groups, with 200 to 600 associate members. This group is engaged in rivalry with *Nuestra Familia*, a group from the farms, and the *Black Guerrilla*, which represents the blacks in prison. LA EME maintains a working relationship with the *Aryan Brotherhood*, who are white neo-Nazis.

These groups have evolved in the past decade for self-protection while in prison. It is estimated that 300 murders have been committed by these groups.

Figure 11-6   Splinter groups.

philosophy cite a ritual in torture. The same book orders members to vengeance rather than turn the other cheek. Followers of these cults believe in and practice such activities. These practices are violations of statute law and as such must be investigated and prosecuted. Another example would be the California People's Church, where drugs and ideologies of social vengeance led to senseless murders.[7] Yet other groups are formed around ethnic identification (Figure 11-7).

COMMON MILITANT GROUP STRATEGIES

In order to establish proper intelligence and enforcement techniques, enforcement officers need to know what they are up against. The following list of activities gives some of the more common group methods. When an organized group begins establishing a target area, it will:

1. Identify the geographical target area. Pending elections, ethnic composition of the community, and economic conditions are common determiners.

[6]*Criminal Justice Digest, Special Report on Terrorism*, 2, 7 (July 1974), 2.

[7]Approximately 800 members of this church committed suicide or were murdered in Guyana in 1978.

Intelligence files bulge with information on hundreds of gangs formed around ethnic heritages, beliefs, and friendships. The following are cited as examples:

Groups such as the *Hells Angels, The American Indian Movement, the Crips,* a black Los Angeles gang, *The Whiters* and the *Longos,* who are basically Chicano groups, all contribute to crime and political corruption in the community.

Oriental groups on the West Coast have in many instances gained a reputation much like that of the Italian Mafia in the early 1900s. These groups include Korean, Vietnamese, and Japanese engaged in extortion for protection. The Chinese groups tend to identify with six families or companies from mainland China. These six companies tend to exercise control over the fraternal guilds or *tongs*. There are three predominate tongs in California: the *Bing Kung,* the *Hop Sing,* and the *Suey Song*. The enforcement groups for these *tongs* belong to the guild but are somewhat under the control of the *Wah Chings,* which has emerged as the most powerful Chinese gang. Other groups, however, under a peace agreement exercise control over their own turf and operate under the direct control of the six companies.

Figure 11–7 Other militant groups.

2. Make contact with people who have vocally or in written form expressed a desire to achieve the common objective of the confederations or militant groups.
3. Move some into area, if no contact people are available. Schools serve as a convenient instrument in retaining flexibility of contacts.
4. Have contact people train a group to implement a plan for obtaining objectives. This technique is regularly used by the Black Panthers, the Muslims, and other groups.
5. Insure that this group is easily influenced by contact people. For example, the Black Berets maintain contact with jail inmates through the distribution of "care" packages.
6. Have contact with people who will influence the power structure. This is especially apparent in minority pressure groups.
7. Have an organized group that will influence the average person and some organizations through confrontation efforts.
8. Pick a volatile subject to pursue, such as skirmishes with the police, labor disturbances, and student unrest.
9. Have an organized group make demands of public agencies. May be in the following order, depending on the subject pursued:

      A. Public schools—for media visibility
      B. Churches or other public gatherings—for media visibility
      C. Post-secondary educational institutions—media visibility and societal pressure
      D. Public-supported service organizations
      E. City and/or county governments
          1. Law enforcement agencies
          2. Courts
          3. Jails and other retention facilities
          4. Welfare agencies
          5. Fire fighters
          6. Others
      F. Private enterprise
          1. Coercive threats
          2. Boycotts
          3. Physical damage

10. Have an organized group bring charges because all demands are not met.

11. Have an organized group create physical disturbances to bring more pressure to bear and revitalize media visibility, as well as the creation of unstable and sympathetic attitudes within the community.

12. Bring pressure to bear in the following ways:
      A. Court injunctions
      B. Hearings before special commissions, such as the Civil Rights Commission

The splinter groups have begun to organize. When national social situations create a vacuum, these groups move in to promote ideologies that may be contrary to popular thought using illegal methods. It is only the latter that interests the police. If law enforcement does not maintain an adequate intelligence network within these groups, the same violent scenes of the past will be repeated across this country for the next decades.

How much intelligence must be gathered from these groups and how it is obtained will become a political question of the future. Unless Congress and courts establish adequate legal guidelines, good law enforcement will become a political footnote and the losers will be the average citizens who need protection from this form of organized criminal activity.

SUMMARY

There is a large number of groups whose ultimate goal is the violent overthrow of the present form of government in the United States. Other organized groups seem more interested in personal aggrandizement and

money collected from constituents than in a cause. Whatever the purpose of these militant groups, there is need for an approach to comprehensive intelligence gathering on the part of law enforcement agencies. There is little question that intelligence on these mobile groups is far too vast an undertaking for local law enforcement. Thus, it has been suggested that cooperative military, federal, and civilian intelligence are necessary to get the job done.

The social pathologies that cause militant behavior have been mentioned, and conclusions have been drawn that traditional police activity will have little impact on militant criminal behavior.

Abstracts of the history of various groups have been presented so that an officer may identify a number of active militant groups and see how they have evolved.

QUESTIONS FOR DISCUSSION

1. What are some of the qualities of militant activities that cause them to be classed as organized crime?
2. What are some of the basic pathologies that cause militant behavior to be unresponsive to punitive control?
3. According to many militants, there is a fine line between a Marxist philosophy and a philosophy where human values are placed above those of capitalism. Explain.
4. Intelligence gathering, especially in the area of political philosophies, is done for the purpose of protecting the innocent as well as for the prosecution of the guilty. Explain.
5. Is it important to understand the heritage of an organization in relation to its militant activities? Explain.
6. Local participation in intelligence gathering has increased dramatically with the evolution of militant groups. Explain.

PART IV

INTERNAL AGENCY OPERATION

This part of the text addresses organizational, administrative, and communications problems encountered in enforcing the law against organized crime. In addition, some general principles for enforcement methods are discussed.

12

ORGANIZATION AND MANAGEMENT PROBLEMS FOR ORGANIZED CRIME CONTROL

LEARNING OUTCOMES

1. Establish an overview of key problems involved in organized crime enforcement.
2. Know the difference between the federal and local response to organized crime enforcement.
3. Be aware of the key issues of management for enforcement agencies.
4. Identify the different organizational structures that bring about more effective management of enforcement units.
5. Begin to develop an individual philosophy about enforcement strategy and ethics.

Organizational structure and management processes are of paramount importance for effective enforcement. Although the types of crimes and manner in which they are committed may be fairly consistent throughout the nation, organizational techniques for enforcement are not consistent enough to limit these crimes. In order to arrive at effective organization and management procedures, we must regard organized crime violations as a problem with national priorities. There must be a high degree of state participation, and identification of individual crimes from a local perspective so that appropriate laws, policies, and procedures may be planned. Organized crime is a concern for all levels of government and must be recognized as such if proper policies and procedures for enforcement are to be developed.

In order to study the best methods for organized crime control, we will discuss the following concepts: (1) planning for organizational efficiency in controlling organized crime, (2) policy development for organized crime enforcement, and (3) special administrative problems for more effective control of organized crime.

PLANNING FOR ORGANIZATIONAL EFFICIENCY

Two diverse philosophies should be reconciled prior to planning. Local law enforcement is geared toward the *violation-response* approach, the federal effort toward the *attrition* approach.[1] Both are proper concepts because each performs a necessary function at the level of use; therefore, enforcement organizations at all levels must be made to accommodate both methods. As criminal structures are created with layer upon layer of leader insulation from criminal acts, methods must be devised that will literally rip the criminal organization at all levels of activity. No single method will be successful.

Organized crime is a combination of variables, some of which exist as fact and some of which are created as diversionary activities; thus, the enforcement organization to counter such activity will vary from city to city. For example, two important variables are illegal markets and the type of law enforcement exerted.[2] Logically, one will influence the other as to the amount and type of enforcement needed. Other variables may be the types of criminal penetration into legitimate business and sociopsychological factors associated with the individual criminal. The form and function of the organization engaged in organized crime will be guided by the interaction of these and other variables.

Organizational methodology, structure, and function will depend on which variables are selected by the enforcement administrator as being most important. The following suggestions identify factors that will influence organizational structure and processes.

The organizational concept of accountability is paramount. The separation of power through "checks and balances" is an excellent method in making an enforcement organization responsible for its sphere of apprehension and prosecution. For example, in many states no higher unit of government is accountable for seeing that the lesser units of local government perform. Thus, there is little or no accountability for seeing that laws are adequately enforced and prosecuted.

The identification of ecological factors as they relate to organized criminal activities is also important. For example, the geographic, political, and cultural environment serve as indicators for the level of enforcement activity required.

In enforcement agency structures, there are built-in organizational safeguards that can increase the degree of efficiency and minimize the presence of

---

[1] Annelise Anderson, *Organized Crime: The Need for Research,* Organized Crime Programs Division (LEAA, U.S. Department of Justice, Washington, D.C., 1971), p. 2. The *attrition* approach reflects a concern with organized crime as an institution rather than a collection of individual violations. This is confirmed in a study from the National Advisory Committee on Criminal Justice Standards and Goals, *Report of the Task Force on Organized Crime* (Washington, D.C.: U.S. Government Printing Office, December 1976).

[2] Nowal Morris and Gordon Hawkins, *The Honest Politician's Guide to Crime Control* (Chicago: The University of Chicago Press, 1970), p. 211.

170

corruption. Enforcement policies must be developed within the organization that will allow for the enforcement of statutes within imposed limitations. This type of planning should be projected through policy and procedure manuals.

There are fairly standardized techniques of management a department should strive for in order to obtain the maximum enforcement effort sanctioned by community sentiment. These techniques should be stated in writing and employees oriented to their proper use. The techniques for managing an organized crime unit are, in most instances, contained in general principles of administration. There are, however, some unofficial techniques that must be passed from one generation to the next. Training programs for this should be planned and implemented.

The complexity of the various state statutes makes planning difficult. The large numbers of statutes make it impractical to cite each violation in determining how to plan for an efficient organization. Federal, state, and local statutes will have different wording and different court interpretation. Organizational processes will vary from state to state. In many instances, what one state permits another prohibits. In the law, the elements of organized crime are neither singular nor nationally accepted, but are an unstructured mix of ingredients based upon the formal and informal pressure groups at the state and local levels. This problem will be somewhat alleviated when states begin to adopt model laws similar to the statutes in the 1970 Organized Crime Control Act (see Appendix B).

An important factor in structuring an enforcement organization is the types of crimes committed by the criminal confederations. Obviously, an investigation into securities will differ from one dealing in vice crime and will call for a different degree of sophistication in personnel and organizational structure. An organization structured to emphasize civil action will be different from one oriented toward criminal prosecution.

Several important methods for pursuing organized crime await research. An example is double or triple damages in suits by victims of organized criminal activities. Identifying whether the criminal engaged in organized crime can be enticed to testify if guaranteed safety and economic security is another. Research is needed on postprosecution results; it may produce evidence that will show a need for enforcement organizations of a substantially different nature.

The factors that influence planning grow as new techniques are developed. The organizational structures in this chapter are offered as examples for organizations moving into more active enforcement.

Structuring the Organization

When structuring an organization to conduct investigations relating to organized crime, certain control measures may be initiated within an organization to make it more efficient. Obviously, not all control techniques

will apply to all organizations, because personnel management ideologies and community needs are unique and diverse. Basically, within the organizational structure there are built-in safeguards that can increase the degree of efficiency and minimize the presence of corruption. Fairly standardized management rules and techniques have been developed to provide a degree of internal "checks and balances."

The Federal System

The Justice Department contains the nucleus of agencies that exert pressure on organized criminal activity. Each of the divisions and bureaus holds a key to a coordinated national effort, and no single agency can be successful without the cooperation of every other agency. The administrative interrelationship among the agencies is shown in Figure 12–1.

Other departments have units that must share in the responsibility for certain types of organized crime control. For example, the Bureau of Chief Postal Inspector maintains liaison with other enforcement agencies. The Secret Service, Internal Revenue Service, and Bureau of Customs are all active in minimizing the effect of organized criminal activities. Both the Treasury Department and the Department of Justice must commit extensive resources if there is to be any impact on criminal confederations.

The machinery established at the national level has been built around the "strike force" concept, with several departments of government represented on each of the strike forces. In 1981, fourteen task forces were in the process of prosecuting 1500 cases. About 38 states have special units for the investigation of organized crime cases; they are part of the state attorney general's office.

As the federal strike forces are pressed into service, local forces are organized to assist in the follow-up investigations that result from task force prosecutions. Local task forces specializing in burglary rings or drug operations have been very successful in their operations with the federal strike forces.

Regional Systems

One important organizational change that promised increased efficiency and cooperation was the multistate compact idea. The multistate compact offered unique advantages of topography, cultural similarities, and cost sharing of information gathering and dissemination. The six New England states reported a higher level of strategic intelligence with a multistate unit. However, the problem of coordination could not be overcome. The organizational scheme of the New England compact is found in Figure 12–2. Today it is largely inoperative.

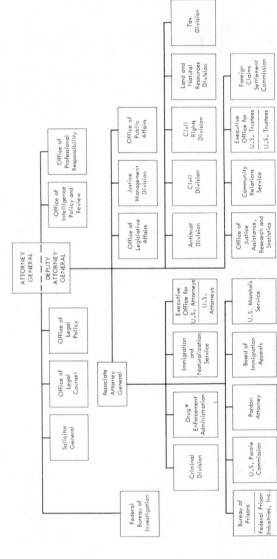

U.S. DEPARTMENT OF JUSTICE

Figure 12–1 The organization of the Department of Justice, from the U.S. government reorganization manual. All organized crime efforts in the federal government are coordinated by the National Council on Organized Crime, which was created by Executive Order on June 4, 1970.

Transferred to The Federal Bureau of Investigation, January, 1982.

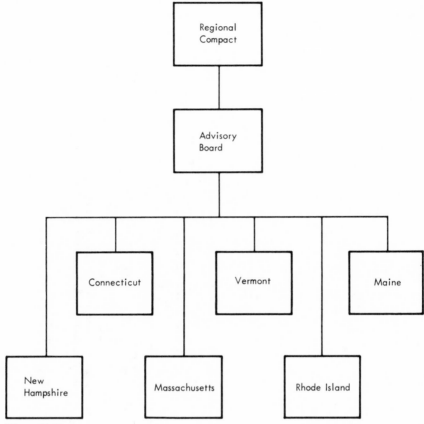

Figure 12-2

State Plans

There have been fifty state methods for combating organized crime, only a few of which are reviewed here.

The Texas plan..   The Texas Organized Crime Prevention Council is a committee of select individuals composed of concerned citizens and other members of the criminal justice system. It is part of the governor's office, and is a sounding board which is used to develop, initiate, and implement ideas. The theory behind this type of organization is sound, and only time will tell whether such a system can help in establishing statewide policy. The organizational structure is shown in Figure 12-3.

The Texas Department of Public Safety is unique in state organizations. While its statutory authority exists on a statewide basis, it is charged with "criminal law enforcement in cooperation with local authorities." Because there is limited enforcement authority within the attorney general's office,

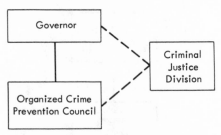

Figure 12–3 The Texas plan for organized crime control.

local corruption, unless it is overt, receives little attention. This is in dramatic comparison with California, where the attorney general functions as an overseer of local enforcement activities.

The Texas Department of Public Safety intelligence and organized crime unit maintains close liaison with the major cities and serves as a clearinghouse for information. Yet, there is no effective statutory responsibility in the state to control organized crime.

Regional Metropolitan and Intelligence Groups

The same information exchange system is used in several states, such as Michigan and Ohio. California maintains this information coordination through its Criminal Information and Identification System and New York, through New York's State Identification Intelligence System.

Within a state, the most viable enforcement organization has been developed through a regional concept—the consolidation of efforts within the major metropolitan areas to include satellite cities. In 1981 the director of the FBI announced that the entire ruling hierarchy of the Los Angeles organized crime family was convicted of racketeering and extortion charges. This was the result of cooperation among regional units. The assignment of U.S. or district attorneys for legal assistance has made this type of organization a potent force against organized crime.

In the metro squad concept, the district attorney, the sheriff's office, and local bedroom cities furnish people to pursue organized crime investigations that cross boundaries. This cooperative approach eliminates problems frequently encountered with groups moving out of the city limits when the "heat" is on in the city. Figure 12–4 illustrates the organizational structure of this concept.

The second metro concept has some inherent problems because it places the district attorney in an enforcement as well as a prosecutorial position. Investigators are assigned to the unit from a local agency. This places the district attorney in both a supervisory and prosecutorial role, thus minimizing conflict with the traditional enforcement attitude toward prosecution. How-

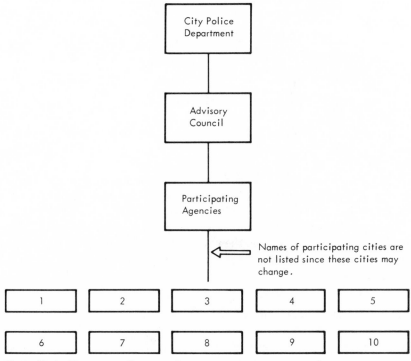

Figure 12–4 The metropolitan squad concept.

ever, this concept does violate the separation of power principle. The organizational structure is shown in Figure 12–5.

One advantage of this system is that a multicounty area comes under the jurisdiction of the district attorney and the organized crime unit. This concept expands the "metro squad" into a regional unit and enhances exchange of information, coordination of investigations, and the ability to move beyond city and county limits to combat crime that inevitably springs up in the suburbs when enforcement pressure is exerted within the city.

POLICY DEVELOPMENT

Merely because enforcement becomes regionalized or national in scope does not remove the threat of corruption. As law enforcement activities extend from the executive branch to the judicial branch and into the elective process, the likelihood of corruption increases. When identifying efficiency within local police systems, an important organizational key lies in the overlapping of enforcement units that serve as a "check and balance" for other units of the system. For example, an internal security, internal affairs, or personal unit overseeing the conduct of officers is necessary if a department has been lax or has failed to investigate organized criminal violations.

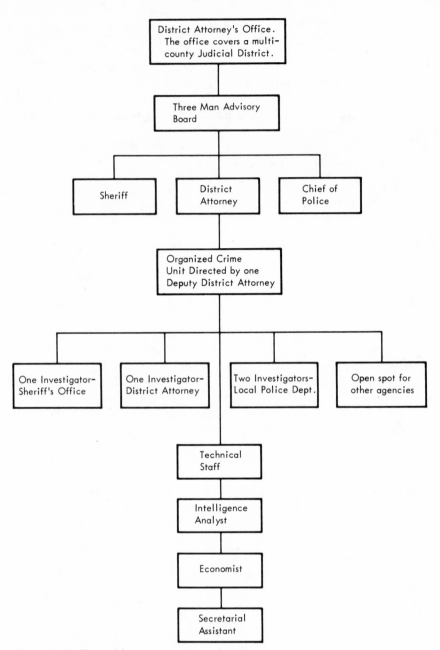

Figure 12-5 The multicounty concept.

Determining Community Needs

In the formulation of broad policies, the law enforcement administrator should carefully assess many factors in determining a community's needs. A few basic guidelines are cited here:

> What is the character and makeup of the community with reference to economic and industrial development?
>
> What is the extent and type of organized crime in the community?
>
> What is the community sentiment; do public and official goals coincide to offer guidelines for a sound policy?
>
> What is the past history of enforcement for vice and other crimes of an organized nature in the community? Political structures rarely make vice reform a continuing process; political corruption is rarely investigated at the local level of government.
>
> What are the physical facilities available for organized crime enforcement; does the physical plant include equipment necessary for complex investigations?
>
> How can personnel needs be met and fiscal support found? Organized crime units are frequently considered unnecessary expenditures. Political factions can eliminate all organized enforcement effort through budget manipulation.

The police chief can, in part, dictate the degree and effectiveness of enforcement through the administrative structure of his department. Although a chief of police may delegate the authority for vice and other organized crime enforcement tasks, the ultimate responsibility for the success of an enforcement policy belongs to the chief. The police administrator should have rigid policies regarding the enforcement of all statutes pertaining to organized crime.

Use of Personnel

Formal and informal pressures make the allocation of personnel a matter of administrative judgment. Organized crime enforcement, while utilizing all the basic organizational techniques, must also make special provisions to ensure that the following criteria are considered.[3]

> All violations, with particular emphasis placed upon vice violations, should be strictly enforced.
>
> Intelligence officers should be oriented to the political dangers inherent in the job, community, etc.[4]
>
> Organized crime violations should be an enforcement function of all officers.
>
> The techniques of enforcement should be within the rule of law.
>
> Sensational or emotional crimes are no justification for deviating from the laws of legal arrests and procedures.

[3]Changes to emphasize organized crime instead of vice have been made.

[4]Intelligence functions are the backbone of the organized crime unit. Some departments may have special units designated as an organized crime unit and utilize intelligence as a staff service.

An officer enforcing organized crime statutes cannot moralize. The statutory laws are explicit and serve as his guide for strict enforcement.

A policy of personnel transfer in and out of organized crime units may be desirable. Although this may appear to create inefficiency, this should not be the case in a well-organized unit.

All violations reported to a department should be in writing.

All investigations made by a unit should be recorded in writing as the investigation progresses.

Records should be protected but should not be so secretive as to render the information useless. This problem is discussed in Chapter 13, where reference is made to the policies of the SEARCH Committee.

Not only supervisors, but the operating organized crime investigators must know the reasoning behind a policy. If the officers understand the policy and the reasons behind its formation, they will be better able to accept responsibility for rigid enforcement.

The organized crime investigator is primarily an independent operator while in the field; therefore, special instruction on department policy toward this type of enforcement is mandatory. Many departments recognize this need and actually have supervisory ranks operating in conjunction with or in direct control of one or two officers.

Policies for Expense Accounting

Intelligence officers are, as a general rule, supplied money from official sources to conduct investigations. Most organized crime prevention operations are supplied with funds to pay for information. The expenditure of this money requires that for every dollar spent there must be (1) a signed receipt from the expending officer, (2) a designation of the amount spent, (3) the reason for the expenditure, and (4) a record of any complaints, arrests, or other case dispositions made as a result of this expenditure.

In most agencies at the local level, the informer will be paid on a "piece basis." In state and federal agencies, the informer may be employed on a full-time basis. This type of expenditure runs into thousands of dollars, but in most instances will be more effective in securing organized criminal intelligence.

Unit commanders usually have some latitude in determining how the money is spent. The policy governing the expenditure of "secret service money" by a department or agency must be closely audited. Political office seekers are quick to audit the expenditure of these funds.

The example of such an accounting system presented here is adopted, in part, from a memorandum from the Law Enforcement Assistance Administration, Department of Justice, addressed to operating organized crime units:

Confidential expenditures will be authorized for subgrants at the State, County, and City level of Law Enforcement.

The funds authorized will be established in an imprest fund controlled by a bonded cashier.

The Agent or Officer in charge of the investigation unit to which the imprest

fund is assigned must authorize all advances of funds up to $500.00 to Agents or Officers for the purchase of information. Payments in excess of $500.00 must be approved by the head of the law enforcement unit to which the subgrant is made. Such authorization must specify the information to be received, the amount of expenditures, and assumed name of the informer.

There must be maintained, by the investigation unit, confidential files of the true names, assumed names, and signatures of all informers to whom payments of confidential expenditures have been made. To the extent practicable, pictures and/or fingerprints of the informer payee should also be maintained. A sample signature of the informer will be obtained and attached to the informer identity sheet.

The Agent or Officer shall receive from the informer payee a receipt of the following nature.

On 25 percent of the contacts, when payments are made, a second Agent or Officer will appear as the witness to the transaction.

On 10 percent of the meetings, the Agent or Officer in charge shall be present to verify the payment to the informer.

The signed receipt from the informer payee with a Memorandum detailing the information received will be forwarded to the Agent in Charge and/or the Supervisor of the Unit.

The Agent in Charge and/or the Supervisor of the Unit will compare the signature on the receipt with the signature on the informer identity sheet.

The Agent in Charge and/or the Supervisor will evaluate the information received in relation to the expense incurred.

A certification of payment to the cashier will be made on the Purchase Voucher form and will be approved by the Agent in Charge and/or the Supervisor on the basis of the report and the informer payee's receipt. Final approval before submission will be by the Chief of the Criminal Law Enforcement Division, i.e., Project Director.

The Agent in Charge and/or the Supervisor will prepare a quarterly report showing the status and reconciliation of the imprest fund and itemizing each payment, name used by informer payee, information received and use to which information was put. This report will be furnished to the Director of the Agency or Chief of the Department upon request.

All of the above records necessary to support, document and verify expenditures are subject to the record and audit provisions of the concerned agency/department with the exception of the true name of the informer.

For practical implementation and application within the bounds of these guidelines, the following procedures will also be in effect in the disbursement of confidential funds.

Usual procedures as outlined will be followed in applying for reimbursement. This procedure shall consist of:

Explanation and breakdown on Weekly Activity Report.

Detailed investigative or Intelligence Report and/or a Memorandum "keyed" to the expenditure, along with an additional Memorandum explaining in detail the expenditure involvement.

The submission of a signed Purchase Voucher form.

The completion of and submission of an informer identity sheet "coded" to the informer's identity.

The Commander of the Division or Bureau will approve the expenditures involved by signing the appropriate Purchase Voucher.

The Agent or officer in charge of the Unit will then approve these

expenditures by signing the Purchase Voucher as approved by the Supervising Agent.

The Purchase Voucher will then be submitted to the Chief of the Agency or Department for his approval prior to being forwarded to Accounting.

The Purchase Voucher will reflect the expenditure number and the appropriate budgetary unit as assigned by the Accounting office.

Filing Procedure—Adequate files will be maintained and are to include:

Weekly Activity Reports reflecting activity and expenditures.

Monthly Mileage Reports reflecting miles traveled.

Travel and/or Per Diem Travel Record.

Informer Identity Sheet (coded and complete as practical).

Informer Signature Card.

Accounting Ledger to be maintained by the Unit Accountant reflecting all expenditures in detail by name, date and key code number, adequately cross indexed in order to readily provide a full justification and/or explanation of expenditures involved.

One copy of the Puchase Voucher will be filed.

The informer receipt will be maintained in the informer's file.

SPECIAL ADMINISTRATIVE PROBLEMS

A few key administrative problems have been selected for discussion. The five cited here are issues that arise in most law enforcement agencies when dealing with organized crime. They are (1) the structure of administrative subunits to ensure lines of authority, responsibility, and channels of communication; (2) supervisory responsibility in planning operations; (3) informal groups within the formal organization; (4) goals for the officer; and (5) the violator and officer relationship.

The Structure of Administrative Subunits

The personal philosophy of an agency head will dictate how to organize an agency for effective control. The illustrations given here are only four of many variations that may exist in the organizational hierarchy of a department.

The chief of police in small and medium sized departments may have intelligence officers and supervisors reporting directly to him. This line of command is shown in Figure 12–6. In larger departments, this authority is

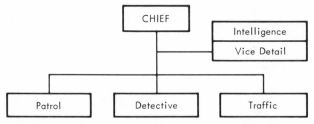

Figure 12–6 Small centralized vice and intelligence unit.

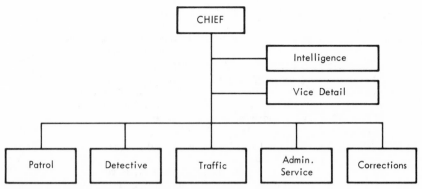

Figure 12-7 Large centralized vice and intelligence unit.

usually shared with the division or precinct commanders, as shown in Figures 12–7 and 12–8. If this authority is delegated, the chief should have one or more units to ensure that the policies are being carried out. The organizational structure of a department helps to ensure policy compliance. In Figure 12–9, the overlapping of unit jurisdictions serves as a check on other units enforcing laws dealing with organized crime.

Supervisory Responsibility in Planning Operations

While most activity will result from individual action, there are times when large-scale activities become necessary. These operations must be carefully planned and coordinated, and minute details must be given to participating enforcement officers. An important facet of an investigation is to assign overall responsibility to one person.

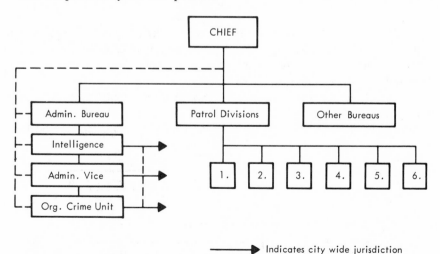

Figure 12-8 Large decentralized vice and intelligence unit with separate organized crime unit.

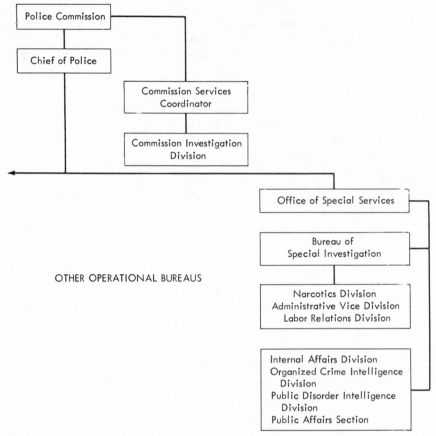

Figure 12–9 Basic structure of the Los Angeles police units designed for organized crime control.

The political ramifications of an action should be anticipated and all possible loopholes closed. Special attention must be given to the safety and conduct of officers when a large group operates. A plan detailing where each officer will be stationed or positioned during every phase of an operation is important. The location, physical features, numbers, and types of suspects anticipated, as well as special evidence to be seized, should be discussed before the entire group of investigating officers.

The importance of expertise in organized crime investigations mandates an ability for informal leadership. Planning and the stimulation of personal and professional pride are the criteria for a successful supervisor.

Informal Groups within the Formal Organization

No other work or assignment will so readily create small cliques within any formal organization as vice and organized crime enforcement. Two or three

working members of a unit will evolve into a working team unto themselves. This type of informality may enhance the individual's morale but it will, in the long term, destroy discipline and the formal operational structure. The supervisor of these units should be aware of these situations and keep all members of the unit working in close cooperation. He may do this by:

Making sure all information coming to the intelligence or organized crime unit is made available to every member of the unit, unless its being revealed will materially interfere with the investigation.

Having current investigation findings in written form on complaints so that information may be made available to all investigators assigned to the case.

Being sure, through staff meetings, that current knowledge possessed by the entire unit is disseminated to every other unit of the department working on organized crime.

Providing shift overlap for units that are organized into day and night shifts. This will bring the crews going off duty into contact with those coming on duty.

Being a group leader in brainstorming sessions on how to execute difficult investigations. Generally, a fixed location where activities are being conducted will be known to some unit members. They will be able to detail approaches, warning devices, and means of entry to a location.

Determining whether past information may also support probable cause for arrest.

Assuming the role of a training officer. With court decisions, department policies, and division enforcement techniques constantly changing, training should be a daily function of the supervisory officer.

Directing the staff in establishing the tempo of the investigations, establishing debriefing techniques and coordinating the information that will go to staff and into a national system. The supervisor should be sure that interpersonal contact and contact with the public is maintained for the good of the agency and public it serves.

Goals for the Officer

The most logical approach for effective organized crime control is to work on the apex of the confederations. It must be realized that the intelligence or organized crime unit officer at the local level is restricted in scope. The local officer will usually find little difficulty in identifying and arresting individual gamblers, bunco artists, and drug users. It is when he or she attempts to climb the ladder of the criminal hierarchy that he or she encounters difficulty. As the "small violator" becomes a "big violator," much more time is required for the investigation, more money is necessary for undercover work, and avenues of investigation will close because of influential contacts by the individual being investigated. Although it is desirable to apprehend the "big violator," the pressure of making cases just to maintain a semblance of control will restrict the number of "big cases" on which an organized crime unit will work.

Violator and Officer Relationship

The relationship between an organized crime member and the officer is usually congenial and friendly because each feels dependent upon the other for mutual assistance. A congenial relationship does not imply deals and collusion; however, many officers have found they are unable to keep the relationship on a friendly yet professional basis. The criminal violator is most anxious to encourage close relationships because this necessitates a trade of information. Frequently, that trade of information may be detrimental to the investigation. The officer must be cautious of what he or she tells an informer or criminal acquaintance. The officer should get information, not give it.

The vice, intelligence, and organized crime unit officer will spend years on the borderline of semilegal associations. The bookie, bunco artist, loan shark, and racketeer of all descriptions will be daily contacts. Without these contacts the officer will be ineffective. However, the problem of association is one of selection and of administrative transfers. Records of corruption and dishonesty in enforcement agencies will show that these acts are preceded by lax policies that permit these associations to continue over long periods of time.

DEVELOPING A PHILOSOPHY FOR ORGANIZED CRIME CONTROL

The ultimate goal for establishing policy and organizational concepts is to arrive at an enforcement philosophy to which a department may subscribe. The development of a sound philosophy should precede the development of policy and organization. However, with organized crime enforcement, there has been no pragmatic philosophy established.

The individual concerned with vice control and other organized crime violations must identify and establish his or her own philosophy. Whether an officer recognizes it or not, every person concerned with control of this type of human criminality has a philosophy upon which he or she relies in doing the job. It is neither systematic nor integrated. Most frequently, it is illogical, inconsistent, and contradictory. What one reveals outwardly is likely to be inconsistent with the philosophy he or she uses in practice. There must be some logical coordination between the dynamics of these activities and the philosophy of the individual in the enforcement of organized crime.

There are many reasons why an officer's philosophy and practices are illogical and inconsistent. Organized crime personnel deal with complex problems in complex surroundings. As many critics have pointed out, the enforcers cannot be completely rational about their actions because it is impossible in this type of control to solve all the conditions of rationality. It is impossible for them to know all the facts about the situations they face. They

cannot conceive all the ramifications that may result from situations they must deal with from day to day. They are not usually aware of the vast range of alternatives to be given consideration. Their knowledge of the goals to be achieved is limited, and that lack of knowledge for the ultimate results is critical to a compatible solution.

If the law officer is to deal adequately with complex organized crime problems, he or she must simplify them, put them in logical contextual frameworks of understanding, and relate them to a system over which he or she has some degree of control. He or she must analyze the problems in terms of ideas and of values that are significant to him or her. To do a good job, the officer must depend upon a philosophy. This section is an effort to assist the officer in understanding his or her philosophy by presenting a broad group of ideas upon which the individual may then base a systematic enforcement ideology.

A person may utilize the term "philosophy" in any one of its many meanings. For the purpose of this text, it has been viewed as "a system of ideas" that does two things. First, it attempts to define what is true—when certain crimes are legalized, the inevitable decay of society will result; or legalized gambling corrupts the whole of society. What our philosophy alleges to be true may not be subject to empirical proof, and sometimes it may be wrong. Yet it is important to describe the complex nature of reality in these terms.

Second, a philosophy should attempt to determine what questions are important, ask them, and rule out others. This is a decision the individual officer must make. Fequently, he or she must decide on the basis of indecisive rules of law and group pressures. Of course, not all questions have equal value for the individual. "Natural law" students, who think it is important to ask what values the moral order of the universe would impose upon them, or a casuist, who might ask what precedents existed for handling a situation, will arrive at different conclusions from a given set of facts. In order to evaluate each crime situation, and even more accurately the general concepts of organized crime control, this chapter has covered a broad spectrum of ideologies. Not all have been adequately treated, but they should serve to help the individual develop a set of values in making decisions. Each reader must establish, develop, and implement his or her own categorical set of values. For example, an officer must reconcile in his or her own mind that contracting with a street bookmaker is in fact, contracting with a national organization. The officer must carefully weigh evidence that shows labor union influence in settling issues repugnant to his or her own viewpoints. When an officer finds political and legal corruption, does he or she become a participant, or does he or she follow an individual code? The questions, of course, remain unanswered until the problems present themselves.

A citizen is faced with the same challenges. If citizens are weak, corrupt, or indifferent to organized crime, they can hardly expect law enforcement,

judicial officers, and political officers to be different. The criminal justice system is a reflection of the people it serves.

SUMMARY

Dynamic management processes are keystones in the effort against organized crime. Correct planning processes have been avoided until recently simply because no one took sufficient interest in the "victimless" crimes. When comprehensive planning comes into general use, a number of organizational concepts need to be studied and expanded. For example, there must be established a clear accountability in law and management procedures for all levels of control. In addition, ecological predictors will indicate the amount of enforcement for organized crime in local areas. An important organizational task is to refine the policy and procedures manuals utilizing accepted management practices. There is need for the standardization of laws simply because criminals move across state lines.

Local option, if there is to be effective control, is a dead issue. There is a need to structure the organization around regional units, and to devise special strategies for organized crime control. Key policy issues in organized crime enforcement are expense accounting, basic unit structure supervisor responsibility for planning, and the control of informal employee groups. Each officer must establish goals and a philosophy as he or she works in the enforcement of all laws and in association with violators.

QUESTIONS FOR DISCUSSION

1. Organized crime prevention units have unique organizational problems that deserve special attention. Identify them.
2. Do the two philosophical approaches to organized crime control (violation response vs. attrition) influence the organization and operations of an enforcement unit?
3. Does the precise identification of variables that influence organized crime in a particular area of the country dictate the type of enforcement needed?
4. Why is "accountability" such a critical factor in the organizing processes?
5. The basis upon which effective organizations will be established on a national scale will be consistency in law. Can the 1970 Organized Crime Control Act serve as a model?
6. Discuss the concept of "checks and balances" and identify how effective organizational structure makes it function.
7. Identify the advantages of the multistate compact; the disadvantages.
8. Discuss the importance of the state role in organized crime control.
9. What are the strongest arguments for making organized crime units regional?
10. Identify five key administrative problems that must be solved for the operation of an effective organized crime unit.

13

INTELLIGENCE GATHERING AND DISSEMINATION

LEARNING OUTCOMES

1. Gain an overview of the need for domestic intelligence gathering.
2. Understand the complexities and the processes of intelligence gathering.
3. Know the legal and social ramifications of loosely controlled intelligence systems.
4. Develop techniques to perfect intelligence-gathering methods.
5. Recognize analysis as a necessary ingredient of an intelligence collection system.

The heart of any program designed to control organized crime is the intelligence gathering process.[1] How these processes take place under constitutional safeguards poses special considerations for enforcement agencies. The intelligence gathering processes have a different significance at each level of enforcement. Developing a modular system to deal with this difference is necessary. The requirements of an effective system first and foremost must guarantee individual confidentiality and rights as well as the rights of society. With the growth of effective data processing intelligence gathering systems, there are few physical limitations for collecting information. In reality, the data gathering capability of present systems is far greater than that which is needed and desirable for an effective enforcement network. To illustrate practical intelligence gathering processes, the following areas are considered: (1) ethical considerations in data gathering, (2) intelligence records organization, and (3) common methods for data collection.

---

[1]Intelligence may be defined as information that has some degree of verification. For a complete discussion of agency intelligence, see Don R. Harris, *Basic Elements of Intelligence*, LEAA, U.S. Department of Justice, September 1976.

ETHICAL CONSIDERATIONS

Mass civil intelligence gathering in the late 1960s and the early 1970s brought to light a dramatic need to carefully evaluate who should be in the business of data compilation and the type of data that is needed to ensure public safety without violating the freedoms and rights that have been guaranteed the individual under constitutional government.

Civil intelligence collection quickly takes on many aspects of military intelligence gathering. This poses many philosophical, legal, and ethical problems for the law enforcement officers who must ultimately do the field intelligence work. Methodology for intelligence investigations, no matter how clearly spelled out, is subject to ethical oversights, abuses, lack of administrative direction, and legal questions.

In an article in the *Saturday Review,* Ralph Nader illustrated in "The Dossier Invades the Home" how privacy is being invaded and how information that is being collected is abused. He showed that by selecting bits of information from hundreds of sources, information systems are thus developing a pattern of life style. The privacy of the individual has vanished. There is no question that good intelligence does precisely as Nader says. Some form of control must be implemented for both civilian and governmental intelligence networks. We need an intelligence gathering capability that will protect society and its members.

Because intelligence gathering is modified by individual values and priorities, an attempt is made here to cover the broad general approaches of standardized intelligence gathering as outlined by statute and as practiced by operating agencies. These basic procedures must be followed in order to establish national computer capability. For example, standardized coding forms must comply with those from the National Crime Information Center, and all data gathered should be coded to conform to the format shown in Appendix D.

In order to safeguard automated records, a national committee entitled Systems for Electronic Analysis and Retrieval of Criminal Histories (SEARCH) has developed comprehensive guidelines for use in information and intelligence gathering. This system has been implemented through the Interstate Organized Crime Index, with 230 member agencies and 16 terminals.

General Guidelines of the SEARCH Committee

The most carefully thought out guidelines regarding the problems of publicity and release of information have come from this federally sponsored group for civilian data gathering. The objectives in the report published by

the project staff are threefold:

1. To construct a fundamental working document that enumerates potential security and privacy problems and presents solutions for the guidance of participants on Project SEARCH during the demonstration period.
2. To provide a dynamic framework of essential elements of security and privacy for any future national system that may develop as a result of Project SEARCH.
3. To outline the kinds of security requirements and self-imposed disciplines that participants have, by their own initiative, levied upon themselves and their colleagues in Project SEARCH.[2]

The issues identified regarding security and privacy are these:

1. Unintentional errors. From typographic errors to mistaken identities, there is always the possibility that the data finally stored in the system will be incorrect, without any intent to make it so.
2. Misuse of data. Information can be used out of context or for purposes beyond the legitimate criminal justice functions, by persons who are actually authorized access and by those who acquire the information without authorization.
3. Intentional data change. The data maintained can be destroyed or modified to accomplish the same objectives as described under misuse, or to restrict the proper and effective performance of criminal justice functions. It has been suggested that organized crime may attempt to penetrate the system for this purpose.[3]

In identifying these issues, the committee has implemented and is working upon a number of recommendations that will assist in establishing national guidelines.

A code of ethics
Development of model administrative regulations
A resolution to limit the information
Content of the central index
Acceptance of the principle of post-auditory evaluation and feedback
Education and training for participants

These guidelines will dictate how state and local agencies will be standardized to provide information flow back and forth to all agencies. There is reason to believe some federal agencies will not be committed to this

[2]*Security and Privacy Considerations in Criminal History Information Systems* (Project SEARCH Staff, California Crime Technological Research Foundation, Sacramento, California, 1970), p. 1.

[3]*Security and Privacy Considerations,* p. 5. These concepts are still viable and serve as guides for an evolving criminal justice intelligence network. SEARCH offered basic guidelines, and the systems that have evolved throughout the country follow the pattern it recommended.

system in theory or in fact. These guidelines point up reasons for believing that "hard core" intelligence information will still be transmitted from person to person by those engaged in law enforcement. In spite of weaknesses that may exist in a computerized system, it is still the only hope for developing an adequate system for information retrieval and dissemination.

Prior to the development of an intelligence gathering system, all persons, both civilian and government, should be informed of the security and privacy problems associated with massive data gathering. The SEARCH committee has drawn up guidelines that should serve as a model for the development of a data-based system.

Security and Privacy Recommendations

These policies on data content have been recommended by the committee and can serve as guides for a department and for the field officer. *Data included in the system must be limited to that with the characteristics of public record.*[4] In substance, these would be:

The fact, date and arrest charge; whether the individual was subsequently released and, if so, by what authority and upon what terms.

The fact, date and results of any pretrial proceedings.

The fact, date and results of any trial or proceeding; any sentence or penalty.

The fact, date and results of any direct or collateral review of that trial or proceeding; the period and place of any confinement.

The fact, date and results of any release proceedings.

The fact, date and authority of any act of pardon or clemency.

The fact and date of any formal termination to the criminal justice process as to that charge or conviction.[5]

These recommendations pertain only to public records. Data not falling in this category will be discussed later in this chapter.

If these data are to be part of the public record, the committee recommends information should be:

Recorded by officers of public agencies directly and principally concerned with crime prevention, apprehension adjudication, or rehabilitation of offenders.

Recording must have been made in satisfaction of public duty.

The public duty must have been directly relevant to criminal justice responsibility of the agency.[6]

[4]Justin J. Dintino and Frederick T. Martens, "The Intelligence Process, A Tool For Criminal Justice Administrators," *FBI Law Enforcement Bulletin*, June 1979, pp. 6–10. This article emphasizes the need for strategic intelligence capabilities and how intelligence is used into policy and decision strategies.

[5]*Security and Privacy Considerations*, p. 16.

[6]Ibid., p. 11.

Participants should adopt a careful and permanent program of data verification, in the following manner:

> First, any such program should require participating agencies of record to conduct systematic audits of their files, in a fashion calculated to insure that those files have been regularly and accurately updated. Periodic programs of employee re-education should also be required, so that every record custodian and clerk is fully conscious of the importance and necessity of faithful, conscientious performance. Appropriate sanctions, as described later in this chapter, should be available for those whose performance proves to be inadequate.
>
> Second, where errors or points of incompleteness are detected, the agency of record should be immediately obliged to notify the central index (if the change involves data stored in the index) and any other participating agencies to which the inaccurate or incomplete records have previously been transmitted.
>
> These procedures will be conducted by systematic audits. The agency of record shall maintain a file of all participants to which the inaccurate or incomplete records have previously been transmitted.
>
> The agency of record shall maintain a file of all participants that have been sent records. Within a state, a record shall be kept of all agencies to which the System's data has been released.[7]

The Fair Credit Reporting Act, effective April 1971, has imposed restrictions on the release of information. In addition, all known copies of records with erroneous or incomplete information are to be corrected.

> Purge procedures shall be developed in accordance with the Code of Ethics. Each participating agency shall follow the law or practice of the state of entry with respect to purging records of that state.[8]

The purposes of these procedures are:

> To eliminate information that is found to be inaccurate or at least unverifiable.
>
> To eliminate information that, because of its age, is thought to be an unreliable guide to the subject's present attitudes or behavior.[9]

How such procedures are initiated is still the subject of study. A model state statute for protecting and controlling data in any future system should be drafted and its adoption encouraged. How these statutes will evolve is still a part of the on going SEARCH Project. Basically, the proposal is that in any

[7]Ibid., p. 20.
[8]Ibid., pp. 11–12.
[9]Ibid., p. 20.

system, a minimum control should be assigned a governing board that will have the authority to:

Monitor the activities of the participating state agencies.
Adopt administrative rules and regulations for the system.
Exercise sanctions over all agencies connected with the system.[10]

Other general guidelines as proposed by the SEARCH Committee are as follows:

Direct access to the system should continue to be restricted to public agencies which perform, as their principal function, crime prevention, apprehension, adjudication, or rehabilitation of offenders.[11]

Under the general standards described above, the following classes or public agencies may be permitted direct terminal access to Project SEARCH and any future system:

Police forces and departments at all governmental levels that are responsible for enforcement of general criminal laws. This should be understood to include highway patrols and similar agencies.
Prosecutorial agencies and departments at all governmental levels.
Courts at all governmental levels with a criminal or equivalent jurisdiction.
Correction departments at all governmental levels, including corrective institutions and probation departments.
Parole commissions and agencies at all governmental levels.
Agencies at all governmental levels that have as a principal function the collection and provision of criminal justice information.

Definitional questions as to users should be presented for resolution to representatives of all the participating states in the system. In order to limit access, the following restrictions should be made:

1. Participating states should limit the number of terminals within their jurisdiction to a number they can effectively supervise.
2. Each participating state should build its data system around a central computer, through which each inquiry must pass for screening and verification. The configuration and operation of the center should provide for the integrity of the data base.

Participating agencies should be instructed that their rights to direct access encompass only requests reasonably connected with their criminal justice responsibilities. Requests from outside the criminal justice community to

[10]Ibid., p. 35.
[11]Ibid., pp. 12–15.

examine data obtained through the system should be honored only if the receiving agency is authorized access by local law, state statute, or valid administrative directive. Efforts should be made to limit the scope of such authorized access. The security and privacy staff should study various state "public record" doctrines and begin prompt efforts to obtain appropriate exemptions from these doctrines for the system's data.

The use of data for research should involve the following restrictions:

> Proposed programs of research should acknowledge a fundamental commitment to respect individual privacy.
>
> Representatives of the system should fully investigate each proposed program.
>
> Identification of subjects should be divorced as fully as possible from the data.
>
> The research data should be shielded by security system comparable to that which ordinarily safeguards system data.
>
> Codes or keys identifying subjects with data should be given special protection.
>
> Raw data obtained for one research purpose should not subsequently be used for any other research purpose without the consent of system's representatives.
>
> Security and data protection requirements should be included in any research contract or agreement.
>
> Nondisclosure forms should be required and the system should retain rights to monitor and, if necessary, terminate any project.

The following are minimum requirements for control of data dissemination:

> Data received through the system should be marked and readily identifiable as such.
>
> Heads of agencies receiving information should sign a copy of an appropriate recommended nondisclosure agreement.
>
> Educational programs should be instituted for all who might be expected to employ the use of the system data.
>
> Users should be informed that reliance upon unverified data is hazardous and that positive verification of identity should be obtained as quickly as possible.
>
> Users should be clearly informed that careless use of this data represents unprofessional conduct, and may subject the user to disciplinary actions.
>
> The central computer within each state, through which all data inquiries should pass, will screen all inquiries to exclude those that are inconsistent with system rules.

Rights of challenge and redress include the following:

> The citizen's right to access and challenge the contents of his records should form an integral part of the system consistent with state law.[12]

---

[12]The Freedom of Information Act has not brought government records from behind closed doors, as was originally intended. There are nine categories of exemptions for disclosure, and these have been sufficient to protect law enforcement files from disclosure.

Civil remedies should be provided for those injured by misuse of the system where not provided for by state law.

Organization and administration include these points:

The system participants should elect a board of directors (governing body) to establish policies and procedures governing the central index operation.

The system should remain fully independent of noncriminal justice data systems and should be exclusively dedicated to the service of the criminal justice community.[13]

A permanent committee or staff should be established to consider problems of security and privacy and to conduct studies in that area.

The permanent staff should undertake a program to identify differences among the states in procedures and terminology, and disseminate information concerning these differences to all participants.

A systems audit should be made periodically by an outside agency.

From the guidelines that have been presented here, the law enforcement officer is in a position to analyze those procedures that are acceptable and ethical.

Publicity and Release of Information

Organized crime information gathering, if not rigidly regulated, will be subject to much valid criticism. The investigations surrounding organized crime produce information on persons who have high community visibility and political influence. Basically, two different approaches serve to control and regulate the dissemination of intelligence information. First are those persons who are interested in keeping intelligence gathering rigid and dissemination legal, factual, and ethical. Second are those who stand to benefit from a minimum amount of information being revealed regardless of how legally and how ethically the information was gained. Because of this second group there will be many pressures to suppress valid information that should be considered public knowledge. Civil suits, delays in fiscal funding, and other tactics are the most common ways to hamper investigations and information releases.

Determining what guidelines will be necessary for the release of information will require extensive study. The following guideline, although not following the procedures of all major intelligence units, is fairly representative and is cited as a logical guide.

Category 1. Information for the internal use of NYSIIS only—cannot be released to other agencies.

---

[13]Information of a noncriminal nature is frequently the most important strategic intelligence. If the system is to perform as a comprehensive data system, methodology to assimilate noncriminal data must be studied.

Category 2. Information releasable to specific agencies—restriction placed on use by donor.

Category 3. Information releasable to any participating agency.

Category 4. Information releasable to any criminal justice agency.[14]

To further safeguard intelligence data, it can be classified as S—sensitive, or E—extra sensitive.[15] Both classifications are designed to ensure against information getting to the wrong people.

In reality, intelligence information, if it is to be effective, must be regarded in a different way. Much intelligence information, such as verified criminal associations, illegal business transactions, and many other illegal activities that are now classified should be designated as open to the public and subject to analysis by intelligence experts. If verified, this information should then be published by interested news media. Historically, intelligence records have been dead files providing little tactical value.

With ethical considerations far from resolved it is, however, appropriate to analyze the intelligence records system to determine what information is being gathered and how it is processed.

INTELLIGENCE RECORDS ORGANIZATION

Policy makers at all levels of an organization are finding that a systematic information processing unit requires special administrative consideration.[16] In order to keep a system compatible with advances in technology, the organizational hierarchy is constantly changing to keep the intelligence processes within normal channels of communication and under the administrative direction of the management structure. Historically, law enforcement administrators have been able to maintain control of information through records distribution, staff meetings, and training sessions. With the infusion of federal money into local departments for highly specialized intelligence and organized crime units, the older methods cannot control the necessary processing of information coming to a department.

[14]New York State Identification Intelligence System, *Security System for Organized Crime Intelligence Capability* (NYSIIS, Albany, 1970), p. 6a. These classifications are still valid and in principle concur with The Privacy Act of 1974. This act has two dimensions. First, it called on government to police itself, requiring agencies to limit their recordkeeping activities and to prevent disclosure of information except under special circumstances. Second, the law set up procedures under which individual citizens could gain access to their records and challenge those that were inaccurate.

[15]Ibid., p. 7

[16]Harris, *Basic Elements of Intelligence,* p. 9.

In an intelligence records system, three distinct kinds of information will be generated:

1. Services to an agency head that will assist in making broad decisions concerning the impact of organized crime upon the total agency operation.
2. Information concerning the criminal clientele directly concerned with operations of specialized units in an agency.
3. Information that concerns an agency's operation and relationship with other criminal justice groups.

Information coming to an agency that reflects managerial processes may concern such matters as these:

1. Identifying staff functions through development of reporting policy. For example, all intelligence personnel should be able to report directly to the chief. Thus, information is not "filtered."
2. Separation of function in allocating responsibility for work to be performed. For example, in most cases, intelligence will not be a "personnel" or "internal affairs" function. Intelligence may assist as a service unit, but it should not have the responsibility for everyday enforcement activities. (This may vary with the size of an enforcement unit.)
3. Division of labor within a unit should be explicitly set out in policy and procedures manuals. Where there is an overlap of function, it should be deliberately designed to offer a "check and balance" to the system.
4. External relations, both within and outside an agency, is a key managerial consideration. There are techniques for the forced flow of information that must be pursued. For example, mandatory reporting and distribution, staff brainstorm sessions, and training so extensive that an officer accepts liaison and communication as a responsibility rather than as an occasional luxury.

The authors assume that agency managers will be aware of intelligence dangers and strengths. Thus, emphasis here will not be upon management processes, but upon the processing of information about the criminal clientele, which begins at the international level.

The Intelligence Establishment by Harry H. Ransom contains a comprehensive analysis of the national intelligence network. With the success of the Central Intelligence Agency and allied units in international intelligence, there is pressure to develop a similar system for domestic intelligence. The National Crime Information Center (NCIC) is the logical organization to eventually make the decisions concerning who will utilize the system. The following section is an endeavor to project the type of information that may evolve from present systems.

To adopt any automated system will ultimately be demeaning to human dignity and a threat to individual liberty, as described in Arthur Miller's *The Assault on Privacy*. Before a domestic intelligence system is fully developed, there will be many hard decisions and much soul searching. Areas for discussion will be (1) the rationale for intelligence collection, (2) identifica-

tion of functional concepts for a records system, and (3) common methods of data collection.

The Rationale for Intelligence Collection

The intelligence processes are basically the developing of techniques to collect, evaluate, interpret, and synthesize information into an estimate that can be used by decision makers. In illustrating the various types of domestic data gathering functions, we should keep in mind that the present NCIC data gathering applies only to the solution of a crime. A fact that assists in interpreting other facts or strategic intelligence information that has little or no relationship to a crime or a series of crimes under investigation is not presently entered into NCIC. This lends some assurance, for whatever it may be worth, that NCIC is an operational file rather than one designed for intelligence. Thus, any intelligence generated from the NCIC file is a secondary function. This system may offer some security to individual citizens. In actuality, this fragments the intelligence system to such an extent that much of the data needed for strategic and operational activity lie untapped.

The history of military intelligence, with a greater degree of sophistication, has had the same growing pains as that presently being experienced in domestic intelligence gathering. Questions regarding the controlling political body, the structure for gathering data, and the dissemination of selective facts are still unanswered problems. Both the police and the public fear any intelligence apparatus because there are no laws and guidelines to say what type of information and dissemination capability an intelligence system should have.

Historically, domestic intelligence on criminals, including business monopolies and conspiracies, has been segmented and suppressed for political and military reasons and in general has been of little value.

The development of national data has appeared to take this approach. The Federal Bureau of Investigation, in accepting administrative control of NCIC, has indicated that it will develop intelligence internally from its own agents and operators and from data acquired from operational data, which is a part of NCIC. The SEARCH Project has claimed the area that is identified as "subject in process." Present data processing units are not focused on collecting information for pure strategic intelligence. Perhaps the most effective national organization for generating intelligence information is the Law Enforcement Intelligence Unit (LEIU). This unit, an ad hoc group of law enforcement agencies, exchanges information on an informal basis from local and state intelligence files. Although LEIU has done much to promote the exchange of information, there is neither adequate financial support nor statutory responsibility for a great degree of expertise in the strategic intelligence field.

Identifying Functional Aspects of a Record System

With improved recordkeeping systems and the utilization of an integrated computer system, organized crime records will become an integral part of a centralized records system. The inquiry will be limited to key stations and codes so that confidential information will not be given to unauthorized sources (see Figure 13–1). In the past decade hundreds of automated systems have been developed for cities and regions. Systems such as TRACER, developed by the Norfolk, Virginia, Police Department, are examples of systems that serve the tactical operations of a multicity region.[17]

Information on organized crime can be entered into a records system from a number of sources (refer to Appendix C):

1. Information on arrestee, location, and type of crime charged will come from booking records.
2. Information on complaints, suspects, and location will be taken from the complaint form.
3. License and permit information, on at least a regional basis, will automatically be entered from agencies concerned with the licensing function. For example, if the city clerk's office issues business licenses, data on ownership, type of business, etc., would become a part of the information system.[18]

The system will be designed so that certain violations occurring at given locations will be entered into the system and upon proper inquiry the system will supply a complete background file on a subject or location under investigation. When a location file is queried by an authorized intelligence officer, all recorded information on a given address will immediately become a part of the investigation. Background inquiry such as this should include a current photo of those connected with the business enterprise. Known associates from arrest reports, intelligence reports, and from field interrogation cards will assist the officer in investigating organized crime.

Information on all complaints, electronically checked against past complaints on the location, suspects, and arrestees, will come to the investigator as part of the preinvestigation for a business enterprise or location being checked. In addition, vehicles, utility hookups, business licenses, or permit records will be checked when a new organized crime complaint comes to an intelligence unit.

Bringing speed and flexibility to intelligence records will undoubtedly be the greatest accomplishment in organized crime control during the next ten

[17]J. W. Nixon and Ellen Posivach, "TRACER: Computerized Service for the Criminal Justice System," *FBI Law Enforcement Bulletin,* December 1978, pp. 7–11.

[18]James W. Stevens, *State and Regional Information Systems: The Criminal Justice Component* (Institute of Urban Studies, The University of Texas at Arlington, February 1970), pp. 10–20.

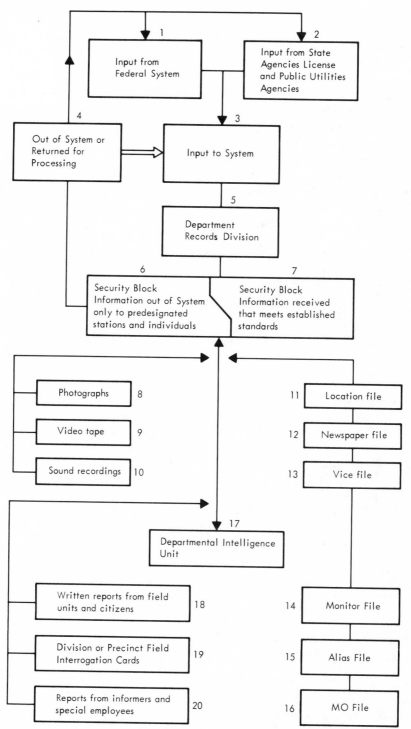

Figure 13–1 Configuration of system security for information entering and leaving the system.

years. Direct access to past police history, methods of operation, and current illegal activities for use in investigations will support better prosecutions and improve the management information system. This information will focus on improved investigations and on better cases for prosecutions.[19]

Organized criminal records will no longer be separate entities but will be part of an integrated criminal justice system. In a data processing system, records of a confidential nature will be more secure than is now possible in a manual records system. The police administrator should begin planning for an integrated computer records system with intelligence records as an integral part of a centralized system. This concept has been part of most sophisticated intelligence information systems.

The extent and depth of inquiry on organized criminal intelligence will be limited only by the sophistication of the system and the accuracy of information entered into it. Remote inquiry stations can be programmed to receive only specific information; thus, the central storage unit can be protected against indiscriminate inquiry and will even note the source of an unauthorized inquiry. Godfrey and Harris indicate that computer technology has progressed to the point that multiple users can concurrently access a common data base. In such a system each individual user can get all the information he is allowed to see, and any information entering the system is safeguarded from the public disclosure.[20] The proposed intelligence process is shown in Figure 13–2.

Common Data Collection Methods

Most Americans today have their profile recorded in several computer banks. This is the end result of all types of automated data gathering. Information gathering on all persons is a practice that will not be easily remedied by legislation. As long as private industry and government pour millions of dollars into computer hardware, it is unlikely the indiscriminate collection of data will cease. Data collected by private business and government are dissimilar, yet each bit of information gathered goes to make up a comprehensive file of interrelated facts. All information collected by business and government is available to the other, through legal or illegal means. Both data gathering systems are equally dangerous in terms of the uses being made of the collected data. It is not the purpose of this book to debate morality or legality in terms of the information collected. Unless the law specifically prohibits certain acts of information gathering, it is presumed that both private business and governmental agencies will utilize techniques

---

[19]All systems in the NCIC net can be designed to receive all the intelligence information generated by the criminal justice system.

[20] E. Drexel Godfrey and Don R. Harris, *Basic Elements of Intelligence: A Manual of Theory, Structure and Procedures for Use by Law Enforcement Agencies against Organized Crime* (LEAA, Department of Justice, 1972), p. 275a.

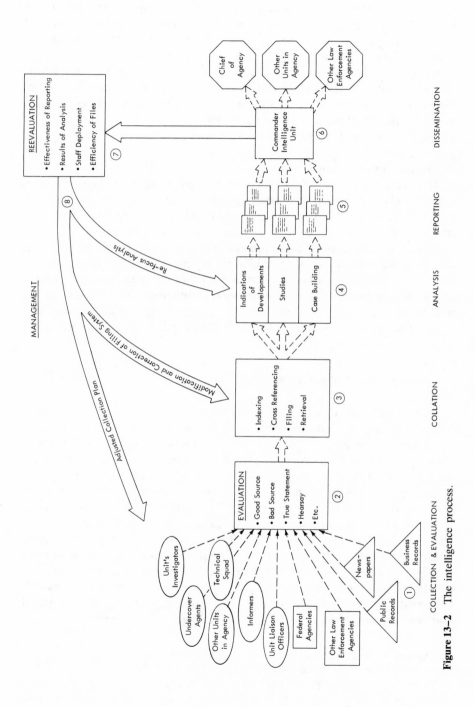

Figure 13–2 The intelligence process.

that are necessary to maintain a place in the business world or that law enforcement believes is necessary to equalize the technological advantage held by the criminal engaged in organized crime.[21]

A legal methodology with a realistic chance for success must be established if there is to be a sound basis for public agencies to be in the data gathering business. Techniques used by the criminal must dictate the countermeasures imposed by law enforcement agencies. As we discuss the role of law enforcement in information gathering, it is important to observe a few of the information gathering techniques used by sophisticated criminal groups that ultimately must be countered by law enforcement.

Criminal use of information technology. Organized criminal conspiracies are not concerned about constitutional guarantees such as "the right of the people to be secure in their persons, houses, papers and effects against unreasonable searches and seizures." They are interested only in desired results and that is what they get for the money they spend. The criminal conspiracies are not in the least worried about the Fair Credit Reporting Act. They will, in spite of legal restrictions, get desired information through apparently legitimate sources. In order to counter this type of activity, it is going to be necessary for law enforcement agencies to have the same advantage, in terms of technology and legal guidelines within which to work.

In order to show how the criminal may utilize information gathering devices, these brief illustrations are cited:

> Consumer fraud practices are so common as to defy individual identity. For example, price fixing, securities manipulation, and other forms of theft are dependent upon the flow of massive amounts of information. Cooperative wholesale grocery associations, for example, frequently do not rely upon supply and demand, but upon monopolies in fixing food prices.
>
> Banking institutions are prime candidates because loan sharks are often tied in with legitimate lending institutions. Usurious rates and other credit dodges fluctuate on computer information. Credit information such as financial status and assets are for sale to criminal organizations through some credit reporting associations. This same information is available to extortionists, promoters, and others. No laws presently in use or proposed can stop or slow this practice.
>
> Wire services that furnish gambling information are important. Information such as the opening line and closing line on sports activities use computer services for carrying coded messages. These services are all provided on a contract basis as a part of a legitimate business enterprise such as sports networks and data transmission of seemingly innocent business data.

[21]U.S. Department of Treasury publishes *Statistics of Income* and the Internal Revenue Service uses files from the income tax returns to prosecute individuals in organized crime.

Information on swindled securities, antitrust violations, and sophisticated theft operations are dependent upon automated information gathering and transmission.

Information obtained by surveillance may be used for bribery, extortion, and shakedowns in a large number of ways. This type of activity is extremely effective when dealing with political figures and those who hold positions of trust. Any situation that demands additional persuasion can secure it through the use of surveillance instruments and data gathering techniques.

The only way law enforcement can counter these types of operations is to have more advanced equipment and better technical personnel than that possessed by the criminal. The problem of dealing with criminal conspiracies is not going to be solved by laws that are unenforceable and procedures and guidelines that no one will follow. Eventually appropriate investigative techniques must be employed to counter equipment used by syndicate operations.

Countermeasures by law enforcement agencies.   Decision making in organized crime control is based upon data secured through the intelligence function. In order to make these vital decisions, governmental agencies need not receive carte blanche authority to pursue investigations without legal safeguards. They do need, however, a succinct set of rules to pursue an effective investigation. It is important to identify the procedures that are legal and to establish the basis upon which administrative decisions and court cases are to be decided. Investigators rarely need to know all the personal habits, traits, and information about an individual for court prosecution. In the decision-making area, however, it is important to assess this type of information. Some is available to criminal leaders through certain kinds of private business transactions. It seems ironic that the legally designated agents of government are prohibited from securing comprehensive information.

The countermeasures by law enforcement have been the subject of many abuses. There can be no question that information on innocent persons has gone into intelligence files under the auspices of national security. A man in public life will have his name entered into intelligence files on many different occasions. The prime question should not be whether his name is in fact in the file, but whether or not the information gives a true and accurate picture of what transpired at that given time.

Analysis of Collected Data

Law enforcement has been weak in the analysis and linking of collected data. For the overall analysis of data, one or more persons must be trained as an analyst. This person must be capable of developing patterns, networks,

connections and new areas of organized crime penetration from the file records and the incoming raw information. Without the analyst, the information flow cannot be utilized effectively. Without the analyst, much of the incoming raw information will remain just that.[22]

The analysis procedure consists of three steps:[23] (1) summarize, (2) compare, and (3) explain. Using the computer, an important new technique in analysis has emerged. This is called *linking,* and the technique determines the presence or absence of links among individuals.[24] The data base usually consists of such information as investigation reports, arrest records, informant reports, financial statements, and newspaper articles.

The linking analysis is completed in six steps: (1) Assembling the information, (2) abstracting information relevant to individual relationships and affiliations, (3) preparing an association matrix (an array of the relationships among a set of individuals, noting the strength of the links), (4) developing a preliminary link diagram, (5) incorporating organizations into the diagram, and (6) refining the link diagram. With more prosecutions under the RICO statute, this phase of analysis will become vital in the proof of a case. The issue of entering a person's name into an intelligence file is not as important as the absolute accuracy of such information.

The nature of the intelligence process does not necessitate massive collection of data by law enforcement officers. The data are available in hundreds of published documents and from persons who are interested in revealing information about an enemy. The real need is for clear-cut lines of policy and law in order to control the collection and dissemination of such information.

All types of information concerning some individuals have been collected indiscriminately by both government and business; there is little question that the individual's right of privacy has been violated by the forces who collect the information. There must be a closer look at how intelligence is collected and who is doing the collecting. How intelligence is processed and the role of the intelligence establishment must also be identified if logical laws to regulate its proliferation are to evolve. Intelligence gathering has lived under a cloak of secrecy, not through necessity, but because of vested interests and a blatant disregard for the right of the public to know what is being done.

SUMMARY

A great number of legal and moral issues must be resolved before comprehensive intelligence gathering can be achieved. Some techniques for control have been advocated by the SEARCH committee for effective data gathering and public protection.

[22]Godfrey and Harris, *Basic Elements of Intelligence,* p. 7.

[23]Ibid., pp. 27–37.

[24]W. R. Harper, "Application of Link Analysis to Police Intelligence," *Human Factors,* 17, 2 (April 1975), 157–64.

It becomes apparent as the development of automatic data processing evolves that there is danger to the individual's right of privacy. This danger, if not curbed by rigid, realistic guidelines, will in the hands of the wrong individuals destroy our free society.

The SEARCH committee reports are designed to offer guidelines for how an effective computerized intelligence system should be developed and function. The design and organization of intelligence records is a key factor in getting maximum usable information from select bits of intelligence. Every step, process, and structure of an intelligence function should be designed for the maintenance of maximum security, accuracy, and a control that will provide for the check and balance system. Information must be developed into a records system that can be properly manipulated and made available to field units where it can provide some beneficial impact. If one step or procedure is weak, the entire system is subject to failure.

Many computer systems operated by private businesses and governmental bodies fail to provide adequate safeguards. As methods of data collection evolve a warning should be issued concerning computerized intelligence. Unless control standards are established, maintained, and enforced, intelligence information will be used against the attainment of justice. Computerized systems that will give the necessary intelligence data and provide protective safeguards must be developed.

QUESTIONS FOR DISCUSSION

1. Why are ethical considerations as important as statutory regulations in the collection and dissemination of intelligence information?
2. Identify major standards as established by the SEARCH committee. How will they affect the intelligence network?
3. Identify the major components of the Fair Credit Reporting Act and assess its value for protecting the citizen.
4. Identify a set of basic rules for the classification of information. Is the classification scheme too secretive or too lax in security?
5. What are the three basic forms of intelligence generated by a good records and reporting system?
6. Explain how basic organization structure influences the control of intelligence through a "check and balance" system.
7. Will an automated records system offer greater security than a manual system?
8. Explain the concept of "synthesizing" intelligence. How does it relate to linking?
9. Identify factors that should cause concern about excessive intelligence gathering.
10. Assess the priority for accuracy of information being entered into an intelligence storage system.

14

METHODS FOR ORGANIZED CRIME CONTROL

LEARNING OUTCOMES

1. Gain an overview of accepted methods for organized crime enforcement.
2. Recognize organization and management techniques that can be applied to crime control.
3. Know common control techniques for organized crime at the community level.
4. Understand techniques for field officers and how they affect organized crime control.
5. Know about commissions responsible for establishing policy leading to organized crime control.

There are a number of ways in which the control of organized crime should be pursued. Each of the ways brought out in this text must look to both the citizen and street patrol officer to ensure its success. As illustrated in Figure 14–1, these ways may be described as: (1) education and the development of awareness throughout the community, (2) civic action groups and crime commissions, and (3) punitive enforcement.

EDUCATION

The most positive approach for controlling organized crime is to inform the police and citizens of the magnitude and implications of organized crime in a community. When officer and citizen know the intricate route of money placed on a $2 bet, they will be reluctant to support or condone such an organization. When officer and citizen are aware of and understand that

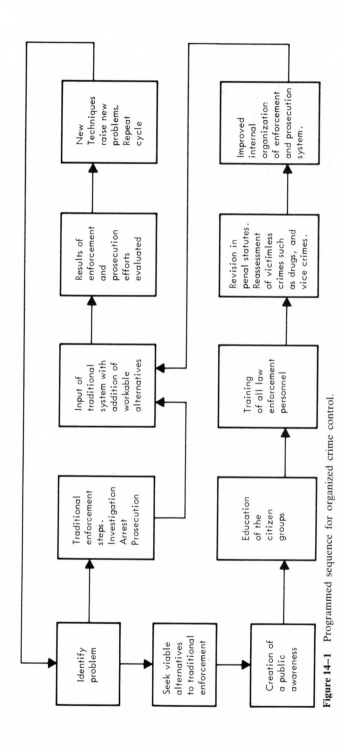

Figure 14-1 Programmed sequence for organized crime control.

certain businesses are controlled by mobsters and illegal monopolies, economic sanctions will assist in bringing them to a halt.[1]

This type of positive action is based on the premise that legislators have decriminalized the activities society will tolerate. Obviously if activities such as gambling are legalized, they cease to be a law enforcement problem.

Education of the police and general public holds the greatest hope for control of organized crime. Every state and national plan should concentrate on such education. A few law enforcement investigators placed about the state and the nation will have little impact on the problem unless they generate a core of police and citizens so knowledgeable about the techniques of organized crime that "street pressure" will force the confederations out of business. The federal government has initiated efforts in this direction with the police through the Law Enforcement Assistance Administration. Two major centers now have training programs dealing with organized crime. They are located at Miami, Florida, and Sacramento, California. Both include high-echelon organized crime orientation for police officers.

Model Programs

Model long-range programs have been drawn up for states, to function under the direction of the governors. Through federal, state, and local financing, a variety of organized crime training programs are offered for all local officers. States are also identifying organized crime problems and are moving toward the education of citizens as a means of control for organized crime.

Some model plans could counter organized crime if properly implemented.[2] But the first step is still extensive training for criminal justice personnel.

Training should be structured to reach all personnel involved in organized crime control. For example, seminars open to the police, prosecutors, and judges should be offered throughout the state. These seminars should be followed by presentations to business groups and interested citizens. Following these sessions would be intensive in-service training for specialists engaged in the arrest and prosecution of organized crime offenders.

Because organized crime has such an impact on the economic and social structure of a community, the authors contend that education is the only technique that will have a limiting impact upon organized criminal influence

---

[1]*America, Inc.,* by Morton Mintz and Jerry S. Cohen. Copyright © 1971 by Jerry S. Cohen and Morton Mintz. Reprinted by permission of the publisher, Dial Press Inc., New York.

[2]Robert G. Blakely, Ronald Goldstock, and Charles H. Rogouin, *Rackets Bureau: Investigation and Prosecution of Organized Crime,* Washington, D.C.: U.S. Government Printing Office, March, 1978.

in a community.[3] The federal effort of zeroing in on individuals and finding some statute on which to prosecute can quickly degenerate into persecution. The local approach of identifying a violation and searching for a culprit is equally absurd. The only way a confederation will be weakened is through pressure exerted by all levels of government through approved enforcement techniques. Public education is the only vehicle that can effectively translate many efforts into action.

The commission approach is partially an educational medium and partially an enforcement technique. Thus, considerable emphasis in organized crime suppression should be on the use of the crime commission.

CIVIC ACTION GROUPS AND CRIME COMMISSIONS

Organized crime can be controlled, but only with full citizen support to reveal the criminal acts that are most covert. The rackets, which were revealed years ago by the Kefauver Committee, still exist simply because citizens have not taken it upon themselves to force necessary action to bring about prosecutions. There are basically two types of civic action groups. They may be classed as civic action citizens' groups and those established under the framework of government.

These two methods of suppressing organized crime are different; however, both look to the citizen as a main force for crime suppression. Civic action groups are usually ad hoc structures that attack a single problem, whereas the crime commissions are legally constituted bodies of government and should have a more lasting impact on the overall organized crime problem.

Civic Action Groups

The ultimate in prevention of any type crime is an aroused citizenry. No agency of government can be better than the citizen it represents; thus, civic action groups are potent forces in an overall organized crime suppression effort. Civic groups historically have been the catalyst for reform movements. Public demand for stricter law enforcement and removal of covert vice crimes has had an impact upon local organized crime. The prime problem with public participation in ad hoc groups is their short life and the difficult problem of coordination with public agencies. Ad hoc groups of citizens formed not through political necessity, but through community pride, offer sporadic hope for organized crime control.

[3]Two recent articles addressed this problem, but neither arrived at definitive ways in which we should be addressing organized crime. D.C. Smith, Jr., "Organized Crime and American Life," *Society*, 16, 3 (March–April 1979), 32–38. S. L. Hills, "Organized Crime and American Society," *Midwest Quarterly*, 9, 2 (January 1968), 171–82.

There are nine recognizable signs that organized crime is moving in on a community:

Social acceptance of hoodlums in decent society.
Your community's indifference to ineffective local government.
Notorious mobster personalities in open control of businesses.
Deceptive handling of public funds.
Interest at very high rates to poor risk borrowers (the juice loan).
Close association of mobsters and local authorities.
Arson and bombings.
Terrorized legitimate businesses.
Easily found gambling, narcotics and prostitution.

Figure 14–2 The nine danger signs of the social cancer known as organized crime, as identified by the Chicago Crime Commission.

One example of the type of commission that has been relatively effective is the Chicago Crime Commission. In operation for several decades, the Chicago commission has been a forerunner in the publication of a limited number of syndicate activities. This crime commission must be judged as an effective device for the revealing of certain criminal activities. An example of this commission's work is shown in Figure 14–2.

These comments on the role of the crime commission have been taken from statements made by various members of the National Association of Citizens Crime Commissions.

Increased public understanding. Crime commissions can contribute materially to better public understanding and public rejection of organized crime.

Planned citizen involvement. The citizens' involvement should be programmed and planned rather than allowed to be dissipated on short-term projects of limited value.

Generation of community initiative. The commission should examine the criminal justice functions and make recommendations to enforcement agencies for system improvement.

Examination of basic political systems. Commissions should require ethics bills and recommend civil service careers in many areas now in the "spoils" domain.

Involvement of organized business. Chambers of commerce and professional associations should encourage the stimulation of programs and seminars to educate and develop blueprints for action within business enterprises.

Expanding the system to include civil sanctions. Criminal law alone cannot curb organized crime. Civil justice for the purpose of reaching the racketeer who moves into the legitimate business field must be explored.

Encouraging cooperation among criminal justice agencies. While there has been no endorsement of the "task force concept," those in the commissions indicate a need to coordinate the efforts of the federal agencies, as well as the different units of local government, including the police, courts, and correction agencies. These recommendations are shown in Figure 14–3.

CITIZENS CRIME COMMISSIONS' RECOMMENDATIONS
FOR ELIMINATING ORGANIZED CRIME

1. The citizens crime commissions must be free from political involvement, thus, financing from private sources is desirable.
2. Have a commission in all major cities to act as an investigative "watch dog" representative of the public interest.
3. Expanded criminal intelligence is rapidly becoming a major function of citizens crime commissions.
4. A dedication to create a climate of communitywide support for innovative programs in juvenile and correctional programs.
5. The business community is encouraged to use the extensive files, research, and consultation services of the citizens commissions.
6. The commissions have interest in legislative changes, although not a lobbying agency, they are effective in having input into initiation of new laws.
7. Conduct periodic surveys of criminal justice systems to determine if the best form of justice possible is being rendered.
8. Encourage public information campaigns for special anti-crime programs and with continued emphasis upon organized crime.

Figure 14–3 Citizens crime commissions' recommendatons for eliminating organized crime. (These goals and statements have been extracted from various speeches made by crime commission members and from position papers.)

Citizen Groups Established under the Framework of Government

There are increasing pressures to fix the responsibility for organized crime control in multijurisdictional organizations, although some experts recommend keeping the hearing or exposure process separate from the enforcement function. Which method becomes more effective will probably depend upon the effectiveness of such groups as the Pennsylvania Crime Commission. It was created in 1968 with the power to subpoena witnesses, to have access to public records, and to make changes and recommendations for legislative action. The report published as a result of investigations during the first two years of this organization should serve as a national model. The publication, entitled *The Report on Organized Crime,* although generally circulated among police agencies, should be published in volume and circulated among all the citizens of the state and perhaps even nationally.

The true effectiveness of this type of group brings us full circle to the realization that politics enters into the selection of the citizen representative. For example, the grand jury is selected in many states by judges or other ranking elected officials who obtain a rubber stamp approval of their appointees. In many instances, the grand jury is kept busy detailing terrible conditions in the jail or other public buildings, returning indictments against run-of-the-mill criminal violators, and puttering with other tasks until the year expires and new appointments are made. Grand jury reports can be the "comedy books" of government ills.

If grand juries are to perform an adequate function, the members should be selected from the general tax rolls, like regular jury members; tenure should be increased to a minimum of two years, with power and staff support to continue certain investigations; and the printing of a report for public consumption should be required. The political nature and lack of budget for operations makes present grand juries relatively ineffective against organized crime.

Crime commissions come in a variety of forms and in many differing degrees of effectiveness. A crime commission with or without legal structure is going to be worthless unless its findings are followed up with intensive investigation and prosecution. The crime commission consisting of ad hoc citizen representation is of questionable value unless its members can forget political vindictiveness, petty jealousies, and personal aggrandizement.

The legally structured crime commission as an adjunct to a grand jury is in a position to render valuable aid to law enforcement. Unfortunately, this type of commission depends upon a strong grand jury. Most grand juries are replaced every year, and because of a restricted budget for investigators, very few organized crime prosecutions are obtained through information furnished by the jury.

Special committees or commissions that have revealed much about organized crime are the congressional subcommittees at both the national and state levels. Information produced from these organizations, although circulated widely for political purposes, has done much to create public awareness. Here are examples of such committees:

> Wickersham Committee, 1928—An early appraisal of crime conditions in the United States
>
> Kefauver Committee, 1950–51—National hearings on all types of organized crime, emphasis on gambling
>
> McClellan Committee, 1957–60—National hearings on all types of organized crime, emphasis on labor rackets

But these and other congressional hearings have had limited success in revealing the operation of the national confederations.

Punitive Enforcement

The primary emphasis, we think, should be upon punitive enforcement. This method is emphasized because the methods of crime prevention previously discussed cannot be totally effective. Local law enforcement officers fully understand that punitive enforcement cannot be a final solution to organized crime. But until better solutions are developed, punitive methods will be used. Officers are aware that without intensive punitive enforcement at all levels of government, there will be little hope for controlling organized crime. Local law enforcement is by and large willing to accept all available assistance at state and national levels. Let us look more closely at the role of the field officer at the local level.

Role of the field officer. In modern departments, the field officer is heavily involved in organized crime enforcement. If a patrol officer is lax in observing violations, overlooks gambling and prostitution, and fails to make reports regarding suspicious actions, he or she is contributing to the success of organized criminal groups. The role a field officer has in controlling organized crime may be identified as the following:

> The collection of facts and the funneling of these facts to specialized units in a department. A field officer through observation can obtain names, addresses, automobile and license numbers of suspects and establish patterns of movement on confederation members living in a district.
>
> The detection of patterns, modus operandi, and other traits that relate to organized crime activity.

The bringing of information to light that will bring about a thorough investigation.

Reduction of personnel through arrest to cause the organization to be more cautious and to minimize victim contacts. The field officer should be in a position to take action on all violations.

Field contact with willing and unwilling victims to develop leads through associates, and to gather other types of information not available to intelligence officers.

Association with local businesspeople so that if these businesses are pressured by racketeers, owner and operators will have the confidence and trust in the officer to report these threats or pressures. The officer then, in turn, refers the material to intelligence officers.[4]

Identification of those who are local organized criminals as opposed to those who have national confederation connections.

The field officer, if well trained in the methods of organized criminals, becomes a field investigator of street activities, many of which ultimately furnish support evidence on top-level hoodlums. If organized crime is to be controlled, the enforcement pressures must come from both street-level and specialized investigatory personnel.

IDENTIFYING ORGANIZED CRIME:
HOW THE PATROL OFFICER FUNCTIONS

Because of new and better information from studies about organized crime, we are able to identify at least three types of crimes that may be considered of an organized nature: (1) the common physical crimes such as burglary or robbery, when one or more persons is involved in the planning, execution, or disposition of the spoils of a crime; (2) those crimes that are socially destructive such as embezzlement, consumer fraud, and other crimes classed in the "white collar" category, and (3) the activities of the traditional "syndicated" or confederated groups who are organized for the sole purpose of pursuing illegal gain. It is the latter category that we normally refer to as organized crime, but the first two classifications should be identified as being of an organized nature in specific instances and considered in the police effort. White collar crime has been discussed in a previous chapter; here we will look at how common physical crimes relate to traditional organized crime.

---

[4]This association also works against the field officer who, through such close contacts, may be tempted to connive with such persons to subvert the laws and overlook violations. When contacts with hoodlums are frequent, the entire enforcement process may succumb to bribery and corruption.

The Common Physical Crimes

The field officer lives daily with these crimes, which are viewed by most departments as being individual violations by an antisocial individual. In many instances, they are organized from the basic inception to the final execution of a given violation.

The field officer should pursue the investigation of every crime with the idea that more than one individual may be involved. Crime reports, arrests records, and follow-up investigation should meet the same rigid processes of analysis as the investigation of traditional organized criminal violations. The complexity of organized crime, as described by Donald R. Cressey, is shown in Figure 14–4.[5]

As the three classifications of organized crime are analyzed, it becomes apparent that very few crimes are not suspect. It is the intent of these

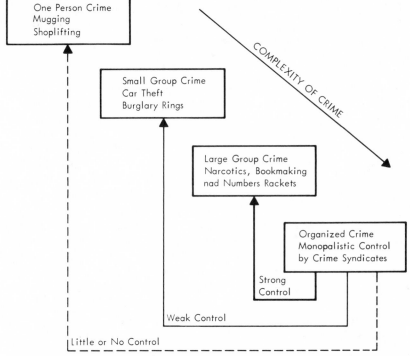

Figure 14–4 Degree of control of various crimes by confederations.

[5]Presentation of Professor Donald R. Cressey, University of California, Santa Barbara, at the Third Organized Crime Law Enforcement Training Conference, sponsored by the Law Enforcement Assistance Administration, U.S. Department of Justice, at the University of Oklahoma, Norman, March 4, 1970.

classifications to cause the field officer to see the possible connections that may arise from a stolen car case or a simple house burglary where merchandise is stolen. What is being asked is that the officer, in enforcement and reporting procedures, consider that some form of organization may exist.

The field officer will be in contact with criminals in this category and unless the criminal activities are investigated and documented, there may be no link to organized crime. Each violation has unique characteristics that may cause it to be of an organized criminal nature:

> Burglary, not normally associated with organized crime, has these loose ties of an organized nature. The common burglar needs a "fence" for merchandise. The fence may become the apex of an organization predicated upon theft. When there is a receiver or fence, burglaries may be considered as being organized at the street level. The fence or receiver of stolen property may operate behind loan and pawn shop fronts, or may be in the secondhand business or moving and storage business. He may be a loan shark, in the construction business, or in dozens of trade businesses that can use the stolen merchandise. (It is not uncommon for a building contractor to have a boxcar of lumber, shingles, or pipe stolen from his supply and eventually end up buying them back at a reduced rate.) Burglars will loot warehouses, docks, and airport storage facilities, all of which must have a pipeline to a market. According to news reports, approximately $5 billion in merchandise were stolen from air terminals alone. The rate of burglary clearance was less than 25 percent. There is a vast armada of thieves who appear to work alone, but who in reality are working for the large organizations. Burglary is a major supporting crime for confederations.

Organization may be present in activities of gamblers, loan sharks, and receivers of stolen property. In investigating a crime scene, a field officer may detect the type of criminal activity by the traits of the job. For example:

> The type of merchandise taken—boxcar loads of merchandise, large hauls of furs or jewelry, stock, bonds or other merchandise—may indicate a need for a fence. Large quantities of office machines may be transported interstate and sold in areas that have not been a part of the mandatory crime reporting system, have very ineffective local law enforcement, and are not a part of the National Crime Information System.

The method of operation may, with the introduction of sophisticated data processing systems, become an effective identifier for gang activities. For example:

> One highly organized group, probably not affiliated with any national organization, successfully used a pipe wrench on the front door of the

victim's home to gain entry. It was later discovered that these thieves had successfully operated in 12 states, with more than 30 suspects involved.

With the computer systems now being developed, the investigators would have immediately identified the trademarks of the participants. This points out to the field officer that every burglary should be investigated with the possibility of identifying organized activity.

Shoplifting is a unique and common form of theft. It should also be approached with the thought of organized involvement. Again, the receiver of stolen property is the key culprit. The field officer who reports the violation is a critical link in identifying those professionally involved in shoplifting and those who are occasional thieves.

The gangs concerned with robbery, although not organized to the extent it had been in the 1930s, still have field units who hit select targets. Postal vehicles, armored cars, and large jewelry consignments have been the prime targets of well-executed action.

Traditional Confederation Crime

The primary thrust of this section is to relate common crimes to the traditional syndicated crimes. Although the traditional organized crime per se may not be the major problem, one of the avowed purposes of this text is to outline how the officer and the citizen must approach the enforcement of such crimes in order to minimize the impact of organized crime on society.

The field officer's approach to the control of organized crime is the strategy called *violation-response*. This strategy means that when there is a violation of the law, there is an attempt to identify, prosecute, and convict the persons committing the offense. This, as Anderson explains, is the traditional way for local officers to respond to organized crime. The other strategy is the *attrition* approach used by the federal government. This is directed toward finding a statute for which sufficient information exists to prosecute and obtain a conviction.[6]

There is no question that the most effective approach is the latter strategy. Both strategies are used frequently by local officers, including field officers, to the extent that prosecution and not persecution is the ultimate end. The field officer should utilize both strategies for apprehending organized crime violators. A conclusion drawn by many local officers is that organized crime will not be eliminated by the arrest of a few top-level members, or many top-level members, but will be successful only when the entire body of the organization is torn apart by massive coordinated efforts that will chop off the head of the organization and "rip the guts" from the entire organization. One without the other is doomed to failure.

[6]Annelise Anderson, *Organized Crime: The Need for Research* (Organized Crime, Programs Division LEAA, U.S. Department of Justice, 1971), p. 2.

SUMMARY

This chapter briefly discusses three different methods for approaching the control of organized crime. Chances are that the average community will be using the third choice cited in this chapter, that is, punitive control by criminal justice agencies. There is no attempt to play down the importance of punitive control. In principle, this type of enforcement looks good; in practice, punitive enforcement alone has no chance in controlling organized criminal activities.

The method with top priority has been identified as educaton for both the police and the public. Education of all police officers and the public must be the predominant thrust if there is to be an impact upon presently structured organized crime. But this method alone will have little impact on organized crime; education must be coordinated with the efforts of punitive enforcement.

The training and education of a few specialized officers cannot of itself make a workable system. The average citizen in cities throughout our country must be deluged with factual information about the corner bookie, the prostitute, the junkies, and the lotteries that support confederations. Crimes without victims are oriented toward the emasculation and robbery of an entire social structure, not toward just a single victim.

The citizens' war on crime offers some hope. Organized citizens are making their presence known through crime commissions and other activities. The National Association of Citizen Crime Commissions has 21 national affiliate units. These units serve as intelligence sources and action initiation groups. They are not vigilantes. In an attempt to deal in true facts, civic action groups have the potential for being effective because they may probe into any area of criminal misbehavior. The governmental commissions are usually established to investigate specific crime areas. Both types would be more effective if there were longer active tenure. This would create a sustained interest in setting and obtaining long-range goals.

To the extent that education and citizen committees fail, punitive enforcement is the final step in controlling organized crime. But one method of enforcement alone is not sufficient; all must apply. Each of the three methods working together will produce results in the control of criminal confederations.

QUESTIONS FOR DISCUSSIONS

1. Give logical arguments that will substantiate why there must be citizen involvement in the control of organized crime.
2. Cite a number of techniques for bringing the citizen into play against criminal confederations.

3. What are some of the disadvantages in having citizens playing active roles against organized crime?

4. Identify and cite the state requirements for grand juries. How can these units of government be made more effective?

5. Cite some recent statements from local citizen crime commissions. How can they be made more effective?

6. Review the efforts of the national crime commissions. Why have the findings from these commissions not had a greater impact on organized crime?

7. Identify what you believe to be the model role of the field law enforcement officer.

8. Review how traditional crimes, such as burglary and shoplifting, tie into operations of crime confederations.

9. Explain why the federal approach to organized crime control strategy (attrition) cannot solve the local organized crime control problem without also using the violator-response method.

10. Identify other techniques that can be used against organized crime. How do we rid society of organized crime?

PART V
EDUCATION AND TRAINING

This part surveys problems yet to be answered or solved.

During the past decade, more and more agencies have educated and trained their officers to recognize the dynamics of organized crime. But commitment to training and education in this field is lacking.

In retrospect, the trends of the past decade are not encouraging. Intelligence files have been compromised. Public support has not materialized because of adverse police public relations, and enforcement efforts have moved from local action to spotty politically oriented action to meet the publicity needs of a politician seeking a higher office. The political manipulation of organized crime enforcement has moved from the local level to state and federal levels because of the flow of money into the enforcement apparatus. Whether honest enforcement will prevail over vested interests remains to be seen.

15

EDUCATION AND TRAINING FOR ORGANIZED CRIME CONTROL

LEARNING OUTCOMES

1. Have an overall impression of the need for and the importance of education and training in organized crime enforcement.
2. Gain some insight into the type of training and education needed.
3. Develop some curriculum techniques for both agency and citizen use.
4. Recognize the importance of education and training of the right type at the appropriate level.

One of the weakest links in the struggle against organized crime is education and training at the local level. Public administrators, who are aware that organized crime exists in their community, are not spending sufficient time in educating and training citizens, law enforcement officers, and other members of the criminal justice system. Consequently, local persons with an interest in curbing organized crime are left to their own resources in securing information about those engaged in organized crime. If there is to be a favorable impact upon organized crime in a community, the transmittal of technology about these crimes must come to both the members of the criminal justice system and the citizen in an accelerated manner.

There are three modes for transmitting information to those concerned with organized crime control. They are (1) education in academic institutions, (2) specialized training for police officers, and (3) greater public information. To implement one mode of learning without the other two will not produce a desired level of information about the criminal confederations. Neither the citizen nor enforcement officer will have sufficient expertise to expose and apprehend the violators.

EDUCATION IN ACADEMIC INSTITUTIONS

The proper place to transmit technology about a social problem of great magnitude is in the academic classroom. Unfortunately, teachers of the social sciences and government classes are not knowledgeable about the functions of organized criminals. In past years, largely because of money available under the Omnibus Crime Bill, educators have suddenly discovered that teachers should have an orientation on the drug problem. Hours have been spent teaching teachers about pharmacology and other general information concerning drugs. Rarely has a teacher been offered the opportunity or transmitted knowledge about the relationship of drug traffic to the total organized crime picture and the deleterious impact of drugs on the society. This fragmentation of instruction leaves the average citizen and police officer without factual knowledge about organized criminal influence on the total crime picture. Traditionally, education and training concerning organized crime have been restricted to a select number of officers who have been assigned vice and intelligence responsibilities. The general administrative attitude, particularly among departments, seems to be that only a limited number of officers should deal with organized crime. Many police department personnel have no more knowledge about this type of crime than a member of the general public.

Academic instructors are rarely qualified to teach these concepts. These courses should be taught at the high school and junior college level in order to obtain a broader base of exposure for all citizens. A course in technical education dealing with drugs and other organized crime should be available to students at this level of education. How such a course is structured will depend upon the instructor. However, the course should be built on broad social concepts and on how organized crime influences the social and economic structure of a community.

There has been little effort to provide organized crime information in educational programs. Consequently, the government has found it necessary to support high-level training courses as part of organized crime action programs. But it does little good to develop field operations in a department if specialized personnel are the only officers committed to intelligence gathering and prosecution of organized criminals. Police organizations generally tend to exclude organized crime as a high priority. This omission is due in part to a lack of knowledge and in part to political considerations.

An educational institution could offer one of the best sources of conceptual information for local officers and citizens. Academic institutions are usually defensive about their failure to have such instruction. The institution usually states that it has no qualified staff to teach such courses. Nothing could be further from reality. Disciplines such as accounting, economics, business management, computer sciences, and mathematics are staffed with persons

who can contribute within the framework of their particular expertise. The subject of organized crime has been studied extensively in small segments in each of these disciplines. It is the responsibility of the educational program to bring these studies into focus. In addition, the enforcement field, primarily at the federal level, has qualified experts who are available to make supportive technical presentations. The educational institutions should be utilizing this talent.

A broad listing of subjects for organized crime study might include the topical categories shown in the following outline.

Projected College Outline for the Study of Organized Crime

An academically oriented course in organized crime may include, but should not be restricted to, these areas:

I. What is organized crime?
    A. The traditional definition and the new concepts for identifying organized crime.
    B. Should organized crime and drug enforcement be fragmented?
    C. How do traditional concepts of organized crime avoid the tie to street crimes?
II. An overview of organized crime in Western societies.
    A. Some history as it relates to current problems. Defining organized crime as it now exists in contemporary society.
    B. The impact upon political subdivisions of nations. The need for control.
    C. The present status of international relationships in curbing organized crime. How it influences fiscal policies.
III. The national problem with organized crime.
    A. The national effort for control of criminal activities.
    B. The political and fiscal ramifications in curbing organized crime.
    C. The national social and political climate. How it influences effective enforcement.
IV. The politics of government and organized crime.
    A. The systems—where does organized crime flourish?
    B. Political restraints, such as conflict of interest laws, political donations, and so on.
    C. Trends in corruption in the political system at all levels of government.

   V.   What is the citizen's role and obligation in organized crime?
- A.   Identify the impact of organized crime in low-income neighborhoods.
- B.   How does organized crime enforcement reflect on all law enforcement?
- C.   What social factors mandate a citizen's participation in organized crime control?

  VI.   How are units of government organized to challenge criminal inroads?
- A.   The regional concept for the organization of enforcement units.
- B.   The gathering of legitimate and legal information.
- C.   How do governing bodies organize to obtain political and citizen participation?

 VII.   The legal system—fighting organized crime.
- A.   New laws, the national trends.
- B.   State laws, state court, and enforcement weaknesses.
- C.   How the prosecutorial function should be strengthened.

VIII.   The impact of organized crime on local enforcement agencies.
- A.   Prevailing concepts in how organized crime should be challenged.
- B.   The issues of corruption, how to maintain a system of checks and balances.
- C.   What does society want and how can an effective effort be made against select crimes?

  IX.   Conceptual issues for police administration.
- A.   How can organized crime be identified so that law enforcement will receive citizen support?
- B.   The role of the police in initiating new laws and administrative procedures for a city.
- C.   How does a department relate to the citizenry in organized crime control?

   X.   Victimless crimes.
- A.   What is the rationale for enforcing such crimes? Is this a realistic approach for contemporary society?
- B.   Are moral crimes, such as prostitution, pornography, and homosexuality, crimes that police should be prosecuting?
- C.   How should laws be changed to make such crimes consistent in scope nationally?

  XI.   White collar crimes.
- A.   Scope of unreported crimes and the effect upon business.

B. How can a tighter control be exerted over these crimes?
C. How valid are news media exposés? How dangerous?
XII. Focus upon concepts for total social involvement in organized crime control.
A. Pros and cons of the citizen crime commissions.
B. Involving citizens in programs for crime prevention.
C. A study of ideologies in how organized crime can be reduced.

SPECIALIZED TRAINING FOR THE LAW ENFORCEMENT OFFICER

Policy makers at the national level are beginning to recognize the need for a federal effort in organized crime control, as shown in the increased use of the RICO statute in enforcement. In addition, intense and highly select training offers the only solution for bringing police, probation officers, courts, and corrections personnel information about what the influence of organized crime is doing to the social structure. It does little good to train the police if judges are not made aware of the problems. Therefore, there should be an orientation course designed for all units of the criminal justice system. The days of generalizations and vague references to what has happened in the past are no longer a valid source for training and instructional material.

Members of the criminal justice system should be informed about cases that are occurring now. Concise briefs on cases that have been investigated and/or adjudicated should be widely circulated. Associates, political manipulations, and so on, should be a part of current information published by national and state criminal justice units. It is an indictment of our system that the news media become a primary source of reference for intelligence specialists and researchers who might contribute to a solution of the problem. Until widespread release of intelligence information becomes the practice rather than the exception, hoodlums will find shelter in administrative weaknesses.

There has been national momentum to train key enforcement personnel. The Law Enforcement Assistance Administration is supporting national, state, and local training efforts. Because of this support, more and more training programs are standardizing the curriculum along the following lines.

Organized Crime Training Outline

I. A broad overview of organized crime.
A. Overview of organized crime internationally and nationally.

    B. The structure of criminal syndicates.
        1. The function of the criminal confederations.
        2. Location of organized crime activities.
        3. Identified members of the criminal confederations.
    C. Organized crime family patterns (international and national).
    D. History and development of organized crime at state and local levels.
II. Statutes relating to organized crime.
    A. The Omnibus Crime Bill of 1970—pertinent statutes.
    B. Other federal laws relating to organized crime.
        1. Federal revenue code violations.
        2. U.S. Code violations.
            a. Stock market manipulations
            b. Labor
            c. Smuggling
            d. Bankruptcy laws
            e. Interstate conspiracy violations
            f. Wire services
            g. Interstate commerce
            h. Loan sharking
    C. State, county, and city laws.
    D. Civil laws utilized to control organized crime.
    E. Law enforcement agencies—areas of jurisdiction in the system (federal, state, local).
III. The intelligence system.
    A. Case preparation—interview and interrogation.
    B. Patterns of organized crime established by intelligence.
    C. The structure and ethics of intelligence systems. Manual versus automated applications.
    D. Information collection: strategic and tactical intelligence.
        1. The federal agencies and state systems.
        2. Undercover agents.
        3. Informants.
        4. The uniformed officer and special units.
        5. Records and filing systems.
            a. Analysis
            b. Evaluation
            c. Dissemination
        6. Undercover operations.
        7. Development and utilization of informants.
IV. Utilizing technology for investigations.
    A. Communications.
        1. Law enforcement intelligence units.

2. Computerized intelligence devices.
B. Electronics.
    1. Wiretapping.
    2. Electronic surveillance.
    3. Intercept and "jumper" devices.
C. Photograhy.
    1. Still and motion pictures.
    2. Infra red—holograph.
    3. Closed-circuit television, remote monitors.
D. Other devices.
    1. The polygraph—special uses.
    2. Heat sensors—remote stakeouts.
    3. Special antiriot control equipment for militant activities.
V. Organization and supervision in organized crime units.
    A. Organizational techniques.
        1. Effective reporting.
        2. Checks and balances.
        3. Special reporting techniques.
    B. Supervisory responsibilities.
        1. Planning strategy.
        2. Assessing and interpreting intelligence.
        3. Personnel problems.
VI. Gambling.
    A. Gambling—national history and techniques used.
        1. Lotteries.
            a. Bolita.
            b. Numbers and policy.
            c. Football, basketball, and baseball cards.
        2. Floating dice and card games.
        3. Bookmaking—on- and off-track systems.
    B. Local gambling.
    C. Prostitution.
    D. Legalized gambling.
        1. Skimming of profits.
        2. History of legalized gambling in United States and England.
        3. Impact of legalized gambling on community.
    E. Organized crime involvement in abortion.
VII. Drugs and organized crime.
    A. History of illegal drug use.
    B. Physiological and psychological aspects.
    C. International, state, and local laws.
    D. Drug identification.
    E. Techniques of search.

VIII.   Infiltration of organized crime into business and labor.
    A.   Legitimate business infiltration.
       1.   General technique of identification.
       2.   Loan companies, banking institutions, and leasing operations.
       3.   Loan sharking.
       4.   Extortion.
       5.   Hijacking.
       6.   Operations and public utilities service.
    B.   Labor racketeering.
    C.   Special frauds, such as the liquor industry, real estate, credit cards.
    D.   Stock market.
    E.   Income tax investigations.

Topical areas in this outline have been taken from established training programs from throughout the United States.

CONCEPTUALIZING TRAINING AND EDUCATION PROGRAMS

An example of how a curriculum evolves is shown in Figure 15–1. This example of computer crime and countermeasures shows training levels, types of schemes, sources of evidence, and the appropriate levels of information and the type of institution in which the materials should be presented. This same model could be applied to any subject.

Figure 15–2 carries the plan one step further and gives a sample outline of a 40-hour course. This material is presented at the applied skills and conceptual skills level at Long Beach City College, Long Beach, California. The same principles of curriculum structure would apply to any subject area.

SUMMARY

It is apparent that in organized crime units throughout the country there is a need for better education and training. There are indications that large law enforcement units are operating around the clock without sufficient knowledge to have any effect upon the incident of organized crime. This need is apparent not only among the specialized intelligence and organized crime units, but also among influential citizens' groups, prosecutor units, and court judges. Recognizing these deficiencies, federal and state agencies are attempting to focus on specialized training.

The topical outlines suggested in this chapter are offered only for

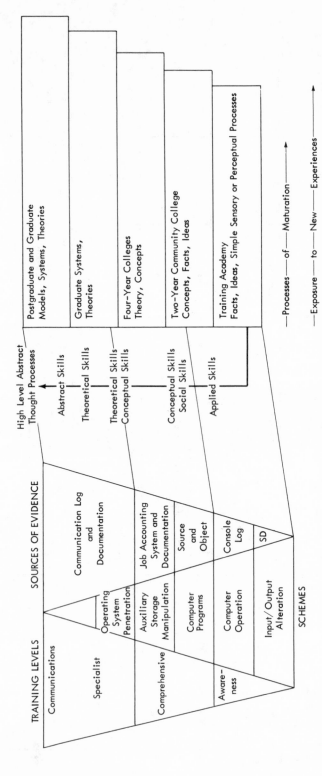

Figure 15–1   Computer crime schemes related to appropriate levels of training and education. The training levels, schemes and sources of evidence are from Bill Colvin. "Computer Crime Investigators: A New Training Field," *FBI Law Enforcement Journal,* July 1979, pp. 9–12.

Time	SATURDAY APRIL 19	SATURDAY APRIL 26	SATURDAY MAY 3	SATURDAY MAY 10	SATURDAY MAY 17	SATURDAY MAY 24	SATURDAY MAY 31	SATURDAY JUNE 7
8–9 A.M.	Registration, introduction, defining computer crime (P)	Systems organization (L)	Fraud and manipulation, theory and practice (L)	Administrative control, output control (P)	Internal audit (P)	Investigative processes, flow charting (B)	Special investigative tools (L)	(L)
9–10	Overview (P)	Systems organization (L)	Administrative control, internal/external policies, business conduct (L)	Administrative controls, error, correction controls (P)	Internal audit (P)	Investigative processes, flow charting (B)	" (L)	(L)
10–11	State of the art (L)	Vulnerabilities of the EDP systems (L)	Administrative control, personnel practices and procedures (L)	Computer security (hardware) (L)	Legal aspects (B)	Investigative methods (L)	" (L)	Case study (P)
11–12	Data processing systems Terminology (L)	How criminals use the system (P)	Administrative and internal controls (P)	Computer security (software) (L)	Legal aspects (B)	Investigative methods (L)	" (P)	Review and critique (P)
12–1	Computer terminology (L)	" (P)	Administrative control processing (P)	Communication and data base systems safeguards (L)	Legal aspects/ privacy (B)	Investigative methods and case studies (L)	" (P)	Final examination (P)

Figure 15–2 A 40-hour course in computer fraud and countermeasures.

orientation. Each agency has its own unique problems. For example, in many areas of the country auto theft by organized groups will take precedence over prostitution or bookmaking. Elsewhere, thefts from airports or from seaport installations may be the prime problems. What we are attempting to emphasize is the importance of getting information out to those who may assist in eliminating organized crime.

QUESTIONS FOR DISCUSSION

1. Discuss the reason why education and training is one of the weakest links in the struggle against organized crime.
2. Name three modes of transmitting information relating to organized crime control to concerned persons.
3. Why is the high school and college a desirable location for transmitting information regarding the social problems relating to organized crime?
4. In the past, to what group of people has organized crime education and training been restricted? Why?
5. Discuss the national interest and actions taken to train key enforcement personnel. Explain.
6. In developing a training curriculum, what are three contributing factors to the type of training required?

16

IN RETROSPECT

LEARNING OUTCOMES

1. Have an awareness of the efforts that have been applied to control organized crime during the past decade.
2. Review the important ideas and concepts contained in this text.
3. Develop some suggestions about an effective enforcement philosophy for the future.

For the past four decades there has been a great debate on defining organized crime by educational novices, and pleas from law enforcement agencies that organized crime is coming to town. While this debate has been going on, crime has become organized and is now firmly entrenched in every prosperous city in this country. During the debate, criminal confederations have quietly built an empire of stocks, property, and political clout. A decade ago it appeared the debate had ended and that through massive funding and planning there would finally be a national movement to eliminate organized crime. A new dimension in planning emerged with the creation of a National Council on Organized Crime. The council was to formulate a national strategy against organized crime and to coordinate federal control efforts. The objective of this council was to determine the thrust of organized crime control efforts by all agencies of the criminal justice sytem in the United States. The results have not been encouraging.

What happened in the decade of the 1970s that emasculated the plans for punitive and nonpunitive enforcement efforts against organized cartels? Where are the plans for economic and administrative sanctions against businesses that support or are controlled by the confederations? The plans, much like those of the 1950s and the 1960s, seem to fade away when enforcement efforts go beyond the talking stages. It seems that enforcement

efforts against criminals are of great political advantage and of tremendous public interest. It remains that way until sanctions begin to affect friends of friends who know someone of influence. At that point, enforcement becomes unpopular and stops.

Since World War II some of the healthiest organizations in the United States have been the individuals and cartels that form organized crime confederations. These organizations have prospered and expanded for many reasons. Our political system, while offering generous liberties, must at some time face the reality that liberty is laced with responsibility. A republic is dependent upon citizens who assume responsibility for their acts. This responsibility is individual and institutional. If the responsibility is not met by both, there is little hope that liberty, as we have experienced it, will continue. The protection of liberty must begin with the politician, the representative of the justice system, and the individual citizen. When one part of this triad fails to maintain integrity, the entire system is subject to failure.

The more one studies the facets of organized crime, the greater the conviction that very little can be done about it unless there is an awakening of citizens who, in turn, must hold all elements of government accountable for the eradication of organized crime. From legislation, through police, courts, and corrections, accountability can come about only if the laws are realistic, consistently enforced, and fairly adjudicated. In order to show how to achieve this accountability, we have tried to illustrate how organized crime evolves from street crimes of a vice nature and the more traditional crimes of burglary, robbery, and theft.

We have attempted to be realistic in believing that some organized crime problems would cease if certain violations now classed as crimes were legalized or placed under government control. This feeling, however, has not been supported by the experience of off-track gambling in many states nor of casino gambling in Nevada or New Jersey. In these cases, organized crime either owns or operates the casinos outright. Who is kidding whom about organized crime in these two states? In other states that are under some government constraint on gambling, organized crime operates side by side with the legal systems that have been established. The state offers little competition for organized crime.

In discussing the political and legal relationship to organized crime, the authors are dealing in areas that are not well documented with empirical research. The instances cited are examples of common knowledge to those who have worked in criminal intelligence or know of instances that have been published in news sources. We hope that by stressing the areas of politics and the legal system as being the keystones to the control of organized crime, citizens, through citizen pressure groups and through the ballot box, can pressure the greedy and the dishonest into the open. The ABSCAM investigations are a warning to citizens that unless they insist upon clean government, it will never be a reality.

In the remaining part of this chapter, we will comment upon each chapter. We will focus on some of the changes that have occurred or failed to occur, new information, and, in some cases, our personal opinions.

PUBLIC AWARENESS AND PROGRESS AGAINST ORGANIZED CRIME

Organized crime and the community seem to have a workable accommodation, with citizens taking a live and let live attitude. The greatest problem in organized crime enforcement is the failure of the community to acknowledge that organized crime actually exists. Politicians claim that organized crime does not exist in their community, police chiefs pleading for larger budgets say that organized crime is beginning to move into the community, and defense attorneys throw in a complete disclaimer about the existence of organized crime. So, the buck is passed from one agency to another, because there is little or no accountability. The grand jury might be an effective force against organized crime, but it is empaneled for a year and it is kept busy evaluating jail conditions and returning indictments. There is a need for a statewide grand jury that might serve two or three years or on a continuing basis, with new members rotating into the jury at alternate years. There needs to be some plan for the work of the jury.

Research and community awareness techniques have hardly been used effectively. Research in the past decade has been a rehash of that of the 1960s without many useful findings. Field procedures that are written in a law school using standards of exposure rather than experience do not contribute much to the field of enforcement. The limited research of the 1970s has brought little in the way of results. This may not be the fault of the researcher, because we believe it has been demonstrated that research on organized crime cannot be effectively conducted by the standard questionnaire survey method.

One needs only to read and listen to the news media to know that organized crime exists in some far off city, usually in another state. Local news media do not name names about people and organizations who are involved locally in organized crime. If they did, economic sanctions in the form of withdrawn advertising or huge lawsuits might result. When reporters do not have confirmed proof of a relationship or event, they tend to ignore the story.

The community is not without protection; each year there is some progress made against organized crime. The system operates in spite of the pessimistic views voiced about the control of organized crime. For example, in 1980 long-time Mafia leader Carlos Marcello was indicted on 14 counts of insurance fraud. Also named in the indictments, using RICO leverage, were three officials who were "well connected" in Louisiana state government. The same

year brought federal indictments to nine of California's Mafia leaders. Other states have been active in reporting some success against organized crime figures.

It appears that many bodies are being removed from circulation; but the assets of the individual, gained from the fruits of organized crime, are not being seized as mandated by Congress in the RICO statute. Understandably, this broad statute is going to encounter future difficulties and receive some adverse court rulings. Until this happens, federal efforts should be pursued with much vigor.

The role of the prosecutor has been touched on lightly. While the prosecutor's offices is a key position in the prosecution of organized crime, most officers will reflect the temperament of the community. The prosecutor, whether at the federal or local level, is in a position to gauge the efforts being put forth by the criminal justice system in combating organized crime. As an officer of a court, the attorneys can determine the temperament of the judge, assess the efficiency of the police investigator, and know whether there are adequate laws for successful prosecutions. From their positions they are able to say whether specific cases will be prosecuted, and eventually they are a determining factor in the final sentence and disposition of a case.

The opportunity for corruption is ever present, and the same criteria guide the prosecutor as guide the police officer and the defense attorney. From experience of case investigators, it would appear that the prosecutor is the least vulnerable in the trying of a case; however, deciding whether to prosecute and whether to allow a plea bargain opens many kinds of options for corruption.

PROSTITUTION AND GAMBLING

The discussion of vice crimes have been given priority because these crimes are most susceptible to control with citizen cooperation. While gambling may have fallen to second place as a leading moneymaker for organized crime, it is still the leading moneymaker for the old, established organized crime families. Gambling does not have the stigma of drug distribution, so those engaged in gambling are an echelon higher in the social structure of organized crime. The experiment in legalized casino gambling in New Jersey has gone as expected. The Atlantic City gambling casinos figured heavily in the ABSCAM investigations when the Justice Department probed bribery of congressmen and state and local government leaders. The attorney general of New Jersey indicated that casinos cannot exist without being an attraction to organized crime.

While the 14 states that now have a lottery view it as a way to finance government, contribute to charity, and aid the elderly, it has not raised revenues as expected. The "something for nothing" attitude will eventually

undermine the enforcement of illegal gambling. It is only a matter of time until organized crime runs the state system, or runs a parallel system along side the legal system. Gambling money in any form is too easy to be passed up by the confederations.

Prostitution and allied crimes are addressed as a social rather than a law enforcement problem. Punitive enforcement cannot eliminate or even control prostitution, although it has been fairly successful in the area of organized prostitution. There is a strange dichotomy regarding prostitution. The moral majority are actively working against the crime of prostitution, while feminists and younger people do not look at prostitution as a violation that should be addressed by law enforcement. Organized crime is allied to prostitution, although not all prostitutes are a part of organized crime. Groups of prostitutes still follow the harvests, prostitutes are still in "houses," and new and innovative ideas like dating services and massage parlors can be traced to organized affiliation.

DRUGS

The issues of drug distribution have been the same for the past three decades. Basic methods of distribution are the same; only the quantity and the site of the drug origin changes. The Unites States' borders are sieves, and users in this country seem to have a voracious appetite for drugs, since they consume all available merchandise. The drug problem grows in relation to the permissiveness of the community; the organization flourishes in the struggles over political and administrative strategies. There are few prospects for a permanent solution to the problem.

The present state of drug usage in this country has grown from individual permissiveness to lack of support for law enforcement and the decriminalization of key narcotic laws. Hundreds of ideological groups spent the 1960s and the 1970s turning people on. As the "turn ons" became national crazes, contraband such as cocaine and marijuana became hot market items. As consumption among upper class groups grew, those charged with enforcing the statutes became benevolent toward drug users and peddlers. The public failed to support law enforcement by permitting unrealistic search and seizure laws; laws that delayed enforcement action so drastically that many police agents just gave up trying to enforce liberalized marijuana laws; restrictive laws governing interrogation; and laws restricting the use of informants. All have combined to discourage arrest except in the most obvious cases. The public attitude toward drugs is reflected in apathy on the part of law enforcement officers who work endless hours on a case, then have it manipulated through the court system by delays and the procedural ploys of highly paid lawyers. This does not mean that we believe the police should be operating without guidelines; we mean that the law should be consistently and universally applied.

When a narcotic such as marijuana is decriminalized and the penalty for the possession of small amounts is lowered to a misdemeanor, it changes the law of arrest under which an agent must operate. It also changes the attitude toward the enforcement of the law. The decriminalization of marijuana laws in many of the states has made the police "arresting pimps" for the legal fraternity. Many officers, as in the days of Prohibition, are releasing small violators rather than arresting them and having them be fleeced by the legal fraternity.

Bureaucratic infighting among the major drug enforcement units has allowed the large drug confederations to operate without pressure. To have an enforcement unit operate effectively means that information must be gained from some source and that information then diligently pursued in an investigation. Often this information is gained outside the drug sphere. Also, when this information has to pass from one agency to another, the "hotness" or urgency of the information and the diligence in pursuing the investigation is lost. This seems to be a human and administrative frailty. Administrators and planners should have been able to foresee this split between Customs and the Drug Enforcement Administration when the Customs Agency Service was arbitrarily transferred to DEA. It is safe to say that the contacts made by the present Customs Service will not soon become a major factor in DEA-based cases. When DEA agents work big peddlers and leave behind street and mid-level peddlers, they are depriving themselves of the best information sources. Information about big peddlers does not move between big peddlers and enforcement officers. DEA administrators should realize that information comes at the street level and at border entry points. The failure to keep these contacts is shown in the drastically reduced quantities of heroin seized during 1979 and 1980. For example, in 1972 seizures amounted to 635 pounds, in 1979 seizures totaled 122 pounds. Covert purchases dropped from 645 pounds in 1976 to 160 pounds in 1979. These reductions were in the face of much increased peddling activities.

Political decisions have affected enforcement along the southern coast of the United States. These decisions have focused major enforcement attention along the Florida border. In the meantime, Alabama and Louisiana have opened their borders. What is happening in these states is similar to what has been happening in southern California for the past two decades.

The strategy of putting DEA agents in foreign countries, with a program to eliminate narcotics at its source, will serve its purpose well if governments will cooperate and political encounters can be minimized.

The solution to the drug problem is not going to be easy; there are just too many people benefitting from the profits of narcotics. A large force of professional personnel live on narcotic and allied violations. Crime is a big business, and big business generates a flow of money that supports many professional people. We do not mean to imply that drugs are allowed to flow with permission; we merely mean that all-out efforts are just not exerted to eradicate the problems. The average narcotics violator is easy to apprehend

and simple to prosecute. Drug peddlers are not known for their intelligence, and the "mules" who do the actual transportation are sacrificed to the system by the money bosses. Thus, the chance to get at the head of the organization is very small.

It does little good to attempt to re-invent the wheel in drug enforcement. As long as the market exists, there will be no effective control. Alcohol and narcotics share a similar future. Legalize them, and the profits are localized in a few hands. Decriminalize use, and the legal profession shares in the profits. As long as huge profits flow into political and legal sources, little impact will be made in curbing the flow of drugs into and within this country.

The domestic transporters of narcotics could suffer if the RICO statue were applied in massive enforcement efforts. The real value of RICO is its use as a lever against middle- and lower-level drug dealers who, in order to avoid forfeiture of property and other assets, will cooperate with federal agents. By injecting fear and mistrust into sales and distribution systems, the enforcement officer is working from a power position. As long as the courts will support RICO, there can be many effective enforcement actions. But these actions will never reach the top money sources, simply because they do not become involved in the transactions. RICO will, however, deter the big organizations from a wide-open operation. This statute should affect the drug peddler much as excessive search and seizure restrictions have affected the enforcement agent. That is, the action will be slowed because of the restraints, but it will not cease.

PORNOGRAPHY

Pornography is another activity that in time will closely parallel the drug trade. The laws are indecisive about pornography and, as a result, enforcement has been inconsistent or nonexistent. For example, as early as 1976 an attempt by the City of Los Angeles to ban newsrack nudity was voided in appellate court. This court ruled that the law violates the First Amendment guarantee of free expression. In Jacksonville, Florida, an ordinance that prohibited the showing of films in which nude persons appeared and that were visible to the outside public were struck down. Nudity is no longer an issue when it is difficult to get a prosecution on explicit sexual acts and other hardcore pornography.

The lax attitude of the courts has caused the business of pornography to spiral. In mid-1981 there were about 2 million videocassette recorders in use in the United States, and about half of all the video cassettes sold were "adult title." Pay TV has caused a surge in porno programming that has raised many ethical and moral questions. While many of the "image conscious" corporations are in a dilemma about "adult programming," organized crime has moved in to fill the void in both production and distribution. Eventually the

market for porno may rival that of illegal narcotics and become the number one moneymaker for the confederations.

BUSINESS FRAUD

This text has touched only briefly on the magnitude of frauds and swindles relating to business and to the confederations. There are whole books devoted to explaining these intricate frauds and swindles. The web of private business interests, the influences of confederation-dominated unions, and other conceptual relationships have not been cited in detail because there are many rumors about these relationships but there is not much hard research evidence on how confederations work with legitimate businesses.

Local law enforcement does not become involved in all business frauds. Most big fraud cases are handled by state attorneys general or by a U.S. attorney and their investigators. Thus, the importance to local law enforcement is minimized.

Labor's ties to organized crime are another problem. In 1981, Roy Williams, president of the Teamsters Union, and four top associates were under federal indictment for eleven counts of bribery and wire fraud. Whether these indictments are politically motivated because of the union's position against the government's regulation of the trucking industry is not clear. But how unions such as the Teamsters were infiltrated by associates of organized crime became obvious in a Senate Permanent Subcommittee on Investigation hearing. This hearing showed that Roy Williams, despite being indicted in 1962, 1972, and 1974, suffered no convictions. In one hearing, Williams took the Fifth Amendment 23 times. This kind of government case preparation and legal loopholes had made him a folk hero to the rank-and-file members of the union. Why should his constituents object to a little association with organized crime?

In an Associated Press story, the Del E. Webb Corporation of Phoenix and Las Vegas was accused of dealing with mobsters hidden behind a complex screen of stock transfers, joint ventures, partnerships, and secret ownerships. The relationships shown in this investigation are a classic example of how legitimate business enterprises become "slaves" to those who control the money.

MILITANT GROUPS

The policing of militant groups has become a major activity for local police agencies. Gang intelligence groups and SWAT teams to deal with militants have become commonplace in local agencies.

These gangs are not only local and regional, but national and international

in scope. Many of the listed gangs have good international connections in narcotics and other criminal enterprises. Thus, local police become not only enforcers of local and state laws, but also necessary intelligence links for group actions against the national government.

There is little question that this country is in for a period of violent actions by these groups. If these groups are met with the tough laws available, terrorism will be restricted to isolated instances. If the groups are met with permissiveness and weak resolve, we can expect increased terrorist activity during the future.

ORGANIZATION AND MANAGEMENT OF ENFORCEMENT

A section of the book has been devoted to organization and management concepts to point out that dozens of different structures may be established and function equally well. In identifying some supervisory and management techniques, we are also pointing out the major weaknesses of organized crime control groups in operation today.

Some criticism has been leveled at certain crime control efforts by federal and state agencies primarily because organized crime is not eliminated by the arrest of one or two thousand known members of the confederations. The establishment of organized crime is too heavily insulated to cease because of efforts exerted at the top. The effort must be multidirectional and with full public revelation so that "fixes" do not take place prior to or after trial.

In discussing technology, such as intelligence gathering, there has been an attempt to stress safeguards. There has been some conceptualizing on intelligence processes, and how the information is applied to crime control. From a national perspective, the last decade has not produced much valid empirical research; the studies cited are restatements of old problems.

Since the Watergate scandal, law enforcement agencies have been reluctant to collect the type of domestic intelligence data that is worthwhile. Government spying, after the indictment of two FBI administrators associated with "black bag" operations, has been closely limited and controlled. The guidelines developed in 1976 carry cautionary measures that are being put to work at the present time. The intelligence networks are again geared up for increased activity against organized crime and subversive activities from abroad.

SUMMARY

One major reason why organized crime flourishes so widely is the social chaos surrounding the laws that govern such activities as sexual misbehavior and gambling. The conflicting history of such activities as pornography and

obscenity has been offered in some depth so that the citizen and the enforcement officer can understand the complexity of requiring arbitrary social conformity through law. As social attitudes have changed, the laws have not been flexible in meeting these changes. This dichotomy is shown in the fact that 36 states permit some form of gambling. Yet the new laws governing organized crime are designed to make taking bets a major federal felony. There is little congruity in how the problem should be reconciled among the various units of government.

Because there are so many diverse philosophies on what crimes should be enforced, this text cannot be expected to furnish but a few solutions and/or suggestions for organized crime control. But a look at the historical background on a few of the more common crimes may help the reader to view a crime, even though it be minor, as another instrument in making organized crime strong.

APPENDIX A
CATEGORIES OF CRIMINAL ACTIVITY ENGAGED IN BY ORGANIZED CRIMINALS

Crimes that fit into this category might be, but are not limited to, the following categories:

Crimes normally conducted by organized groups:

Racketeering by monopoly or extortion
Planned bankruptcy
Black market or prohibited products

Crimes by persons operating on an individual, ad hoc basis (or crimes conducted with a common scheme and thus classed as organized crime):[1]

Purchase on credit with no intention to pay, or purchase by mail in the name of another
Individual income tax violations
Credit card frauds
Bankruptcy frauds
Title II home improvement loan frauds
Frauds with respect to social security, unemployment insurance, or welfare
Unorganized or occasional frauds on insurance companies (theft, casualty, health)
Violations of Federal Reserve regulations by pledging stock for further purchases, flouting margin requirements
Organized or unorganized "lonely hearts" appeals by mail

Crimes in the course of their occupations by those operating inside business, government, or other establishment, in violation of their duty of loyalty and

[1]Herbert Edelhertz, *The Investigation of White Collar Crime: A Manual for Law Enforcement Agencies* (Washington, D.C.: U.S. Government Printing Office, April 1977).

244

fidelity to employer or client:

Commercial bribery and kickbacks by and to buyers, insurance adjusters, contracting officers, quality inspectors, government inspectors, auditors, and so on

Bank violations by bank officers, employees, and directors

Embezzlement by business or union officers and employees

Securities fraud by insiders trading by the use of special knowledge, or causing firms to take positions in the market to benefit themselves

Employee petty larceny and expense account frauds

Frauds by computer, causing unauthorized payouts

"Sweetheart contracts" entered into by union officers

Embezzlement by attorneys, trustees, and fiduciaries

Fraud against the government
  A. Padding of payrolls
  B. Conflicts of interest
  C. False travel, expense, or per diem claims

Crimes incidental to and in furtherance of business operations, but not the central purpose of the business:

Tax violations

Antitrust violations

Commercial bribery of another's employee, officer or fiduciary (including union officers)

Food and drug violations

False weights and measures by retailers

Violations of Truth-in-Lending Act by misrepresentation of credit terms and prices

Submission or publication of false financial statements to obtain credit

Use of fictitious or overvalued collateral

Check-kiting to obtain operating capital on short-term financing

Securities Act violations to obtain operating capital, false proxy statements, manipulation of market to support corporate credit or access to capital markets, and so on

Collusion between physicians and pharmacists to cause the writing of unnecessary prescriptions

Dispensing by pharmacists in violation of law, excluding narcotics traffic

Immigration fraud in support of employment agency operations to provide domestics

Housing code violations by landlords

Deceptive advertising

Fraud against the government:
  A. False claims
  B. False statements:
    1. To induce contracts

2. AID frauds
3. Housing frauds
4. SBA frauds, such as SBIC bootstrapping, selfdealing, cross-dealing, or obtaining direct loans by use of false financial statements
C. Moving contracts in urban renewal

Labor violations (Davis-Bacon Act)

Commercial espionage

White-collar crime as a business, or as the central activity:

Medical or health frauds

Advance fee swindles

Phony contests

Bankruptcy fraud, including schemes devised as salvage operation after insolvency of otherwise legitimate businesses

Securities fraud and commodities fraud

Chain referral schemes

Home improvement schemes

Debt consolidation schemes

Mortgage milking

Merchandise swindles:
A. Gun and coin swindles
B. General merchandise
C. Buying or pyramid clubs

Land frauds

Directory advertising schemes

Charity and religious frauds

Personal improvement schemes:
A. Diploma mills
B. Correspondence schools
C. Modeling schools

Fraudulent application for, use, and/or sale of credit cards, airline tickets, and so on

Insurance frauds:
A. Phony accident rings
B. Looting of companies by purchase of overvalued assets, phony management contracts, self-dealing with agents, intercompany transfers, etc.
C. Frauds by agents writing false policies to obtain advance commissions.
D. Issuance of annuities or paidup life insurance, with no consideration, so that they can be used as collateral for loans
E. Sales by misrepresentations to military personnel or those otherwise uninsurable.

Vanity and song publishing schemes

Ponzi schemes

False security frauds

Purchase of banks, or control thereof, with deliberate intention to loot them

Fraudulent establishment and operation of banks or savings and loan associations

Fraud against the government:
  A. Organized income tax refund swindles, sometimes operated by income tax "counselors"
  B. AID frauds
  C. FHA frauds
    1. Obtaining guarantees of mortgages on multiple-family housing far in excess of value of property with foreseeable inevitable foreclosure
    2. Home improvement frauds
Executive placement and employment agency frauds
Coupon redemption frauds
Money order swindles.

APPENDIX B
ORGANIZED CRIME CONTROL ACT OF 1970

The Organized Crime Control Act consists of Title 18 United States Code, Sections 1961–68, and three other sections. These statutes show the guidelines implemented by Congress to combat organized crime. Only major titles are cited; refer to the U.S. Code for full details.

Title I. Grand juries.   Special grand juries under the jurisdiction of district courts to sit for periods of 36 months.

Title II. General immunity.   Provides "use" immunity rather than "transaction" immunity for an organized crime witness.

Title III. Recalcitrant witness.   Authorizes a maximum 18-month civil commitment with respect to witnesses who refuse to testify.

Title IV. False declarations.   Abandons the two-witness and direct evidence rule and authorizes a prosecution for perjury and false declarations based on irreconcilably inconsistent declarations under oath.

Title V. Protected facilities for housing government witnessses.   Authorizes the attorney general to protect and maintain federal or state witnesses and their families.

Title VI. Depositions.   Authorizes the government to preserve testimony by use of a deposition in a criminal proceeding.

Title VII. Litigation concerning sources of evidence.   Omits limits on the disclosure of evidence illegally obtained by the government.

Title VIII. Syndicated gambling (five parts).   Prohibits the obstruction of state or local law enforcement by making it unlawful for two or more persons

to conspire to obstruct the enforcement of law with the intent to facilitate gambling.

Unlawful to engage in conspiracy to gamble in violation of state law by five or more persons, having a gross revenue of more than $2000 per day.

Unlawful to engage in the operation of an illegal gambling business. If inferentially established, property used in violation of the provision may be seized.

A Presidential Crime Commission is established to review gambling and enforcement policies and to recommend alternatives.

Makes possible enforcement of Parts 1 and 2 by court-ordered electronic surveillance. This surveillance is not preempted by state law.

Title IX. Racketeer influence and corrupt organizations.   Makes unlawful the receipt or use of income from racketeering activities.

Prohibits the acquisition of any enterprise engaged in interstate commerce through a "pattern" of "racketeering activity."

Proscribes the operation of any enterprise engaged in interstate commerce through a "pattern" of "racketeering activity."

Title X. Dangerous special offender sentencing. Section 1001.   Authorizes extended sentences of up to 25 years for dangerous offenders.

Title XI. Regulation of Explosives. Section 1102.   Establishes federal controls over interstate and foreign commerce in explosives.

Title XII. National Commission on individual rights.   This commission is designed to conduct comprehensive study and review of federal laws and practices relating to special grand juries and other rights as authorized by law or acquired by executive action.

Title XIII. General provisions.   If parts of the act are held invalid, provisions of other parts are not affected.

APPENDIX C
REGULATIONS THAT CONTROL NCIC COMPUTER OPERATIONS

DATA FILES

The NCIC (National Crime Information Center) contains data on stolen vehicles, missing license plates, lost or stolen guns, lost or stolen articles that are individually serially numbered and valued at $500 or more, wanted persons, and stolen or missing securities (including stocks, bonds, money orders, currency). Criteria for data input are stipulated by the NCIC operating manual. For instance, the following general provisions govern entries made by control terminals.[1]

Vehicle File

It is suggested that unrecovered stolen vehicles be entered in file within 24 hours after the theft.... An immediate entry should be considered in instances where the place of theft is in proximity of a state line.

Missing vehicles will not be entered in file unless a formal police theft report is made or a complaint filed and appropriate warrant issued charging embezzlement, etc.

Vehicles wanted in conjunction with felonies or serious misdemeanors may be entered into file immediately.

License Plate File

Unrecovered stolen license plates will be entered on the same basis as stolen vehicles provided all plates issued are missing.

[1]The following criteria for entry have been abridged from the *Operating Manual,* pp.6–8, of the National Crime Information Center, Washington, D.C., U.S. Department of Justice, 1968.

Gun File

Serially numbered weapons (stolen or lost).

Weapons recovered in connection with an unsolved crime for which no lost or stolen report is on file may be entered in the file as a "recovered" weapon.

Article File

Individual serially numbered property items valued at $500 or more. Office equipment (adding machines, typewriters, dictating machines, etc.) and color television sets may be entered regardless of value.

Multiple serially numbered property items totalling $5,000 or more in one theft.

Any serially numbered property items may be entered at the discretion of the reporting agency if (1) the circumstances of the theft indicate that there is a probability of interstate movement, or (2) where the seriousness of the crime indicates that such an entry should be made for investigative purposes.

Wanted Person File

Individuals for whom federal warrants are outstanding.

Individuals who have committed or have been identified with an offense which is classified as a felony or misdemeanor under the existing penal statutes of the jurisdiction originating the entry and felony or misdemeanor warrant has been issued for the individual with respect to the offense which was the basis of the entry. Probation and parole violators meeting the foregoing criteria should be entered.

A "Temporary Felony Want" may be entered when a law enforcement agency has need to take prompt action....

Securities File

Stocks, bonds, money orders, currency, etc., will be stored in this file.

These criteria for data input serve as the basis for all agency decisions regarding information that will be processed for entry into the national system. Whereas in some cases restrictive, the provisions provide a fairly flexible working basis for the identification of the major items of data with which law enforcement agencies are concerned.

In regard to these criteria, two primary characteristics should be noted. First, the criteria provide that items of data be uniquely identifiable. Articles

that cannot be identified or distinguished as unique cannot be entered, because no point of reference for an inquiring agency is provided. A vehicle must have a license number or identification number; a person must have a name; a gun must have a serial number; currency must have a denomination and serial number. In other words, each data entry must include an identifier that will allow discrimination between like objects.

Second, the system will take information on criminals or wanted persons, but will not take information on crimes. When a criminal offense is committed, no entries can be made unless article, person, vehicle, etc., associated with the crime can be identified positively. This prevents the inclusion of data that would be useless in the solution of crimes and gives evidence to the fact that the NCIC is an operationally based system designed to serve administrative and operational needs, rather than a research or data gathering system that would aid in management control.

RETENTION PERIOD OF NCIC RECORDS

In addition to the control terminal updating or purging provisions to be discussed at a later point, the NCIC has regular purging provisions to keep files current. General regulations have been formulated for discarding data that would be useless after a longer period of time. The decreasing probability of a need for locating particular items of data makes it possible to purge the files periodically, based on a standardized retention period. The following general rules apply to items of data for which no locating information has been received by the NCIC:

Vehicle File

Unrecovered stolen vehicles will remain in file for the year of entry plus 4.

Unrecovered vehicles wanted in conjunction with a felony will remain in file for 90 days after entry. In the event a further record is desired, the vehicle must be reentered.

Unrecovered stolen VIN plates, engines and transmissions will remain in file for the year plus 4.

License Plate File

Unrecovered stolen license plates not associated with a vehicle will remain in file for one year after the end of the year during which the valid period of the plate expires.

Gun File

Unrecovered weapons will be retained in file for an indefinite period until action is taken by the originating agency to clear the record.

Weapons entered in file as "recovered" weapons will remain in file for the balance of the year entered plus 2.

Article File

Stolen articles uncovered will be retained for the balance of the year entered plus one year.

Wanted Person File

Persons not located will remain in this file indefinitely until action is taken by the originating agency to clear the record (except "temporary felony wants").

The data items when purged according to these rules are stored on magnetic tape for future reference. They are not totally purged from the files on the NCIC, but are simply shifted from the active files to inactive files. The same process applies to data files on located property or persons, which are governed by the following rules:

Vehicle, License Plate, and Article Files

Records concerning stolen vehicles, vehicles wanted in conjunction with felonies, vehicle parts...[license plates, and articles] will remain in file for a period of 10 days subsequent to the date of recovery, as shown in the message clearing the record, and then automatically removed.[2]

Gun File

Records concerning stolen or lost weapons will remain in file for a period of 10 days subsequent to the date of recovery....

Records of "recovered" weapons will be removed from file immediately upon receipt of a stolen report concerning that weapon.

[2]*Operating Manual,* pp. 8–9.

Wanted Person File

Records concerning wanted persons shall remain in file for a period of 30 days subsequent to the date of apprehension, as shown in the message clearing the record, and then automatically removed.[3]

Periodic validity checks of NCIC data files are requested of control terminals. Appropriate data are furnished to control terminals which, in turn, check data entries against original agency records. Quarterly checks are made of data in the vehicle and license plate file; and annual check is made of data in the gun file. No provisions are presently established for frequency and scope of validity checks of the wanted person file, and no validity checks are required of data in the article file because of purge criteria covering this file.

MESSAGES AND DATA REVISION

The NCIC computer will accept six types of messages and make appropriate types of changes in the active files. These include:

Record entry—places a new record in file.

Record modify—adds data to or changes a portion of data previously placed in the NCIC file by a record entry. May be made only by agency originally entering the record.

Record cancel—cancels a record for reasons other than recovery of property or apprehension of a wanted person, i.e., record later determined to be invalid, withdrawal of prosecutive action, etc. May be made only by agency originally entering record. Cancel messages are not to be used for any purpose other than that stated above.

Inquiry—requests a search of the NCIC file against information available to the inquiring agency.

Locate message—shows a temporary change in record status. The message is sent by an agency which has located an item of stolen property or wanted person previously entered in the system.

Record clear—records recovery of stolen/missing property or apprehension of a wanted person, the subject of a previously placed record in the NCIC. May be made only by agency originally entering record.[4]

The NCIC, in turn, will transmit three types of messages to control terminals. These include: (1) acknowledgements of messages other than inquiries, (2) replies to inquiries, and (3) administrative messages. Administrative messages concern operating aspects of the system sent to system

[3]*Operating Manual,* pp. 9–10.
[4]*Operating Manual,* pp. 30–38.

participants. Control terminals, however, cannot send administrative messages to NCIC through terminals.

Messages sent to NCIC by control terminals are to be prepared off-line, except for inquiry messages that are prepared on-line.[5] Off-line preparation allows adequate time for verification of data entries by originating agencies to ensure accuracy. On-line preparation of inquiry messages provides instant response to operating needs for information checks. Because inquiry messages are the only type that require immediate response from the NCIC, this pattern of messages provides an effective operational basis for accurate input while allowing immediate response to operational needs.

SCOPE OF DATA IN NCIC FILES

The scope of data in computer files either limits or increases the chances for a variety of types of searches. In the NCIC data format most of the data relevant for search purposes are provided. The vehicle file requires the following items of data on stolen vehicles, vehicle parts (as appropriate), and vehicles involved in felonies (to the extent that data is available):

License plate number
License plate state
License plate year of expiration
License plate type
Vehicle identification number
Year
Make
Model
Style
Color
Date of theft
Originating agency case number

In addition to this basic data on the item involved, the record as contained in the NCIC files includes a message key that instructs the NCIC and its participants as to the intent of the message, an originating agency code, and a NCIC record number. The record provides space for later inclusion of the

---

[5]Off-line is defined as "a system...in which the peripheral equipment is not under the control of the central processing unit." On-line refers to "a system...in which information reflecting current activity is introduced into the data processing system as soon as it occurs. Thus, directly in-line with the main flow of transaction processing." See *Automatic Data Processing Glossary, Datamation* magazine, 1968.

date the item is located or the record is canceled, the locating agency, and a locating agency case number. A "miscellaneous" field is provided for relevant information or for extension of data not totally contained by established fields. (For instance, when a license plate number exceeds eight digits, the full number must be inserted in the "miscellaneous" field.)

Inquiries concerning stolen vehicles, felony vehicles, stolen parts, and stolen and/or missing license plates are processed as follows:

1. Inquiries should be made by complete license plate number and state of issue and/or complete vehicle identification number, or vehicle part number in instances involving engines and transmissions.

2. When inquiry is by license plate number only and positive response is received, it is necessary to match the remaining identifying data in the NCIC record with the plate being inquired about before taking further action. In this instance, search is by plate number only; thus, multiple "hits" may ensue.

3. Uncommon circumstances may indicate a need for a special off-line search, e.g., for all vehicles of a particular year and make; for a particular model or color; etc. Such requests must be kept to a minimum and only requested where communicated to the NCIC off-line.[6]

Data items on stolen or missing license plates are identical to that on stolen vehicles listed above, with the exception of the six data items descriptive of the vehicle.

Record entries on stolen or missing weapons include the following data items:

Serial number
Make
Caliber
Type
Date of theft or missing report

The data entry also provides for a message key, an originating agency number, an originating agency case number, a NCIC number, and a miscellaneous field for date weapon is located or record is canceled, the locating agency, and the locating agency case number. A "recovered" weapon is identified by a code included in the message instructions to the NCIC.

In addition to the normal identifying data field for locating information, the article file entries include the following fields; type, serial number, brand name, and model.

[6]*Operating Manual*, p. 45.

Data records on wanted persons are more extensive than those required for other items. Fields of data include:

Name	Operator's license year of
Sex	expiration
Race	Offense
Nationality	Date of warrant
Date of birth	Originating agency case number
Height	License plate number
Weight	License plate state
Color hair	License plate year of expiration
FBI number	License plate type
Fingerprint classification	Vehicle identification number
Miscellaneous number	Year
Social Security number	Make
Operator's license number	Model
Operator's license state	Style
	Color

Provision is made for locating information, a NCIC number, and originating agency identification. In addition, the message key may be coded with "A" if the subject is known to be armed, with "S" if the subject is known to possess suicidal tendencies, and with "Y" if both describers apply.

Duplicate entries on persons will be accepted by the NCIC, if the originating agencies are different. "The agency making the second entry will receive as a hit the record already in file at the time the second entry is acknowledged. Should the entry contain data concerning a vehicle or license plate that has already been entered in the vehicle or license plate file, the agency making the entry will be furnished the record in file at the time the wanted person entry is acknowledged."[7]

Inquiries of the wanted person file are governed by the following provisions:

1. Inquiries may be made by name and at least one of the following numerical identifiers: complete date of birth, FBI number, miscellaneous number, social security number, operator's license number, and originating agency case number.
2. Inquiries may be made by using message code "QW" with license plate number, license plate state, and/or vehicle identification number. In this instance it is not necessary to use a name.
3. Special circumstances may indicate a need for a search by name only. These

---

[7]*Operating Manual*, p. 62. A "hit" as used in this quote refers to a positive response from the system that a person, vehicle, or object is wanted by some agency. The requesting agency is then provided the information that a record exists and relevant information on the person, vehicle, or object.

can be made off-line but...must be...requested only where extreme circumstances warrant.[8]

NCIC EXTENSION AND DEVELOPMENT

The NCIC system has grown and matured since its inception in 1967. Each state and adjoining foreign countries now access this system. This type of system supports strategic and tactical intelligence capabilities to each NCIC terminal. For example, if strategic intelligence were requested on a certain vehicle ownership, this could be traced through the system. The ability to keep car and owner together is often important intelligence information. In a tactical intelligence application, this system has been instrumental in curbing the flow of stolen cars into Mexico, which in turn resulted in the curbing of narcotics flowing back into the United States.

The advisory group of the NCIC was reportedly considering extension of active files to include "missing" persons in its wanted persons file to facilitate location of such persons through normal activities. The advisory group was also considering storage of criminal identification records. "Such records of arrests and dispositions could be entered or retrieved instantaneously in the NCIC real-time system" and would aid in the NCIC's criminal justice statistical program.

OTHER NATIONAL SYSTEMS

Two other national communication systems are the Law Enforcement Teletype System (LETS) and the National Driver Register Service (NDRS). Law Enforcement Teletype System is simply a teletype connecting system between law enforcement agencies throughout the United States and is primarily devoted to the exchange of general information among police departments. It can supplement NCIC by providing the means for verification of entries, for notifying originating agencies of arrests and dispositions, and for sending administrative messages from control terminals to NCIC.

The National Driver Register Service (NDRS) consists of a computer-based file of "dangerous drivers." Its reason for being is explained by the following statements:

> The purpose of the National Driver register is to provide a central driver-records identification facility containing the names of drivers whose licenses have been denied, suspended or revoked for any reason other than

[8]*Operating Manual*, pp. 63–64.

a denial or withdrawal of a license for less than 6 months due to a series of nonmoving violations. It was established by the United States Congress to assist each State in locating all the records available on these drivers, regardless of where in the United States they may have established these records.[9]

The basic file is established from reports sent to the NDRS by each state and serves each state by providing information on requests concerning drivers—within twenty-four hours of receipt of a request for a license search.

The file is theoretically useful to a large number of state and local officials. These include:

Driver license administrators—for checking on individuals who request to be licensed by the state.

Police—developing complete accident reports (by providing background information on individuals involved in accidents).

Prosecutors—may need driver information to determine whether to file first- or second-offense charges.

Judges—need driver information to determine appropriate sentences after conviction.

School administrators—need driver records in the section of driver education teachers.

Other public authorities—need driver records on job applicants and on employees.

Insurance firms and transportation companies—need complete records for identifying poor risks among applicants for automobile liability insurance and for employment as truck and bus drivers.

Only state and federal officials can obtain information directly from the NDRS, but information can be made available to other officials who need it.

[9]U.S. Department of Transportation, *The National Driver Register: A State Driver Records Exchange Service* (Washington, D.C.: U.S. Government Printing Office, September 1967), p. i.

APPENDIX D

STANDARD CLASSIFICATION NUMBERS FOR CRIMES RELATED TO ORGANIZED CRIMINAL ACTIVITY

SOVEREIGNTY	**0100**
TREASON	0101
TREASON MISPRISION	0102
ESPIONAGE	0103
SABOTAGE	0104
SEDITION	0105
SELECT SCV	0106
MILITARY	**0200**
DESERTION	0201
IMMIGRATION	**0300**
ILLEGAL ENTRY	0301
FALSE CITIZEN	0302
SMUGGLE ALIENS	0303
HOMICIDE	**0900**
KILL—FAMILY—GUN	0901
KILL—FAMILY	0902
KILL—NONFAM—GUN	0903
KILL—NONFAM	0904
KILL—PUB OFF—GUN	0905
KILL—PUB OFF	0906
KILL—POL OFF—GUN	0907
KILL—POL OFF	0908
NEG MANSL—VEHICLE	0909
NEG MANSL—NOT VEH	0910
KIDNAPPING	**1000**
RANSOM—MINOR—GUN	1001
RANSOM—MINOR	1002

RANSOM—MINOR— STGARM	1003
RANSOM—ADULT—GUN	1004
RANSOM—ADULT	1005
RANSOM—ADULT— STGARM	1006
HOSTAGE FOR ESCAPE	1007
ABDUCTION—FAMILY	1008
ABDUCTION—NONFAMILY	1009
SEXUAL ASSAULT	**1100**
RAPE—GUN	1101
RAPE	1102
RAPE—STGARM	1103
SODOMY—BOY—GUN	1104
SODOMY—MAN—GUN	1105
SODOMY—GIRL—GUN	1106
SODOMY—WOMAN—GUN	1107
SODOMY—BOY	1108
SODOMY—MAN	1109
SODOMY—GIRL	1110
SODOMY—WOMAN	1111
SODOMY—BOY—STGARM	1112
SODOMY—MAN—STGARM	1113
SODOMY—GIRL—STGARM	1114
SODOMY—WOMAN— STGARM	1115
STAT RAPE	1116
ROBBERY	**1200**
ROB BUSINESS—GUN	1201
ROB BUSINESS	1202

ROB BUSINESS—STGARM	1203
ROB STREET—GUN	1204
ROB STREET	1205
ROB STREET—STGARM	1206
ROB RESIDENCE—GUN	1207
ROB RESIDENCE	1208
ROB RESIDENCE—STRGARM	1209
FORC PURSE SNATCH	1210

ASSAULT   **1300**

ASLT AGG—FAMILY—GUN	1301
ASLT AGG—FAMILY	1302
ASLT AGG—FAMILY—STGARM	1303
ASLT AGG—NONFAMILY—GUN	1304
ASLT AGG—NONFAMILY	1305
ASLT AGG—NONFAMILY—STGARM	1306
ASLT AGG—PUB OFF—GUN	1307
ASLT AGG—PUB OFF	1308
ASLT AGG—PUB OFF—STGARM	1309
ASLT AGG—POL OFF—GUN	1310
ASLT AGG—POL OFF	1311
ASLT AGG—POL OFF—STGARM	1312
ASLT SIMPLE	1313

ABORTION   **1400**

ABORT OTHER	1401
ABORT SELF	1402
SOLICIT SUBMIT ABORT	1403
SOLICIT PERFORM ABORT	1404
ABORTIFACIENT SELL	1405

ARSON   **2000**

ARSON BUS—LIFE	2001
ARSON RES—LIFE	2002
ARSON BUS—INS	2003
ARSON RES—INS	2004
ARSON BUSINESS	2005
ARSON RESIDENCE	2006

EXTORTION   **2100**

EXTORT THREAT PERSON	2101
EXTORT THREAT PROPERTY	2102
EXTORT THREAT REPUTATION	2103

BURGLARY   **2200**

BURG SAFE—VAULT	2201
BURG FORCED—RES	2202
BURG FORCED—NONRES	2203
BURG NO FORCED—RES	2204
BURG NO FORCED—NONRESS	2205
BURG TOOLS	2206

LARCENY   **2300**

POCKET PICK	2301
PURSE SNATCH	2302
SHOPLIFT	2303
LARC PARTS FM VEH	2304
LARC FM AUTO	2305
LARC FM VEH TRANS	2306
LARC FM COIN MACH	2307
LARC FM BLDG	2308
LARC FM YARDS	2309
LARC FM MAILS	2310

STOLEN VEHICLE   **2400**

VEH THEFT SALE	2401
VEH THEFT STRIP	2402
VEH THEFT FOR CRIME	2403
VEH THEFT	2404
VEH THEFT BY BAILEE	2405
VEH RCVING	2406
VEH STRIP	2407
VEH POSS	2408
TRANSPORT	2409
AIRPLANE THEFT	2410

FORGERY   **2500**

FORG CHECKS	2501
FORGERY	2502
COUNTERFEIT	2503
COUNTERFEIT—TRANSPORT	2504
COUNTERFEIT TOOLS	2505

PASS COUNTERFEIT	2506		COCAINE	3533
PASS FORGED CHECKS	2507		SYNTH NARC—SELL	3540
POSSESS COUNTERFEIT	2508		SYNTH NARC—SMUG	3541
			SYNTH NARC—POSSESS	3542
FRAUD	**2600**		SYNTH NARC	3543
CON GAME	2601		NARC EQUIP	3550
SWINDLE	2602		MARIJUANA—SELL	3560
MAIL FRAUD	2603		MARIJUANA—SMUG	3561
IMPERSONATION	2604		MARIJUANA—POSSESS	3562
FRAUD CREDIT CARDS	2605		MARIJUANA—PROD	3563
NSF CHECKS	2606		MARIJUANA	3564
FALSE STATEMENT	2606		AMPHET—MANU	3570
			AMPHET SELL	3571
EMBEZZLE	**2700**		AMPHET—POSSESS	3572
			AMPHET	3573
STOLEN PROP	**2800**		BARBIT—MANU	3580
STOL PROP THEFT SALE	2801		BARBIT—SELL	3581
STOL PROP THEFT			BARBIT—POSSESS	3582
TRANSPORT	2802		BARBIT	3583
STOL PROP THEFT	2803			
STOL PROP TRANSPORT	2804		**SEX OFFENSE**	**3600**
STOL PROP RECEIV	2805		SEX CHILD	3601
STOL PROP POSSESS	2806		HOMOSEX GIRL	3602
STOL PROP CONCEALED	2807		HOMOSEX BOY	3603
			INCEST MINOR	3604
PROPERTY DAMAGE	**2900**		INDEC EXP MINOR	3605
DAM PROP BUS	2901		BESTIALITY	3606
DAM PROP PRIV	2902		INCEST ADULT	3607
DAM PROP PUB	2903		INDEC EXP ADULT	3608
			SEDUCE ADULT	3609
			HOMOSEX WOMAN	3610
DANGEROUS DRUGS	**3500**		HOMOSEX MAN	3611
HALLUC—MANU	3501		PEEPING TOM	3612
HALLUC—DIST	3502			
HALLUC—SELL	3503		**OBSCENE MATERIAL**	**3700**
HALLUC—POSSESS	3504		MANU OBSCENE	3701
HALLUC	3505		SELL OBSCENE	3702
HEROIN—SELL	3510		MAIL OBSCENE	3703
HEROIN—SMUG	3511		POSSESS OBSCENE	3704
HEROIN—POSSESS	3512		DIST OBSCENE	3705
HEROIN	3513		TRANSPORT OBSCENE	3706
OPIUM—SELL	3520		OBSCENE COMM	3707
OPIUM—SMUG	3521			
OPIUM—POSSESS	3522		**FAMILY OFF**	**3800**
OPIUM	2523		NEGLECT FAM	3801
COCAINE—SELL	3530		CRUEL CHILD	3802
COCAINE—SMUG	3531		CRUEL WIFE	3803
COCAINE—POSSESS	3532			

BIGAMY	3804
CONTRIB DELINQ MINOR	3805
NEGLECT CHILD	3806
NONPAY ALIMONY	3807
NONSUPPORT PARENT	3808

GAMBLING	**3900**
BOOKMAKE	3901
CARDS—OP	3902
CARDS—PLAY	3903
DICE—OP	3904
DICE—PLAY	3905
GAMBLING DEVICE—POSSESS	3906
GAMBLING DEVICE—TRANSPORT	3907
GAMBLING DEVICE—NOT REGIS	3908
GAMBLING DEVICE	3909
GAMBLING GOODS—POSSESS	3910
GAMBLING GOODS—TRANSPORT	3911
LOTTERY—OP	3912
LOTTERY—RUN	3913
LOTTERY—PLAY	3914
SPORTS TAMPER	3915
WAGERING INFO—TRANSMIT	3916
EST GAMBLING PLACE	3917

COMMERCIAL SEX	**4000**
KEEP BROTHEL	4001
PROCURE PROSTITUTE	4002
HOMOSEX PROST	4003
PROSTITUTION	4004

LIQUOR	**4100**
MANU LIQUOR	4101
SELL LIQUOR	4102
TRANSPORT LIQUOR	4103
POSSESS LIQUOR	4104
MISREPRESENT AGE	4105
LIQUOR	4106

DRUNK	**4200**

OBSTRUCT POLICE	**4800**
RESIST OFF	4801
AID PRIS ESC	4802
HARBOR FUGTV	4803
OBSTRUCT CRIM INVEST	4804
MAKE FALSE REP	4805
EVIDENCE—DESTROY	4806
WITNESS—DISSUADE	4807
WITNESS—DECEIVE	4808
REFUSING AID OFF	4809
COMPOUND CRIME	4810
UNAUTH COMM W PRISONER	4811
ARREST—ILLEGAL	4812

FLIGHT—ESCAPE	**4900**
ESCAPE	4901
FLIGHT AVOID	4902

OBSTRUCT JUDIC (CONGR., LEGIS.)	**5000**
BAIL—SECURED BOND	5001
BAIL—PERSONAL RECOG	5002
PERJURY	5003
PERJURY	5004
CONTEMPT COURT	5005
OBSTRUCT JUST	5006
OBSTRUCT COURT	5007
MISCONDUCT—JUDIC OFF	5008
CONTEMPT CONGR	5009
CONTEMPT LEGIS	5010

BRIBERY	**5100**
BRIBE GIVE	5101
BRIBE OFFER	5102
BRIBE RECEIVE	5103
BRIBE SOLICIT	5104
CONFLICT INT	5105
GRATUITY GIVE	5106
GRATUITY OFFER	5107
GRATUITY RECEIVE	5108
GRATUITY SOLICIT	5109
KICKBACK GIVE	5110
KICKBACK OFFER	5111
KICKBACK RECEIVE	5112
KICKBACK SOLICIT	5113

WEAPON OFFENSE	**5200**
ALTER ID ON WPN	5201
CARRY CONCLD WPN	5202
CARRY PROH WPN	5203
EXPLOS—TEACH USE	4204
EXPLOS—TRANSPORT	5205
EXPLOS—USE	5206
INCEND DEV—POSSESS	5207
INCEND DEV—USE	5208
INCEND—TEACH USE	5209
WPN LIC	5210
POSSESS EXPL	5211
POSSESS WPN	5212
FIRE WPN	5213
SELL WPN	5214

PUBLIC PEACE	**5300**
ANARCHISM	5301
RIOT—INCITE	5302
RIOT—ENGAGE	5303
RIOT—INTERFERE FIRE	5304
RIOT—INTERFERE OFF	5305
RIOT	5306
ASSEMBLY—UNLAW	5307
FALSE ALARM	5308
HARASS COMM	5309
DESECRATE FLAG	5310
DISORDERLY COND	5311
DISTURB PEACE	5312
CURFEW	5313
LOITER	5314

TRAFFIC OFF	**5400**
HIT RUN	5401
TRANSP DANG MATL	5402
DRIV INFLU DRUGS	5403
DRIV INFLU LIQ	5404
MOVING TFC	5405
NONMOVING TFC	5406

HEALTH—SAFETY	**5500**
DRUGS ADLTD	5501
DRUGS—MISBRAND	5502

DRUGS	5503
FOOD ADLTD	5510
FOOD—MISBRAND	5511
FOOD	5512
COSMETICS ADLTD	5520
COSMETICS—MISBRAND	5521
COSMETICS	5522

CIVIL RIGHTS	**5600**

INVADE PRIVACY	**5700**
DIVULGE EAVESDROP INFO	5701
DIVULGE EAVESDROP ORDER	5702
DIVULGE MSG CONTENTS	5703
EAVESDROP	5704
EAVESDROP EQUIP	5705
OPEN SEALED COMM	5706
TRESPASS	5707
WIRETAP—FAILURE REP	5708

SMUGGLE	**5800**
CONTRABAND	5801
PRISON CONTRABAND	5802
AVOID PAYING DUTY	5803

ELECTION LAWS	**5900**

ANTITRUST	**6000**

TAX—REVENUE	**6100**
INCOME TAX	6101
SALES TAX	6102
LIQUOR TAX	6103

CONSERVATION	**6200**
ANIMALS CONSERV	6201
BIRDS CONSERV	6202
FISH CONSERV	6203
LICENSE CONSERV	6204

VAGRANCY	**6300**

APPENDIX E

CUE SHEETS

TM-(L)-2506/000/01

EVENT REPORT CUE SHEET[1]

Item 1.   Event Report
_____
            (Type of Report)

Reporting Officer:
Item 2.   /   /
            _____
            (Name)   (Serial Number)   (Division of Assignment)

Item 3.
_____
            (Type(s) of Crime: Insert from list of crime classifications:
            Indicate attempt or conspiracy to commit. If more than one
            crime involved repeat "Item 3," followed by the additional
            classification for each crime.)

Date and Time Reported:
Item 4.
_____
            Month/Day/Year   Example: 12/6/66.
            (Use 24-hour designation. Example: 1315)

Location of Occurrence:
Item 5.
_____
            (Type of Premises)

Item 6.
_____
            (Address: Number   Street   City)

Time of Occurrence:
Item 7.
_____
            Month/Day/Year   Hour/Minutes (Use 24-hour clock)

Item 8.   People (Use People Cue Sheet[s])
Item 9.
_____
            (Approving Authority: Inserted by Reviewer)

Item 10.
_____
            (Clearance: By Arrest, Other (State), Unfounded)

Item 11.
_____
                        (Property Description)

Item 12.
_____
            (Event Number: Blank if new report; if follow-up information,
            insert number of original report.)

Item 13.   (Narrative)

1 This form is taken as a sample from the Los Angeles Police Department, Phase
I. Operating System Description, Technical Memorandum TM (L) 2506/000/01. (Santa
Monica, Calif.: Systems Development Corp., 1965), pp. 77-81. This example is cited only
as a theoretical model and does not imply that it will be adopted by any department
for official use.

These three forms are cited as examples only. Every department accessing a state computer network and in turn NCIC will use an approved form. Comprehensiveness and format may vary from agency to agency.

December 31, 1965   TM-(L)-2506/000/01

PEOPLE CUE SHEET

Item 8. _____ / _____ / _____
                (Name: Last name first)   (Role)   (Crime)

Descriptors

A. _____
   (Sex/Descent)

B. ____/____/_____
   (Birth date)

C. _____
   (Place of Birth)

D. _____/_____
   (Height/Weight)

E. _____
   (Hair)

F. _____
   (Eyes)

G. _____
   (Complexion)

H. _____
   (Residence address)

J. _____
   (Residence telephone)

K. _____
   (Occupation)

L. _____
   (Address of employment)

M. _____
   (Telephone number of
   employment)

N. _____
   (If suspect arrested, booking number)

P. _____
   (Nickname or alias)

R. _____
   (Driver's license number)

S. _____
   (Social Security number)

T. _____
   (Vehicle description)
   1. _____
      (Year/Make)
   2. _____
      (Body style)
   3. _____
      (Color)
   4. _____
      (License number
      (state, year))
   5. _____
      (Other identifying features)

U. _____
   (Clothing)

W. _____
   (Other identifying
   characteristics)

X. _____
   (Other suspect information)

(Items A through M relate to all roles; items N through X relate
only to suspect.)

BOOKING REPORT CUE SHEET

Item 1.　Booking Report
_____
　　　　　(Type of Report)

Reporting Officer:
Item 2.　　　　　　　/　　　　　　　　/
_____
　　　　　(Name)　　　(Serial Number)　(Division of Assignment)

Location of Occurrence:
Item 3.
_____
　　　　　(Location of booking)

Time of Occurrence:
Item 4.　　　　　　　　/
_____
　　　　　(Month/Day/Year)　　　(Hour/Minutes)

Police Department Booking Number:
Item 5.　(Automatically Assigned)
_____

County Booking Number:
Item 6.
_____
　　　　　(Insert if known)

Charge(s):
Item 7.
_____
　　　　　(If warrant, insert number; include type of charge: Misdemeanor,
　　　　　felony, other.)

Identifiable Personal Property:
Item 8.
_____

People:
Item 9.　(Use People Cue Sheet[s])

Other information on the booking report which may be retained
in the System:

　　　　Emergency notification information
　　　　Vehicle impound information
　　　　Evidence booked information
　　　　Special medical problems information
　　　　Amount of money in prisoner's personal property
　　　　Other articles of personal property
　　　　Probable investigative unit (probably will not be determined
　　　　　　by reporting officer)
　　　　Location crime committed and date, time arrested, and
　　　　　　arresting officers (better input from event or arrest report)
　　　　Name of searching officer
　　　　Name of booking officer

BIBLIOGRAPHY

This partial bibliography includes publications from 1960 to the present. Articles and short research reports may be secured from the National Criminal Justice Reference Service, Box 6000, Rockville, Maryland 20850.

Albini, Joseph L. *The American Mafia: Genesis of a Legend.* New York: Appleton-Century-Crofts, 1971.

Allen, Edward J. *Merchants of Menace—The Mafia, A Study of Organized Crime.* Springfield, Ill.: Charles C Thomas, 1962.

Allsop, Kenneth. *The Bootleggers and Their Era.* Garden City, N.Y.: Doubleday, 1961.

Anderson, Annelise G. *The Business of Organized Crime: A Cosa Nostra Family.* Palo Alto, Calif.: Hoover Institute Press, 1979.

Becker, Jay. *The Investigation of Computer Crime.* Seattle: Battelle Law and Justice Study Center, 1978.

Bequai, August. *Computer Crime.* Lexington, Mass.: D.C. Heath, 1978.

Bequai, August. *Organized Crime: The Fifth Estate.* Lexington, Mass.: D.C. Heath, 1979.

Bequai, August. *The Cashless Society: EFTS at the Crossroads.* New York: Wiley, 1981.

Bers, Melvin K. *The Penetration of Legitimate Business by Organized Crime: An Analysis.* Washington, D.C.: U.S. Department of Justice, LEAA, 1970.

Blakely, G.R. "On the Waterfront—RICO (Racketeer Influenced and Corrupt Organizations) and Labor Racketeering." *American Criminal Law Review,* 17, 3 (Winter 1980.)

Blakely, G.R., and C.H. Rogovin. *Techniques in the Investigation and Prosecution of Organized Crime: The Rackets Bureau Concept. General Standards for the Operation of Organized Crime Control Units.* Washington, D.C.: U.S. Department of Justice, LEAA, 1977.

Blakely, G. Robert, Ronald Goldstock, and Charles H. Rogovin. *Rackets Bureau: Investigation and Prosecution of Organized Crime.* Washington, D.C.: U.S. Government Printing Office, March 1978.

Bullough, Vern L. "Streetwalking—Theory and Practice." *Saturday Review,* September 4, 1965.

Buse, Renee. *The Deadly Silence.* Garden City, N.Y.: Doubleday, 1965.

Carroll, John M. *Secrets of Electronic Espionage.* New York: Dutton, 1966.

Chamber of Commerce of the United States. *Deskbook on Organized Crime.* Washington, D.C.: An Urban Affairs Publication, 1969.

Chamber of Commerce of the United States. *Marshaling Citizen Power against Crime.* Washington, D.C., 1970.

Chamber of Commerce of the United States. *Mafia.* Greenwich, Conn.: Fawcett, 1972.

Cook, James and Jane Carmichael (part 3). "The Invisible Enterprise," *FORBES,* September 29–November 24, 1980. Four-part series.

Doherty, Bill. *Crime Reporter.* New York: Exposition Press, 1964.

Dolci, Danilo. *To Feed the Hungry, An Inquiry in Palermo.* London: Macgibbon and Kee, 1959.

Dolci, Danilo. *The Outlaws of Partinico.* London: Macgibbon and Kee, 1960.

Dolci, Danilo. *Waste.* New York: Monthly Review Press, 1964.

Drzazga, John. *Wheels of Fortune.* Springfield, Ill.: Charles C Thomas, 1963.

Dulles, Allen W. *The Craft of Intelligence.* New York: Harper & Row, 1968.

Dulles, Allen W. *The Secret Surrender.* New York: Harper & Row, 1966.

Edelhertz, Herbert. *The Nature, Impact and Prosecution of White-Collar Crime.* Washington, D.C.: National Institute of Law Enforcement and Criminal Justice, May 1970. ICR 70–1.

Edelhertz, Herbert. *The Investigation of White Collar Crime: A Manual for Law Enforcement Agencies.* Washington, D.C.: U.S. Government Printing Office, April 1977.

Ernst, Morris L., and Alan U. Schwartz. *Censorship, The Search for the Obscene.* New York: Macmillan, 1964.

Etzioni, Amitai. *Men and Organizations.* Chicago: Rand McNally, 1965.

Gardiner, John A. *The Politics of Corruption: Organized Crime in an American City.* New York: Russell Sage, 1970.

Geis, Gilbert, and Robert F. Meier. *White Collar Crime: Offenses in Business, Politics and the Professions.* New York: Free Press, 1977.

Geis, Gilbert, and Ezra Statland, eds. *White Collar Crime: Theory and Research.* New York: Sage, 1980.

Godfrey, E. Drexel, Jr., and Don R. Harris. *Basic Elements of Intelligence.* Washington, D.C.: U.S. Department of Justice, LEAA, 1972.

Goulden, Joseph C. *Truth Is the First Casualty.* Chicago: Rand McNally, 1969.

Gramont, Sanche de. *The Secret War.* New York: Putnam, 1962.

Halper, Albert, ed. *The Chicago Crime Book.* New York: World, 1967.

Harris, Don R. *Basic Elements of Intelligence: A Manual for Law Enforcement Officers.* Washington, D.C.: U.S. Government Printing Office, September 1976.

Hill, Albert F. *The North Avenue Irregulars: A Suburb Battles the Mafia.* New York: Cowles, 1968.

Hilsman, Roger. *To Move a Nation.* Garden City, N.Y.: Doubleday 1967.

Homer, F.D. "Conflicting Images of Organized Crime." In *Critical Issues in Criminal Justice,* R.G. Iacovetta and Dae H. Chang. Durham, N.C.: Carolina Academic Press, 1979.

Homer, F.D. *Guns and Garlic: Myths and Realities in Organized Crime.* Purdue: Purdue University Press, 1974.

Horan, James D. *The Mob's Man.* New York: Crown, 1959.

Ianni, Francis A., and E.R. Ianni. *A Family Business: Kinship and Control in Organized Crime.* New York: Russell Sage, 1972.

Jennings, Dean. *We Only Kill Each Other: The Life and Bad Times of Bugsy Seigal.* Englewood Cliffs, N.J.: Prentice-Hall, 1967.

Kahn, David. *The Code Breakers: History of Secret Communication.* New York: Macmillan, 1967.

Kefauver, Estes. *Crime in America.* Garden City, N.Y.: Doubleday, 1951.

Kelly, R.J. "A Study in the Production of Knowledge by Law Enforcement Specialists." Ph.D. dissertation, New York University, 1978.

Kennedy, Robert F. *The Enemy Within.* New York: Harper & Row, 1960.

Kennedy, Robert F. *The Pursuit of Justice.* New York: Harper & Row, 1964.

King, Rufus. *Gambling and Organized Crime.* Washington, D.C.: Public Affairs Press, 1969.

Kinsey, Alfred C., Wardell B. Pomeroy, and Clyde E. Martin. *Sexual Behavior in the Human Male.* New York: Saunders, 1948.

Krauss, Leonard, and Aileen MacGahan. *Computer Fraud and Countermeasures.* Englewood Cliffs, N.J.: Prentice-Hall, 1979.

Landesco, John. *Organized Crime in Chicago.* 2nd ed. Chicago: University of Chicago Press, 1968.

Law Enforcement Assistance Administration, Organized Crime Program Division. *The Role of State Organized Crime Prevention Councils.* Washington, D.C., 1970.

Lewis, Jerry D., ed. *Crusade against Crime.* New York: Bernard Geis, 1962.

Lewis, Norman. *The Honored Society.* New York: Putnam, 1964.

Lyman, Theodore R., Thomas W. Fletcher, and John A. Gardiner. *Prevention, Detection, and Correction of Corruption in Local Government.* Washington, D.C.: U.S. Government Printing Office, November 1978.

Maas, Peter. *The Valachi Papers.* New York: Putnam, 1968.

Madison, Charles A. *American Labor Leaders.* New York: Ungar, 1962.

Martin, Raymond V. *Revolt in the Mafia.* New York: Duell, Sloan, and Pearce, 1963.

Matthews, John D. *My Name is Violence.* New York: Belmont Books, 1962.

Maxwell, Edward. "Why the Rise in Teenage Veneral Disease?" *Today's Health,* 1965.

McClellan, John L. *Crime without Punishment.* New York: Duell, Sloan, and Pearce, 1962.

McGovern, James. *Crossbow and Overcast.* London: Hutchinson, 1965.

McLaughlin, Donald. *Room 38: A Study in Naval Intelligence.* New York: Atheneum, 1968.

Messick, Hank. *The Silent Syndicate.* New York: Macmillan, 1967.

Messick, Hank. *Syndicate in the Sun.* New York: Macmillan, 1968.

Messick, Hank. *Lansky.* New York: Macmillan, 1971.

Miller, Arthur R. *The Assault on Privacy: Computers, Data Banks, and Dossiers.* Ann Arbor: University of Michigan Press, 1971.

Mollenhoff, Clark R. *Tentacles of Power: The Story of Jimmy Hoffa.* Cleveland: World, 1963.

Mori, Cesare. *The Last Struggle of the Mafia.* New York: Putnam, 1963.

Moscow, Alvin. *Merchants of Heroin.* New York: Dial Press, 1968.

Municipal Police Administration. Chicago: International City Managers' Association, 1961.

National Advisory Committee on Criminal Justice Standards and Goals. *Organized Crime, Report of the Task Force on Organized Crime.* Washington, D.C.: U.S. Government Printing Office, December 1976.

National District Attorneys Association, Economic Crime Project. *Insurance Fraud Manual.* Chicago, 1981.

New Mexico Governor's Organized Crime Prevention. *Annual Report, 1979.* Albuquerque, 1979.

New York State Commission of Investigation. *Racketeer Infiltration into Legitimate Business.* March 1970.

Norton, Augustus R., and Martin H. Greenberg. *International Terrorism: An Annotated Bibliography and Research Guide.* Boulder, Colo.: Westview Press, 1980.

Oyster Bay (New York) Conference on Combating Organized Crime, 1965. *Combating Organized Crime.* Albany, 1966.

Pace, Denny F. *Handbook on Vice Control.* Englewood Cliffs, N.J.: Prentice-Hall, 1971.

Pace, Denny F., and Jimmie C. Styles. *Handbook on Narcotics.* Englewood Cliffs, N.J.: Prentice-Hall, 1972.

Pantaleone, Michele. *The Mafia and Politics.* New York: Coward-McCann, 1966.

Penkovskiy, Oleg *The Penkovskiy Papers.* Garden City, N.Y.: Doubleday, 1965.

Pennsylvania Crime Commission. *Report on Organized Crime.* Harrisburg, Pa.: Office of the Attorney General, Department of Justice, 1970.

Platt, Washington. *Strategic Intelligence Production: Basic Principles.* New York: Praeger, 1957.

Ploscowe, Morris. *Organized Crime and Law Enforcement.* New York: Crosby Press, 1952.

Project SEARCH (System for Electronic Analysis and Retrieval of Criminal History), Committee on Security and Privacy. *Security and Privacy Considerations in Criminal History Information Systems.* Sacramento, Calif.: Project SEARCH staff, California Crime Technological Research Foundation, July 1970. Technical Report No. 2.

Puzo, Mario. *The Godfather.* New York: Putnam, 1969.

Quebec Commission de Police. *Organized Crime and the Business World* (Crime Organise et le Monde des Affaires), Quebec, Canada 1977.

Ransom, Harry Howe. "Intelligence, Political and Military." *International Encyclopedia of the Social Sciences,* VII, pp. 415–21. New York: Macmillan, 1968.

Ransom, Harry Howe. *The Intelligence Establishment.* Cambridge, Mass.: Harvard University Press, 1970.

Reber, Jan, and Paul Shaw. *Executive Protection Manual.* San Francisco: Assets Protection, 1980.

Reckless, Walter C. *The Crime Problem.* New York: Appleton-Century Crofts, 1961.

Redston, George, and Kendall F. Crossen. *The Conspiracy of Death.* Indianapolis: Bobbs-Merrill, 1965.

Reid, Ed, and Ovid Demaris. *The Green Felt Jungle.* New York: Trident Press, 1963.

Salerno, Ralph. *The Crime Confederation: Cosa Nostra and Allied Operations in Organized Crime.* Garden City, N.Y.: Doubleday, 1969.

Schabeck, Tim A. *Computer Crime Investigation Manual.* San Francisco: Assets Protection, 1981.

Schiavo, Giovanni. *The Truth about the Mafia.* New York: Vigo Press, 1962.

Schur, Edwin M. *Narcotic Addiction in Britain and America.* Bloomington: Indiana University Press, 1962.

Sciascia, Leonardo. *Mafia Vendetta.* New York: Knopf, 1964.

Seidly, John Michael. "'Upon the Hip'—A Study of the Criminal Loan Shark Industry." Ph.D. dissertation, Harvard University, 1969.

Sheldon, Jonathan A., and George Z. Weibel. *Survey of Consumer Fraud Law.* Washington, D.C.: U.S. Government Printing Office, June 1978.

Sondern, Frederic. *Brotherhood of Evil, the Mafia.* New York: Farrar, Straus and Giroux, 1959.

Spergel, Irving. *Racketville, Slumtown.* Chicago: The University of Chicago Press, 1964.

Sterling, Claire. *The Terror Network.* New York: Holt, Rinehart and Winston, 1981.

Stratton, John G. "The Terrorist Act of Hostage Taking: Considerations for Law Enforcement." *Journal of Police Science and Administration,* June 1978, pp. 123–34.

Swanson, C.R., and L. Terri. "Computer Crime Dimensions, Types, Causes, Investigation." *Journal of Police Science and Administration,* September 1980, pp. 304–11.

Treback, Arnold S. *Drugs, Crime and Politics.* New York: Praeger, 1978.

Trubow, George. *Privacy and Security of Criminal History Information: An Analysis of Privacy Issues.* Washington, D.C.: U.S. Government Printing Office, 1978.

Tully, Andrew. *Treasury Agent.* New York: Simon & Schuster, 1958.

Turkus, Burton, and Sid Feder. *Murder Inc.* New York: Farrar, Straus and Giroux, 1951.

Tyler, Gus. *Organized Crime in America.* Ann Arbor: University of Michigan Press, 1962.

United Aircraft—Corporate Systems Center. *Definition of Proposed NYSIIS Organized Crime Intelligence Capabilities.* Farmington, Conn., 1966.

U.S. Department of Justice. *Cargo Theft and Organized Crime: A Handbook for Management and Law Enforcement.* Washington, D.C.: U.S. Government Printing Office, December 1972.

U.S. Department of Justice, LEAA. *Intergovernmental Cooperation in Organized Crime Control: Examples of States' Activities.* Washington, D.C.: U.S. Government Printing Office, 1979.

U.S. Department of Justice, LEAA. *The Investigation of White Collar Crime: A Manual for Law Enforcement Agencies.* Washington, D.C.: U.S. Government Printing Office, April 1977.

U.S. General Accounting Office. *War on Organized Crime Faltering, Federal Strike Forces Not Getting the Job Done—Department of Justice.* Report to the Congress by the U.S. Comptroller General, 1977.

U.S. Senate. *Organized Criminal Activities, South Florida and U.S. Penitentiary, Atlanta, Ga., Hearings before the Senate Permanent Subcommittee on Investigations.* Part 3, 95th Congress, 2nd Session, October 24–25, 1978.

Walker, Bruce J., and Ian F. Blake. *Computer Security and Protection Structure.* Stroudsburg, Pa.: Dowden, Hutchinson and Ross, 1980.

Walsh, T.J., and R.J. Healy. *Protection of Assets Manual.* San Francisco: Assets Protection, 1981.

Westin, Alan F. *Privacy and Freedom.* New York: Atheneum, 1970.

Wheeler, Stanton. *On Record: Files and Dossiers in American Life.* New York: Russell Sage, 1969.

Wise, David, and Thomas B. Ross. *The Invisible Government.* New York: Random House, 1964.

Wyden, Peter. *The Hired Killers.* New York: Morrow, 1963.

Wykes, Alan. *The Complete Illustrated Guide to Gambling.* Garden City, N.Y.: Doubleday, 1964.

INDEX